Tor Books by Joanne Bertin

The Last Dragonlord
Dragon and Phoenix
Bard's Oath (forthcoming)

Dragon
and Phoenix

Joanne Bertin

A TOM DOHERTY ASSOCIATES BOOK
NEW YORK

Hi, Mom—
this one's for you!

This is a work of fiction. All characters and events potrayed in this book are either products of the author's imagination or are used fictitiously.

DRAGON AND PHOENIX

Copyright © 1999 by Joanne Bertin

A Tor Book
Published by Tom Doherty Associates, LLC
175 Fifth Avenue
New York, Ny 10010

www.tor.com

Tor ® is a registered trademark of Tom Doherty Associates, LLC

ISBN: 0-812-54542-7
Library of Congress Catalog Card Number: 99-37456

First edition: December 1999
First mass market edition: November 2000

Printed in The United States of America

0 9 8 7 6 5 4 3 2 1

With thanks to:

The Navajo people for their good humor and patience with a traveler in their land, and their generosity in sharing the beauty of that land with strangers.

Jennifer Lindert, who gave me crash space and hospitality while I was on the Navajo Reservation.

Dee "Ardelis the Bloodthirsty" Dreslough and Paul Galinis for letting me use parts of their names, real and SCAdian, for characters.

And once again—and always—the biggest thanks of all to Sam Gailey for fixing my computer every time it tried to get me, and for keeping me (more or less) sane.

Prologue

The old dragon stirred as something blazed like a shooting star through his dreams.

Something new. Something . . . unbelievable.

He drifted toward waking. In all his long life he had never known such a thing. He trembled with joy. The waters of the deep lake above him rippled, echoing his movement.

Then, like a morning mist, the thought was gone, hidden once more from him.

He sank back into sleep, to dream the centuries away.

One

Lura-Sharal was dead.

Shei-Luin bowed her head as her sister's body was carried away for burning, borne upon a litter of ebony by four burly eunuchs. A cloth of the imperial gold silk covered the girl's slight form. What did it matter?

Lura-Sharal was dead.

Shei-Luin knew she should be proud of that mark of the emperor's favor. But all she wanted was her elder sister back. What would she do without the wise and gentle words of Lura-Sharal guiding her?

She watched as the litter disappeared through the door. Tears streamed down her cheeks; she wanted to run screaming after it, to hurl herself upon her sister and beg Lura-Sharal to tell her it was but a jest, to hold her, to sing and dance with her once more. She yearned to run away and ride the wide open plains again as Zharmatians with Yesuin, their childhood friend.

Ah, Phoenix, if only they could all be free once more . . .

But now Yesuin was a hostage to the uneasy peace between his father's tribe and the Jehangli.

And Lura-Sharal was dead.

A hand came down with jarring force upon Shei-Luin's shoulder. She jumped, and looked up to find Lady Gei's masklike face hovering over her.

"Come," the lady said. Her voice held no sympathy. "Come; the Phoenix Lord has seen you and grants you the favor of his company. For you are also of the seed of Lord Kirano; it is time to do your duty, girl. At thirteen you are old enough."

"But I am n—" Shei-Luin broke off. To speak the truth

would be to close the path she suddenly saw open before her. Shei-Luin turned her head to hide her slip of the tongue.

The fingers on her shoulder tightened like bands of steel. Empty inside, Shei-Luin went where they led. Eyes filled with jealousy and hatred followed her as she went deeper into the perfumed sanctum of the harem to be made ready.

And afterward . . .

She bowed her head. But only for an instant; she would not shrink from her fate or from Xiane Ma Jhi, Phoenix Lord of the Skies. For she knew a thing that no one else alive now remembered.

She stared straight ahead, her eyes dry now.

Two

Dragonlords—those who are both *human and dragon.* *They come to Jehanglan. They will bring war to the Phoenix.*

So said the rogue Oracle. And the words of an Oracle were truth.

But now his Oracle was dead. She would never See for him again.

Lord Jhanun pondered the prophecy once again. Had he known the girl had a weak heart, he would not have ordered that she be given such a large dose of the forbidden drugs. But her words had been so tantalizing . . .

His fingers smoothed the piece of red paper on the desk, discovering its texture, gauging its precise weight. Each piece of *sh'jin* paper was subtly different. A true disciple revered such individuality.

He made the first fold. "This is a true thing, these—" he hesitated over the uncouth foreign word—"Dragonlords?"

He glanced at the man who knelt a few paces before the desk.

"It is, lord. There are a certain few, far to the north, who are born with the joined souls of dragon and human," Baisha said.

Fold, crease, fold. "And these weredragons—they are able to change forms as do the weretigers that haunt the mountains?" Jhanun asked.

"Yes, lord. But they may change form whenever they wish, not just at the full moon."

Jhanun ran one end of his long mustache through his fingers and shuddered. Abomination! He must calm himself, else the paper would sense his disturbance. Fold, fold, a quarter turn of the sheet . . . "The creature now beneath the mountain—it is not one of these . . . ?"

"No, lord; it is a northern dragon, else it would have Changed and escaped as a human."

"I see," Jhanun said, thinking.

One alone—the Hidden One—means the end of the Phoenix. But four will give you the throne—

A pity the girl died with those words; more would have been useful. How was one more dangerous than four? he wondered. He would get no more; he must gamble with what he had. The crisp red paper hummed as he slid a thumbnail along a crease.

Jhanun said, "The Phoenix must live. You will lure these unnatural creatures to the sacred realm. You know the prophecy; you know what must be done and the best way to do it."

After all, according to the prophecy, the vile creatures were coming no matter what. He would merely make certain that it would happen in the most advantageous manner—for him.

Turn, fold, crease, fold.

Baisha smiled to the precise degree allowed a favored servant to his master. The hands resting on his thighs suddenly turned palm up. They were empty. Then he pressed them together and brought them up to touch fingertips to forehead. Then he laid them palm up in his lap once more.

This time a silver coin lay in one hand.

The Jehangli lord nodded in understanding; the creatures would be tricked. "You're certain they will come?" asked Jhanun.

"Yes," Baisha replied. "They will come, the noble fools."

"So be it." He studied this, one of his three most faithful and trusted servants.

Pale skin, yellowed now, wrinkled and lined; a bald head fringed with thin white hair bleached by the powerful phoenix of the sun: a *baisha*, a foreigner indeed.

The Jehangli lord went on, "I raised you from slavery. I covered you with the hem of my robe though you were not one of the children of the Phoenix. I gave you what your own people denied you.

"Now I give you this task. The journey will be long and hard, the task difficult. Do not fail me." A final fold, a last crease, and a paper lotus of a certain style lay before Jhanun.

"It will be done, lord. I will bring you the required number of Dragonlords." Baisha rose and bowed. His eyes burned with fervor. "I know what will bring them. I won't fail you."

Stirred by such devotion, Jhanun rose from his desk and came around it. Bending slightly, he rested his fingertips on his servant's shoulders, a mark of great favor. "I know you will not fail. Now go; there's much to be done." He let his hands drop once more to his sides.

Baisha bowed once more, backed the required three steps, then turned and strode to the door.

With a satisfied smile, Jhanun folded his hands into his wide sleeves.

It was beginning.

Shei-Luin fanned herself as she watched the tumblers with their trained dogs and monkeys performing in the open space between the two gazebos. She sat by the railing of the Lotus Gazebo in the choicest spot, as befitted her current status as favorite concubine. Her eunuch, Murohshei, stood at her left shoulder, keeping the lesser women from crowding her.

The Lotus Gazebo and its companion, the Gazebo of the Three Golden Irises, stood in the heart of the Garden of Eternal Spring. Winter never came here; the leaves of the plum and peach trees never withered from cold, the bright green of the grass never turned sere and brown. The might of the Phoenix ruled here, a gift to its royal favorite, the Phoenix Lord of the Skies. Or so said the priests who chanted here at the solstices.

To one side sat the Songbirds of the Garden. A group of boys and young eunuchs chosen for the incredible purity and beauty of their voices, their sole purpose was to sing for the emperor whenever he chose to visit the Garden. They were silent now, except for giggles as they watched the performers. They were, after all, just boys.

Shei-Luin hid a smile behind her fan as she glanced at the youngsters. Many rocked back and forth, holding their laughter in lest it disturb his august majesty in the Gazebo of the Three Golden Irises. One boy eunuch, Zyuzin, the jewel of the Garden, had both hands clapped over his mouth as he doubled over in mirth; his three-stringed *zhansjen* lay forgotten on the grass before him as he watched.

For one of the tumblers ran in circles, waving his arms and crying exaggerated pleas for mercy as a lop-eared, ugly, spotted dog chased him. Each time the dog jumped up and nipped at the man's bottom, the man would grab his buttocks and leap into the air, squealing like a pig with a pinched tail.

The Songbirds giggled and pinched each other in delight.

A loud, braying laugh shattered the air. Shei-Luin winced delicately, careful that no one should see it, and looked into the opposite gazebo.

Xiane Ma Jhi hung over the railing, laughing as the ugly dog persecuted its master. He called encouragement to it, slapping the shoulder of the man standing by his side and pointing at the tumblers. The man grinned and said something in return.

Shei-Luin's heart jumped at the sight of the second man. He was Yesuin, second son of the *temur* of the Zharmatians, the People of the Horse, the Tribe; Yesuin, once her childhood love and now hostage to his father's good behavior. How she'd cried when he first came to the palace, knowing what it meant to him to lose the freedom of the plains. She'd remembered all too well what she'd felt when the walls of the imperial palace closed around her. But his misfortune had become her salvation.

Between the Phoenix Emperor and Yesuin was a certain resemblance; the concubine who had borne Xiane had been a woman of the Tribe.

Yet such a difference! Yesuin was all fire and grace; Xiane . . . *Bah; Xiane does not bear thinking about,* Shei-Luin told herself. *He looks like a horse and brays like an ass.*

As if he sensed her thoughts on him, Xiane looked across the lawn into the gilded structure where Shei-Luin sat with the other concubines and their eunuchs, the only males allowed there beside the emperor himself. Their eyes met. He made a great show of licking his lips and leering at her. Shei-Luin's stomach turned; she knew that look. Unless he drank himself into oblivion, he would come to her chamber tonight.

She pretended modest confusion and hid behind her fan, gaze lowered. Later she would send Murohshei to bribe Xiane's cupbearer into seeing that the Phoenix Lord's wine bowl was kept full.

The other concubines tittered. Shei-Luin considered ordering them all flogged. But no; she had not the power for that yet. She must become *noh*, a servitor of the first rank; she must give Xiane an heir.

An heir that he could not give himself. But she had found a way; for she alone knew the ancient secret of the palace. And then . . .

The scene before her changed. The tumblers and their

animals gave way before the female wrestlers that were Xiane's current mania. Shei-Luin sat up straighter.

Not because she enjoyed the wrestling. Far from it. She thought these women hideous beyond belief. They were as ugly as the women soldiers who guarded the harem; big women, solid as oxen, and muscled like them, too.

But this was the fourth troop of wrestlers in the past span and a half of days, and if Xiane remained true to form . . . She watched the women, naked save for loin clothes and breast bands, grapple and struggle with one another, and waited as patiently as she could.

At last! Xiane stood up. A servant ran to take the robe he shrugged from his shoulders. The loose breeches beneath came off next and the emperor of Jehanglan stood clad only in his loincloth. He vaulted over the railing, calling over his shoulder, "Let's have some fun!"

Laughing, the other young men in the gazebo followed suit. For once they were freed of the restrictions of the imperial court, where every move was ancient ritual, every word and glance noted, debated, dissected for insult or weakness.

Only in this garden and among the troupes of entertainers that he delighted in, could the emperor of Jehanglan, Phoenix Lord of the Skies and Ruler of the Four Quarters of the Earth, relax. Shei-Luin felt a momentary pang of sympathy. The Phoenix was cruel, setting this man upon the Phoenix throne instead of making him a performer.

But that moment was lost as she watched Yesuin run lightly across the lawn to stand beside the emperor. Her heart hammered in her chest; it was a wonder that all could not hear it.

They might almost be brothers, they look so much alike standing together!

But similar as the men were in build, it was the thought of Yesuin that thrilled her. The memory of Xiane's body on hers made her feel ill. It amazed her, how differently she could react to two men so much alike.

Neither was tall but both were well-made and athletic.

Xiane's skin was the paler, legacy of his imperial father, and smooth; Yesuin's scarred here and there from the battles he'd fought before coming to the imperial court as hostage. Some of the courtiers cast glances of mixed admiration and disdain at the sight of the scars; when those gazes fell upon the Zharmatian's thigh and the brown birthmark there, they were pure contempt.

So the People of the Horse don't kill their children for every little blemish, Shei-Luin thought fiercely, dismissing those contemptuous glances with an unconscious flick of her fan. *They're not the cowards you are. They don't fear your demons.*

She watched him, and him alone, as he wrestled first with the women, then with any of the courtiers brave—or foolish—enough to challenge him. She knew what was to come.

It happened all in a heartbeat. Yesuin and Ulon, one of the courtiers, rolled across the lawn as they grappled; Yesuin caught his opponent in a choke hold. As if by chance he looked over Ulon's head and into the Lotus Gazebo where no man's gaze but the emperor's might fall. Shei-Luin was ready.

She dropped the fan. *Tonight*, she mouthed, quick as a thought. He blinked. Then Ulon twisted, and he and Yesuin rolled away once more.

It was enough. She would be ready.

Three

As he warmed himself by the brazier at his feet, Haoro, priest of the second rank, received the messenger in the outer room of his private quarters in the Iron Temple.

Before kneeling to Haoro, the man bowed to the small

image of the Phoenix that adorned one wall of the plainly furnished room. Reaching into his wide sleeve, the messenger carefully withdrew a single sheet of rice paper, folded in the form known as Eternal Lotus. A *red* lotus. It was exquisite. Every graceful line spoke of a master *sh'jer*'s touch.

So, Haoro thought as the man held out the message with both hands, careful to never let it sink below the level of his eyes, *it is time*.

He took the paper lotus and held it up, admiring it. His uncle had exceeded himself this time. He would have to congratulate Jhanun. With eyes only for the flower resting on his palm, Haoro tossed the man a token and intoned a brief blessing. "You may refresh yourself at the inn of the pilgrims," he said negligently. "You also have my leave to attend the dawn ceremony tomorrow in the inner temple if you wish. Tell the lesser priests I said so."

Joy spread over the messenger's face. To be allowed to hear the Song without having made the full pilgrimage beforehand was a rare privilege. The man knocked his forehead against the floor three times. "Thank you, gracious lord!"

He crawled backward, touching his forehead to the floor now and again, until he was at the door. Then the man stood up and left.

The moment the messenger was gone, Haoro cupped the paper lotus in both hands.

By this one's color, he knew its message as if it had been set before him in the finest calligraphy.

Be ready.

So—the time had come for the realization of the ambitions he and his uncle shared. *And what*, Haoro pondered, *has my revered uncle devised for his part?*

No matter; he would find out when his uncle made his pilgrimage to the Iron Temple. Jhanun would never set his schemes to paper; this would be for Haoro's ears alone. Again he wondered what his uncle had planned. Whatever it was, it would be bold.

The priest looked once more at the lotus. Had the messenger guessed the import of what he'd borne? The Eternal Lotus was by custom worked only in paper of the purest white. Therefore, this one could not exist.

With a thousand regrets, Haoro let the masterpiece drift into the brazier and watched it burn.

Many spans of days after he started his journey, Baisha stood beside a crude dugout canoe on a desolate beach on the northern shore of Jehanglan. He rubbed his forehead as if he could rub away the lingering effects of the illness that had delayed him. Damn that he'd ever caught the shaking sickness! It had made him late to leave Jehanglan.

"You are certain the Assantikkan ship will be leaving shortly?" he said to the trembling man the temple soldiers had forced to kneel before him. "Answer me or they die." He jerked his head.

"They" were the man's terrified family—a wife and a babe in arms—standing behind him within a ring of more soldiers. Swords pricked the hostages' throats.

"Yes, lord," the man stammered. "They never stay very long—a few hands of the sun. You must hurry." He tried to look back at his family. A soldier seized his long black hair and yanked his head around again. Tears of pain filled the man's frightened eyes.

It mattered not to Baisha. He looked over to the priest from the Iron Temple. "Did your master give you what I need?"

The priest nodded and reached within his robes. When he brought out his hand again, a crystal globe filled it. Inside floated a golden image of the Phoenix. The captive whimpered at the sight of it.

Baisha took it and hid it away inside the ragged and salt-stained robes he had donned a little while ago. "The rest?"

Once more the priest reached into his robes. This time he brought forth a jar of ointment. "Smear this upon your face and hands, and all other exposed flesh. It will redden and irritate the skin so that you'll look as if you've spent days drifting in the boat. Remember to smear some upon your lips, as well; they must be swollen and cracked as if from lack of water."

Grimacing, Baisha took the jar and removed the oiled paper lid. So he must look as wretched as he felt. With a sigh, he scooped some ointment out and smeared it on his bare arm. The priest signaled the acolytes who flanked him to aid.

Soon Baisha was ready. He stepped into the dugout; two soldiers ran to catch the sides and push it out to sea. Baisha picked up the single paddle and set to work, cursing under his breath. The damned ointment was doing its work quickly and too well.

The priest called out, "What about these cattle?"

Baisha barely glanced over his shoulder. "Kill them, of course. We want no witnesses."

He ignored the anguished screams behind him and bent to his work.

Four

To rule the heart of the Phoenix Lord—that was power. Yet what was power if one lived confined? Though the bars of the cage were of carved jade, banded with gold and hung with silk, they were still bars.

Shei-Luin *noh* Jhi turned from the screened window. Her silk-shod feet padded softly against the floor as she went once more to read the message on the desk.

Such an insignificant bit of paper; the merest strip that would fit around the leg of a fast messenger pigeon. But all the world hung in its words.

The emperor is dying. Come at once—Jhanun.

Shei-Luin studied it, tracing the words with a long, polished fingernail. Her finger paused over the signature: *Jhanun*. Just that. No title, no seal, not even an informal thumb print.

Were I as stupid as you hoped, Jhanun, it would have worked. And you would have wrung your hands over my death, vowed vengeance against whoever used your name, and grinned like the dog you are in private.

She could well believe Xiane claimed he was dying; that did not surprise her. A stomachache from green mangoes and Xiane Ma Jhi, august emperor of the Four Quarters of the Earth and Phoenix Lord of the Skies, squalled that he was poisoned.

She'd seen it too often to be frightened anymore.

But whether Xiane was dying or not, it would mean her death to approach him before her time of purification from childbirth was over. Which was exactly what Jhanun wanted. He had lost much of his former influence over the Phoenix Emperor since Xiane had become enthralled with her.

Was Jhanun mad that he thought she would obey—or did he think her a fool? No matter. He would learn. She was not to be taken by such ploys. Fool he was, to place such a weapon in her hands; if Xiane saw this, Jhanun would not escape banishment a second time. She would keep this safe to use one day if necessary.

But that the emperor's former chancellor thought to order her as though she were still a simple concubine—that was arrogance.

And arrogance was not something she need tolerate. Not even from one as powerful as Jhanun *nohsa* Jhi—Jhanun, second rank servitor of the Jhi. Not when she herself was *noh*, first rank. Not when she was the mother of the Phoenix Lord's only "heir," born just three weeks ago.

A cloud of black hair spilled over her shoulder as she bowed her head at a sudden thought. Her hand clenched on the fan beside the note.

Was all well with her son? Xahnu was with his retinue in the foothills of the Khorushin Mountains, sent there to avoid the lowland fevers that carried off so many children every hot season. He should be safe. Even those as ambitious as Jhanun or the faction he headed would never dare harm the emperor's heir—the Phoenix would destroy them.

Even so, she wanted her baby by her side. Tears pricked at her eyes.

No! She must not be weak. Her breath hissed through clenched teeth. She must be the coldest steel—especially if the emperor were truly dying. There would be a throne to seize did that come to pass. A throne that Shei-Luin already had ambitions for.

And Jhanun must be taught a lesson. That he thought to fool her by so transparent a trick angered her. He must be removed from the game that was the imperial court. Without him the Four Tigers would be masterless, scuttling in every direction and none, like a centipede with its head chopped off. They would cease their endless attempts to manipulate the weak-willed emperor. More importantly it would end their attempts to depose *her*.

"Murohshei!" she called. Her voice rang in the airy pavilion like a bell. At once she was answered by the slap of bare feet against the polished wood floors of the hall as her eunuch obeyed the summons.

Murohshei—slave of Shei. Idly she wondered if even he remembered what name he had carried long ago, before being given to the then-child Shei-Luin for her own.

The eunuch entered the room. He fell to his knees before her, forehead pressed to the floor. She stood silent a moment, pale hands clasped before her, holding the fan of intricately carved sandalwood and painted silk like a dagger.

"Murohshei." Her voice was clear and sweet.

The eunuch looked up at her.

"Murohshei, I desire the head of Jhanun."

"Favored of the Phoenix Lord, Flower of the West," Murohshei said. "It shall be done. However long it takes, it shall be done." He touched his forehead to the teak floor once more.

Shei-Luin smiled. She imagined Jhanun's head on a pike outside her window. It would look very well indeed.

Then, as it had done all too often of late, the earth trembled violently. Shei-Luin staggered, would have fallen had not Murohshei sprung to her aid.

The Phoenix was angry once again.

Five

The dragon flew rapidly to the north, urgency in the rapid beating of its wings. Soon it dwindled to little more than a speck in the brightening sky.

Maurynna paused in the doorway to the balcony, wondering which Dragonlord was abroad so early and with such pressing need. She knew it for one of her kind and no truedragon; whoever it was, he—or she—was much smaller than her soultwin Linden's dragon form. And even he, she'd been told, was no match for a truedragon.

She finished wrapping the light robe around herself and continued into the new day, considering what this early-morning flight might mean.

She'd caught only a glimpse, just enough to tell her that the dragon was dark, either black or brown. Jekkanadar or Sulae, perhaps? She knew they were both black in dragon form; but then so were a few others. If brown, well, there were too many it might be to hazard a guess. Maurynna pursed her lips in frustration. She was too new at Dragonskeep to know her fellow Dragonlords by sight in both of their forms.

Ah, well; no doubt she would find out eventually. She would put it from her mind and enjoy the early morning. It had always been her favorite part of the day.

The thought brought back a memory of the sea and the

feel of her ship beneath her feet; she pushed it away and concentrated on what was before her. This was her life now.

The mountain air was still cold with the passing night; she shivered but made no move to go back inside. Instead she marveled at the colors of the mountains as the light spread across them, reaching bright fingers across the great plateau to the Keep.

First came the grey of the mountains' granite bones peering through their skin of earth. Then, as the growing light flowed down the mountainsides, it revealed the pine forests standing guard between frozen peaks and living valley below, hidden now in the morning mist. Below their windswept green ring blazed the autumn leaves of maples, oaks, aspens, and many other trees Maurynna couldn't name, turning the valley walls into a tapestry of frozen fire that inched downward day by day.

Autumn in Thalnia, her home country, never announced itself with such a fanfare of color, nor did it begin so early. Maurynna refused to think of what was to follow: snow that would bury the passes until the spring, trapping those who could not fly inside Dragonskeep. She would *not* think of that; she would think only of the beauty before her.

Remember how you dreamed of this when you were a child listening to Otter's tales before the fire.

How she'd dreamed, indeed—and now it was real. Joy blazed in her heart. She, Maurynna Erdon, was one of the great weredragons.

Maurynna Kyrissaean, a sleepy voice corrected in her mind. *Your dragon half would not like to be neglected*, the voice added with a chuckle. *She's a most opinionated lady—for all that she won't speak to me, Rathan, or anyone else.*

Maurynna made a wry face at the reminder, then concentrated; mindspeech was another thing new to her. *I'm sorry. Was I shouting again?* As always when she used mindspeech, she felt what she could only describe as an "echo" buzzing in her skull. It made her want to open her head and scratch.

Only a little; no further than me, anyway. You're doing much better. What are you doing up so early, love?

On the heels of his words, her soultwin Linden Rathan padded out onto the balcony in his bare feet. Linden's long blond hair was tousled, his dark grey eyes still heavy with sleep. He rubbed at them, yawning. Maurynna caught a glimpse of the wine-colored birthmark that covered his right temple and eyelid—his Marking. He wore only a pair of breeches against the chill.

Maurynna shivered at the sight and shrank into her robe.

One eyebrow went up as he smiled. "Are you cold? Silly goose, did you forget you could call up a heat spell now? Come here."

She went happily into his arms, turning in them so that she could look out over the mountains once more. Sometimes there were advantages to forgetting one was a Dragonlord, she told herself smugly as she pressed her back against her soultwin's broad chest. Linden must have called up a heat spell even before getting out of bed. Someday such things would become second nature to her, but for now she was content to stand with Linden's chin resting on the top of her head, his arms warm around her, and gaze out at the mountains that were her new home.

Yet try as she might, she could not think of them as home. They were beautiful, yes. But they were not the refuge of her heart. She admitted it to herself: she wanted the *Sea Mist* back.

I'd only just become a captain, she thought sadly. *It was still all bright and shiny and new.*

And the thought of being trapped in the Keep for the long northern winter nearly made her scream in panic.

Though she knew it would do her as much good as beating her head against the proverbial stone wall, she had to try once more. "Must we stay here? I'd like to see my family and friends in Thalnia one last time. I never had a chance to say good-bye to them."

Linden sighed and rubbed his cheek against her hair. "I'm sorry, dearheart, but you know what the Lady has decreed. She's concerned because you can't Change; she feels it's safer for you here. Besides, there is the matter of Kyrissaean."

Ah, yes; the matter of Kyrissaean. The recalcitrant, irritating, inexplicable dragon half of her soul. Who refused to speak to any Dragonlord or even another dragonsoul, yet always lurked in the back of Maurynna's mind. Who would not let Maurynna Change, who kept her earthbound and chained to the Keep.

Damn Kyrissaean. It would be long and long indeed before she forgave her draconic half.

Maurynna fumed. "I hate being coddled. And you're coddling me—all of you."

"Yes," Linden agreed equably. Maurynna wondered if he guessed how tempted she was to kick him for it. "We are; I am," he went on. "It's been far too long since there was a new Dragonlord. And I waited far too long for you, love. Bear with us."

And if you all drive me into screaming fits because you're smothering me? Then what? But she held her tongue; the last thing she wanted to do was fight with Linden first thing in the morning. Especially not when he nibbled her neck so gently.

Eyes closed, she let her head fall back against his shoulder to make it easier for him. His hands slid upward. Oh, yes; a fight could wait at least until after breakfast.

But when, much later, they reached the great hall where the meals were served, something drove all thoughts of argument from Maurynna's mind.

A young man stood with his back to her. As tall as Linden, though not as broad of shoulder and chest, he conferred with Tamiz, one of the *kir* servants. His hair glinted red-gold in the late morning sunlight that poured through the tall, narrow windows. He wore it in the Yerrin fashion, as Linden did his: shoulder length save for a long, narrow clan braid hanging from the nape of his neck and down his back. But where Linden's braid bore the four-strand pattern of a noble and was bound with the blue, white, and green of Snow Cat clan, this man sported Marten clan's black and green tying off the three-strand braid of a commoner.

Curly, reddish hair was common among Yerrins, and Marten a large clan. It might be anyone. Still . . .

Tamiz nodded, a sudden grin appearing on her short-muzzled face. She beckoned the man to follow. The set of shoulders and head was distinctive, but it was the horseman's walk that gave him away beyond a doubt.

"Raven!" Maurynna gasped. Then, louder, "Raven—what are you doing here?" She ran across the wide floor.

Raven stopped, looked back over his shoulder; his face lit up at the sight of her. "Beanpole!" he cried as he caught her in a hug.

Maurynna hugged him back, forgetting that she was now much stronger than she had been as a truehuman.

"Ooof!" Raven wheezed in surprise.

"Oh, gods, Raven—I'm sorry. I forgot," Maurynna said, laughing in delight. What was her best friend in all the world doing here?

Raven avoided her eyes. "So did I," he said at last. "I'm sorry, Your Gr—"

Maurynna went cold. Not from Raven. Please—not from the boy she'd traded black eyes and heartfelt secrets with all her life. She couldn't stand it.

"Finish saying it, lad, and you'll be lucky if all she does is knock you down," Linden said as he came up. He clapped Raven on the shoulder. "Remember me? We met when you were a child. When did you arrive?"

"Late last night, Dragonlord." Raven bowed, then stared a moment before blurting out, "But you're not as tall as I remember, my lord."

Linden laughed. "And you're not as little as I remember. You'll certainly not be sitting in my lap anymore. Otter warned me a while ago that you'd grown. Speaking of him, isn't your disreputable great-uncle awake yet?"

"I kept him up last night," Raven said with a smile.

"No excuse for him—not today," Linden said. "Lazy

wretch. Tamiz, if Otter's playing slugabed this fine day, tell him I said you could pour a bucket of cold water over him to rouse him. Dragonlord's orders, in fact."

Tamiz laughed and went off. There was a wicked glint in her eye.

Oh, my—she wouldn't, would she? Maurynna turned back to find Raven staring at her.

"So it's true," he said.

"Yes." She swallowed. Why was her mouth suddenly so dry?

Linden said nothing, only shifted so that their shoulders lightly touched.

"I used to tease you about your eyes, that they were a Marking because they were two different colors," Raven said. His voice was flat and tight. "I never thought I was right." A long silence, then, "You won't ever come home again, will you?"

There was pain in the words, and resentment. But what hurt most were the unshed tears she heard. Raven shifted his gaze to Linden. A long look passed between them.

"Ah," said Linden at last. In her mind he said, *I think there was more on Raven's side than just friendship, love. You two had best talk. Take him to an out of the way corner; I'll see that you're not disturbed.*

Confused, Maurynna said, *What do you mean, 'more than—'*

Talk to him, Maurynna.

And Linden left them alone. Maurynna studied Raven; it was like facing a stranger. "This way; we can talk over here." She hoped she didn't sound as lost and lonely as she felt.

He followed her without speaking. She led him past the Dragonlords and visitors dining at the tables to one of the little alcoves that opened off the great hall. Cushioned benches lined the walls, a cozy place for friendly confidences. It seemed a mockery. She took a seat; Raven hesitated as if unsure whether he should sit in the presence of a Dragonlord.

Maurynna glared at him. He sat. Not as close as he once would have, but not as far away as she had feared.

A stiff silence hung over them for too many long, awkward moments. Then Raven asked again, "Will you ever come back?"

Maurynna bit her lip. "They'll have to let me go sometime—I hope."

Raven started in surprise. "They're keeping you here against your will?"

She shrugged. How to explain this? And should she? She knew that Dragonlords kept secrets from truehumans lest those few against the weredragons find a weakness to exploit.

But this was Raven. She made her decision and damn anyone who disagreed. "Not quite. The Lady says it's for my own safety. The Lady would likely also say I shouldn't tell you, but . . . I—I can't Change at will. Something . . . happened the first time. It was agony and it's not supposed to be. Now Kyrissaean, my dragon half, won't let me become a dragon. She stops me whenever I try. Did you hear what happened in Cassori a few months ago, the regency debate?"

Raven nodded. "Yes, we got the news when the *Sea Mist* came home to Stormhaven. How the Dragonlords had been called in as judges, how you'd gone to trade there and that you'd become—" His voice nearly broke. A moment later he went on, "I heard it from Master Remon himself."

The breath caught in Maurynna's chest at the mention of Remon, her former first mate. She wondered what he'd thought when the Cassorin ship caught up to him with its astonishing news. Never mind that; what had the poor man thought when he'd discovered she was missing from the *Sea Mist*? She tried to imagine how Remon had felt those few months ago, when he'd walked into her cabin only to find it empty, the open window bearing silent witness to his captain's disappearance.

Raven continued, "Great-uncle Otter told me more last night; that's why we were up late. But he didn't tell me everything; he said some was your tale to tell me if you wished."

It was a moment before she could say, "We didn't discover the problem, you see, while we stayed in Casna. Then, because Linden's Llysanyin stallion, Shan, had escaped from Dragonskeep and made his way to the city looking for Linden, we decided to ride back. It seemed the best thing. Shan made it plain he wouldn't tolerate another rider and Linden was afraid I'd overreached myself on my first flight. The other two Dragonlords who had served as judges with Linden, Kief Shaeldar and Tarlna Aurianne, agreed. They flew home the day we set out.

"All seemed well, but one day on the journey Linden wanted to show me something from the air. It was to be a short flight, nothing difficult—and that's when it happened. I couldn't Change again."

Maurynna swallowed against the memory; even remembering that pain made her queasy. "Not that time, not the other few times I've had the courage to try. It's never happened before in anyone's memory, and there's no mention of such a thing in any of the records. Both the Lady of Dragonskeep and her soultwin Kelder, as well as the two archivists, Jenna and Lukai, all of the *kir* recorders, Linden and I have spent candlemarks searching them. I keep hoping there's an answer. . . ."

"I'm sorry for that," Raven said. "Truly sorry." Then, "You and . . . Linden Rathan . . ."

The pain was back in his voice. Maurynna suddenly understood. "Raven—did you . . . did you think that we would . . . ?"

He turned bright red. "Um, ah—yes. I did. We got along so well, you see. And we always made up after a fight. We wouldn't have to get used to another person's ways, either of us."

"Raven, you don't really consider *that* a good reason to get married, do you?" The thought boggled her. She had certainly never felt that way.

Raven said, "It's better than some."

She had to admit that he was right; indeed, it was a better reason than many she'd heard.

But it still wasn't enough.

"It seemed so simple. We've always been comfortable together," he finished plaintively.

If she'd had something to hand, she would have thrown it. Marry her because she was comfortable, like a pair of old boots? Because it was the easy way out? She considered hitting him but remembered her new strength in time. "What!"

From the corner of her eye she could see heads turning to look. She didn't care. "Oh, for—! Raven, yes, I love you, you idiot, but as a friend." She relented at the hurt in his eyes. More gently she said, "Don't you see? We would never have had a chance. Even if we had married, I would've had to leave you once I'd Changed the first time. Try to understand; I don't just love Linden. He's part of me—literally. That's what being a soultwin means. I would have had to go to him no matter what."

He nodded. His voice shook when he spoke. "I'm trying . . . to, to understand. I do here," he touched his forehead. He continued, "But I'm having trouble here," and laid a hand over his heart. "I'd always thought we'd marry, then go to my aunt in Yerrih. You know she wants me to help her raise and train her horses."

The words shocked Maurynna. Not *his* plans; she'd known about *his* plans for years. But she'd never known of his plans for *her*.

Feeling the walls of the Keep closing in, she got slowly to her feet. Suddenly there wasn't enough air to breathe. "You thought I would give up the sea so easily? That I could?"

She couldn't believe it. Raven of all people should know what having her own ship meant to her. He had dreams as well. "Hang it all! Don't any of you understand?"

Maurynna bolted from the alcove and out of the great hall. Through the halls of the great Keep she ran, ignoring those who called to her, running like a deer from the hounds, running from those who wanted to bury her alive.

It was silly and childish—she knew that. But neither could she sit still any longer. She'd suffocate.

One of the postern doors was open to the fresh morning air. Maurynna went through it like a bolt of lightning looking for a target.

She didn't stop until she reached the paddocks behind the Llysanyins' stable. A leap that she wouldn't have even considered trying a few short months ago carried her over the fence to her Llysanyin stallion's yard. She landed, nearly lost her balance, but caught herself before she sprawled facedown in the dirt.

Boreal trotted to her, snorting concern over his person's agitation. Maurynna buried her face in his mane and wrapped her arms around the dappled grey neck, fighting back tears of frustration and anger.

I can't be a proper Dragonlord, I can't be a ship's captain at all, and everyone wants to either wrap me in wool like some glass bauble or drag me off to fulfill their dreams. Damn it, it's not fair!

Boreal draped his head over her shoulder and pulled her closer. Encouraged by the intelligent animal's sympathy, she drew breath to recite her list of grievances.

With my luck, the horse will be the only one who understands. The sudden thought made her break into a wry, hiccuping laugh.

"Thank the gods," a lilting—if ironic—voice said behind her, "you're not crying after all. I had wondered about that from the way you fell on Boreal's neck. For alas and alack, little one, you're a wee bit large for me to cuddle on my lap for comforting."

Raven hunched miserably on the bench and stared at the stone floor. He'd well and truly made a mess of it. He hadn't thought Maurynna would take it like that.

The worst of it was that he wasn't quite certain what he'd said wrong.

The arrival of two figures at the entrance to the alcove

caught his attention. One was a silent Linden Rathan; the big Dragonlord's face was unreadable. The other was his great-uncle, Bard Otter Heronson. And he was anything but silent, blast him.

"You always did have a way with words, lad," his kinsman said cheerfully.

Raven reminded himself of the penalties for wringing a bard's neck. Then he reminded himself of the penalties for helping a kinsman out of this life. It was barely enough. "Thank you," he snapped.

"Did you really come all this way just to fight with Rynna once more?" Otter asked, all wide-eyed innocence.

"No," Raven said. "No, I didn't, curse you." Then, remembering the reason he'd journeyed here, he bit his lip in worry. Looking once more to Linden Rathan, Raven said, "Dragonlord, I came here as an escort. The man I guided claims that a truedragon is held captive in Jehanglan!"

"What?" Otter exclaimed. He shook his head. "Boy, you missed your calling—you should have been a bard!"

Linden Rathan's eyes went wide. "A truedragon? That's impossible."

Raven shook his head. "No, Dragonlord. It's true. My word on it. There's a truedragon prisoner in Jehanglan— and they're destroying it."

It was not often that the full *Saethe*—the Dragonlords' Council—met in such haste and need. But the few words the Lady had had last night with this stranger had prompted her to call this gathering, and to send her soultwin Kelder winging north.

The members of the *Saethe* filed into the Council chamber. As each entered, they looked curiously at the one seated to the Lady's left. She knew what they saw—a man obviously ill, his hair hanging lank around the parchment-colored skin of his face, a heavy shawl wrapped around bowed shoulders—and wondered what her fellow Dragonlords thought, what rumors were flying about.

When all were present, the Lady stood and said, "This is Taren Olmeins, a Kelnethi who was shipwrecked in Jehanglan. He has been a slave there these past thirty or so years. But recently he learned something that prompted him to a desperate move: to escape Jehanglan and bring us word of a great wrong done there."

She waited for the murmurs to die down. Good; judging by the surprise in faces and voices, there had not been many rumors—yet. She found herself wondering what a certain small Dragonlord might have heard.

"And what is this wrong?" asked Kyralin Sanraelle.

"Taren, I think it best if you tell them yourself," the Lady said.

Taren bowed his head and, using the arms of the chair, pushed himself up. For a moment the Lady feared the effort would be too much for him. She stretched out a hand to stay him.

He turned a smile of dazzling sweetness upon her. "Nay, Lady, do not worry about me. This illness and I are very old enemies. It is but a weakness that will be made well by seeing justice done."

A murmur of approval ran around the table at Taren's gallant words. The Lady saw the members of the *Saethe* lean forward to catch this unlikely hero's tale.

"As your Lady has already told you, my lords and ladies, I was shipwrecked in Jehanglan many years ago, and taken as a slave. It was a hard life and cruel, for my master was not a gentle man, but I didn't dare the Straits of Cansunn— what the Jehangli call the Gate of the Phoenix—once more. For though life may be hard, it's still sweet, and I feared that I would not pass those waters a second time and live.

"So I lived my life as content as I could be, acting as an overseer of one of the salt mines my master was in charge of for the imperial court. For, you see, all salt there belongs to the Phoenix Emperor. Those mines are a favorite place to send those who have somehow offended the throne. Those so punished often don't live long; the labor is hard.

"So it was that one day a renegade priest came to work

the mines. Because he was both learned and old, I begged for him to work under me as a clerk. To my surprise, my request was granted. We became good friends and Taorun told me many things I never knew before—such as the true source of the power behind the Phoenix Throne."

Taren paused and wiped his brow with a trembling hand. The Lady signaled her personal servant, Sirl, the only one allowed in this meeting. The *kir* brought forth a goblet of rich Pelnaran wine already poured against such need. He offered it to Taren with a bow. Taren whispered a barely audible "My thanks" and sipped.

A faint trace of color came to his cheeks. Taren drank again and went on, his voice a little stronger, "Your Graces, have you ever heard of the Jehangli phoenix? It is said to be a giant bird, more beautiful than the dawn, that lives for a thousand years. When those thousand years are past, the phoenix builds a great fire upon Mount Rivasha and casts itself within. There it is consumed by the flames and is destroyed—or so it seems. For from the ashes of the old, there rises a new, young phoenix.

"Taorun told me that, a little more than a thousand years ago, one of the Jehangli Oracles—children who have a gift of true prophecy—told a Jehangli noble how he might found a dynasty to last for all time. For there is a short span of time, before its feathers have hardened enough for flight, that a young phoenix might be captured if one has power enough.

"Taorun wouldn't tell me all, for he still held to the deepest of his oaths, but that noble did capture a young phoenix, and thence became emperor. The anchor of that prison of magic was a fell beast, Taorun said, a creature of nightmare. He had seen it once, and feared to speak of it. But I was curious, and one night, I admit, I plied him with rice wine to loosen his tongue. At last he described the 'horrible monster' chained beneath the Iron Temple of Mount Kajhenral.

"My lords and ladies, can you imagine my horror when I realized he spoke of a northern dragon? He didn't know what it was, for there are no dragons in Jehanglan. And worse yet . . ."

Taren stopped, biting his lip, as if what he would say next was too painful. Silence filled the room. At last he drew a shuddering breath and went on in a whisper, "I said nothing of this to the young man who brought me here, for I feared it would upset him too much. His friend, you see, is a Dragonlord.

"But Taorun also told me that in the oldest records, there were reports that the creature had been seen to change from man to dragon!"

Silence turned to uproar.

One arm still about Boreal's neck, Maurynna looked around, laughing in truth now. While "little one" was the traditional endearment for the newest Dragonlord—which she was—its use by this particular weredragon was always a delightful absurdity.

Lleld Kemberaene perched on the fence like some red-capped bird, eyeing her with exaggerated innocence. "Ah. That's much better. Yes, it would look silly, wouldn't it? All of you trying to fit into my lap."

The tiny Dragonlord stood up on the top rail and walked along it as easily as if she walked the road leading to the Keep. She sprang into the air, somersaulted, then landed in the paddock and stretched to her full height, roughly that of a ten-year-old child—a somewhat undersized ten-year-old.

Maurynna applauded; Boreal stamped a foot and snorted in appreciation.

"Thank you, Your Grace, and noble Llysanyin steed," Lleld said, bowing with a flourish.

Maurynna knew that before Lleld had Changed for the first time, the other Dragonlord had been a tumbler and a juggler in a band of traveling entertainers. "You've lost none of your old skills, have you?" she asked with a touch of envy, remembering her own awkward landing. Would she herself be so lucky, or would she forget how to read wind and wave if immured in Dragonskeep for too long? A sudden need to hear the crying of gulls shook Maurynna to her soul. Her breath caught in her chest once more.

"No, I haven't forgotten," Lleld said. "Too useful when traveling as a truehuman." She tossed back her mane of fiery red hair. "Is Linden being an ass again?" the tiny Dragonlord demanded, hands on hips.

Maurynna swallowed against the lump in her throat and half smiled. "That's not entirely his fault, Lleld, and you know it. Though I do wish he would argue with the Lady on my behalf; she won't listen to me.

"No," Maurynna continued. She paused to start a braid in Boreal's long black mane. "This is something different. A friend of mine from before I Changed—my oldest friend, we grew up together—is here. I—I had never realized that he expected we would one day marry. I suppose I should have; I just never thought of him as anything beyond a friend."

"You wouldn't have," said Lleld. "Our dragon halves know we're waiting for someone else and hold us back. We have to be pushed into a marriage."

The braid tangled somehow. Maurynna picked at it. "As Linden was, centuries ago."

"Just so." Lleld cocked her head. "But I'd guess that you weren't grieving for your friend's hurt feelings, not the way you looked when you came over that fence. So what is it?"

Tangle turned to knot under fingers suddenly grown clumsy. Maurynna said bitterly, "My *best friend* Raven was another one who thought to keep me from the sea." The betrayal hurt. It would, she knew, for a long time. She explained Raven's erstwhile plans for them.

Lleld listened, shaking her head in disbelief. "Rynna, we've got to find you a way to sail again. For the sake of the gods, you were captain of your own ship! I freely admit I don't understand why you wish to leave the mountains— I've never heard of a Dragonlord or a truedragon who didn't love them—but, blast it all, it's not fair to you."

Despite the comfort of hearing her own feelings echoed,

sudden misgivings danced down Maurynna's spine as a wicked smile crept across the little Dragonlord's face. She'd known Lleld for only a couple of months, but on the journey to Dragonskeep she'd heard many a story from Linden about the madcap bundle of trouble that was the smallest Dragonlord. "No one that tiny," he'd complained again and again, "should have that much mischief in them."

"Lleld," Maurynna said in alarm, for if even half of Linden's stories were true, this Dragonlord was known as "Lady Mayhem" with good reason. "What are you planning now?"

"Oh, nothing," Lleld said airily. Then, "Did you see Kelder flying north this morning? I've an idea about that."

Something else to worry about. Lleld and her "ideas"— or "wild guesses" as the others called them when they were being polite—were all too well-known in the Keep. And, as Lleld gleefully reminded Linden at every opportunity these days, sometimes she was even right.

Now Maurynna knew which Dragonlord she'd seen this morning. Yet what errand could send Kelder Oronin, soul-twin to the Lady of Dragonskeep, winging north so urgently? All she could think of to say was a weak, "Oh?"

Lleld needed no further prompting. She launched enthusiastically into her latest incredible theory. Maurynna could only shake her head as she listened, too stunned to protest.

A shadow swept over them, was gone. They looked up; Maurynna recognized the Dragonlord she'd seen flying north candlemarks ago. The sight of Kelder Oronin hardly slowed Lleld down. She continued lecturing.

Then even the voluble Lleld was stricken silent.

Maurynna gasped. As five giant shapes flew in close formation not far overhead, a second shadow slid over them, this one taking heartbeats to pass by. Their hair whipped about their faces in the sudden wind. Boreal snorted in fear and quivered under Maurynna's arm.

"I thought they hardly ever left their mountains," Maurynna whispered in awe.

"They don't," Lleld said. Her eyes looked ready to pop from her head. "So what are they doing here?"

Six

Shei-Luin slipped through the tunnels of the palace like a ghost, her slippers of heavy felt making no noise to betray her upon the smooth wooden floor. Now and then she paused when something in a conversation caught her ear. She would listen for as long as it interested—or profited—her. Then she would be away again. She hadn't much time before she must be in the gardens, and she must still bathe and dress. What if Xiane should take it into his idiot head to come to her chambers before the gathering in honor of Riya-Akono's feast day? The edge of danger just made this, her only freedom, more exciting. She giggled behind a hand.

These hidden passages were *her* palace, ever since she had discovered them when Lura-Sharal was mistress of the chambers of the favorite concubine. She and her sister had explored them together until Lura-Sharal's death.

Now those chambers—and the secret they held—were hers. She spared a moment to wonder which emperor had had the tunnels built, and why, as she put her eye to the secret peephole in her sleeping chamber.

It was empty save for Murohshei guarding the proper entrance and her maid, Tsiaa. Shei-Luin released the catch and slid the door open.

Murohshei leaped to his feet and helped her pull off the old Zharmatian tunic and breeches she kept for her secret expeditions. Tsiaa clucked at the dirt on her hands and scrubbed at one cheek.

"Into the tub with you, Favored One," the maid scolded. "Aiyee, that you should run about like a Zharmatian hoyden! What a trial you are to me! See how white my hair is because of you?"

But the scolding words were affectionate. Shei-Luin patted Tsiaa's cheek and said with false innocence, "But I *am* a Zharmatian hoyden, Tsiaa! Don't you remember?"

She laughed and ran to the bathing room ahead of the only woman she named friend.

Moments later, Tsiaa was scrubbing her back. Shei-Luin heard Murohshei setting out the new robes that Xiane had sent for this day, the finest she'd ever had.

For today was the first time that Xahnu would be taken from the near fortress that was imperial nursery and shown to the court.

Especially to one member of the court.

The tumult had died down at last. Now there were a dozen discussions going on and what sounded like a hundred disagreements. Taren, sitting once more, leaned back in his chair and closed his eyes.

Just as the Lady wondered if she should have him escorted back to his rooms, she felt something brush against her mind. Recognizing that touch, she held up her hand; when she had the attention of most of those in the room, she tapped her two middle fingers against her forehead— the Dragonlords' signal for mindspeech. The last of the clamor died away.

I am here, Jessia, the mindvoice said.

I thank you, Morlen, for coming so promptly.

Thee are welcome. The others and I will await thy coming in the Field.

The voice faded from her mind. The Lady stood. "Early, this morning I sent Kelder north to request Morlen the Seer to come and lend us his counsel upon this matter. He's here."

Nodding approval, the rest of the *Saethe* also rose from their chairs. The Lady beckoned Sirl, who came at once. She said, "Taren, we must go to the Meeting Field. Sirl will help you, if you will."

Brow furrowed, Taren said, "Meeting . . . ? Lady, who is this Morlen?"

"One of the wisest of the truedragons, and a good friend to the Dragonlords. I value—Taren, is something amiss?" she demanded, for the look that filled the man's face verged on panic.

"I would rather not. . . ."

Nebulous suspicions rose like ghosts. The Lady asked, "And why not?"

"Because . . ." A sudden, shy smile of unbelievable sweetness greeted those suspicions and made them tawdry. "Because I'm but a slave, the lowest of the low, and not fit to meet one of the lords of the sky, Lady. I'm unworthy."

Touched, the Lady said, "You are a slave no longer, and that you were will be of no importance to one such as Morlen. What does matter is your bravery in finding your way to us so that this wrong may be righted. But I wish him to hear the tale from your own lips. He may have questions for you that I cannot answer."

For a moment she thought he would refuse; his eyes would not meet hers. Then, so quietly that had she been truehuman she doubted she would have heard him, Taren said, "As you wish, Lady," and drew the shawl closer as if seeking comfort in its warmth.

As she watched him shuffle from the room, leaning heavily on Sirl's arm, a belated realization struck her: the man was unused to dragons of any sort! Of course he was frightened; most truehumans were, save those born and bred at the Keep.

It was clearly too long since she had moved in the world outside Dragonskeep. She followed, shaking her head and thinking.

"Explain," Linden said shortly. He was in no mood to be generous with this boy. He didn't know what Raven had said to his soultwin, but he'd seen her face as she bolted from the hall. The boy had upset her badly.

And now he was trying to tell them a tale wilder than a

drunken bard's. Linden folded his arms across his chest and waited.

First the boy flushed with anger; then his face went dead white. He'd heard the challenge, then. Well enough; let him make good his wild words.

Raven slowly stood up. He crossed the short distance between them, halting a bare pace from Linden. Hands gripping his belt, he stared hard into Linden's eyes, his face set in lines of fury.

Linden returned the glare. Yet for all his anger, he had to admit the lad had courage. There were few willing to risk the anger of a man as large as he was, even those who mistook him for a truehuman. But to challenge a Dragonlord, one known to be inhumanly strong and fast, took more bravery than most had. Or, Linden allowed, far fewer wits.

But whatever other faults he might have, Raven did not look stupid. He did look ready to try his luck in a fight. Linden made ready to catch the fist he was certain was coming. From the corner of his eye, he saw Otter raise his hands as though to push them apart.

Instead, Raven earned Linden's grudging respect by keeping his temper on a tight rein and replying calmly—if in a voice hard with anger—"As you wish, Dragonlord. I don't know if Maurynna's told you aught about me, or what you remember from meeting my father so long ago, but he's a wool merchant in Thalnia now."

Linden nodded. "I remember." And he did, very well; the memory was still bright and clear. What seemed so long ago to Raven's truehuman perception of time was not long ago at all to him. "You were three, perhaps four years old. It was before he left Yerrih for Thalnia; he thought he could do better there, Thalnia being so much closer to Assantik. Did he succeed?"

"Yes," Raven said. "And that's why I'm here today and not someone else—if someone else had even believed Taren.

"Just before Maurynna left Thalnia late last spring, my father sent me to the highlands to bring home the wool

sheared from our flocks there. I was furious; he had promised that I could go with Rynna and my great-uncle on
board the *Sea Mist*. But at the last moment our factor, Black
Oak—he who was to fetch the wool and bring it to Tanlyton—became ill. Instead of sending my stepbrother, Honigan, who was eager for it, my father insisted I go in Black
Oak's stead."

A spasm of anger passed over Raven's face. "I don't
think Black Oak was ever ill; nor was there any reason to
pass over Honigan for the trip. I think my father was afraid
I'd never come home once I was so close to Yerrih. So he
broke his word to me."

Linden mindspoke Otter. *Would he do that?*

*Which one—Raven or Redhawk? In truth, a good chance
for either. The boy hates the wool business and is no trader.
He has a gift for working with horses and an aunt in Yerrih
who's eager to welcome him and that gift. And as for Redhawk . . . Much as it grieves me to say this of a kinsman,
yes, he would break his word to the boy. He wouldn't think
such a promise binding; he would say he knows what's best
for the lad.*

Despite his irritation, Linden felt a sneaking sympathy
for Raven. He'd trained horses long ago and still kept his
hand in here at Dragonskeep. And although he and his own
father had fought like snow cat and wolf, at least his father
had appreciated his talent and let him do what he loved.
Besides, Linden thought wryly, *Da made a good profit from
it*.

Raven continued angrily, "I did my duty. I brought the
wool train to Tanlyton, the big port on the southern coast,
and saw it into the hands of our Assantikkan partners,
House Mimdallek. In return, they gave into my hands a
madman—so they said—who'd been picked up drifting in
a dugout boat in the Straits of Cansunn."

Otter frowned. "Cansunn. It sounds familiar somehow."

"Cansunn?" Linden said, surprised. He knew he'd heard
of the Straits. But it was another name that niggled at his
memory, something Jekkanadar, Lleld's soultwin, had said

long ago as part of a story from his past. What was that
tale . . . ?

Part of it came back: that the deadly waters between Assantik and the fabled land of Jehanglan were considered
unlucky even to name. That only madmen and the favored
few attempted to sail them. That the madmen never came
back and sometimes the favored ones didn't, either. And
this Taren was found there?

Now he remembered the other name. "The Haunted
Straits?"

"The same," Raven answered. Bit by bit the anger faded
from his voice as he went on, and the tight set of his shoulders relaxed. "It's a long story, but eventually Taren came
into the hands of a Mimdallek friend of mine, Iokka, the
one who bought the wool from me. He had to be rid of
Taren before anyone in Assantik found out about him. So
he brought the man with him when he set sail for Thalnia."

Why? Linden wondered. *And why not just kill the man?
It would have been simpler.* "It was that important? So why
trust you with the secret?" he asked, keeping the skepticism
from his voice with an effort.

A shrug. "Iokka was desperate; he had other things on
his mind. We've helped each other before. He had little
time and less choice."

"And this Taren is the one you escorted here?" Linden
asked. In Otter's mind he said, *If his father is so against
Raven's getting anywhere near Yerrih, it's surprising he let
the boy go.*

I'm wondering about that, was the slow reply.

Ah. Aloud, Linden said, "So it was Taren who told you
about the . . . truedragon held captive in Jehanglan?"

This time he couldn't keep the doubt from his voice.
Bind a truedragon? No and no and no yet again. Such a
working wouldn't need a band of mages. It would need an
army of them.

And that was an impossibility. There was truth behind
the old children's tale about the six silly mages arguing the
best way to churn cream into butter. Mages were a noto-

riously independent and fractious lot. One might as well try herding a business of ferrets as convince a band of mages to agree on a working; it would be as likely to succeed, far less frustrating, and much more amusing.

No, this was the stuff of a madman's ravings. It had to be.

"You think me a fool for believing there's a truedragon held captive in Jehanglan, don't you?" The anger was back.

Linden drew breath to answer, not certain how to soften his words or even if he should. But before he could speak, another voice broke in.

"If that's the tale, Raven, then there are more fools about than you, I think."

Maurynna came up to them, Lleld a scant half pace behind. The smallest Dragonlord's eyes were wide, and for once she was silent. Indeed, she looked too stunned to speak.

That did not bode well. Not at all. Linden drew a deep breath.

Maurynna finished, "There's five truedragons just landed."

With Murohshei and Tsiaa following, Shei-Luin went to the wing of the palace that housed the imperial nursery. The guards at the entrance gaped at her; then, remembering that such as they were not allowed to look upon a concubine of the emperor's, they looked away in confusion. When one made to drop his pike across the entrance to block it, she struck his wrist with her fan.

"I come for my son," she said coldly.

The pike moved aside slowly.

But one of the women inside had heard. Lady Hami, wife of Imperial Minister Musahi, came to the door.

"You're not supposed to be here," she said with a frown. "Lord Xahnu's nurse will bring him to the gardens."

"No," Shei-Luin said. "I shall bring my son myself. Now stand aside, so that I may go to him."

"But—!"

Shei-Luin stared her down. Though Lady Hami's lips thinned to a tight line, she moved aside. Shei-Luin entered the nursery.

The main chamber was a bright room, with walls painted with images of the Phoenix. In one corner sat musicians, playing softly to soothe whatever childish tantrums might arise. Maids scurried about, picking up toys.

Standing in the center of the room, directing the maids, stood Xahnu's nurse, a woman of middle years. She held the Phoenix heir on one hip.

Xahnu caught sight of his mother and crowed with delight. The nurse turned, frowning when she saw Shei-Luin.

"I'll take my son," Shei-Luin said, holding out her arms. Xahnu lunged for her.

The nurse pulled him back. "It's not done so," the nurse huffed. "I am his nurse, and—"

Shei-Luin smiled, all silk and steel. "And I say that this day is a holiday for you. Give Xahnu to me. Or must I speak with the Phoenix Lord?"

Fear entered the nurse's eyes then; it was well known in the palace that Shei-Luin was the jewel of the emperor's eye. One did not make an enemy of the First Concubine— not if one could avoid it. She passed Xahnu to his mother.

Shei-Luin kissed her son's forehead as his sturdy arms wrapped around her neck. "Come, little phoenix, today is a day of celebration," she crooned to him.

As they left the nursery, Shei-Luin wondered if she could talk Xiane into letting her visit Xahnu. By custom, the concubine-mother of an heir was not allowed to visit, and thus influence, the future emperor.

Xiane's own mother had been allowed to raise him, but only because she'd been a favorite of the old emperor, and because Xiane had had two older brothers; no one had ever thought he'd become emperor.

As Shei-Luin carried the precious weight of her son through the halls, she vowed to see that custom changed.

*   *   *

"May the gods help us all," Linden said, realizing what the arrival of the five truedragons might mean.

Otter said slowly, "It could be true?"

"It would seem the truedragons think so," Maurynna answered. "Else, from all I've heard of them since coming here, I see no reason they would leave their mountain holds otherwise."

"One of them is old Morlen the Seer," Lleld said, her voice barely audible.

"What!" Linden exclaimed. "Morlen? But why is he— why are any of them here?" If it hadn't been for the shock in Lleld's eyes, he would have suspected her of having him on.

"I don't know," Maurynna said. "We just saw them come back with Kelder."

"Kelder?" Linden asked, confused now. When had Kelder gone to fetch truedragons?

Maurynna frowned. "Didn't you see him—oh, of course not. He was out of sight by the time you came out on the balcony this morning. And then I forgot because—" She stopped.

Linden hoped his face was not as red as his soultwin's.

Otter coughed and hid a smile behind his hand. Raven's lips thinned to an angry line. The stunned look left Lleld's face; a knowing grin replaced it.

"You were . . . distracted?" she sniggered.

"Lleld!" Linden said in warning. It didn't stop her snickering. He ignored her in the hope that she would stop. If the gods were kind it might even work.

And rivers would flow uphill.

Perhaps—"I owe you an apology, Raven. I'm sorry. If you're willing, I'd like to hear the full story, as much as you know about the captive truedragon," Linden said to the young Yerrin.

That did the trick. If there was one thing Lleld prized above all else, it was news; she turned greedy eyes on Raven. "The captive truedragon—you know about it?"

Linden held up a warning hand. "Lleld, not so fast. We've still no proof—"

Lleld ignored him, reached up and caught Raven's elbow. "Have you broken your fast yet, lad? No? I'm Lleld Kemberaene. Here, come and tell m—tell us everything as you eat."

Surprise banished the smoldering anger in the boy's face. "As you wish, Dragonlord," he said politely to Lleld as she propelled him to a table.

It was a while before they were all settled and food was brought to them. Then Jekkanadar arrived and they had to find a place for him as well, Lleld excitedly telling him about the truedragons. At last they were ready. To Lleld's obvious frustration, Raven began eating. At Linden's nod, Otter took pity on Lleld and acquainted her, Maurynna, and Jekkanadar with what he and Linden already knew.

At one point while his great-uncle spoke, Raven picked up a slice of bread from the serving platter and looked around; without a word and hardly taking her eyes from Otter, Maurynna pushed one of the three little clay jars on the table to the young Yerrin. The blue-glazed one, not the green jar with rose-hip jam or the brown with elderberry in it. Raven accepted the jar without examining the contents and dribbled honey onto his bread. It was plain that that was what he'd expected.

It filled Linden with unreasoning jealousy that Maurynna would know Raven's wants, that she would be so aware of him, that Raven would accept it with no surprise. *Don't be stupid*, he told himself. *Of course she knows what he likes on his bread, just as he no doubt knows what she likes with hers. They grew up together, damn it!* The cold reasoning did little to douse the fire of resentment. He glared at the younger man.

Raven chose that moment to look up from his food. First surprise, then a smug half smile lit his face. *Soultwin you may be, Dragonlord, but even you cannot erase what went before*, that smile seemed to say. And when Maurynna laid her hand on the green jar, Raven said, "Rose-hip?"

She smiled as she ladled a good-sized dollop of jam on her bread, and said, "Of course; what else?" before turning her attention back to Otter.

Otter finished his tale and turned to his own food. Linden felt the tickle in his mind that meant Otter was trying to mindspeak him. He opened the contact.

No bard is he, diving into his meal like that, Linden said in half-hearted jest, struggling to keep jealousy from coloring his mindvoice. That he didn't quite succeed was evident in the puzzled look in the bard's eyes.

Luckily Otter chose not to ask any awkward questions. *Not even an inkling of it,* was all he said. *Any true bard with an audience this eager would have starved before disappointing them. Ah, well.* He scooped up a spoonful of frumenty and ate with relish.

One's enough for any family, Linden replied.

Linden, is all well? Otter asked, pausing before eating another spoonful.

Linden ignored the question. Silence fell over the table as they ate.

When Raven did start talking, it was so sudden that most of them jumped. "House Mimdallek had Taren from certain, ah, merchants who occasionally have business in northern Jehanglan."

Linden raised an eyebrow. Well and well; it seemed that some not of the favored—and no doubt official and heavily taxed—few made it to and from Jehanglan.

"Merchants, my ass," said Lleld. Then, with relish, "Smugglers! What fun." She rubbed her hands together in glee.

Raven blinked in surprise at the little Dragonlord, then laughed. All at once Linden saw the little boy he'd played with years ago.

"Gilliad al zefa' Mimdallek," Raven continued, "is the Second of her House in Nen dra Kore, the Assantik port on the Straits. She's both greedy and superstitious; one was nearly the death of Taren, the other saved him. She got Taren out of Nen dra Kore before House Mhakkan—and

her own First, Bendakkat—found out about him. House
Mhakkan is a very powerful House, the only one that trades
with Jehanglan; the only one allowed to—officially. They
hold the imperial grant.

"Taren was passed through Mimdallek hands the length
of Assantik and shoved onto a ship bound for Thalnia. My
friend Iokka brought Taren to me in Tanlyton; he and all
the others along the line were convinced Taren was mad.
He sounded it, too."

"Lucky for him," Jekkanadar said. "It's ill fortune to kill
a madman."

"Just so, Dragonlord. Likely that was all that stopped
Gilliad from ordering Taren killed—that and the fact that
in betweeen his bouts of raving he'd invoked Danashkar to
avenge him if she had him killed. It stayed Gilliad's hand,
but must have burned her toes, as Iokka says, not to have
had Taren's throat cut somewhere along the line. She
wishes her associations with these particular trading partners to remain very, ah, discreet."

Otter snorted. "I can imagine."

Linden rubbed his chin. "Is it so important?"

Maurynna, next to him, nearly choked on her tea.
"Very," she said.

Raven rested his elbows on the table and said kindly—
too kindly—"Why, Dragonlord; surely you must know
about the Dawn Emperor's grants of—"

Before Linden could pin the snide brat's ears back for
him, Lleld broke in with, "Obviously he doesn't and neither
do I. I've never been to Assantik, I don't think Linden has
either, and neither of us was ever a trader. So, hang it all,
just *why* is it important? And who is Danashkar?"

"Danashkar," Jekkanadar said, "is a particularly nasty
Assantikkan demon you don't want angry with you. He's
not invoked lightly. The mad are his children, and he'll
hunt you down if you kill one of them. All the stories agree
you're lucky if you take only a few years to die in his
domain. I'll let one of those who understand trade explain
the emperor's grants."

Smirking at Linden, Raven began an answer, but jumped in his seat and shut his mouth again. He darted an angry glare first at his great-uncle to his left and then across the table at Maurynna. Linden generously hid a satisfied grin behind his mug of tea.

Maurynna said, "For the most part, the Dawn Emperor doesn't interfere with the great trading Houses. It's the Council of Ten which, as my Assantik 'cousin' of sorts complains, writes the laws and causes all the problems. But sometimes an emperor will, for reasons best known to him or her, grant a House the rights of trade for a particular commodity, or with a particular port.

"My family is allied with House Bakkuran for trade, Lleld, and that same 'cousin' once told me that a very, very long time ago, the empire of Jehanglan closed itself off from the outside world."

Jekkanadar nodded agreement. "A long time to truehumans, yes; it was not long ago as Dragonlords reckon time. It happened in my father's time; he was a child but he remembered. Even at the campfires of the lowest was told the tale of how an emperor of Jehanglan closed his land against the world and became the first Phoenix Lord. No one knew why. From what I understand, it's still not known."

Raven whistled. "You Changed that long ago, my lord? But that's—"

"A little more than a thousand years ago," Jekkanadar finished. "As Dragonlords go, I'm still considered young, my friend.

"The realm of Assantik was in chaos from decades of the Wars of the Witch Kings, the armies still battling back and forth across the land when I first Changed. I was only a goatherd then, but even the most humble of us were caught in the fighting." Jekkanadar paused and absentmindedly fingered the thin scar running along his dark cheek. "It was almost a hundred years later that one man took the throne and his children and children's children held it after him. That was Nerreklas the Black, first emperor of the Third Dynasty.

"Nerreklas's great-great grandson tried to break Jehanglan's isolation. He was greedy, and the tales of Jehanglan's wealth had not lost in the telling over the years. He raised a navy to conquer them. That navy was destroyed.

"Only one sailor returned from the Straits of Cansunn. Tied to a spar, he was found by a fishing boat and brought before the emperor. He lived long enough to pass on the message he had been given, then died."

Jekkanadar stopped. His last words hung on the air.

"And?" his soultwin demanded at last.

"What was the message?" Maurynna asked at the same time.

"Oh, well done," Linden heard Otter whisper under his breath. "Give me this man and I'll make a bard out of him." The words were so soft that only the unnaturally keen hearing of a Dragonlord would have heard them. From Jekkanadar's wink, Linden knew he'd heard them as well.

"The message? Let me see if I can remember. . . . Ah! I have it!"

Good thing, too, Linden mindspoke Otter, *or else Lleld would have had his hide for boot leather, the tease.*

Jekkanadar continued, his voice low and menacing, "From the tales I heard when I went back to Assantik many lives of men afterward, it was plain that the man was under some spell, kept alive until he could deliver his message. For he said, 'Those who challenge the Phoenix, shall die by the Phoenix's might,' and fell dead, the flesh rotting from his bones in that instant."

"Eeyahh," Lleld said with a grimace. "That's gruesome."

Her soultwin smiled, pure wickedness. "That's how I heard it. It's best told around a campfire in the dead of night, though. One can imagine all sorts of awful things then." He hitched one hand across the table like a monstrous spider, fingers veering this way and that as if they searched for something. "All *sorts* of things creeping up on you out of the darkness beyond the firelight."

A long moment of silence; then, "Feh," said Lleld, pushing her plate away. "I don't think I'm hungry anymore."

Linden wholeheartedly agreed.

Four of the truedragons stood together to one side of the Field; they were the guard of honor, made up of kinswyrms of the fifth and largest truedragon, one honored and venerated among his kind and the Dragonlords.

Morlen the Seer swung his long neck around as the Dragonlords and Taren approached. *Well met, little cousins,* Morlen said. *And good day to thee, truehuman Taren Olmeins; we thank thee for thy sacrifices in bringing us this news.*

Taren's face turned an alarming shade of grey. *Be gentle with him, Morlen*, the Lady said privily to the Seer. *Like most truehumans, he's terrified of dragonkind, and has been ill as well.* Aloud she said, "Taren, please tell Morlen all you told the *Saethe* earlier."

Once more Taren Olmeins recited his news. But this time he told it quickly, the tale skinned and cut to its bones. Now and again the Lady elaborated in mindspeech for Morlen's benefit.

When the man was done, Morlen thought for a time, then asked, *Have thee any idea who it might be, Jessia?*

Taren's gaze darted between them.

The Lady replied, "Kelder and I talked it over last night. While Taren says that the captured dragon is a Dragonlord, it's not proved to our satisfaction. We all know, old friend, how false tales can spring to life. It could well be a truedragon. More of your kind have disappeared than of mine. That's why I asked you to come.

Still, the tale could be true. Besides the many truedragons that have gone missing, there are a few Dragonlords who have disappeared over time, Dragonlords that thee have no idea what befell them. This could be any one of those. But I agree—this is most likely one of my kind.

"I tell you, the one beneath the Iron Temple *is* a Dragonlord!" Taren interrupted. His hand flew to his mouth as if to chastise his tongue for its rudeness. A faint flush of color crept into his cheeks.

The Lady nodded, accepting the tacit apology. "It's possible. And there's one we consider more likely than any of the others, for he was fascinated with exploring new places before . . ."

*Before his soultwin, Carra, died. Thee should not look so surprised, Jessia; thee were thinking of Dharm Varleran, were thee not? I remember him wandering the northern wilds after her death. I spoke with him then; Dharm talked of releasing his hold on life so that Varleran would come into his own, and he would be free to follow Carra to the other side. It would also explain a Seeing I had long ago; I could not understand it then, for it was confused and faint, but now . . . *

"If it is Dharm, then this is the concern of the Dragonlords."

No, Jessia, even if this is the one we once knew as Dharm Varleran, then Dharm has already gone on to the other side. That means it is Varleran who is imprisoned—and if that is so, it is the concern of the truedragons. And even if it is not he, there are truedragons it might well be. As thee said, we have also had our disappearances. Either way, I think we must claim this burden. I will bring it before our council, and we will decide what must be done.

A gasp from Taren brought her attention back to the man. "You will send Dragonlords, will you not?" he demanded of her.

She frowned at him, surprised by his vehemence. "Lord Morlen has claimed this—"

"No! Where he's kept, the truedragons wouldn't be able to reach him. You must send Dragonlords!"

Then, as if his last outburst was too much for him, Taren staggered and would have fallen had not Sirl caught his arm. "I apologize, I have no right to speak so. It's just . . . I—I must lie down," he whispered.

The Lady nodded and beckoned to Sirl. She watched the *kir* help Taren back to the Keep. "Now why . . . ?"

Morlen chuckled in her mind. *Did thee not say he was terrified of my kind? Perhaps he feared thee would send him as our guide and that one of us would mistake him for a rabbit one dark night.*

Once again the Lady spent a rueful moment reflecting that she had forgotten too much about truehumans—especially if a truedragon had to remind her of their foibles!

"What of Taren's claim that you won't be able to reach the prisoner?"

Where one dragon has gone, others may follow. This is not the task of thy kind, Jessia. Let us hope it need never be.

"I suggest you stop pushing your luck, young man," Otter said as he entered the chambers that were his whenever he came to Dragonskeep. He pushed the door closed behind him. "That was cowardly; you know Linden won't clout you because you're my great-nephew, and Maurynna's friend."

Raven looked up from sorting through his packs, his eyes flashing in anger. "Ah—because he's a Dragonlord I'm supposed to be so careful of Linden Rathan's feelings? Just lie down and accept that he's stolen my lass from me? I thought you always said he preferred being treated like any man, not like some godling. Well and well, I'm treating him better than any other man who'd taken Maurynna from me. I haven't Challenged him, have I?"

Otter shook his head in disgust. Was the boy really such a fool? That wasn't the Raven he knew. "You ass. Do you really think you'd have a chance against Linden in a duel? Likely he could have scrubbed the stable floor with you even before he'd Changed. Or did you forget that he's a warrior trained from the cradle, O my idiot nephew, and you a trader with but a few tricks with the sword? Remember those he was a mercenary under—the woman who became the greatest queen Kelneth ever had, and the man whose reign as High Chief was a golden age for Yerrih. It would have been no contest even then. Now, of course, he could merely pick you up and throw you into a wall to have done with it.

"But never mind that. I wasn't talking about Linden. I was talking about Maurynna. Don't think she didn't notice you sniping at Linden all morning long. Just a short while before I left them she was planning to have a little . . . talk with you."

At least the boy had the sense to wince at that. There was hope for him yet. A flaying with the sharp edge of Maurynna's ire was not a thing to court. Nor would she hesitate to clout the fool boy, either, as the young idiot knew well. She'd done it many a time back in Thalnia.

"Rest easy; Linden was talking her out of it when I left them. Why, I don't know. I've always told him he's too easygoing." Otter crossed over to his favorite chair and sat. He looked down at Raven squatting over his bundles on the floor and tugged his beard in frustration. "Didn't you listen to a single blasted word of the tales I told you and Maurynna when you were both sprats? Linden didn't 'steal' Maurynna from you. They were given to each other by the gods more than six hundred years ago."

The bard sighed. "If you only understood how lonely he was, waiting for his soultwin to be born, afraid it would never happen."

" 'The Last Dragonlord,' " Raven quoted softly. "He was named so in the stories, wasn't he?"

"You remember that much at least," Otter said. "And don't you dare tell me you'll be as lonely as that pining away for Maurynna. It's not the same thing as missing literally half your soul. Not at all."

A sheepish grin told him Raven had indeed been clutching that bit of romantic idiocy to his bosom.

"Ass," Otter said again, but this time with affection. "There's someone else for you, you'll see. And just for my curiosity—did you tell your father and stepmother you were coming here?"

Raven bit his lip. After a moment, he said, "No."

"They must be worried sick—especially Virienne—wondering what's happened to you," Otter said quietly.

"The letter should have reached them by now. Remember how desperate I said Iokka was? You'll understand just how much when I tell you that he agreed to give that letter into Da's own hand in return for my getting Taren as far away from Assantik and anyone in House Mhakkan as I could," Raven said smugly.

Otter laughed until the tears came. The boy wasn't the trader his father was, thought the bard, but that time he'd driven the bargain of a lifetime. "That was cruel, lad," he said with real admiration.

"Iokka thought so, too," Raven said with a grin. "But I kept my part of it. House Mhakkan doesn't trade this far north. And how could I trust poor Taren to anyone else? There he was, ill with the shaking sickness and so glad to have someone he could speak Yerrin to once more—" He stopped, cursing himself.

"He's Yerrin?" Otter asked, surprised. Taren wasn't a Yerrin name.

"Yes," Raven said. The words came reluctantly. "Taren Willowson is his real name—

"Willowson?" Otter interrupted, tugging at his beard. "There's something—bah! It's gone again; getting old, I guess. But my apologies—go on."

"His mother was Kelnethi, but his father was Yerrin and he was raised in Yerrih. Mountain Eagle clan. He's as Yerrin as you or I, or Linden Rathan for that matter. It's just—"

Suspicions sprang up in Otter's mind at Raven's hesitation. "No clan braid? He's outcast, then?"

"It was cut off in Jehanglan; he was a slave there. Please don't tell anyone he's Yerrin," Raven pleaded. "He wants to pass as Kelnethi. Though it wasn't his fault, he feels his honor in his clan has been broken. He's ashamed to face them. That's why he asked no word be sent to his kin."

"I see," Otter said. And he did. Unconsciously his hand groped for the long, narrow clan braid hanging down his back. He sighed in relief. Silly, that; of course it was still there.

Gods—not even your worst enemy will cut off your clan braid. Your head, perhaps, Otter thought. *But not your braid.*

The mere thought made him queasy. To cut off a clan braid was to brand one as *parna*, outcast, unclean. It was done to break a man or woman's spirit, declare them dead to the clan and to all honor. "But of course the Jehangli wouldn't know," he said. But whether to reassure himself or Raven, he wasn't certain.

"They did. He'd told them, you see, what it meant. They cut it off anyway," Raven said. He looked ill. "Taren said they laughed when they did it."

"Oh, gods," said Otter, sickened. Never mind that it wouldn't mean the same thing to the Jehangli as it would to any Yerrin, even anyone in the Five Kingdoms. The thought still turned his stomach.

Raven grabbed his packs and pushed to his feet. His voice rough, he said, "If it's all the same to you, Greatuncle Otter, I'd like to switch to that outside sleeping chamber. I like the view from the window. But it's a long way down, isn't it?"

"Very," Otter said. "This end of the Keep is built right on the edge of the cliffs. Nothing between you and the valley floor but thin air and lots of it. Don't get any ideas about sneaking out that way as you used to do when you'd slip out to the big fair at Stormhaven."

Raven laughed. "I always thought you knew about that. Thanks for never giving me away to Da."

Otter watched his grandnephew stride from the sitting room. Aye, the boy was hurt now but he'd recover. He was young and, though he'd deny it hotly, had never been desperately in love with Rynna. There was some other girl whose life Raven would make miserable, Otter thought with a smile.

Raven's disembodied voice floated in from the small sleeping chamber. "He's calling himself Taren Olmeins.

That was his mother's name. Never let on that you know he's Yerrin, please; he'll feel like an outcast around you because you're a bard, and he doesn't deserve it. He's a fine man, risking his life to help that dragon."

"You're too late, Lleld," said Nevra, one of the *kir* guards barring the way to the Meeting Field beyond the Keep.

"What do you mean?" Lleld asked. Blast it all, she knew she should have tried sneaking in from the other side. There was a well-hidden trail through the rocks there so narrow that only a child—or a very undersized Dragonlord—could fit through it. A pox on Jekkanadar for tricking that promise out of her! Now how was she to know what the truedragons had discussed with the *Saethe?*

She tried to see past the stocky guard. "Where's the one from Jehanglan—Taren?"

Nevra said, "The truehuman went back to the Keep some time ago. He didn't look at all well. The Lady and some of the *Saethe* are still talking with Morlen and the other truedragons, but most have left. The council is over, they told us."

Damn, damn, damn! "So what did they say? Is there really a truedragon held captive in Jehanglan? Or is it one of us? Either way, who is it?" Lleld demanded in an agony of frustration. How maddening! She could see the truedragons and a few Dragonlords talking, too far away for even another Dragonlord to hear what was discussed. "What do the truedragons say?"

Nevra shrugged. "The truedragons are keeping their own counsel. My guess is they'll— There they go!"

Five mighty forms erupted from the ground. Wing stroke after powerful wing stroke gained them the upper air. As she watched them rise, an idea came to Lleld.

She raced away. A quick run along the paths seaming the plateau of Dragonskeep brought her to the stone stairway leading to the wide landing cliff. She raced down it, leaping from step to step like a demented mountain goat.

The landing cliff was empty; no one had thought to balk

her this way. She let herself flow into Change. Scant moments later Lleld, now a small dragon the fiery red of her hair, launched herself from the cliff.

It wasn't long before she had the truedragons in sight. She followed at a discreet distance.

What on earth are they doing? Lleld asked herself in surprise a short while later. For the truedragons had flown only until they were out of sight from the ground at Dragonskeep, and were spiraling down to land in a meadow that she knew was nearby. *They* must *be stopping to discuss something. Perhaps I could sneak in—*

Sneak in? How? You'd glow like a beacon fire against that green grass. Then all one of them has to do is sit on you, and it will be all over, Jekkanadar said. *Remember your promise.*

It was only for the council in the field, she complained but veered away. It would be just too embarrassing to have her soultwin arrive and drag her off. Especially in front of truedragons. And he'd do it, too.

But one way or another, curse it, she'd find out what was going on.

Seven

Bless Lady Riya-Akono, Shei-Luin thought. On this one day of the year were all women honored; on this one day of the year could the concubines of the harem mingle freely in the palace gardens with the lords and ladies and courtiers.

Besides, she had always felt a special kinship to the Lady. Were they not both of the West? True, the legends said nothing of where Lady Riya-Akono was from, but it must have been the western lands, for it was only there that two names were used. Then there was the Lady's bravery and resourcefulness. That, as far as Shei-Luin was concerned, was the final proof. Jehangli women had no spine.

Yes, it was only right the Lady of the Moon be honored.

As it was only right that she held the place of special honor among the Phoenix Lord's women. The courtiers and the lords and their ladies made way for her as Shei-Luin walked with studied nonchalance through the exquisite beauty of the gardens. For by her side Tsiaa now carried little Xahnu, her son and heir to the Phoenix Throne. Behind her walked Murohshei.

Her son—though not Xiane's. She turned to gaze fondly at her child. Dressed in robes of the imperial yellow, little Xahnu looked solemnly about him, dark eyes big in a face already losing its baby roundness. His hair shone glossy black in the sun as he gifted her with his sweet child's smile.

Shei-Luin's heart flamed with love for her son. He was worth every risk she'd taken in conceiving him. She thanked the Phoenix that she'd been able to bear this child to the man she loved—the same man who walked toward her now with Xiane's arm around his shoulders. Shei-Luin sank gracefully to the ground at the emperor's approach. Her servants did the same. She watched them through lowered lashes.

They were nearly to her when a flash of black and red buzzed around Xiane's head. To her astonishment, he turned as white as bleached silk and jumped back, shaking. Yesuin swatted at the insect. It flew off.

She heard Yesuin murmur soothingly, "Only a fly, Xiane, the kind that looks like a bee. Don't worry. All's well."

And what means this? Shei-Luin thought in astonishment. *Phoenix! Don't tell me the man is afraid of a little bee!*

It was all she could do to hide her contempt as the color crept back into Xiane's cheeks.

A moment later it was as if nothing had happened. "Have you seen my son yet, cousin?" Xiane brayed as he threw

his arm around Yesuin's shoulders once more and led the
Zharmatian hostage to where she waited, eyes lowered now.

Shei-Luin dared to look up. She met Yesuin's eyes.

"Handsome, isn't he?" Xiane went on.

"Just like his father, my lord," Shei-Luin said.

Xiane laughed in delight. "Ah, Precious Flower! Tell me,
Yesuin, am I not a lucky man? A healthy, handsome son
and the most beautiful woman in Jehanglan is his mother
and my concubine. What man could ask for more?"

Yesuin said, "You are indeed lucky, my lord." There was
a touch of pain in his voice that Xiane, she knew, would
never hear.

Indeed, even now the emperor turned to clap his hands
for everyone's attention. "To the Garden of Eternal
Spring!" he called. "I have arranged for a special treat in
honor of my son!"

Shei-Luin lowered her eyes once more. It would not do
to burst out laughing. But even as the laugh bubbled to her
lips, it died. There had been more than simple pain in Yesuin's voice. But what?

Her breath caught in her chest as she thought she recognized it.

It—it could not have been remorse. Could it?

Maurynna couldn't decide who was the more annoying,
Linden or Raven. How dare Raven snipe so at her soultwin!
It wasn't as if he had any claim on her beyond friendship.
As far as she knew, Raven never had approached her Uncle
Kesselandt to seek her in marriage or had asked his father
to do so. So what right had he to act so proprietary?

She grabbed Boreal's saddle and blanket from their rack
and his bridle from its hook, and went out to the paddock
for the second time that day. The stallion trotted up at her
whistle. "How about a nice, long ride, boy? Before I kick
a certain best friend in the ass for being such a pain in
mine."

Boreal's ears flicked back and forth as he tilted his head

at her. But he came up and stood quietly as she smoothed the saddle blanket over his back.

Linden was almost worse, Maurynna thought. Raven deserved a good thumping or at least a severe dressing down. Yet Linden had refused to do it.

But it was herself she was most annoyed with; she'd let Linden talk her out of pinning Raven's ears back. She set the saddle down carefully on Boreal's back, fuming as she fumbled with buckles and straps she still wasn't at home with; one of the stablehands usually saddled Boreal for her. At least she didn't have to worry about getting a bit into his mouth.

Her mind insisted on going over the argument yet again. . . .

"Why?" she'd demanded. "He was trying to start an argument with you all morning long. Why didn't you just rake him over the barnacles and have done with it?"

"Because," Linden replied, "I understand how he feels. He's lost you, Maurynna; lost you completely and he knows it."

"He never had me to begin with," Maurynna snapped back, "save as a friend. I was never *his*, damn it all. If anyone owned me, it was my House. Only they had the right to order my life. And damn Raven anyway for expecting me to blithely give up my ship and follow him to Yerrih."

Linden opened his mouth, shut it again.

"Don't say it," she warned him. "I didn't try to get back to the *Sea Mist* because of the Lady's orders. Now that I'm a Dragonlord, she is to me what Uncle Kesselandt is to House Erdon—the Head of this, my new 'House.' "

She stalked around the room, then stopped and rearranged the apples in the big pottery bowl with a violence that sent two of them flying onto the table. She scowled at them, then grabbed one and bit into it, tossing the other back into the bowl; she resumed prowling as if she might find the source of her ill humor lurking in a corner and squash it. All at once she stopped. "Linden, would you have made me give up the *Sea Mist* if the Lady hadn't?"

"Made you? No," Linden had said, shaking his head slowly. "Tried to convince you to—yes." Then, "I'm sorry, but I would have."

She'd walked out of their chambers at that. He hadn't followed. . . .

The last buckle was done; Maurynna swung into the saddle and gathered up the reins. "Let's be off, shall we?"

Boreal broke into a trot.

Very well then, Lleld thought. *No doubt Morlen and the other truedragons wouldn't like it if I barge in on them. But what if I just happen to meet them as they fly north again? Just out for a bit of exercise, that's all, and such a coincidence if I should run into them on their way home.*

She swung wide of the valley so that no one inside would see her and dashed north as fast as her wings could take her.

So here she was, riding their favorite trail—alone.

In truth, not quite alone, Maurynna had to admit. But special as Boreal was, he was not the company Linden was.

Or usually is. How hard, Maurynna wondered, *would he have tried to talk me into giving up my ship?* She was perversely glad she'd closed herself off to him when she'd felt him "searching" for her earlier. She was not ready to talk to him yet. And perhaps would not be for some time. She would see.

The trail grew steeper. Maurynna concentrated on lifting herself from the saddle slightly to ease Boreal as he surged up the incline. *That's right; get up into a half-seat—No! Don't stand in your stirrups*, she could "hear" Linden say as he always did at this point.

This was the worst bit of the trail—especially coming back down—but the mountain meadow on the other side was worth the trouble. In a few moments it would open before her, a green haven of lush grass and wild flowers, cupped within a circle of ridges. She and Boreal would drink from the spring that bubbled from a cleft in the sheer stone at one side, then she'd strip the Llysanyin's tack from him and let him wander while she scrambled over the tumbled boulders at the edges of the meadow. There were imprints of seashells in some of the rocks. She had hopes of someday finding a perfect one small enough for her to take back. She didn't feel quite so far from the seas that she loved, somehow, among these rocks; those same oceans had once been here.

She tried not to think of how these trips usually ended when Linden was with her. Instead she concentrated on the ride. Just around this bend in the trail, and down again—

Boreal stopped, neighing in surprise. He spun halfway around, ready to bolt, before Maurynna threw off the paralysis of astonishment that had briefly claimed her. "No!" she cried and clamped her legs around him, holding him. She knew that if Boreal fell prey to his fright, she'd never stay on him, not on this trail. "Don't be silly—they won't eat you!" She hoped the stallion listened.

Boreal stopped, hooves braced wide, trembling in every limb, but now set as immovably as the boulders around him. Maurynna patted him on a shoulder suddenly dark with sweat, and dismounted. It seemed courteous, somehow.

The five truedragons seemed even more surprised than she. Almost as one they reared back, heads well up, watching her as she approached, leading the stallion by the reins. Boreal followed, reassured now that he was not to be dinner.

There was something wrong, Maurynna realized, in the wary poses, the uneasy glances they cast at each other. She stopped, unsure what to do next. Surely these lords of the sky could see she was no threat?

Greetings to thee, the largest said at last.

"Greetings, my lord dragon," Maurynna replied. "I hope I'm not disturbing you, my lords."

The truedragon who had spoken came forward a few steps. That would be Morlen the Seer, Maurynna guessed.

He was huge, larger than any living creature she'd ever seen; she wondered if even the fabled great whales of the far northern seas could compare to this truedragon. The slanting light of the sun washed over his dark green scales. The other four came up until she stood ringed by truedragons. She looked at each one in turn, tilting her head far back to do so. Boreal crowded her back, no doubt having second thoughts about the wisdom of all this.

Like Dragonlords, the truedragons were various colors. Morlen was a deep moss green; of the others, two were brown, another a deep sapphire blue; the fourth was the color of amethyst and Maurynna knew she looked upon the flower of dragonkind, Morlen's granddaughter, Talassaene.

A sudden—memory?—of a white-haired young woman with violet eyes overwhelmed Maurynna. Someone she didn't recognize, had never met, but knew nevertheless. The gaze of the violet eyes haunted her. She knew that if that woman—Who is she? And how do I know her?—had been a Dragonlord, she would have been the color of the truedragon standing here. . . .

Maurynna shook her head to clear it of the unbidden image, and returned to her study of the first truedragons she'd seen close up. As with Dragonlords, their belly scales were the color of old ivory, and their eyes shone with ruby fire. They were utterly beautiful and dangerous beyond anything she'd ever met with.

She faced Morlen once more.

No, thee do not disturb us, Morlen said. His mindvoice was kind, if perplexed. **We have merely paused on our journey back to our own mountains.**

Ah; no doubt they were discussing whatever they'd learned from Taren, then. It would account for their initial wariness; she'd surprised them. Still, the smoke curling from the nostrils of two of the other truedragons sent chills up her spine. The magic that made her a Dragonlord was proof against all harm from fire—all, that is, save dragonfire. If these were so minded, she would die here and no one would be the wiser.

Should she mindcall Linden? To what end? He could do nothing against the likes of these; even the smallest of these truedragons was larger than he was. If the gods meant her to die here nothing would help her. She swallowed, her mouth suddenly dry.

But the look in Morlen's eye was as kind as his mind-voice had been. With a grunt he settled himself in the long grass and continued to study her; the others followed suit. She wondered what went through Morlen's mind.

I am Galinis, one of the other truedragons suddenly said, the brown one to Morlen's left. *These others are Aeld, Aumalaean and Talassaene,* the truedragon contin-ued, pointing with his chin sunwise around the circle, nam-ing the other brown, the blue, and the amethyst dragons. *Aeld, Aumalaean, curb thy fires. They are not needed. And thee are . . . ?*

Before Maurynna could introduce herself, Morlen spoke again.

I see thee, the huge truedragon said. His mindvoice was slow, thoughtful. *But I do not see thee.* Once again he studied Maurynna.

Behind her Maurynna felt Boreal shift, likely sensing her growing uncertainty. Swallowing hard, she took her cour-age into both hands and asked, "What do you mean, my lord?"

These old eyes see thee here before me quite plainly. Morlen stretched out a forefoot capable of crushing a draft horse and touched her cheek with one claw tip, a touch as light as a child's kiss. *I can touch thee. But thee are not there when I look with just my mind. It is as if thee have a cloud wrapped around thee. But because I know thee are here, I may speak to thee.*

There was a hint of—fear? awe?—in the truedragon's mindvoice. No, that couldn't be right. Nothing as insignif-icant as she could inspire such feelings in one so huge and powerful and ancient. Still, Maurynna had the feeling that if he could have, Morlen would have wrinkled his brow in deep thought.

Talassaene, the dragon to Morlen's right said, *Grandsire, perhaps she is the one.*

Morlen swung his great head to face his amethyst-scaled companion. Their gazes locked; Maurynna made no move lest she disturb the silent communion. Then Morlen turned to her once more and said, *So. Are thee, then, the newest Dragonlord? The one none of us sensed?*

"Yes," Maurynna said. "I am Maurynna Kyrissaean."

Ahhhhhh.

The exhalation surged like a wind through her mind. Behind it Maurynna thought she caught a glimmering of understanding. But of what?

Little cousin, Morlen said, *I must admit to a great deal of curiosity about thee and thy dragonsoul. I wish to speak with thy dragon half, Kyrissaean. Will thee allow this? There is no danger to thee, but I would not enter thy mind so deeply without thy permission.*

Maurynna smiled halfheartedly. "My lord Morlen, if you can get Kyrissaean to speak with you, then have at her!" she said with a wry laugh. Maybe this lord of truedragons could talk some sense into her idiot dragon half.

The great head tilted; Morlen looked puzzled. Then, *Very well, little cousin. Perhaps it would be well if thee sat down; it is best if thee can relax.*

Maurynna had her doubts that she would be able to relax while someone she didn't know went into her mind, but she was willing to try. She sat cross-legged in the long grass; at a grunt behind her she turned to see Boreal lowering himself to the ground, crosswise to her. "Thank you, Boreal," she said as she leaned back against him and closed her eyes.

Morlen's touch was gentle, like kitten's whiskers tickling her mind. Maurynna nearly laughed. But in the next instant, agony blazed through both mind and body.

Kyrissaean shrieked in rage, lashing out at Morlen, at the other truedragons, at Maurynna. The breath froze in Maurynna's lungs; she fell to the side, thrashing upon the ground, struggling for air. But the pain only grew worse and breathing impossible. The world turned grey.

Linden knocked on the door to Otter's chambers. The voices inside broke off their conversation. Then came the crisp click of boot heels crossing the floor; a moment later the door swung open.

"Hello!" Otter said in surprise. "What are you doing here, boyo?" He stood aside.

As Linden entered, Raven paused in the doorway of one of the three sleeping chambers off the sitting room of Otter's suite.

Oh, Gifnu's hells, Linden thought sourly. *He would have to be here now.*

"I'm looking for Maurynna," he said. "Is she here?"

"No," Otter said. Then, "Can't you tell where she is? I thought soultwins always knew where each other were, what was happening, that sort of thing."

Raven leaned against the door frame, arms crossed before his chest, listening. Every line of his body screamed insolence.

Linden pressed his lips together in annoyance before answering, "I tried searching for her before. But she's angry with me and shut me out. Since she's not here I'll look to see if Boreal is in the stables; if he's not, then I can guess where she went." The next irked him no end to admit to before that smug grin. "I—Maurynna seems to be unusually aware of me," Linden began.

"So I remember," Otter said, a faraway look on his face. "Even before you two were joined she knew that something was wrong with you back in Casna."

"Just so. For her it's as if she looks through a spyglass; for me, it's as if she's hidden in a fog. Nothing is clear and sharp. I don't understand why it's like this. But . . . Damn it all, I'm feeling . . . nervous? Apprehensive? I think something's worrying her but I don't *know*, blast it."

A satisfied light came into Raven's eyes, and Linden knew the boy had some scathing comment ready. And if

the young pain in the ass came out with it, Linden also
knew this time he'd pin the boy's ears back for him and
make him eat those words. Maybe Maurynna was right. He
took a deep breath, ready to cast restraint to the winds.

And found himself suffocating. He clutched at his chest.

Thee must come at once!

The words exploded in Linden's mind. He staggered under their force; only instinct made him put a hand out, catch
himself on a wall before he fell. The world went grey before his eyes and he knew he was about to black out. Then
suddenly he could breathe once more. He gasped for air,
grateful for the sweet feel of it in his lungs.

"Gods help us! Linden, what's wrong?" Otter cried as he
ran to support Linden. Even Raven, eyes wide and frightened now, came to help.

Linden shook his head. "I don't know. It's—" Unable to
continue, he tapped his forehead with the two middle fingers of one hand.

"Ah. I see. Not now, Raven." The bard waved his great-
nephew to sputtering silence.

Who? What? Linden said to the presence he still felt in
his mind.

Morlen the Seer, the voice said. **Thy soultwin is ill,
perhaps dying; we do not know what is wrong with her.
Come quickly!** The fear in the truedragon's mindvoice was
sharper than an eagle's talons.

Linden thought his heart would turn to ice. *Where are
you?* he made himself ask with a calmness he didn't feel.

**A mountain meadow. It is shaped like a bowl and filled
with wild flowers.**

He knew at once where Maurynna was. Now to get to
her as fast as possible. He staggered for the door, only to
fetch up against the wall once more, his legs shaking. He
cursed. Dear gods, it would take too long to get to the
landing site on the cliffs—especially like this. Then he remembered where in Dragonskeep Otter's chambers were
located.

A deep breath and the worst of the weakness passed.

Linden pushed off from the wall, knocking both truehumans aside. "Something's wrong with Maurynna," he said, desperately recalling the layout of Otter's rooms. A moment later he ran for the sleeping chamber Raven had come from.

Fear beat at Linden as he raced through the small room. He threw the mullioned window open and jumped onto the wide ledge.

The cliff here dropped straight down as if it had been sliced with a knife. The wind whipped his hair into his eyes; he shook it free. Far, far below his sharp eyes caught the glitter of a stream like a thread.

Behind him he heard Otter yell, "No, Linden, you can't! You've said yourself that's too dangerous!"

Gathering himself, Linden gave a mighty leap straight out. His only chance was to get far enough away from the cliff so that the wind wouldn't blow him into the sheer rock wall.

He fell like a stone through the crisp mountain air.

Eight

Xiane's special treat was yet another troupe of entertainers. At least this time she was spared the female wrestlers, though these might be worse, she thought; they were entertainers from the northern lands, hideous to look upon with their pale, fish-belly skins, and hair ranging in color from yellow to brown like animal pelts. When the trained pony finished his counting tricks, and before the rope could be set up for the ropewalkers, Shei-Luin took Xahnu from Tsiaa and walked off with him. Such a thing was never done, she knew, by the noble ladies of the court. Even children who were not imperial heirs were usually given

over to maids and servants to raise until such time as they
had manners and wit enough to hold a conversation with.
But Shei-Luin cared nothing for what the meek court ladies
did. She had been a woman of the Plains—as Xiane's own
mother had been.

And that, she knew, was a large part of her fascination
for Xiane. For he was obsessed with all things Zharmatian;
she was grateful for that even as she used it to her advantage. It meant he treated Yesuin as an honored guest, not
as a prisoner. It also meant that, if she were careful not to
go too far, she could pressure Xiane in ways that no proper
Jehangli woman would even dare to think of. Even as she
twisted him around her finger, he begged for more.

Only Murohshei followed, for he was her shadow. Shei-
Luin took herself deeper into the garden. From time to time,
she paused to listen. Xahnu snuggled against her; she nuzzled him lovingly. He was such a good child.

"Listen," she said, and kissed him, "and I will tell you a
story, little phoenix. Hear now the tale of the lady we honor
today. I will tell it to you just as it was told to me.

"Long, long ago Lady Riya-Akono, wife of the cruel
Dragon Emperor, fled to the moon and rained silver arrows
down upon her husband so that she might save the people
of Jehanglan. But the Dragon Emperor survived her arrows.
Hot for vengeance, he raced along the magical bridge that
she had used to reach the moon, seeking to kill his empress."

She paused. Nothing—yet. So she went on with her tale
because Xahnu seemed to enjoy it.

"Waiting until the Dragon Emperor was nearly to her,
Riya-Akono slashed the bridge with her father's old sword,
knowing what it meant. For though the Dragon Emperor
tumbled to his death, thus ending his cruelties, Riya-Akono
had marooned herself upon the moon. But even knowing
what would be her fate, the empress had not hesitated. And
that is why the throne of the empress is known as the
Throne of Riya-Akono.

"Therefore, upon this day and no other, the temple choruses sing the praises of the Lady of the Moon. On no other day is the moon mentioned, only the Phoenix of the Sun."

She sang what she could remember of the hymn to the Lady of the Moon. Xahnu squealed in delight. She laughed softly at him. "Remember—she was of the West, as are we."

At last she heard what she had waited for: a voice softly humming a Zharmatian love song. She stopped in a little grotto formed by jasmine bushes. Their sweet scent welcomed her; she plucked a flower and teased Xahnu with it. The child gurgled with delight as he snatched at it. Murohshei stood guard at the entrance, his powerful bulk between her and the world.

Moments later, he stepped aside without a glance at the man who slipped past him. Shei-Luin handed Xahnu into the arms that reached for him.

Yesuin cradled the boy against his chest; Xahnu looked up into his father's face and cooed.

"He knows," said Shei-Luin.

"I know you had sent me word that he looked like me, but . . ." His voice broke. Then, recovering himself, "We're lucky, you know, that Xiane took after his mother. Else . . ."

He shook his head. For a time he was silent; Shei-Luin watched him as he lost himself in the wonder that was their son. Her heart brimmed with love for these two.

Then Yesuin said, "My love, I thank you for this most precious of gifts, but . . . We cannot go on."

Shei-Luin's heart turned to ice. "What do you mean?" she demanded.

"Betraying Xiane this way. . . . Shei, he's been good to me. He's become my friend. To trick him like—"

"You'll abandon me to him?" Shei-Luin blazed. "Leave me to a man with no idea what a woman wants or needs, a man clumsy as an ox, who falls upon me as if he were the village bull forcing himself upon a cow? A man I despise to the depths of the earth! The coward is afraid of a tiny insect!"

Yesuin bit his lip, then said, "Shei, he has good reason. But I can't—"

She cut him off. "A friend Xiane may be to you—and for that alone, I make certain he receives as much pleasure as I have to give him—but I'm the one you love. Will you never dare the tunnels to see me again?"

Oh, Phoenix; if she lost Yesuin . . .

For a moment she thought he would say the unspeakable. But then she saw in his eyes that she'd won as she was certain she would. She leaned toward him.

"Lady," Murohshei said in an urgent whisper. "Someone comes this way."

They must not be caught together! Shei-Luin snatched Xahnu from Yesuin's arms and hurried from the jasmine bower.

She was not quick enough. Even as she left the shelter of the bushes, Lord Jhanun appeared in the path before her.

He said nothing. Yet she saw his eyes go from her son's face to beyond her shoulder where Yesuin still stood among the jasmine, then back to Xahnu. A slight smile twisted his mouth.

Then he bowed and turned away, still without a word.

But Shei-Luin had seen the light of an idea dawn in those cold eyes and wondered.

"Think you he'll betray us?" Yesuin said as he joined her. His hand reached protectively for her.

"No. For he tried to turn Xiane against me once before and was nearly banished," Shei-Luin said. "Nor will he cause another to do it for him. Nothing would come of it. Jhanun has no proof, and knows well that Xiane will never put me aside without a compelling reason. Bah—Xiane would have to stumble upon us himself before he would believe such a thing. No, Jhanun will say no word of this, for should a certain message come to light, Xiane *would* banish him for certain. But then what . . . ? Go; we must not take any more chances."

She wondered, as she returned to the main part of the Garden, what did run through Jhanun's treacherous mind.

*   *   *

Ican'tbreatheIcan'tbreatheIcan'tbreathe! Maurynna's mind screamed. She lay on her back, fighting for air, barely seeing Morlen's and Boreal's heads hovering anxiously over her as her vision faded in and out. Then the world exploded in pain.

I'm dying was her final thought as she spiraled into darkness.

This was insanity. But he'd had no choice; Maurynna might be dying. The air rushed past Linden as he tumbled through emptiness. Gods help him if the wind that always blew here smashed him into the cliff. . . .

Linden forced himself to empty his mind of fear, ignore that he might well fall to his death even if he completed Change. For one long, terrifying moment nothing happened. He couldn't Change.

Then he felt his flesh dissolving, turning into mist. As always, Change itself was frightening; but this was an old terror, welcome in its familiarity. And with it came an end to his falling.

But the reprieve was short-lived. One heartbeat he was a red fog hanging in the air; the next, a dragon and plunging down once more. He spread his wings open. For a moment he thought the sudden jerk he felt as the unceasing wind caught them would snap them like kindling; they were wrenched back until he was certain they would be torn from their sockets.

He fought to extend his wings again—if he could. As his muscles screamed in protest, he forced his wings open once more, frantically angling himself away from the cliff.

It worked. The wind spun him away from the rock. But before he could heave a sigh of relief, the treacherous wind gusted once more, sending him tumbling straight for the cliff wall. Once again he snapped his wings shut lest they be crushed against the rock face.

Falling once more, he twisted in midair, gaining a little more room. And now he had no choice; he must either fly—if he could—or fall to his death in the valley below. Yet he wasn't quite far enough from the cliff. . . .

When he came out of the garden paths, Lord Jhanun beckoned one of his servants to him. When the man reached him, the Jehangli lord whispered, "Send for my niece, Nama, who lives in Yalunreh."

The man blinked in surprise but would not ask any awkward questions, Jhanun knew, though a thousand of them danced in his eyes.

"At once, my lord." The man bowed and withdrew.

Jhanun paused to study a particularly exquisite chrysanthemum. He stroked the white petals in appreciation of its beauty and wondered, as he often did, how fared his Baisha and, therefore, his other plan.

Then he remembered the words of the rogue Oracle and took pleasure in them.

Linden spread his wings once more.

One wing tip scraped along the cliff, leaving a streak of blood on the pale granite, that pain lost amid the greater of his wrenched muscles. Linden angled into a glide, caught the wind that such a short time before had nearly killed him, and swooped up, away from the valley floor that was now dangerously close.

Well enough; he was no longer falling. But could he move his wings to fly, or could he only glide? Nothing for it but to try. Linden clenched his jaw, his long fangs grinding as he forced his aching wings into first one downstroke, then another and another.

He climbed into the sky, slowly, painfully, concentrating so hard on keeping his protesting wings in motion that he hardly noticed the two white-faced men in the window. Bit by bit, Linden gained altitude. The moment he was clear of the plateau, he pushed his abused wings to take him as fast as possible to the meadow. He ignored the blood dripping from the injured wing tip. All that mattered was reaching Maurynna in time.

*   *   *

Otter and Raven crowded together on the wide ledge of the window, watching in horror as Linden plunged toward the ground. Just when Otter was certain it was too late, Linden dissolved into the familiar red mist that flowed into the ghostly form of a dragon. Before he could blink, the mist solidified.

"Gods help us!" Raven yelped as a dragon the wine red color of Linden's birthmark appeared below them.

A tiny part of Otter's mind chuckled in amused sympathy; he remembered the first time he'd seen Linden Change from man to dragon. The rest of him prayed that Linden's wings didn't snap.

For one long, horror-stricken moment he thought it had happened; the great wings shot out to their full extension and were immediately wrenched back. Then, more slowly than Otter wanted to see, the wings inched out once more.

Otter breathed, "Thank the—No!" He watched in fear as the wind caught Linden and nearly smashed him into the cliff. The next few moments were pure hell as Otter watched Linden tumbling through the air.

Then the great wings spread once more. It looked to Otter as if one wing tip struck the cliff, but he couldn't be certain.

Linden glided a short way. Otter remembered to breathe again. Then the powerful wings began a stiff, heavy pumping. The red dragon lurched in the air but stayed aloft.

"He must have wrenched them badly to be flying like that," Otter said, limp with relief. "Still, he's lucky. He's so very lucky."

They watched the red dragon climb and disappear over the edge of the plateau.

"What do you mean?" Raven asked. His voice was subdued and there was none of his earlier hostility.

Otter put a hand up, found he was sweating profusely. He wiped his forehead. "While it's not their favored method of beginning a flight, a Dragonlord can leap from a high enough place and Change midway. It's only truly safe, though, if the air is calm. Yet even a wind isn't bad if it's steady and mild, and blowing in the right direction.

"But the wind at this end of the plateau never stops. Worse yet, it shifts with the blink of an eye. It's enough to blow a Dragonlord into the cliff wall. That's what nearly happened to Linden. And if it had . . ." Otter couldn't complete the sentence. He sagged against the wall, trying not to think about what would have come next.

"Oh," Raven said. Then, after a short silence where it looked to the bard as if the younger man argued with himself, Raven continued, "He did that only because of Maurynna, didn't he?"

"Yes. I think he was afraid it would take too long to reach an open spot—the landing cliff, say—where he could Change and launch himself safely." Otter wanted to ask, *Would you have taken such a risk?* but decided that would be too heavy-handed. Leave such blatant idiocies to the boy's father. He had faith that Raven could read the writing on this wall—now that his nose was shoved into it.

"What's wrong with her?" Raven asked.

"I've no more idea than you, lad," said Otter. "We'll just have to wait and find out."

"Couldn't he have told us? Gods damn it all, but I'll go mad wondering," Raven said with quiet, heartfelt fury.

Otter could only agree.

Now what? Lleld wondered as she circled—oh, so innocently!—far to the north of the ridge that just happened to have a certain mountain meadow on the other side of it. The sight before her so astonished the smallest Dragonlord that she stopped, hovering in midair, her wings beating furiously to hold her place.

It was the last thing she had expected: Linden racing up from the south for that same meadow. Even stranger, he flew clumsily, with none of the powerful grace she associated with his dragon form. He skimmed the lower southern ridge with barely enough room to clear it and disappeared into the bowl of the meadow.

Her curiosity tortured her. Why was Linden flying like that? Had the truedragons summoned him for some reason? What was happening?

She ground her fangs in frustration. If only she dared enter the meadow herself. . . .

The Songbirds were singing as Shei-Luin neared the main garden again. As always, the incredible purity of their voices caught her with their beauty. She stopped to listen. Even Xahnu seemed entranced, for he stopped fidgeting in her arms and listened as the melody faded and Zyuzin the Jewel began a lover's ballad.

She glanced over her shoulder at the sound of a sudden intake of breath. Murohshei stood as if spellbound, his face filled with a yearning that she'd never seen before. It startled her, and for an instant she regretted she must disturb him. But this could mean their lives, Yesuin's, and, more importantly, the life of her son. She would stop at nothing to protect Xahnu. Nothing.

She beckoned to Murohshei. He came to her and she set Xahnu in his arms as if she were tired. As she leaned forward, she whispered, "That message from Jhanun—the one that tried to trick me—move it from my rooms to the tunnels for safekeeping when—"

A braying laugh from inside a nearby grove of peach trees cut her off.

Shei-Luin closed her eyes. *Not Xiane again!*

Pain brought Maurynna back to the world, an intense, blazing pain that racked the muscles of her upper back. *What?* she thought blearily, unable to understand the *why* of it. But she welcomed the discomfort, for it ended both the agony that had sought to consume her very bones, and the death grip on her breathing.

She opened her eyes with a groan. Morlen and Boreal, now standing, peered down at her, their heads silhouetted against the blue sky. She sat up slowly, wondering if her head really would shatter. At last she was upright, hunched in a shaking ball, but sitting. The tide of pain in her head ebbed. Boreal snuffled her anxiously.

Little cousin, are thee well? Morlen asked gently.

His mindvoice hurt; Maurynna's very thoughts felt bruised and battered. But she was able to say, "I think so. But what . . . ?"

I do not think Kyrissaean wanted to speak with me, Morlen said with dry understatement.

Maurynna leaned against one of Boreal's sturdy forelegs and laughed weakly despite the pain. "It would seem not, my lord."

'Ware! Galinis shouted. *Look to the sky!*

Maurynna looked up in time to see a red shape drop like a thunderbolt from the sky. Although she had only seen Linden in his dragon form twice before—she suspected he'd not Changed out of consideration for her—she recognized him immediately.

Bellowing in rage, Linden swooped low over the group of truedragons. He landed, smoke curling from his nostrils, long fangs bared to fight. To Maurynna's horror, blood dripped from a wing tip, fell smoking onto grass that curled and died. There was a mad gleam in Linden's eyes.

"Linden, no! Please!" Maurynna cried, fear gripping her heart. *He can't hear me*, she realized in horror. But when she tried mindspeech, the torment that lanced through her head nearly felled her again. She couldn't reach Linden!

The red dragon charged Morlen. The four smaller truedragons leaped forward to face Linden, ready for battle.

"Morlen! Stop them!" Maurynna screamed.

The thunder of fire rumbling down six dragon throats filled the air as the great wyrms prepared for battle. No one heard her.

"Gods help him," Maurynna whispered, "else he doesn't have a chance."

Xiane it was, emerging from the grove. And from the look on his face, he had but one thought in mind. Her stomach turned even as she knelt.

"Precious Flower!" he called as he loped up to her. His smile was huge, displaying long white teeth like a horse's. "I found you—now you must pay a forfeit!"

She made herself smile at him. "Forfeit, my lord? Pleasure, rather!" Shei-Luin raised her hands to meet his.

He pulled her up with easy strength. "Come with me."

"But Xahnu—" she countered.

"Murohshei can take him back to Tsiaa. *Come.*"

There was no arguing. Her hand held firmly in Xiane's grasp, she followed as he led her deeper into the vast gardens than she'd ever been before.

They emerged from an ordered arranging of jasmine, roses, and other fragrant shrubs, dotted here and there with little groves of peach, pear, and artfully arranged almond trees, into a woodland glade.

Shei-Luin caught her breath. It was almost too perfect, but the artist who had designed the gardens so long ago had arranged trees, moss, rocks, and water with a delicate, restrained touch, and then had had the wisdom to let nature take its course.

A miniature deer raised its dripping muzzle from the spring-fed pool and gazed unafraid at them. They stopped to watch it.

"I found this part of the gardens when I was a child," Xiane said, low-voiced. "There's still much I haven't explored, the gardens are hu—"

He gasped and ducked almost before Shei-Luin heard the telltale angry buzzing. Once again his face turned deathly white.

The coward is afraid of a tiny insect!

Shei, he has good reason.

Shei-Luin suddenly understood. Her hand flashed out, closed on the red-and-black striped insect darting at Xiane's face, and crushed it. Pain like a burning needle lanced through her palm. She cried out and instinctively flung the dead bee away, then looked down at her hand. Already there was an angry red swelling in the center that ached abominably.

Xiane snatched her up in his arms and began running. "We must leave," he said, his voice shaking. "That was a red bee. If the others smell their dead sister, they'll be after us."

Shei-Luin said nothing, but cradled her aching hand and her new knowledge to herself.

Oh, the hell with it; I must *know! I never promised Jek-kanadar I wouldn't go to the meadow, after all.*

Executing a neat flip, Lleld stooped in a long slanting dive; the ground sped away beneath her. She held the dive until the last possible moment, then began flying south as fast as she could, cursing under her breath that she had been at the far northern edge of her circling.

He'll be killed if I don't stop this.

The thought gave Maurynna new strength. "Boreal," she ordered. "Help me up."

The stallion lowered his head. Maurynna grabbed onto his long mane. "Now!" Boreal pulled her straight up. She staggered forward a pace or two. The Llysanyin walked with her.

"Linden! Linden, for the sake of the gods, will you listen!" She wàved frantically, trying to get Linden's attention, but she was behind the line of truedragons. He couldn't see her. He didn't know she was alive and well. He'd die under the claws of the truedragons for nothing. "Linden!" she screamed.

Nothing. Then . . . The mad charge stopped. He'd heard her! As the red-scaled head swung around, eyes frantically searching among the truedragons, Boreal seized the back of Maurynna's tunic in his teeth and dragged her forward between Galinis and Morlen.

At once a red mist surrounded the solitary dragon, shrank, disappeared, and Linden faced the truedragons in human form.

She stumbled into his arms, held him tightly, glad to feel them around her even though their grip was painfully tight.

After a time she became aware of a growing wetness under her left hand and she remembered the blood she'd seen.

"You're hurt," she said, pulling back from him a little. "How? What happened?"

"Never mind that," said Linden raggedly. "What happened to you?" His face was stark white and etched with fear.

"I . . . I don't know," she answered.

It was my fault, Morlen said. His wings drooped. He sagged onto the grass; the others lay down as well, their relief at avoiding battle plain to see.

His mindvoice dismayed, Morlen continued, *I wished to speak to Kyrissaean. I told thy soultwin that there would be no harm to her. I thought I spoke the truth.*

"There should have been no danger," Linden said. "Speech with a dragonsoul has been done before and no ill came of it."

Maurynna rested her head on Linden's shoulder. "Until Kyrissaean, damn her." She held back tears of frustration. If she could only get at her dragon half and have it out with her! "At least she didn't half kill me when Rathan tried to speak with her."

Little cousin, Morlen said. His mindvoice was the barest whisper. *I have endangered thee—*

"My lord Morlen," Maurynna said. She refused to cry in front of the truedragons; it was a matter of pride. But if Morlen continued apologizing, cry she would. "This is not your fault. *Please.*"

Thee are kind, Morlen said, bowing his head to her. She wondered if he sensed her fear. *I thank thee.* The Seer heaved himself to his feet once more; sunlight sparkled over his moss green scales. The other truedragons rose as well.

Maurynna stood transfixed as Morlen towered over her. He bent his neck so that the tip of his muzzle touched her forehead as if in benediction. His scales were pleasantly cool against her skin.

I do not See as clearly as I once did, little one, and I

am not quite certain just what *thee are, but I think that thee will be important to us someday. I would stay to make certain thee are well, cousin, but we have grave news to bring to our kin. We may not delay any longer. Fare thee well, Maurynna Kyrissaean.**

The great head snapped up. Linden grabbed Maurynna and tugged her back as the truedragon spread his wings. The others followed suit.

"We must give them room," he said and pulled her into a stumbling run. Boreal loped alongside them as they ran to the side of the meadow.

Maurynna stood at Linden's side, arms tight around him once more, breathing much harder than she should be and shaken by Morlen's final words. From the feel of his mindvoice, she suspected that he'd spoken only to her that time. She watched the truedragons crouch in preparation to jump.

Fare thee well, little cousins! came a chorus of draconic mindvoices.

With a mighty heave of his hind legs, Morlen launched himself into the air. Even from where she stood Maurynna could feel the backwash of air from the great wings as Morlen left the earth behind. Then Galinis and Talassaene sprang into the air after their leader, followed by Aumalaean and Aeld when the way was clear.

What did he mean? Maurynna wondered as she watched the truedragons fly away.

Nearly there. Lleld somehow forced her wings to beat a little faster. Time to angle up once more. . . . In another moment she would crest the ridge line and then she'd see—

"Aaaaaaaaaahh!" Lleld screamed—the most she could do in dragon form—as she pulled up short and tumbled backward through the air.

For five enormous shapes had appeared as if out of nowhere in front of her. Only her small size had averted a disaster; Lleld was as nimble as a swallow, a tumbler in the air as well as on the ground.

Still, it was a close thing. The sapphire blue truedragon

she'd nearly collided with bellowed in angry surprise. Scarlet flames erupted from his mouth. Lleld clamped her wings to her body and dropped like a stone until she was out of range.

Those flames had come too close for comfort.

Your pardon, my lords! she yelled. *I didn't know you were—*

The truedragon roared and dove after her; his eyes shone with berserker rage. Lleld neatly reversed within her own length and prepared to fly for her life.

Enough, Aumalaean! Douse thy fires. It was naught but an honest mistake, and no harm was done, said Morlen the Seer. *Little cousin, do not fear!*

Lleld looked back over her shoulder, watched as Aumalaean struggled with his temper, saw when his leader's command won. His jaws snapped shut with a sound like a portcullis crashing down. He glared at her, eyes glowing like red-hot coals.

Despite Morlen's reassurance, Lleld waited until the smoke pouring from Aumalaean's nostrils became mere wisps before she joined the truedragons in their circling. It would be humiliating in the extreme to return to the Keep with a scorched tail. She'd never hear the end of it.

Morlen said, *That was a pretty piece of flying, little cousin.* His mindvoice was amused. *And if thee are well—which thee seem to be—then we will continue our journey to our homes. We bear desperate news.*

There is a truedragon held captive in Jehanglan! Lleld crowed to herself in triumph. To Morlen she said respectfully, *I am indeed well, my lord, and I thank you for the compliment.*

Then we will be on our way. But I would ask thee to see to thy fellow Dragonlords, whom we left in the meadow. I think they are well enough now, but . . .

Dragonlords? Not just Linden, then. And "well enough now?"

Lleld thought furiously. The only thing that would bring Linden in such haste was something threatening his soultwin. So Maurynna was down there, too; she must have ridden out. But what was the threat? Certainly not the true-dragons, even if Aumalaean was a crabby sort of fellow. And how did Linden get hurt? She couldn't wait to find out.

It will be my pleasure, my lord.

Was that a muffled laugh she felt in her mind? Before she could say anything, the five truedragons turned as one and flew north.

My thanks, little cousin, came faintly into her mind. This time there was no mistaking the laugh. Lleld snorted; twin curls of smoke drifted up from her nostrils.

What was so funny? she thought irritably. Then she remembered the charge laid upon her and brightened. This was going to be better than a bard's tale.

There were no surprises this time when she crested the ridgeline. Just Linden, Maurynna, and Boreal in the meadow below. Lleld tucked her wings and dived. Her very scales itched with the need to *know*.

Distant bellows of rage reached their ears.

"What is it?" Maurynna asked. Her body tensed beneath Linden's arm and one hand flew to her belt dagger.

"Something attacked the truedragons," Linden said grimly. He moved away to give himself enough room to Change, cursing as his abused muscles protested.

"Don't even think of it, you idiot!" Maurynna yelled. "You're hurt." She grabbed the front of his tunic and jerked him close until their noses nearly touched. "Whatever it is, there's nothing one lame Dragonlord can do to help five truedragons, do you hear? We'll mindcall all the others—"

Linden glowered at her, annoyed at the reminder of his injuries. It didn't help that she was right, blast it all. But it irked him beyond belief to be helpless when—

A distant flicker of motion beyond Maurynna's shoulder caught his eye. For a moment he couldn't believe what he

saw; then, *Idiot—who else would it be?* he said to himself.
He began laughing.

Maurynna drew back a little as if she thought him mad
and it was contagious. She did not, he noticed, let go of
his tunic. "What," she began, then looked over her shoulder.

"Trust Lleld," Linden said with a grin, "to be the first to
get the news."

Maurynna watched, barely containing her burning anger as
Linden awkwardly peeled off his tunic and presented his
injured back for Lleld's inspection. *She* should be the one
doing this for him, not Lleld, not any other Dragonlord, not
even any truedragon. Damn Kyrissaean for this latest insult.

She winced in sympathy at the painful slowness of his
movements. Gods, but he must have wrenched every muscle in his back and shoulders to be moving like that. And
how did he do it? That he wouldn't tell her did nothing to
mend her ill temper or ease her throbbing head.

Well and well, that must mean it was some pretty bit of
idiocy he knew deserved a tongue-lashing. Or even a be-
laying pin to the side of the head, she thought sourly. Just
as a reminder not to do whatever it was again.

Whatever he did, he did it for you, part of her mind
chided. She squirmed at the thought. *Morlen must have
mindcalled him.*

Lleld finished her inspection of the deep scrape down
Linden's back. *That*, she said, *was stupid, Linden. You
know better than to jump from there.*

So he'd told Lleld what he'd done and not her? Her
sympathy took wings. Maurynna promised herself the pleasure of keelhauling Linden if she ever got him on board a
ship.

"Just get on with it, will you?" Linden growled over his
shoulder.

For the first time Maurynna heard a dragon laugh, a deep
houf, houf, houf punctuated by tendrils of smoke from
Lleld's nostrils. Then Lleld opened her mouth; blue-green

flames rushed over teeth like daggers and bathed Linden in their Healing fire.

When she was done, Linden stretched. From his look of relief Maurynna knew that the Healing had taken; there was not even a mark showing where the scrape had gouged the fair skin.

I'm not a Dragonlord, Maurynna thought, blinking back sudden tears. *Not really. All I have are the "little magics." What good are heat spells and coldfire? So what if I can stick my hand in a roaring fire and not get burned? I can't Change, I can't fly, I can't Heal my soultwin myself. If Lleld hadn't come—*

She pushed to her feet. *I'm nothing but a fraud.*

Morlen's words came back to her; she shook her head in bitter disbelief. *How could I, the least of the Dragonlords, the "little one," be important to truedragons?*

Desperation overcame her. She bowed her head and willed herself to Change.

Taren poured himself another goblet of the Pelnaran-wine that Sirl had so thoughtfully left for him. If he'd known he'd have to face truedragons, he would have refused to leave Jehanglan! He gulped half the wine down.

Yet it seemed his fears that they could "see" into a man's soul were without cause. They had believed him just as the Dragonlords had, just as that fool boy had.

Still, he'd best keep to his plan of isolating himself as much as possible. A blasted curse this illness might be, but exaggerating it gave him an excuse to play the hermit.

A fit of shivering took him and he grimaced. Not that it was it all a sham; his blood was too thin now for these mountains. He took another sip and swore.

What if the cursed truedragons *did* go to Jehanglan?

Maurynna rode back down the mountain, sick and shaking. Instead of Changing, she'd only succeeded in enraging Kyrissaean further; her draconic half had lashed out in fury. The pain had been too much; Maurynna had fainted.

Now she clung to the saddle, certain that only the care Boreal took of her kept her from falling off. Boreal insisted on frequent rests; how he knew each time she felt ready to faint, she didn't understand. She was just glad he did.

Linden, watching over her from the air, landed, Changed, and helped her down yet again. She sprawled on the grass, gasping. "How does Boreal know?"

Linden said, "He feels it in the way you sit him. Even from above I can see you slump just before he stops. Are you certain you don't want me to walk beside you?"

She shook her head and wished she hadn't. Suddenly the world doubled in front of her eyes; she shut them. "Don't be silly; not with those boots. Your feet would be a mass of blisters by the time we got back. Besides, Lleld should have gotten home by now and sent Shan on his way."

"Then why don't we stay here until he does reach us? You're dead white, love." He knelt beside her and gently stroked her forehead. "I could try to ease you by taking some of this onto myself. But I don't dare; I don't know what Kyrissaean would do at my interference." His voice was a tangle of frustration and worry. "But promise me that you won't try Changing again. Not until we know why Kyrissaean behaves as she does."

Damn Kyrissaean anyway, Maurynna thought. *Linden waited so long and look what he gets as a soultwin: a sorry excuse for a Dragonlord no matter what Morlen says.* "I promise." The words were bitter and hard in her mouth.

If she thought about it anymore she'd cry. "I hope Shan gets here soon," she said to change the subject.

Nor was it long before the big black stallion cantered up the trail. He stopped before them, snorting, and snuffled Maurynna. Next he touched noses with Boreal; a moment passed and Shan snorted once more, seemingly satisfied with whatever had passed between them.

"Ready?" Linden asked.

"Ready enough," Maurynna said. "The rest helped, but by all the gods, I just want to lie down in my own bed."

Linden helped her into the saddle and vaulted onto

Shan's bare back. The sight of him seated comfortably atop the big stallion brought back memories of riding behind him in Cassori barely more than two months ago; it seemed like another lifetime. A time before she knew she was Linden's soultwin, before she knew she was a Dragonlord.

Shan danced up beside her. Linden smiled, and she knew he was remembering that ride as well. "If you get too dizzy," he said, "we can ride double on Shan again."

"I can do it," Maurynna said. Silently she vowed she would ride into Dragonskeep without help.

"Where are they?" Raven snapped. "Haven't you heard anything yet?"

"No," Otter said. "Not yet." And that worried him.

Raven swore and slammed a fist into his other palm. "You can mindspeak Linden Rathan, can't you? So why don't you?"

"Because, first, I can't really mindspeak him. The most I can do is concentrate very hard if I wish to speak mind-to-mind with him and hope he 'feels' it; and I can only do that much because we've been friends for so long. I also have to be relatively close to him," Otter said in exasperation. "And secondly, have you considered that distracting him might prove dangerous? We don't know what's happening, after all."

"Just so," Raven said. There was a note in his voice that Otter didn't like. "We don't know."

It took all the willpower Maurynna had to keep her vow. More than once she nearly gave in, but the thought of the Lady's reaction kept her in the saddle. It was bad enough being confined to the Keep like some delicate hothouse flower; let word reach the Lady that she was too ill to ride—and why—and the Lady would no doubt order her to their rooms. And that, Maurynna knew, she could not stand.

Still, when they finally reached the Keep, Maurynna's head ached so badly she could not open her eyes; the light hurt, sounds were much too loud and hammered at her skull, and her sense of smell was far too acute, even for a Dragonlord.

Linden helped her down. She sagged against him, unable to protest when he picked her up and carried her off, leaving the Llysanyins to the grooms. She closed her eyes and clutched the neck of his tunic to anchor herself as the world spun around her.

Sudden coolness and a dimness she could sense even through closed eyelids told Maurynna they were inside the castle of Dragonskeep. She counted the stairways as Linden climbed them: one, two—she sighed with relief as they reached the third. Almost there. Then—

"Rynna!"

The call was desperate—and far too loud. Maurynna was certain Raven's voice had shattered her skull. She couldn't stop a whimper of pain.

"Rynna—what's wrong?"

Linden growled, "Get out of the way, boy. Can't you see she's ill?"

Raven snapped back, "Of course I see that. But what's wrong with her? I have a right to know. You never said before you threw yourself out of my window."

The words took a moment to penetrate the shroud of pain in her head. Linden had done *what*? He could have died! No wonder he wouldn't tell her before.

She opened her eyes. She caught a glimpse of Raven's salt-white face glaring at Linden, heard Linden's wordless snarl of anger; then the world danced before her and she was certain she would be sick.

"Raven—go away," she managed to say. All she wanted was her bed. All else had to wait—even explaining to Linden in no uncertain terms that he was never to do anything like that again or she'd kill him herself. She swallowed hard, eyes squeezed shut once more, and her stomach, thank all the gods, stayed in its proper place.

A gasp, then retreating footsteps. Once more Linden strode upward, then down the hall to their rooms. He laid her on the bed. When she tried to sit up, groping blindly at her boots, he said, "Let me do that."

Maurynna fell back against the pillows as he tugged her boots off. "Windows," she whispered, covering her eyes with her hands.

"The light hurts?"

"Yes." She heard him pull the window hangings into place; the sudden darkness was blessed relief. "Thank you."

She felt him sit down on the bed.

"I've mindcalled Fiaran," he said softly. "You remember him, don't you? He's the Keep's Simpler. I described your symptoms and he's making up an infusion for the pain. He'll be here soon, love. Try to rest until then."

"I will." She let her mind drift, refusing to acknowledge the pain, hoping it would go away. The encounter on the stairs came back to her.

I have the right to know, Raven had said as if he were her soultwin, not Linden.

She considered that. *No, Raven, you don't have the right. You're a friend—my best friend—but Linden is the other half of me. I wish you would understand that.*

Raven—go away.

She'd ordered him away.

Raven still couldn't believe it. Ordered him away as if he meant nothing, as if all the years of their friendship had never been. As if she didn't care that he loved her.

It was all that bastard Linden Rathan's fault. It had to be. She'd only known the Dragonlord for a few months; how could that so completely take the place of a nearly lifelong friendship?

His great-uncle's words tried to come back to him: *they were given to each other by the gods more than six hundred years ago.* He pushed them away. Pushed away all his great-uncle had ever told him about soultwins, what it meant, even while deep inside he knew its truth.

He strode down the hall in a white-hot rage. As he surged around a corner, he nearly ran into Otter deep in conversation with a slender, brown-haired young man. The stranger turned a mildly surprised face to him.

Raven took the man for one of the few truehuman servants in the Keep until his great-uncle said, "Kief Shaeldar, may I present my grandnephew, Raven Redhawkson?"

Raven nearly choked in surprise even as he bowed low. *This* was one of the Dragonlord judges who had settled the regency debate in Cassori? The man looked as meek as a merchant's clerk. Then Raven noticed the six-fingered hands.

And there was something else that surprised Raven, though he could not ask his great-uncle in the presence of a Dragonlord.

"Ah," said Kief Shaeldar. "You're the one who brought Taren to us, aren't you?" When Raven nodded, the Dragonlord continued dryly, "I'm not certain whether to thank you or not for that; I, for one, have had rather enough excitement lately."

Raven thought back to the night before. As soon as he'd been taken to his great-uncle, he'd insisted on hearing from Otter the entire story of Maurynna's adventures in Cassori. It had taken until near dawn.

And knowing now what he did, he could well understand this Dragonlord's understated preference for a bit of quiet. He almost forgot his anger in appreciation of Kief Shaeldar's wry comment.

Raven grinned. "My apologies, Your Grace, but I couldn't think what else to do with him."

Kief Shaeldar laughed. "A fair hit. I suppose he is our problem, isn't he, seeing that we're intermediaries between truehuman and truedragon. Now I must be off. Good day, gentlemen."

Otter bowed as the Dragonlord took his leave; Raven followed suit. When they were alone, Raven said, "I noticed you called him by both of his names. I thought you were friends with him."

"On friendly terms, yes, but not close, though I've called him just "Kief" in extreme situations. We're not friends as

I am with Linden, Lleld, Jekkanadar, and a few of the others. Remember, the doubled name—human and dragon—is as much of a title as 'Dragonlord' or 'Your Grace.' I would never presume to address another Dragonlord by a human name alone unless he or she gave me permission. Rynna, of course, is an exception; we were friends before her Change."

Raven screwed up his face in thought. "After breakfast today, both Lleld Kemberaene and Jekkanadar Surael gave me permission to use their human names."

"I'm not surprised; they're both like Linden, very easygoing with truehumans," Otter said. There was a look of speculation in his eyes.

Raven met that look. "Linden Rathan didn't."

Otter's eyebrows went up. "Why should he? You were certainly less than gracious to him, my fine lad. No, my boy, that right you're going to have to earn. Are you going back to the rooms?"

Raven, who had planned to do just that, said, "No."

"Good luck that I ran into you, then. I was going to wait there for you."

"Why?"

"To tell you that all was well with Maurynna. Aside from a violent headache, she seems well enough."

Raven gaped at him. "How did you know?" he demanded.

"Linden just mindcalled me, of course," Otter said in surprise. "Didn't you think he would? He knew we were concerned for her as well."

Raven's fury returned. So Linden Rathan had mindcalled his great-uncle to reassure Otter, but had never thought of him? And didn't he consider one Raven Redhawkson good enough to use his human name alone?

Damn Linden Rathan anyway.

"How thoughtful of him." Raven pushed past his great-uncle. He called back, "I'm off to see how Taren is faring. I don't know when I'll be back to the rooms."

*   *   *

Linden drew the square of fabric from the bowl of cool water and wrung it dry, then handed it to Fiaran. The Simpler took it, expertly folded it into thirds, then laid it across Maurynna's forehead.

"There," said Fiaran. "How does that feel?"

"Good," Maurynna whispered. "Thank you."

"You're very welcome. Now try to sleep." The portly Simpler rose from his seat on the edge of the bed and beckoned Linden to one side. "I've done all I can for now," he said in a low voice. "I'll leave the infusions with you. You know which are which?"

"Yes," Linden said; then, just to be certain, "The flask with the blue glaze is for pain; no more than five drops in wine every three or four candlemarks. The green is if she begins vomiting again."

"Just so. She'll not want to eat much for a day or two, I'll wager, and be warned that it would be best if you ate elsewhere. I've known the smell of food to turn someone's stomach when they've a sick headache like this. But if she'll drink it, hot broth would be good for her. Oh, and keep the room dim; that seems to help. And now I'm off. I'll stop in again in a few candlemarks, if you like."

As he walked the Simpler to the door, Linden said, "I would appreciate it, Fiaran. Have you any idea how long . . . ?"

"This will last? Not really. This is one of the worst attacks of this kind that I've ever seen. Give her a few days, though, and she should be right as rain." The Simpler paused in the doorway, frowning thoughtfully. "Though why rain should be right or wrong, I've no idea. I shall return later, Linden."

Linden shut the door behind Fiaran and smiled.

Tsiaa fluttered around her like a distracted hen, fussing over the poultice she had ready and didn't dare apply. Resting comfortably among the pillows of her bed, Shei-Luin watched, amused, as her maid wavered back and forth, torn between the need to tend to the swollen hand and fear of the man who held it cradled in his own.

At last Tsiaa took a deep breath and quavered, "Phoenix Lord . . ."

Xiane looked up. Tsiaa showed him the poultice.

The Phoenix Lord of the Skies stared blankly at her for a moment, his mouth hanging open like an idiot school-boy's, before saying, "Oh!" and jumping to his feet. He laid down Shei-Luin's hand with a gentleness she hadn't thought him capable of and moved aside. Tsiaa bent to her work.

Xiane turned to the door. Murohshei sprang to open it lest the emperor sully himself with such petty labor. And, Shei-Luin suspected, to get Xiane out of here that much sooner so that they all might relax.

The emperor paused in the open doorway, regarding her. His long face held a seriousness that Shei-Luin had never seen before.

Phoenix! she thought in astonishment. *For once, Xiane looks like an emperor!*

"I know what you did," he said quietly. "And I will not forget it, Precious Flower."

The door closed.

Nor will I, my lord, Shei-Luin thought. *Nor will I.*

When he returned to his mansion, Lord Jhanun gave orders to call back two particular servants from their quarters outside the city. Then he bathed and took his dinner in his study. It would take time, he knew, for the message to reach them, and they would wait until dark before coming. The fewer who saw them, the better; there were always officers of the army in the imperial capital. One might recognize these two men, and that would be fatal to his new plans. Whether Baisha succeeded or not, Jhanun meant to have the Phoenix Throne. Jehanglan must be saved from the impious ones who would destroy her.

After the evening meal was over, Jhanun's house steward

entered the study. "Is there anything else you require, my lord?"

"The gatekeeper has been warned?"

"Yes, lord. The instant Nalorih and Kwahsiu are here, he will let them in."

"Is everything ready for my journey tomorrow? I wish to leave as early as possible; after this foolishness of worshiping a woman and the moon, I wish to make offerings at the Iron Temple. That damn feast day should be abolished. Only the Phoenix is worthy of worship."

"My lord's piety is well known, and much admired. All is in readiness, lord."

"Good. Then bring me a pot of fresh tea and that will— Wait! I almost forgot. Have the Jasmine Hermitage made ready for my niece, Nama; I've sent for her. When she arrives, engage the finest tutors for her. She is to be made ready for the imperial harem."

Only the merest elevation of the steward's eyebrows betrayed his surprise. He bowed. "It shall be done as you command, lord. I will bring the tea." He bowed once again and left.

When the tea arrived, and the evening incense had been lit beneath the image of the Phoenix, Jhanun opened the new package of *sh'jin* paper resting on his desk and pulled out a sheet at random. Setting it before him, he inspected it closely, finishing by running his fingertips over it. He could not find a single flaw.

Guildmaster Joon had been right; this was some of the finest stuff ever produced by the papermakers' guild for the gentle art. This would be a joy and a privilege to work with. And to give such fine material the honor it was due, he must meditate between each fold to insure the proper serenity of mind. He closed his eyes for a time to find the still center of his thoughts.

When he was ready, Jhanun made the first fold in the pattern known as the Dancing Phoenix.

* * *

The painful tale was told.

Blast Linden Rathan. There must be some way he could get back at the bastard, Raven thought as he tugged at the neck of his tunic.

The room was hot and stuffy. The windows were shut, their hangings pulled tight, and a roaring fire burned in the hearth. Hanging in the air were the acrid scents of illness and medicines and the bitterness of Raven's heart.

Taren was seated as close to the fire as safety allowed, eyes shut, and a thick shawl wrapped around his shoulders.

Raven mopped his face with a sleeve and considered pulling his tunic off. The place was near as hot as an Assantikkan steam bath, he thought.

"So she sent you away," Taren said into the silence.

"Like a dog being kicked," Raven said. His anger rose again.

The wrinkled eyelids opened. Taren's blue eyes held only sympathy. "I grieve for you that one has come between you and the girl you love. I remember how much you spoke of her. Your devotion moved me."

Raven looked down, embarrassed. In truth, the stories he had told were mostly of the scrapes he and Maurynna had gotten into as children. He hadn't really been baring his heart—had he? Or had Taren listened to the silences between the words, as the saying went?

The older man shook his head now. "How sad it comes to naught—and for what?"

For what indeed? Raven thought, angry again.

"And nothing you can do, either. Or is there?" Taren said.

"Of course not. They're soultwins," Raven said.

"Ah." Taren smiled oddly. "Of course not," he echoed. He settled himself deeper into his chair and closed his eyes once more. "Forgive me; I am but poor company this day. I must rest again." His head drooped.

Raven shut his teeth on the question that had leaped to his tongue. Instead he watched the fire and thought about *how* Taren had spoken when he'd repeated Raven's objection; the same words and so different a meaning.

Was there a way around a soultwinning? Or a way of *ending* one?

It was late when two men robed and cowled like Walker priests slipped into Jhanun's study. They waited, motionless as stone, for him to acknowledge them.

Jhanun did not look up from his contemplation of the paper figure resting on the desk before him. He had never, he thought, created such a masterpiece. The little phoenix might almost fly away. Every fold, every crease, was perfect, as if the paper would not allow mistakes. He would obtain as much of this batch as he could.

But now he must turn his attention to business. "Did anyone recognize you?" he asked the two men.

"No, lord," Kwahsiu said. "Who pays attention to low-rank priests? No one recognized us."

"It's as he said, lord," Nalorih added. "Rest easy. What service is it our privilege to perform for you?"

"You're both familiar with the emperor's appearance?"

They had steadier nerves than the steward; neither betrayed any surprise at the odd question, though Kwahsiu, as was his wont, grinned now and again as if he found the world impossibly funny.

Said Kwahsiu, "Very, lord. When we were still officers, we were both assigned to the palace for a time, and we often rode escort for the Phoenix Lord when he rode to the woods where he hunts."

"Good. This then, is how you may serve me: I desire that you seek a man who looks enough like Xiane Ma Jhi to be his brother and bring him to me. Slave, free man, a captured Zharmatian—I care not. Just find such a one, and as quickly as you can."

Rubbing his crooked nose, Nalorih said slowly, "This may take some time, my lord. Likely we will need to find someone half-Jehangli and half-Zharmatian as the emperor is."

Jhanun nodded. "I understand. I know this task is difficult, but I also know that if it is possible, the two of you can do it."

The renegade officers bowed. "We thank you, lord," said Kwahsiu. "We will not fail your trust."

"Good. I wish you to leave as soon as possible. Take horses from my stable." Jhanun raised a hand in dismissal.

The men bowed once more, then turned to the door. They were almost to it when Jhanun bethought himself of something crucial.

"Wait!"

They stopped, Nalorih's hand on the latch. "Yes, lord?" they said as one.

"The man you look for—I care not if he is whole or crippled, but he must *not* be a eunuch, either made or natural. Do you understand?"

"We do, my lord," Nalorih said after a moment. The corner of his mouth twitched.

Kwahsiu had no such restraint. He grinned hugely. "Don't worry, my lord. We'll make very certain of it."

Despite Tsiaa's cooling poultices, the pain in Shei-Luin's hand kept her awake. She snapped at Tsiaa when that good woman offered her a cup of balm and ginger tea to help her sleep.

In a fit of pique, she sent Murohshei to find one of the lesser musicians among the eunuchs. She wished she dared send for Zyuzin or one of the other Songbirds, but they sang only for the emperor.

The only good thing about this damned bee sting, she thought crankily when the eunuch left, was that it gave her a reason to fend off Xiane's attentions that night; he'd practically apologized when she'd pleaded weakness and pain.

Let some other concubine put up with him.

She waited in petulant annoyance for Murohshei's return. But when he did come, not only did one of the lesser musicians accompany him, so did Zyuzin. The boy's round face was streaked with tears.

"What is this?" she asked, astonished, as Zyuzin knelt before her, forehead touching the floor.

Murohshei waved the other musician to the outer chamber. When he was gone, Murohshei said quietly, "Xiane has decreed that the gardeners in charge of that portion of the gardens be executed for negligence. But—"

Zyuzin sat up. "But they didn't *know* that the bees were there, lady," he wailed. "How could they? Until a few days ago, they took care of the water gardens! They're new to that part of the gardens. If they had known, they would have asked—" Here the boy broke down. He covered his face with his hands.

Moved by the piteous sobbing, and more confused than ever, Shei-Luin asked, "How does he know this?"

"They're his relatives—two uncles and a brother. That was how Zyuzin's talent was discovered; he came to the gardens to learn the trade from them, and the Songmaster heard him singing as he planted water lilies." Murohshei's broad forehead wrinkled. He said, "Lady—Flower of the West—only you. . . ." His soft voice broke. "Lady—please. It will break the boy's heart. I fear he won't sing again."

Murohshei's eyes begged her more eloquently than any speech. *Faithful Murohshei—he has never before asked me for anything but the chance to serve me with all his heart.*

Shei-Luin nodded. "I shall speak to Xiane tomorrow."

Zyuzin whispered from behind his hands, "They are to die at dawn."

Shei-Luin closed her eyes and sighed. She knew what must be done. "Murohshei, prepare me for the emperor. I will go to him now." She stood.

Zyuzin stared up at her in awe. "Lady, thank you, thank you! But you would go to the emperor—when he didn't send for you? No other concubine would dare!"

She smiled mischievously at him. *"I,"* she said, "am not just any concubine. Xiane will be delighted to see me. I shall tell him only he can comfort my pain."

As Murohshei helped her into her best robe, he asked, "Do you think the Phoenix Lord will grant this?"

Holding out her hand so that they could see the swollen palm, she said, "After today? Yes. Go back to your bed, Zyuzin, and dry your eyes; your kin are safe."

She swept out of the room as regally as an empress.

It was late the next morning before she returned. As she entered her sleeping chamber, Murohshei looked up from the flowers he was arranging in a bowl of water as he did every day for her.

"Have my ladies prepare my bath," she told him wearily. She sank into her favorite chair.

"At once, my lady." But he hesitated in the doorway. "Favored One . . . ?"

She was tired, but not too tired to find a smile to reassure him. "The little songbird will still sing, my Murohshei."

He bowed. "Thank you, Flower of the West." Simple words, but she heard his heart behind them.

Nine

Once again Linden saw Fiaran to the door. "My thanks for coming to see Maurynna so often these past few days."

The barrel-shaped little Simpler hugged his scrip of medicines to his chest. "It was my pleasure, Linden—not that I wish her or anyone else here at the Keep ill. But were it not for visitors and servants, I'd have nearly nothing to do. You Dragonlords are such a disgustingly healthy lot," he complained with a wink. "All I get are your occasional headaches and colds."

"Runny noses and short tempers, eh?" Linden said. He chuckled. "I guess we are a disappointment. But you've another patient now, don't you? The man who escaped from Jehanglan."

Few at the Keep had yet seen the mysterious traveler; he'd arrived ill and had been bedridden well-nigh ever since, with no visitors allowed but Raven and the Lady and Kelder. Linden had never even caught a glimpse of the man.

And if *he* wondered about Taren, Lleld must be eaten alive with curiousity.

"If I may ask, Fiaran, why haven't you come to one of us to Heal the man? You know we'd gladly do it," Linden asked.

"I thought of that first thing. But when I mentioned it to Taren, he refused. Said he'd had a Healing done once for a broken arm and was miserably sick for a week, with hives on top of it. It was something we were warned about at the College," Fiaran said, referring to the College of Healer's Gift where Healers and Simplers were trained. "Some unlucky folks are like that; a Healing or some food that the rest of us can tolerate makes them sicker than that proverbial poor dog."

Linden rubbed his chin, thinking. "My sister Fawn couldn't eat strawberries," he remembered aloud. "Same thing happened to her—hives, I mean. She loved strawberries, too."

"Isn't it always the way? Poor girl. But Taren's bad luck means I've something more than sore throats and sneezes to attend to for once."

"Jekkanadar says it's something common in Assantik," Linden said.

"Yes, that shaking sickness they have. Makes you miserable for a tenday or two, more if you're unlucky, then goes away until the next time, whenever that is. Seems it's common in Jehanglan as well from what Taren said. I've some infusions that ease the worst of it, and I left one brewing. So I must get back to it, but I'll come by later to see how Maurynna's feeling. I think she could try some real food this evening."

"She'll be glad to hear it. She's getting tired of sops and broth, and of staying in the room." Linden raised a hand in farewell as the Simpler set off in his peculiar rolling gait. He went back into the suite of rooms that he and Maurynna shared. At the door to the sleeping chamber, he paused, thinking about what Fiaran had just told him of Taren. Poor beggar, unable to tolerate a Healing.

Linden shook his head in sympathy and slipped into the darkened room to sit at the bedside once more.

"Your friend is still not well?" Taren asked as he poured wine for both of them.

"Not yet," Raven answered. "Though my great-uncle says she's feeling better. Thank you," he said as Taren handed him a goblet. He laid the bridle he was mending for Lleld in his lap and sipped. "This is good!"

"It's Pelnaran; the Dragonlords drink only the best, it seems. So your great-uncle was allowed in to see her and not you?" The voice was full of gentle indignation for him.

"Um, no. But Linden Rathan told him and not me," Raven said. He didn't mention that he'd not stopped by the rooms to inquire as had his great-uncle. The less he saw of Linden Rathan, the better.

In the lull that followed Raven silently stewed over the injustices of life. He ran a thumb along the cheek strap of the bridle. Was the stitching coming loose by that buckle?

Taren said, "It must be boring for you, then, with your best friend ill. A pity you've no one else besides your great-uncle to speak with when I'm too ill for visitors."

Raven brightened. "But I do have. There's Chailen, the head groom, for one; I don't think I've ever met anyone who knows so much about horses. Then there's Lleld and Jekkanadar. They've even taken me riding on some of the mountain trails."

"They're also grooms?"

"No," Raven answered with proud wonder. He glanced down at the bridle once more. Yes, that stitching needed replacing as well. He put down his goblet and took up the sewing awl with its length of heavy waxed-linen thread. "They're Dragonlords: Lleld Kemberaene and her soultwin

Jekkanadar Surael. This is her Llysanyin Miki's bridle in fact."

A sharp hiss of breath greeted his words. Raven looked up in surprise. "Is something amiss, Taren?"

For there was an eagerness in Taren's face and a glitter in his eyes that Raven had never seen before. It made him vaguely uneasy. Yet Taren's next words did nothing to explain the mystery.

"So—you have *four* Dragonlords as friends?" Taren asked.

Raven shrugged. "I don't know as I'd call Linden Rathan a friend."

"But you know *four* Dragonlords?" Taren persisted. His eyes shone.

Frowning, Raven said, "Put like that . . . Yes, I do know four— Taren, what is this about?"

Taren's incredibly sweet smile brushed away his uneasiness. "Just that so many truehumans never even see a single Dragonlord in their lives—and you know four. Most would name you fortunate, Raven Redhawkson."

"In three of those cases I wouldn't argue," Raven muttered.

"I should like to meet these four Dragonlords you know, Raven. I should like that very, very much," Taren said softly.

"As soon as Maurynna is better, I'll ask them," said Raven, pleased that he could do something for the man. Taren had been a patient listener. "Will that do?"

"That will do very well indeed."

As always at dinnertime, the great hall was filled with the buzz of conversation and the clink of dishes. It was usually a cheerful noise. But tonight there was an undertone of speculation, a kind of uneasy anticipation.

Maurynna rubbed the back of her neck; she felt as though the air hummed like a plucked harp string. Her unease brought Kyrissaean to the fore more than her usual wont.

Maurynna could feel her draconic half watching, waiting behind her mind. It made her brain itch.

It didn't help that this was the first night that she'd felt well enough to dine in the great hall. For the past four days she'd stayed in the rooms, waited on by their *kir* servants, Varn and his wife Wyone, and hovered over by Linden and occasionally Fiaran.

Fiaran she hadn't minded; the poor man was pathetically grateful to have a patient. Maurynna thought he must get bored to tears in Dragonskeep, so she had drunk his potions without complaining. Indeed, most were quite tasty. Fiaran gave his few patients no cause to complain.

Linden, on the other hand, had *fussed*. Unceasingly. He had refused to leave her side until, in a fit of exasperation, she'd heaved a pillow at him and threatened to follow it up with a bowl of stew. Only then was he convinced she wasn't about to die.

Now she wondered what rumors had spread about her illness. Too many people stopped her as she and Linden passed, inquired after her health, looked at her as if she would shatter with a touch. By the time they reached their table, Maurynna was tired from pretending to feel better than she did. But she would not falter; let the Lady hear there was nothing wrong with her and wonder over that.

At last they reached the table they usually shared with Lleld and Jekkanadar. The other Dragonlords were already seated and with them was Otter. Pleased smiles greeted her.

"Where's Raven?" Maurynna asked. "And, for the sake of the gods, do *not* ask me how I'm faring!"

Mouths snapped shut all around the table.

"I don't know," Otter said after a moment. "After I left you a little while ago, I went back to my rooms and told him you'd be coming to dinner tonight. Then I went to my chamber to change that broken harp string and, well, nap. When I woke up, he was gone. No note, either."

Is he avoiding me? Damn him for an idiot, Maurynna thought as she took her place. *I can't believe he's sulking somewhere because I wanted Linden, not him, by me after that encounter with Morlen and the other truedragons. Oh, Raven,* why *won't you understand?*

More Dragonlords passed by. Each asked her how she felt. Maurynna fixed a smile on her face and assured every one she was well, thank you. A sick headache, nothing more, and yes, Fiaran's medicines had helped. Yes, wasn't it a good thing that there was a Simpler at the Keep? One couldn't expect a full Healing from one's fellow Dragonlords for every little ache and pain, after all.

At last everyone seemed satisfied she wasn't going to fall dead in front of them and left her alone. She slumped in her chair.

Linden reached over and rubbed the back of her neck. *Tired already, love?* His dark grey eyes were sympathetic.

Gods, that feels good, she said and leaned into his strong fingers. *A little, yes. Kyrissaean is very awake tonight and that's always draining—no, don't stop!*

But at a sudden buzz of conversation, Linden's hand had dropped away; he looked to the high table where the Lady sat. Maurynna craned her neck to see what had caused the stir.

With a shock she recognized Raven slowly approaching the high table. He walked beside a frail-looking man, one hand under the man's elbow, guiding his faltering steps to the seat at the Lady's right.

As the glow of the coldfire hovering over the table fell on him, Maurynna thought the man's face looked like a ball of crumpled, yellowed silk, all lines and creases and wrinkles. What was left of his hair—the top of his head was completely bald—was white and thin, cut unusually short.

When Raven made to leave, the man caught his arm. A brief discussion ensued with the Lady and Kelder. At its end, Raven took the seat on the other side of the man. He looked half embarrassed, half pleased, and wholly stunned to be at the Lady of Dragonskeep's own table.

"At least he wore his best tunic tonight," Otter sighed. Then, slowly, "So that's Taren Olmeins."

"The one who escaped from Jehanglan?" Lleld asked. For a moment Maurynna thought the little Dragonlord would climb onto the table for a better view.

"The same," Otter said. "I recognize him from Raven's description. It would seem that his tale is taken as truth if he's asked to grace the Lady's table."

A Dragonlord seated at another table leaned over. "Bard Otter, that's your grandnephew, isn't it?" Merlet Kamenni called.

"It is indeed, Dragonlord," said Otter.

"Ah; then no puzzle who the other man is." The Dragonlord nodded. Her single thick braid of brown hair swung over her shoulder. "Odd that he hasn't appeared before now."

"A flare-up of an old illness, Your Grace, that Taren brought with him from Jehanglan, Raven told me. I would venture that this is the first night Taren's been well enough," Otter said.

Seeing Merlet's brow furrow in consternation, Maurynna called, "It's nothing contagious, Merlet. It's also known in the south of Assantik where the swamps are. I forget the Assantikkan name for it—" She looked to Jekkanadar.

"*Degwa n'soor*," he supplied, turning in his seat to look at Merlet. "The 'shaking sickness.' The attacks sometimes last a tenday or so at a time. Raven said Taren was ill most of the ride north. It comes and goes, very nasty, but as Maurynna said, not contagious."

Merlet looked relieved. "He was lucky to have your grandnephew looking after him, Bard Otter. Now, I suppose, we all wait on what the truedragons decide."

"It would seem so, Dragonlord. But this waiting worries me," Otter said.

"As it does all of us," Merlet said bleakly. "May the gods guide them," she finished and turned back to her companions.

"From her lips to the gods' ears," Linden muttered.

Maurynna made the sailors' sign for luck under the table. May the gods listen very hard indeed for once.

Then the servers came forth from the kitchens, moving among the tables bearing heaped platters of food. By an unspoken agreement, the conversation turned to other, less distressing, subjects.

The Lady, Kelder, and the guests at the high table had left long before. So had most of the other Dragonlords and visitors throughout the hall. Only a few small groups lingered here and there over the cheese and fruit that ended meals at the Keep.

Maurynna carved slices of the sharp yellow cheese that was their favorite while Linden cut up an apple for them. He had just handed her half to her when a truehuman servant approached the table.

"Dragonlords, Bard," the man said, "the young truehuman who sat at the Lady's table this evening sent me to say that Taren Olmeins would like to meet his—Raven's—friends and great-uncle this night. He asked if you would be willing to go to Master Olmeins' quarters in a candlemark's time."

Maurynna thought Lleld would whoop aloud.

"Yes! Yes, indeed, Melian," the little Dragonlord said, all eagerness. "We'll all be there—won't we?" She turned to Linden, sudden misgiving in her eyes.

Maurynna heard Linden's quiet grunt. "Friends, eh? I wonder," he said for her ears only, "if that's meant to include me."

"If it isn't," she told him fiercely, "then I shall box Raven's ears for him no matter what you say." To Melian she said, "Yes; we shall certainly all go. Tell Raven Redhawkson that, please: we will *all* go."

Melian bowed. "As you wish, Dragonlord," he said and went off on his errand.

As soon as the door to Taren's rooms opened, a wave of heat billowed out and enveloped them. Linden blinked in surprise; good gods, so this was what his sick room in Cassori must have been like the night Healer Tasha decided to sweat that poison out of his system! He felt renewed sympathy for Tarlna and Kief, who had assisted Tasha. They had certainly downplayed the unpleasantness when they'd described it to him.

Raven beckoned them. As eldest, Lleld went in first; Linden saw Taren struggle to rise from his chair by the fireplace. He sank back with a grateful sigh when Lleld said, "There's no need for that, Taren. We're all friends here. I'm Lleld Kemberaene."

Linden happened to catch Raven's eye just as Lleld said "friend." An ironic look passed between them.

"Then come and sit down, my friends, and make yourselves comfortable," Taren said. He smiled.

It was a wonderful smile, one that welcomed you as a heart friend, that said "All is well in a world that has you in it." It was a smile you couldn't help answering.

Lleld introduced the other Dragonlords and Otter as they settled themselves. Raven played the host and poured wine.

When all were served, Taren gallantly inquired after Maurynna's health, brushing aside his own illness as unimportant when asked. "It comes and goes, goes and comes. Yes, it's worse than usual this time, but I'm fortunate to be here where I have such good care."

They talked for a while of little things; to Linden's amusement, even Lady Mayhem restrained herself, listening while Jekkanadar and Taren fell into a discussion of similar phrases between Jehangli and Assantikkan. Words, Linden knew, were a passion with Jekkanadar. As they spoke, Taren constantly played with a loop of white beads; Linden recognized them as Assantikkan "worry beads," though these were not the usual blue-glazed beads that he had seen before. Perhaps this was the Jehangli variety; more had crossed the Straits long ago than just words.

"Despite the differences, it's clear that there was once a great deal of contact between Jehanglan and Assantik," Jekkanadar said when they'd finished dissecting one particular adage.

"So I see now, Your Grace. I knew some Assantikkan,

but until you told me the older forms of those words, I never realized how alike some phrases were in both languages. Indeed, my lord, now I wonder who had which sayings first," said Taren.

It had to come at last, Linden supposed; Lleld had been restrained too long—a most unnatural state for her. She said, "If you don't mind my asking, Taren, how did a Kelnethi come to find himself in Jehanglan?"

From the corner of his eye, Linden saw Otter twitch as if the bard was about to speak. But then a glance flashed between great-uncle and grandnephew, and Otter nodded and looked down. Linden wondered, but said nothing.

Taren smiled ruefully. "I don't mind, my lady, though I don't come off well in this tale. Seeing me now, on the wrong side of my middle years and ailing, you might find it hard to imagine me as young, impetuous, and headstrong. Foolish, you will no doubt find easier to believe." He paused while they laughed at this sally against himself.

"But all those things I was—especially foolish—and I fell in love with a girl. Alas for me—and well for her, I daresay—she was a sensible girl. She refused my suit. And I, certain that my life was over, began wandering.

"I lived the life of a vagabond, going first here, then there, until I found myself in the port of Tanlyton in Thalnia. I was down to my last few coppers with no hope of earning more, and wondering where my next meal was to come from, when I overheard two sailors talk of how their ship needed more hands. I signed on and rue the day I did, for a madness seized her captain and he dared the Gate of the Phoenix—what you call the Straits of Cansunn."

"The Haunted Straits," Linden murmured.

"Just so, Dragonlord. They are haunted in truth—by Death. Our ship foundered in a storm."

Maurynna said, "All the others . . . ?"

Taren looked away, his face creased in pain.

"I'm sorry," Maurynna whispered.

"Perhaps they were the lucky ones," Taren said softly. "The Jehangli . . . Dragonlords, *you* must go and free that poor dragon. Not the truedragons. From what I know, his suffering is much worse than mine was, and my life was hell."

"This is the affair of the truedragons," Lleld said in surprise. "Even if it was Dharm, he's surely passed on, leaving Varleren behind as a dragon."

"No," said Taren. "No. Dragonlords must do this thing. *You* must do this. You *four*." His eyes shone and he trembled.

Looking at him, Linden wondered if the man had a touch of the Sight—or merely another touch of fever.

"Taren, I promise you this," Lleld said. "If you are right, then Dragonlords will go. And if I can manage it, it will be the four of us."

"Your Grace," Taren said, bowing to her from his chair, "you've no idea how happy you've made me."

A little more than a tenday after meeting Taren for the first time, Maurynna went down to the stables. She wound her way through the halls until she came to Boreal's stall. Leaning over the stall door, she whistled softly.

Boreal raised his head, grain dribbling from his lips. The Llysanyin crossed his roomy stall and blew gently at her. His breath was sweet with grass and oats. She stretched a hand to him, wiggling her fingers. He met it and she rubbed his nose with her knuckles for a moment before he returned to his dinner. She rested her arms along the top of the stall door.

She watched the stallion eat, lost in a waking dream, letting the warm scent of horse flow over her. A stable, she decided, was a comforting place to be. Almost as good as a ship.

Footsteps approached. A glance told her it was Raven. She shifted a pace to make room for him to lean against the door with her and rested her chin on her laced fingers. Another sideways glance made her smile.

For Raven's mouth hung open as he stared and stared at the dapple-grey stallion. She remembered how she'd felt the day she'd met Shan. For here was a thing out of legend and song: a Llysanyin. One of the children of the wind, the mount of a Dragonlord.

"Gods, he's beautiful. Just *look* at him! And he really belongs to you?" Raven managed to say at last.

Boreal's head came up at that. The stallion turned his head so that one large, dark eye regarded Raven without blinking.

"Say, rather, that I belong to him," Maurynna said. "For it was he who picked me, not the other way around."

Boreal nodded sharply. One large, feathered hoof stamped as if to emphasize the point. The stable floor vibrated; like all his kind, Boreal had legs like young tree trunks.

Raven's eyebrows went up. Maurynna laughed at his chastened expression.

"Yes, he understood all that. Mind what you say about any of them."

"I'll remember that. My apologies," he said to Boreal.

Boreal tilted his head as if debating with himself, then nodded once more. Then he was all horse again, dropping his nose into his feed bin and whuffling in the corners, his clever upper lip digging out the last stray bits of grain. His tail swished contentedly. Maurynna blew him a kiss.

"You've met Miki and Hillel, haven't you?" she asked, naming Lleld's and Jekkanadar's Llysanyins.

From the corner of her eye she saw Raven nod. "True, but I'm still trying to imagine *you* with an ordinary horse, let alone someone like *him*."

She laughed and thumbed her nose at him, then rested her chin on her hands once more so that she could watch Boreal.

From the other halls in the warren that was the stables came the the sounds of the grooms and stablehands working, talking to each other and their charges. She and Raven were alone in this row of stalls. There was no speech between them now, but they were old enough friends not to fill every moment of silence.

Maurynna was content. It seemed Raven had finally accepted that they were no more than companions. She'd hardly seen him lately, for he'd spent most of his time closeted with the refugee from Jehanglan. Perhaps Taren had talked some sense into him. If so, she thanked the man.

Together they watched as Boreal pulled wisps of hay from his haynet. Then—Was it her imagination or had Raven inched closer? Maurynna decided imagination.

Raven asked, "What's his name? I heard it once, I think, but it won't come to mind. And did you choose it? There's no way he could have told you what he calls himself."

She nodded. "I did choose it. His name is Boreal."

"Why that?" said Raven.

She admitted sheepishly, "It was the name of Bram Wolfson's horse."

Now it was Raven's turn to laugh, which he did, loud and long. At last he wiped his eyes and said, "Of course; you would still remember those stories about him and Princess Rani. But why didn't you name him after Rani's horse? You would never let anyone else be her when we played at being them and their mercenaries as children."

"Because her horse was a mare and Boreal made it clear he didn't want to carry a mare's name, the silly creature."

Boreal flicked his long tail at her. "Stop that," she said, smiling fondly.

Raven grinned at her, his eyes still laughing. Then something crossed his face, something she couldn't put a name to, it was gone so fast. "How do you know that it was Boreal? I don't think my great-uncle ever told us."

She blinked in surprise. "Linden told me, of course. How else? Remember—he knew them. And he doesn't forget them."

"I see."

The silence fell between them again. But it was no longer comfortable; if she could touch it, it would spark. She sighed, lost in thoughts turned gloomy.

What happened next took her by surprise. It shouldn't have; she should have been expecting something like this.

Raven was no more one to give up on a dream than she was.

Before she could think what was happening, his arm was around her waist, his mouth seeking hers. Shocked, she did nothing—could do nothing.

At least, not at first. Then she pulled away, exclaiming in surprise. One hand shot out and seized the front of his tunic. Before she knew what she did, before she remembered her Dragonlord's strength, she lifted and heaved. Raven flew backward through the air.

Luckily it was not one of the stone pillars that broke his fall. Instead he landed in one of the piles of fresh bedding that would be used when the stablehands reached this row. Still, for one moment Maurynna's heart leaped into her throat. Raven lay so still in the pale golden straw that she was certain she'd killed him.

Then he was on his feet. He said nothing at first; simply stared, his bright blue eyes flashing with a rage she'd never seen in them before. "That wasn't necessary," he said at last, his voice too quiet and cold as ice.

Maurynna shook her head. "I'm sorry; I—I didn't mean to do that. I forget . . . Raven, you shouldn't have—"

He turned on his heel and strode off. As he reached the intersection with the main aisle of the stable, he nearly collided with Linden turning the corner.

Raven halted, a heartbeat's hesitation as if he would speak to Linden. Or strike him. But Raven did neither; just shoved past his startled rival and stalked off.

Maurynna wrapped her arms around herself. She felt cold and sick. True, she and Raven had quarreled aplenty in the years they'd grown up together. But never had she seen him so coldly angry.

And gods help her, she could have seriously injured him. She had no business forgetting her unnatural strength. She was a Dragonlord now, no matter how inadequate. She slumped against the stall door, waiting for Linden to ask what had happened.

He didn't. He already knew—or at least guessed. It was

there in his eyes. "Raven still refuses to understand, doesn't he?" was all Linden said.

His voice was quiet. Only one who knew him well would hear the anger lying beneath the calm surface like a reef beneath a glassy sea.

Maurynna heard it clear as a ship's bell. "He's not one to give up," she pleaded for Raven's sake. Or for the sake of the memory of their friendship; she wasn't sure which. "I should have realized it long ago. I could have told him then . . . Are you . . . going to do something?"

Please don't, she silently begged him.

His dark grey eyes held no hint of his thoughts as he stood motionless before her. Maurynna waited for his answer. It was long in coming.

"No," Linden said with a sigh. "It would only make things worse, I think. I just hope the boy comes to his senses soon. Besides, you've already made it plain to him that he's wasting his time."

"Wha— How did you know?"

A sudden twinkle woke in Linden's eyes as he jerked a thumb back over his shoulder. "Maurynna-love, he was wearing half that pile of bedding on his back."

She couldn't help it. She fell into his arms, laughing.

The last of his ceremonial rings in place, Haoro flexed his laden fingers and grimaced. As usual, the rings pinched. He scowled at the acolyte who had dressed him. The boy blanched and cowered.

Before Haoro could lash out at the unskilled oaf, another acolyte entered the room.

"Holy One," the second acolyte said. "Your uncle, the most gracious Lord Jhanun, wishes to see you before the ceremony."

Haoro sighed. Was it truly already a year since he'd received the red lotus? It felt more like only days since his uncle's last pilgrimage, the one that revealed to him his uncle's plan. Trust his uncle to combine piety and business.

Haoro wished for at least another year. "Very well; escort

him here and then take this clumsy one and make certain
he knows how to properly dress a priest. Beat it into him
if you must."

The second acolyte looked surprised, bowed, and left.
Haoro pinched the bridge of his nose between forefinger
and thumb. Truly, he must control himself; a beating, indeed! Such crude punishments were not his usual method.
It was the thought of seeing his uncle again, he mused. It
would rattle anyone.

The acolyte returned, leading Jhanun. After bowing the
Jehangli lord into the room, he left once more, this time
followed by the shaking boy.

When they were alone, Jhanun said, "You have your
priests in place?"

Haoro nodded as he adjusted the rings.

"You're certain it will work?"

"Oh, yes," the priest said. "I read through the old records
of the original ceremony that bound the beast here and created the Stones of Warding at the other three quarters. It
should work even better with a source of power at each
quarter. A *nira* need not undergo the kind of torment that
all have gone through since the binding. And if your Baisha
is correct—"

"He knows of what he speaks." The words snapped out
like the crack of a whip.

Haoro bowed his acceptance of the reproof. "Then it will
be easier to keep these creatures imprisoned in their human
form than the beast beneath our feet."

"Are your priests in place at the other three Temples of
the Warding? And are you ready to move against Pah-Ko?"

This was the question Haoro had been dreading. "The
priests are in place and ready, but . . ."

"You are not." Cold eyes black and hard as obsidian
bored into his. "I suggest you remedy that, nephew, and
quickly. You must be ready to step into Pah-Ko's place as
I step into Xiane Ma Jhi's when Baisha returns. I must start
my return journey for the capital tomorrow. Soon after I

reach there, I expect to receive news that *you* are ready. Is that understood?"

Pressing his lips together to hold back a retort, Haoro bowed in acceptance once more. "I understand, exalted uncle. But it's not easy finding a weapon to use against Pah-Ko. He's well loved. And now I must go to the temple for the ceremony."

"Ah, yes. I look forward to the singing."

With that, Jhanun left.

Haoro glanced down at his robes to make certain nothing was amiss, smoothing them automatically. Suddenly one hand clenched on the priceless silk, creasing it.

It *would* work, binding the Phoenix within a Warding anchored by four of these . . . Dragonlord . . . creatures. And it would be a binding that would last a thousand thousand years in truth, not wear thin like the one holding the fell beast in the vast cavern below the temple. For wearing thin it was; sometimes even he felt the torments the beast endured, and he was not the *nira*.

But he would be. No longer would his family have to beg for whatever favors Jhanun deigned to toss their way.

Lord Jhanun closed his eyes and let the incredible beauty of the singing wash over him.

Ah, Phoenix, if I ruled Jehanglan, I would see that you are properly honored—not like that impious, decadent wretch who sits upon the throne. Give me the throne, give me power, and I will use that power to spread your worship throughout the world.

He would see that the old ways were brought back. And when they were, never again would a concubine be allowed to gain influence over an emperor such as that little whore Shei-Luin had. Women would know their place.

He shuddered. To think that the daughter of the Blasphemer held such a high position in the court sickened him. No wonder there were earthquakes, fires, floods, drought, and any number of disasters. The Phoenix was right to be angry; that Kirano's get was the mother to the heir made a mockery of the Phoenix's sacrifice.

If only the emperor had listened to him and set the creature aside. If only she'd fallen for his little trick. . . . But no; the girl was cunning as a serpent.

All of which reminded him that he must return to the capital as soon as possible. If nothing else, he must keep a finger on the pulse of the court.

But for now, he would let the holiness of the Phoenix fill him.

Haoro listened with the others, impatient for the ceremony to be over. No, he had to admit to himself: not impatient with the ceremony, but impatient with himself. For he had yet to find the chink in the armor of the high priest, *Nira* Pah-Ko. He had yet to implement his part of the plan. Which he must, ere his uncle's man returned.

As if the thought of the *nira* was a lodestone, Haoro's gaze traveled to where the older man watched the ceremony from his private balcony, attended by acolytes, his new Oracle, and servants. By habit, Haoro dismissed all but the *nira* as beneath his notice.

Then something caught his eye: the mute boy by Pah-Ko's side, the one who replaced the old Oracle when the other had outgrown his gift. The search for the new one had been long and hard; Haoro remembered hearing that the boy had been found in a family of salt-mine slaves two hundred *ta'vri* away, and that he was an Oracle of exceptional strength.

What was his name again? Ah, yes—Hodai.

But it wasn't the boy himself that drew Haoro's attention; he looked like any common brat. No, it was the expression on the boy's face. Haoro had never seen such hunger. As the chorus welled up into the final, triumphant chorus praising the Phoenix of the Sun, it hurt to see such raw desire.

Haoro knew he had found his key.

* * *

Shei-Luin looked up from her book as Murohshei entered, carrying a *zhamsin*. She blinked in surprise, for following him was Zyuzin the Songbird, and *he* struggled with a large pottery jar. It was crude work, the kind of jar that poor people used, but Zyuzin beamed as if he carried something precious. She and Tsiaa exchanged a baffled glance. At Shei-Luin's nod, the maid ceased her sewing and came to watch, kneeling behind and to one side of her mistress.

Moving as carefully as he could with his awkward burden, Zyuzin knelt before her. Murohshei knelt to one side, facing them both. He looked, Shei-Luin thought, like one who knew a delightful secret.

Zyuzin set the jar down and, resting one hand on its lid, said proudly, "Flower of the West, I have a gift for you. Please forgive the humble jar it comes in; it was the best my family could afford."

Intrigued, Shei-Luin asked, "What is this, little songbird? Surely no one would send flowers in a sealed jar."

"Ah, but most of my family are not gardeners, Favored of the Phoenix. Only two of my uncles and one brother are gardeners—the ones whose lives you saved. The rest live a few *ta'vri* outside of the city." His round, solemn face broke into a smile. He patted the jar like a proud parent with a precocious child. "This is red bee honey."

Shei-Luin nearly dropped the book. Behind her Tsiaa gasped. Red bee honey was esteemed throughout Jehanglan for its delicate flavor—and known for its rarity. She had learned more of them since that day in the garden; Xiane had been right to fear. Red bees were aggressive creatures; disturb them and the entire hive attacked you—a habit, she discovered, that was used for a gruesome purpose.

Jehangli lords were not supposed to have the right of death over their servants; death was for the emperor alone to mete out. But a favorite way around that restriction was to send the hapless offender to raid a hive of red bees. If one were fast enough, one could outrun the furious bees after him—it was said.

"Your family gave you this honey?" she asked. At his

nod, she studied the plain red clay vessel. It hadn't even been smoothed; the marks of the potter's fingers were plain to see. If this was the best jar they could afford, how could they afford red bee honey? "Is it from the hive that was in the garden?"

"No, Favored One, not from that one; that hive was destroyed. This is from my family's own hives. They are beekeepers, you see," Zyuzin said, "and among the few who can keep red bees. Another uncle and my grandfather can hum them to sleep. They sent the honey to show their gratitude for saving Padlen, Vui, and Akaro."

Shei-Luin was touched. This must be a large portion of their harvest; Zyuzin's family would have a lean year. She would send them much fine millet and dried meat, and a bolt or two of sturdy cloth. "I thank them for their generosity," she said. "But you have already repaid my help with your beautiful songs in the garden."

Zyuzin blushed and lowered his gaze modestly. Murohshei smiled.

A thought came to Shei-Luin. "We should share this with his imperial majesty," she said.

Panic filled Zyuzin's face.

"Don't worry, little songbird, I will find a more appropriate jar," she said, then laughed as the young eunuch heaved a huge sigh of relief. "And we'll keep a good amount for ourselves; it shall be our secret, yes?" she added with a conspirator's wink.

Laughter greeted this "plot" against the emperor.

Xiane will be pleased with this, she thought. He had a child's cravings for honey and other sweet things. Each time he had some of this, he would think of her. And that was just what she wanted—to be in the forefront of Xiane's thoughts.

She must remember Zyuzin's family and their bees.

Ten

Hodai stood in the shadows watching the chanting priests. Here, in this little hall that opened onto the *nira*'s small private balcony, the young Oracle could hear the singing without being seen himself. The voices of the chorus soared like birds amid clouds of incense as they paid tribute to the Phoenix. Four times a day the great chorus raised the power: at dawn, the nooning, sunset, and midnight when the power of the sun phoenix was at its lowest. Four times a day Hodai came if he could, with his master the *nira* or without him—mostly the latter now; Pah-Ko was too ill and tired—and each time Hodai listened with all his heart.

The thought of his master, tormented with the pain of keeping the great beast imprisoned, darkened Hodai's heart for a moment. Then he remembered where—and especially when—he was.

Sunrise. The return of the phoenix of the sun.

The ceremony of dawn was the best of all. It seemed the voices were more beautiful now than at any other time, more joyful as they welcomed the sun phoenix once more to the world to bathe it in warmth and light. He imagined the voices as the colors of dawn, all red and apricot and copper and gold. His heart thrilled.

The chant swelled up now into the Song. It had no other name, did the Song, and needed none. Sung only to welcome the sun phoenix from the little death of night, it was the most wonderful thing he'd ever heard, the most wonderful thing in the world. He liked to imagine that when the foreseeings came upon him and he could speak, that at those times he heard an echo of those perfect voices in his own.

As always when he heard the Song, something in him beat against his chest, fluttered in his closed throat like a butterfly against a shuttered window. He wanted so much to sing—he who grunted like an animal. But perhaps, just perhaps, this time the Phoenix had heard his prayers. . . .

He took a deep breath to soar into beauty with the others. But once again all that came out was a horrible croaking. "Guh," he tried. "Guh-uh-uhk."

Hodai moaned and buried his face in his hands. He slumped down along the wall. Were his prayers never to be answered? Surely he served the Phoenix well! He wept in defeat.

He was crying so hard he only noticed the footsteps when they stopped in front of him. Hodai looked up, frightened, scrubbing at his tear-soaked cheeks.

One of the senior priests, Haoro, looked back at him, a gentle smile like a benediction arranged across his face. Hodai knew Haoro, knew that smile, knew the lie of it. But before he could scuttle away, Haoro put out a foot to block him.

"It grieves you, doesn't it, child, that you cannot sing? I've seen your face, Hodai, during the great festivals when the full chorus hymns the sun phoenix. I have seen the grief and longing there and I grieve with you."

Hodai hiccuped in astonishment. Haoro had noticed him? Hodai the Insignificant? Oh, Hodai knew well enough that he was important to Pah-Ko. He was Pah-Ko's Oracle. But he could never prophesy for Haoro. Or anyone else, for that matter; whoever became *nira* after Pah-Ko would need his own Oracle. An Oracle found his or her tongue for only one master.

No, this must be a trick. Another thing Hodai knew only too well was how sincere Haoro could appear, even as he plotted a rival's downfall or made a mockery of an unfortunate servant—such as a certain Oracle. Hodai gathered himself to bolt.

"I'm sorry, Hodai, for your pain—but I can help you."

He collapsed in mid-spring. Caught in an ungainly

sprawl on the floor, he looked up at the priest. *Why do you do this? Do not mock me.* But as always the words caught against his teeth and died there. "Ah-wuh?" he begged miserably.

Haoro knelt so that their eyes were level. In his panic Hodai forgot to breathe. What was the priest doing, coming down to him, a slave? And the look in those black eyes, so full of grief, Haoro's weeping heart there for anyone to see.

Hodai saw. He knew he shouldn't trust; such tears meant no more than those a *kaiwun* snake was said to shed before poisoning its prey. But he also knew that Haoro did not lie. Haoro didn't need to; he simply used truth as a weapon.

No, he shouldn't trust. But Haoro had said he could help him.

And Haoro does not lie.

Hodai stared beseechingly at the priest.

"Yes," Haoro said. "I can help you. I can order the healing power of the Phoenix to be summoned; you know that. What is wrong with your voice can be undone. But in return, Hodai, I need *your* help."

What? Hodai asked with his eyes. Anything; anything for a voice, and to lift his voice in the Song.

Haoro smiled. "Just a little information, boy. That's all. Just a little . . . information." He leaned closer. "This is what I want you to listen for," he said and whispered in Hodai's ear.

Hodai's heart sank within him. He couldn't; he just couldn't. But then the Song came to its triumphant, beautiful ending. One voice rose above the others, heartbreakingly pure, like a shaft of sunlight through clouds.

To sing like that . . .

"Do you understand what I need?" Haoro asked.

Hodai nodded.

"And you will do it?"

Long moments while his heart thudded in his ears, his emotions warred within him. Then Hodai nodded. Once.

"Good," Haoro said and rose. "Good."

There were no longer tears in his eyes. Only victory.

Eleven

A few days after his return from the Iron Temple, as he returned from a meeting with other like-minded nobles, Lord Jhanun drew open the curtains of his litter at the sound of unfamiliar noise in the courtyard of his mansion. The yard seemed full of strangers.

"Halt!" he called to his bearers.

They stopped, and he drew the curtain back farther. A closer look revealed that there were not so many people as he'd thought; just a few older men bearing swords or spears grouped around two women, one veiled. An old travel cart that had seen better days a lifetime or two ago was disappearing around the corner, one of his grooms leading the patient ox drawing it. A stripling youth—the driver, no doubt—trotted after.

An air of genteel shabbiness hung over the little group clustered together. Robes were tidy but patched, the colors faded, and the piping frayed. The leather of the scabbards was worn, in some places down to the wood beneath. The guards saw him watching and bowed. So did the women.

Ah—his niece, Nama, was here. Jhanun signaled the bearers to set the litter down. He stepped from it and waited.

The little circle of guards opened and the women came forth. The veiled one led; the other, a woman of middle years, followed. Her face was bare since she was but a servant.

Nama bowed deeply to him. "I am here as you commanded, uncle," she said. Her voice trembled.

Jhanun reached out and flipped the veil back from her face. The maid drew breath in a sharp hiss; her hand darted forward as if to undo his action. She quailed and fell back only when he turned a fierce glare on her. But her eyes blazed anger at him for this insult.

The maid, Jhanun thought, would have to go. She was too protective. Even now she stood, her fingers twitching as if they ached to curtain her lady from curious eyes and importunate stares. It was well he'd prepared for such an eventuality.

But it was his niece's reaction that Jhanun sought. Did the girl show any flash of spirit over such a gross insult? Any spark of rebellion in the dark eyes?

None. Only fear and confusion looked back at him. She cringed slightly as if expecting a blow. That was well, very well indeed. Nama was still the trembling little mouse he'd remembered. His plan could go forward; she would never say a word of what had been done to her.

"Welcome, niece," he said, his voice warm. "Come; I will show you myself to your new home."

He turned and set out, striding swiftly. A moment later he heard her scurry after.

"You've been avoiding me, Hodai."

The voice came from behind like an attacker in the dark. Hodai gasped and jumped. He whirled around, his heart beating wildly; one hand flew to his throat. Beneath his shaking fingers the gold of his slave's collar was hard—as hard as the eyes of the man who faced him.

Haoro stepped out of a wall of shadows. Or had the man woven them around himslf in a cloak of darkness? For the shadows fell away and scuttled off like insects. The servants' tunnel was once more lit with the warm, yellow light of the oil lamps set in their niches along the walls. It was dim, but nowhere was there anything like the inky pool of darkness from which Haoro had emerged.

Hodai looked desperately up and down the narrow passageway. He'd thought he was safe here, that Haoro would never stoop to using these back ways. They were for the lowest slaves. Even Hodai had the right to use the main passages through the temple.

But he'd thought here be safe he'd. . . .

Haoro's hand snapped out quick as a striking snake. The long, cold fingers seized Hodai's chin, tilted his head up to meet eyes like black jade. Part of Hodai was mildly surprised that the priest's hand was covered with skin like anyone else's; he'd half-expected to feel scales rasp against his flesh.

The rest of him was terrified.

"Well?" Haoro said. "Have you nothing to tell me, boy?"

Hodai shook his head frantically. Or tried to; the priest's fingers held him in a grip like a vise. He waved his hands in fright.

"I know he questions the Rule of the Phoenix, boy. I *feel* it. Why else do so many messages pass between him and the Seers of the Zharmatians and the Tah'nehsieh? I don't believe it is just for the sake of learning as your master says. Yet Pah-Ko is clever; he doesn't speak his true mind to us lesser priests, or tell us what lives in his heart.

"But you. . . . I know he says things to you that he would say to no one else, would not dare say to anyone else. Who would you tell? So few others know the Oracles' finger speech." He smiled, a bare twist of the lips, and his voice dropped, soft as silk and cold as jade. The priest continued, "As I do. Ah—you didn't realize that, little Oracle? But I do know it. So tell me; tell me everything."

Hodai forced his trembling fingers to move. *Nothing. Master say nothing bad.*

Haoro's fingernails bit into Hodai's face; the boy's eyes filled with tears. He squeezed them shut.

"Look at me!" the priest demanded.

Whimpering, Hodai met the black eyes boring into his. They burned with a coldness that seared both mind and soul, tearing him apart as they raged through every corner of his being.

After an eternity Haoro released him. Hodai fell back against the wall, gasping. In his terror he'd forgotten to

breathe. The world danced grey and dim before his eyes.
His thin chest heaved as he gulped down great draughts of
air.

"You tell the truth," the priest said. "Pah-Ko has said
nothing in your hearing. But he will, Oracle. He will. And
when he does . . ."

Haoro turned the full brilliance of his smile upon the
mute. "When he does and you have told me of it, then shall
you have your reward, brave little Hodai. Then shall you
sing. Listen."

From the empty air came a ghostly singing. The voice
was faint and clear, and more beautiful than even the voice
that led the Song. Hodai trembled at the sound and
stretched out his hands as if he could snatch it from the air.

Without another word the priest disappeared back into
the shadows he'd come from. The singing ended. Hodai
slid down the wall into a huddled ball on the floor. He wept.

How could he betray the man who'd been father and
mother to him?

He remembered the voice promised him.

How could he not?

The compound of her uncle's city mansion was huge, Nama
thought as she pattered along behind him. There was the
main house itself, then a number of little houses, many in
their own gardens, here and there. Houses for guests? Favored servants? She had no time to stop and look.

Nor did she want to. She might meet someone's eyes.
For she did not dare rearrange her veil; her face was still
bare to any man's gaze. From the corner of her eyes she
could see servants stop and stare. To her utter humiliation,
some of the men leered at her once Jhanun was past. Phoenix help her, did they think she was some courtesan of
Jhanun's? She wished the earth would open and swallow
her. She wished the Phoenix would strike her dead with its
holy fire and spare her this shame. But all she could do
was hurry after her uncle with her head bowed and her eyes
brimming with tears she dared not shed.

At least Moya was with her. She could hear the maid and a few of her uncle's servants following close behind.

Please let us get there soon! And please *don't let uncle stay very long.* Once there, and they were alone, Moya would hold her while she cried.

By the kindness of the Phoenix, it proved to be only moments more before they reached their destination, a place so far away from the other houses that it might almost not be part of the compound. Jhanun paused before a gate set in a palisade of stout bamboo higher than a man's head. He reached into his sleeve and drew out a key. It turned in the lock without a sound. He pushed the gate open and led her inside.

Nama paused in the gateway. A single glance made her forget her fear and confusion. The place was enchanting!

Jasmine vines grew in wild abandon along the fence, softening its harshness and perfuming the air. Other flowers grew everywhere, a riot of color to delight the eyes. A little stream meandered through the landscape, singing merrily to itself as the sunlight glinted on its waters. A small foot-bridge arched over it. Beyond lay a house, also small, but perfect as a jewel in its setting.

Entranced, Nama took a few steps forward into this un-expected haven. She clapped her hands in delight.

Like some nightmare echo came the sounds of the gate swinging shut and Moya's cry. Nama spun around; from beyond the gate came sounds of a scuffle.

"Lady! My lady!" Moya wailed. "Let me go to my lady!" Her cries grew fainter.

"Moya!" But there was no answer. Nama thought she would faint from sheer terror. "Uncle?" she whispered.

"She'll be sent home with your guards. You no longer need the services of an inferior maid," her uncle replied with a lift of his eyebrow. "I have engaged a better one for you." He lifted a hand and gestured.

Nama looked. The door to the little house opened; a woman came out. Though her clothes were of the plain cloth of a servant, they were elegantly cut, and worn with such regal assurance that they might have been silk brocade. From her perfect hair to her elegant slippers, this was a maid fit for a lady of the court.

But her expression was as hard and grim as a stone wall, and her eyes held no welcome, only cold indifference. She was a big woman, as tall as some men. Nama's spirit quailed at the sight of her.

"That is Zuia," Jhanun said. "She will see to your needs. In two days, after you have rested from your journey, the first of your tutors will come. Now go."

Nama hesitated, frightened by the grim-faced woman.

"Go." Her uncle's voice was soft, but cold as a knife blade against the throat on a winter night.

Moving through a cloud of despair, Nama crossed the little bridge.

Twelve

The Lady of Dragonskeep woke from a dream. Tears slid down her cheeks as she sat up in bed, careful not to disturb Kelder. She brushed the tears aside.

Gods, what a sad dream, so full of grief and regret! Yet she couldn't remember what it had been, just that a voice bearing all the sorrow in the world had threaded a way through her mind. She drew a shuddering breath.

Then, quietly as dusk falling, the voice was back in her mind. Her waking mind; no dream this time.

Fear seized her. She knew that voice. *Morlen? Morlen, what's wrong?*

We have decided what must be done, Jessia.

One of you has volunteered to go to Jehanglan to free the captive? But if so, why was Morlen so— The Lady bit her knuckle. Was it Talassaene? That would explain—

No, my friend. I tried to take that task upon myself, for if I had understood that Seeing so many years ago, perhaps much misery could have been avoided.

Sorrow gusted through her mind like a storm, then the truedragon went on, *The others would not hear of it. Instead—*

A flood of grief brought fresh tears to the Lady's eyes. She cried silently, caught up in Morlen's emotions. *Then what . . . ?*

We go to war, my dearest friend. Even I, for although my magic is not what it once was, I cannot abandon my people. So in a few days . . . That I have lived to see this wretched day! Jessia, heart friend—I beg thee to pray for us. I fear we shall have need of it, for there is worse yet.

She listened as he told her his fears, and grew cold inside.

Nira Pah-Ko sat by the window, watching the early morning mist swirl through the valley below. His breathing came loud and harsh in the stillness of his tower room. He was not an old man, but looked like one, limbs twisted and wasted from containing the power that nourished Jehanglan. Deep, deep within his tired bones he felt the pain of the captive chained in the caverns below the temple.

He was the *nira*, the focus, the linchpin of the holy prison that held the dark beast; he was the living sacrifice for Jehanglan. It had been an honor to be chosen so many years ago, but it was a hard one.

It happened to every *nira*, Pah-Ko reflected as he shut his mind to the latest surge of pain. Agony in the beginning, it had become easier to ignore with long practice; the priest shut the thought from his mind that the jolts came stronger these days, harder to put aside. He did not like what that might portend—that and the earthquakes to the east that the runners spoke of.

"The signs are bad," he wheezed aloud to the colorful finches in the cage by his chair and to the child crouched on the floor before him. "All bad. The emperor is weak, sinful. Were he righteous, all Heaven and Earth would be in harmony. Instead he skimps on the ceremonies when he even bothers to attend them, and fails to honor his ancestors properly." He shook his head sadly. "That I should have lived to see such days, Hodai," he said to the boy at his feet.

The boy nodded, his great eyes fixed on his master, but offered no comment. The finches hopped from perch to perch in their cage of gilded bamboo. "Beee, beee, beee," they buzzed and flocked to the side of the cage, hoping for a treat.

Pah-Ko fumbled in the dish on the table. With difficulty he made his crooked fingers scoop up a small quantity of seeds and cast them into the bottom of the cage. Like tiny, animate flowers, the finches jumped down and pecked eagerly at the seeds. As the *nira*, he was entitled to have nightingales sing for him as the emperor did; but their sweet song seemed to torment Hodai and he would not add to the young slave's pain. He kept finches instead, and enjoyed their impertinent ways.

Poor, poor child; he wants to sing so badly and cannot even speak.

The boy made the signs for *pretty* and *greedy* and smiled.

"Aren't they, though? There's fire and flood, drought and disease—but you don't care, do you, my little jewels? The land is racked by earthquake, the runners bring tales of two-headed calves born in the villages along the *sian* lines, dead men have been seen walking, and there are rumors of blood filling temple courtyards—but what is that to you?" Pah-Ko said.

He waggled a finger at them. One or two turned a saucy eye on him, but the rest snatched greedily at the seeds. "Ah," he said, amused as his favorite, Little Jade, fluttered back up to the nearest perch and watched him, bright green head cocked to one side. "This though, you should care about."

The boy tilted his head much like the finch, listening. His face grew serious and something like fear filled his eyes.

•

The priest lowered his voice though there was no one else in the room. "My powers are fading, Hodai, and Haoro eyes the feathered mantle of the *nira*—*my* mantle. And if Haoro becomes *nira*, then— Bah! His family was always greedy, and now they are poor; a dangerous combination. And the honor—and power—it would bring to his mother's brother, Jhanun . . ."

Hodai nodded, hesitantly at first, then vigorously. His clever fingers said, *Bad power*, then made his private sign for one of the other senior priests, Deeh.

"Yes," the priest wheezed and began coughing. At once Hodai jumped up, fetched him a cup of bitter tea and helped him drink. When the fit had passed, the young slave arranged a blanket over him, then knelt before him once again. "Yes," Pah-Ko repeated, relishing the warmth of the thick wool. "Bad power indeed. The Phoenix should choose Deeh. It would be better."

Agreement washed across Hodai's face like a flood. He signed, *Haoro does not lie. But Deeh speaks truth.*

Pah-Ko looked out of the window once more at the mist. *Such simple words and so true*, he thought. *Is it not bad enough that Haoro's paternal grandfather was so deep in the plans to overthrow the Imperial Palace? The family was stripped of nearly everything—and rightly so. But now there's the chance that they may come into power again. The old emperor was too lenient; he should have destroyed them. At the least Haoro should never have been allowed to rise in the ranks of the priesthood. Maybe it is a mistake that when a man is chosen to be the* nira, *so much wealth and power is heaped upon his family. But if not, what sane man would accept?*

Pah-Ko was honest with himself. Anything that benefited Jehanglan could be endured—especially when it brought fortune, rank, and honor to one's kin. He would never have agreed to become the *nira* years ago had it not been for the benefit to his family. It was a sacrifice any Jehangli man of good conscience would make; the well-being of one's family was all.

Now his brother was a duke and a sister had been a concubine of the old Phoenix Lord, retired now in honor to an estate of her own with many servants. Another sister married an Imperial Judge. His parents' ashes—honor of honors!—were interred in the great Temple of the Phoenix itself and incense burned to their souls every day. He had done well by his family; it had been a small price to pay to lift them from their abject poverty.

Another surge of pain; he hid it as well as he could from Hodai. Pah-Ko shifted carefully in his chair. *I hope Deeh is the one chosen. He's an orphan; Haoro has a family of jackals ready to leap upon Jehanglan—if only his mother wasn't one of Jhanun's sisters!*

Nor was the choice of his successor all that disturbed Pah-Ko these days. The uncomfortable doubts which plagued him of late raged in his mind like crows tormenting a trapped fox.

"It's all unraveling," he muttered. Hodai leaned against his knee, offering silent comfort; Pah-Ko stroked the sleek black head. "All of it. Our temple's reverend ancestor, Gao-lun, said that the reign of the Phoenix would last a thousand thousand years. Now it's only a few handfuls more than a thousand years, and the world disintegrates before my eyes. And what of my other Oracle's prophesy, Hodai, that said to bring the seed of Lord Kirano to the Phoenix Lord? Shei-Luin has borne a fine son to Xiane Ma Jhi, and still there's calamity!"

The boy fluttered his hands anxiously and his dark eyes filled with fear. He grunted in an effort to speak.

With difficulty, Pah-Ko caught the hands beating at the air like frightened butterflies. "No, no, don't worry, child. It wasn't even your prophecy. You Oracles only tell us what you see, and you see the truth. All we mere mortals can do is try to follow the Phoenix's divine words. But are we in truth doing that?"

A tiny sob escaped the boy. He rested his head against Pah-Ko's knees. One hand came up, searching.

Pah-Ko caught and held it, willing comfort and peace to

the shaking boy. He thought, *I must be more careful what I say to Hodai; sometimes I forget how young he is, with all the self-doubts of the young. He has so much wisdom for a child.*

He sat, staring out of the window. The crows of doubt returned to pick at his mind. Suddenly he said, "Some say the first *nira* was wrong to do what he did. Some also think the binding *should* be undone. Eh, Hodai—shall we ask Little Jade what he thinks? Bestow your wisdom upon us, O tiny wise one!"

Hodai's hand clenched like a vise. It jerked once.

"Beee," the little finch said. "Beee, beee, beee."

Pah-Ko nodded wisely. "You agree the Phoenix should be free? Good! And what is that? Yes; I now think the poor beast below us should be set free as well, may the Phoenix forgive me my heresy."

The boy's hand, suddenly cold, slid like a dead thing from his grasp.

Linden came out of the bathing room, working his fingers through the wet, unbound length of his clan braid to untangle it. Steam rose gently from his naked body as he wandered through the sleeping chamber, humming. Maurynna, content to be warm and lazy under the blankets, watched with appreciation as he paused before the fire to fight with a particularly recalcitrant knot.

I don't think I'll ever tire of just watching him, she thought. Then she smiled. *Or of—*

A sharp tapping at the chamber door interrupted the pleasant train of thought. She sat up in suprise.

"Linden? Maurynna?" Varn, their *kir* servant called through the door; he had learned better than to just walk in, poor fellow. His voice had an edge to it that Maurynna had never heard before. Alarmed now, she snatched up the nightgown that had fallen to the floor the night before and yanked it on.

"Yes. Come in," Linden called when she was ready. He turned to her. She had his breeches ready and tossed them to him. He pulled them on as Varn slipped into the room. Maurynna jumped off the bed and went to her clothes chest at the foot of it. She grabbed the first tunic and breeches that came to hand, and stood up to listen.

The usually cheerful *kir* was frowning. "I thought you might want to know," he said, "the *Saethe* is meeting. Now."

This early? Why, half of them must have been rousted out of bed, Maurynna thought in surprise.

"Why?" Linden asked.

"I don't know for certain," said Varn slowly.

"Kitchen rumor, then," Linden snapped.

Maurynna remembered Linden once telling her that nine times out of ten, whatever came out of the servants' quarters was correct.

Varn nodded. "Word is that the truedragons suspect it's either Dharm Varleran or a truedragon named Pirakos in Jehanglan. That Morlen had a Seeing: it will take magic or magical beings to free the captive, so asking a band of truehumans to invade is out, even if they could get into the kingdom."

The *kir* paused; he rubbed his short-muzzled face. The next words came out as barely more than a whisper. "Word is that it will take them a few days to make ready, but . . . The truedragons . . . The truedragons are going to war." Tears slid down his furred cheeks.

"Gifnu's bloody hells," Linden swore softly. He turned away.

Tunic and breeches slipped from Maurynna's fingers, and she put her hand over the icy pit where her stomach used to be.

"Dear gods, no," was all she could say.

Thirteen

It was beginning.

Sulae Shallanan, in dragon form to bring medicine to an isolated family of *kir* shepherds, saw them first. She mind-called the other Dragonlords at the Keep. The word spread from them, and soon everyone who could was outside, watching.

"Here they come!" someone cried. The sky to the north grew black across the narrow mountain horizon. Many wept openly. Such a thing had not happened in centuries, not since the shaman's war that unleashed the wild magic that had created the Dragonlords. No one had ever wanted to see it again.

The truedragons were going to war.

Linden stood with Maurynna, Otter, and Raven. Taren stood to one side. Fear etched the man's face. Fear and . . . anger.

Aye, well might Taren be angry. For Linden was angry as well, that the truedragons should try this way first and go so much against their natures. But who were any of them to tell the great lords of the sky their business?

The truedragons were nearly overhead now. Like a swarm of monstrous locusts they came on, one after another. The sky grew dark overhead as they passed over and those upon the ground watched in silence. But all too soon the pale blue of the autumn sky reappeared.

"Morlen couldn't stop them?" Maurynna whispered.

"No." Lleld came up. "He was outvoted." For once Lleld did not look happy to be the bearer of tidings. Her brown eyes brimmed with tears. "All save the very old, the very young, and the infirm are with their army."

"And Morlen?" asked Maurynna. "I thought I—" Her voice shook.

"And Morlen, love," Linden said. He stroked her hair. "I recognized him."

"He wouldn't leave the others to face this danger; though he's old and his magic isn't what it once was—his words, I heard the Lady say—it's still strong. He doesn't agree with this plan, but he won't desert them," said Lleld. Her voice quivered, and she turned her face away to watch the truedragons once more.

"May the gods help them," Otter said after the last truedragon disappeared beyond the range of mountains to the south of Dragonskeep.

"And see them safely home," Linden said. To himself he said, *I had no idea there were so few of them. Gods help us all, what if the Jehangli magic is stronger than theirs?*

It could mean the end of the truedragons. He shut his eyes against the thought. "Avert," he whispered against Maurynna's hair. "Avert."

His master slept. Hodai stood in the doorway and listened to Pah-Ko's deep, even breathing, broken by an occasional whimper brought on by surges of the pain that was a *nira*'s constant companion. He was glad his master could find even this much relief in slumber. That Pah-Ko napped also meant Hodai could go outside to play for a time.

Like a bright-eyed mouse, Hodai left the chambers of the *nira* and slipped through the halls of the temple complex that crowned Mount Kajhenral. Whenever he couldn't avoid being seen, the little Oracle trotted purposefully along, knowing that if he seemed to be on an errand for the Holy One, no one would stop him.

Not even Haoro. Hodai pattered down the curving stairs that led to the back exit by the temple storerooms.

But as if the thought were a summoning, Haoro was standing at the bottom of the stairs, talking to one of the lesser priests who oversaw the storerooms.

"I wish more of the new incense to be sent to my rooms. The scent is most pleasing."

Hodai stumbled to a halt. He tried to turn around, but in his terror, his legs betrayed him. They gave way and he sat with such force that a pained grunt forced its way out.

Haoro instantly looked up the stairs and saw him. The Oracle could only stare back, too frightened to move. The priest studied him for a moment that went on and on as Hodai's blood pounded in his ears like thunder. He thought he would faint. When he saw the smile that crept at last across Haoro's face, he nearly did.

Haoro *knew*.

With a flick of his hand, Haoro dismissed the lesser priest. The man hurried away. Hodai willed his legs to stand, to run, but they had all the strength of melted·wax. He could only watch the priest mount the stairs toward him, each stride as slow and deliberate as a stalking tiger's.

"You've something to tell me."

Hodai trembled. *No!* he wanted to shout, to jump up and run away. But the gift of speech was not his, nor would his body obey him. The best he could do was lock his fingers together so hard it hurt and vow not to—

The priest's hand gestured. Once more the ghostly, beautiful voice sang in the air. Once more the sound smote Hodai to the heart. He listened hungrily; it died away too soon, leaving him aching for more.

"That can be yours, Hodai. Yours for as long as the phoenix lives."

Still under the spell of the voice, Hodai unclenched his hands and, like one in a trance, began forming words with trembling fingers.

When Hodai was done, Haoro said, "Yet he has said nothing of actually undoing the binding?"

Hodai shook his head vigorously, his paralysis of terror finally breaking. *No,* he signed again and again.

"Then I shall let him dig this tiger pit a little deeper for himself." To Hodai's relief, Haoro continued up the steps past him. The young Oracle stared rigidly ahead, willing Haoro far, far away.

But the reprieve was cruelly short. For Haoro, stopping just behind him, said, "You're loyal to Pah-Ko, aren't you, little Oracle. For this didn't happen today, did it?"

Hodai stiffened. How did—?

"I always know, boy. So don't think to warn Pah-Ko, Hodai. For if you do, I'll know that as well. And then you shall die. Do you understand?"

Hodai nodded stiffly, still not daring to turn his head. Not until the last echoes of footsteps were long gone, and his buttocks were nigh as cold as the stone he sat upon, did Hodai dare to move.

When he did, he trudged back up the stairs, all thoughts of play forgotten, as empty inside as a ghost.

Taren sat close to the fire after a dinner few had the appetite for, a heavy shawl over his shoulders and a blanket covering his lap. His sallow face looked even yellower in the firelight. The string of white worry beads flashed as they slipped endlessly through his fingers.

Jehanglan must be warm indeed to have thinned Taren's blood so much, Linden thought as he leaned on the mantel near the former slave's chair. He looked across at Otter, who wore only a woolen tunic and breeches against the chill of the autumn night. *Even Otter is comfortable, and he's older than Taren.*

His gaze traveled among the others ranged throughout the chamber. The bard sat in the chair on the other side of the fireplace from Taren, his face grave, studying the goblet in his hand. His harp leaned against the far wall. Linden wondered if Otter would have the heart to sing tonight. Raven sat on a low stool by his great-uncle's knee, resting his chin in his hands, staring into the fire. He looked troubled.

Lleld and Jekkanadar were curled up together in the room's only double chair. The little Dragonlord's fiery red head rested on her soultwin's shoulder; Jekkanadar put his arm around her. Neither spoke.

In the centuries I've known her, I've never seen Lleld upset like this. I know I've often wished that she weren't quite so . . . exuberant, but damn! If this is how that wish is answered, I'll take her ten times worse than she was before.

Maurynna sat cross-legged on the floor nearby. She picked at the long silken fringe of the Assantikkan sash she wore belting her tunic, braiding and unbraiding it. Her goblet of wine sat untouched by her knee.

"I can't believe they're going to try it," Lleld said, breaking the heavy silence.

Linden sipped his wine. "They couldn't just leave Pirakos or Varleren or whoever it might be there. What else could they have done?" He held up a hand against the anger that blazed in the red-haired little Dragonlord's face. "No, I don't agree it was the right thing to do. I just don't see how else—"

"That's because you still think like a soldier," Lleld snapped. "There are other ways of getting to the honeycomb than running your head into a bees' nest."

"What would you suggest?" Linden countered.

Lower lip sticking out, Lleld said, "I don't know. But there has to be a better way."

Raven looked up. "I'd never really thought about how many truedragons there were before today. But there seemed far fewer than I thought there would be. Why?"

Linden looked to the two older Dragonlords. *I wondered about that myself. Do you think a number of them have chosen to pass on?*

Perhaps, came the slow answer from Jekkanadar. *And if so, what does that mean?*

Not something I like the sound of, said Lleld.

Linden agreed with her and said aloud, "We're not certain. Perhaps the Lady knows."

No one spoke; the others looked as grim as he felt. *What is it that Maurynna says when she's angry or upset—*

"Black dog on my shoulder?" Well, that black dog is prowling this room, he thought. The silence grew, leavened only by the crackling of the flames.

It went on so long that when Otter spoke, Linden jumped, almost spilling his wine.

"Taren." The bard was no longer studying his goblet, but his face was even graver than before. "Taren, what will the truedragons face? What kind of magic do they have in Jehanglan?"

The soft clicking of the worry beads stopped. "They don't have magic as we have it here," Taren answered. "There are no mages. Nor do you find someone such as a milkmaid, say, who can make the butter come with a word. You understand me? Odd little talents."

Maurynna said, "Mm—yes. The little magics that sometimes crop up. There's a sailor like that on board my Aunt Maleid's ship. No matter how wet and tangled the ropes, how tight the knot, it will all come free at his touch if he wills it. My uncles have been trying to lure him away from Aunt Maleid for years." She smiled. "But she also has the best ship's cook."

Welcome laughter at that; the gloom filling the chamber eased a little. But Taren's statement bothered Linden.

"No magic at all?" he said. "How is the land protected, then? For protected it is, from all I've heard."

Taren shrugged and turned a benign smile upon him. "I was but a lowly slave, Dragonlord. All I know is that I was told there is no magic in Jehanglan, that the Phoenix protects the land with its holy might. I never heard of any mages; there are no stories about them, either."

A land without magic. It seemed inconceivable to Linden. There was magic everywhere—wasn't there? Images of a world without it filled his mind; he wasn't certain he wanted to live there. In the back of his mind a voice said, *Did you live in such a place, you would have died six hundred years ago.*

Not a comfortable thought, that; the skin down his back crawled and he shivered. He muttered, "Goose walking over my grave." Then, louder, "Are there no creatures of magic, then, in Jehanglan? Surely the Phoenix is a creature of magic. What about dragons, say, or anything else?"

The firelight danced on Taren's bald pate as he shook his head. "No dragons. The priests of the Phoenix temple teach that the dragons were evil and the Phoenix killed them all long ago."

"What do priests from other temples preach?" Otter asked.

"There are no other temples."

The others looked at each other in astonishment.

Otter persisted. "You mean there's only one way to worship? No choice of gods to believe in?"

"The Zharmatians—a tribe of horse herders who roam the Western Plains—believe differently. So do others that the Jehangli name barbarian, such as the Tah'nehsieh. But they're few and powerless, small groups of no importance."

A gesture of dismissal, and the clicking of the worry beads began again. "Sometimes the soldiers of the priests descend upon a village and take one or more of the children back with them. No one knows why those children are chosen. Males are given to the temple to become priests. I don't know what happens to the girls."

"And I don't think I like Jehanglan," Lleld muttered under her breath.

By unspoken agreement, the talk drifted onto other, easier, subjects for a time.

The cliff beckoned him. Crawling on hands and knees to the edge, Hodai looked over. Already the valley below was wreathed in darkness.

But it was no darker than his heart. He had betrayed the man he loved like a grandfather, and who loved him as a grandson. He remembered the first time they'd met, how kindly the *nira* had treated him. He had given his heart then to the man.

He deserved death. But he was young, and the thought of dying frightened him.

Then the wind sang among the rocks below, and in it he heard an echo of the Phoenix's voice. *His* voice—someday.

Hodai crept away.

Taren's head nodded; the next moment he was drowsing in the manner of a man much older, light and easy, as quick to wake as to dream. Linden held a hand out to Maurynna.

"Come," he whispered as he pulled her up from the floor. "I've a wish to learn more of Jehanglan."

Jekkanadar heard, whispered in turn, "Ah. You're thinking the same thing, perhaps, as I?" He pointed at the ceiling.

Linden smiled. "Indeed, yes."

He led the way from the room, Maurynna's hand warm in his own. Lleld tucked the shawl a little tighter around Taren's shoulders as she passed him on her way to the door. Once in the hall, Jekkanadar took the lead, scattering a handful of coldfire ahead like scouts.

"Where are we going?" Linden heard Raven mutter to Otter.

"The library," said the bard. "I'll wager Lukai and Jenna are still awake and presiding over their kingdom."

Jekkanadar grinned over his shoulder. "You'll not find anyone willing to take that wager, bard, in all of Dragonskeep. We know our archivists too well."

Taren listened as the soft footsteps vanished down the hall. With an oath, he flung the shawl to the floor. *Damn* them for asking so many—and such searching—questions. As tired as he was of feigning illness, he was glad he had such a trick to fall back on. He would play it as often as he needed.

A sudden shiver reminded him that it was not all a sham. The sickness still had its claws in him. He picked up the shawl once more and wrapped it around his shoulders.

These were the four. He *felt* it. These would give the throne of Jehanglan to his master—if the cursed truedragons didn't succeed in their mission.

But they cannot succeed. The rogue Oracle said nothing of such a calamity.

Taren paced the room, giving vent to the foulest curses he knew. The truedragons must fail, he told himself again and again. If they did not, it would completely negate Lord Jhanun's Oracle. And that could not be.

Yet no Oracle, not even a *nira*'s, saw everything.

Damn the truedragons.

He hoped whichever way it went, it would be over soon. This waiting was driving him mad.

Jekkanadar led them down the hall to a wooden door. He pushed it open, revealing a narrow stone staircase. It curved around and around; with each step Linden's feet found the smooth hollows worn in the stone treads, testimony to the many Dragonlords who had sought knowledge or simply quiet in the centuries since Dragonskeep was built.

And how many of us have come this way biting our fingernails because we didn't complete the lessons our tutors had set us? he wondered, remembering when he was new to the Keep and learning the languages of the Five Kingdoms. He could smile about it now, but old Brithian—his tutor for Pelnaran—had been a terror; a ghost of long-ago apprehension tweaked Linden as he reached the final step. He paused to shut the door at the top of the staircase before following the others down the hall.

They filed into the library. Jenna, the archivist, sat at a table near a window; she looked up in surprise from her book. Lukai, her truehuman counterpart, came out of one of the small rooms used for lessons, feather duster in hand. He blinked owlishly at them. *Kir* and truehuman looked first at each other, then stared at the newcomers in frank astonishment. The only other occupants were two truehuman men, each at a different table.

Of those two, one was clearly one of the scholars who sometimes journeyed to Dragonskeep; the floppy, four-cornered cap of an academic lay by his elbow. He scowled briefly at the interruption and bent over his books and scatter of parchment notes once more. He muttered to himself, pulling his small oil lamp closer. Dragonlords held no interest for him, the set of his shoulders said.

The other man also looked up at their entrance. He wore a bard's torc. Linden heard Otter's startled but quiet "What's he doing here?" as Otter slowly raised a hand in greeting.

At first the stranger did nothing, merely staring coldly at Otter. Then the man nodded and went back to his book.

Someone you know? Linden asked. *And no friend, either, by the look of it.* There had been venom in that look. To himself Linden thought, *Who would bear Otter such animosity?*

Otter replied, *Yes to both; he's a fellow bard, one of the Masters at the Harpers College; doesn't usually travel much. I've told you about him.* His lips were a grim line.

Linden suddenly knew who it was. *Leet?* he asked. That would explain much.

Yes. A welter of emotions twisted beneath Otter's unsteady mindvoice. *I wonder what—*

Otter broke off as Raven spoke.

"Good gods!" Raven exclaimed, staring about him. "I had no idea there were so many books in the world!"

A disgruntled snort came from the scholar's table. Leet read on as if he hadn't heard anything.

Linden looked around the room, remembering his own astonishment at his first sight of the library of Dragonskeep. Shelves lined the walls, filled with books, some in gaily colored bindings, most in sober brown; some were the gifts of kings and queens, some the presented works of grateful scholars who had found long-sought-after knowledge in the collection, others acquired by Dragonlords on their travels. The gentle, slightly stuffy scent of old leather welcomed him; he'd forgotten what a haven this had been when he'd first come to Dragonskeep, a hillman fresh from the mountains of Yerrih, awkward and nervous and frightened at what he'd become.

Jenna chuckled softly. Rising, she said, "There may well

be no other collection like it, young truehuman. Kingdoms may come and go, but there has always been the library of Dragonskeep—and the Keep itself, of course." An impish smile twitched over her short-muzzled face. "It's late in the evening to be looking for a little reading, my friends. Shall I guess what you've come for?" She laid a hand upon the page she'd been studying.

"Bother," said Lleld. "Someone's been here before us, then?"

Another, louder, snort from the scholar.

Lukai blinked; his large, watery eyes crinkled with amusement. "Many someones, Lleld. Indeed, we were surprised we haven't seen *you* before this. And we've missed you, Jekkanadar. We found some words in an old history of Assantik that we'd like your help with."

"Here," said Jenna. She shut her book and patted it. "Let's take this into one of the lesson rooms and leave Master Pren in peace."

Since the volume looked heavy, Linden picked it up for the frail *kir* archivist and followed her to a small room off the main library. Once they were all inside, Jekkanadar shut the door behind them; the others sat. Linden placed the book before the two archivists and took his own place by Maurynna.

Before anyone could speak, Jenna nodded at Raven. "You're the one who brought Taren Olmeins to Dragonskeep, aren't you, young truehuman?"

"I am," Raven admitted.

"When we heard the news," Jenna said, "we remembered this book and began reading."

"Do you know every book in the collection?" Lleld asked.

Kir and truehuman smiled. "Yes," they said together.

"You see," Jenna explained, "they're old friends to us."

"Old and well trusted," Lukai said. "How may we help you?"

"Tell us about Jehanglan," Lleld said. "We know that the

Phoenix Emperor closed his kingdom. It happened in Jekkanadar's father's time."

"True," Jenna said as Lukai nodded. "And from then until a hundred or so years ago, no one traded with Jehanglan save a rumored few smugglers, and not many of those, either. Then an envoy came to the Dawn Emperor, saying that his brother emperor of Jehanglan wished to beg a favor of him, for there had once been much contact between the two kingdoms. It was the first word from the Phoenix Kingdom."

"Odd," Linden said. "Why change their minds all of a sudden?"

Though her eyes were full of old stories, Jenna said only, "Silk."

Dragonlords and truehumans looked at each other.

"Silk?" Maurynna echoed.

"Just so," said Lukai. "It is all here in this journal by Lady Ardelis of Kelneth. She was a great traveler and seeker of odd bits of information. She visited the Assantikkan court perhaps a year or so after the pact was signed. Here; let me read this to you." He pulled a kerchief from his sleeve and dabbed at his eyes. "I beg your pardon, but the dust upon these old books . . ." he muttered as he carefully turned the pages.

"Ah! Here it is. Lady Ardelis wrote: 'Today I saw a most strange ship come in to the port of Nen dra Kore. It's not like our northern cogs, nor even like to the galleys of the Dawn Emperor. I've not the knowledge of ships to say anything more detailed than that it's not like anything I've ever seen before. Every inch of it is painted and carved as if the sight of the good bare wood were an offense to the eyes. A veritable rainbow of colors it was! And looming over all upon the sail is the image of a great, fiery bird; yet flying from the mast was the triangular pennant of an Assantikkan trading house—House Mhakkan, my escort, Merreb, said.

" 'I was told that this was one of the ships from fabled Jehanglan. When I remarked that I'd heard it was closed to outsiders, Merreb said that had once been so. But it seems some time ago the silkworms of Jehanglan were wiped out by a plague or some such thing, and the Phoenix Kingdom was desperate for silks and silk brocades. It is all their nobles and rulers wear in court. Now, it so happened that before Jehanglan shut itself off from the world, there had been a great trade between the two countries, even to the establishing of temples to each other's gods to accommodate the traders, and that silkworms were exported from there to Assantik at one time.

" 'While they never did quite as well in Assantik as in their homeland, the silkworms had prospered well enough that the Assantikkans could spare silk to sell to Jehanglan—in return for certain trade concessions. The Phoenix Lord agreed and the Dawn Emperor granted the right of trade with Jehanglan to House Mhakkan, who controls much of the production of silk here.

" 'All this I was told by Merreb, factor to House Azassa, who spat whenever House Mhakkan's name was mentioned.' "

Lukai ran a finger down the page. "Here Lady Ardelis noted—with great delicacy—that she later heard that the Dawn Emperor owed much to House Mhakkan."

"Which meant they owned him," Raven said bluntly. "Knowing what I do about that House now, the emperor likely had to give Mhakkan the grant. They would have brought him down otherwise. I wonder what hold they had over him? Whatever it was, they haven't lost any of that power over the years; much the opposite. They're stronger than ever and still greedy as hell. Now they control *all* of the silk production in Assantik. Trust Mhakkan to be in the right place at the right time even then." He shook his head, looking disgusted. It was plain Raven had no more love for House Mhakkan than the long-dead Merreb of House Azassa.

"I understand better now," Linden said, "why Gilliad al zefa' Mimdallek wanted Taren out of there." He stared at the books lining the walls without seeing them. "No, House

Mhakkan wouldn't take kindly to someone using smugglers and taking trade from them, would they? Perhaps even opening a new route. What if someone found a way around the Haunted Straits? And if it were known there was such trading—" He looked over at Lleld.

"The emperor would have to stop it, wouldn't he, because whoever did it violated an imperial order," finished Lleld.

Maurynna nodded. "Exactly; he would have no choice but to destroy that House. And that is not something Gilliad al zefa' Mimdallek would want. For when the Dawn Emperors destroy a House, it is absolute. Ships, warehouses, merchandise, wagons, homes, everything that House has. Their fields are salted, their livestock slaughtered. Adults are killed and the children sold into slavery. Even the name of that House is stricken and may never be used again."

"It's happened?" Linden asked.

"Oh, yes," Maurynna said. She shivered. "It's happened."

"Taren," said Linden, "is a very lucky man indeed to still be alive, then. Good thing for him that Second is so superstitious."

Lleld, chin in hand, asked, "Does Lady Ardelis say what the Jehangli trade for besides silk? There must be more than that."

Muttering to himself, Lukai thumbed through the journal once more. "Hm, hm, know it's here somewhere. . . . Ah— 'they trade for silks'—which we knew—'and cochineal and murex dyes, myrrh from Assantik, muttonfat amber and the gum of the sweet balsam tree that both come from the north, as well as other dyes and incenses and gemstones. Wheat and a few other grains, and Assantikkan dates, oranges, and ginger. Yerrin horses as well when they can get them—Merreb said the Jehangli are as passionate for horses as any Yerrin—and, oddly, troupes of traveling entertainers. Those are the only outsiders allowed to travel in Jehanglan. Perhaps the Jehangli have no jugglers of their own? I thought that odd and asked the reason.' "

The aged parchment crackled as Lukai's careful fingers turned the page with loving care. He went on, " 'But I fear I will never know why. None of the players, Merreb said, ever speak of what they saw; it's as if once they leave the shores of Jehanglan behind, their memories of the place fall away from them. He has tried speaking to the members of more than one such troupe, he said, and none recall what happened there.' "

Lukai blinked up at them. "The list goes on for a bit more; shall I continue?"

"No," said Lleld. "I think I've heard enough." She slouched in her chair.

The archivist nodded and carefully shut the book once more.

Linden shifted uneasily in his chair. Not one tumbler who had traveled Jehanglan could remember what he or she saw there? That was not something he liked the sound of; it stank of magic—the magic that was not supposed to exist in Jehanglan. He looked around the table. The others, when they met his glance, shook their heads or grimaced, made equally uneasy by the reading.

All but Lleld. She gazed over everyone's head, chewing on a thumbnail. At last she said, "Only traveling entertainers?"

"That's what Lady Ardelis wrote," Lukai said. "I would guess it's the same yet."

"Oh," was all Lleld replied. "Indeed."

Once the tunnels had been her secret and Lura-Sharal's, one of the very few they had managed to keep from Lady Gei's prying. Lady Gei had a nose for secrets like a rat did for food, Shei-Luin thought as she turned into one particular passage. Thank the Phoenix she no longer had to worry about the mistress of the harem. The woman avoided her now the way a cat avoided water. Shei-Luin paused for a moment just inside the entrance.

The tunnel felt like a tomb. Dust lay thick beneath her heavy felt boots, muffling each cautious step. The silence wrapped around her like a cocoon shrouding a silkworm. After what seemed like forever, Shei-Luin reached her goal.

She laid trembling fingers upon the latch. It had been years since she'd dared come to this place. She dropped her hand, afraid; reached out once more, hesitated; then, in a sudden burst of determination, she pushed the hidden catch.

Click.

A tiny sound, no louder than a cricket's chirp, but it might as well have been a thunderclap the way her heart jumped. Shei-Luin held her breath and listened.

Nothing. No one cried for the guards, no one called out, "Who's there?" Not even the hiss of silk brocade as someone turned to listen. Just silence, heavy and oppressive as the air before a summer storm. Shei-Luin let her breath out in a long, ragged sigh.

She slid the door open.

The room was huge; dark shapes loomed in it like monsters from a nightmare. Shei-Luin held up the tiny lantern she used to light her way in the tunnels, and stepped forward a few paces. The nearest shadows retreated before the glow, revealing an ornately carved chair and a tambour frame. A closer look told her the chair was of ivory inlaid with gold and jewels. She ran her fingers over it in wonder. How could she have forgotten this?

The carving on the back of the seat caught her eye: a woman standing upon the moon, a sword in her hands, but her head bowed in grief. Shei-Luin bowed to the image.

Then she wandered through the room, marveling anew at the riches here, riches matched only by the emperor's chambers. It was all as she remembered from the night she and Lura-Sharal found this room. They had not dreamed of such a prize when they had discovered the long-forgotten tunnels only a few days before.

Shei-Luin wrapped her arms around herself and closed her eyes, the better to listen to the darkness. Memory welled up. . . .

Whispers darting through the dark room, soft and secret though there was no one else to hear them.

"The emperor likes you," Shei-Luin giggled, "but he looks like a horse."

"Hush—he does not." Even in the pale moonlight Shei-Luin could see her sister blush.

"What—doesn't like you or doesn't look like a horse? He does too like you. Hasn't he called for only you these past three moons? Do you really think you are . . . ?"

Joy lit the beloved face. "Yes."

"Then this room"—Shei-Luin waved a hand at the opulent chamber—"will be yours. You shall be empress."

"I—empress? There hasn't been an empress for a hundred years. Don't be sil—" Lura-Sharal broke off in a fit of coughing. She buried her face in her sleeve to stifle the sound.

Frightened by the violence of the paroxysm, Shei-Luin threw her arms around her sister's shoulders and supported her as she sank to the floor. At last the fit ended; Lura-Sharal's hand fell away in exhaustion.

Blood stained the sleeve.

"You told me you were getting better," Shei-Luin sobbed, horrified at the amount of blood. There was much more than usual. Much, much more.

"I thought so, too," Lura-Sharal gasped. "We must go back."

They never returned to the imperial chambers. Three weeks later, Lura-Sharal was dead. And not even the hawk-eyed Lady Gei ever guessed Lura-Sharal's final secret.

Tears leaked from beneath her closed eyelids, and her chest heaved in a sob. Shei-Luin bit her knuckles against the sadness that consumed her, but couldn't stop crying. It was three years ago today that Lura-Sharal had died.

At last the storm of tears ended. She wiped her eyes and looked around the chambers of the empress one last time.

"I will make this mine, sister—I swear it!—and burn incense to your soul each day," she whispered.

An instant later the room was empty but for its ghosts.

*　　*　　*

The only light in the sleeping chamber came from the leaping flames in the fireplace, dancing red and yellow and blue in the darkness. A log settled and spat a burning coal onto the hearth.

Linden picked it up and rolled it in his hand before tossing it back into the fire. He turned at the strangled yelp from the bed behind him.

"Surely you're used to that by now," he said, smiling. "You've done it yourself." He pulled off his tunic and tossed it onto one of the clothes chests at the foot of the bed.

Maurynna sat up, back against the headboard, hugging her blanketed knees. Long black hair spilled over her bare shoulders and down her back.

"True," she said. "But I have to make myself. I still think that fire should burn me. I don't know if I shall ever get used to it."

He sat down on the edge of the bed and worked his boots off. "You will. It takes a while, that's all," he said.

"Linden—" Her odd-colored eyes were huge in the dim light. "Linden, I'm worried for the truedragons. I've heard so much about the magic that guards Jehanglan. . . ."

"And if Taren's right? That there are no mages?"

She tossed a stray bit of hair back over her shoulder. "Maybe their mages stay hidden. He was a slave; maybe they lied to him. Maybe—oh, I don't know. But I'm frightened. I've heard too many stories. Almered knew someone on board a ship that was lost in the Haunted Straits."

Her hand stretched out to him. Linden caught it, yielding when Maurynna pulled him to her. There was a desperate feel to the hands that stroked his back, to the lips that sought his.

He answered it with his own feeling of unease, seeking refuge in Maurynna's arms.

Haoro met with certain of his fellow senior priests in the night-shrouded grounds of the Iron Temple. When they were certain that no one lurked nearby, they gathered in a circle, a small lantern in the center the only light. Wrapped in robes and cowls against the night chill, only their faces showed, floating like ghosts in the lamp's glow.

He told them of Hodai's confession.

"Phoenix help us!" one said, shocked. "No wonder there have been so many calamities! Isn't it bad enough that the emperor fails in his duty? But for the *nira* to doubt—!"

"Next he'll be sending for Kirano the Blasphemer," another said bitterly.

Hands flashed in the gesture to avoid misfortune. After a silence, the first speaker said, "So now what, Haoro? Do we move against him, though we haven't much proof, just the boy's word? It won't be easy."

No, it wouldn't be, Haoro thought. While pious, these men had no desire for the role of *nira*, nor had they the stomach to attempt deposing Pah-Ko unless they were certain of success. They came from poor families who could not protect them. He, on the other hand, had Jhanun as a shield—and he was the only one who wanted the feathered mantle. When it came time, they would support him.

"We don't move openly against him—yet," Haoro said slowly. "First, let us see if he says more. If we could get a younger priest or one of the older acolytes to ask Pah-Ko's advice for his own doubts, then pretend to sympathize with Pah-Ko's . . ."

The others nodded.

"It might work."

"I'll keep my eyes open for such a one."

"There are one or two who might do among those acolytes who see to the incense on the main altar."

"Sound them out, then," Haoro ordered. "We'd best get back; soon it will be time for the midnight ceremony."

They scattered like a flock of startled crows, each taking a separate way back to the temple.

Linden lay in bed with one arm tucked behind his head, the other across the blankets pulled up to his chest. He

ignored the cold night air on his bare shoulders and arms;
there was too much to think about and it might help him
stay awake. Beside him Maurynna breathed deep and easily, sated after their lovemaking, curled so that her back
pressed against his side. He guessed she was already asleep.
Which didn't help him; he wanted nothing more than to fit
himself around the curve of her warm body and drift away.
But now he needed to think.

He blinked and yawned. Damn; something Taren said
tonight was bothering him. But he couldn't put a finger on
just what, and now he was growing too sleepy to chase it
down. But it was something important, very impor . . .

*. . . He was in the great hall at Dragonskeep. Nothing
strange in that, but standing beside him was his sister's
husband, Fisher. Although one part of his mind told Linden
that Fisher had died centuries before, it seemed right that
his brother-in-law was here.*

*"Shall we go hunting today?" Fisher asked. "I've some
fine new ferrets that will do well after rabbits, I'm thinking." He patted the reed basket slung from one shoulder
and grinned. From inside came an eager scratching and
chuckling.*

*Linden grinned in return. If there was one thing Fisher
was always ready to do, it was hunt with his ferrets. Linden
wondered if Fisher's well-known fondness for rabbit stew
was the result of ferreting or the cause of it.*

*"Let's," he said. "There's a warren in the apple orchard
that's been after the young trees. I'll warn you, though, it's
a fair walk."*

*But when they passed the gate of Dragonskeep they
found themselves in that orchard. Yet, with the logic of
dreams, Linden was not surprised. Things were as they
should be. Fisher set the ferrets' basket on the ground.*

*"Be ready, Linden," Fisher warned. "We'll have to herd
the lot of 'em into the rabbit holes."*

*Before Linden could ask him what he meant—surely the
basket could hold no more than one or two ferrets, and
where were the nets for the rabbit holes, anyway?—Fisher*

threw back the lid and pushed the basket over. Ferrets poured out and raced about, leaping and dancing. The breathy, staccato ah-ah-ah *"laugh" of excited ferrets filled the air. Already there were far more than the basket could have possibly held, and still the slinky animals bounced out.*

"Quick! Quick! Herd them down the holes!"

Linden stood bewildered amid the army of sleek, leaping bodies playing around his feet. "Herd ferrets? Are you mad? There's too many!"

"Aye!" *Fisher roared in glee.* "A whole business of 'em! Better yet—an army of 'em! And there's more."

With that, he upended the basket and the last few ferrets tumbled out. There were six of them, all wearing little robes with magical sigils. They sat up on their hindquarters in a line before Linden, front paws crossed solemnly over their stomachs. One, a white ferret, fixed ruby red eyes on Linden and said, "We have agreed upon the best way to churn butter." *Then the white ferret-mage waved a paw, and all of the cavorting ferrets were garbed in robes. The next instant, the entire business raced down the rabbit holes.*

Linden could only gape in astonishment. "What the— Fisher, I don't—"

"Understand," Linden muttered. He shook his head and pushed up onto his elbows. Darkness pressed around him. From the fireplace came the dull red glow of embers.

"Mmm?" Maurynna rolled over and slid an arm around him. After a huge yawn she asked sleepily, "Did you have a nightmare?"

Blinking the sleep from his eyes, Linden said, "No. It was a very silly dream, actually. My sister Fawn's husband, Fisher, was in it, and hundreds of ferrets as well. And there was a ferret who was a mage—no, there were six ferrets who were dressed as mages are in children's tales, with those foolish robes with the magical symbols on them that no self-respecting mage would wear. Then the next moment all the ferrets wore them and they ran down some rabbit holes."

Maurynna chuckled. "That does sound silly—but fun. I wonder why you dreamed that."

"So do—"

His mouth went dry. In his mind he was back in the great hall with Raven and Otter, hearing Raven's tale of a captive truedragon, remembering his thoughts that day.

He suddenly understood his dream. The Jehangli had learned how to herd ferrets.

For once Linden was up before Maurynna. After dressing quietly, he left their rooms and went to the Lady's chambers. The door opened to his knock; Sirl, the Lady's servant, looked surprised to see him. The elderly *kir* bowed.

"Dragonlord," he said, gesturing Linden to enter. "May I help you?"

"Is the Lady awake yet?" Linden asked.

Kelder Oronin, the Lady's soultwin, appeared at the door of the inner chamber. "We're awake, Linden, and about to break our fast. Will you join us?"

"For a mug of tea, perhaps. I want to get back before Maurynna wakes up," Linden said as he followed Kelder into the private chambers of the ruler of Dragonskeep.

The Lady stood by the table. She wore a heavy robe against the chill, dark blue with green ivy vines embroidered upon it that emphasized the icy whiteness of her skin and hair. It reminded Linden of the robes the ferret-mages had worn in his dream.

"Lady," he said. When he made to kneel to her, she stopped him with a wave of her hand. He bowed low instead. "I'm sorry to disturb you so early."

The Lady's smile was warm, if a trifle wry. "I hope nothing's amiss, is there? Or are you come once more to argue that Maurynna be allowed to travel?"

"Not this time." Linden returned the smile as Sirl handed him a steaming mug. "Though I do wish you would reconsider, Lady. She's used to the freedom of the sea; to be bound to the Keep is hard for her. She's afraid of being trapped here for the winter, I think. I hear it in her voice sometimes."

Sympathy filled the pale eyes. "Does she know what a champion she has for her cause?"

"No, Lady." Linden sighed and drank. "I'm afraid to raise her hopes each time I come to you lest she grow bitter with repeated disappointment. I beg you to reconsider, though."

The Lady shook her head. "Not until she can Change, Linden. She would be too vulnerable away from here. Surely you've not forgotten how close the Fraternity came to destroying you and Tarlna in Casna."

In all honesty, it was no more than the truth; Linden bowed his head in acknowledgment of that. The Cassorin regency debate had provided the ancient enemies of the Dragonlords with a rare opportunity for a magical attack on the three judges.

It had very nearly succeeded. Kas Althume, the mage who had masterminded it, had proved the equal of Ankarlyn the Mage, the greatest foe the Dragonlords had ever faced before. His murderous attack upon Tarlna Aurianne was thwarted only by the intervention of her soultwin, Kief Shaeldar.

Linden was very nearly next. Had it not been for the self-sacrifice of a former lover of his, Sherrine of Colrane, Linden knew he would have died by Kas Althume's magic. The Fraternity had come too close to winning that skirmish in the war to destroy all Dragonlords.

Still, being a full Dragonlord had not helped *him* that time. It might not help Maurynna, either. But this was not the moment to argue the point. That was not what he'd come here for.

"I don't agree, but we both know that, Lady. This morning I'm here for a different reason." He licked his lips and prayed he was wrong. "Lady—do the truedragons know what they face in Jehanglan?"

The Lady exchanged a quick glance with her soultwin. "What do you mean?" she hedged.

"That although Taren thinks there's no magic in Jehanglan, there is; the phoenix itself must be a creature of magic, after all. That the Jehangli priests are, in truth, mages. That being of the same religion, those priestmages all work to the same end—in effect, an army of mages."

"So you've unraveled that knot as well, have you? Yes, Linden, they know. And went anyway, knowing full well what they may face. They couldn't leave whichever dragon it is in torment."

Linden groaned. "May the gods help them."

"With all their might," the Lady replied, her words heavy with foreboding. "I fear the truedragons will need it."

Fourteen

We will rest here, said Morlen. *Scatter in small bands so that we will not be too much of a burden for this land.*

The Assantikkan wilderness called the Samarrakh was vast, but it was not a rich land, Morlen knew. Did they all congregate in the same area, both dragons and land would suffer. There would not be enough large game to feed the dragons well, and what there was would be decimated.

It will take us time to regroup, one of the younger hotheads objected. *And that is time wasted. Let us go on to Jehanglan!*

Morlen fixed the culprit with a glare. *I lead, Nalarae, not thee, and I say that we will rest, for we need it. We have come far. Yes, it will take time for all to return here. I deem it a necessary setback. Or would thee have us come to Jehanglan too weary for whatever might face us?*

Nalarae grumbled, but gave in. He flew off, a small group of his friends with him. Others did the same; soon only a few dragons were left.

Talassaene said, *Rest thee here, grandsire. Galinis and I will hunt for thee.*

Morlen, grateful for the chance to rest his tired wings, nodded and sank to the hard, bare earth. *I am too old for this,* he thought, *as are too many others. But we have lived good, long lives; it is the young ones who break my heart. How many of us will never see our mountains again?*

The frenzied beating of tiny wings against the thin bamboo bars of the cage woke Pah-Ko. He blinked in confusion at the frantic sounds. The finches squawked madly as they threw themselves at the bars again and again.

"Earthquake?" Pah-Ko wondered sleepily.

"Ahhhhh. *Ahhhhhh!*" The strangled noises came from the other room.

Pah-Ko threw the covers back. Hodai! The boy was in the throes of a prophesy!

The *nira* lurched to his feet. Now the tables were turned; now he was servant to the slave. Pah-Ko snatched up the bowl and bottle of ink that always rested by the little shrine to the Phoenix and carried them into the other room.

The pallet bed on the floor was empty. The boy stood stark naked in the middle of the room, the first rays of sunlight bathing his body, his dark eyes huge but seeing nothing. His mouth worked; the grunts that emerged became clearer. Pah-Ko could almost hear words in them.

Pah-Ko set the bowl down by the finches' cage. He fumbled at the stopper of the bottle of ink, got it free and filled the bowl. Then he went to Hodai and, resting his hands gently on the boy's shoulders, guided him to the table and tilted the boy's head so that the vacant eyes looked into the ink. He knelt by the boy's side, looking up into those empty eyes, praying he'd been in time.

The eyes focused; Pah-Ko silently blessed the Phoenix. Hodai stared at the bowl of ink as if he saw the secrets of the heavens inscribed there. His mouth worked; the words fought to come out.

Then the voice of the Phoenix belled out from the young

Oracle's lips like a song, wild and clear and free.

"Dragons," it sang. "Dragons flying swiftly to Jehanglan. They would bring death to the Phoenix."

Pah-Ko's soul froze within him. He wanted the Phoenix free, not dead! "How long do we have?"

Hodai's face worked. "Dawn two days hence."

The golden voice slid away in a whisper on the last word. Pah-Ko knew the prophecy was over.

With a sureness of movement that belied his pain-twisted limbs, the priest stood up and caught up the robe at the foot of the sleeping pallet. He tossed it over the naked boy; the chill of dawn was still in the air. Then he strode to the door like a much younger man, calling to the temple soldier standing guard outside.

There was much to be done and little time to do it.

Maurynna was busy writing a letter to her cousin Maylin, so Linden went wandering. He came across Lleld on her way to the great hall. Having nothing better to do, he fell into step beside her.

"Hello, lit—" She broke off with a wry grin.

"Hah—can't call me that anymore, can you?" Linden teased. During the more than six hundred years he'd been the youngest Dragonlord, tiny Lleld had delighted in calling him by the traditional nickname.

"Hmph," she snorted. Then, cheerful again, "Ah, well—at least Maurynna's still taller than I am."

"Not hard, imp." Linden jumped back from a quick little fist and followed Lleld into the hall.

"Hunh," Lleld said thoughtfully, nodding at the far end of the hall. "Something amiss, you think?"

Linden glanced over. There, sitting by the hearth, was Otter. The bard wore a thoughtful frown.

"You look perplexed," Linden said as they joined Otter by the hearth, sitting on the opposite bench. "Can't think of a rhyme?"

"I'm not rhyming," said Otter, "but perplexed I am. Do you remember Leet?"

"Leet?" Lleld asked. She snapped her fingers. "Ah! Would that be the other bard who was in the library that night?"

"The same."

"A, um, friend of yours?" Lleld asked delicately.

Otter smiled wryly. "Ah—no. Long ago he was one of my rivals for Jaida, another bard. When she chose me, Leet took it hard. And when Jaida died in childbed, he blamed me, of course."

The look in Otter's eyes said that Leet was not the only one. "Jaida was such a little thing; we knew it was foolish to try, but she wanted children. So," Otter admitted, "did I."

Linden knew that desire; had known it for some six hundred years. And knew that, as Dragonlords, it was unlikely that he and Maurynna would ever have children. Their kind did not breed easily.

Likely just as well, he told himself. *Else, with our life-spans, the world would be awash in Dragonlord get.* Still, it hurt.

He said, "I never felt comfortable asking, but . . . You never wed again. Wasn't there ever—"

"No," Otter said. His voice was tight. "No. I started traveling again then, and that's no life to build a family on."

Linden didn't argue. Instead he thought of the times Otter had journeyed to Thalnia, remembered how the bard yearned to go more often, and now understood why. For in Thalnia were two children that took the place of the child who had died with Jaida. Maurynna still spoke fondly of sitting before a fireplace with Raven, listening to Otter's tales.

After a while, Otter went on, "I can't say Leet and I are enemies anymore, but I can't say we're friends, either. Indeed, I think he's always avoided Dragonskeep before because he knows I come here often. That's why it was so odd seeing him in the library. But odder yet was what he was reading."

Lleld sat up straighter. "Oh? Wasn't he investigating collections of ballads or something like?"

"No." Otter tugged his beard; the perplexed look was back. "I thought the same, but it wasn't. I went to visit him in his room a little while ago. We may not be friends, but we're both bards. We should exchange whatever news we have. But the servants told me he left very early this morning. Then, I don't know why, I thought to see what ballads he'd been studying; professional curiosity, I guess."

"Of course," Linden murmured.

Otter flashed him a look, then laughed and spread his hands, acknowledging defeat. "Very well, then. It was curiosity plain and simple. Jenna found the books Leet had read during his stay, and we looked through them. They're rather gruesome."

Linden raised his eyebrows. *That* was unexpected. "Indeed?"

"A Lord Culwen of Cassori had an unappealing interest in blood magic, hauntings, murderers, and the like; he hunted out the old stories and wrote them down. Gruesome reading, as I said, if you can work your way through all his blatherings to the stories themselves. Somehow his books ended up here."

Otter twitched as if with a sudden chill. "You know the kind of tales I mean—the ghost wolf of Lachlan forest, Grey Carra, the Creeping Hand—all those 'scare small children into nightmares' kinds of tales. Culwen seemed especially fond of the stories about Gull the Blood Drinker."

"I *wish* he'd been only a story," Lleld muttered.

"He was no myth, Otter," Linden said to Otter's suprised look. "The man existed and truly did murder all those people. I remember hearing about it when they caught him; it was only about two hundred years or so ago."

Otter shuddered. "He really drank blood to keep himself young? Oh, gods, that's sickening."

"Indeed. Worse yet, the man enjoyed torturing and killing those people." Linden rubbed his chin. "Well and well—let's hope that witch spruce they planted over his grave still keeps his soul pinned down. Thing should be huge by now if those trees really do feed on evil as the stories say."

"But why would this Leet be reading about such things? To write a song about one of the tales?" Lleld asked.

"Not he," Otter said. "Something like that would be beneath him. Tales of valiant kings and beautiful queens, heroes in battle, or star-crossed young lovers—*royal* young lovers—are more his style. A pity he never spoke with Taren, if Culwen's work was the kind of thing he liked."

"What do you mean?" Linden asked.

"Taren and I have talked now and again about Jehangli legends. Some are *very* eerie," the bard said. "Yet, somehow, this still doesn't feel right."

Lleld sighed. "How very strange about Leet. I daresay we'll never know why, will we?"

"Not likely," Otter agreed. "I'd be the last person he'd confide in."

"Damn," said Lleld. "I hate not knowing."

"Are the pigeons ready yet?" Pah-Ko asked Deeh as he watched the scribes finishing the last few message strips. Each bore the same cryptic words: *Grey Lands—send on.*

"The pigeon girl is putting them into their baskets now, Holy One."

Said Pah-Ko, "Good. Then I shall await them upon the tower." He gestured, and two sturdy male servants hastened to him. They formed a chair with hands and forearms; he sat, bracing himself with a hand on each man's shoulder. He hated moving about the temple this way, but he was in too much pain these days for the long walk to the tower and its steep stairs. They set off, Hodai pattering along behind.

When they reached the top of the tower, the pigeon girl was already there with her helpers. Little baskets covered most of the small floor of the tower. Gentle cooing filled the air; Hodai smiled in delight and knelt by the nearest, peering inside the tiny opening in the lid.

The girl and her helpers bowed when they saw the *nira*. Pah-Ko had the men set him down. The air up here was brisk; it revived him, though he knew that if he stayed too long, the cold would settle in his twisted joints.

Just then one of the scribes arrived, carrying the narrow strips for the pigeons' legs in a small, open box. The girl took one and bound it to the leg of a pigeon an assistant gently withdrew from its basket.

"Where, Holy One?" she asked, cradling the pigeon in her hands. It snuggled contentedly against her.

Pah-Ko said, "The temple at Mount Rivasha."

The pigeon girl nodded, then held up the sleek bird before her face. The pigeon turned its head to meet her gaze with one dark eye. They stood so for many moments, the girl trilling softly to the bird. Then she tossed it into the air. It circled once, then flew away as swiftly as an arrow. Once it reached Rivasha, and its message was read, Pah-Ko knew more pigeons would be sent out to the next temples in the relay, and on and on until every temple in Jehanglan, large or small, was alerted.

Her assistants had the next bird ready, a message already bound to its leg. Once again Pah-Ko named a temple; once again the girl communed with her charge, impressing its destination upon it.

"Holy One," Deeh said quietly, "it grows colder. I beg you, go inside where it's warm, and rest. You'll have need of all your strength when you go into the Grey Lands tonight. I know the destinations."

The younger priest was right; journeys into the Overworld, the place between waking and sleeping where only a trained mind could venture, could be tiring, especially when one spent a great deal of time there.

As he would do, when each temple received the message in its turn, and each head priest went into the trance needed. Nor did it help that the tidings he bore were dark.

His heart heavy within his breast, Pah-Ko beckoned his

bearers once again. "To my rooms," he said. "Come, Hodai."

As they paced the halls to his rooms, the *nira* wondered how many would die—and if he would be one of them.

What will happen to poor Hodai then?

Fifteen

Morlen did not understand it. And he liked it even less.

The great truedragon rose above the army of dragons nearing the coast of Jehanglan in the cold dark before sunrise and floated on the currents of air that offered themselves to his wings. He hovered and thought as his kindred passed below him. The more warlike, Aumalaean and Nalarae chief among them, were already venting their flames.

Talassaene veered off from the band and spiraled up to meet him. In the waning starlight her amethyst-hued scales looked black.

Thee are troubled, his granddaughter said.

I am, he said. *I know we have no other way to free Pirakos or Varleren, but for dragonkind to war . . .*

At least it is not with our kind, she said. *For that small mercy we can thank the gods. These truehumans had no right to do what they did, to use Pirakos's or Varleren's magic that way, and to imprison him and the other one, the phoenix.*

Her words rang in his mind with righteous anger. He sighed in agreement. *True. And it is also true that truehumans sometimes seek our blood for their black mageries. For all that, though, I am still not happy with what we do. But more than that, I feel something is wrong, very wrong. I should be able to sense whichever dragon it is. Yet try as*

*I might, I cannot tell just where he is. I have an idea—but
only that. I do not have knowledge. And that troubles me
greatly.*

Thee think he is warded, then.

I know he is warded. But still . . . Morlen shook himself until his scales rattled. *Still I should sense him.* He
stretched his wings and flew once more to the head of the
army.

Talassaene raced after him. *Thee worry too much.*

Perhaps. But something was wrong, and until he knew
what it was, he would continue worrying. And watching
with eyes and with magic.

The *nira* stood before the altar in the holiest of chambers
in the temple of Mount Kajhenral. It formed the symbolic
linchpin of the fell beast's prison as he, *Nira* Pah-Ko, was
its living one.

Radiating from the base of the altar the symbols of power
were arrayed in gold, the sacred metal of the Phoenix. Already the ones beneath his bare feet were warm, humming
with power. Clouds of incense curled around him.

His Oracle crouched against his right leg; Pah-Ko did
not need his eyes to know that Hodai was caught in the
grip of the Phoenix. He felt the child tremble and twitch.

The *nira* stood, eyes shut, running mental fingers over
the latent power of the lesser priests, allowed this once in
the room with him. Throughout the empire the priests had
been alerted to aid in this ceremony from their own temples. The ones here with him were the fortunate ones, privileged to be at the ceremony's very heart. Chief among
them stood Deeh, the man Pah-Ko felt was Jehanglan's
only hope when he died at last.

When Hodai's breathing changed, Pah-Ko laid his hands
upon the altar. Carved with its brother stones from a single
enormous boulder of white quartz found in the caverns below more than a thousand years ago, it was the largest of
the Stones of Warding; the others rested in temples to the
south, east, and west. Now it pulsed under his hands, draw-

ing energy from the magic of the unholy—*unfortunate*, his mind amended—creature chained in the cavern below.

Pah-Ko began the chant. One by one, in a carefully orchestrated dance of voices, the others joined in. In his mind's eye, the priest imagined the voices as threads, filaments in a tapestry that only he could weave.

With one part of his mind he reached into the Overworld, the Grey Lands that were normally only visited in dreams or trance. As he waited for the rising power from the other temples, he felt first one, then another, presence in the Overworld.

Are you certain you wish to do this? a disembodied voice asked. Pah-Ko recognized Zhantse, the Seer of the Tah'nehsieh, and a gentle adversary.

This is not the Way, another voice snapped in his mind; Ghulla of the Zharmatians, this one was, and less gentle. *Let them have their kinswyrm.*

Let it end now, Zhantse urged. *Admit it, Pah-Ko—you have been considering freeing both dragon and phoenix.*

So I have, Pah-Ko agreed heavily. *But not this way; this is too abrupt. Calamity upon calamity will fol—*

Ghulla said, *There is no gentle way of doing this. The wild magic has been imprisoned far too long. Let things unfold as they should.*

I do what I must, Pah-Ko replied. *I protect Jehanglan.* He turned his mind from them, for now he "saw" the strands of power raised by the other temples. Zhantse and Ghulla lingered a moment longer, then disappeared. Though he knew they were right, Pah-Ko was relieved; he needed all his attention for the task before him.

Thread by thread he wove the magic to protect Jehanglan from the coming invasion. It was hard controlling so much power—power that seemed to fight him. What if he failed? The backlash would kill him and everyone else in this room. Sweat trickled down his back at the thought of Hodai's charred, blackened body.

The tapestry of power began to unravel. Here and there a voice faltered. Hodai whimpered in terror.

Gasping, Pah-Ko cast the hideous image of his Oracle's death from his mind and seized the threads of magic. Once more the voices returned, true and strong, swelling in a chant that carried him before it. The hands of his imagination flew swift and sure, warp and weft growing, growing, until the image of the Phoenix filled his mind, shining like the sun.

And like the sun it both warmed and burned. He bore the pain without complaint. He was the *nira.* He would hold the power. Forever, if needed, until his Oracle bade him unleash it.

Or until it reduced him to ashes.

Shei-Luin woke as the man beside her stirred. He rolled over and slipped an arm around her waist.

"Beloved," she whispered in his ear as she pressed herself against him. "The dawn comes soon."

Yesuin's eyes blinked open. "And I must go back through the tunnels once more. I hate it when we have to leave each other, Shei-Luin." He nuzzled her neck.

"And I hate it as well. But come, my love, we still have some time for us." She slid her hand down his body and stroked him.

He was on her in an instant. Shei-Luin laughed softly and met him as a tigress would her mate.

Images, horrible images, like nightmares in his waking mind.

Morlen closed his eyes for a few heartbeats as he flew and let his senses range outward, seeking an essence that he once knew. It came in tantalizing bursts, never enough to satisfy, never enough to be able to say, "There!" and race arrow-swift to a destination. But now and again he caught something, something that shone out like sunlight from behind scudding clouds and was gone again as quickly. *Here*, it said. Barely enough to give him a direction; yet it sufficed. It had to.

He angled his wings and turned.

* * *

The chanting continued, welling up around him like a fountain. Pah-Ko held the power of the Phoenix steady; though it seemed the flesh would melt from his bones any moment, he would not let the power slip away from him again.

Their goal: one peak rising above many dropping sheer into a narrow valley that wandered between the mountains. It put Morlen in mind of Dragonskeep, though there was no castle here, but a complex of buildings of an unfamiliar design instead.

But similar though it was, what he felt from this place made that resemblance a mockery. For now he sensed the captive's full agony, the pain of a dragon kept from wind and sky and freedom for a millennium and more. A dragon chained to the ground like an animal. Nay, not even that—chained *under* the ground, away from the life-giving sun and air, unable to fly among the moonlit clouds and the winds of dawn.

Fear and rage and terror blasted into Morlen's mind. He reeled under the onslaught, battered by the madness underlying all else in the maelstrom that was the captive's thoughts.

But underneath the storm, Morlen sensed a tiny thread of a mind he once knew: Pirakos, a truedragon. So much for the old tales of Jehanglan, Morlen thought.

Savemesavemesavemesavemesaveme. Terrifying, tangled visions of smothering beneath tons of earth, chains so tight they scored through scales into the tender flesh beneath. The frantic need to soar on the winds once again. A nightmare spectre: a great golden bird that filled the sky, emerald eyes filled with hate, fire dripping from its wings, sinking its talons into his breast, tearing, ripping ... (*No! Not mine—Pirakos's!* Morlen's mind cried.) A sick, raging need to bathe in the blood of that enemy, to crush its heart beneath vengeful claws.

But even worse than the madness was the fleeting moment of lucidity.

Destroy me. It is the only way.

Could a dragon weep, Morlen would have done so. His old wings, already tired, faltered in grief.

Bellows of horror exploded around him. Morlen was not the only dragon blasted by Pirakos's torment. Flight after flight of the great wyrms dove for the mountain, screaming their rage in the breaking dawn.

So suddenly that the *nira* jumped, a new voice added itself to the chant. It rose above the others like pure molten gold above the dross of its refining. There were no words in its song but none were needed. High and wild it rang, heart-breaking in its sweetness. It was the cry of the Phoenix that Pah-Ko had been blessed to hear in his most precious dreams. He trembled at its beauty.

The voice paused and its absence was pain. Suddenly it rang out once more; this time there were words in it.

"It is time," Hodai sang. "Unleash the Phoenix."

It had never been like this. Yes, making love with Yesuin had always been pure joy, but this!

There was power here; she felt it. Felt it rising in her, felt it in the thrusting of the man who took her.

It was rising and there was naught she could do to stop it. Nor did she want to.

Shei-Luin surrendered herself as she had never done before.

A Seeing burst into flame inside his mind. Never before had one come upon him like this; this was the purest agony, like dragonfire inside his head.

Back! Morlen cried. *Back or we are undone! They know!*

But it was already too late. Far too late. For the air above the dragons rippled and the colors of the dawn melted together. Like a ghost came the shimmering figure of an enormous bird like none Morlen had ever seen.

The Phoenix of Jehanglan.

Its wings spanned the sky; emerald eyes glittered in rage. It was both beautiful beyond words and terrifying beyond imagining. Then, shrieking, it fell upon them, fire trailing in streamers from its wings and tail.

As was her custom before breaking her fast, Jenna went to the library to open the window hangings. To her astonishment, a lone figure sat at one of the tables, poring over a book. It was rare indeed that anyone came here so early.

Even more astonishing was *who*.

"Good morning, Jenna," Lleld said, looking up from her book.

By the redness of the little Dragonlord's eyes and the slump of her shoulders, Jenna guessed that Lleld had been here most of the night. She also recognized the book that had captivated Lleld's interest: the journal of Lady Ardelis the Traveler.

Before Jenna could reply, Lleld shut the book and carried it back to its proper place.

"Did you find your answer?" Jenna asked, wondering what the question had been.

"Yes," said Lleld. "I did."

Morlen had never known such agony.

And he'd barely been touched in the strange bird's onslaught. Others had not been so lucky.

For the fire that dripped from the Phoenix's wings clung and burned through scale and flesh and the muscle beneath if one caught the full force of it, then ran through the bones like the harvest-fires the truehumans set to clear the fields of dead straw when the grain was in. Like that straw, bone turned to ash.

Many—too many—dragons died in the first attack, tumbling through the air like shooting stars, ending their lives in a shower of ashes on the cold, hard earth below. The rest scattered in confusion.

All but Aumalaean. Spouting red flames, he flung himself straight at the Phoenix. For a moment Morlen thought the rash young dragon might succeed; Aumalaean's claws tore into the Phoenix's breast—

And passed through. As did the rest of Aumalaean, unable to stop his headlong flight. With a scream of agony the like of which Morlen prayed he'd never hear again, Aumalaean burst into flames. He fell, tumbling end over end through the cool air of dawn, burning like an oil-soaked torch. Then, mercifully, his screaming ended. Moments later he crashed into the ground.

One final thrust, and it was over.

Yesuin collapsed on her, his chest heaving, his body hot and sweaty against her own. Shei-Luin lay gasping. Her hands roamed blindly over her lover's body.

Then Yesuin rolled off of her and fell heavily to the cushions. His eyes were closed as he fought to catch his breath.

She turned her head on the pillow to look at him. Her gaze devoured him, willing herself to remember everything about him at this moment, the line his dark, heavy eyebrows made, how a strand of his long black hair curved around one high cheekbone.

How she loved this man. . . .

A sudden swift, sharp pain in her womb made Shei-Luin sit up, hands clasped to her belly. "Oh!"

At once Yesuin was on his knees beside her. "Shei—what is it?"

Wonder stayed her tongue. For beneath her hands, it was as if a sun glowed in her womb for an instant and she *knew*. Joy bubbled up inside her.

"Yesuin," she whispered, hardly able to speak for sheer happiness, "I am with child again. It happened just now—I know it!"

"Are you certain? Can such a thing—"

An urgent knock at the door interrupted him. "Lady," Murohshei called, low-voiced, "someone comes!"

At once Yesuin was out of the bed. He snatched up the clothes he'd let fall to the floor the night before and was running for the entrance to the secret tunnels before she could say a word. She saw the red-and-gold lacquered panel slide back under his fingers, watched mutely as Yesuin disappeared into the dimness beyond and the panel slid shut once more.

All that was left was the knowledge of what lay under her spreading fingers, and what it might bring her.

At last Morlen understood what they faced. This was not the Phoenix itself. This was a Sending built of magery, a concerted effort of a kind he'd thought impossible, using the magical forces of the Phoenix and Pirakos to fuel it. His heart went cold within him.

Mages did not band together, work to one end this way. They wouldn't; they couldn't!

But the deadly proof filled the sky before him. The ghostly bird wheeled and the balefire lashed out once more. Once again the dragons scattered before it. A few more were caught. They fell, burning, to their deaths as had the others before them. The Phoenix turned on the largest band of survivors. They fled.

It was hopeless. The dragons were doomed. Despair washed over Morlen. They could not succeed against an enemy they couldn't even touch. Their only hope lay in retreating beyond the range that the priestmages could project the Sending.

Retreat! Now! Get beyond the mountains! Morlen roared to his kindred wyrms. For a feeling rose in him now that if the dragons could but win to the red lands they had passed over earlier, they would be safe. He remembered the welcoming feel of that land, sent it on to the others.

One by one they responded, halting their panicked, fruitless dodging, and raced for the mountains as fast as they could. Some faltered in the air, barely able to fly. Others dashed in to help, heedless of their own safety, risking death as the Phoenix swooped down once more.

It singled out a pair of dragons; with a cry of despair Morlen saw it was Lurione, one of the youngest dragons, gravely wounded—and Talassaene, her amethyst scales glittering like jewels in the light of the newly risen sun. He struggled to reach them in time; in time to do what, he didn't know. But he was too old, too tired, and wounded besides.

And there was nothing he could do, anyway. That knowledge hurt the most.

Yet somehow Talassaene, her claws gripping the younger dragon, twisted in the air and tumbled into a dive. The lash of the Phoenix's fire missed her body by scant inches. For a moment Morlen thought she would win free unscathed; then the streamer of fire slewed around and caught her across the back and wings.

She cried out but kept hold of Lurione and by some miracle kept to the air. Staggering as she flew, Talassaene nevertheless dodged out of the Phoenix's range and continued toward the mountains, still bearing Lurione.

Relief flooded Morlen; she would be safe. He turned his attention to the other dragons, urging them on. They obeyed, flying as fast as they could for the mountain barrier to the red lands.

Once more the Phoenix dove after them. The last stragglers' wings beat frantically in what Morlen feared was a futile attempt. He cried out a warning as it loomed over them; one of the dragons, despair filling her ruby eyes, looked over her shoulder at the Phoenix closing in. Then, just as the fire from its wings reached for the dragons, the Phoenix disappeared. Like the haze above a fire, it vanished, leaving the clean blue sky behind.

Morlen went weak with relief. The gods only knew why their enemy had disappeared—had the mages reached the end of their power?—but he didn't question it, only blessed it. Now he must get his kindred to safety.

The flight was pure nightmare. His pain increased with each beat of his injured wings. Yet he couldn't give in to it, couldn't rest; nor could he allow any of the others to do so. Morlen didn't know how the Jehangli had known of the dragons' attack, or even how long they had known of it.

There might be troops waiting below to kill or capture any wounded dragon setting down.

They must keep flying. Morlen begged, pleaded, bullied, and cajoled his kinswyrms along when they would have given up. He would not allow it.

At last they were over the mountains. *Rest,* he sent to the others. *Here we are safe.*

Agony! Death!

The old dragon twisted and thrashed in his sleep, his dreams now a torment. He moaned, all unknowing, and-fled the nightmares that stalked him, sinking deeper into his mind.

The waters of the lake swirled around him as if to wash away the pain.

It was Heilan, one of Xiane's eunuchs kept to run errands to the harem. Shei-Luin received him after donning the proper robes.

"The Phoenix Lord wishes to ride to the Pavilion of the Three Pines this day, lady," Heilan said. "He desires that you ride with him."

Despite his condition, the eunuch kept his gaze firmly upon her embroidered slippers. It was a moment before Shei-Luin noticed; her mind was still full of what had happened earlier.

But when she did notice, she raised her fan to hide a smile. While it was true she was currently the emperor's favorite, she was still only a concubine, and a palace eunuch was free to look upon her. Indeed, the eunuchs were the only males in the palace free to gaze upon the faces of any woman, noble or otherwise.

Any woman, that was, save those of the highest rank, such as the mother of an emperor, his sisters, or . . . his empress.

She was not Xiane's sister, and certainly not his mother. But that Xiane's eunuch unconsciously treated her with such respect told her how his master truly thought of her.

She let the fan fall away with a graceful gesture. "Tell the Phoenix Lord that it will be my greatest pleasure to ride with him this day, and that I thank him for this mark of his favor," Shei-Luin said. Then, greatly daring, she went on, "And tell him I also thank him for thinking of the Pavilion of the Three Pines. It is very . . . romantic there," she added, her voice low and silky.

A moment later she nearly laughed aloud. Though the eunuch's gaze stayed firmly on the toes of her slippers, the tips of his ears had turned bright pink.

"You will repeat to your master what I said—and *how* it was said," Shei-Luin ordered with impish delight. She knew Heilan was an uncanny mimic.

The ears turned red. "I will, Light of the Emperor's Eyes." The eunuch crawled backward to the door, then stood and left on his mission.

Pleased, Shei-Luin rose from her chair to allow Tsiaa and Murohshei to undress her for her bath. "Use the jasmine perfume; it's Xiane's favorite."

Though once Xiane received her message, she doubted she'd have need of any perfume. They might not even get away from the palace this day.

She thanked the Phoenix for this gift of chance.

The dragons rested on the small plateau they had found. Few were unscathed; most bore at least some small wounds; some were gravely hurt. And too many of those were hurt beyond saving. Some, like Lurione, died before they could be helped.

Indeed, Morlen suspected Lurione had died before ever reaching this poor sanctuary. It was a mercy, he thought, that Talassaene had fainted as soon as she'd touched the earth. She did not yet know her sacrifice had been wasted. He looked upon his granddaughter once more and wondered how she had brought herself to this place, let alone carried Lurione, she was so gravely wounded.

The dragons did what they could for their kindred, exhausting themselves by repeated uses of their Healing fire.

Morlen aided where he might. But for him all that he could do was not enough; and draining him further was the fore-knowledge that the dragons could not stay. If they lingered the priestmages would find a way to send the ghost Phoenix after them once more. And that would mean the end of them all. They *must* leave.

The Seeing sapped what little strength he had left. *I am old and useless,* he thought bitterly, watching a nearly spent Galinis bathe Talassaene in Healing fire once more. The blue-green flames enveloped her, slid around her uncon-scious body—and died out in a flicker. Galinis's head sank to the ground, his eyes dull with exhaustion.

I have done what I could, the younger dragon said. Even his mindvoice shook with weariness. *I can do no more.*

Thee have wrought valiantly, said Morlen, afraid it wasn't enough. Talassaene had not regained consciousness. *Rest now; we must leave with the night.*

Groans greeted this announcement. *Why?* a dragon named Beracca asked plaintively. One eye was seared shut, never to see again.

Galinis lifted his head. *A Seeing?*

Yes.

Sighs gusted through his mind, and their resigned accep-tance followed. They would rest while they could. Morlen stretched out beside his granddaughter, willing her to live.

The *nira* was still dazed, having regained his senses only moments before. He blinked like an owl forced out into the day, unable to make sense of his surroundings. Giving up, he sagged against the arms that supported him—one of the acolytes allowed in to help. Another held a cup of tea out to him.

"Drink, Holy One," the young man said. His face was pale and his eyes wide and frightened. Whether it was be-cause of what had transpired in this place, or for the place itself, the *nira* could not say.

His confusion passed; with each moment memory came

back. But he was still weak and in pain. Pah-Ko waved the
cup aside. "Where's my Oracle?" he whispered, holding
aside the welcome relief of oblivion by sheer force of will.

"Here, Holy One."

The voice came from behind him. Pah-Ko half turned in
the shelter of the encircling arms.

A young priest of the lowest rank cradled Hodai against
his chest. Hodai's eyes were shut, black lashes stark against
the ashy hue of his face. An acolyte gently wiped the boy's
mouth with a damp cloth. There was a red stain upon it.

Pah-Ko gasped in dread. His heart jumped and hammered jerkily in his chest. One withered hand stretched out.

"Rest easy, Holy One," the young priest hastened to say.
"He bit his lip, that's all. He sleeps now from exhaustion."

"Ah. Ahhh." Pah-Ko relaxed. "Take him to my chambers
and put him in his bed—" He wrinkled his brow in thought.
"Yalin, is it not?"

The young priest beamed, pleased that his name was
known to one so high. "Yes, Holy One. I will take him
there now."

"Stay by him until he wakes." As the young priest bore
his precious burden away, Pah-Ko turned his attention to
the events around him. For the first time he noticed the
sour stink of voided bowels beneath the fragrant incense.
Then he saw the still, covered forms that littered the floor
of the chamber.

But other forms were not so still. Pah-Ko heard wild
mutterings as the junior priests struggled to hold down their
thrashing brethren.

"What is this?" Pah-ko asked the one who still supported
him.

"The backlash. . . . It was too much for some of them.
Their brains are fevered, it seems. Whether they will recover . . ."

"Who?"

The youth rattled off a few names, but the only one that
penetrated Pah-ko's befuddled mind was Haoro's. So—
Jhanun's devious nephew was no longer a player in the

great game of the temple. Pah-ko wondered how long the reprieve might last; forever, he hoped.

But what price had they paid for it?

"Deeh?" he gasped.

For an answer, the acolyte pointed to one of the shrouded forms, one whose dead hand had slipped from beneath its covering. A simple braided band, the kind popular among the countryfolk, encircled the wrist, its bright colors vivid against the greying skin beneath.

Pah-Ko recognized the band. *Phoenix, please—not Deeh.* But it was; he knew it in his heart. It was too much. *Why Deeh and not Haoro? How many of the best have died across Jehanglan to keep the empire safe?* he wondered as he spiraled down into the welcome darkness.

Dusk—the gate of night had come at last. Morlen watched as the sun inched below the western horizon and the shadows flowed together, and the air around them and the red stone below them grew cold with the passing of the day.

It was time.

With a rattle of scales and wings, Morlen rose. All around him heads came up as the exhausted dragons roused. So spent were they, they had not posted even a single sentry.

But some dragons did not move. As Morlen went among those, he saw that many had died. Others yet lived; but the spark of life within them was so faint, he knew they could never fly.

He came back to Talassaene. By her side rested Galinis, one wing spread over her as if he would protect her. Her head came up as Morlen gently touched the tip of his nose to hers. Galinis drew his wing back.

Grandsire. Her mindvoice was the barest whisper.

My heart, it is time to leave, he said gently.

She tried to stand. Before Galinis could help her, she fell to the ground once more. *Grandsire, I cannot. Please; I am afraid. . . .*

I will help thee, fly by thee. Thee will reach home,

Morlen said, knowing he lied and willing to risk everything to make those words truth.

Thee know it would be fruitless. And I do not fear death. I do fear what these priestmages would do to me should they find me still living. Please, I beg thee: do not let them do to me what they did to Pirakos. For I know they would.

With a supreme effort, she raised her head and tilted it far back. The light of the first stars twinkled on the amethyst scales of her throat.

The other dragons too hurt to fly did the same, baring their throats to their companions.

Save me, Grandsire.

With a howl of rage and grief, Morlen slashed across Talassaene's throat with his razor-sharp claws. Her blood gushed hot and smoking onto the red stone as her long, graceful neck crumpled to the ground.

All around him other dragons did the same for kith and kin, granting them the mercy of a swift death.

Wild with grief, Morlen flung himself into the air. The others followed.

Heartsick, hurt, and weary, the dragons retreated from Jehanglan.

Sixteen

A gloom hung over Dragonskeep. From the lowliest kitchen boy to the Lady herself, all walked wrapped in a shroud of apprehension. There was no word yet from the truedragons to ease their minds.

What laughter there was these days was forced and brittle. But there was little of it; no one had the heart for jests. The battlements of the Keep, usually deserted, played host to an unending stream of visitors, their gazes turned to the south.

The watchers rarely spoke to each other. They stood, *kir* and Dragonlord and truehuman, cloaks wrapped tight against the cold mountain wind that blew around them, and watched and waited.

Days passed, but still no word came. Eyes strained to see anything, the merest speck in the distance that might give them hope. And no one saw anything save the occasional hawk circling against the pale blue sky.

To his surprise, Linden often saw Taren on the battlements, his expression tense, standing watch as often as his health permitted. Sometimes Taren stood alone or leaning on a servant; most times Raven stood by him, lending his young strength to the sick man.

Once Linden came upon Taren alone. The man shook, his teeth chattering and his cloak wrapped tight as a shroud around his thin body. He leaned heavily against a staff.

"You should be abed," Linden said in concern as he came up behind Taren.

The man turned; his face looked grey in the waning light. "I must watch," he said. "I must know."

He looked away once more. The wind whipped between them; Linden brushed tears of cold from his eyes.

"It's my penance," Taren said, so softly Linden wasn't certain he'd heard correctly. Then, louder, Taren said, "There will be many deaths of this. And I'm to blame; I didn't think . . ." Taren shook his head.

Linden laid a hand on the man's shoulder. "They'll come back," he said with a confidence he didn't feel. "And Pirakos with them. You'll see."

"Yes," Taren said. His eyes glittered in the failing light. "Yes. We will see."

With the privilege of an old and faithful servant, General V'Choun entered the Garden of Eternal Spring without invitation and went straight to the emperor's gazebo. He sketched a bow to Xiane as the Phoenix Lord looked up from the game of dice he played with Yesuin.

"You look grim," Xiane said in surprise.

"I am, Majesty. Here; read this." He held out a folded sheaf of papers. "Pah-Ko was too rattled to even seal these."

His long, horsey face awash with curiosity, Xiane took the papers. V'Choun watched his emperor's face grow pale as he read. Without a word, he passed the message to Yesuin.

"An attack of . . . dragons?" asked Xiane of the air. "But how?" he went on in bewilderment. "The dragons are all dead!"

"No, Majesty," V'Choun said. "Not all the dragons. Did you not read that these had wings? They are northern dragons, come to right the wrong that was done to one of their kind."

Laying the note upon the table, Yesuin said, "Xiane, what more proof do you need? You read of how many priests died, did you not?"

Xiane nodded.

"That was not because of the battle they waged; Pah-Ko could have easily controlled that power. No, this was the Phoenix itself taking this chance to strike back at those imprisoning it," Yesuin said.

V'Choun sighed. "I'm afraid I've come to agree with him, great lord. Pah-ko dared not write it for all to see, but I know him of old and I can read what he does not say. It's past time for the Phoenix's death, Majesty, and the Phoenix knows it. Even that great being must live by the Way of All Things."

Said Yesuin, "You know he's right."

Xiane turned a look of anguish upon him.

V'Choun said quietly, "Other reports have come in from across the countryside. Sudden floods where there has been no rain, ghosts heard wailing in the cemeteries, the earth shaking and hurling down temples—but only temples— springs spouting fire or blood instead of water, and worse. And all happened the day of this attack, Xiane."

Ashen-faced, Xiane stood. "I must think on this," he said, and left the gazebo. He called, "Cousin, come with me."

Yesuin sprang up, then paused a moment. Turning to V'Choun, he said, "You know what we ask of him, don't you?"

"Yes," said V'Choun heavily. "The end of the Phoenix dynasty. *His* dynasty. Otherwise, it's the end of Jehanglan."

"I know," Yesuin said softly. "But Xahnu . . ." He followed Xiane into the garden.

V'Choun sat down and stared unseeing at the dice on the table. He knew what was needed. So did the emperor. But would Xiane have the courage to undo the mistake his father had made?

A sliver of moon rode high in the black sky. This night Merlet Kamenni stood the watch the Dragonlords had set by unspoken agreement. She paced the battlements, looking ever to the south, and twisted her single thick braid around and around her hand.

A shadow slid across that sliver of moon. For a moment Merlet couldn't believe her eyes. She rubbed at them, certain they played her a trick.

But no—there came another and another. Throwing off her cloak, Merlet let herself flow into Change.

They're back! she cried to all inside the Keep. *The truedragons have returned!* She leaped into the air.

As she arrowed into the night sky, she thought, *But, dear gods, there are so few of them.*

Maurynna sat atop Boreal early the next morning, watching as the drovers herded cattle into the Meeting Field. The frightened animals lowed as they milled about in confusion. Somehow they knew they were doomed.

The first Dragonlord dove out of the sky, seized one and bore it aloft. She recognized Kelder Oronin in his dragon form. The herd panicked, but before they could stampede, a second Dragonlord flew in from the opposite direction. Once again a frantic cow was carried away.

She watched as the herd was decimated animal by animal. Only two Dragonlords could carry more than one cow at a time: Linden, and another Yerrin Dragonlord almost as large, Brock Hatussin. And even they were hard put to do it, Maurynna saw.

Lleld, riding Miki, joined her. It was small comfort that there was at least one other Dragonlord who could not help; Lleld was too small to carry a struggling cow safely. But at least she could Change.

By way of conversation—and to take her mind from her inadequacies—Maurynna said, "It will be a lean winter." For though this was certainly not all the cattle of Dragonskeep, it was a goodly number.

But what else could they have done? The truedragons waiting in the mountain meadow before going on to their homes in the north were too weak to hunt for themselves. They must eat or die.

"So it will," Lleld agreed, then added, "For some—but not all. Shall we be off?"

All during the ride to the meadow, Maurynna wondered what Lleld had meant. But she dared not ask. There were some things it was much safer not to know—at least where Lleld was concerned.

Seventeen

He's here; Morlen the Seer is here.

The word spread through Dragonskeep like the wind. Raven heard it down in the stables where he was helping Chailen, the head groom, with a young mare just delivered of her first foal. It had been less a tenday since the return of the truedragons. No one had expected to see Morlen so soon.

* * *

The mare was frightened; the birthing had been difficult, and now she wasn't certain who this little stranger was. Or even if she wanted anything to do with it.

"A pity she's but a horse and not one of the Llysanyins," the *kir* grunted as he rubbed the foal down with a handful of clean straw. "It would be just a matter of explaining things to her. And if she still wouldn't accept it, why then, I'm sure her dam, granddam, and all her aunties would explain it in their way."

Raven stroked the mare's neck, soothing her, coaxing her toward her new son. "They truly understand that well?"

"They do indeed. I'm not saying you could discuss with 'em whether there are nine manifestations of the goddess or three or twenty-seven, as I understand some scholars waste their time with, but everyday things . . . Oh, yes; they understand. Too cursed much sometimes." Then, to the foal, "No, little idiot—not the straw! You're too young to eat that. Let's get you to your dam."

Raven soothed the nervous mare as Chailen helped the gangly-legged colt across the stall. She trembled under his hand but stood steady as he murmured to her.

"Good, good, hold her steady," Chailen grunted softly as he guided the foal to its proper dinner.

There was a tense moment when the mare started as the eager nose butted her udder, but Raven made much of her, crooning endearments and encouragement. He knew the instant she accepted the colt; one moment she was rigid beneath his hands; the next, she relaxed and whickered softly to her new baby.

Raven grinned, heady with the joy of knowing that all was well with dam and foal. He followed Chailen out of the birthing stall.

The *kir* blew out a relieved breath. "Well done, Raven. You've definitely got the touch with horses. I don't think that mare would've stood so quiet for anyone else. Thank the gods that's ended well; I don't need an 'orphan' on my hands." He reached up and clouted Raven on the shoulder.

"Any more like you at home? I could use another half a dozen or so," Chailen said, laughing. "Let's get a bit of fresh air."

Raven followed him, pleased by the head groom's praise. He'd never met anyone before as knowledgable about horses as this *kir*. "No, just me—likely to my stepmother's relief. I was a handful, she likes to tell me now. But at least she always knew where to find me."

"The nearest barn, eh?" Chailen said. "Aye, you've the touch. No question about that."

Together they wandered to the back paddocks. A mixed herd of Llysanyins and horses waited in the largest paddock. They milled impatiently, the Llysanyins stamping their feathered feet. Raven watched a stablehand—this one truehuman—swing up onto one of the horses. Even bareback she had a good seat, he noted absently. "She's bringing the herd up to pasture?" he asked.

"Katha?" Chailen asked. "No, she's going just to open the gates. The Llysanyins herd the horses along, see that they all arrive without mishap. But a two-foot still has to work the latches; unfortunately Aewin the smith has yet to devise a gate latch that only a Llysanyin can undo."

Raven shook his head. "Can't be done. If it can be opened by teeth and lips, there's a horse somewhere that can figure it out. I've even met some of them."

He watched as Katha slipped the gate latch; watched as the herd poured out of the gate; whistled softly to himself as the Llysanyins took up positions around the ordinary horses. Each went to a certain place as if according to some prearranged plan, working together like a well-drilled team. With a thunder of hooves, the Llysanyins led the horses up the mountain, a laughing Katha in their midst.

"They're truly amazing," he whispered to himself. He watched them as long as he could, lost in a dream.

He came back to himself when Chailen bellowed almost in his ear, "Ho, lad! Where to so fast?"

Raven looked around in time to see a running *kir* young-

ster veer off from whatever errand he was on to come to a
skidding halt before Chailen.

"Haven't you heard, Chailen?" the youngster panted.

Chailen frowned. "Heard what?"

"Morlen. Morlen the Seer is here. In the Meeting Field."
The answer came in short bursts between heaving breaths.
A few longer breaths and, "He's asked all the Dragonlords
to meet with him, not just the *Saethe*. That's the Dragon-
lords' council, sir," the young *kir* explained politely to
Raven. Then, once again to Chailen, "I must be off now."

Chailen waved him on; the youngster ran off.

"The Meeting Field?" Raven asked.

Chailen pointed. "There; the other side of the plateau.
It's where the Dragonlords meet with any visiting truedragons. I wonder what will come of it this time," he said,
shaking his head. "Ah, well, it's back to work for the likes
of me. And you?"

Raven said vaguely, "Back to the Keep, I think, for
breakfast," and left.

But food was the furthest thing from his mind. Filled
with a curiosity he couldn't explain, Raven wandered up
the flagstone path to the Meeting Field.

At first he stood at the back of the crowd; when no one
objected to his presence—*to be honest*, he said to himself,
*I don't think they even notice me, they're so intent on Mor-
len*—he wormed a way through, looking for Maurynna and
a closer view of the truedragon.

But he couldn't find Maurynna and didn't dare go any
closer to the front of the crowd. Still, he was close enough
to hear the red-haired little Dragonlord as she made her
speech.

"We need traveling entertainers to get into Jehanglan,"
Lleld was saying as he came within hearing. "A troupe can
go anywhere; no one pays any real attention to them,
they're nothing except when there's a show. No doubt it's
the same in Jehanglan as in the Five Kingdoms. And traveling entertainers are the only northerners allowed deep into
Jehanglan."

"Perhaps so, Lleld," the Lady said, "and no doubt we could find a troupe willing to go there, and work you into it. But you are not going as the only Dragonlord to Jehanglan, and that is final. Nor am I willing to ask truehumans to take this risk for us."

Lleld waved a hand impatiently. "We don't need a troupe. We could make our own."

Murmurs of amusement and dissent rumbled through the gathered Dragonlords. The Lady shook her head, smiling.

Wait, Morlen said, startling everybody. *I would hear more of this plan.* He swung his great head around to study Lleld. The little Dragonlord met his gaze unflinchingly. *Go on, little cousin.*

"I can tumble, walk the tightrope, and juggle. You all know that. Jekkanadar can juggle, too, and do some of the easier tumbling. I'll teach him everything I can, and teach the same and some other things to whoever else goes."

Hmmm . . . the great mindvoice rumbled. *It has its merits, Jessia.*

The gathering waited while the Lady considered Lleld's words. At last she said slowly, shaking her head, "I don't know. . . . Morlen, this will take much thought."

"I can do it," Lleld insisted.

Another Dragonlord, a woman with blonde curls tumbling down her back, spoke up. She said, "But will you be able to teach whoever does go enough for a show?"

She came forward, limping slightly. Raven recognized her from Maurynna's description as Tarlna Aurianne, one of the other two judges with Linden Rathan in Cassori a few months ago. She had, he remembered Maurynna saying, a withered leg as her Marking.

That explained the limp. Now Tarlna Aurianne reached the front of the crowd and turned to face the conclave. "Remember—the members of a real tumbling troupe have been practicing for years, since they were children. Can any of us learn those kinds of skills so quickly? And no doubt the Jehangli have their own such bands of entertainers.

What could a troupe of half-trained Dragonlords offer to set them apart from those?"

Raven saw heads nodding around him, heard murmured words of agreement. And even from where he stood he could see the frustration in the small Dragonlord's eyes. Though he wasn't certain her plan would work, he felt sorry for her; if only there was something he could do to help. . . .

The image of the Llysanyins guiding the horses up the mountain sprang up before his mind's eye.

"Use the Llysanyins." The words were out of Raven's mouth before he thought about them. One part of his mind was aghast that he dared speak up in a Dragonlords' council; he wasn't even supposed to be here. Still, what was done was done. He might as well go on. "I've seen a lord's crack troops ride intricate formations for show on the parade ground. It's impressive as all get out; just think what a group of Llysanyins could learn."

The Lady searched the faces before her. "You that spoke—you're Raven Redhawkson of Thalnia, aren't you? The one who brought Taren here. Come forward, young sir." Her voice was cold.

More murmurs, some with an angry undertone that said, *What has this truehuman to do with our councils?* Someone in the crowd laughed. It was not a friendly laugh. Raven swallowed his fear and made himself walk along the path that opened before him to the Lady's icy stare.

Lleld caught his eye; she mouthed, *Good try. Thank you.*

"He's right," a deep voice behind him suddenly said. Raven jumped; he hadn't expected support from *that* quarter. He looked back over his shoulder.

It was indeed Linden Rathan who eased out of the crowd; he who fell in step beside him, speaking so that all could hear as they made their way through the crowd to stand before the Lady of Dragonskeep.

They stopped but a few feet from her. Linden turned to face the conclave. "I've seen what Raven speaks of, and it could well be a spectacle to build a performance around. It takes years of intensive training to teach an ordinary horse the movements—and nine out of ten horses can never learn above a certain level. That's why you don't see a traveling show with something so intricate. Usually the most you'll get is a horse trained to 'count' or sit on command, some simple thing like that.

"But with Llysanyins, now. . . . It would be an easy matter to explain what's needed and devise something with them. And they don't even need to be ridden for it." Linden Rathan hooked his thumbs into his wide leather belt, his face thoughtful. "Think how impressive that will look."

Raven dared a sideways glance; he met Linden Rathan's steady, dark grey eyes. "Thank you, Dragonlord," he murmured.

The corner of the big Dragonlord's mouth quirked up. "It's a good twist on Lleld's plan, Raven," he said quietly. "Tarlna was right. None of us would be able to learn enough to put on much more than a performance fit for some second-rate fair. But a spectacle of performing Llysanyins . . . ah, now, that would be something to see. Remember what Lady Ardelis wrote? This could get us free passage anywhere if the Jehangli do indeed prize horsemanship as much as we Yerrins."

Linden Rathan's words surprised Raven. *So he still thinks of himself as Yerrin; I would have thought he'd forgotten us by now, he's so far above us.* Somehow the idea made him uncomfortable; it left a nagging taste in his mind that he had done the big Dragonlord some wrong.

No; it was he *did me the wrong.* But it still vexed him. He turned his attention back to Lleld.

"It's a wonderful idea!" Lleld was saying now. "Just the thing; believe me, I know."

"I don't think this is wise," the Lady snapped.

Morlen's big head hovered over them, going from one to the other as the argument went back and forth. It was clear that the two women had forgotten the truedragon even as he considerately spread a wing to shield them from the sun. The carrot-topped little Dragonlord's hands described extravagant circles in the air, and the regal Lady, white of hair and skin like the Frost Queen of legend, shook her head to Lleld's unbounded—and overconfident—enthusiasm. Raven was certain he saw a twinkle in the truedragon's ruby eye.

"Ah," Linden Rathan said quietly. "Lady Mayhem will have her way." To Raven's confused "Who?" he explained, "Lleld."

Lady Mayhem; well and well, Raven could see why that might be. He grinned at the nickname. "But what makes you think—"

"Morlen's nodding whenever Ll—hush!"

It is a good plan; the only one I can see that might work.

A sadness that knew no bounds filled the words, spilled over into Raven's soul. His breath caught on a half-choked sob. He'd never imagined such heartache. And on its heels came bitterness: *For our plan certainly did not.*

Raven thought of all the truedragons who had died to save their brother. Morlen's grief washed over everyone like a wave of sorrow. Someone behind Raven wept quietly; his own eyes burned with hot tears.

Into the heavy silence the Lady said, "But who should go? There's grave danger there; if you're right, Seer, the Jehangli priestmages can sense the presence of dragonmagic. Surely they would sense Dragonlord magic as well. How, then, are we to answer this riddle? Magic is needed to free Pirakos, but no truedragon or weredragon may approach his prison. A truehuman may approach safely but has not the magic needed to free your kinswyrm. We're caught in a cleft stick, Morlen, and I see no way out of it."

Yet there is one who is the answer to your riddle, Jessia, Morlen said.

Their gazes met, locked like two warriors testing each other for a weakness. The Lady looked away first.

"I don't know," she said heavily. "I must think on this."

She went from them then, alone, back to the castle of Dragonskeep. When Kelder made to follow, she bade him stay with a gesture. The conclave dissolved into small groups, discussing, wondering, debating, arguing.

Raven wondered of whom Morlen spoke, and why the Lady looked so unhappy.

Xiane sat stiffly upon the Phoenix Throne. His face schooled to the mask expected of the emperor, he let his gaze wander the audience room. Ministers and courtiers lined the walls, either waiting their turn to be presented to him and make their reports, or simply to see and be seen in this place of power.

Before him knelt Lord R'sao, minister of the imperial salt mines. R'sao droned on and on. Xiane sneaked a glance at Lord Musahi, his old tutor and now Imperial Minister, who sat in his accustomed place at the little desk by the throne. Musahi's writing brush flew across the rice paper before him as R'sao spouted figures dry as a cloud of dust.

Thank the Phoenix for Musahi. Xiane knew the Imperial Minister would present him with a report that cut through the layers of flowery language to the heart of each matter. Xiane let his gaze wander again.

The room stretched out before him. Beams of dark, carved wood arched overhead, stark against the gold leaf that covered the ceiling they supported. Their bases divided the red-lacquered walls into bays. And in each bay hung a golden image of the Phoenix.

Are V'Choun and Yesuin right?

The thought chilled him. It was especially frightening that V'Choun now believed the heresy—or seemed to. That Yesuin did, Xiane had known for years and accepted of the man he'd come to love as a brother. Of course the barbarian tribes called for the release of the Phoenix; it was the power of the Phoenix that lent strength to the armies of Jehanglan. Without that power . . .

So Yesuin naturally wanted to believe in the heresy of the Way. But V'Choun? Xiane knew he'd been friends with Lord Kirano the Heretic—Shei-Luin's father—before Kirano was exiled; he had not realized that the old general shared Kirano's beliefs.

That the two men he trusted most in the world thought this way shook Xiane badly.

If only there was someone who believed as strongly in the sacrifice of the Phoenix as I do—did?—to stand beside me.

Xiane knew he was, in many ways, a weak man. He feared that V'Choun and Yesuin, who had been more like father and brother to him than his blood kin had been, would wear him down by the sheer strength of their belief. He felt their questioning like tiny cracks in the dam of his own beliefs.

If only ...

Lord R'sao ended his report. Xiane surfaced from his inner turmoil long enough to raise the sandalwood fan in his hand in the ritual gesture of dismissal.

R'sao knocked his head against the floor three times, then backed away on hands and knees to the prescribed distance before standing and bowing deeply. Xiane waited dully for the next minister's report.

If only ...

The great doors at the far end of the room swung open, surprising everyone. Who dared interrupt the reports of the ministers to the Phoenix Lord? For once decorum was forgotten; those standing along the walls craned their necks and jostled each other like peasants at a cockfight to see the interloper. Xiane, while grateful for a break in the deadly dull routine, felt his stomach clench with fear.

Not another invasion!

But to his unbounded astonishment and relief, the figure that entered was Shei-Luin's eunuch, Murohshei. Following him were some of the lesser eunuchs of the harem. A few steps into the room, the eunuchs knelt and cast themselves upon their faces, awaiting his pleasure.

Hissing whispers spread scandal from minister to courtier and back again. It sounded like a nest of angry snakes. Xiane snapped his fan up and brought it down against the arm of the throne with a violent motion. The fan shattered with a resounding *crack!* that rang through the room.

The whispers stopped at once. Pale faces turned to him, terrified at this show of imperial temper. Xiane let the remains of the fan fall from his hand. The fragrance of sandalwood filled the air.

"I trust there is a good reason for this intrusion, Murohshei?" he said, his voice carrying in the leaden silence.

Jaws dropped and eyes fairly bulged all along the hall. From the corner of his eye, Xiane saw many of the elder lords grab at the breasts of their robes as if the shock of the emperor deigning to address a mere eunuch in public was too much for them.

Murohshei raised his head. "Indeed there is, Phoenix Lord. May my lady approach you?"

Hope blazed up in Xiane's heart. Shei-Luin was daring, but this was not a thing she would do for a jest. Could this mean—"Yes," he answered, somehow keeping his voice steady.

The eunuchs rose. A slender figure, heavily veiled, appeared in the doorway behind them. As the guard of eunuchs formed around her, the veiled woman walked forward. Murohshei dropped back to walk in his proper place, one pace behind his mistress.

Down the long stretch of the audience room came the strange group. They moved with slow dignity, ignoring the scandalized faces lining their path. Straight to him they came, until at last the lesser eunuchs stepped to one side or the other and knelt, foreheads touching the floor. Shei-Luin came to the first step leading up to the Phoenix Throne and knelt there. Murohshei dropped to his knees just behind her.

Xiane almost forgot to breathe as he stared down at the slight figure swathed in the finest silks. To approach him so, here in the audience room, took a courage unthinkable in a woman. But clearly *this* woman had the spirit of a tiger.

This woman had the strength to hold him firm against the doubts V'Choun and Yesuin planted in his heart. And if she brought him the news he hardly dared hope to hear . . .

"Speak," he said, finding his tongue at last.

"Phoenix Lord of the Skies," Shei-Luin said, her sweet voice muffled by her veils, "I bring you joyous news. By the grace of the Phoenix, I am with child once more."

Xiane's head spun. Another child? Another son, perhaps? Joy blazed up in his heart. Heedless of the ritual of the audience chamber, Xiane stood up. Amazed at his own daring, Xiane came down the nine steps that led to the throne, his heavy, stiff robes forcing him to a majestic walk when he wanted to leap from step to step.

At last he stood before Shei-Luin. A movement of the veils told him she had tilted her head back to look at him. His hand trembling, Xiane swept the veils away. The Flower of the West gazed up at him, her dark eyes wide.

"Give me another son," he told her, his voice low and intent, "and I will reward you beyond your wildest dreams."

A buzz of speculation filled the hall as those nearest the throne passed his words on.

Her smile dazzled him. He wanted nothing more than to drown in it. And somehow he knew that there would be another empress in Jehanglan after more than a hundred years.

At dinner that night, Otter looked across the table and said, "Raven told me earlier what you're planning, O Lady Mayhem, and you've been eyeing me throughout dinner. You want a bard for your little scheme, don't you?" He raised his goblet to his lips.

"Yes, I do," answered Lleld promptly. "Thank you for volunteering, Otter."

When Otter choked on his wine, she wheedled, "Think of the songs you'll be able to write about it—the only bard ever to go to the fabled Empire of the Phoenix!"

"If my great-uncle goes, so do I," Raven said, pounding that same great-uncle's back as the stunned man coughed and wheezed.

"Done!" said Lleld. "You're the fourth—myself, Jekkanadar, Otter, and now you." She looked down the table at Linden and Maurynna. "We need at least two more Dragonlords and their Llysanyins."

"No," Linden said, appalled. "For the sake of the gods, Lleld, Maurynna can't even Change!"

"And that's just why she must go, Linden," Jekkanadar said. "Believe me, Lleld and I discussed this for a long time after we came back. You heard what Morlen said to the Lady—that there's 'one who is the answer to your riddle.' Who else can that be but Maurynna? Because we at Dragonskeep *know* she's among us, we may mindspeak her even though we don't sense her presence.

"But the Jehangli priestmages won't know about her, so how can they sense her when even you, her soultwin, barely can?"

"No," Linden said again, desperately this time, for what Jekkanadar said made terrifying sense. "No and no and—"

"Yes."

The quiet interruption stopped him cold. Stunned, Linden turned to Maurynna. Her face was white and set.

"Yes," she said again. "I have to go, don't I?"

"No, you don't," Linden began. Then her gaze locked onto his. He had never seen her eyes so hard, so cold, so filled with determination.

She said to him, "I have to go," her eyes still fixed on his. Now there was a hint of desperation as well.

He understood. This was not just for the captive dragon's sake. This was for her own sake, as well.

He could go to the Lady, demand that she forbid Maurynna to leave, knowing that the Lady looked for any excuse to do just that.

With a sinking heart, he realized it was the one thing he couldn't do. Maurynna was not a child to be forbidden something, nor was he her jailer. It was not for him to tell her what she might and might not do when it touched her sense of honor, of right and wrong, no matter how dangerous it was, no matter how much it frightened *him*. He had no business living her life for her; he was her soultwin, not her master.

"So you do, love," he said at last. Then, because he had to have this much, "But I'm going with you!"

As if she'd planned it this way all along, Lleld said, "Good, that's settled. Now, since Otter looks oldest, I think he should be our 'leader'...."

Lost in his fears, Linden listened with only half his mind as Lleld bubbled on with her plans for all of them. Maurynna listened intently.

Gods help her, she can't even Change! What was Morlen thinking?

He had only one forlorn hope. "Remember—the Lady may yet say 'no' to all of this," Linden said.

"The Lady might," said Lleld. "But Morlen won't. You'll see."

Eighteen

Have thee reconsidered, Jessia?

The voice was gentle but firm. Much as she wanted to, she could not ignore it. Instead she fenced with it, seeking time, seeking . . .

She was not certain what she sought. It worried her, this indecision; it was a new thing for her. She scolded herself: *You're the Lady of Dragonskeep; you cannot afford such things.*

Then, to the truedragon, *You don't give me much time to reconsider, Morlen*, she countered.

Thee have had since yesterday morning in the Meeting Field, the voice rebuked her gently. **How much longer must Pirakos wait?**

So little time. . . . The thought drifted across her mind.

Just so. Pirakos has so little before the darkness claims him utterly. And if Lleld Kemberaene's plan is to succeed, her troupe must have whatever time there is to practice. And thee know who must go.

The Lady sighed and paced the tower room. The truedragon was right, of course; if they were to have a chance, Lleld's band must learn as much of the Jehangli language as possible, learn new skills, devise a show with the Llysanyins and each other. She paused by the window overlooking the plateau.

A grey day to match her mood. Soft clouds hid the sun; soon the autumn rains would begin in earnest. Mist hid the valley below.

Don't you understand, she wanted to cry to him. *I* must *know more about Maurynna. She may well be the last of us!*

The thought that her kind might be ending was like cold steel in the Lady's heart.

Jessia?

Why could none of us sense her? Why was there so long between Linden and Maurynna with no other hope? Or were there others, others who died without our knowing they had ever been born? she asked herself. *Why, Morlen? I have a thousand whys.*

I understand, dear friend. But I have no answers for thee.

It's too dangerous for her; she can't Change. I can't allow her to go. The Lady clenched her fists as if the gesture could hold Maurynna back from any harm.

She must. I have Seen it. She is the only one who has dragonmagic and casts no more of a magical shadow than a truehuman.

She had no answer to that simple truth. Maurynna had to go; the girl was the only one who could approach Pirakos's prison—in theory.

You would have me risk her for a 'perhaps,' the Lady said angrily.

Thee would keep her buried here against her will.

The harsh words lashed at her mind like a whip. The Lady turned her face away as if from a slap.

He continued, *She is a sea hawk, Jessia, caged and beating against the bars. I felt it those few moments I was in her mind. It would be too easy for her to fall into despair if she is without hope of freedom. This is not only for Pirakos now, my Lady of Dragonskeep. It is for Maurynna herself.*

You would have me send her out defenseless against the world? So shall it be, Morlen. And on your head be it if she dies.

And with those bitter words she closed her mind to him.

"Sirl," she called. When her servant appeared, the Lady said, "Call the *Saethe* into session, please; we will meet in the Old Tower a candlemark from now. And ask Lleld, Linden, and Jekkanadar to attend."

She would protect Maurynna as long as she could.

Sirl bowed and went off on his errand. The Lady stared out of the window, her heart as grey as the mist.

Still no change.

Swearing under his breath, Lord Jhanun flung the message into the fireplace. It caught and blazed up in a brief moment of glory.

So Haoro is still abed with brain fever, and Pah-Ko still rules at the Iron Temple. Damn!

It was beneath him to pace like a tiger, though he wanted to. A Jehangli gentleman of the old school did not give way to his emotions so. Discipline was required in all things.

Could his rogue Oracle have been wrong? Had he misinterpreted her words? It couldn't be; somehow victory would be his in the end, for victory was the due of the righteous. *His* due.

Still, it was just as well that he had another arrow in his quiver. Catching up the little carved stick that hung by the gong in its stand on the mantel, he struck a single clear note.

Almost before the echoes died away, his steward came into the room. "Yes, my lord?"

"My niece's tutors report to you. What have they to say of her?"

"They say that she progresses well in her studies, my lord. Her calligraphy improves, as does her playing of the *zhansjen*. She is becoming well versed in the womanly arts of embroidery and perfumery. While she has little talent for pen and ink drawings, Master Kialen, her drawing instructor, says she has exquisite taste in others' work."

"Good," Jhanun murmured. "Good; that is how it should be for a woman. Go on."

The steward continued his dry recitation. "Her poetry, while adequate in attention to the forms, is not very original. She can, though, carry on a lively and intelligent conversation about both the classics and the more recent popular works."

"Decadent works, you mean," Jhanun said in disdain. "But still, it's well that she can. Xiane is very fond of the work of some of these young upstarts."

He stroked his long mustache, thinking, while the steward waited patiently. Suddenly, he said, "Does she play *ulim-choi* yet? I ordered that she be taught, though women usually don't play it."

"She's learning, my lord."

"And how does she play?"

The steward waggled a hand in the air. "She has been taught the rules, my lord, and has a good grasp of the theory. But she's a very timid player. She doesn't take chances."

"Therefore she loses each game." At the steward's nod, Lord Jhanun smiled. The way one played the ancient game of war and strategy often gave valuable clues to one's character. He did not want Nama to be a bold, ruthless player. That would not suit his plans at all. "Very, *very* good."

*　　*　　*

The members of the *Saethe* met once more. The Lady watched them file in and take their seats, a great weariness upon her. She could see only two other choices before her, and neither gave her any joy. First, they could leave Pirakos to his fate—and that was unthinkable. Second, she could send some other Dragonlords to slip into the country. That would be possible, she knew; but they could never approach the truedragon's prison without alerting the priest-mages. So what use sending them?

Maurynna was the only choice. Because she couldn't Change and Jehanglan was a closed land, only Lleld's plan had a chance of succeeding.

Last of all came Linden, Jekkanadar—and Lleld.

"No doubt you've guessed why you're here," the Lady said to the three. "Lleld's plan is our only hope."

They nodded.

"So," she said to Lleld, "you've won."

The little Dragonlord met her gaze steadily. "Have I?" Lleld countered. "I think not."

The Lady considered that. "That's true. No matter how this ends, no one wins this game. But hear now the rules you must play by—"

And if they are not met? she asked herself.

Then we must leave poor Pirakos to his fate, came the answer.

"First, if certain help is not forthcoming . . ."

A few flowers, hardier than their fellows, hung on stubbornly, but for the most part the garden at Dragonskeep was slipping into the bareness of winter. Only the trees still delighted the eye with their colorful leaves; most still clung to the branches. The rest crunched underfoot as Taren wandered the meandering paths with Raven, Otter, Lleld, Linden, Maurynna, and Jekkanadar. Wondering why he'd been invited, he listened, at first politely, then with growing excitement, as Lleld explained her scheme.

He applauded. "A wonderful idea—traveling entertainers!"

"Could we go in as traders?" Maurynna asked him. "I'm certain that if the Lady asked, the Dawn Emperor would be only too glad to order House Mhakkan to take us on one of their ships."

Raven chuckled. "Wouldn't that burn their toes?" he murmured.

Shaking his head, Taren said, "Yes, but as traders—even under the protection of House Mhakkan—you wouldn't be allowed to leave the foreigners' quarter in Jedjieh, the only port that trades with the outer world. Only entertainers are allowed to travel within Jehanglan."

This will make it easier for my lord Jhanun. I'd not looked forward to arranging the kidnapping of these four from Jedjieh! But once they're in the middle of nowhere, my lord's house troops can take them.

How kind of these fools to make his work easier. "A wonderful idea," he repeated with heartfelt sincerity.

Jekkanadar asked, "I've been wondering, Taren—will we be allowed to carry weapons in Jehanglan? I know Linden will want to bring his greatsword, Tsan Rhilin, and I'd certainly feel better if we were armed."

He needn't lie or even stretch the truth for this one. "Entertainers aren't allowed to carry swords. The best you'll be allowed are long knives," said Taren. Of course, all these four had to do was Change, and what need of weapons after that?

Then an idea came to him, so audacious he nearly stumbled. But if it worked . . .

"There is a thing I must tell you, my friends," he said. "Once in Jehanglan, you'll not be able to use your magics. Legend has it that Dragonlords can speak mind to mind—is this so?"

"Yes," Lleld said after glancing around at her fellow Dragonlords. "We can."

"Don't, once we're in Jehanglan," Taren said earnestly. "For the priestmages can detect magic, even though they don't call it that, and speaking mind to mind—or especially Changing—will bring them upon us like a pack of wolves."

Looks of varying degrees of astonishment met this announcement.

" 'Us?' " Maurynna said. "Taren, you don't mean—"

He smiled sweetly at her. "Yes, I intend to come with you."

"But aren't you afraid of being taken for a slave again, Taren? What if someone recognizes you?" Lleld said.

"Don't worry about me; all will be well. Jehanglan is large, and we'll be nowhere near the salt mines," Taren said with perfect truth. "I must be with you to guide your steps. Again—don't worry about me. I do this of my own free will."

Nineteen

The gardens of the Assantikkan emperors were as beautiful as story had them. Sulae Shallanan admired them, running her fingers along a fragrant jasmine flower. Though she herself was Assantikkan, she had never seen the lauded gardens while she had lived in this land; donkey herders were not invited to visit Dawn Emperors.

Dragonlords were, especially when they came on urgent errands from the Lady of Dragonskeep. She smoothed the black silk of her gown and nodded to the servant. "I'm ready," she told him.

The man bowed deeply. As deeply, Sulae suspected, as he would for the Dawn Emperor himself, judging by the awe she'd seen in the man's eyes. An emperor was something seen every day; a dragon who alighted in a courtyard and Changed into a woman was not. The servant went off on cat-soft feet and a swirl of silk robes. Sulae wandered the garden as she waited.

When the Dawn Emperor came, it was a surprise. There

were no attendants, not even the awestruck viziers who had greeted her earlier when she'd landed. There was only Chakkarin himself, striding swiftly and decisively along. She studied him as he approached her.

Tall and slender like most Assantikkans, with his hair in the traditional "hundred braids" of royalty, Chakkarin reminded Sulae of his great-grandmother, an adventurous woman who had made the journey to Dragonskeep long, long ago as truehumans reckoned such things. His black beard was short and neatly trimmed, flecked here and there with grey. More grey showed at his temples. Lively eyes danced in a dark, lean face.

So very like Famissa, he is. The thought gave her pleasure. Chakkarin's ancestress had been a delight, a young woman with a quick, agile mind and a talent for *riyudal*, a kind of traditional Assantikkan poetry. Sulae, on the other hand, was a listener who appreciated the nuances a master could bring to the complicated form. Famissa had been one of her few truehuman friends.

Famissa's great-grandson came before her, studied her for a moment. Then a warm smile lit his face and he bowed. "Dragonlord," he greeted her. "Sulae Shallanan. It is an honor and a pleasure to meet you, Your Grace."

Sulae made him a courtesy. "You lend me honor, Your Majesty," she said. "I thank you for it, and for agreeing to meet me upon such short notice."

"We rarely hear from Dragonskeep this far south, Your Grace, so I'm delighted at this unexpected visit. Your message said that you had a request from the Lady, yes?"

Sulae nodded. "Yes. The *Saethe* met three days ago; my mission is the fruit of that."

"And this mission is something urgent and private, your message also said. That's why I suggested we meet here." He waved a hand at the garden. "No chance of eavesdroppers." He offered her his arm. "Shall we walk in the gardens, then, my lady?"

She threaded her arm through his. "Let us, my lord."

As they wandered deeper into the garden, the Dawn Emperor said, "Word came to me that dragons—many dragons—were sighted in the wilds not long ago. Hunters were the first to see them; they sent the word on. The dragons hunted and rested, then went on. The next word came from the coast—dragons landed with the dusk and left long before the dawn.

"Then, only a day later, they returned." Chakkarin stopped walking. His voice dropped. "And there were far fewer than before. Dragonlords or truedragons, my lady?"

"Truedragons."

"And those that did not come back?"

Sulae Shallanan took a deep breath. "Dead. Most in a magical battle with the Phoenix. Those too wounded to fly were killed as a mercy by their kin rather than be left in Jehanglan."

His eyes closed a moment and he shuddered. "May the gods have mercy," said Chakkarin. "Has this visit something to do with that tragedy?"

"Yes," said Sulae. She slid her arm from his and began walking again, arms folded tight against her chest to hold back the tears. She did not speak. She could not. He kept pace silently.

When she was in control of her emotions once more, she waited until they were well away from the garden borders where a spy might hide. When she judged they had reached a safe place, she stopped, finger to lips, listening. Chakkarin stood motionless.

No; no sounds that should not be here in the quiet garden. Only a distant cicada thrumming in the hot, sweet-scented air, and the nearby hum of bees, sleepy and content. Sulae knew that if anyone was close enough to overhear them speaking quietly together, she would hear their breathing with her unnaturally sharp hearing.

The Dawn Emperor tilted his head in inquiry.

Sulae smiled at him. "We are indeed alone, my lord. We may speak now. First I have a question for you, Your Majesty: do troupes of entertainers still travel to Jehanglan?"

She nearly laughed aloud at his look of astonishment.

Whatever the poor man had expected, it certainly wasn't this.

"Why—yes," he finally managed to say in bewilderment. "More than ever in the last ten years or so; Xiane Ma Jhi, the present Phoenix Lord, delights in jugglers and tumblers and the like, and many of his lords follow his taste. There is always demand for new entertainments. House Mhakkan frequently puts together large troupes by combining smaller ones or sometimes certain performers from various troupes."

That fit with what Taren had told the *Saethe*. And Lleld had guessed right for once. No, Sulae amended, Lleld had guessed right *again*; she would be pleased. The Lady would not. Though the Lady had agreed to Lleld's plan, Sulae had heard the reservation in her voice when she'd bade Sulae undertake this mission. The least setback, and the Lady would dismiss the whole idea.

But what other chance did Pirakos have? For once the Lady was wrong. *And may the gods have mercy on Pirakos that his best chance is one of Lleld's mad schemes.*

"Good. Very good," she continued. "Hear then, the favor the Lady of Dragonskeep would ask of you. In the spring there will come a ship bearing a very special troupe of entertainers, my lord. The Lady asks that you give them what aid they might need, see that when the time is right they are taken to Jehanglan, and safely brought away again."

The Dawn Emperor slid a glance full of speculation at her. "That's all?"

"That's all," said Sulae.

"And will you tell me what this is about, Your Grace?"

"It's better you do not know, Your Majesty."

It was plain his curiosity was eating the man alive; just like Famissa, he was! But the emperor of Assantikkan did not beg or even cajole. He did look very frustrated. Sulae gave him a smile but nothing else.

His mouth curved in a wry grin. "You drive a hard bargain, Your Grace. May I hear the tale when it is over?"

"Done," Sulae said as she clapped her hands in the ancient signal of a sealed bargain. She held out her right hand, palm up.

"Done." He placed his own palm over hers. She was pleased to see his expression did not change at the sight of her webbed fingers. He was *very* like his great-grandmother; she wondered if he composed *riyudal*, as well. She would ask when she returned.

He said "I will see to it that all is prepared for these . . . entertainers. How long will you favor us with your presence, my lady?"

"My errand is done and time is short," Sulae said with regret. "I must return to Dragonskeep immediately." ·

"Then may the gods go with you," Chakkarin said, "and the wind sing under your wings, Sulae Shallanan. Come back and tell me the tale when you can."

"I will," she promised. "I will."

Hodai trotted behind two priests, listening as they discussed the conditions of their fellows injured in the dragons' attack. They paid no attention to him. It was surprising, he mused, how many thought him deaf as well as dumb.

No matter; it served him well from time to time, as it did now.

"What about Nisse?" one priest asked.

"His attendants said he opened his eyes yesterday. They hope he'll recover soon, as Teurun and Cham did. That's how it goes, it seems. If they come out of that unnatural sleep, they live. If not, they go the way Domhiou did—straight to the Phoenix. And the longer they stay asleep, the less likely they'll come out of it."

The first speaker clucked his tongue. "Who else still sleeps? One never hears anything at the hall for the pilgrims." He looked, Hodai thought, like a wet hen.

The other rattled off a list of names, but the only one Hodai noticed was Haoro's. He looked down at the floor to hide a smile as the speaker went on.

"And it's said his uncle is furious, though no one knows

why. It's not as if uncle and nephew were close, though Lord Jhanun comes here often on pilgrimage, and the two of 'em talk for hours. From all I've heard, Lord Jhanun disapproved of his sisters' marriages, and never did a damn thing to aid their families when they fell on hard times."

"I've always heard Lord Jhanun is a very pious man," the wet hen said as they turned down another set of hallways.

"Then why doesn't he go to Mount Rivasha instead of here? It's holier, and much closer to the capital where he spends most of his time," his friend complained, his voice fading with distance. "That cold face of his gives me the chills."

Hodai went past the turn. Now he no longer bothered to hide his smile. He should, he decided, see if he could visit Haoro's sickroom. He wanted to see for himself that his master's enemy still slept like one dead.

At another crossing of hallways, Hodai turned and trotted on.

Twenty

Sulae had finally returned from her mysterious errand; not even her soultwin had known where she'd gone, she'd left in such haste. Or perhaps that was just Janno's defense against Lleld's rampant curiosity. If it was, Linden couldn't blame him.

But now Sulae was back. And after a short consultation with her, the Lady had sent for Linden, Lleld, and Jekkanadar.

The meeting was short and stormy. When it was over, the Lady was angry, Lleld elated. Jekkanadar said nothing.

Linden didn't know whether to be pleased or afraid as he left the Lady's quarters.

For a time he wandered the halls of Dragonskeep, lost in thought, until he found himself staring out a window.

Another grey day; they would have to leave Dragonskeep and the north very soon now or risk being snowed in because Maurynna, Otter, Raven, and Taren couldn't fly.

And that meant they had to find mounts for the three truehumans. Llysanyin mounts. Linden hoped it wouldn't prove an impossible task. He reached out with his mind to warn Otter.

Shei-Luin lolled among the pillows of the bed as Tsiaa painted her toenails with henna paste. She'd forgotten how tired she got during the early stages of pregnancy. She closed her eyes, letting herself drift off. If Yesuin dared the tunnels tonight, she wanted to be awake for it!

A mumble of voices brought her back from the near shore of sleep. Blinking, she pushed herself upright as Murohshei entered her chamber. His expression was so odd, it alarmed her at first. Then she realized he was trying not to laugh.

"What is it?" she asked suspiciously.

"Flower of the West, his Imperial Majesty sends you this delicacy," Murohshei said. That done, Murohshei stepped to one side and bowed low as another eunuch—one of the oldest Shei-Luin had ever seen, and that meant one of some importance—entered the room. At the sight of the pale yellow robe and sash of deep gold that marked a body servant of the emperor, Tsiaa went to her knees and bowed to the eunuch. He ignored her.

In his hands he bore a covered tray of gold; the handle of the lid was a phoenix. Honor of honors—this was one of the emperor's own dishes. An aroma of cooked meat wafted from it. It threatened to turn Shei-Luin's stomach; she swallowed again and again until the weakness passed.

The emperor's eunuch shuffled forward and set the tray on the little table that Murohshei hastily placed by the bed.

Then the old man knelt and knocked his forehead against the floor. Finally, he uncovered the tray. Upon it lay an odd-shaped, unappetizing lump of *something* in a sauce of cloud mushrooms. The smell filled the room in a burst of gamey richness.

Shei-Luin clapped her hand over her mouth. She would not vomit! After a moment, she could lower her hand enough to ask, "What is it?"

The eunuch's head bobbed up, revealing a nearly toothless grin. His voice high and quavering like an old woman's, he said proudly, "Tiger liver, Flower of the West. Tiger liver to insure a male child, and a strong one. His Imperial Majesty hunted it himself just for you, as his father did for his mother. I had the honor of presenting that one as well."

Shei-Luin closed her eyes. She despised liver. Trust Xiane not to remember—or had he even thought to inquire after her dislikes? That tiger liver was a traditional viand for the mother of an imperial heir did not comfort her. She could only thank the Phoenix that she had somehow escaped it the first time. This time, though . . .

She would have to eat the revolting thing, and under the benevolent gaze of Xiane's eunuch, who would report back to Xiane.

Think of the throne of Riya-Akono.

That thought was all she had to sustain her. Opening her eyes once more—but averting her gaze—she motioned to Murohshei to bring eating utensils.

The old eunuch beamed as proudly as if he'd caught the tiger himself. Murohshei cut off a small bit and fed it to her. Somehow she choked it down.

Whatever I must do to become empress for my children's sake, I will do. No matter what it is.

Linden slipped into the small chamber off of the main room of the library; he sat in one of the chairs near the door. Maurynna flashed him a wink. Kharine gave him an absentminded salute, her attention on her pupil. He spared a quick glance for the banded candle burning in its holder on the table.

It was near the sixteenth candlemark; Maurynna's lessons for today should be over soon. He watched her, black head bent over the book between her and Kharine, reading aloud softly. Now and again the *kir* tutor would interrupt, correcting a pronunciation here, explaining a word there when the reading faltered. At those times Maurynna took quill pen in hand and jotted down notes on the sheet of parchment before her.

She continued reading. Her accent was good, Linden realized, much better than his. She had easily caught the proper pronunciation of *arolan*, the common tongue of Dragonskeep. He, on the other hand, had never rid himself of his Yerrin mountain accent—not that he'd seriously tried. Sometimes it was useful to let people think he was the country bumpkin he sounded.

But Maurynna's ease with the finer nuances of the Dragonlord's language revealed her privileged upbringing. No doubt as a scion of a wealthy trading family, she'd had tutors to teach her at least some of each language of the Five Kingdoms as well as Assantik, and to make certain she sounded as much like a native as possible.

How she must have surprised those same tutors with her quickness, Linden mused, thinking of the innate Dragonlord talent for languages. *Just as Bram and Rani were when I learned their mercenaries' tongue, the* meijas, *so fast.*

It was, he reflected, amazing what a band of soldiers from different countries could cobble together for a common language. A mongrel thing it had been, bastard child of five languages and a dozen dialects, but it had worked as well as the Dragonlords' cultured language, centuries in the making. He lost himself in memories of the past as the soft voices murmured in conversation. The shutting of the book brought him back from his half drowse.

"Very good, Maurynna," Kharine said. "Keep on like this and you'll easily pass for one born to Dragonskeep." She closed the book and tucked it into her scrip lying on the table.

Maurynna smiled. "Only because I have such a good teacher." She stood up and stretched a little. "Ahh, I'm stiff!"

Shouldering the scrip, Kharine smiled in return and started for the door. "A ride would do you good; it was a long lesson today." She nodded pleasantly as she passed Linden. He saluted her in return.

When they were alone Linden said, "She's a good tutor, isn't she?"

Maurynna said, "Very. She's patient and has a way of explaining things so that they stick. I enjoy the lessons with her much more than some of the others."

He grinned, knowing that she spoke of her tutor for courtly Assantikkan. Gaddo could indeed be a stuffy prig. "Then I'm sorry to say that your lessons with her must cease for now," Linden said.

"Wha—why?" Maurynna asked in dismay.

"You're to have double lessons with Gaddo." He laughed at her look of horror. "Love, you're too easy to tease! No, it's because from now on you'll be studying with Taren," Linden replied, turning serious. "All of us—that is, you, Lleld, Jekkanadar, Otter, Raven, and I—will be studying with him."

He nodded as comprehension dawned in her eyes. "Just so. The Lady has consented at last to Lleld's plan."

So; it was to happen even as Lleld wished. The Lady rubbed her forehead, seeking to banish the headache forming behind her eyes.

Sirl approached her where she stood by the window in the dining room of her private quarters. "Lady, Taren Olmeins is here in answer to your summons," he said. "Do you wish to see him now?" The *kir*'s tone chided, *You should rest*, and his eyes were stern.

The Lady smiled at him. There was no greater tyrant than a faithful servant. "Yes," she said. "I'll see him now." She held up a hand as Sirl pursed disapproving lips over his fangs. "I promise you; it will be short. A request of him, nothing more."

The tilt of Sirl's head told her he would hold her to that. He went off to fetch Taren.

The Lady rubbed her forehead again. Once this was done, she would send for Fiaran, the Keep's Simpler; perhaps the herbalist would have something for her aching head.

Sirl entered once more, Taren close behind. The truehuman bowed to her in the Kelnethi manner, hand on heart. It surprised her a little. She knew his history, knew that he'd been raised a Yerrin.

But a Yerrin without a clan braid thanks to the Jehangli. I suppose that he must needs play the Kelnethi at all times lest he forget his role. To him, she said, "Welcome, Taren. I wished to tell you of the decision the *Saethe* has come to."

His eyes grew brighter.

"Dragonlords will indeed go to free Pirakos according to Lleld Kemberaene's plan. They need to learn the language, though."

He stared blankly at her for a moment. "You wish me to teach Dragonlords to speak Jehangli?" Taren asked in disbelief.

"Yes," said the Lady. "Lleld asked for it and for once she and I agree."

The alarm that filled Taren's face surprised her. It seemed to her a logical request; surely the man had expected this.

"But, Lady, it's a very difficult language, and I shall be with them to act as interpreter. What need that they learn it?" he said.

"Because one never knows what the gods might see fit to ordain. You will find the Dragonlords at least to be able students; it's a talent that we have. As for the two truehumans, Otter Heronson and Raven Redhawkson, who will also go, teach them what you can." A thought occurred to her; it would explain his hesitation. "Will this be too great a strain for you, Taren? I would not have you make yourself ill again but I deem this necessary. And while we all greatly appreciate your willingness to accompany Lleld's troupe as interpreter, you might wish to reconsider. I would not have you returned to slavery."

Alarm shaded into fear. "No, Lady! I must return," Taren exclaimed. He licked his lips. "I—I must see this through. There are many pitfalls. I know the people, the customs. I must return to Jehanglan with the Dragonlords."

Moved, the Lady said, "You are a brave man, Taren. Thank you."

Taren smiled his sweet, beautiful smile. "I simply do what I must, Lady."

Otter sat in one of the solars in Dragonskeep, his small traveling harp in his lap. His fingers played over the strings while his troubled thoughts chased each other. No particular songs, just the random meanderings that always soothed him.

It seemed others found them comforting as well. Dragonlords wandered in and out of the solar; most listened for a time, then left. Some stayed, eyes closed, letting the music take them where it would. Most wore peaceful smiles.

Would that he could be so easy in his mind. "Unsettled" was a mild description of how he felt at the moment. A *very* mild description. Lleld often had that effect even when she wasn't the bearer of disquieting tidings. And the news of the Lady's capitulation had been disquieting indeed.

Add to it Linden's request a short while later that he tell Raven and Taren to be ready for a trip to the upper pastures, and it was a wonder that the music flowing from his harp didn't twist everyone else's nerves into the same jangling knots as his own. Raven had been eager; Taren pleaded fatigue and well-nigh fled to his chamber.

Taren might have the right idea, Otter thought gloomily. He knew what the trip to the pasture meant, even if Raven didn't. It was the first step of their journey; a first step that might be doomed to failure.

Nama laid her writing brush down. She rolled her shoulders to loosen them, then examined the papers before her. Sheet after sheet was covered with painted characters. She picked up the last one and eyed it critically.

Yes, her calligraphy *was* improving. Uncle would be pleased—she hoped. It was not easy, living up to the example he set; as a proper Jehangli noble, he was well-versed in all the gentle arts: poetry, painting, calligraphy, and, most of all, *sh'jer*. She would never be able to fold paper with such depth of spirit, she thought wistfully.

Once more she took up her writing brush. Choosing a fresh sheet of paper, Nama copied out a short poem by one of her uncle's favorite poets:

> *White winter tiger*
> *That brings autumn's old men down*
> *Falls to spring's children*

She wondered if she dared give it to him as a gift. No, it was such a little thing, compared to all he had done for her, that she hadn't the nerve. Still, she must show him how grateful she was for his generosity; she must work harder with her tutors, so that she would be worthy of the noble marriage he promised her.

If only she didn't have to stay within the confines of this little house and its tiny grounds, hidden away within his mansion's compound. Uncle Jhanun was so old-fashioned! It would be nice to see other people besides Zuia the Cold and the tutors. She wondered if anyone else even knew she was here. No one ever came to visit.

Nama rolled her shoulders once more and prepared to practice her calligraphy anew.

The clicking of the worry beads was loud in the quiet of his room. Taren paced the floor, the string of beads looping endlessly through his nervous fingers.

Of all the cursed bad luck! The last two things he'd thought he'd have to face—teaching the damned Dragonlords Jehangli and riding one of their blasted horses—and both in barely more than a candlemark. .

Still, he should have read that trail even before it was blazed. Both things followed the decision to send the Dragonlords as logically and inevitably as thunder followed lightning. This farce of playing the humble, heroic, ailing near-hermit was dulling his wits. And that was the one thing he could *not* afford. Here he had no weapons save those same wits.

The beads moved so quickly now, their clicking sounded like the little bones in a Zharmatian rattle. It was not a comforting resemblance. Taren dropped the beads into his belt pouch. He did not stop pacing.

So—what could he do? Teach them nonsense words? No, he'd likely trip himself up; at least one would remember that *oogfa* didn't mean the same thing as it had two days before, may they writhe under the Phoenix's claws. Gallant fools Dragonlords might be, running to that dragon's rescue, but they were not stupid.

Teach them some obscure Jehangli dialect instead? He knew a few from his work for Lord Jhanun. A lovely idea, but one that had two edges; the first time they realized that most Jehangli couldn't understand them, nor could they understand most Jehangli, the game would be up.

No, he'd have to teach the damned weredragons to speak proper Jehangli. The thought left a sour taste in his mouth.

One problem, if not solved, then disposed of. Next was the matter of riding a Llysanin. True, he'd tricked truehumans, truedragons, and Dragonlords thus far, but dumb animals might be another matter. Taren remembered how his brother's hound had growled and bared its fangs whenever it saw him. A wise beast—far wiser than its master had been.

So how—?

The answer was so sudden and so simple that Taren nearly laughed aloud. *Baisha* might consider a Llysanin no more than his due, but Taren, the former slave, would never dream of riding a Dragonlord's mount.

To celebrate, Taren sauntered over to the table and poured a goblet of Pelnaran wine. This, he thought as he watched the dark red wine cascade from the flask, would be the only thing he'd miss about the north.

He raised the goblet in a toast to himself and drank. Then he called to his servant in the outer room, saying, "I would ask you to carry a message to His Grace, Linden Rathan, please. . . ."

The smell of rain hung heavy in the air tonight; the herd would be coming in early. Linden led the new troupe out to the pastures in the soft dusk. Balls of coldfire lit the way around them, dancing in the chilly air.

Linden stopped at the gate. He called down one of the bobbing globes to shed more light on the gate latch. Lleld and Jekkanadar leaned on the top rail of the fence, gazing into the pasture; Maurynna followed their lead. Behind him Linden heard Otter clear his throat for what seemed the dozenth time since they'd turned onto the trail leading to the upper pastures. He looked back.

"Out with it," he said, one hand resting on the latch. "What's wrong?"

Great-uncle and grandnephew exchanged a long look. Raven jerked his head abruptly at his great-uncle as if to say, "*You* explain," and studied an elderberry bush by the stream that ran through the pastures. But for all his seeming nonchalance, Linden saw the tension in the young man's stance, the shoulders tight and rigid beneath the blue cloak, how the long hands clenched by his side.

Otter slid an unheeded—and sour—glance at his grandnephew. "*You're* the one who's so eager for this, I'll remind you."

Raven ignored him. His whole attention now focused on the rabbit settling under the bush as if to forever burn it upon his memory. Linden doubted if he'd ever found a rabbit so fascinating before in his life, or would again.

"I'll remember this, boy," the bard muttered and gave in. "Ah, Linden—while Shan has let me ride him a few times, I know that the Llysanyins will usually only bear Dragonlords. Are you certain that . . . ?"

Linden raised an eyebrow in amusement. "That we'll find some willing to bear you two? No, I'm not certain. That's why we're here. I'll admit it would be simpler if, like Taren, you two insisted on riding ordinary horses. But we need at least one more Llysanyin with us; Miki is so little that she'd look silly in a *caelah*."

"What's that?" Maurynna asked.

"Yerrin for a kind of dance for four people; it also refers to a performance of four horses," Linden said.

"Now, Otter and Raven—first I'll explain to the herd what we want; then you two will walk among them. They will choose, not you. Remember that." He pushed the gate open and led the way inside. "And remember that most— if not all—will choose *not* to."

The mixed herd of Llysanyins and horses, led by Shan, Boreal, and Lleld and Jekkanadar's mounts, Miki and Hillel, ambled down the hill toward them. Once all the troupe were inside, Linden latched the gate carefully once more and went to meet the animals. Shan came up eagerly, stuck his nose under Linden's cloak and sniffed his belt pouch.

"No apples," Linden said.

The stallion's ears went back.

"Stop that, silly," Maurynna said as she joined Linden. She paused to rub the black nose. "There weren't enough for everyone; it would have been rude." Boreal came up and rested his chin on her shoulder. Miki and Hillel joined their people as well.

Shan's ears flicked back and forth, allowing as how that might be so but he expected one later in private. He permitted Linden to scratch along the crest of his neck; Linden smiled and perversely went for the most ticklish spot at the base of the mane. Shan's nose reached skyward and his trembling upper lip stretched out and out. He looked remarkably silly.

Linden surveyed the mixed herd before them. There were two Llysanyins missing, a granddam and one of her many grandsons. Linden decided to give them a little more time. The mare had been the last mount of Mercen Evraene before he died, a Dragonlord who had also been a bard. Perhaps, when she saw Otter's red bard's cloak . . . Linden could only hope.

He continued rubbing Shan's neck. The two missing Llysanyins did not appear. When he judged enough time had passed, Linden stopped, his hand resting on the stallion's shoulder.

"Enough. We've come to you on serious business," he announced.

Every Llysanyin who had been cropping grass or otherwise occupied stopped, their attention now on Linden. Many looked at the truehumans in the party and then at each other. As always, Linden wondered just how much the breed could think; he could have sworn many of those exchanged looks said *What have truehumans to do with us?* Some herded the ordinary horses away. This was not their business and they would be a distraction.

When the herders returned, Linden began, all the while keeping an eye out for the two missing Llysanyins. Still not here, but he could wait no longer. "You saw the truedragons fly south, didn't you?"

Heads nodded. The Llysanyins waited.

"You saw when they returned."

A number of heads turned away. Linden knew the intelligent Llysanyins would have seen—and likely understood—what it had meant when the beaten and crippled remnant of that once-proud army had passed by on their way home. And no doubt many Llysanyins had listened as their Dragonlord partners or the stablehands discussed the matter before them.

"It's been decided that Dragonlords will now go to faroff Jehanglan to help the captive truedragon Pirakos. And that's where we need your help." Now he saw the missing two standing on the edge of the small Llysanyin herd and pitched his voice to carry to them. "We need two Llysan-yins willing to carry truehumans"—some Llysanyins immediately turned away; well and well, Linden admitted to himself, he'd expected it—"and willing to pretend to be nothing more than ordinary horses." He paused to let the remaining Llysanyins consider his words.

Shan, Miki, and Hillel were used to such subterfuge, he knew; Linden did not always travel openly as a Dragonlord, and neither did Lleld and Jekkanadar. Inexperienced Boreal would follow their lead and learn quickly.

The granddam and her grandson moved a little closer. Linden's hopes rose with each slow step; they were the only two who seemed interested. They were striking animals, black with iron grey manes and tails. Linden had seen many such before, but those had been true greys whose coats and manes had lightened to white with passing years. These two had kept the unusual coloring; Linden didn't think anything but a Llysanyin could.

They were set off by more than their unusual coloring as well. Chailen, the head groom, called them the closest things to hermits he'd ever seen among horse or Llysanyin. They cared little for the company of others, preferring to always graze by themselves, pointedly moving away if any Llysanyin or horse came too close. And always they moved in unison as if sharing a single mind.

"Odd animals," had been Chailen's considered judgment. That from a *kir* who had worked with Llysanyins and their many quirks since he was a youngster.

Let us hope that "oddness" extends to carrying truehumans, Linden thought. "There is more you should know," he continued. "There will be a voyage aboard a ship."

More Llysanyins left. Miki tried to scuttle away; Lleld grabbed her tail. The little blood bay mare hung her head.

"You'd think we were threatening you with the knacker," Lleld said in disgust. "This will be fun."

Miki stared over her shoulder at her person.

"Truly," Lleld coaxed. "We're going to be performers again."

While the promise cheered Miki, Linden saw many heads go up in consternation. "Lleld Kemberaene," he announced, "will tell you what else you need to know."

Though she was startled, Lleld quickly recovered as Linden knew she would. She vaulted into a handstand on Miki's broad back, then eased down until she sat. When every Llysanyin eye was on her, she began.

Trust Lleld, Linden thought as he stepped back, *to make a performance of this.*

Do you think any of them will agree? Maurynna said in his mind as Lleld exhorted the Llysanyins. As always there was the odd hum in the back of her mindvoice. This time it was stronger than usual; Kyrissaean must be very alert tonight.

I truly don't know, love; none of them look very enthusiastic, Linden admitted.

In truth, the Llysanyins looked very *un*enthusiastic. Some wandered off. Others stayed, Linden suspected, merely to be polite. Not one looked as if they'd ever dreamed of running away with a band of traveling entertainers. Granddam and grandson stared intently first at Lleld, then at the truehumans; their noses touched for a long moment as if they discussed something. But a heartbeat later they dropped their heads and grazed. Linden's hopes plummeted.

When Lleld finished, Linden waited to see if any Llysanyins would step forward. None did. As one the two grey-maned blacks rose on their hind legs, pirouetted, and trotted away. With a sigh, Linden beckoned Otter and Raven forward. Perhaps one or two of the Llysanyins would change their minds when face-to-face with the men.

"Go," Linden said. "Walk among them."

Otter hesitated a moment; Raven went into the center of what was left of the herd. Otter followed, his scarlet bard's cloak pulled close. Linden retreated and motioned the other Dragonlords to do the same.

The Llysanyins studied the two men. Linden's hopes soared for a moment when one young mare looked deep into Raven's eyes and touched his shoulder with her nose. But then she turned away; it was plain she'd done nothing more than wish him luck.

The rain began and the group of Llysanyins melted away. Some went to fetch the horses to drive them to the stables. Others stood by the gate, waiting for one of the two-foots to unlatch it for them. Lleld, still mounted on Miki, went off to oblige them. Horses and Llysanyins poured through the gate and set off for the warmth and dryness of the stables in a flood of tossing heads and cavorting bodies.

Full darkness fell as Dragonlords and truehumans kept to their places, waiting for the press of horseflesh to be well away. Concerned that Otter would have difficulty picking his way in the rainy dark, Linden tossed a few more balls of coldfire into the air, mindspeaking the other Dragonlords to do the same, and led the way to the gate. Immediately more bright globes burst into existence like tiny suns, dancing in the rain. A dozen or so swirled in the air and strung themselves in a line to guide the truehumans from the pasture to the gate.

Raven and Otter joined them. No one said a word. Linden urged their Llysanyins through the gate. As soon as all, two- and four-foots alike, were outside the pasture, Linden latched the gate shut. They started down the trail to the Keep, Shan, Boreal, and Hillel to the fore.

Lleld hopped down from Miki and slapped the mare on the rump. "Go on," she said. Miki trotted ahead to join the others. The Llysanyins were soon out of sight.

They trudged along without speaking, wrapped in gloom.

"Why?" Raven asked at last. Coldfire lit his wet face. Rain? Or tears? The pain in his voice was a thing that cut, sharp and hard and edged like a knife. "Do they truly look down on truehumans so?"

Linden had no answer for him. He didn't think anyone knew, or ever would know.

Then Jekkanadar spoke; a ball of golden coldfire illuminated his dark, narrow face. "I don't think that's it." His words had the shy hesitation of a belief spoken aloud for the first time. "They bond strongly, very strongly, with their riders."

"I've seen it with Shan," Otter said. "But what has that to do—"

The coldfire drifted away into the night. "You can live as long as three hundred years—maybe more. Think of the pain of giving your heart to someone who will live but a fraction of that time. How many times can you do it without that heart breaking? Nightsong already gave her heart once."

They went on, drawing cloaks closer against the wet cold. Linden wondered if Jekkanadar had touched on the truth.

Lleld said with unaccustomed soberness, "After all, it's why so many Dragonlords can't be friends with truehumans. It hurts too much."

"We come and go so quickly, don't we?" said Otter. He spoke as a man who had lived many years and, knowing he was near the close of a truehuman's allotted span, accepted that truth.

"Like moths in a flame," Lleld whispered.

Walking beside Linden, Maurynna made a small choking noise. Was this the first time she had truly understood what being a Dragonlord meant? That she would outlive everyone she had known in her life as a truehuman; all of her friends, all of her family, every truehuman she now knew would be dust, and she would remain unchanged. That she would see every child not yet born to kith and kin grow old and die, and their children after them. He flipped the edge of his cloak aside and reached for the hand that he knew would be searching for his. Cold fingers closed around his as though they would never let go.

We have each other, he told her, pouring as much comfort as he could into the words.

Thank the gods, came the heartfelt reply.

Raven stopped short and held up a hand. "What's that?" he asked sharply.

Linden halted, as did the others. He'd been so caught up

in the conversation and Maurynna's distress that he hadn't heard anything amiss. Now he did. After a moment he identified the sound.

"Hooves," he said. "Running horses."

"And they're getting louder," Maurynna said. "They're coming toward us—our Llysanyins?" The doubt in her voice said she didn't believe it.

"Trouble ahead?" Otter asked quietly.

"I don't know," Linden said and sent his globes of coldfire ahead of them. The others bade theirs join his. They waited in a tense group on the path.

For another moment the sound continued straight for them. Then the horses went to either side—two, Linden decided by the sound—and swept out and around once more.

New hope sprang up in his breast. "Look!" Linden cried.

Just ahead of them, from either side of the trail, two Llysanyins burst into the light. Their bodies were as black as the night, but their grey manes and tails shone in the glow of the massed coldfire. They raced headlong at each other; at the last possible moment they sat back on their haunches and pivoted swiftly to face the waiting group. Moving as one, they raised their forelegs off the ground, a slow controlled movement. Then both leaped straight up, hind legs kicking straight back at the apex of the leap, in flight for one magical instant.

Linden watched in awe. He knew what he saw and that Raven would as well: the *aelarhan*, the battle maneuver meant to decapitate a foot soldier or unhorse another rider, a maneuver both deadly and beautiful—and damned difficult.

The Llysanyins came down, each in the place it had leapt up from, creatures of the earth once more. The tall stallion went straight to Raven; his granddam followed more slowly but went without hesitation to Otter.

For once the bard was too stunned to speak. As for Raven—Linden had to look away from the naked joy that filled the young man's face as he laid a hand on the stallion's neck. It was too much like trespassing.

The first thing he saw was Lleld dancing in the rain. Her red hair was plastered to her skull and her cloak flapped around her like the wings of some drunken bird.

"Oh, well done!" she cried. She caught Jekkanadar's hands and swung him around in a circle. "We have our troupe! We have our troupe!" she sang.

A few days later, on a day when the sun shone strongly enough to warm even Taren's bones, Lînden brought him to the mountain pasture to select a horse for him.

"Are you certain you don't even want to try?" Linden asked.

"No, Dragonlord," the man said with a self-deprecating smile, "an ordinary horse is good enough for the likes of a former slave like myself."

"That was hardly your fault," Linden said more sharply than he meant to.

"Who would argue with the will of the gods?" Taren countered gently, his mildness a reproach. "Not I. I'm content, my lord, that you pick out a sturdy, sensible beast for me."

Contrite, Linden said, "Shan and I will do that."

So he went off, hand resting on the big Llysanyin's neck as he told Shan what he was looking for. The stallion knew the horses as well as any two-foot ever could, even Chailen who had eyes for little else than his charges. Between them they would find a "right fine" horse for Taren, as the hillmen of Yerrih would say.

"Well?" Otter asked in a low voice.

Linden stepped to one side, drawing Otter out of the press of people making their way into the great hall for the evening meal.

"I tried to talk him into trying for one of the Llysanyins," Linden reported, "but he refused. Felt even one of the half breeds was too good for him. So an ordinary horse it was. A solid gelding, strong and sensible, with good paces and hooves like iron. Even Chailen approved the choice, and that's saying something."

Otter's eyes crinkled as he grinned. "So it is. And here comes your lady-love, looking for you; we'd best go in to supper."

Linden caught the hand that Maurynna held out to him and pulled her close, sliding an arm around her waist. Otter flanked her other side as they went to their accustomed table. Her nearness comforted him, but his thoughts were far away.

Bit by bit, Lleld's mad scheme was becoming reality. Bit by bit, their danger grew.

Twenty-one

The day after a mount was found for the last member of her troupe, Lleld was climbing the stairs to the library to read more of Lady Ardelis's book when a gentle "tug" at her mind made her stop. One hand on the banister, she asked *Who—?*

It is I, Morlen, little cousin. I have a news of a Seeing for thee. Will thee hear it?

Lleld's breath caught in her chest. *Of course, my lord!*

I do not think thee will like it; and Jessia will like it even less. It is also very clouded; something blocks my vision somewhat.

Oh, dear; that did not sound at all encouraging. Lleld said, *And what is this Seeing, my lord?*

She listened, and as she listened, her heart sank. Morlen had been right. She didn't like it at all. The Lady might well have second and third thoughts about letting them go. And Linden . . . !

She would think about that later. When Morlen was

done, Lleld asked, *Have you told the Lady about this yet?*

A long silence, then an embarrassed, *No.*

Lleld waited.

She is already very angry with me, Morlen said.

Lleld indulged in the luxury of grimacing because Morlen couldn't see. So she was to get stuck with this bit of dirty work, was she?

Well and well, this whole thing had been her idea from the beginning. She supposed she couldn't complain.

But she certainly wanted to. Instead, she said, *I thank you for this news, my lord. While it's true it's not clear, anything we can find out is of great help to us. And yes, I will tell the Lady.*

A sigh of relief gusted through her mind. *I thank thee, little cousin Lleld. I only wish I could do more to aid thee. May the gods go with all of thee, and the winds sing under thy wings.*

She felt him withdraw from her mind. She slumped against the wall, trying to find a way out of this thornbush of unpleasant choices. But no matter what way she thought of, all involved getting scratched.

Ah, hell—she might as well get it over with. Grumbling under her breath about cowardly truedragons, she mindcalled the Lady, Jekkanadar, and, after a long moment of hesitation, Linden.

Then she turned and trudged back down the stairs as slowly as she could. Perhaps she didn't have the luxury of cowardice, but she certainly didn't have to rush into having her head bitten off.

"What!" Linden roared the instant Lleld finished relaying Morlen's news. "Maurynna go alone to that damned mountain? Are you mad, Lleld?"

"No, Morlen is, if anyone is," she pointed out. "And he didn't say she had to be alone. He just said that you couldn't go with her as we'd orginally thought you could. You always knew that you wouldn't be able to go inside the mountain with her, Linden."

"Yes, I knew that," he snarled. "But I always thought I'd be able to go at least most of the way with her—even up to the mountain, though not inside. And now you tell me she must go alone?"

"She won't be alone, not really. I told you he said that there was help waiting there for her."

Linden just glared at her. By the gods, Lleld thought, she'd never seen him like this. She'd rarely seen Linden lose his temper in all the time she'd known him. She'd never thought him capable of such anger, such fury. But there he sat, his dark grey eyes cold and hard.

"But Morlen didn't say she must go alone *to* the mountain, Linden," said the Lady unexpectedly. "Surely one of the truehumans can go with her."

Lleld nearly fell over at this sign of support from such an unexpected quarter. She'd never be surprised at anything else again.

"That's true," Jekkanadar said.

She caught his eye. *Otter?* she asked him privately.

Who else? Do you *want to rub his nose in it?* he replied dryly.

Ah—no. "It's a capital idea. Otter can go with Rynna, and—"

"No," Linden said in a tone that brooked no arguments. "Not Otter. And this is why. . . ."

Maurynna wondered what news had come that Lleld called Otter, Raven, and her to the quarters she and Jekkanadar shared. Perhaps now they would see the final details of their mission settled. She also wondered why she hadn't been called to the meeting with the Lady. That, she thought, did not bode well.

Even worse, Linden hadn't mindcalled her to tell her about it; she'd only found out when she returned to their quarters and heard the news from their servants.

She looked from Lleld to Jekkanadar to Linden, who looked like a storm about to break. "You three were closeted with the Lady for a long time. Have you decided the final details? Will Linden and I have to split off from the rest of you because four Dragonlords would likely alert the priestmages?"

No one said anything.

Uneasy now, Maurynna asked, "You *have* decided the last details?"

Lleld would not meet her eyes. "Um, yes. There's only one way to do it, Rynna. I don't like it. Jekkanadar doesn't like it."

"And I bloody well don't like it, either," Linden snarled. His hand clenched; the pewter goblet he held crumpled like eggshell. He cast it aside. Wine splashed across the table like a gout of blood. With a vicious curse he kicked his chair over backward and strode out of Lleld and Jekkanadar's quarters.

Maurynna sat back, shaken by the violence of his actions. She had never seen Linden like this. She cast a quick glance at Otter, looking for enlightenment; he had known Linden for more than forty years. Was this flash of temper a common thing? But the bard looked as astonished as she felt.

Uncertain, she half rose from her chair. "Lleld, Jekkanadar—what . . . ?"

Jekkanadar caught her wrist to stay her. Maurynna looked down at the dark brown hand clamped over the still-pale patch of skin where the rank bracelet of a sea captain once had rested. Suddenly she knew what was coming next. "I have to know what's wrong with Linden," she insisted, seeking to forestall Jekkanadar.

"I can tell you what's wrong with Linden," said the Assantikkan Dragonlord. "Linden's frightened for you. For as you pointed out, we must split up once we are in Jehanglan."

Lleld said, "You'll have to leave us, Maurynna. Or we have to leave you. As far as we—and Morlen—know, you're the only Dragonlord who can approach Mount Kajhenral without lighting every alarm beacon—so to speak—for miles around. Linden will stay with the troupe; we'll create a diversion."

Part from Linden? For the gods only knew how long? Perhaps to never see him again?

No. No and no and no yet again, she tried to say. As short a time as they'd been together, they were already entwined like two trees that had grown around each other. The thought of being apart from him hurt—frighteningly so.

But it had to be done. There was no other way; she could see that. A wave of desolation passed over her. "I'm to go alone?"

She might as well. No one else could make up for the loss of Linden. . . .

But Lleld shook her head. "No, you'll need someone to watch your back if nothing else. We've talked it over and decided that the best person to go with you is Raven."

Maurynna whipped around to face him. If he'd known about this, blast him, or had any sort of hand in separating her from her soultwin, she'd—

If Otter had looked surprised before, Raven looked stunned now. This was as much of a shock to him as it was to her. Maurynna bit back the harsh words that had jumped to her tongue.

"Me?" he sputtered. "But why?"

"Because Rynna is still far from an expert rider," Lleld said bluntly. "She'll need someone who's experienced with horses with her, someone she—and we—can trust. Most importantly, she needs someone whose presence won't blow a war horn right in the ear of the priestmages. That leaves out any of us. We had considered your great-uncle, you know, but it was decided that the one who went needed to be young enough and strong enough to stand the pace Maurynna must set. In other words, Raven—you."

"Is that why Linden Rathan's so upset?" Raven challenged. "He's jealous that I won over my great-uncle?"

Lleld's brown eyes narrowed. In them Maurynna saw a contempt and anger that she'd never seen the little Dragon-lord display before. Her lip curled.

But before she could say anything, Jekkanadar spoke.

Somehow, though his voice was gentleness itself, it was all stinging rebuke. "It was Linden who insisted it be you, Raven Redhawkson. In deference to his feelings, Lleld and I had suggested that Otter go with Maurynna. But Linden argued in favor of your youth and stamina, your knowledge of horses. And he reminded us of another thing.

"Like Healers, bards must be free to travel safely upon their business since it's to the benefit of all. Therefore, their persons are sacred. But in return for that immunity, neither may they do harm to others. Otter is forbidden from killing save in the last extremity of self-defense. To help Maurynna, you may well have to cut a man's throat from behind." He cocked his head. "Have you ever killed, Raven?"

Raven stared at the table. "No," he said. "Never."

Jekkanadar nodded. "It's not an easy thing, believe me. Even to save your own life, it isn't easy. I know. I hope you can do it if it becomes necessary. Have you any idea how hard it is for Linden to entrust the other half of himself, the half he loves more than anything, to a boy who isn't a blooded warrior? Who never even trained as one? Linden was a soldier; now, as a Dragonlord, he's more than the equal of any man in speed and strength. He's the best guard possible for Maurynna. And he can't do it.

"Once we're in Jehanglan, they daren't mindspeak each other once you two split off from us. He won't even know for certain what's happening to the two of you. Do you wonder that he's angry and upset? And you put it down to common jealousy." Jekkanadar made a noise of disgust and turned away.

No one else spoke. Unable to stand the tension in the room—or the miserable expression on Raven's face—Maurynna left. This time neither Lleld nor Jekkanadar tried to stop her.

Once out of the other Dragonlords' quarters, Maurynna paused in the hallway, letting her mind seek Linden. She could feel him close by, a seething tangle of anger, resentment, and, yes, jealousy. But overriding it all was a wretched, helpless fear.

All will be well, she mindspoke him. She stretched her perception of him a little more and knew at least in which direction he'd gone. She went after him.

A heavy mental sigh, then, *If the gods are kind. Maurynna-love, you've no idea how this hurts.*

She pushed open the door leading to the narrow staircase that spanned this end of Dragonskeep. Linden sat across one of the steps, back against the wall, his long legs sprawled out before him. He looked up, his handsome face weary, and swung around, making room on the step for her.

"I do know," she said, sitting beside him. "Do you remember the night I Changed? When you were facing Kas Althume at that altar? All I knew was that I had to be with you, that somehow *I* had to protect *you*. Part of me knew that was silly; I still thought I was a truehuman then. You were once a soldier and now a Dragonlord. What help could an untrained truehuman give you?

"But it didn't matter. I had to be there." She rested her head against his shoulder. "I was lucky; I was able to be with you."

"And a damn good thing you were; I wouldn't like to think what Kas Althume would have done with his first plan thwarted," Linden said.

"For which I still thank Sherrine," Maurynna said with some reluctance. Although the young Cassorin noblewoman had saved Linden from Kas Althume's black magery by sacrificing herself, there had been no love lost between the two women. Instinctively one hand twitched toward the eye that Sherrine had once cut open with a whip.

Instead Maurynna made it rest atop the other one on her knees. Linden would know why she touched her eye. She would not bring back those memories for him. Not at this moment.

He covered both of her hands with one of his and squeezed. "Ah, love, it wouldn't be so bad if Raven knew more. If only I could choose who went with you," Linden said. "If only I could reach back in time. . . ."

She knew whom he thought of: his cousin, Bram Wolfson, leader of the mercenary troop Linden had belonged to. The man who'd helped Rani eo'Tsan to her throne in Kelneth, who in his turn had become High Chief of Yerrih. Rider of the first Boreal and the hero of many of the ancient stories and legends Otter had told Raven and her when they were children.

A shiver took her. To her, Bram and Rani were legends from the distant past, stories for a winter's night by the fire. But the man sitting beside her, who even now slipped an arm around her shoulders and pulled her closer, had known them, had fought beside them. He had been a legend himself in her eyes.

And now they were soultwins.

And she would have to leave him.

Is nothing ever to go right for us? she demanded of the gods. They didn't answer. She said, "Tell me the rest of the plan."

"Nothing much more to tell. Once we're in Jehanglan, we'll have Jehangli guides—rather, guards, I'll wager—with us. Somehow or another we'll have to make them think you and Raven have been sent back to the port. Taren says he can convince them of it; it's not unheard of. Or tell them you ran away together, I don't know. We'll toss those dice when it's time. It's already been decided that you two won't have any important part in the show. Chailen tells me that Otter's mare, Nightsong, has rounded up two more of her offspring. Lovely bite marks they had, he said. They won't bear truehumans, but they'll take the places that Boreal and Raven's Stormwind would have played in the performance. That way the Jehangli won't have any excuse to send us home after you disappear. We can continue to create a diversion and—perhaps—be there if you need us."

She considered that. "Once we separate, it's up to Raven and me."

"Just so," Linden said. "It's up to you."

Gods help her; she didn't want this kind of responsibility. She wasn't even a real Dragonlord.

He rose, pulled her up to lean against him. She buried her face against his neck, content to take this moment. His hand stroked her hair.

The door above them creaked open slowly. They looked up.

It was Raven. At the sight of them in each other's arms, his blue eyes burned; for a moment Maurynna thought he would fly at Linden. Then something changed in his face and the anger fell away.

"Dragonlord," he rasped and stopped. Clearing his throat, Raven went on, "From the stories my great-uncle told us when we were little, I know that you were a soldier." He paused. His mouth worked as if what came next was hard.

"True," Linden said into the silence.

What is this all about? Maurynna wondered.

Raven took a deep breath. "I'm not. I'm not what Maurynna needs for this venture. I'm just the best you've got here and now. But I—I . . ." He drew himself up. "Linden Rathan, I know I can't learn it all, it would take too long, but will you teach me what you can of fighting?"

At first Maurynna thought Linden would refuse, he took so long to answer. His hand ceased stroking her hair. Then—

"I'd do that gladly, Raven," he said quietly.

Raven's chin went up. "Thank you, Dragonlord. I'll do my best."

Linden smiled, a sad little half twist of his lips. "I know that. That's why I insisted on you. And, seeing as we're all in Lady Mayhem's little mess together, it's Linden. I'll work you hard, make no mistake, but I'm fair." He held out a hand. "Done?"

Maurynna wanted to cheer when Raven came down the few steps and caught Linden's hand in a firm clasp.

"Done . . . Linden," Raven said. "When do we start?"

"Tomorrow," said Linden. "Early." His smile turned to pure little-boy wickedness; it was a look Maurynna knew well. "Very, *very* early. And you, love"—he smiled down at her upturned face—"are included."

Her outraged, "What!" brought only laughter. She fumed at him; he only laughed more. "Damn you," she muttered. "You know I don't like that sort of thing."

"I'll rest the easier for it, love, if I know you can defend yourself to your utmost," he said, no longer laughing. "Yes, you know a bit; it's not enough." His hand clenched on her back. "It's not enough," he whispered.

The workday was ended at last! Liasuhn went from table to table, bucket of clean sand in one hand, stiff-bristled brush in the other. With a practiced motion, he dumped a fine sprinkling of sand across each wooden table and scrubbed it with the brush until it was clean. A final few swipes sent the last of the sand to the dirt floor.

Only one table still had customers at it: two men, agents for an incense merchant, who had come in frequently the past span of days. Jolly fellows they were, too; quick with jokes, and generous. They always left him a little extra when they paid for their bowls of soup and millet. Liasuhn smiled and waved his brush at them.

"You're in a hurry tonight," one said. He grinned and waved Liasuhn over to join them.

With a glance over his shoulder to make certain his father was still in the kitchen, Liasuhn pulled up one of the drum-shaped stools and sat with them.

"I am," he confessed. "There's a dice game in the back of old Saji's fish shop in a bit. The old man is away from the village tonight, so his apprentices are making the most of it. Old Saji's a real bastard."

The other man, he of the crooked nose, laughed. "You lose, brother; it wasn't a wench after all."

The first speaker pulled an exaggerated frown. "Hell—I was certain it was a girl, handsome lad like that. But even *I'm* not right all the time," he grumbled, and flipped a coin from the pocket in his sleeve at his friend. His ever-present smile returned an instant later, showing no hard feelings.

An idea came to Liasuhn. "Do you like to gamble?" he asked.

"Shall we wager on where the sun will rise tomorrow?" the cheerful one countered.

Liasuhn grinned. "Want to come to the dice game with me? We could use a few more players."

"Lad, we'd love to. I'm Kwahsiu, by the way, and this ugly fellow is my old friend Nalorih. You're Liasuhn, yes? Thought I'd heard your father call you that. And just so you don't make a complete liar out of me, how about the three of us go find a lusty wench to take us all on after the game?"

Liasuhn nearly swallowed the wrong way. He could rarely afford a prostitute, even at the rundown sty known as the Silver Parrot. But the thought of having a woman tonight made his face grow warm. "I'd like to, but . . ."

"Afraid you won't have the coin?" Nalorih said sympathetically. "We could skip the game."

Liasuhn squirmed uncomfortably on the stool and sighed. "Even if . . . You see, my . . . Oh, damn."

"Say no more," said Kwahsiu, spreading his hands. "We understand. Your father has forgotten how the juices flow when a man is—?"

"Eighteen," Liasuhn filled in, pleased at being called a man. His father still thought of him as a child.

"Eighteen," Kwahsiu echoed. "No doubt he can't get it through his head you're not a boy anymore. And I'll wager he's stingy as a crab with your allowance, am I right?"

Another sigh. "Yes. Very."

Kwahsiu rolled his eyes. "Think of it, brother," he said to Nalorih. "All those poor wenches deprived of this handsome lad. It's a crime, it is, and one that I think we must remedy in the name of charity to the poor girls. Why, look at him—looks enough like the emperor to be his little brother, doesn't he?"

"He does indeed."

Liasuhn looked down modestly. He confessed, "Chiyual, our old village priest, said much the same once—he'd seen the emperor at one of the big temples while he was on pilgrimage. Chiyual said it was because I took after my grandmother. She was Zharmatian."

Kwahsiu's eternal smile grew wider. "I thought it might be something like that. Well now, Liasuhn, why don't you get this last table cleaned and we'll be off? Never mind the dice game; I think I know just the wench for us."

Taren sat by a window in his quarters watching the last of the sunset paint the sky. His master, he thought, would enjoy this view. A moment's thought, and Lord Jhanun would compose a poem comparing the scarlet-streaked sky to, to—well, to *something*. And he would listen, and realize how true, how *apt*, the words were, that that was just what the sky looked like.

"What," he mused aloud, "might Lord Jhanun—"

He broke off as his servant entered. "Sir, Lleld Kember-aene would speak with you. She asks if you are well enough to receive her."

May the gods damn it all! What the hell do these people want now?

"Of course!" he said, turning a delighted face to the *kir*. "My friends are welcome anytime!"

When the little Dragonlord came in, Taren rose from his seat like a man much older.

Her forehead wrinkled in concern, Lleld Kembaraene said, "Oh, Taren, I'm sorry. Are you not feeling well to-day?"

"My friend, the sight of you eases all my pains," Taren said, bestowing a smile upon her. When she answered it with one of her own, he asked, "And to what do I owe the pleasure of this visit, Lleld?"

"We need a map of Jehanglan," she said. "Can you make one for us? One of the scribes can help you if you need."

Damn. He'd been afraid it would come to this. Like the teaching of the language, it was something he couldn't lie about. If one of these cursed creatures took it into his or her head to ignore his warning against Changing and flew over enough of Jehanglan, they'd soon see any errors. No, this was another thing he must do without trickery.

In a tone of mixed admiration and surprise, he said, "Ah—what a fool I am! I should have thought of that long ago. Of course I shall make a map for you. It will be my pleasure."

To see you in chains, he finished to himself.

Never had he even dreamed of going to such an expensive brothel! This was the only good one in town, the one used by any lords and rich merchants passing through when the captains of their river barges stopped to take on supplies. The bed was covered in silk, there were pen-and-ink drawings on the walls, and the cups they drank good rice wine from were of fine white clay. No broken bedframe here, no holes in the wall for the rats to wander through. There were even fresh flowers in a vase by the bed, and the woman was young enough and pretty, and had all her teeth.

Liasuhn could not believe his luck in meeting these men. He hoped they truly would take him on as an apprentice as they'd hinted they might. Then he, too, could learn to be an agent for a successful merchant! No more dishing out millet and cleaning tables. . . .

At a low, throaty moan, he nearly dropped the dice in the game he and Kwahsiu ostensibly played while Nalorih took first tumble with the woman. Without his willing it, Liasuhn peeked. It seemed the wench was certainly giving Nalorih his money's worth. Liasuhn looked away, embarrassed.

The thought of bedding a woman with someone else present both repelled and excited him. He gulped down more wine. It hit his stomach with a burn that went straight to his head. He sneaked another quick look; Nalorih certainly didn't seem to care that he had an audience.

Kwahsiu poured a little more wine into his cup with a wink and a grin that said, *Not too much, now!* Liasuhn raised the cup in a toast and drank.

Once again, the wine went straight to his head, and this time rubbed off the last edges of his fears and inhibitions.

Forgetting any manners, he watched openly now, breathing heavily. The dice lay forgotten on the table.

Sight and sound and scent nearly overwhelmed him. It was much too hot in the room. Liasuhn opened the neck of his robe. It didn't help.

When Nalorih finally rolled off the woman, and she turned on the bed and beckoned him with a smile, Liasuhn nearly tore his clothing in his hurry to undress. She laughed as he flung himself on her.

As he took the woman in a frenzy of lust and wine, Liasuhn heard Kwahsiu say with a laugh, "He's certainly no eunuch, is he, brother?"

Liasuhn grinned drunkenly. No, he certainly wasn't, and set about proving it with a will.

Twenty-two

A few days later, in answer to Lleld's mindcall, Linden and Maurynna arrived in time to find Jekkanadar at the door to the library. He paused, hand on the latch, waiting for them. Maurynna waved a greeting.

"Lleld is already inside, and Otter and Raven on their way," he said. "They should be here soon." He pulled the door open and went in.

They followed. Once more Master Pren sat at his table; he favored them with a glare and a sniff before bending over his books again, the quill pen in his hand quivering as if indignant at yet another interruption.

The door to the study room—now a planning room— opened. Jenna peered out and beckoned them to enter. "You're moving much more easily today, Maurynna. Not so sore anymore?"

"Not anymore—though no thanks to this brute," Maurynna said, giving Linden a mock frown. But the practice sessions were getting easier, she had to admit.

They filed in. Lleld and Taren stood side by side at the far side of the table, bending over a large sheet of parchment that stretched across it; books weighed down the four corners. Taren drew a finger across the parchment, explaining something in an undertone to the little Dragonlord. Her fiery red head nodded in understanding.

What they studied was upside down to Maurynna, but she could guess what it was. Lleld's next words confirmed it.

Lleld looked up as Jekkanadar came around the table to join her. "It's finished," she said. "Taren's map. Come look."

Her heart thudding, Maurynna made her way around the table, Linden right behind her. Somehow, this made things more real. As if before had been part of one of Otter's tales, but now . . .

It took a moment to orient herself, even accustomed as she was to sea charts. Seeing the southern tip of Assantik at the *upper* edge of a map disconcerted her. This was much farther south than she'd ever thought to journey.

Jehanglan sprawled across the sheet, a full calf's hide. Large areas were marked; desert, mountains, plains, and others. There were cities shown in red and the inked lines of rivers like veins running blue through the Phoenix Kingdom. One mighty river ran from a range of mountains at the edge of a northern desert through the heart of Jehanglan to the sea in the southeast. Its name was scribed along the length of it.

"The Black River," Linden read aloud.

"The blood of Jehanglan," Taren said. "And here is the heart of that country—Mount Rivasha, the home of the Phoenix." He pointed to a drawing of a cone-shaped mountain with what looked like flames spurting from it. It lay in the center of the area defined as Jehanglan. There were smaller figures around the mountain, a series of little squares.

Buildings? Another look and Maurynna wondered if the other squiggles were indeed flames. Could the "phoenix" of Jehanglan be merely an active volcano? Was the truedragon held prisoner in an effort to ward off an eruption?

Then the great fiery bird Morlen told us of is simply how the Jehangli imagine the power of that volcano. Would that make any difference to their quest?

"Where is Pirakos held prisoner?" she asked.

The crooked finger swept north, traced one of the lines of mountains seaming that part of the map. "Here; the Iron Temple at Mount Kajhenral."

"The Iron Temple? Is it truly made of iron?" Jekkanadar broke in. "And what does 'Kajhenral' mean?"

"No, the temple isn't made of iron." A thoughtful look on his face, Taren scratched his head. "Do you know, I never asked why it was called that. I just accepted it. But I can tell you the rest: Kajhenral-cha'a Choor is the full name; it means the Place of Dragons, the Place of Nightmares." Taren smiled the sweet smile that was so striking in his sallow, wrinkled face. "The character for dragon—kajhenral—is the same as for nightmare. The Jehangli are fond of such word games."

"Humph," was all Lleld said as she studied the map once more. Then, pointing to a spot on the northeastern coast, "And is this the port where we shall land?"

"Jedjieh. Yes; there we will find a sponsor and guide," he said.

"Aren't you afraid of being made a slave again, Taren?" Linden said.

"No." Again the sweet smile. "Jehanglan is large; there is room to hide, even for a bai—even for an outlander."

Studying the map a little more, Maurynna noticed that north of the range of mountains that included Mount Kajhenral, and west of a smaller river far to the west that ran parallel with the Black River for a good portion of its course, there were no cities or villages marked. The rest of the map was dotted with them.

"What's here and here?" she asked, pointing to them.

Taren frowned. "Barbarians live there," he said shortly. "They are as nothing."

Linden, Maurynna noticed, gave Taren an odd look. "What are their names?" he asked.

Taren's lips pursed as if he disliked the taste of the words. He stabbed a finger at the northern mountains. "Here live the Tah'nehsieh. Their land is dry and barren, and they live in caves, it is said." His finger dragged a reluctant way to the western portion of the map. "And here are the People of the Horse, the Zharmatians."

" 'People of the Horse?' " said Linden. "And why are they called that?"

"They're nomads, wandering with their herds from place to place in the grasslands. They live in tents and once waged war against the Jehangli. They're barbarians." His teeth clicked shut on the last word as if he no longer wished to speak.

"So there's peace now?" Linden prodded.

Taren smiled thinly. "The *temur's* favorite son is a hostage in the imperial court. There is peace."

There was something different about Taren, Maurynna thought, an edginess she'd never seen before. She guessed Linden saw it as well, and was as curious as she, for he opened his mouth to ask another question. But before he could, the door opened, and Otter and Raven slipped in.

Lleld looked up. "Good. Now that we're all here, I shall tell you what the Lady told me earlier.

"Linden and Maurynna—both of you must memorize the map. The rest of us must become as familiar as we can with it, but you two are the most familiar with maps and such, I think. We won't be able to bring this with us once we reach Jehanglan."

Maurynna nodded, as did Linden beside her. Lleld's words made sense. Linden was used to memorizing maps from his days as a mercenary, she knew; she was used to memorizing sea charts. A captain never knew when she might be deprived of them. It was best to know by heart where the reefs and rocks were.

And once she and Raven were on their own, she would not be able to consult with Linden. Her hands curled into fists; she would sail that passage when it came, not one moment before.

"What else?" Linden said.

The little Dragonlord tilted her chin up. "That if there's any fighting, you—as the most experienced—are to be in charge."

Again, Maurynna thought, that made sense. So why was Lleld staring at Linden with such challenge in her eyes?

After a moment, Linden said, "There's more to it than that, isn't there?"

"Yes. *You* are in charge of anything 'military'; *I* am in charge of the mission." Lleld folded her arms across her chest.

"You?" Linden said, his deep voice incredulous. "You, Lady Leap-Before-You-Look? Not Jekkanadar the Sensible?"

Jekkanadar's smile as he nodded was wry. Lleld's was smug. "Just so," she said. "The Lady tried to name Jekkanadar as leader. But Morlen said I was to be; he mindspoke the Lady early this morning. So there."

"Oh, gods," was all Linden said. It seemed all he *could* say. "Oh, gods."

Maurynna thought of the stories he'd told her about Lleld and silently agreed. *I will be important to the truedragons and Lady Mayhem is to lead this quest. Has Morlen gone mad?*

"And we leave for Casna," Lleld said, "three days from now."

"Lord Jhanun, this message arrived a few moments ago by pigeon."

Jhanun raised his free hand for silence, then dipped his slender brush in ink. Pausing to make certain the moment was right, he swept the brush across the paper on the little portable drawing table before him. A few quick strokes and the figure of a plum tree appeared, sparse and delicate.

He studied it, looked up at the living model before him, then back to his painting. It was good; it was very good, but he feared he had not quite caught the essence of the tree.

Still, many would call it the work of a master. Jhanun knew better. "Yes?" he said, looking over his shoulder.

His steward came forward, a small bit of paper in his hand. Jhanun took it, read "Apprentice found," and smiled.

Then he selected another sheet of paper and studied the plum tree once more. Perhaps this time he would understand its true nature.

Twenty-three

The journey to Casna, the great port city of Cassori, went swiftly and uneventfully. Linden hoped it was a portent for the rest of the trip.

They reached the city gate just as dusk was falling. Unlike the last Dragonlord visit here, this time they entered the city without state, riding in as merely another group of travelers.

Just as Linden preferred it.

The guards stopped the band as they did all those seeking entrance. The harp case on Otter's back, the red of his cloak, and a flash of his bard's torc were assurance enough for the guards; they waved the travelers on and retreated to the fire in the gatehouse.

While he silently thanked the gods for it, the casual attitude rankled the mercenary in Linden's soul. *They've been at peace for so long, they've gotten soft. Ah, well; better that than war and distrust.*

He drew the hood of his cloak close as if against the chill—though by the standards of Dragonskeep far to the north, it was merely cool—as they passed through the gate and into the streets, lest some attentive guard or citizen recognize him from his previous visit. It had, after all, been only a few months since the regency debate. At least this time the Dragonlords' presence was . . . unofficial.

He'd had more than enough pomp and ceremony during that other visit to last him a century or two. He was well pleased to make a way without fanfare to the house of Maurynna's kin—and now his as well—here in Casna.

Gods, it was good to have kinfolk again. But better yet a soultwin. He shifted his weight in the saddle. Shan moved sideways enough to let Linden's leg brush lightly against Maurynna's as they rode side by side.

She flashed a mischievous grin at him. "Aren't you going to miss your old quarters?" she teased. "That house you were lent in the noble's section is much larger than my aunt and uncle's new home, I'll wager."

"True," Linden said, smiling in return. "But the beer wasn't as good."

"You couldn't complain about the wine cellar, though," Otter called back from just ahead of them.

Linden agreed, laughing. Trust the bard to have appreciated the wine there; though truth be told, it had been superb. But he still prefered Elenna's beer.

He looked over his shoulder. Raven and Taren rode just behind, with Lleld and Jekkanadar bringing up the rear with Jhem and Trissin (or the Two Poor Bastards, as Chailen called the other Llysanyins pressed into service) on leads. Lleld caught his eye and waved. Her eyes darted from side to side; Linden guessed she was wondering which corners in the daytime might support a performance by a juggler and a tumbler. He knew she and Jekkanadar had done it before while traveling unheralded.

"Do you have the directions to their new house?" Lleld asked.

Maurynna drew a folded sheet of parchment from her

belt pouch. "Yes," she said and rode forward. "They were in Maylin's last letter. Here, Otter—I think you know Casna better than any of us."

"At least Casna nowadays," said Jekkanadar, looking around. He pointed to a group of buildings. "If I remember rightly, there was a green for sheep there some eighty years ago. And that street's new."

"Hrmm, hrmm," Otter muttered as he peered at the parchment in the dim light. Nightsong ambled along, the reins loose on her neck. "Thank the gods Maylin writes a nice, clear hand; this light is terrible. Now where . . . ?"

"And where's the little fountain that was here only a century or so ago? Things change so quickly," Lleld complained.

Linden smiled as Raven nearly choked at that remark. Even Taren, always calm and unruffled, boggled a little.

"Ah! Now I know where to go," Otter announced. The bard led the way through the streets of Casna, guiding them unerringly to the Vanadins' new home, a reward from Prince Rann. The rest followed, holding to their roles as servants and fellow players.

Linden grew uncomfortably warm within the closeness of hood and cloak. He wanted to throw back the hood at least, but there were still too many people out. So he rode on, feeling sweat trickle between his shoulder blades. He hoped Elenna had plenty of that good brown ale left.

At last they were at the house. They clattered into the courtyard, larger than the old one, the Llysanyins and Taren's gelding crowding together companionably. Lleld and Jekkanadar slipped the halters from the Two Poor Bastards. The door opened, and a man Linden didn't recognize stood in it, the warm lamplight from the house streaming out around him.

"Who is it?" the man called, squinting into the darkness.

As Linden threw his hood back, Maurynna cried, "Uncle Owin! You're here this time!" and clambered down from Boreal.

The man descended the three steps. "Rynna?" he said,

his voice filled with delight. "Is that really you? What are you doing back in Casna?" He held his arms out.

She threw herself into them, hugging her uncle. "I'm so glad you weren't on another trip," she said. "I missed you the last time."

Linden swung down from Shan as her uncle replied, "And I missed you—and quite a bit of excitement, they tell me." He held Maurynna from him and looked up at her with wondering eyes.

Then Owin must have caught a glimpse of Linden's approach from the corner of his eye, for his head turned. Linden saw his eyes go wide as the man guessed who he was.

"Dragonlord," Owin said formally. Then his face melted into a smile and he held out his hands. "Kinsman. Welcome once again to my house."

His heart glowing, Linden caught the proferred hands. They were warm and steady and strong, much like the man himself, Linden thought. "Thank you," he said, finding it a little hard to talk. He cleared his throat. "Again—thank you."

Then a delighted shriek from the doorway caught everyone's attention. "Rynna! Linden! What are you doing here?," and Maylin was trying to hug both of them at once. She stepped back, pushing her brown curls back from her face and laughing. "Otter! You're here as well? And who—"

She broke off so suddenly that Linden looked around in alarm to see what was wrong. But all he saw were the others, still mounted, as Otter swung down from Nightsong's saddle: Lleld, Jekkanadar, Taren, and—

No. Raven had dismounted. He stood with the light from the house illuminating him, glowing in his red hair. He was watching with a closed expression as Maurynna greeted her family.

And, Linden belatedly realized, watching as they greeted *him* as kin. No doubt Raven had thought to stand here one day, meeting these people as Maurynna's husband. Instead another man was in "his" place, here not just as husband, but as something far, far more.

Soultwin.

It was all there in the boy's face. Then, with an abrupt movement, Raven was astride Stormwind once more.

"I've decided to stay at the inn with the others," he said. To his credit, Raven's voice did not betray him—much.

"But Raven—" Maurynna began.

Linden hastily mindspoke her, allowing Otter to "eavesdrop" to forestall any comment from the bard. *Let him, love. This is rubbing his nose in it, seeing me with your family.*

She nodded almost imperceptibly.

"Well enough, Raven. I think we should be off, then," Lleld said, entering the conversation. With a nod at Taren, she continued, "It's been a long day's ride. I say we save the introductions for tomorrow and leave you two and Otter to the gentle care of your family, Rynna." She flashed a mischievous smile at Owin and Maylin, who looked up at her, curiosity writ large across their faces. Who, after all, would dare tell a pair of Dragonlords what to do as this seeming child did?

A hand flashed up in salute and Lleld wheeled Miki around. Jekkanadar followed with a wave and a grin of his own.

Good thinking, Lleld, Linden thought in amusement. *Two Dragonlords in your yard are surprise enough—but four?*

After them went Taren, slumping now in his saddle, weariness in every line of his body. Raven followed close behind. His back cried out his smoldering anger.

As the sound of trotting hooves disappeared into the darkness, Maylin said, "That was your friend Raven, Maurynna? The one you grew up with in Thalnia?"

"Yes," said Maurynna.

"You never told me he was handsome."

For a moment Maurynna looked surprised. "Is he? D'you know, I'd never even thought about it. He used to be terribly gawky. Has he come out of it well, then?"

"*I* think so," said Maylin with a smile like a cat's.

Linden heard Otter's snort of laughter and touched the bard's mind.

Oh, gods—do you think I should tell my poor idiot of a nephew he might as well surrender now? said the bard.

Linden replied, *What do you mean?* though he had a fair idea. He hid a grin.

Boyo, you've no idea how determined that young lady can be. Remind me to tell you about my encounter with her at the kitchen table the last time we were in Casna. What Maylin sets her sights on, she gets. Otter's shoulders shook in silent laughter. *She's more than a match for Raven.*

Maylin said, "The three of you must be hungry. I'll set out bread and cheese and ale for when you've finished with the horses." She turned away, still smiling, and walked lightly back to the house.

Her father cleared his throat. "Ah, the stable is full," Owin began. "There's a public stable nearby, but—"

"If it's agreeable to you, uncle," Linden said, "we've grain for them, and they could stay in your garden tonight."

Owin's face glowed at "uncle," then creased in concern. "Won't they wander off?"

"No, Uncle Owin," Maurynna said. She caressed Boreal's neck. "They're Llysanyins."

"Oh," said Owin, eyes wide. *"Oh."*

"Just so," Linden said, smiling at the awe in his new kinsman's wondering gaze. He caught up Shan's reins. "Come along, crowbait. Let's get you settled; I want that bread and ale." He led the snapping stallion into the garden behind the house.

"How do you like this room?" Maylin asked as she dropped the bundle of blankets on the bed much later.

Maurynna looked around, shaking her head in wonder. "It's lovely with these carved beams! And look at the tiles around the fireplace; I've never seen such a pretty pattern. It's so different, isn't it?"

"From the old house? Yes, much larger and brighter.

Kella and I can each have our own room now. But, d'you know, sometimes I miss the old house. We haven't rubbed all the hard edges off of this one yet, so to speak. But when Prince Rann offered . . ." She shrugged. *Who were we to refuse a prince?* the lift of her shoulders said.

"We could have put up all of your friends," she went on, "even if we'd had to double up a bit. At least your friend Raven. . . ." she said with careful diffidence.

Maurynna snorted. "I'm glad he's staying at the inn tonight. He's being an ass," she snapped.

"Oh?" Maylin paused as she spread the first blanket. "Do tell."

"Maylin, you will not believe this. . . ."

Maylin sat down, ready to listen, until Linden should interrupt them.

It had been a joyous reunion, but now everyone else had retired to bed a candlemark or more ago. Linden and Maurynna stood, arms tight around each other, in the garden. The new house was so different from the old, familiar one. Bigger, richer, but without the well-lived-in feeling of the old.

At least the garden felt more familiar, filled with roses—now fading with the autumn—and a well like the old one, even to the moss growing on the stones. A single ball of coldfire hovered nearby, its light shining like crystal in the frosty air. Maurynna's head rested on Linden's shoulder; he stroked her hair. The Llysanyins stood together close by, heads down and hipshot, drowsing. He was glad they'd slipped out for a final look at the horses.

They stood together with no need for words between them.

Maylin sat by her window overlooking the street and brushed her hair. It had started out a dull day, but what an ending! It was good to see Rynna and Linden and Otter again. She wondered how long they were staying; when she'd asked them, they'd danced nimbly around that question with no real answer.

More importantly, *why* had they come?

Yawning, she laid down her brush. She'd get it out of them soon enough; time for bed now. But as she stood up to tug the window hangings closed, a flash of movement from the street below caught her eye.

She pressed her face to the glass to get a better look. A shadowed figure slipped around the side of the house into the alley that separated the Vanadin's home from the next.

Oh, for—! Fuming, Maylin left her room and pattered barefoot along the hall, and then down the stairs. At the door, she snatched her cloak from its peg by the door and threw it over her nightgown. Then she pulled back the bolt, eased the door open, and slipped outside.

Of all the idiotic . . .

She stalked through the gate and around the corner.

"Remember the last time we stood in a garden by a well?" Linden said softly.

"Gods, yes," Maurynna said with feeling.

"Was your silver well spent?" he teased, remembering how he'd come upon her just after she'd tossed a coin to the moon's reflection in the well to make a wish.

He felt her smile against his shoulder. "Indeed," she answered. "There I was, worried about finding my dockhand again and lo! A Dragonlord found me instead." A moment's pause; then, dryly, "I was, to say the least, surprised."

He laughed, remembering her face, and suddenly crushed her against him. She clung to him with equal fierceness. No matter how long it took, Jehanglan would come all too soon. Once again he would be without his soultwin, as he had been for so many long centuries.

Who knew when they'd be together once more?

She found him hiding in the shadows as he peered over the garden gate. A murmur of soft voices from inside the garden drifted wordless on the night air, revealing who stood inside. She could guess where they were, too: near the well.

Cloak drawn tight around her, Maylin watched Raven watching Maurynna and Linden. She knew he had no idea she was there; how could he? All his attention was for the two standing by the well. When he shifted to get a better view, the moonlight limned his face.

She sighed. There was no mistaking the stubborn jut of his chin. Maurynna was right; Raven was not one to give up a notion, no matter how idiotic it was. And this one was foolish indeed.

Besides, she had her own notions that required him to change his. She might have her work cut out for her, but she would prevail. Maylin was certain of it. It just might take a bit longer than she wanted.

First she had to get him to notice her—*truly* notice her. She crept up behind him.

Then she poked him.

His nerves were good even if his manners needed mending. For though Raven jumped a good handspan or two into the air, he made no sound. He did, however, whirl around in a fighting crouch when his feet touched ground once more, his hand flying to his belt dagger. Maylin saw with satisfaction that he had the grace to look embarrassed at the sight of her. There was hope for him yet.

"Are you done with being rude?" she whispered.

He glared at her, but followed when she pointedly turned and walked away.

When they were at the beginning of the alley, Maylin said, "I thought you'd gone to the inn."

Raven shrugged and made no explanation. He muttered, "It's not fair."

"Fair?" Maylin said. She had to tilt her head far back to look him in the face. It was a decided disadvantage; however, Maylin had never let that stop her before. She folded her arms across her chest. "*Fair?* Since when is anything in life fair? Not that 'fair' has anything to do with this. If you'd take the time to look beyond the tip of your selfish nose, you'd see how right they are for each other. They belong together, Raven."

"I'd thought Rynna and I would . . ." He trailed off.

"In-*deed?* And did you ever discuss this with Rynna? No? Then don't get all into a snit that she didn't follow the story you'd written—not when you didn't tell her the tale." She rested a hand on his arm. "Raven, please; look at them and truly see them, not what you want to see."

He shook her hand off and stalked away.

"Where are you going?"

"Back to the inn." But after three long strides he stopped. Half looking back over his shoulder, he said, "Blast you. Why do you have to be right?" Then he was off again before she could say anything else.

Maylin walked slowly to the gate leading to the courtyard in the front of the house and passed through. Shutting the gate behind her, she leaned against it, lost in thought until the chill of the autumn night drove her inside once more.

Raven walked quickly through the streets of Casna. *Curse* the girl! She was right and they both knew it.

Maurynna would never be his.

The next day was spent quietly. Word was sent to the palace of their arrival, a privy message for the eyes of Duke Beren, regent of Cassori. A short, cryptic note came in return, bidding them await a visit that evening from one who would arrange what they needed.

So when the early autumn darkness fell, they met in the front room of the Vanadin home. Linden looked around the table; to his left was Otter, then Raven, Elenna, and Owin. Next came Jekkanadar and Lleld, with little Kella on her new heroine's other side. Lleld had spent the day teaching the girl a few tumbling tricks, and now the child wanted nothing more than to run away and join their troupe. Judging by the look in her mother's eye, Kella might well be tied down when it came time for them to leave—just in case. Maylin sat nearly opposite Raven; Linden noticed her eyes rarely left him. He, on the other hand, seemed hardly to notice her.

Only Taren was absent, having pleaded fatigue earlier. They'd left him resting at the inn.

"Why can't I come with you?" Kella asked Lleld for perhaps the hundredth time. "I did well, didn't I? I want to learn juggling next."

"Perhaps next time, sweetheart; this time we're for a long journey to visit Rynna's other kin," Lleld said.

Kella sighed. "I never get to go anywhere. Bother; well then, I shall teach Rann what I've learned today the next time I play with him."

Linden said in surprise, "You play with Rann?"

"At the palace," Kella told him proudly. "We have fun. He's my best friend."

How did this miracle come about, Linden wondered. He would have thought the Cassorin aristocracy too rank-proud to stand for their prince playing with a merchant's child. Then he realized: commoner though she was, Kella was bloodkin to one Dragonlord and marriage-kin to another. That would be good enough for even the most snobbish Cassorin noble.

He found himself suddenly wishing they were not traveling in disguise. He would have liked to go to the palace with Kella and see the little Cassorin princeling again. Surely the boy was in better health now that his traitorous uncle Peridaen, and Peridaen's mage, Kas Althume, were no longer slowly poisoning him.

But in the end it was Peridaen who saved the child when Kas Althume would have slain him, a part of Linden's mind reminded him.

So he did—and died in Rann's stead, Linden said in amends to Peridaen, silently thanking the man.

On the heels of the memory came a knocking at the door. After a glance at the Dragonlords, Owin went to answer it himself.

Linden heard the door open, heard a mutter of voices

and a low exclamation of surprise. Then came the sound of running feet, and a boy dressed in the livery of a servant pelted into the room and flung his cloak to the floor. Linden stood up in time to catch the child as the boy launched himself at him.

"Dragonlord! Linden Rathan! You came back!" And Prince Rann was in Linden's arms once more, arms tight around his neck.

But what a Rann this was! The little boy Linden had left behind was thin, sickly, and pale, only beginning what promised to be a long recuperation from his illness. This lad was sturdy and hale, with rosy cheeks and a glow in the brown eyes that peeked out from beneath thick bangs.

"Ooof! Gods help us—look at you, boy!" Linden laughed as he ruffled Rann's brick red hair. "This is wonderful!" He hugged the boy in return.

As he had done once before, Linden balanced Rann on one hip. Rann waved to Maurynna.

"Hello, Captain Erdon!" the boy began, then stopped in confusion as she laughed and held up a hand in greeting. "I mean, Maurynna Kyrissaean. Hello, Bard Otter."

"Hello, boyo," Otter said with a wink.

Rann beamed.

Owin and another man entered, the latter with a rueful grin. He, like Rann, was dressed in a servant's livery. It was a moment before Linden recognized him as a supporter of Duke Beren in his bid for the regency a few months ago. What was the man's—ah; he had it.

"Lord Tyrian, I'm pleased to see you again. And thank you for bringing Rann."

The man's face lit with pleasure at being remembered. Then the rueful expression was back. "Don't ask me how he found out you were coming, Your Grace, but find out he did, and wouldn't give poor Beren any peace until he was allowed to come along tonight."

"Well, I for one am glad," Linden said as he pulled up his chair once more. "But I think we need to get down to business right away. It wouldn't do for Rann to be missed at the palace." He sat; Rann curled up in his lap, head on Linden's shoulder. Linden heard the boy heave a sigh of pure happiness; he wrapped an arm around the child and wished they didn't have to leave Cassori so soon.

There was a general murmur of agreement on the need for haste. The mugs were refilled with Elenna's ale, a new one poured for Lord Tyrian.

Then Lleld once more took over as leader of the expedition. "We need," she said after introducing herself and the others Tyrian didn't know, "swift passage to Thalnia for ourselves and one other who is not with us tonight. We must be there before the winter storms strike—and Maurynna says we've not much time until they do."

"Why not Change and fly there?" Tyrian asked innocently.

Only a sharp intake of breath from Maurynna broke the sudden silence. But Tyrian knew his business; Linden saw the man's eyes dart from one Dragonlord to another, seeking an answer to a very different question.

Then Otter said, "Because we wish to travel together, my lord, and neither my nephew nor I—nor the other man with us—are Dragonlords. Besides, there are the horses to consider."

"Of course," said Tyrian with a look of chagrin. "How silly of me to forget you're truehuman."

Otter laughed. It sounded genuine; but then, Linden thought, it would. Otter was a bard down to his fingertips, and well used to dissembling.

"A pity, that," the bard said, "considering what the voyage here from Thalnia was like. I'd just as soon pass up another trip at sea. But at least this time I shan't be at the mercy of a certain mad sea captain." He blew Maurynna a kiss, his eyes twinkling.

Her answering smile was tight and brittle but convincing enough. Tyrian, however, still looked a touch . . . Wary? Suspicious? Linden shifted Rann in his lap as if readying for battle.

But Tyrian let the silence stretch on as he watched his

forefinger trace a pattern on the table. Linden relaxed again.

Abruptly the Cassorin said, "May I ask, Your Graces, why this hasty voyage and why such secrecy?" Once more his gaze flickered from Dragonlord to Dragonlord.

But if Otter was an old hand at dissembling, Lleld was more experienced yet. She smiled brightly at Tyrian and laid her small, pale hand on her soultwin's darker one. "Sometimes, my lord, even Dragonlords get tired of Dragonskeep. The truth be told, Jekkanadar and I were *bored*. Add to that Maurynna and Linden's decision to visit Rynna's family in Thalnia, and that Otter and his kinsman Raven—good friends to us, both—are also bound for there, and you have a good excuse to go a-wandering." She turned to smile up at Jekkanadar a moment before continuing, "As for secrecy, why, this is no visit of state and we simply wish to avoid any unnecessary fuss. Linden, I know, had enough of that his last time here."

Tyrian covered a cough that sounded suspiciously like a chuckle.

Maurynna said, "And as for haste, my lord, well, the decision to go south to Thalnia was made late. I was a sea captain before I was a Dragonlord; I remember only too well what it's like to be caught in a winter storm at sea. I've no wish to repeat the experience. I want to be off as soon as possible."

Well done, Linden said, letting amusement color his mindvoice. *Spoken as convincingly as Otter or Lleld could have done.*

The best way to lay a false trail is to tell the truth, Maurynna replied. *All I just said is nothing more than that. The Lady was late in letting us go. He doesn't need to know who made the decision. And those storms are no joke.* She rubbed her forehead as a spasm of pain crossed her face. *I can't . . . continue. . . .* Her mindvoice grew fainter. *Kyrissaean . . .*

But Linden had felt the dragonsoul's presence buzzing like an angry horde of wasps in Maurynna's first words. Her skull must feel as if it were splitting.

Rest easy, love, he said in concern as the color drained from her face.

"Maurynna Kyrissaean?" Prince Rann whispered, stirring uneasily in Linden's lap. When no answer came the small, worried face turned up to him. "Is she well?"

"Just tired, lad," Linden reassured him quietly. "That's all." To Lleld he said, *End this quickly*.

And for once, bless her, Lady Mayhem did as she was told.

A soft knock sounded at the door. "Here's the meadow-sweet tea you asked for," Maylin said from the other side.

Linden opened the door and Maylin scooted in, a steaming mug held carefully before her. She paused a moment to stare openmouthed at the globes of coldfire illuminating the room before remembering her mission and bringing the mug to Maurynna, sitting propped up in the bed. "Haven't we done this before?"

"So we have," Maurynna said with a weak smile. "Thank you." Her hands shook as she took the mug. Linden reached out to help her, but she shook her head and drank.

"I don't know if I shall ever get used to seeing these," Maylin murmured, reaching out to touch one of the glowing white globes. Her odd-colored eyes were wide. The coldfire bobbed under her tentative finger like a cork in water, returning to its place when Maylin dropped her hand.

"I know what you said downstairs," she began in a voice as ordinary as if she discussed the weather, "but I also know it was a lot of nonsense. You're not really going to visit the Erdons. You're on a mission of some sort—and a dangerous one, too—aren't you?"

Linden exchanged a swift and startled glance with Maurynna. He began, "Nonsense; what—"

Maylin put her hands on her hips and stared at him, one eyebrow raised.

He admitted defeat under that withering tell-me-another-one glare. "How did you know?"

"Because lighthearted as you all seemed, from time to

time one or another of you would suddenly grow serious," Maylin said. "And . . ." She waved a hand vaguely. "I just knew."

There was no answer to that.

"Where?" Maylin finally asked.

Maurynna said, "Do you remember the carved jade box from Sherrine's wergild? The one I gave you?"

Maylin's jaw dropped. After a false try or three, she gasped, "Jehanglan? You're going to Jehanglan? But *why*?"

"To do the impossible," Maurynna said, her eyes dark and haunted.

Twenty-four

Lord Tyrian had wrought most efficiently. It was only four days later that a vessel was ready for them.

Maurynna studied the area and their ship. She'd never been to this end of the dockyards on the Uildodd River. It was not an area frequented by reputable merchants.

But, she thought, looks were deceiving. To a casual glance, the dock appeared well-nigh abandoned, in poor repair and little used. Yet her practiced eye noted that despite the dirt and grime, the wood and ropes were in good—very good—condition. More importantly, so was the ship tied to the dock, a nondescript cog named the *Swan's Heart*.

She nodded to herself. It made sense. Any ruler might have need of a ship to send on delicate—and very private—business and a place to berth it. And she'd wager that although the crew of the *Swan's Heart* looked the worst band of cutthroats she'd ever seen, no doubt every last one was sworn to the crown, knew how to hold his tongue and, above all, could outsail the very gods.

Satisfied that they were in good hands, she waited with the others: Uncle Owin and Aunt Elenna; Maylin and Kella; Otter, Lleld and Jekkanadar. Linden and Raven were on board settling the animals. Even Rann was here with Lord Tyrian, both again disguised as servants, coming up as the travelers waited to board. Taren stood slightly to one side, looking absorbed in his thoughts. Maurynna wondered if he regretted agreeing to return to Jehanglan.

The breeze shifted; the smell of docks and river disappeared. Now came the clean tang of salt air, the promise of freedom and the sea. Once more her horizons would be limitless, the blues of water and sky meeting level and open, and not the jagged fence of mountains surrounding Dragonskeep. A living ship would dance beneath her feet again.

So why did she feel so miserable? It was what she had longed for more than anything all this time.

Wasn't it?

The sea breeze teased at her hair and gamboled around her, but gave her no answer. Sighing, Maurynna looked up to watch Taren's horse rise into the air as the workers strained against the wheel working the cables. Kella and Rann, each holding one of her hands now, stared, their mouths *O*s of wonder. The gelding hung, quietly miserable, in its canvas belly sling. At least it was much less trouble than the Llysanyins had been. They were not amused by the thought of a sea voyage. At the sight of the ship they had balked, one and all. Shan had even tried to kick Linden when the canvas sling was wrapped around him on the dock. Only Linden's speed had saved him; for once Shan hadn't been in jest. Miki had been quicker with her teeth, though. Linden, Maurynna thought, would have a spectacular bruise on his shoulder by tonight.

If Linden ever finds out who told the Llysanyins about seasickness, he'll skin me alive.

The crane swung out over the water, Taren's horse looking more wretched than ever. Then it was in position over the ship. Slowly, carefully, the men turning the great wheel reversed direction. The gelding descended into the hold, the open hatch waiting like a mouth to devour the hapless animal. Maurynna shuddered at the image as the beast disappeared from sight.

Linden climbed out of the hold a few moments later. He called something down to the sailors below, then started across the deck. Maurynna saw Captain Hollens stop him; Linden listened, rubbing his sore shoulder. A glance at the river and she knew what the captain's message was. Then Linden nodded and strode down the gangplank.

"They're settled?" Maurynna said as he joined her.

"After too damned much fussing, yes," Linden grumbled, wincing as he massaged his shoulder. "Blast Miki; I didn't think she'd try something like that." He glared at the little mare's rider.

Lleld stared off into the distance, whistling softly.

"None of that when we're aboard," Maurynna said sharply. At Lleld's look of surprise, she softened her tone. "It's bad luck to whistle on board a ship if you don't need a wind. And at this time of year we won't." She half turned at the sound of more footsteps coming down the gangplank.

It was Raven—an unscathed Raven. Maurynna saw him hide a smirk at Linden's discomfort and squashed an urge to kick him for it. Instead she merely narrowed her eyes, waiting until he noticed her glare.

When he did, he squirmed under it to her almost complete satisfaction. That would wait until she was able to have a few private . . . words with him.

Then she heard Linden say, "We must board now; Captain Hollens said that the tide is turning and we must be away," and it seemed her entire family was hugging her at once, murmuring good-byes, wishing her a safe voyage, bidding her to come back soon. She fought back tears and said whatever meaningless assurances came to her tongue, keeping up the pretense that this was merely a pleasure trip.

Suddenly, like a whirlwind, Maylin was before her. Odd-colored eyes met odd-colored eyes. Hands caught hers; how did such a little thing as Maylin have such strength in her grip? Maurynna surrendered to it.

"Come back," Maylin whispered fiercely. "All of you. Safely." The burning gaze darted to Raven. "Come back to me."

Then Maylin spun away and Linden's hand was on her shoulder. "Time to go, love," he whispered so that only she might hear.

She nodded, unable to speak; gods knew when she'd see these dear people again. Or even if she ever would. Linden handed Rann back to Tyrian and caught her hand in his.

Somehow she got up the gangplank without shedding the hot tears that were suddenly filling her eyes. Then came the familiar ritual of casting off. Though this time she had no part in it, it comforted her, with its very familiarity. She stood at the railing with the others, waving to those left behind until she could see them no more. One by one her fellow travelers left until she stood alone.

She did not leave the aft rail until darkness fell and Linden came for her. She woke then, as if from a dream, to the wild, briny scent of the ocean, the endless song of the waves.

Somehow it was no longer enough.

Magic. . . . Magic upon the water. . . .

The thought wove itself through the old dragon's dreams like a broken bit of river weed tumbling along a current. And like a bit of weed, it slipped through his grasp when he tried to snatch at it.

But it had been there. He knew it, in this slumber so deep it was like a little death. This water he slept in brought him tidings from waters far away, for, in the beginning and the end, all waters were one.

There would be more.

They were in luck. Late in the sailing season as it was, Maurynna had fully expected that they would encounter at least one early winter storm in their passage. But the gods seemed to smile upon their journey. For the weather was as mild and calm as even Otter could wish for, and the trip an easy one with a good wind following them, speeding them on their way.

The only ones who "complained" were the Llysanyins stuck below deck. Not because they were ill, thank all the gods—Maurynna couldn't think of anything worse than being seasick and unable to vomit, a thing no horse could do—but because they could not enjoy the sun and air on deck as their two-foots did. Maurynna was glad Linden had thought to ask for a store of apples for the trip; there was much to be said for bribery, she decided one day, as she groomed a contentedly munching Boreal.

The voyage was a bittersweet thing for her. True, she was at sea again. True, Linden was with her. And with them were some of the people she cared for most in this world.

But this was not her ship. And ahead lay separation from her soultwin. She made herself forget that. These days were a gift, a pleasant dream, something caught out of time that she treasured moment to moment.

Yet, be they waking or sleeping, all dreams must end. This one did the day the docks of Port Stormhaven came into view. By courtesy of the captain, the Dragonlords and their companions stood on the quarterdeck with him and the steersman.

Stormhaven was as beautiful as ever, Maurynna thought. The sight of the golden city glowing in the afternoon sunlight made her eyes burn. Rank after rank of buildings fanned out from the harbor in a semicircle, marching up the side of the limestone cliffs that formed the northernmost part of the great Thalnian plateau, cradling the blue water at their feet.

"It's beautiful," Linden said. "I can see why you missed it."

She nodded, unable to speak for the sudden wave of homesickness that took her. She had been so afraid she would never see this again—or else come too late to see her family. Would she, her mind asked, see echoes of faces she knew now in children born centuries hence?

Thank the gods I could come here while everyone I know is still alive.

It was hard to stand aside as they came in to dock. Maurynna had to bite her tongue so as not to usurp Captain Hollens's proper place. Not that he did anything *wrong*, it was just that there were so many little things that she would have ordered differently.

But at last they were alongside the Erdon family's own docks, the sailors leaping ashore to make fast the lines of the *Swan's Heart*. The dockhands converged on the ship like bees to honey. More than one looked in some alarm at the band of cutthroats manning her.

One moment Maurynna stood with the others in the middle of the deck; then, somehow, she was at the rail, leaning dangerously far out, hoping to see a familiar face on the crowded dock.

There! Maurynna waved frantically. "Keronis," she called and waved again. "Keronis!"

Keronis looked up. He shaded his eyes and searched to see who had called him. His face lit at the sight of her and he waved excitedly. But then, to Maurynna's surprise, his expression changed; her cousin turned and ran to the main warehouse that housed the dockside office.

"What?" she murmured, confused.

"Who was that?" Linden asked.

"One of my far too many cousins here that I told you about," she said, trying not to let her uneasiness show.

She waited in an agony of apprehension as sailors and workers made fast the ship. Was she in that bad odor with the family that Keronis would turn tail and run as if suddenly finding himself nose-to-nose with a leper? Didn't they understand that she had had no choice but to abandon her ship? Surely her old first mate had explained things to them!

The moment the sailors ran out the gangplank, Maurynna swarmed down the ladder leading from the quarterdeck, leaving Linden behind. He sprang after her with an exclamation of surprise.

But Maurynna was already across the lower deck and halfway down the gangplank. Her heart thudded against her ribs; it was hard to breathe. The next moment her foot trod Thalnian soil once more. Come what may, she was home again. Tears stung her eyes.

And now she saw more familiar faces among the workers. She smiled at them, but it died as they moved back, eyes wide, clearing an area around her and the others who had joined her. As if by magic, an avenue opened up between ship and main warehouse. Hurrying down it were her Uncle Kesselandt and various aunts, uncles, and cousins, their faces white and agitated.

Maurynna stared in bewilderment and growing fear; she had never seen Kesselandt like this. Not even an angry king could shake the Head of House Erdon's composure—as she had seen on one heart-stopping occasion.

But her proud uncle, now ashen-faced and sweating, stopped before her. His gaze darted over her, roved among the others she felt against her back; "Your Grace," he said. Once again his gaze settled upon her though he would not meet her eyes. He licked his lips nervously. "Your Grace," he said, and began stiffly to kneel upon one knee before her. The other Erdons and the workers followed suit.

"No," she whispered. Now the tears threatened to spill over.

Behind her she heard Otter growl, "Kesselandt, you ass! *Don't.*"

Before a single knee came to rest upon the planks of the dock, a jeering voice rang out. "You call that bargaining, what you did for your last trip, dear coz? The price you paid for that lamp oil! Pathetic!" Breslin said as he swaggered along in the other Erdons' wake. "Maybe it's just as well you've given up trading."

White-hot anger burned the tears away. "Oh, indeed?" Maurynna yelled, dodging around her uncle and advancing on her least-favorite cousin as her family scattered before her. "I suppose you think you could have done better? Have you any idea how many merchants were in Casna at that time? Those wretches at the Cassorin lamp oil guild had so many people desperate for a cargo, any cargo, that they could charge whatever they wanted!"

Breslin smiled blandly into the teeth of her wrath. "Then you should have waited," he said, "as I did. Came in just after all the foolishness in Cassori was over and damn well robbed those idiots who'd held off selling. What were they thinking—that a market like that would go on forever? Idiots. Downright grateful to me, they were, for taking the stuff off their hands."

He looked past her to Linden, whom she felt standing at her back, dismissing her as he'd always done. "Linden Rathan, I presume?" Breslin said politely, one supercilious eyebrow raised, and bowed. "Welcome to the Erdon compound, Dragonlord." His puzzled gaze lingered on Taren, Lleld, and Jekkanadar, not certain what to make of them. He regally inclined his head, then nodded to Otter and sniffed affectedly at Raven.

Raven returned the compliment.

Years of humiliation at Breslin's hands came to a boiling point. "Why, you . . ." Maurynna snarled, her hands itching to wrap themselves around his throat. "I suppose you think getting a good deal on a few barrels of lamp oil makes up for running the *Fortune's Child* on a sandbar, don't you? I *told* you that bar had shifted, but you knew better, didn't you?"

"You did *what*, Breslin?" Raven called from behind her. "I hadn't heard about that one."

That shattered Breslin's aloof pose. "You shut up!" he yelled back, beefy fists raised. "Stay out of this!"

Raven laughed.

From the corner of her eye Maurynna saw Linden come up beside her; ready, no doubt, to protect her should Breslin throw a punch. Annoyed, Maurynna pushed him back, hardly noticing the shocked gasps around her. "Oh, no, you don't. You stay out of this, too." For the first time she had the strength to defend herself against her biggest, brawni-est—and most detested—cousin. She'd give the bully the drubbing of his life. Her own fists came up—

Only to drop at a familiar bellow. "Children! Stop that!"

Silence fell over the crowd. Maurynna dared a glance over her shoulder. She caught sight of Kesselandt bearing down on them. Otter and Raven were laughing like mad-men, blast them, as they explained to the bewildered Drag-onlords and Taren what was going on.

Uncle Kesselandt sputtered like a teakettle about to boil over. Ordinarily the sight of him, face dark red with anger, would have terrified her. Now it just felt like home.

But he ruined it when he stopped, clapped a hand to his mouth, and then quavered, "Dragonlord, I—I'm sorry. I should not have spoken to you—"

Please, she wanted to beg, *don't make me feel like a stranger, as if I don't belong here as well*. But she saw in Kesselandt's eyes and the eyes of the aunts and uncles and cousins behind him that it would never be the same again.

"Uncle," was all she said. "I'm still me. Truly I am." It was no good. They looked, she imagined, like sparrows who'd returned to their little nest only to find one of their eggs had hatched an eaglet. "I'm still Rynna," she faltered, defeated by their frightened eyes.

"Pity," Breslin drawled.

Kesselandt turned on him in indignation.

She fumed. Trust Breslin to remain the same: a large pain in the ass. She glowered at him.

He winked. Before she could say anything—her aston-ishment nearly choked her—the superior look was back in place. Breslin turned on his heel and walked away amid incredulous murmurs.

But he had served his purpose. Kesselandt was too fu-rious at him to remember to bow and scrape before her—for the moment at least. Her uncle went after Breslin, still sputtering in anger.

*   *   *

Once the family had gotten over the shock of their runaway returning with fellow Dragonlords in tow, Maurynna's kinfolk had rallied well—even if a few still looked somewhat poleaxed, Linden thought.

After a hasty consultation with Kesselandt and the senior aunts, uncles, and elder cousins in port, Maurynna came back to where the rest of the troupe (save Raven, who'd left with her) waited in Kesselandt's office in the main warehouse.

Linden made room for her on the edge of the desk. She sat down beside him. There were signs of strain around her eyes.

"Where's Raven?" Otter asked.

Maurynna said, "For his sins, Breslin was set the task of overseeing the unloading of the horses. Raven went to . . . supervise him." Her face was the very image of innocence.

Otter snorted. "Needle him, you mean. Not that Breslin doesn't deserve it a hundred times over."

"Just so. Anyhow, messengers have been sent off and a Mousehole is being made ready for us," Maurynna reported. "We can move in tomorrow. Tonight we'll stay elsewhere."

"A *what*?" Lleld asked. She shook her head as if uncertain she'd heard correctly.

Linden wasn't certain he had, either. A mousehole? They were to guest in a . . . *mousehole?* No; there must be something wrong with his ears. He looked over to Otter. The bard just shrugged his shoulders and nodded, grinning.

"A Mousehole," Maurynna repeated. "It's what the guesthouses in a House's compound are called. I've no idea why; they just are."

"Mousehole," Jekkanadar echoed softly. His brow furrowed and he looked thoughtful.

"How odd," Lleld said. "I've never stayed in a mousehole before." She looked as bemused as Linden had ever seen her.

Points to you, love, he told Maurynna. *For once it's Lleld who's baffled.*

"And I'll warn you now," Maurynna said, hiding a smile. "They're planning a welcoming feast tonight. Luckily, on such short notice it will be rather small—for an Erdon affair. That will be in the Great House."

"And that is?" prompted Lleld.

Maurynna answered, "The biggest dwelling in a House's compound. There's almost always one large house—often an estate on its own—where the Head lives."

The conversation shifted as Lleld demanded more about the way the great merchant families of Thalnia lived. "What are the compounds? It sounds very military."

"Not at all," Maurynna said. "Or at least, not anymore. They started during the Interregnum, the Years of Chaos, as houses and warehouses were built behind palisades where the the biggest and most powerful merchant families—the Houses—and their hired mercenaries lived and guarded the merchandise from attacks. It was a grim time.

"Since then, the compounds have grown beyond their original walls. Each House owns land in its home city. Most is bought, some ceded by royal grant. On that land are the Great House and the Mouseholes, and a number of smaller but very fancy homes for the senior members and their immediate families, plus some more modest dwellings for the married juniors. The homes are usually close by each other, and the whole area is known as that family's compound even if there are no longer walls setting it off from the rest of the city. Everything is owned by the House in common.

"As I said, it's the senior members of a family—those who make the decisions—or juniors with families, that live within its compound. If we're not given houseroom by a senior, we unmarried juniors must find lodging where we can, often sharing a couple of rooms with two or three others. I was lucky. Since I was the only female among the younger cousins, I had a garret room to myself in my Aunt Maleid's house." Maurynna paused. "It was very small, stifling in the summer and freezing in the winter, but it was mine."

And then I got my own ship. . . . She didn't say it aloud but the unspoken words hung in the air. Her expression grew dour.

Linden drew breath to speak, then let it out in a sigh. What could he say? She'd lost the wild freedom of the sea and was barred from the sky. He had no words to console her. Guilt pricked him. Perhaps she'd come to this pass because of him. Had First Change come upon her too soon because he'd needed her in dragon form? Was that why Kyrissaean tormented her so—being forced to awaken before the dragonsoul was ready?

His mood was so dark that when Jekkanadar chuckled, Linden bit back angry words just in time.

For it was plain that Jekkanadar was not laughing at him or Maurynna. "Mousehole," he said in delight. "Who would have thought? But it makes sense, of course, don't you think?" he appealed to them.

Linden exchanged puzzled glances with Maurynna before looking around to find the others as much in the dark as he.

Now Jekkanadar laughed aloud. "I'm sorry; of course you wouldn't know. It's just a guess, but . . . There's an archaic word in Assantikkan, so old I'd nearly forgotten it. *A'mhausool.* Even when I was young it was hardly used anymore.

"A hundred years before the Wars of the Witch Kings, when justice was dealt out by the priests and priestesses of the goddess Kirakki, at each temple there was a sacred area designated as a kind of sanctuary—the *a'mhausool.* All disputes were brought before the priests, anything from an argument over the ownership of a pig to a border war between two nobles.

"Anyway, built upon the *a'mhausool* were lodgings that any plaintiff might use no matter what their rank. Pigherder or duke, all were equal before Kirakki. One could stay in a nearby inn, of course, but there one risked a knife between the ribs. Only at the *a'mhausool* were you truly safe.

"That is, until the high priest Hannakulan used his power

as Kirakki's judge on earth for personal gain. It led to the destruction of the temples and set the stage for the Wars. It was," Jekkanadar said, "a very dark time."

Taren said thoughtfully, "The Zharmatians have a goddess K'rahi; she has something to do with their Seers. Another instance of ideas and words traveling between Jehanglan and Assantik, think you?"

"Truly?" Jekkanadar said, his eyes lighting with interest. "We'll have to discuss this further another time. But let me guess, Maurynna," he continued. "Any guest staying in a Mousehole is sacred, yes?"

Maurynna nodded. "Even if he were your House's worst enemy, if the Head gives him guestright in the Mousehole, you may not harm him." She tilted her head. "I'd always wondered why a guesthouse would be called that. But that does make sense; there are a lot of words from Assantikkan mixed in with Thalnian." Her smile grew. "But what a silly thing for that poor word to change into."

"Indeed," Jekkanadar replied. "Introduced in dignity the gods only know how long ago, only to be mangled in that peculiarly Thalnian way with words."

Maurynna thumbed her nose at him.

"Mangled along with a cartload or ten from every other language I've ever heard," Linden teased, tugging a lock of Maurynna's hair, pleased that her grey mood had passed—at least for now.

For a festive gathering conceived and launched on the spur of the moment, the Erdons did themselves proud, Linden thought.

The Great House was one of the richest dwellings he'd ever been in; it would have done credit to a duke of the realm. Even this, the smaller of the two feasting rooms, easily could have held twice as many people as could come on such short notice.

Standing by a table laden with food and drink, Linden waited as an awestruck young servant filled his goblet with wine. Under the eagle eye—and no doubt the ready scoldings—of the watching house steward, the boy offered it up to him in the proper fashion, left hand beneath the base, right thumb and forefinger touching the stem just enough to steady it.

Linden took it from him. "My thanks, lad," he said.

The boy beamed; then, sensing the steward's iron gaze, replied, "You're welcome, Your Grace. May I offer you anything else?" He gestured at the many platters filled with savory tidbits and sweetmeats.

Even for an impromptu banquet such as this, the Erdons had many resources and, Linden reflected, one hell of a cooking staff. He considered the choices, then cast a glance over his shoulder.

Just as he thought: another bunch of Maurynna's relatives had cornered her and were talking all at once. Angling for preferred trading status with the Keep, no doubt. He saw Maurynna's lips thin into a grim line.

Idiots. Couldn't they read the signs that a squall was brewing? *He* could, and he'd only known Maurynna for a few months. A long-ago comment of Rani's about a fellow officer came back to him: "He's not only stupid enough to stand behind a kicking mule—he's fool enough to paint a target on his rump as well."

Now Maurynna's eyes narrowed. The squall was imminent. And still they persisted, the greedy idiots.

Time for a rescue. *Hold them off for a little longer, Maurynna-love*, he mindspoke her. *They'll stop as soon as I get there.*

A heartfelt *Thank you!* rang in his mind.

Linden turned back to the servant. "Choose for me, will you, lad? Enough for two and bring it to me."

"With pleasure, Your Grace!"

Linden sauntered a way through the group importuning Maurynna. The conversation flagged as the petitioners realized who passed among them. He slipped in beside his soultwin and slid an arm around her waist, smiling blandly at his new—and importunate—kin. The assorted relatives glanced at each other and hemmed and hawed. Hoping they'd take the hint and disperse, Linden said nothing, merely sipped his wine.

His eyebrows went up at the first taste. This was a different wine than he'd had earlier and was one of the best he'd tasted in all his six centuries.

Hm—perhaps there were some discussions of trade he'd welcome.

Maurynna mindspoke him, her words vibrating with mixed annoyance and gratitude. *Thank you for saving me from them. But I'm furious that they'll harangue me and wouldn't dream of doing it to you.*

That's because they've always known of me as a Dragonlord. You're too familiar for them to be in awe of once the first surprise is over.

A pause, then she continued, fuming, *This lot never had the time for me before, either; they certainly do now.*

You're now of a rank that could be useful to them. Get used to it, love; it will never stop. That's why you learn to value the true friends you do find. And ofttimes families are the worst. You should have seen my father and older sibs if you think this lot is bad.

Oh? she asked.

Insisted I get them the right to sell our holding's horses to Dragonskeep—and only them. It did me no good to point out that Dragonlords ride Llysanyins, and if ordinary horses were needed, they were bred at the Keep. Da took it into his head that I was getting him back for all that he'd done to me. Didn't speak to me until almost twenty years later.

He heard her intake of breath at the thought, then a sly bubble of laughter formed in his mind. With it came a thought that he wasn't quite certain he was meant to hear.

I wonder how I could arrange that. . . . Her gaze slid over the group waiting, Linden knew, for him to leave again.

Just then the boy arrived with a dangerously laden plate. Linden took it carefully as Maurynna said, smiling, "Thank you, Temion. You're out of the kitchens now? Good."

To Linden's amusement the boy swelled visibly. Never

mind he'd likely known Maurynna all his life as one of the most junior of partners in the family enterprise. He'd been greeted by a Dragonlord. By name, even. He'd brag tonight in the servants quarters; Linden could see it in his eyes.

Temion bowed low and left. It was, Linden noted, an even deeper bow than Kesselandt would have received. Some of the relatives looked sour at the honor done their erstwhile underling. With another smile and a nod, Linden steered Maurynna away from them before they lost their awe of him and found their greedy tongues again.

They sought out a small bench in an isolated corner of the room. Maurynna settled onto it with a sigh composed of equal parts weariness and annoyance. Her face was set. Linden deemed it best not to say anything; instead he offered her the plate. Barely glancing at the proferred tidbits, Maurynna caught up a small tart. Before he could stop her, she bit into it and ate, staring grimly ahead.

It was worse than he'd thought, Linden realized. For the tartlet she'd chosen had a filling of almond paste, which Maurynna despised. Yet there she sat, not even noticing the too-sweet, sticky filling that usually made her gag.

He decided it was safest not to enlighten her. It wouldn't improve her temper one jot.

Phoenix, but his rear was sore! He'd never ridden so much. But Liasuhn didn't really mind. He was on his way to riches!

Well, he admitted to himself, perhaps not immediately—but one day. One day he would have enough money to eat at the best places and frequent the best brothels, as Kwahsiu and Nalorih did.

A sudden doubt assailed him. Urging his horse alongside Kwahsiu's, he asked, "Your head merchant won't mind your bringing me back, will he?"

Kwahsiu turned to him, his ever-present grin wider than ever. "Not at all," he said. "Why, we were told to keep our eyes open for a likely looking lad. Our master will be delighted to see you. Absolutely delighted."

Liasuhn dropped back to his proper place, a warm glow deep inside. He was destined for greatness, without a doubt.

And someday he would return to his little river town and astonish them all, oh, yes he would. He rode on smiling, lost in a happy daydream, and forgot all about his sore rear.

Twenty-five

Raven woke up the morning after the welcoming feast with a mouth that felt like the bottom of a manure pile. He sat up carefully.

"Ooooh," he moaned—but softly, very softly. His head came nigh to shattering anyway.

He groped, slit-eyed, for the pitcher of water by the bed and splashed some into the mug alongside. He drank greedily. It eased the worst of his thirst, but his mouth still felt as if baby dragons nested in it.

"Feh," he said, swinging his legs over the edge of the bed to put his feet on the floor. The soft pile of the carpet jabbed his feet and his head throbbed. Raven sat, feeling sorry for himself.

Then he remembered, and his aching head suddenly seemed pleasure itself.

For today he had to go home and face his family. His father. Perhaps he'd die of his hangover first.

No, he thought gloomily. *I wouldn't be so lucky*.

Raven heaved himself to his feet and staggered to the small bathing room. It would take a long time to get ready for this.

As if he could ever truly be ready.

When Raven came down the stairs at last, a servant approached him. The man held out a much-folded scrap of parchment. Curious, Raven took it and turned it over; there was no seal to identify the sender. He looked to the servant for an explanation.

"This came for you just a short while ago, young sir," the man said. "One of the boys who hangs about the marketplace to earn a penny or two brought it."

Raven opened the note, all the while wondering what and who would—

The "what" filled him with relief. He read, *Your father and brother are in Weavers Street and look to be there for some time. I'd go see your mother now if I were you.*

The "who" nearly made him choke in surprise. "Breslin?" he said in wonder.

By all the gods, if this wasn't a trick, he'd shake the hand of that obnoxious toad yet.

Raven halted Stormwind in the courtyard before his father's house. He wiped his sweating palms on his breeches and debated riding off again. But then Corlan, one of his many friends among the grooms, appeared. Raven stayed.

"Yer lucky, Raven; the master isn't here right now," Corlan said as he caught the reins Raven tossed him. "Hoy! Isn't this 'un a fine lad? Look at the color o' him! I've never seen the like." He patted the Llysanyin's neck. "He yours?"

"More I'm his," Raven said as he jumped down. "This is Stormwind. He's a Llysanyin from Dragonskeep."

Whatever Corlan had been about to say died in a strangled croak. "Wha—" he sputtered. His eyes grew huge as he stared at the horse that looked calmly back at him. "Gods ha' mercy," the groom got out at last. "So the rumors were true? You did go—And this really is a—" He held the reins as if they might bite him.

Taking pity on the man, Raven said, "He won't eat you, Corlan. Just tell him what you want him to do and he'll do it. Isn't that so, Stormwind?"

The Llysanyin nodded and nudged Corlan's shoulder.

"And just about now I'd wager he'd like a drink—right, boy?" *So would I. . . .*

Stormwind snorted assent. Raven gently pushed Corlan in the direction of the stables. The stunned groom went off like a sleepwalker while Stormwind paced alongside. Just before they went around the corner of the house, Stormwind looked back. And winked.

Laughing now, and brave with it, Raven went into the house to find his stepmother, Virienne.

Taren stood by the window in the room he'd been given in the Great House and looked out, watching the servants as they went in and out of another house across the wide central courtyard. That, no doubt, was the Mousehole they were to stay in.

He wondered if Raven would be returning to stay in the Erdon compound or if he and his father would come to an agreement between them. Taren hoped the former. There was something the boy was not telling of what he knew about Dragonlords, particularly these Dragonlords. Worse yet, without Raven to act as a buffer between him and the Dragonlords, he would have to spend more time with them.

And that was a thing he wished to avoid at all costs, until he knew much more about them. It was said certain of the priests of the Phoenix could smell a falsehood, taste deceit like a foulness on the tongue. Taren had no wish to find out these weredragons could do the same. He remembered stories of Dragonlords from his childhood; they had ascribed all manner of magical powers to these shapeshifters. True, he'd deceived them this far, but it might be only because he isolated himself as much as possible. Which in some ways was a pity; he enjoyed talking with Jekkanadar.

He would continue to stay aloof. He had no intention of risking everything, not unless he had to. Not until he discovered who the Hidden One was.

With a muttered curse, Taren turned away from the window.

*   *   *

The house was cool inside. This early in the cold season, the fires weren't lit during the day. It would be good sleeping weather tonight, Raven thought as he trod the halls of his home.

It was a fine home; not as grand as the Erdon family's, of course, but a fine, comfortable house just the same. In many ways, it was good to be back.

But something no longer felt right. . . .

He paused before the door to the solar. Taking a deep breath, Raven gathered up his courage and went inside.

His stepmother sat in her favorite chair, all her attention on the embroidery in her lap. Her hair, brown shot through with grey, was gathered in a bun at the back of her neck with a pair of hairsticks. Despite the grey, she looked much younger than her years.

By her side stood a little table. Upon it was a basket brimming over with colorful balls of thread. The needle she plied flashed as it darted in and out of the dark cloth. A neck band for a feast tunic, he guessed.

Then she looked up, alerted somehow to his presence.

"Hello, Virienne," Raven said weakly.

She said nothing, simply looked at him.

Wary, Raven came forward. "Didn't you get my letter?" If Iokka had reneged on their agreement . . .

Virienne pushed a loose strand of hair back from her face. "He was furious," she said wearily. "How could you do such a thing to him? He expected you to come back with that shipment and sell it."

"Virienne, how could he break his promise to me?" Raven countered. "How does he justify forcing me into his mold? I'm not a trader; we all know it."

He rubbed his forehead. The willowbark tea he'd choked down earlier had banished his headache, but now it threatened to return with a vengeance and five offspring besides.

Virienne flung her embroidery down on the bench beside her; it fell to the floor. "Ungrateful puppy! You have the world handed to you on a platter and you cast it aside. How poor Honigan would love to have what you do! Instead he must make do with your leavings, take whatever scraps you might throw him when the business comes to you."

The bitterness in his stepmother's voice astonished Raven. Never had Virienne betrayed any jealousy, any resentment of him since her marriage to his father when he was eight. She'd never treated him differently from her son and Raven had been grateful for that. His friends had told him too many tales of wicked stepmothers when it became known that his widowed father was remarrying.

"My leavings?" said Raven, stung by her accusation. "Damn it all, Virienne, as far as I'm concerned Honigan can have the wretched business and be welcome to it!" he yelled.

She rose to face him, her eyes telling him he lied.

It hurt. He said, "I mean that. If Da left the wool business to Honigan, I'd rejoice. I know Da worked hard to make it a success, and believe it or not, it would kill me to see it thrown away. That's the gods' own truth whether you believe it or not. And thrown away it will be if it comes to me. Do you think that wouldn't hurt? To know my lack of skill is what killed my Da's hard work? I don't want that to happen.

"Honigan, now; Honigan loves this trade as much as Da does. He *should* be the one it comes to. He's clever, respected by the other traders. Me—ah, hell, Virienne, they hide behind their hands and laugh when they see me coming along. They know they can shear me closer than any sheep."

He picked up her embroidery from the floor and dusted it off. "Here; it would be a shame to spoil it now, you're nearly finished." He offered it to her, half fearing she would slap his hand aside.

But she took it from him. "Yes; yes, it would, wouldn't it?" she said, the storm gone from her eyes now. Resignation filled them instead. "When we wedded, Redhawk promised me that if I would look upon you as my son, he would look upon Honigan as his own."

Raven laughed, a short, bitter laugh. "A great one for

keeping his promises my Da is, isn't he? You kept your end of the bargain. Did you know there were times when I forgot you weren't my blood mother, forgot that Honigan was but a stepbrother?" He rested his hands on her shoulders and said gently, "Thank you for that, Virienne. Thank you for all the times you've kept peace between the two pigheaded men in this family.

"Now—why don't we sit down, and tell each other all the news?" he said. "I've something that will surprise you, I think," he added, trying to look mysterious.

"It must be about a horse," Virienne said with a smile as she sat once again. "I know that gleam in your eye."

Raven pulled a chair up to share the patch of sunlight that bathed Virienne's and they talked. Virienne insisted upon hearing what Raven had done since he'd left.

Her hand went to her throat at the tale of Taren's suffering and daring escape; she nodded her understanding when Raven spoke of realizing his duty after meeting the former Jehangli slave; wonder filled her eyes as he described Dragonskeep, talked of sitting at the Lady's table, and of seeing truedragons flying overhead.

When he recounted the first meeting with Stormwind, she laughed. "I knew it!" she said, clapping her hands in delight. "I knew there was a horse somewhere! And such a horse!"

But her expression grew grave over the failed mission to free the captive truedragon, and when he told her of Lleld's plan, and that he was part of it—though he did not say just what his part was to be—the color drained from her face.

"Must you?" she asked faintly.

"Yes," he said. "I must. And you must swear to me not to say anything of this to anyone. Not to Da, not to Honigan, not to anyone at all. Just say that I'll be going with the Dragonlords when they travel on. Will you?"

She said, "I swear." Her voice was almost steady. But her eyes held a mother's fear.

Raven nodded. He looked down at the floor and realized the patch of sunlight they'd started out in had long since shifted. They'd talked for a long time, longer than he'd thought. He was lucky his father hadn't come home.

And if he wanted that luck to continue, he'd best leave. Raven stood up, his cloak over one arm. "I must go back now."

Virienne stood as well. "I understand. Raven, what I said before . . . Please don't think I'm just being ambitious for Honigan," she begged him. "Yes, I want him to take over from Redhawk someday—but only because I know that would leave you free for your dreams and fulfill his. What mother could ask more for her sons?"

Raven smiled. "What more can any of us wish for? Just ask Maurynna. She got her dream; now it's my turn."

Her hand flew to her mouth. "Ah," Virienne said. "I'm sorry, Raven; I know that you were hoping . . ."

"It doesn't really hurt anymore," Raven lied. "No doubt you'll want to see her . . . and Linden. I'll bring them here—"

Virienne's eyes widened in panic. "Dragonlords here? Raven, I've no time to plan a feast—"

"Virienne!" he said. "This is Maurynna! Remember her? The Maurynna who broke your favorite, and very expensive, Assantikan teapot when we were ten years old? *Don't* do anything fancy for her. Please. I think she'd finally break down and cry if you did. Yesterday, for the first time in my life, I wanted to hug Breslin."

And I owe him on my own account as well. He decided it would be best not to elaborate. Let Virienne think it was by chance he came when his father wasn't here.

"Breslin?" Virienne echoed in astonishment. "That ill-mannered little—why on earth? I'd have thought you more likely to bloody his nose for him."

Raven nodded. "So would I. But when we made port, Rynna's family behaved as though some stranger had come among them, some princess of the realm that they couldn't even approach. Not one hugged her, and Kesselandt even began to bend the knee to her. I thought Rynna would burst into tears right then and there. But that's when Breslin saved the day, may the gods bless the obnoxious toad. The moment he saw her he started a fight with Rynna as though nothing had changed—especially Maurynna." Raven grinned at his stepmother, knowing how she hated puns.

This one did not slip by her. She grimaced. "Maurynna— Changed. Raven, that one was truly awful, even for you." She swatted him.

Dodging, Raven said, "Friends again, Virienne? Tell Honigan I want to see him, that I'm on his side in this, will you? I—I lost my girl; I don't want to lose my mother and elder brother, too." It had been close, too close to happening. The thought stuck in his throat.

She drew his face down to hers and kissed him tenderly on the forehead as any mother would. "I'll see that you won't, dearest. You're returning to the Erdon enclave? It might be for the best, at least for tonight. I'll try to reason with your father. Go with my love."

He kissed her cheek. "Thank you," he whispered and hugged her hard before letting her go.

Raven let himself out of the small solar and walked slowly through the house, still trying to lay a finger on what was wrong about his home. It felt too small, as if it had somehow shrunk while he was away. He paused by the door to his sleeping chamber. What would he find if he looked? An empty room, his father having ordered even the memory of the wayward son wiped away? Or had his father turned it into a storeroom for wool bales in revenge? After a moment Raven gave in to temptation and peeked inside.

It was just as he'd left it, still smelled of leather oil and sweet woodruff. He sagged against the doorjamb in relief; a thousand memories came back in a rush. The window hangings were open; the last rays of the sun lay like bright fingers across the black and green blanket on the narrow bed, the blanket Virienne had woven for him when she'd first married his father. There was the clothes chest at the foot of the bed, his saddle resting on it, waiting for him to finish repairing the broken stitching. He saw the table desk by the window, the account book he'd been working on the morning he left still open upon it. By the book were a quill and a bottle of ink. He wondered if the ink had dried out; as usual he'd forgotten to stopper it. Everything the same. It all felt so familiar and yet . . . different.

How can it feel strange, he mused, leaning against the frame, *when nothing's cha—*

He was off the doorjamb like a stone from a sling and into the room. Where were his horses? The shelves along the far wall that held his childhood collection of carved wooden horses were empty. He began searching.

It wasn't long before he found them. It was plain they'd been swept off in a fit of temper. They lay on the floor, hidden from sight on the far side of the bed—or, rather, what was left of them. The proud herd was now nothing but bits of splintered wood fit only for tinder.

Dropping his cloak, he knelt by the sorry little pile. Tears stung Raven's eyes as he touched a leg here, a finely carved head there. He knew them all, had a name for each of them, had loved them through the years. The dust was thick upon them—and only them. This had been done some time ago and left as—What? A warning?

His favorite lay at the bottom, a stallion carved of some dark wood that had aged over the years to blackness. It looked, he realized with surprise, much like Shan. Or it had, once; now it was slivers. Clearly this one had borne the brunt of the destroyer's temper.

Da's temper, a voice said in Raven's mind. He wanted to name the voice liar. He knew he couldn't. Not without naming himself liar as well. *And that I will not be.*

Raven was up and moving for the door. He wanted nothing more than to get out of this house; this house that he could never come back to.

This was not home. Not now.

At the end of dinner, a servant came in and whispered something to Uncle Kesselandt. He nodded and dismissed the woman with a quiet, "Thank you."

When she was gone, Uncle Kesselandt said, "The Mousehole is now ready for you. Your belongings have been brought over; I trust that is satisfactory, Your Graces?"

"As long as I didn't have to pack the stuff, it certainly is, Master Kesselandt," said Lleld with heartfelt fervor. "I always forget how much I hate that part of traveling."

Kesselandt smiled.

"Thank you, uncle," Maurynna said.

"You're welcome, my dear."

It was a little stiff; she could almost hear the unspoken "Your Grace" that her punctilious uncle no doubt felt he should add, but it was much more like the Kesselandt she knew than the man who had greeted her on the dock. Someone must have spoken to him.

She thought she could guess who. A glance across the table confirmed it; Linden was nodding in approval at Kesselandt. She wished she dared thank him. But this was not the time or place to try Kyrissaean's forebearance.

Ah, well. She would "thank" him later, she thought, and drank to hide her smile.

Now her uncle looked around the table. It was a small family dinner by Erdon standards: only a dozen or so kin and the travelers.

"Raven isn't staying here with you, Rynna?" Kesselandt asked.

Heads turned this way and that as everyone looked for the young, red-haired Yerrin.

Taren, who had been silent for most of the meal, said, "He told me he was going to his family's house, Master Kesselandt. That was late this morning, just before he left."

Otter glanced over his shoulder to look out the window. "He must be staying there; it's near dusk now."

Maurynna heaved a sigh of relief. *Otter's right. Thank the gods; Master Redhawk must have finally come to his senses.*

Kesselandt said, "Shall I show you to the Mousehole now?"

The Dragonlords looked at each other and nodded. "That

would be well, Master Kesselandt," Lleld said, her gaze lingering on Taren. "It's been a long day for us."

Kesselandt rose and went to the door. The Dragonlords, Otter, and Taren followed.

As the sun slipped beneath the horizon and the air grew colder, Raven wrapped his arms around himself and called himself nine kinds of an idiot for forgetting his cloak. A tree trunk against one's back did little to keep one warm. And to add aggravation to annoyance as the saying went, he was growing cramped, sitting here watching Stormwind crop the grass. Ah, well; the long ride back to Stormhaven would warm him up and ease the kinks in his muscles.

Raven stretched out his legs and groaned. Damn; worse than he'd thought. To compound his misery, his stomach growled, protesting that he'd ignored it all day. But even that wasn't the worst of it.

He felt lost. He hadn't realized how much, deep inside, he'd counted on being able to return home. Was this how a baby bird felt when it was shoved from the nest?

No, he had to admit, he'd not been shoved. He'd jumped—and jumped without looking. What was done was done. His life was his own now. The thought scared the daylights out of him.

It was time to face up to that new life. First he had a thing to see through, and then . . . Well and well, he'd see. Time enough to worry later.

He rose stiffly to his feet, Stormwind's bridle in hand. As always, the sight of it made him look twice; he still wasn't used to a bridle with no bit.

Stormwind's head came up. At the sight of the bridle, he trotted up to Raven and tugged a lock of his person's hair.

"Give over, you big lump," Raven said, laughing. *At least my horse still likes me*, he thought as he tweaked the stallion's upper lip. It made him smile.

"A bit different from your garret room?" Linden teased as he and Maurynna turned around and around, examining the sleeping chamber assigned to them.

It was large and airy and spoke of refined wealth. The walls were of pale wood, the panels matched so carefully that the joints were barely visible. A painted border of vines ran along the walls below the ceiling. They were so cleverly done that at first glance Linden thought them real.

All the furniture had the understated elegance that spoke of money freely spent. The woven hangings on the bed alone must have been a small fortune, he thought.

"Gods, yes," Maurynna said. "Not having much business with any guests of the family, I've rarely been inside one of the Mouseholes, and never to the upper floors. As Lleld would say, 'Coo!' "

Linden caught her around the waist and pulled her to him. "The bed looks comfortable—think we have time before meeting with Lleld and Jekkanadar to find out just how comfortable?" he whispered in her ear.

She laughed and said, "We'll make the time."

He swung her up into his arms. They'd make the time; they had so little of it left together.

They galloped most of the way, the stallion moving light as a cloud along the pale road. The first stars glittered in the evening sky. Raven gave himself over to the pleasure of the ride, laughing aloud as the wind whipped the hair back from his face.

But all too soon the gate to the city lay before them. Stormwind slowed and pranced through it at a more decorous pace. Not far now. . . .

"Damn," he whispered.

"You're late," Virienne said as Redhawk and Honigan entered the room where she waited at the table, the meal arranged before her. "Everything's cold."

"Nothing wrong with cold chicken if there's plenty of green sauce to go with it," her husband said as he took his seat.

She studied him as the little table maid served his dinner. His manner was a mix of well-pleased and distracted, for although he smiled, now and again a tiny frown creased his brow as though something nagged him. Honigan's demeanor, on the other hand, was unalloyed pleasure. It would seem something had gone well today.

Let it be so, she thought. That will make what I have to say go down easier.

She decided not to tell Redhawk about Raven's visit until the meal was over. Instead she listened as husband and son celebrated the good price they'd gotten for the wool from one of their flocks. A flock, she remembered with pride, that had been Honigan's idea to bring in at considerable expense from the highlands of Yerrih. Although Redhawk had been skeptical at first, Honigan had talked his stepfather into importing the little sheep with their long, blue-grey fleece.

Now the gamble had paid off, it seemed, for Honigan said, "Best of all, we've a ready market for it. Mistress Parmale said that she would buy all the wool we could produce. She weaves the cloth for the temple of Duirin, and it's just the color they want for their robes. It will save her the trouble and cost of having the wool dyed, she said, now that old Watt the Dyer is gone and his son Derenel's careless with the work."

"Fool ruins the cloth more often than not," Redhawk said around a mouthful of cold chicken. "Pity to see a good business go to waste like that." A crafty gleam came into his eye. "Tell you what, Honigan—I'll wager anything Derenel's eager to sell; Watt's been in the grave less than a month, and folk are looking elsewhere already. In a few months' time the business will be worth nothing. I'll buy it now, then we'll set you up in charge of the dye works, and Raven in charge of the wool end of things, and we'll grab a fine chunk of the market. What do you say, eh?"

Honigan looked down at his plate. He said softly, "But I'm not interested in the dye works. . . ."

"Nonsense, boy!" Redhawk said, his voice hearty but with an edge beneath it. "I'll buy the damn business, you'll run it, and once Raven's back—"

This was not how she wanted to do it, but the memory of Raven's words and now the disappointment in Honigan's face tricked the words from her tongue. "Raven *is* back," Virienne said.

A silence like the pause twixt thunder and lightning fell over the table. At last Redhawk said, "What? How do you know Raven's back? I heard nothing of it." His voice shook with barely contained anger.

"Have you heard about the Dragonlords?" Virienne countered.

Frowning, Redhawk said, "Aye—there was talk in the market today that Maurynna and her soultwin, the one they called the Last Dragonlord, arrived yesterday. Was Raven with them? No one said anything to *me!*"

"I heard there were two other Dragonlords besides them," Honigan said, catching Virienne's eye. "Who would notice Raven with Dragonlords about?"

"There are two others," Virienne confirmed, "as well as Otter and someone else. As to how I know . . . He came here, Redhawk, earlier today." She took a deep breath. "He's . . . not here to stay."

"Of course he is." A priest declaiming his god's will from the temple stairs could not have spoken with more authority. Or more rigidity.

Virienne sighed. "He said he'll be traveling with the Dragonlords when they move on."

Redhawk slammed his hand down on the table with such force that the plates and silverware jumped. A vein beat in his forehead. "I'll see about that." He stood up.

Maurynna had not meant to eavesdrop as she returned from a late-evening raid on the buttery for a jug of ale and some spice cakes. But her bare feet made no noise on the wood floors as she passed the open window; those standing outside had no warning of her approach. Even so, the voices were low enough that had she been truehuman, she could not have recognized the voices, let alone made out the words.

But a Dragonlord's acute hearing was hers now, and she recognized both voice and words. It was Raven.

Even as she thought *How odd; I thought he'd gone home candlemarks ago*, his words penetrated her mind.

"I can't go home, Master Kesselandt." The words were slurred as if with emotion and exhaustion. "Please . . ."

"No," a crisp voice said. It was not Uncle Kesselandt.

Maurynna's lips drew back, baring her teeth. Uncle Darijen had never been friend to her or Raven. Remembering how he'd nearly convinced Kesselandt she was too young for a captain made her hot with anger all over again.

"With all due respect, sir, I asked the Head of this family—not you."

Despite his exhaustion, there was steel in Raven's voice. Maurynna silently cheered him.

"Insolent pup! I'll see you broken for that."

"Master Kessel—"

Uncle Darijen cut him off. "You set those sails yourself, boy, now live with the course you've chosen. You'll find no help here."

Oh, gods, what that sneering voice brought back. Memories burned through her, all the slights and indignities this uncle had heaped upon her throughout the years. Maurynna set the tray with its ale and cakes down on the floor. Then she took a deep breath and went to find a door.

Linden was wondering where Maurynna had gotten to with the promised ale and cakes when he heard the sound of a horse's hooves rapidly approaching. A late guest? Not likely. Curious who would be visiting at this candlemark and in such haste, he went to the window and twitched the embroidered hanging aside, peering out into a night lit only by stars and a quarter moon.

A servant appeared as the rider pulled up in the central courtyard before the houses. In the light of the torch the servant held, Linden saw the visitor was a man of perhaps forty or so. Every movement, from the way he threw the reins at the groom who came running up, to the angry jerk at the hem of his tunic spoke of fury. Linden wondered anew who came in such haste and such anger. Surely not a dissatisfied fellow merchant?

Lleld joined him at the window, fitting neatly under his raised elbow. "Who is it?" she asked.

"I've a suspicion, but I'm not certain. I can't see his face."

Jekkanadar came to peer around his shoulder. As they watched, the servant pointed at the Mousehole.

Linden looked down at Lleld; she still stared out of the window. Then her eyes met his for a brief moment, eyebrows raised in speculation.

Once again Linden looked out the window. Below, the torchlight played over the man's hair as he crossed the courtyard. At that distance and in such poor light, only a Dragonlord's unnaturally sharp vision could have caught the glint of red. "Oh, hell," he grumbled and let the curtain drop. "I know who it is."

Lleld caught it, peered outside once more; a moment later she said, "That's Raven's da, isn't it? He looks as mad as a bear with a burr up its butt."

"Doesn't he just, though?" Linden said. In fact, he'd never seen anyone meet the old hillman's description so well. "This will not be pretty."

"But why is he here? Raven left this morning to go home," said Jekkanadar.

Linden, too, wondered about that:

Maurynna skirted the moth garden with its sweet-scented flowers. Though it was late in the season for them, a few of the gauzy-winged insects still tended the blooms. They fluttered through the pale moonlight as they paused at one blossom after another, paying court to the white flowers that dotted the shadows.

When she was younger, Maurynna had often sneaked out of her garret room to play in the garden. On soft summer nights when the moon was full, it was a magical place, a place where anything might happen.

But now she strode past without even seeing it. A trailing vine of moonflowers brushed her shoulder. She pushed it aside. Her goal was the knot garden on the far side of the honeysuckle hedge. She hoped she was not too late; the closest door had been on the opposite side of the house from where the three men argued. Under her bare feet the brick walk was rough and scratchy, and the sharp, dry scent of the baked clay contrasted with the sweetness of the flowers and the soil's rich fragrance. The cool night air slid along her cheek like silk.

Lleld cocked her head at him. "Shall we?"

Linden sighed and took a last look around the small sitting room. He'd been hoping for a quiet evening and early to bed, but now . . . For a moment he was tempted to let Raven deal with the mess the boy had landed himself in. Then his conscience prodded him; it was for the sake of a truedragon, after all, that Raven was now in trouble.

He sighed again. The gods only knew where the son was, but he could go reason with the father. "Let's get it over with." He led the way to the door.

Maurynna rounded the hedge and halted. Before her stood three men: Raven, cloakless, his shoulders slumped in despair, but his feet planted wide in defiance, shivering with the cold; Uncle Kesselandt running the fingers of both hands through his hair as he always did when facing a difficult and unpleasant task. And Uncle Darijen, as arrogant as ever, sneering at Raven, snug in a thick wool cloak.

"Getting above yourself, aren't you, boy, playing tagalong to your betters? Did you run crying to Maurynna when your Yerrin kin had the sense to throw you out? And now she's tired of you tagging after her and her soultwin and brought you home like a runaway cur."

Maurynna's fists clenched. Idiot Raven might have been lately, but by the gods he'd been a friend too long for her to let that slander pass. She took a deep breath to steady herself and forced herself to take the first step.

But Darijen wasn't finished; there was yet more venom there. "I suggest you crawl home to your father and beg him to take you back. He might find you a place as one of his shepherds, though I don't see why he should, you ungrateful—"

"Enough," Maurynna said. The words—and the courage to say them—came from somewhere deep inside. She spoke quietly but with a snap like a whip. All three men jumped. "That will be quite enough, Uncle Darijen."

She bore down on them, feeling like a stranger to herself. Who was this woman who strode so confidently along the winding path, ordering to silence a man whose poisonous tongue she had feared all of her life?

She halted in front of Darijen. But as he turned his withering glare upon her, the bold stranger inside quailed beneath the weight of memories. Maurynna's mouth went dry and the words died on her tongue.

She looked to Raven for support—and found none. There was only despair in his eyes.

"Where is he?"

The speaker pushed past the hapless servant who, all unsuspecting of what lay beyond, had opened the door to the sharp knocking. Redhawk surged into the foyer as Linden reached the bottom stair, Lleld by his side. Jekkanadar paused on the step behind them.

Linden quickly glanced around for Maurynna. Luckily she was nowhere in sight; Redhawk would likely vent his ire upon her before remembering what she was now.

Redhawk's eyes lit upon them in that instant. Linden saw that the man's face was red with fury; vengeance glittered in those blue eyes so much like Raven's. Wherever the boy was, Linden devoutly hoped he stayed there. However much a pain in the ass Raven could be, he didn't deserve a homecoming like this.

Redhawk looked ready to storm through the house in his search for his errant son. Two long steps and Linden stood before him as if by chance, blocking his way to the lower reaches of the house. Lleld and Jekkanadar stayed on the stairs, she leaning nonchalantly on the newel post, he against the wall. But Linden knew that if Redhawk thought the tiny woman and the slender Assantikkan no obstacle, the man was in for the rudest awakening of his life. Which, considering his churlish behavior so far, was likely no more than Raven's father deserved.

"Where's my son?" the man snarled, looking at each of them in turn. The riding whip he carried in one hand quivered as if it wished to lash out at one of them.

"Master Redhawk!" the servant gasped. "These are Dragonlords! Please, you mustn't speak to them so."

But if Redhawk heard the warning and the servant's anxiety for him, he gave no sign. Indeed, Linden feared the man was so caught up in his anger that he would strike one of them—and the gods help Redhawk if he did. He had no wish to see a kinsman of friends face what would come of it.

Redhawk took another step as if he would push past Linden. Linden held his ground.

The blue eyes burned with rage, and the whip came up to strike.

Her braver self did not desert her after all. Maurynna went on, "Everything you've just said is a lie, uncle. Raven's Yerrin kin did not throw him out. He never even went to Yerrih—he came straight to Dragonskeep. Nor is he merely a tagalong as you've said. On the contrary, he is an equal traveling among equals. And as far as I'm concerned, Raven stays in the Mousehole as an honored guest with the rest of us, or we will all leave. I'm certain that one of the other Houses would be willing to welcome four Dragonlords and a bard even on such short notice."

She folded her arms and stared coolly at Darijen. Then she turned to Kesselandt. "Uncle? As Raven pointed out before, the decision is yours."

*   *   *

The whip fell, but only to strike against Redhawk's boot. "Where's my son?" he asked once again. His eyes darted everywhere as if to spy out Raven hiding behind one of the sconces on the wall.

Linden shook his head. "I've no idea, Redhawk," he said. "He went home candlemarks ago."

He paused, waiting for Redhawk to recognize him. Surely the man hadn't forgotten meeting him?

Redhawk hadn't. That furious gaze turned on him once again; Linden saw it snap into focus as if Redhawk only now truly saw him.

From somewhere in the house came the sound of a door opening and shutting once more. Some servant running to fetch help? He hadn't the time to wonder.

Redhawk said, "You're Linden Rathan. We met long ago. You—you haven't changed at all, have you?" There was a touch of fear in the words.

It was a fear Linden was all too familiar with. "No, I haven't. Regarding Raven, Master Redhawk, we've not seen him since—"

Voices from behind interrupted him. One was the last Linden wanted to hear at this moment.

Redhawk's face went red with rage; a vein pulsed in his forehead. "Raven!" he bellowed.

Linden turned. Sure enough, Raven and Maurynna were behind him. Both faces were pale.

"Oh, gods," Raven whispered. "I'm in for it now."

But Raven did not, Linden saw with approval, try to hide behind him. Instead the young Yerrin passed him to stand before his father. Linden was less pleased that Maurynna followed, but understood; he knew they were used to facing punishment together.

"Sir?" Raven said.

"You ungrateful whelp!" his father roared. "Is this how you pay me back for all I've done for you?" Redhawk's hand came up; too late Linden remembered the riding crop.

The crop slashed down at Raven's head. But before it

could strike, Maurynna sprang forward with a Dragonlord's speed and caught the hand holding it.

"Master Robinson, no!" she cried.

"Get out of my way and don't interfere, stupid girl!"

For the first time since she'd become a Dragonlord, Linden saw Maurynna truly believe her new rank. He knew that she'd practically grown up in this man's house. He knew that Redhawk was a successful merchant, an important player in the great game these traders gambled at. As a very junior partner in House Erdon, she would have deferred to one of his stature or risked the wrath of her own elders. Hell, the idea of raising her hand to this man would likely never have occurred to her.

But she was no longer that junior partner. Instead of backing down, Maurynna snarled right back, "It's 'Your Grace' now, Master Robinson! And I order you to drop that whip!"

Her words had the force of a slap. Linden saw shock replace fury in Redhawk's eyes, followed by outraged indignation as he glared at Maurynna. The man looked near to choking on the angry words trying to get out.

But the riding crop fell to the floor. An almost inaudible sigh of relief swept the room. Maurynna stepped back, her face pale and set.

"Thank the gods that's over with," said Lleld from the staircase. There was an edge to her voice that Linden had seldom heard.

She stepped down from the stairs to face Redhawk. "I am Dragonlord Lleld Kemberaene, Master Robinson," she said, her voice low with anger. "What is the meaning of this unseemly intrusion?"

They glared at one another, each willing the other to give ground. Though the difference in their heights bordered on the absurd, there was nothing amusing in the confrontation. Someone coming in unaware might have thought it an argument between parent and child at first glance, but there was nothing childlike in either Lleld's fury or the regal way she stood up to the much larger man.

It was Redhawk who conceded. "Your Grace," he said, calmly enough, "I apologize for disturbing you, but my son has defied me for the last time. I simply came to take him home where he belongs, and to face the punishment he deserves." The angry flush receded.

"I think not," Lleld said. She spoke quietly, but her tone brooked no argument. "Raven will be coming with us when we leave Thalnia."

A frown darkened Redhawk's face. "I order you to come home," he said to his son, "and forget this traipsing about like some ne'er-do-well."

"I'm afraid you don't understand. We need him with us," said Lleld.

Redhawk's face grew red again. "With all respect, Dragonlord, I did not raise my son to be a servant."

"No, Master Robinson, you didn't. You raised him to be *you* all over again, instead of one Raven Redhawkson, didn't you?" Lleld snapped.

For a moment it seemed Redhawk might lose all control of himself. But though his fists clenched at his sides, and a vein beat visibly in his forehead, the merchant said nothing.

"But he isn't you, with your interests and your talents. He's himself, with his own very special talents—and we need those talents. Raven is not a servant, Master Robinson, rest assured of that. I can't tell you the *why* of all this, but I can tell you that it is with the heartfelt thanks of the Lady of Dragonskeep and our cousins, the truedragons of the north, that Raven is with us. . . ." She paused to let the full import of her words sink in.

The look Redhawk flashed at his son reminded Linden of Maurynna's kin on the dock.

"And he will stay with us," Lleld finished. "He didn't need this to come with us, Master Robinson, but I think you do: Dragonlord's orders."

A long silence followed in which Redhawk visibly struggled with the final thwarting of his plans for Raven's life. When he finally spoke, his voice seethed with cold fury.

"There is nothing I can say to *that*, is there, Your Grace? After all, I'm but a simple merchant, and you a Dragonlord. So I will just say this: so be it." He bowed to Lleld.

Then he looked once more at Raven. "But to *you*," he snarled, "I say this: I wash my hands of you. From this day I have but one son, and his name is Honigan."

With that, Redhawk stared defiance at each Dragonlord in turn, and sketched them a mocking bow before turning on his heel and striding from the Mousehole without a backward glance.

When the door slammed shut, Lleld turned to Raven, a stricken look on her face. "Oh, Raven! I'm sorry! I just destroyed your life for you, didn't I?"

But Raven said with a sigh, "No, you didn't, Lleld. I did that the day I left with Taren, though I didn't realize it at the time. I do now."

He sounded both sad and resigned, but then a smile twitched at the corner of his mouth. "At least one thing went right."

"What?" Lleld asked.

"Honigan gets stuck with the damned sheep after all, not me."

Linden thought the grin that followed would split Raven's face.

Twenty-six

The next morning, Linden came upon Otter in the solar as the bard sat examining a selection of hand drums on the table before him.

"What's this?" he asked.

Otter looked up. "There's a damned good instrument maker here in Port Stormhaven. I know him from our student days at the Bards' School in Bylith. Mediocre singer, and not much of a harper, but a rare hand at making instruments even then. His eldest daughter does most of the work nowadays, but old Merris still keeps his hand in with these little drums. He always enjoyed these the most, he said. I was there until late last night, catching up on the news and picking these. Raven can drum a bit, you know."

"Ah—so that's why you missed all the excitement."

"Oh?"

"Mm, yes. Redhawk was here, and he had blood in his eye." Linden looked over the drums; there was quite a range, from various sizes of Assantikkan *zamlas* to a couple of Yerrin *taeresans* and their beaters.

Otter groaned and buried his face in his hands. "Tell me," he ordered.

When Linden finished, Otter sat tugging his beard. Finally he said, "Raven's right. It's best this way. Honigan loves the wool business as much as Raven detests it. And now Raven will have no choice but to go to his aunt. I was always afraid he'd never bring himself to fully defy his father, and do what was right for him. He loves Redhawk, and would have suffered rather than risk turning his father against him. But it's done now. When this is over, Raven can go to his aunt." The bard grimaced. "Still, I'd best go talk to Redhawk, see what I can patch up between them; I've done it before. It was good of Lleld to take upon herself the responsibility for Raven's going. Redhawk won't lose face—or too much, anyway—when I finally talk him into accepting Raven back into the fold. That was a stupid thing to say about having only one son. I'll just give him a bit to cool down, though."

"You'll have a few days for it, then, before we leave." Linden picked up a *taeresan* and its beater. Wrapping his fingers around the crosspiece inside the open end of the shallow drum, he tapped on the hide, flipping the beater back and forth as he'd seen performers do—without the same rhythmic, foot-tapping results. It sounded, he thought, pathetic. He kept at it, determined to get it right.

"We've a place to live and rehearse?" Otter asked, taking drum and beater away from him. "Good. And boyo—stick to the harp."

Linden thumbed his nose at the bard, then said, "Lleld told him what we need, and Kesselandt's discussing with the other senior members which of the country estates would be best for our needs."

"When do we find out?"

"Kesselandt sent a messenger to Maurynna earlier. We find out by this afternoon."

Linden waited impatiently for Kesselandt to join them in the solar. The man should be here any moment; then they would learn where they would be staying—and rehearsing—for the winter. He glanced around the room at the other Dragonlords.

Lleld and Jekkanadar bent over a chess board with an unfinished game upon it, studying the pieces. Jekkanadar shook his head.

"I should not want to be White in this game," he said.

"Ah," said Lleld. "But what if White did this?" and moved the horse to illustrate her point.

Jekkanadar stroked his chin. "Hm—perhaps. Perhaps . . ." He fell to studying the board again, his gaze darting this way and that. "But if Black countered with the queen's mage *here*—"

Lleld crowed, "Then take *this*!" as her hand darted to the board.

I hope they remember where they started, Linden thought with a grin. *Or someone will be very surprised at the turn their game has taken.* Lleld was not the most conservative of players at the best of times. Judging by the evil glee lighting her face, the little Dragonlord planned a singularly unorthodox strategy for this bout. He caught Taren watching in dismay.

The smile faded as Maurynna entered the room. Something was wrong; he knew it at once. For she chewed her lower lip now and again, something she did only when nervous. She came to stand with him, but said nothing.

"What is it, love?" he asked.

"Temion just warned me that my Uncle Darijen is in a dangerously foul mood over this. Temion heard him say something about not being a 'peasant to be turned out of his home.'

"I suspect that the estate to be given over to us is the one he uses in the winter. It's a hunting lodge, not all that big as some of the country places go, but it's in the south, where it's warmer. Darijen's the one I told you about last night." Her lips pressed together.

"Ah, yes—the one with the poisonous tongue." The one who'd upset Maurynna so much she'd not slept until near dawn. "Try not to let him bother you, sweetheart. He can't do anything to you. Not anymore."

She didn't believe him, any more than she had last night. Darijen's power over her was too ingrained.

Linden frowned. He wished he could convince her that all would be well. That the old ties of affection still held, yes; but no longer did a newly fledged Dragonlord owe obedience to his or her birth family. That obligation was gone now, replaced by fealty to the ruler of Dragonskeep.

It was a lesson each new Dragonlord had to learn: that the hardest thing of all was to stand up to one's own family. Kings and queens were child's play in comparison.

Old habits die hard. The time-worn adage drifted across his thoughts; cliché though it was, it was still true. So he did the best he could; he slipped an arm around her shoulders and, to distract her, led her to where Otter, Raven, and Taren looked over the drums.

Raven picked up a *zamla* and turned it this way and that. He tucked it under one arm and tapped out a quick rhythm.

"Very nice," he said. "But why are they so plain? Usually *zamlas* have some decoration."

"Merris just finished lacing them," Otter said. "Once we decide which ones we'll take, I'll have Merris do 'em up gaudier than a potted peacock playing in a paint pot."

Try saying that *one quickly*, Linden said to Maurynna, turned his head to catch her eye.

Her mouth twitched. It was a start.

"A shame," Raven said. For once Linden agreed with him. "They're fine instruments."

"I know, and Merris will have a fit when I tell him, but it can't be helped. Remember, we're traveling entertainers, not court musicians. Gaudy it will have to be."

"So you'll have Merris paint your harp as well?" Linden couldn't help saying. "Scarlet, with lots of gold leaf? Some bright green, too, perhaps."

Otter turned an outraged glare upon him. "There are," he announced frostily, "limits."

Linden chuckled, and felt Maurynna's shoulders shaking under his arm. Her dark mood was broken, if only briefly. Well enough, then; it was a start.

"Ahem."

The slight clearing of a throat caught everyone's attention. They all turned to look.

Kesselandt stood in the doorway. Beyond him, Linden could see some of the other senior Erdons peering in.

Only one claimed his attention: Darijen.

The instant Linden saw the man's venomous expression, he knew which estate they'd been given—and that it would be long indeed before Darijen forgave them this slight.

"What was that?" Tsiru's friend, another acolyte, demanded of him.

Tsiru finished dribbling a little water between the lips of the man he'd nursed since the attack by the foul creatures from the north. "What was what?" he asked, turning around.

A quick movement at the door. "That!"

"Oh—that's just Hodai, I'll wager, come to see how Priest Haoro is doing. Hodai!" he called. "You may come in."

A dark head peered once more around the door. Tsiru beckoned, and the little Oracle slipped in as quietly as a mouse. With a shy smile at the two of them, Hodai drew closer to the bed until he looked down into the still face of the man upon it. Only the rise and fall of the chest, and the occasional movement of the eyes beneath the closed lids, showed that the priest still lived.

Hodai bent closer, his hands clasped at his breast, and studied Haoro for a long time. As always, Tsiru wondered just what the Oracle looked for.

At last the boy looked up, smiled his thanks, and slipped out as quietly as he had come.

"Hunh—he do that often?"

"Oh, yes—every few days. Kind of touching, isn't it? I hadn't realized he was so fond of Haoro," Tsiru said.

"I didn't realize *anyone* was fond of Haoro," his friend muttered.

A grumbling from the bed brought them both around. The priest's lips moved, but the words—if there were any— were incomprehensible.

Tsiru's friend jumped to his feet. "Oh, damn! Do you think he heard me?" he asked in an agonized whisper.

"Relax. He's been doing that lately. Mutters a bit, then goes quiet again. Watch."

They did and, as Tsiru predicted, the mumblings soon subsided, and Haoro lay upon the bed like a living corpse.

Tsiru cocked his head. "Still, I have to say this—this time I could almost understand words."

As Otter rode through the marketplace on his way to visit Merris once again, he spied Redhawk standing before a stall and talking with the owner, a stout woman in a long, colorful dress in the Assantikkan style. Her wares filled the table behind them, long sashes in a gay tumble of color like a flower garden gone wild. They were almost as bright as their owner.

Ah, hell, Otter thought—he might as well get it over with. Biting back a sigh, he pressed a rein against Nightsong's neck. The Llysanyin mare instantly turned and forged a way through the noisy crowd.

Coming up behind Redhawk, he said, "Good day, nephew."

Redhawk whirled around. The first emotion to cross his face was pleasure; Otter was certain of it. But then he saw Redhawk remember his uncle was one of those responsible for his son's defection, and the pleasure disappeared.

"Uncle," he said coolly. "I see you're in Thalnia again."

"For a time," Otter replied with equal coolness.

The stallkeeper looked from one to the other, and wisely retreated into her stall, where she busied herself with pulling more sashes from their storage baskets. She tossed them over her arm, where they hung like rainbow snakes.

The passing crowd jostled Nightsong; she snapped a warning, then braced her sturdy legs.

Redhawk frowned at her. "I'm no expert, but isn't that an odd color for a grown horse, black body with grey mane and tail? Don't they usually go all grey?" He peered closer. "And why doesn't she have a bit?"

"The answer to your questions is: because Nightsong is a Llysanyin," said Otter.

At Redhawk's sharp, questioning look, Otter went on, "That's right, nephew. A Llysanyin bearing a truehuman— makes you think, doesn't it? And here's a bit more to think about while you're about it: her grandson, Stormwind, chose Raven."

Redhawk went very still.

Leaning down from the saddle so that he didn't have to shout his words for all to hear, Otter said, "So think twice about disowning the boy, Redhawk. Despite what you seem to think, there's more in this world than sheep and wool. Much more. Someday you're going to be damned proud to call Raven your son."

At a touch of his leg, Nightsong sank down upon her haunches and pirouetted in place, each broad, feathered forehoof stepping delicately. As she paced regally away, Otter turned in the saddle. "My word as a bard on that," he called.

Twenty-seven

The troupe gathered in a meadow near the Erdon hunting lodge; truehumans and Dragonlords sitting or sprawling in a circle on the ground, Llysanyins grazing among them. A gentle breeze frisked among them and played tag with stray locks of hair before whisking off across the field.

They were lucky, Linden thought, watching the long grass dip and bow as the breeze passed over; the weather was still remarkably warm even for a country known for its mild winters.

The passes to the Keep must be deep with snow by now.

He was content to lie back in the grass by Maurynna's side, Shan and Boreal nosing for some choice tidbit behind them, and drowse in the unseasonable warmth. Somewhere close by a late cricket sang of summertime, while on his other side the clicking of Taren's beads came, steady as a heartbeat. The sound was hypnotic.

The idyll ended. Lady Mayhem yawned hugely and sat up. Linden grumbled under his breath; time to get to work, no doubt. He levered himself up onto his elbows.

"Now that we're settled and rested from the journey, shall we see just what talents we have between us?" Lleld said. "I know we've discussed it somewhat already, and everyone's thought about it, but now we begin in earnest. I'll go first.

"I can tumble and juggle, walk a rope, and so can Jekkanadar." She looked to her right. "Raven, you can play the drums that Otter brought along, am I right?"

Raven nodded. "Yes. I can keep time for my uncle, as well as play some fairly complicated Assantikkan dance rhythms, too. Or at least I could at one time; I'll need to practice."

"That's what we're here for."

"And he can sing well enough to come in on a chorus with me," said Otter, next in line. "As can Linden."

"Good! So can Jekkanadar and I, for that matter," Lleld said. "We're not bards, but we can carry a tune."

Maurynna said ruefully, "As I can't even to save my life. But if there's a little *zamla*, I can do a simple beat while Raven plays the more complicated things; we used to do that years ago."

Lleld's face wrinkled up in thought. "Well enough; you two are supposed to just be servants, anyway. So it won't matter to the show when you leave us."

Linden tensed at the words. His eyes met Lleld's.

I'm sorry, Linden, she said in his mind. *But you knew that all along.*

Aye, but that doesn't mean I like to be reminded of it.

She shrugged. "And Linden shall be our strong man. It's what would be expected, given his size."

"But not too strong," Jekkanadar said. He twirled a stem of grass between his fingers and grinned.

Linden tossed a pebble at him. Jekkanadar caught it, scooped up a few more and juggled them.

"Just so," Lleld said, pushing back her red curls with one hand. "You want to astonish an audience, not scare it out of 'em."

The resulting mental image drew a smile out of Linden. His usual good humor at least partially restored, he said, "And don't forget I can accompany Otter on the harp as well as sing. And how about a fire-breather? We might as well take advantage of our immunity to fire."

"Good thinking, Linden; add one fire-breather, then. Coo," said Lleld, rubbing her hands together. "We're a talented lot, aren't we? This is better than I had expected; all this and the Llysanyins will do nicely."

"But what of me?" Taren said. He sat, not quite with them, but not quite apart from them, either. He smiled gen-

tly at Lleld, the string of white beads sliding through his
fingers like a crystalline waterfall. Indeed, Linden hadn't
even thought he was listening; Taren had contributed nothing to the conversation earlier. He'd merely sat cross-
legged, beads clicking, apparently lost in contemplation of
the little meadow pinks before him.

Linden looked at the man in surprise. Taren had never
even hinted he wished to be one of the performers. Linden
had always thought the former slave wanted to stay out of
the public eye as much as possible, that Taren would act
as interpreter when needed but otherwise stay in the back-
ground lest he be recognized and taken again.

And now he was offering to perform in their show?

Linden saw he was not the only one taken by surprise.
Lleld's face showed open-mouthed astonishment.

"Uh," she said. "Um, ah—but what can you do, Taren?
Sing? Juggle? Tumble?"

The restless beads stopped. Taren folded his hands over
them. He shook his head. "Alas, no, lady," he said, his
voice filled with sadness. "At my age? You mock me."

Taren's gaze dropped once more. He opened his hands;
the beads were gone. With a soft click of his tongue, Taren
reached behind Lleld's ear. His hand reappeared, the beads
threaded between his fingers.

"Mock an old man and then steal his worry beads," Taren
said, still with infinite sadness. But now Linden heard the
laugh hiding behind it. "Ah, Dragonlord, you are not kind
to a poor old man."

With that, Taren stretched out his other hand—a hand
that Linden swore was also empty—and reached behind
Linden's ear. This time Taren pulled forth a meadow pink.

He offered it to Lleld. "Yet see? I forgive you."

Lleld whooped with delight as she took the flower. After
a moment of astonished silence, the others laughed and applauded. Linden couldn't help it; although he knew it was
a trick, he still touched the ear from which Taren had
"picked" the flower.

No, nothing else there—thank the gods. Linden joined in the applause and laughter.

When she'd caught her breath again, Lleld said, "Tumblers, jugglers, singers and musicians, dancing horses, fire-eaters, and a conjuror! I think we'll do very well indeed, my friends. Very well.

"And now—to work. Linden, while Jekkanadar and I work on a simple tumbling routine, why don't you take Maurynna and Raven back to the riding ring for some practice with various weapons?"

Elsewhere it was winter. Here, in the Garden of Eternal Spring, the air was warm and mild. A butterfly drifted past, dancing on the perfumed breeze. Birds sang in the little grove of cherry trees that Shei-Luin rested under as Murohshei fanned her. She lay, eyes closed and half drowsing, and sighed in contentment. It was a perfect moment. Murohshei had been right; this was a good place to wait.

For when Xiane received the message she'd sent him that morning . . . Shei-Luin smiled in quiet triumph. She'd been right to go to the palace temple this morning and consult the Revalator of Riya-Akono. A Revalator couldn't always tell a pregnant woman what she would have, but when the Revalator—the closest thing to a female priest in Jehanglan—did, she was almost always right.

Then a voice rose in quiet song, so beautiful that when the birds fell silent, it was as if they did so in homage. Even the breeze ceased playing among the blossoms. Shei-Luin caught her breath, listening.

The song grew louder as the singer approached. It was an old ballad, gently melancholic, about a young man whose heart's desire hardly knew he existed.

The fan ceased moving. Surprised, Shei-Luin glanced up.

Murohshei's gaze darted back and forth as he searched the garden before them. For a moment Shei-Luin was alarmed; then she saw Murohshei's lips curl in a tiny, hopeful smile. She lifted her head enough to see what pleased her eunuch.

It was Zyuzin the Songbird who wandered among the peach trees and hedges of jasmine, singing as he walked. His eyes were downcast, modest as any maiden; as he passed the flowers, the fingers of one hand brushed them as lightly as a butterfly, a lover's secret caress. In the crook of his other arm he cradled his *zhansjen*.

As Shei-Luin watched, amused now, Zyuzin suddenly halted, his hand darting to press against his chest, his eyes wide as if startled to see them. He was, she thought, a very good actor. Only a flash of dimples gave him away.

Shei-Luin sat up and beckoned him. Once more the Songbird's gaze dropped modestly—but not before a delighted glance flashed at Murohshei. A smile creased Zyuzin's face, round as a full moon. He approached quickly, and bowed to her as the mother of the heir.

"Lady," he said. Once more the dimples appeared, this time to stay. "Shall I play for you?"

Shei-Luin nodded, stifling a sigh of regret that he couldn't sing for her. But the Songbirds of the Garden of Eternal Spring raised their voices in performance only for the emperor. Even this much was daring; some of the more conservative ministers would demand that punishment be meted out. But Shei-Luin knew Xiane. Even more, she knew her hold over him—a hold that would only grow now like a *chual* vine overtaking its tree.

So she laid her head in Murohshei's lap once more, listening as Zyuzin settled himself and plucked the strings of his *zhansjen*. Its sweet melody spilled over her.

"Precious Flower!" an all-too-familiar voice brayed from beyond the peach trees. "Preee-cious Flower, where are you?"

For once Shei-Luin didn't wince at the sound of that voice. Indeed, she welcomed it. Murohshei helped her to sit up; she knelt, sitting upright on her heels as was her privilege. Both eunuchs touched their foreheads to the ground. But, like them, she could not look directly at Xiane before others. Such was not her right. Not yet.

But it would be. She glanced through the curtain of her lashes, watching and waiting.

Xiane hove into sight, his robes flapping about his long arms and legs as he made for her, waving a sheet of rice paper in his hand. Ministers trailed after him, their faces registering varying degrees of bafflement and displeasure. Lord Jhanun, she was pleased to see, was the most annoyed of all. She bowed her head demurely as Xiane halted in front of her.

"Is it true, my Flower?" he asked in delight.

She rested her hands across her belly. "It is, Phoenix Lord. I consulted the Revalator this morning. If she is right, I carry another son for you."

A hushed gabbling broke out among the ministers. She peeked at them. Most looked pleased; only one heir could mean trouble, children died so easily. Some looked vinegar-faced at the news; this would give her more power than she had before. But only one betrayed no emotion, and by that Shei-Luin knew that whatever plot Jhanun brewed, she'd thrown a large obstacle in his way. She hoped it choked him.

Fingers slid under her chin and raised her face. She dared to meet Xiane's eyes then.

"I remember my promise, Precious Flower. If this child is indeed a boy, I will make you my empress," Xiane breathed.

Ignoring the surprised gasps of the ministers, Shei-Luin said, "It will be another son for your glory, Phoenix Lord. I'm certain."

I am very certain. Yesuin does not father girl-children.

She smiled up at Xiane. Now would this *chual* vine climb like never before.

Damn, Liasuhn thought as Nalorih and Kwahsiu turned off the road and made for a copse of trees and the travelers' shelter within, *we're this close to the imperial city, and we're stopping to camp instead of pressing on.*

He couldn't wait to see the city of the emperor. While

Kwahsiu had laughed when asked if the streets really were paved with gold, Liasuhn was sure it would be the most splendid place he'd ever seen—certainly a far cry from the little river village he'd grown up in. *We're only a few* ta'vri *away, Kwahsiu said, and that was a while ago. Why are we stopping now? The horses could go on for a bit.*

But he was only an apprentice, so he said nothing, just turned his horse to follow the others. To make up for his disappointment, he grumbled under his breath, careful not to let his masters hear.

When they reached the shelter, Liasuhn was surprised when someone came out. He was even more surprised when Kwahsiu said, "Do you have them?" and the man, instead of being surprised, answered, "Yes."

Nalorih jerked his head at the door. "Go in."

Liasuhn said, "But—"

"Don't argue!" Nalorih snapped. "Move!"

More bewildered than frightened, Liasuhn dismounted and obeyed. As he entered the shelter, the stranger glanced at him, a glance that held no comfort.

Prickles of uneasiness rippled between Liasuhn's shoulder blades. He paused a few steps inside the door, letting his eyes accustom themselves to the dimness. He'd no wish to break his leg tripping over a stool.

First he saw three staffs leaning against the wall. Then something on the rickety table caught his eye. A closer look revealed clothing—three bundles, all the same. He pawed through the nearest. He held up a hooded robe, his confusion growing with every heartbeat.

This was the garb of a Walker priest, one of those who traveled incessantly through the countryside, tending to the folk of places so poor or so small that they didn't have a temple of their own. Priests of the Phoenix they might be, but Walkers were also the lowest of the low, despised by other priests.

The sound of galloping hoofbeats retreating brought him back. For a moment, he thought his masters and the other man had abandoned him here. The thought brought both

fear—what would he do so far from home and alone?—
and a vague relief.

Then Kwahsiu and Nalorih walked through the door, and
relief fled.

"That wasn't fair!" Raven shouted as his wooden practice
sword went flying once more. His face was as red as his
hair. "You're far stronger than any ordinary man, and
you're not holding back!"

Linden sighed. "But I am holding back, Raven. I might
well have broken your fingers, thumb, or even wrist if I
hadn't. But if you persist in letting your thumb slide up as
if you were holding reins instead of a hilt, *anyone* will be
able to knock your sword out of your hand—all they'll
need is the right angle of attack." He ran his fingers through
his hair. "You're too angry to teach at the moment. Why
don't you get one of the weighted metal swords and practice hacking at the leather dummy? That will both
strengthen your wrist, and give you a chance to work off
that temper."

For a moment Linden thought Raven would refuse. But
the younger Yerrin stalked off across the sand of the indoor
riding ring they used for weapons practice. He chose a
sword, and went off to the other end where a well-padded
dummy wrapped in stiff leather and mounted on a stout
pole awaited him.

Shaking his head, Linden turned to where Maurynna sat
on the sidelines, watching. "Your turn, love. Just a quick
bout—we're nearly done for the day—and then you can go
get that bath I know you want."

Grimacing, Maurynna heaved herself to her feet and
picked up her practice sword. She stopped in front of him,
sword raised, knees slightly flexed.

"Good, love, good," Linden said. "Ready?"

"As ready as I'll ever be."

"Good." And with that, Linden's sword swung down at
her head.

To his relief, hers flashed up to block, parry, and dart in

for an opening. He met it, then tested her again and again
and again. Each time she caught his sword on her own. He
knew he drove her hard; sweat dripped down her face. But
by the gods, he'd make damn certain that if she couldn't
depend on Raven, she could rely on herself.

If only he could find some way to go with her. . . .

Taren watched, amused, from the shadows of the stable
aisle that led to the indoor ring. Ah, such gentle barbs he
could slip into the young fool tonight, inflaming his anger
with the big Dragonlord even more. A little more and, if
necessary, he was certain he could get Raven to betray at
least Linden Rathan once they were in Jehanglan.

It promised to be a most amusing evening. He slipped
deeper into the shadows as the session came to an end, but
kept watching. After they put their swords away, Linden
Rathan and Maurynna Kyrissaean exchanged a quick kiss,
and she left the ring by one of the other doors. He went to
the water bucket which sat on the bench by the wall.

Raven still swung at the dummy. But as Linden Rathan
bent to drink, the young Yerrin stopped to watch him. Then
he walked briskly across the sand.

Puzzled, Taren said nothing. But he kept his eyes open.

"So, you've found them," Kwahsiu said. "Put them on."

"But these are the robes of a Walker," said Liasuhn.
"Why do I have to wear them?"

"Don't ask questions," Kwahsiu snapped. "Just put them
on."

Liasuhn had half a mind to refuse until he got an answer.
But Nalorih took a step forward, his expression hard as
granite. Even Kwahsiu wasn't smiling for once.

Suddenly afraid, Liasuhn clutched the robes to his chest
as if they might protect him. What had become of his two
jolly traveling companions? They were gone now, replaced
by men as dangerous as angry tigers.

"Put them on," Kwahsiu repeated.

"Or else," Nalorih said. A knife appeared in his hand. It

looked cold and deadly and hungry for blood. So did Nalorih.

The weapons session over, Linden bent over the bucket
sitting on the bench and splashed water on his face to wash
the dust off.

"Brrrr!" The water, drawn from a deep well, was still icy
cold. Linden pushed his damp hair back from his face and
fumbled, eyes squeezed shut, for the towel. As his hand
patted the bench where he thought it was, his clan braid
slid over his shoulder and tickled his fingers.

Curse it all, where was the blasted thing? He could have
sworn the damn towel was right—

His ears caught the sound of quick, stealthy footsteps
coming up behind him. A sudden prickling along his spine
made him pause, hand still outstretched. The footsteps
stopped, and at just the right distance, he guessed: too far
away to grab at a wrist, but just close enough . . .

Moving slowly and deliberately, Linden straightened,
wiped his eyes with his knuckles, and turned.

He looked down at the sword pointed at his chest; then
his eyes met Raven's. Fury blazed back at him.

Shaking, Liasuhn undressed and pulled the priest's robes
on as quickly as he could. When he was done, Kwahsiu
jerked the hood up.

Nalorih picked up a silk scarf that Liasuhn had dropped.
He tossed it into the air. As it fell, the knife darted out like
a living thing and slashed at the scarf.

For a moment Liasuhn thought Nalorih had missed. But
two bits of blue silk, not one, fluttered to the floor.

The thought of a knife that sharp made Liasuhn's stomach turn.

"Once Nalorih and I have donned our robes, we're all
going on a little journey," Kwahsiu told him. "Stay between
us, keep your face hidden, don't make any trouble, and you
don't get hurt. Understand?"

Liasuhn nodded; his teeth chattered so hard now that he

couldn't speak. But to his relief, Kwahsiu was satisfied with that.

"Good. Very good."

Fury at him, yes, but there was more for Raven himself as the deadly point fell away.

Raven watched him, half defiant, half terrified at the enormity of what he'd almost done. "You could have me hanged for that," Raven said, his voice harsh as a crow's. But he stood straight and proud as he spoke.

"Why? I wasn't in any real danger, was I?"

Raven cast the sword away. "You know I wanted to! Or do you think I'm too afraid to kill a man?" Anger warred with guilt in Raven's face. Guilt won, followed by shame.

"No, I believe that, if necessary, you could kill to defend yourself and Maurynna. But you're not a murderer," Linden said quietly, "nor are you a coward to stab a man in the back." He looked around and caught up the towel. As he wiped his face dry, Linden said, "As for wanting to, I can well believe you thought you did. Just as I once thought I wanted to kill my father when I was young. But we both knew it would solve nothing; you this day, myself so long ago."

Raven stared back at him, shocked. As well he should be, Linden thought; kinslaying was one of the heaviest of sins for a Yerrin clansman. Even threatening kin with a weapon might be cause for expulsion from a clan if the elders decreed it. Linden smiled grimly as he saw Raven's gaze drop to the clan braid that had fallen over his chest.

"No, I didn't raise the blade I held that day, so I wasn't outcast; I wear my braid honestly, Raven."

Linden licked his lips before going on. This was not a thing he was proud of; he had not told anyone since he'd confessed to his sister Fawn centuries ago.

"My Da was always at me, always trying to start an argument so that he could win—as he saw winning. And since he would take the opposite side from me no matter what, of course he never won by convincing me. Gods help me, I honestly believe that had it come to an argument about where the sun would rise the next morning, he would have said 'west' to my 'east' just so he could have a fight. They always ended, you see, with his knocking me into the nearest wall when I wouldn't give in. When you're a child, it's hard to argue when you're crying too hard to speak. That was how he 'won'—until I was big enough to hit back, that is. And if I refused to play his games, he'd keep after me and after me until I broke and fought.

"But one day . . . One day I had a knife that my little cousins had dulled almost beyond hope with digging in the stony ground of our keep. The knife was my eldest brother's, and I knew Oriole and Thistle would get a whipping for well-nigh ruining it. So I took it to sharpen before their father found out. But my father found me first, and started on me, I don't even remember for what now. Whatever it was, he wouldn't give up."

Linden shut his eyes for a moment, caught up in the old anger, the all-too-well remembered feeling of his stomach churning with frustration and fury. He almost forgot Raven was there. His voice sounding distant and hard even in his own ears, Linden went on, "I don't know why that day was different, why that one time of all the times the same thing happened, it was just too much. But may the gods help me, I wanted to slash out at him, to drive him away once and for all. Even if it meant killing him. Instead, I pressed the blade against my own wrist, harder and harder. I wanted to hurt him—but I couldn't. He was my father, no matter how angry he made me. So I showed myself a little of how much it would hurt, and told myself I couldn't do that to my own father."

Linden laughed harshly and shook his head. "I was lucky Oriole and Thistle had done such a good job of dulling the blade. I'd have opened my veins by accident and spilled my life's blood—for what? Some bit of stupidity I don't even remember now."

"He didn't bring you to the clan elders?"

Linden snorted with laughter. "D'you know, I don't think

he ever realized the *why* of what I was doing. Was he too conceited to conceive of someone wishing him ill? Was he too stupid? Or did he just not want to see it, because he would have had to bring me up before the elders at the next clan gathering? He saw only that I was apparently trying to kill myself, and it frightened him, because I think that deep inside, he did love me even though I was a disappointment to him, sickly little thing that I was then.

"But, gods, how I wanted to kill my father in that instant." Linden eyed Raven with a touch of envy as he tossed the towel he still held over his shoulder. "At least you don't have that burden on your soul."

"Some would say what I wanted was as bad," Raven countered.

Linden raised an eyebrow. So Raven wasn't about to let himself off lightly. "Were you set to kill a Dragonlord—or a rival?" The expressions passing over the young Yerrin's face told him what he'd suspected. "So you felt the same way ten thousand other disappointed suitors have felt about their rivals. As long as you do nothing worse than that, no harm done. Stop beating your breast and heaping ashes over your head, Raven. It's over, and I'll say naught about it if you don't, either. Done? Good. Now that's no way to treat a weapon, so why don't you clean it off and put it away, and we'll work together with the wooden swords for just a bit longer."

Raven nodded and went off for the weapon he'd cast aside. He picked it up, staring at it a moment as if it were tainted; then, his gaze still fixed on the blade in his hand, he said, "Do you— Do you think that if . . ." A flush spread across his pale cheeks.

"That if Maurynna weren't a Dragonlord, that the two of you might have wed? Yes, I do; her heart would have been free then." At Raven's quick look, Linden said gently, "She had no choice, you know, nor did I."

"What if, if I had . . ." The blade flashed as the younger man turned it to and fro.

"You would have destroyed her as well."

Raven came back, the sword carefully pointed down and away from Linden.

"I can't stop caring for her just like that," said Raven with a last burst of defiance.

"I don't expect you to," replied Linden. "It's only because you *do* care so much that I'm willing to let her go with you as her only bodyguard."

And if you only knew how much that hurts—and frightens—me, he nearly said. Instead he said as calmly as he could, "Nor do I want you two to cease being friends. That would sadden Maurynna no end.

"Now, once we get the practice swords, I want to work on your blocking. . . ."

Taren leaned against the wall, his knees weak. By the Phoenix, he'd thought that damned young fool would kill the Dragonlord! That would not do. Taren had no love for Dragonlords, but these four must reach Jehanglan so that the words of the Oracle were fulfilled.

Luckily neither man had seen him hiding in the shadows of the doorway. So caught were they in their private drama that he'd been able to retreat with no one the wiser.

Taren pushed away from the wall and left as quietly as he came. Amusing as it was to create mischief between the boy and his betters, Taren knew it had to end. He didn't know why Raven hadn't plunged the sword into the Dragonlord's unprotected back when he'd had the chance, or what the two men had spoken of so quietly and with such passion, but he couldn't take the chance that further veiled baitings and false sympathy might push the younger Yerrin into the murderous folly he'd so narrowly avoided just now.

It would have been deliciously ironic, though, Taren thought with a wry smile, if he'd yelled a warning and so earned Linden Rathan's—and Maurynna Kyrissaean's—undying gratitude.

Damn. He could have made good use of that.

*   *   *

The walk to the imperial city was long and dusty. Though Liasuhn wished for some water, he didn't dare ask if they could stop and search for a stream or spring. His world had changed so rapidly that he scarcely knew up from down anymore. So he licked his dry lips and suffered in silence.

Only once were any words exchanged. Nalorih said, "Think you it will be dark enough when we arrive, brother?"

Kwahsiu looked at the westering sun and replied, "Likely. But we'll take the long route just to make certain. That will also give us a chance to see if anyone follows."

Dark enough for what, Liasuhn nearly cried. And why would anyone follow us?

He wasn't certain he could stand the answer.

The sun was setting as they entered the city he'd waited so long to see. But he saw nothing of its glories; Kwahsiu and Nalorih led him through the poorest quarters in the failing light. They moved swiftly, as men who knew their destination well, but always one or the other was close to his side or right at his back. Once, when Liasuhn hesitated at the mouth of a dark, narrow alley that stank of piss and vomit, the tip of a knife pricked his spine. Liasuhn scuttled forward, heedless of the foul stuff underfoot. At least no one accosted them; a Walker's fighting skill with his staff was well known.

It was almost full dark by the time they came out into a street of dingy shops. Now the pace picked up. They moved swiftly, each new street an improvement over the old as the shops became larger and more prosperous. Many were shutting for the night as they passed. Once, when they passed a shop selling fried bean cakes, Liasuhn's stomach growled, demanding food.

Kwahsiu laughed, saying, "Wait. You'll have better than that swill soon enough. *Much* better."

Liasuhn struggled to understand what was happening to him. Why the disguises? Why must no one see him? Where were they taking him—and for what reason? And why did they threaten him one moment and promise him good things the next?

So fogged was his mind that they were well into an area of walled compounds before Liasuhn realized it. His captors kept to the back ways that the tradesmen used, but even these "alleys" would have been fine roads back in his village. From the way Kwahsiu and Nalorih quickened their pace, he sensed they were near their goal. The thought so terrified him that he nearly broke and ran. Better the knife than whatever horror waited for him.

Somehow they guessed. Before he could do anything, his companions grabbed his arms and dragged him to a gate in a wall. It swung open; someone had been waiting for them. Liasuhn remembered the man from the traveler's shelter. Kwahsiu pushed him and he fell through the gate.

Hands caught him, hustled him along a path lit by paper lanterns. They met no one else. Then they were at a second gate, this one set in a palisade of bamboo. Fighting a way through the tumbling confusion that was his mind now, Liasuhn realized that this must lead to a private guest house within this compound. He'd heard of such things; whoever owned this was a wealthy merchant indeed—or even a lord.

Then they were through that gate as well. The scent of jasmine enveloped him; he had a hazy impression of a dark garden, and heard water somewhere nearby. The gate shut behind him, and Kwahsiu and Nalorih dropped his arms at last.

"Why?" Liasuhn found the courage to ask at last. He rubbed his aching arms.

"You're to do our lord a great service. Come," Nalorih said, and led the way into the garden.

Liasuhn had no choice. He followed, Kwahsiu close behind.

Their footsteps drummed hollowly as they passed over a little footbridge. Liasuhn could make out the darker form of a house against the night. Then a door opened, and light spilled out and across the lawn.

He was almost beyond terror as he went through the

door. Once inside, he stopped in confusion. Was this nightmare or dream? This might be the bower of the Flower
Princess of legend, it was so beautiful. Overwhelmed by
the room, he didn't notice anyone in it until Kwahsiu
yanked his hood back, and a voice said, "Incredible. Were
he older, he could almost pass for Xiane. You've done
well."

Liasuhn gaped at the speaker as Kwahsiu and Nalorin
bowed low to him. The man stared back at him, coldly
amused. One hand toyed with his long mustache. He wore
the brocade robes of a noble; as he moved, the light rippled
over the heavy silk.

"You have been brought here to perform a task for me,"
the lord said. "I think you will not find it onerous. Obey,
and you will be treated like a prince." He turned his head
slightly and called, "Zuia!"

From another room came two women, one herding the
other, younger, woman before her. Liasuhn's heart pounded
in fright when he saw the second. Brocade robes, pale skin,
and soft hands that had never known harsh labor in the sun
marked her as noble—and her face was uncovered. He,
Liasuhn, commoner, had looked upon her. He could die for
that.

Or, worse yet, lose his balls. Liasuhn moaned in terror.

But the lord called for neither his death nor his castration.
Instead he motioned for the first woman—a servant by her
dress—to bring her charge forward. She pushed the young
noblewoman so that she was only a few feet from Liasuhn.
When the girl tried to shield her face from his gaze, the
servant slapped her hands down. Tears ran down the pale,
pretty face.

The lord moved so that he stood off to one side between
them. "This is my niece," he said. "As you see, she is quite
comely, so your duty will be a pleasant one. You will get
her pregnant."

The girl cried out in shock.

At the lord's nod, the servant seized the shoulders of the
girl's robe and tore it from the young woman's body. Only

a silk loincloth now covered her nakedness. She sobbed piteously as she tried to cover her body with her hands.

Liasuhn's jaw dropped. "Whaa—"

"You heard me." The noble moved toward the door as he spoke. The others drifted after him. "Get her pregnant. You know how it's done, of course, or my men would not have brought you here.

"And don't think to play the virtuous hero. She is now a virgin. If she still is when Zuia returns in the morning, it will be very much the worse for you." The quiet menace in his voice sent a shiver down Liasuhn's spine.

With that warning, the noble left. The others followed.

The door shut; Liasuhn heard the key turn in the lock. The girl stared at him with wide, frightened eyes like a deer's, her robe puddled around her feet. For a moment he considered disobeying, she looked so pathetic.

But he remembered the danger in her uncle's voice, cold as steel, and knew what he had to do. Unfastening his robe, he let it fall to the floor. Next he loosened his breeches. They followed the robe.

She wailed and cowered back, one small hand raised to fend him off.

"I'm sorry," he said. Then he reached for her.

Twenty-eight

The months that followed passed in a haze of activity. Almost every day, the troupe practiced either in the meadow, if the weather was good, or in the enormous covered riding ring. Sometimes Lleld declared a holiday, but they were few and far between. They all knew that they hadn't much time.

*   *   *

"So how does a fire-breather breathe fire anyway, O Lady Mayhem?" Linden asked one day after Lleld and Jekkanadar flopped to the ground, tired from a few candlemarks of tumbling and ropewalking. "Were there any in your family's troupe?"

"Eh? Ah, that's right—we have to turn you into a fire-breather in this form. Pity you can't just Change. . . . Yes, we had a fire-breather for a time. He would never tell anyone what he used; said it was a secret of his brotherhood.

"But this is how he'd start." Lleld caught up the waterskin, took a small swig, then, moving away from the others, pursed her lips, and spat the water out in a fine spray. She pantomimed sticking a brand into the mist. When the water was gone, she wiped her chin—for some water had dribbled down it and onto her tunic—and said, "It was something like that. And even if Linden doesn't get it quite right, it doesn't matter. The fire won't hurt him."

"But if we don't know what fire-breathers use for the spray, how—" Taren began.

Linden laughed. "I'm a Dragonlord, remember? If it can burn at all, I can make it burn hotter and faster."

"Cooking oil, then?" Maurynna said.

"Feh," Linden said, making a face. The thought of a mouthful of oil did not appeal to him. A pity he couldn't make water burn, but that was beyond even a truedragon's magic.

Raven jumped up. "I'll get some from Cook," he said, and whistled Stormwind over. He leaped up onto the Llysanyin's bare back and galloped off.

"Hell of a rider," Linden said in admiration, watching.

"If he doesn't go to his aunt after all this is over, I'll kick him," Otter said, chewing on a grass stem.

When Raven returned, Linden took the small flask of oil from him and, catching up a twig from the ground, went to stand a few feet away. He took a small mouthful of the oil, then, with a silent command, set the end of the twig alight. Mimicking Lleld, he spat oil and air out in as fine a spray as he could, and at the same time he touched the twig to the mist, he ordered the oily mist to burn.

The results were spectacular, even from where he stood. From the delighted shrieks, he thought it must look even better from the audience. Some of the oil dribbled down his chin, but no harm done, he thought.

Then the wind shifted, and the fire burned back toward him. A moment later, the oil upon his chin caught fire and dripped down onto his tunic, setting it aflame as well. He ordered the fire to cease, but it was too late. He looked ruefully down at his ruined tunic.

From the sidelines, Lleld remarked thoughtfully, "I think this needs a bit of work, Linden."

Near the end of the winter, Maurynna took her place in the raised seats in the riding ring with Linden, Lleld, Jekkanadar, and Taren. Finally, she thought, Linden, Otter, Raven, and the Llysanyins were about to reveal what they'd worked so hard on all this time. "Where are Otter and Raven?" she asked.

"Down there," Linden said, pointing to the far end of the ring.

Sure enough, both men stood on either side of the open doors to the stable, Otter with a Yerrin *taeresan* and its beater, Raven with an Assantikkan *zamla*, its gaudy strap bright across his chest.

Then Otter began a beat. Maurynna thought it sounded familiar, but it wasn't until Raven came in with the complicated counterbeat that she recognized it.

"The Dance of the Red Ghost!" she said at the same time Jekkanadar cried, "*Takka nih Bahari*! I haven't heard that in far too many years!"

Then she forgot all else as Nightsong, Shan, Hillel, and Jhem entered the ring at a slow, controlled canter. They circled the ring, then, as the beat changed, turned into the circle, met in the center, reared up, and reversed direction.

She gaped in wonder as the Llysanyins danced, obeying no orders, just the beating of the drums. From time to time she was aware that Linden whispered to her.

"That slow trot with the pauses between each step is the *shallinn*; if they stayed in place, it would be called a *ver-allinn*."

At one point the Llysanyins wove a daisy chain, passing back and forth in a slow canter. "Look! They're skipping!" she said.

Muffling his laughter, Linden replied, "They're changing leads with every step."

"I don't care what it is, it's beautiful. All of it's beautiful."

"Let's hope the Jehangli think so as well."

All too soon the spectacle came to an end. The four Llysanyins lined up to face them; as a drum roll signalled the end of the song, they sank down upon their haunches, their forefeet raised. Maurynna recognized it as the menacing pose Shan had adopted last summer when a Cassorin noble had threatened Otter with flogging. They held the not-quite rear—*"Nilurn,"* Linden whispered—then, as the Dance of the Red Ghost ended with the traditional four measured drumbeats, the Llysanyins jumped forward with each beat, their forefeet lashing out but never touching the ground.

Then it was over, and they were horses once more. Shan came to the seats. Linden tossed him an apple from his belt pouch.

"For once, crowbait, you deserve it. That was perfect." He turned to Taren. "How do you think the Jehangli will like it?"

Taren shook his head, his eyes still wide with wonder. "I've never seen anything like it. My lord, be prepared to fend off offers of cartloads of gold for them."

Linden laughed. "We'll fend those off if they come; as long as it opens doors for us, we should do well."

Maurynna saw Lleld climb over the railing and drop down. "Where are you going?" she called as the little Dragonlord trotted to the stables.

"My turn," Lleld called back, "mine and Miki's. Watch."

Maurynna sat back in her seat and took Linden's hand.

"This should be fun," she said.

"More likely terrifying," Linden grunted. "You've never seen Lady Mayhem's act, have you? If she ever slips . . ." He shook his head.

He was not, Maurynna decided a little later, exaggerating. She hoped the Jehangli were not faint of heart. Then she hid her eyes again.

Spring was in the air, in the red buds sprouting on the maple tree outside the riding ring. It was time to move on to Assantik. Maurynna sent word to her kin in Tanlyton to arrange a ship for them. When it was ready, Jekkanadar Changed, and flew to Assantik to remind the Dawn Emperor of his agreement.

Upon his return, he mindcalled Lleld. The troupe gathered together in the field for the last time to await his coming.

"What word?" Lleld asked as soon as her soultwin had landed and Changed once more to human form.

"All is arranged," Jekkanadar said quietly. "As soon as we reach Nen dra Kove, the ship will sail for Jehanglan."

Twenty-nine

"Gilly!"

The shout pulled Gilliad al zefa' Mimdallek from the mental calculations that occupied her mind as she walked. In a bemused way, she noticed she'd passed the tea seller's. She really must pay more attention when she walked.

Then the matter of hearing her name came back to her. She paused, certain she'd imagined it, as the throngs of Nen dra Kove swarmed past her. Then, louder, this time desperate: "Gilliad!"

She turned. One of her cousins, Mossuran al zef Mimdallek, pushed through the crowded street after her, heedless of whom he elbowed aside. She blinked in surprise;
that was not like this particular cousin. Neither was the
frown that darkened his chubby face.

He wasn't supposed to be in Nen dra Kove; his place
was as House Third in the capital city of Zarkorum. Judging
by his evident exhaustion and dust-streaked clothes, Mossuran must have ridden almost nonstop from there. Something was very wrong.

Her former pleasant distraction evaporated. Gilliad
fought her way against the river of bodies that flowed in
the opposite direction. "Mossuran—what is it?" she called.

When he caught up to her he said nothing, just grabbed
her elbow and angled her off to the side. She saw he was
making for a *tekeral*, one of the tiny pockets of parkland
that dotted Nen dra Kove, an oasis of green in the over-
whelming heat.

This one was empty save for two old men sitting on a
bench beneath a huge jasmine bush. A battered game board
lay between them. They didn't even look up from their
game of goats and jackals as Gilliad and Mossuran cast
fleeting shadows across it.

Mossuran led her to another bench, this one under a
stately date palm. He collapsed rather than sat, breathing
heavily. His dark skin was a sickly shade of grey. "That
damned madman's back," he said without preamble. "He's
in Zarkorum."

It took Gilliad the space of a few heartbeats to understand
him.

"What!" She felt sick. What in the ninety hells of Udasah
was that Kelnethi madman doing back in Assantik? In Zarkorum especially? Had he come to tell House Mhakkan that
she traded with Jehanglan in defiance of the Dawn Emperor's grant?

If he did, then that was the end of House Mimdallek.
That was not a thing she would allow, even if she spent
the rest of eternity beneath Danashkar's poisoned claws.

In her fright she must have spoken the last aloud, for Mossuran shook his head.

"I don't think you have to worry about Danashkar any more, Gilliad—if indeed you ever did. I saw Taren Olmeins myself, and he looked as sane as any man that ever I saw."

"You think then—" She couldn't finish.

He met her eyes, and nodded. "He was shamming before. He knew, cousin; he *knew* what strings to tug, just as if we were shadow puppets and he the puppet master. I don't know how he managed the frothy spittle and the bloodshot eyes, but I'm now certain that they were faked. The man is no more mad than you or I." Mossuran drew a deep breath. He turned pleading eyes upon her; his voice quavered as he asked, "So now what do we do?"

She wished for a partner with a little more steel in his backbone than Mossuran, but he was all she had. She explained with a patience that barely hid her own fear, "If he's here to inform on us, we'll have to send the next shipment out as quickly as possible. That will do two things: get rid of the evidence, and get Afrani and his crew out of the reach of the emperor's torturers. Get word to them; tell them to sail north to Thalnia after they've delivered this shipment and bide there for a while."

She was not afraid of the emperor's torturers for herself or Mossuran; their rank within House Mimdallek would protect them against one outlander's word if there was no evidence to be found. But the sailors and farmers were another tale. . . . She did not betray her quietly mounting fear; that would only panic Mossuran. Best to pretend she'd prepared for such a contingency.

"But the hold isn't full yet," Mossuran objected. "And there are more on the way; we weren't supposed to send the ship out for another tenday." His voice was steadier; as she'd known he would, Mossuran took strength from her calmness.

Gilliad sighed, playing her part to the utmost. "Mossuran, it's not as if there will never be more silkworms and mulberry trees. The Tah'nehsieh will understand. I will ride to intercept whatever is on its way from the farms to the secret cove. I will burn it myself if necessary, and tell the farmers to hide in the hill country. If we play this round well, this is merely a setback; we can still destroy House Mhakkan's stranglehold on Jehanglan."

Mossuran nodded. "Very well, then. But what about Taren Olmeins?"

That surprised her. "You have to ask?" she demanded. "He dies."

Her cousin threw his hands into the air. "That's just it, Gilly; there's no way to get to him! I saw him come off a Thalnian ship—one of House Erdon's—myself. He was with a group of people. Three Yerrin men, two young, one much older; a small woman or girl, I couldn't tell which from that distance; an Assantikkan man; and another woman who looked like an Erdon—tall, black hair, with that heart-shaped face so many of them have.

"They were met at the dock by a group of men and spirited away. I recognized one of the men in that group, even out of uniform; it was Barduun al zef Kisharrek—a captain in Chakkarin's personal guard!"

Gilliad swayed. Taren Olmeins under the Dawn Emperor's protection? House Mimdallek was doomed indeed! She caught herself, knew she'd come close to fainting, dug her fingernails into her legs to ward such weakness off.

So much for the Tah'nehsieh shaman's assurances, she thought, *that no ill would befall my House from this. What would Zhantse predict now? The same?* Bitterness filled her, tasting like bile on her tongue.

She stared at the designs painted in henna on the backs of her hands, not really seeing them. One moment they were blurs before her eyes; the next they snapped back into focus. If the worst was come upon House Mimdallek, revenge was all she had.

And she could not have it. But she would do all she could to save her House. She got to her feet.

"Come. There's much to do, and not much time to do it, cousin."

* * *

The Phoenix Lord hunted this day.

Xiane Ma Jhi drew the bow back and sighted. An instant later the string slid off the thumb ring he wore and flew toward its target. He reined in his horse.

The arrow took the buck just behind the left foreleg. It sprang into the air and cried out, then crumpled to the ground.

The other hunters pulled up around him and whooped in congratulations; Xiane smiled at the honest praise. If only he could spend all his time riding through the pine forests like this! There were no lies in the hunt.

"Well done, Majesty!" Yesuin called. He rode up, wine-skin in hand, and held it out with a grin. "As sweet a shot as I've ever seen."

The others, from grizzled general to the tracker's apprentice, all nodded. Their murmurs echoed Yesuin's words. "Well done, indeed!" "Damn nice shot!" "A prize buck!" "Good shooting!"

Xiane took the skin and let cherry wine slide down his throat in a long, bloodred stream. He wiped his chin and handed the wineskin back. "Thanks to you, cousin," he said. "That trick you showed me worked. For once, the string slid off the thumb ring smoothly. The arrow didn't jerk up when it left the bow as it usually does."

Old General V'Choun pulled his long white mustache. "Best get it bled," he said. He motioned to the tracker and his young apprentice.

They bowed and trotted across the clearing, leaping fallen tree trunks. Xiane set his horse to amble after them; the others followed.

Suddenly, when the two servants were only a few *vri* from the fallen buck, the man's head jerked to the left. For a long moment he stared into the thick woods there. Then he screamed in terror, grabbed his apprentice, and ran back. Xiane stopped in astonishment.

"Phoenix help us! Majesty, get back!" the tracker shouted.

Surprise dulled Xiane's wits. "Wha—" he began.

Then he saw it.

A huge green serpent glided from the thick underbrush and flowed across the ground to the buck. Nearly twenty *vri* long, its body was as thick as a man's waist; Xiane had never heard of a snake so large. Once, twice, three times it circled the dead animal. The buck glowed with a golden light; the light flared, hurting Xiane's eyes, and died. Then the snake slid over the carcass and, coiling, settled itself as if on a throne. It stared at the men. A forked tongue flicked from between its scaled jaws, and blood dripped onto the buck.

An arrow whizzed past. In the instant it flew by him, Xiane recognized the colors of the fletching. Trust V'Choun to keep his head; the doughty old army veteran had faced worse, Xiane thought wildly, remembering the general's late wife.

The arrow struck full into the scaled throat—and went straight through the serpent. The snake stretched up and up, and opened its jaws, revealing fangs dripping venom, as if it would swallow the entire hunting party, horses and all.

While the man she named "the Demon" splashed and sang in the bathing room, well-pleased with his past night's work, Nama dragged herself from the bed and pulled on a robe. Then she went to the desk and sat. As quietly as she could, she opened a drawer and slid a sheet of rice paper from under the sandalwood matting that covered the bottom.

Nama counted the days since the last moon, then counted them again, and yet again. Numb, she set aside the paper upon which she'd marked the days and the phases of the moon.

No, she had made no mistake. It was true. Bile rose in her throat, and she buried her face in her hands.

"What is that?" Zuia demanded from behind her.

Nama jumped. She had not heard the maid enter the

sleeping chamber. She snatched at the paper and tried to thrust it back into the drawer.

Rough hands pulled it from her grasp. Nama bit her lip while Zuia studied the sheet. At last the maid laughed softly.

"Your courses are late, aren't they?" Zuia asked.

"Yes," Nama whispered.

"So you are with child at last?"

"Yes." She squeezed her eyes shut, trying not to cry. The thought of bearing her rapist's child made her sick at heart.

A hand slapped her face with enough force to snap her head back. She cried out. The tears spilled down her cheeks.

"Fool!" Zuia spat at her. She thrust the sheet in Nama's face. "You should have told me the moment you suspected. Now Lord Jhanun will have to rush his plans."

Nama cradled her stinging cheek in her hand as Zuia hurried out of the sleeping chamber. She heard the maid leave the house, no doubt to apprise her master of the long-awaited event. Nama slumped in the chair.

If only she could cut her wrists or throat. But Zuia had banished anything sharp from the little house after Nama's first attempt to end her torment. She'd botched it; she'd thought all she had to do was slash the blade lightly across her wrists. Now she knew she must go deeper, much deeper, to where the bright red blood of her heart flowed.

That same day all cords and sashes disappeared from the house lest she hang herself. Nama considered tearing the silken sheets into strips and plaiting a rope. But she would never finish before Zuia returned. Besides, what could she cut the silk with? She wasn't strong enough to rip it. And to touch the sheets that stank of the Demon's sweat from, from . . .

She doubled over and vomited again and again. When she was done, she wiped her mouth and sat up once more.

If only I had a friend to help me end my shame, a friend to bring me a knife, a rope, some poison. . . .

The sound of footsteps—many footsteps—and voices

came to her ears. She recognized Zuia's voice, and her uncle's, among them.

They came, as she expected, into the sleeping chamber. Behind came the two men who had brought the Demon into her life. One bore a sword strapped to his back.

At a gesture from Jhanun, the men continued on to the bathing room. The song ended in a frightened squawk. There came the sounds of a struggle and the Demon cursing the men.

Nama listened as the cursing ended in mid-tirade and the sounds of fighting stopped. As the men dragged the Demon, now bound and gagged, from the bathing room, she was too numb to feel much satisfaction at the terror in his bulging eyes as he struggled helplessly in the powerful hands that gripped his arms.

Now he knew what she had felt all this time. It hardly mattered anymore. Somehow she knew that her torment was not ended, not yet. It would only change form as a silk moth changed from caterpillar to moth.

Her uncle caught her chin in his hand. "Now," he said, "you are ready to become Xiane's concubine."

The giant serpent swayed and hissed. Its cold gaze fixed on the men as if it would hypnotize them as lesser snakes were said to hypnotize small birds.

Xiane stared in stupefied horror. Even his horse stood beneath him as if caught in that same paralysis.

The snake reared back to strike. Before Xiane could blink, it faded. For a moment a ghostly image hung in the air; then—nothing.

But the deer he had brought down was now bloated and black, oozing a foul liquid that killed the grass. The breeze shifted; the stench that rolled over Xiane and the others set them all to gagging. The horses neighed in fear and bucked. The men turned their mounts and raced away.

When they neared the camp, Xiane suddenly said, "This is not a thing to speak of."

"Do you hear that, dogs?" V'Choun said to the trackers.

Hear and obey the Chosen of the Phoenix. If your tongues wag, you shall lose them."

The trackers threw themselves to the ground and knocked their foreheads against the earth again and again. "We will not speak," they promised fervently. "May our worthless lives end before we speak."

"Talk," the general said dryly, "and of a certainty they will end. Painfully."

The camp was quiet that night; there were occasional outbursts of talk, even laughter. But they were forced and unnatural, dying quickly. Instead the men stared into the fire for a time, now and again looking fearfully over their shoulders, sitting close together for what comfort they might find against the darkness lowering outside the campfire's reach. They did not stay long by the fire.

When Xiane and Yesuin retired to the tent they shared, the emperor disobeyed his own command and whispered, "What was it? Did you understand the meaning of the snake?"

"No," Yesuin replied, "save that a snake is of things armored; it could mean war, soldiers—Xiane, if you want to know what this and all the other portents we have heard of mean, you must speak with one wiser than I; I know so little. You must send for Lord Kirano, Shei-Luin's father."

"The Blasphemer?" Xiane said, aghast.

Yesuin regarded him. "Is he?" the Zharmatian hostage asked softly. "Xiane, in your heart—is he truly?"

Nama stared down at the bed.

As always, the sleeping silks were turned down in invitation—an invitation the Demon had been only too quick to accept any time of the day or night.

But now he was gone. Where, she neither knew nor cared. She just hoped it was far, far away.

Yet the bed was still here; the bed, and all the horrific memories it held. It mocked her, that bed, with its welcome.

She stretched a hand out to touch the sheets, recoiled as

memory stabbed her. Perhaps she should sleep on the floor. . . .

And have Zuia find her in the morning, and run to tell tales to her uncle? To hear her uncle berate her for endangering the safety of the child—the *invader*—in her womb? Finally, to let a mere piece of furniture defeat her?

A thousand, thousand noes. She crawled into the bed, her heart hammering, remembering all the nightmare days and nights. Defiantly, she blew out the oil lamp, and lay in the darkness, staring up at the ceiling.

As her eyes adjusted to the night, as her terrified body realized that yes, she was alone, finally, gloriously alone in this bed, Nama ran her hands out as far as they would stretch. They touched no one.

She turned on her side. After a long, long time of starting at every little sound, she fell asleep, wondering how long this reprieve would last.

They argued about it for what seemed like a lifetime. But in the end, Xiane gave in. Yesuin dropped his head into his hands as the Phoenix Emperor ordered a servant to bring General V'Choun to him.

Shei-Luin would be furious with him, Yesuin thought, his heart sinking. For if anyone discovered the truth from Lord Kirano, truth that anyone might have for the asking . . .

Ah, Phoenix; why must it be both our danger and our saving that Kirano follows the Way of the Crane Hermit? If he can turn Xiane from this madness of keeping the Phoenix imprisoned, it will save the land. But Kirano will not lie. If anyone asks him if Shei-Luin—

Yesuin shook his head violently to stop the rush of thoughts. To think such things gave them power.

Only one thought comforted him. No matter what was revealed, Xiane would never cast Shei-Luin aside; the emperor loved her too much.

Loved her as much as *he* did. Yesuin bit his lip against the the pain he must never reveal.

Thirty

Yesuin wished Xiane would *not* tell Shei-Luin about her father. But how did one tell the Emperor of Jehanglan "no" when that same emperor announced his intention of informing his "Precious Flower" that he'd sent for her father because it would "no doubt please her so," just as soon as they reached the palace?

How did you tell that emperor that his "Precious Flower" hated the very mention of her father's name? That his favorite concubine had come to him only because the man the world believed was her father no longer wanted her about him after his true daughter had been sent for?

In short, you didn't. You tricked him.

"Will you really tell her?" Yesuin asked.

"Of course," Xiane said, looking surprised. "She should be very happy, don't you think?"

Yesuin said vaguely, "I thought it would make a nice surprise. . . ."

Xiane laughed his braying, raucous laugh. "Cousin—that's a wonderful idea! A surprise it will be."

Generous, maddening, bumbling Xiane; even after that, he somehow let it slip that he thought of sending for Lord Kirano, and word was carried to Shei-Luin. That he had also let slip *who* had suggested it, was abundantly clear the instant Yesuin slipped into Shei-Luin's chamber from the tunnel. Xiane, he knew, would not come here this night; Shei-Luin was far enough advanced in her pregnancy that, by custom, no man could lie with her. They were safe from discovery.

He, though, was not safe from Shei-Luin. She descended upon him like a storm the instant he appeared.

"Are you mad?" Shei-Luin spat. "You must cease this insanity." Though her voice was low, the rage in it scorched him.

Yesuin reached for her. "Beloved, you must understand. The Way has been perverted; the world cannot go on like this. You've heard the tales of disasters in the land. If the Phoenix isn't freed, it will destroy the earth, even as your father—"

"He is not my father and you well know it!"

Scarlet silk flashed as she evaded him. Even with her belly swollen with child, she was grace itself. Shei-Luin paced like a tiger, her dark eyes blazing. Were he to touch her now, he thought, she would throw off sparks like a cat.

"I understand that you would destroy my son's empire." Back and forth, back and forth. "You speak of disasters! There are disasters only because the man who sits upon the Phoenix Throne is weak and sinful. He doesn't observe custom, and that's the only reason the Way is lost! This nonsense about setting the Phoenix free is just that—nonsense. When Xahnu is emperor, there will be no more disasters. Jehanglan will draw strength from him."

Her voice shook with fury. And more: hate. It was like a knife in Yesuin's heart. She whirled to face him.

"You would destroy what should be my son's—our son's," she said. Her lip curled in disdain. "Or are you so greedy for Jehanglan that you would see her torn apart so that your tribesmen may pick over her bones like the mangy jackals they are? Are you so jealous of your son's fortune—"

He cut her off. "You know it isn't true. What are these lies? And as for mangy jackals . . . You lived in our tents, Shei-Luin. You grew up with me. Surely you don't believe these words."

The same words that ached inside him. Once he'd taken an arrow in the leg; tearing its barbed head out had hurt less than Shei-Luin's bitter accusations. What had happened to the little girl he remembered? Had the imperial court corrupted her so much? By the Mother of the Herds, had he a horse between his knees this moment, he would ride away and never return—just as he and Shei-Luin had dreamed of once. But now he knew she no longer shared that dream. And without her it was dead, ashes upon the wind.

"Do you love me?" she demanded suddenly.

What, can you not see my heart in my eyes? Yesuin thought miserably. *Once you could.* "You know that I do," he said, his pain spilling over. "How can you doubt it?"

"And you would do anything for me?"

Honor held his tongue. The question was not unexpected, but he couldn't answer it the way Shei-Luin wanted.

She eyed him, testing his silence. "Then stop telling Xiane this nonsense that the Phoenix must go free. Tell him you and my father are wrong. *Make him believe you.*"

"Beloved," he said, "don't ask me to do that. Anything will I do for you—anything but that. I must follow the Way."

The silence now was hers, hard as stone and colder than a mountain of ice. At last she spoke. "I'm not your beloved," she said in a voice like steel. Her hands cupped her belly. "Never say that to me again. Ever. I *am* a mother, and I will protect my children—even from you, their . . . father." She spat the word like a curse. "Get out. I never want to see you again."

He knew she meant it. Even as a child Shei-Luin had been a very good hater. There was no appeal; she would not forgive him.

Yesuin turned, stumbling for the door to the tunnel, like a man who has taken a mortal blow and not realized it yet. Somehow he was through it, and shut it behind him, though he had no memory of the deed. He leaned against the tunnel wall, heartsick. Yesuin heard the door to the sleeping chamber open and close, and knew Murohshei went in to comfort his mistress.

And where would he find comfort, he thought bitterly as he picked up the little lamp and set off down the dimness of the tunnel.

Suddenly Yesuin knew he could no longer stay in the palace. He slammed a fist into the ancient wood of the tunnel wall and bit his lip against something that was a curse or a sob. He must ride the plains once more or die.

"Oh, damn!" Lleld fumed, pausing as she tugged a brush through her thick, red curls.

"What?" Jekkanadar asked from the bed.

Lleld turned on the chair to face him. "Linden just mind-called me. He went down to make certain the horses were settled for the night, and found Taren's gelding's off hock swollen. He suspects that it kicked out while being raised from the hold, and smashed its leg against the wood of the hatchway."

"And since neither he nor Raven were there—" Jekkanadar said, running a finger along the scar on his face.

"Because Chakkarin's agents instantly swept us away to this inn, and since it's not known we're Dragonlords—" Lleld added, waving the brush.

"The dockhands were not as careful as they might have been, and somehow forgot to mention this little mishap," Jekkanadar finished. He sat up. "Damn, indeed. How long of a delay?"

"A few days at least. Linden wants to be certain that it's properly healed. The last thing we need is for any of the horses to founder on us." She returned to brushing her hair, and fuming.

After a brief silence, Jekkanadar said, "Have you ever thought of what freeing Pirakos will mean to the Jehangli?"

She laid the brush on the little table. She'd always known that one day, one of her companions would ask her that. It didn't surprise her that it was her soultwin. "Yes," she said, "I have."

"They depend upon the power of the phoenix to rule their land."

"Power that's stolen," she pointed out, "from two creatures, both of whom are innocent victims."

"And if that power is broken, chaos will rule."

"I know," she said quietly, "and I wish there was some way to avoid it. But the Jehangli had no right to do what they did all those years ago, and no right to perpetuate it. I'm afraid they're going to have to take their chances like the rest of us."

Jekkanadar held out his hands as if weighing one thing against another. "To interfere or not interfere—which is truly the right course?" he asked, a wry smile on his lean, dark face.

She shook her head sadly. "Were this a bard's tale, I could tell you. But as is all too often true, there's no black or white. We right what wrongs we may, and do the best we can. It's all anyone, truehuman or Dragonlord, can ever do."

And with that, she blew out the oil lamp and crawled into bed. Jekkanadar wrapped his arms around her, and she fell asleep, still wondering what was right.

Thirty-one

The two men sat their horses and looked out to sea, sheltered from the fierce Jehangli sun in a shallow cave scooped by wind and wave from the cliff wall behind them.

Not that the harsh sunlight would have burned either of them. They were Tah'nehsieh, dwellers in the unforgiving desert, children of the red lands, darker than any Jehangli of the Phoenix Empire. But like all who knew the desert and respected it, they spared themselves and their mounts when they could.

One of the men, both younger and lighter of skin than his companion, sniffed the air. He smiled. Strange indeed was the briny tang, the taste of salt upon his lips. But familiar, somehow, and welcome. Perhaps it called to the northern part of his blood, the worlds his mother had told him of: high mountains covered with forests of pine and oak, maple and beech, then a life at sea. He tried to imagine so many trees standing straight and tall, crowded thickly together, crowned with green leaves. It was beyond him. All he saw in his mind's eye were the scrubby trees he knew, the desert pine and scrub oaks near the *mehanso*. Few and far between were those trees, twisted and stunted by wind and sun and drought.

Then he thought of the Vale, and had an inkling of what a northern forest might be.

The other man said, "Do you see it? The ship? If my Seeing was a true one, it left a few days ago and should be here today."

"No, Zhantse," the young man said. "Not y—'Wait!" He shaded his eyes with one hand. Yes, that was a sail. Once again, his master had Seen truly. Not that he'd doubted; Zhantse's visions were never wrong. Hard to understand sometimes, and sometimes mistaken in interpretation, but in the the end, they were never wrong.

He squinted up at the sun and did some quick figuring. "She," he corrected absently, "not 'it.' All ships are female, my mother says." How something that never lived could be male or female was something he didn't understand. His mother had only laughed, and told him that perhaps one day he'd find out. "She'll be here before the sun drops another two hands in the sky."

He cupped his hands to his mouth and called the news to the men waiting in the shadow of the rocks on the beach below. They waved acknowledgment. Most went back to drowsing in the shade.

But why was the ship here? She'd not been due for another span of days or more. Was something wrong? Had some evil befallen their Assantikkan partner? Zhantse had spoken of an uneasiness underlying the vision. . . .

"I wonder if—" He broke off. The air caught in his lungs as if some giant hand crushed his chest. Cold sweat dripped down his bare back and chest.

Panic swept over him. His mind seized on the image of the mountain's worth of rock mere handspans above his head. It was falling, falling to crush him like a beetle under a sandbear's paw.

Run!

His horse responded to the unconscious squeeze of his knees and bounded into the sunlight.

The sudden glare blinded him; his eyes filled with burning tears in protest. He welcomed the pain they brought. For with them passed the sudden madness, the need to run away. He brought his mare to a skittering halt.

Gasping, he leaned on the pommel of his blanket-covered saddle. Spirits help him, what was wrong with him these days?

"Shima!"

The sharp voice penetrated the fog that clouded his mind after each of these panics. He made himself look around, answer calmly. "I—I'm well." He looked away before Zhantse saw the lie in his eyes.

A deep shuddering breath; he looked at the rock cliff stretching up and up to the sky; looked at the older man still sitting his horse in the dimness of the shallow cave, and knew he couldn't go back in there.

The men on the beach had noticed, damn it; he saw them exchange puzzled glances. His father's milkbrother, Nathua, stood up, a worried frown creasing his brow as he brushed the sand from his short kilt. Shima waved him back. Nathua hesitated, clearly minded to investigate for himself.

Shima held his breath. He did not want to try to explain this to his prosaic clan-uncle. Once more he waved Nathua back. He even found a smile from somewhere. To Shima's relief, Nathua shrugged and sat down again.

The shaman rode out into the sun. "Again?" he said. "The Feeling?"

Shima nodded. "Yes. As if the cliff . . ." He shook his head at the images conjured by his mind. "Each time it's as if everything is closing in on me. I have to get *away*."

"I've heard of such a thing before," Zhantse said. "But usually it's a thing that is with you from childhood, or else brought on by some harrowing exerience. Yet I know that no such thing has happened to you. So why?"

"Indeed," Shima said bitterly. "Why? Why do the Spirits torment me this way? One moment I'm well; the next, out the door, and running for the largest open space I can find."

"And then?" Zhantse prompted.

"And then the feeling disappears, and I feel like a fool." *Or a madman.*

Shima passed a hand over his eyes. *Was* he going mad? He didn't think so. Yet it was said the mad never considered themselves to be.

Perhaps he should throw himself from a cliff before it got worse. He couldn't stand the thought of his parents' pain as they watched their oldest son sink into insanity. A clean death would be better. But something inside him shrank from the idea, driving him further into despair.

Coward.

A hand on his shoulder brought him back. He jumped.

"You are not going mad," Zhantse said. "Yes, I know what you've been thinking. I've known you from a child, remember? I can read you like a hunter reads tracks.

"But just what is happening to you, my young drummer, I don't know. I've tried to See, but . . . Something blocks me; there's a window there, but someone has hung a blanket over it. I have only a vague sense. . . ." The shaman frowned. "There's another path before you. But where it leads, I cannot tell. I *should* be able to See. But I can't; I sense . . . change of some kind ahead of you. And that's all I can say."

Shima rolled his eyes at his master and managed a wan smile. "All life is change, Zhantse. How many times have you told me that?"

Despite his wrinkles, Zhantse looked remarkably young and mischievous when he grinned like that, Shima thought. It usually meant trouble ahead—for a certain spirit drummer at least.

The shaman patted that same drummer's shoulder with a fatherly hand. "So you shall have a little more than the rest of us. You're young; you can stand it," the shaman said cheerfully. He urged his horse down the beach, calling back over his shoulder, "You have always wished for an adventure, Shima. Perhaps one is coming."

Shima made a wry face as Zhantse laughed and danced his brown and white gelding in and out of the breaking waves. It was true he often wished for an adventure like those of the ancient heroes of the tribe. But that didn't mean he really *wanted* one. He sighed and sent his mare after the shaman.

At least he needn't fear another attack while under the open sky.

The Phoenix Lord was in a fine temper, Jhanun thought, as Xiane scowled at the troupe of entertainers cavorting in the gardens for his amusement. One youngster was so frightened by that sign of imperial displeasure that he dropped two of the balls he juggled.

Xiane waved a hand. "Take them away. I would see the performing horses instead." He slouched in his chair, muttering, "I hope these can count better than the last ones."

Sturdy young eunuchs moved in and herded the performers away. Jhanun thought he knew the true source of Xiane's bad temper: the concubine Shei-Luin was far enough advanced in her pregnancy that Xiane could no longer go to her. Indeed, even now, preparations were being made to bring her to the Phoenix Pavilion where, by custom, all imperial children were born.

From his spy among the emperor's eunuchs, Jhanun knew that Xiane had called a different concubine to his bed every night for the past moon, and was dissatisfied with all of them.

The time was ripe. Indeed, he couldn't wait much longer. If Xiane didn't take the bait dangled before him, and soon, Nama would have to be disposed of.

He knelt before Xiane. "Your Majesty," he said. "I see

that you are displeased these days, and I think I understand why." He smiled as one man to another.

One corner of Xiane's mouth curved up.

"I know that we've disagreed," said Jhanun, "on the subject of the concubine Shei-Luin, but it grieves me to see my lord so distressed. Alas that my dear, late wife and I never had a daughter that I could offer you as a concubine to ease your cares. But I have a niece that I have caused to be brought to the imperial capital, and I would offer her to you instead. She's a pretty girl, delicate as a butterfly, and as dear to me as the daughter I never had. Will you accept her?"

Xiane considered for so long that Jhanun thought he would refuse. But at last the emperor nodded.

Jhanun fought to keep from betraying his elation. "You honor me, Phoenix Lord. With your permission, I shall have Nama escorted to the quarters of the concubines right away. She'll be so happy."

Xiane nodded once more, this time in dismissal.

Jhanun rose. *Now how to make certain she is brought to him before it's too late. . . .* he thought as he bowed and backed away.

But as he stepped down from the pavilion, the Phoenix smiled upon him.

"Lord Jhanun!"

Jhanun turned back and bowed. "How may I serve you, Imperial Majesty?"

"When your niece is brought to the concubines' quarters, tell them to make her ready for me tonight," Xiane said.

"With the greatest pleasure, Phoenix Lord."

Yes, with the greatest pleasure do I watch the tiger fall into the pit. Thank you, Xiane.

Shima stood with Zhantse and the ship's captain at the top of a dune. As the captain called instructions to his crew, Shima watched his fellow tribesmen tread the narrow path to the cliffs above, heads bent against the tumplines of their packs. Each man bore on his back one precious sapling. They looked like a line of ants.

But there were so few trees this time. And the Spirits only knew when their Assantikkan partners would dare send more. Or even if they ever would again. If the ship's captain—a man they knew only as the Sailor—was right, House Mimdallek might even now be facing the wrath of the Assantikkan emperor.

The last man reached the top of the cliff where the carts waited. Shima listened to the various sounds: Nathua shouting a final order; the rumble of voices; the creak of the wood as the men swung up into the carts to make themselves comfortable among the young mulberry trees for the ride to the Vale. Once there, the men would pack the saplings in along the narrow trail that was the only way in or out of the Vale.

Shouts; the drivers were urging the horses on. The men began a song, a deep-throated chant to encourage the young trees in their new land. The song rolled down the cliff in a shimmering wave of sound, took wings, and flew, a paean of hope to gladden the heart and spirit. Shima listened as it faded into the distance.

Someday that hope would be realized.

He pulled his attention back when it would follow the song and forced it to pay heed to the Sailor, who spoke once again. It rebelled; the Vale was a pleasanter thought. But Shima was stern.

"As I already told you, drummer," said the Sailor, "the return of this Taren Olmeins . . ." His face twisted in fury. "Gods damn him—and me for being fool enough to pick him up. I should have had his throat cut and dumped him overboard then and there no matter what Gil—"

He stopped short; Shima waited until he mastered himself once again. The man went on, "My . . . supplier is in danger." The angry accusation in his voice was like a blow.

The Sailor spoke good Yerrin, though with a heavy accent. Shima answered him hotly in the same language.

"And we told you when all this began five years ago,

that Zhantse has Seen no danger to your partner."

"What says he?" Zhantse demanded in their own tongue. "I can follow a little, but not enough."

Shima translated; Zhantse shook his head.

"Tell him," the shaman said, "tell him that no act of mercy is wasted. I cannot see what part this Taren is to play, but I know that it will bring about great change. Tell him that even now I See no danger to him or his."

Shima passed the message on to the Sailor. The man still looked grim, but Shima could see in his eyes how he longed to believe. At last the Sailor spread his hands out; acceptance or defeat, Shima could not tell.

"It's in the hands of the gods now," said the Sailor as he shrugged. The amulets woven into his many braids clicked together. "And may your shaman have the right of it."

The unspoken *Or else* hung in the air between them.

"He does," said Shima boldly. *I hope.*

"Your litter is ready, Favored One," Murohshei said.

"At last," Shei-Luin snapped. She clapped a hand to her belly as the baby inside her kicked.

"A strong one," Tsiaa said approvingly. "That's well."

Shei-Luin slanted a dark look from under lowered lids at her maid. But Tsiaa only laughed gently at her and helped her up from her chair.

"I know, I know," the maid said as she smoothed Shei-Luin's robe. "You hate this part of a pregnancy. True, it's uncomfortable, but it will soon be over, my lady, and you shall have another fine son."

They walked the short way down the hall to the courtyard of the concubines' quarters. Waiting by an ornate litter were eight eunuch bearers; they bowed when they saw her.

Shei-Luin leaned heavily upon Tsiaa's arm as they crossed the smooth stone paving. Just as they reached the litter, the gate to the courtyard swung open and another litter and its bearers entered. Shei-Luin stopped and stared in surprise, for the closed curtains of the new litter bore the crest of Lord Jhanun.

"Wait," Shei-Luin said when Murohshei drew back the curtain of her own litter, and Tsiaa made to help her in. "I would see what passes here."

She thought furiously. Lord Jhanun was a widower, she knew. Likely his wife found death a blessing after living with that prig, Shei-Luin thought. They had had no children, so this couldn't be a daughter of the house.

The bearers set the litter down. One drew back the curtain and offered a hand to the occupant. A moment later, a young woman—pretty enough, Shei-Luin thought, in a demure way—emerged. Her scarlet and blue gowns were rich with embroidery; Shei-Luin caught a glimpse of a tiny slipper dotted with seed pearls. There was wealth behind this woman, and Shei-Luin knew whose.

So what plan did Lord Jhanun hatch now?

The woman started across the pavement at the urging of the lead bearer. Shei-Luin looked over her shoulder. As she thought—one of the harem eunuchs now came to meet this new denizen. Shei-Luin turned back; her gaze met the new concubine's, and she almost forgot to breathe. She had never seen such emptiness in another's eyes; it was as if this woman's soul had fled. Even as Shei-Luin wondered if this was no human woman but a fox-ghost come to trick Xiane, the other woman stared up at the palace, and all-too-human despair filled her face.

Shei-Luin watched her disappear into the palace before getting into her own litter. As Tsiaa settled in beside her, Shei-Luin said to Murohshei, "Find out who she is."

"I will, Favored One, and then join you at the Phoenix Pavilion," Murohshei said. He bowed, then untied the cord that held the curtain back.

As the interior of the litter went suddenly dim, and the world shrank to four panels of silk brocade, Shei-Luin heard Murohshei clap sharply. Instantly the litter rose up and up, until it came to rest on eight sturdy shoulders.

Then they set off for the Phoenix Pavilion to await the birth of the next Phoenix heir.

"Psst! Hodai!"

Hodai turned from Haoro's sickbed. He tilted his head in question at Tsiru.

The acolyte looked embarrassed. One hand rested on his lower belly. "Um, ah—I don't think I should have eaten that fish." A look of pain flashed across his face. "Would you watch—"

Hodai flapped his hands at him. *Go! Go!*

"Thanks. I'll remember this," Tsiru said even as he hurried for the door. The *thwap! thwap!* of straw sandals against stone floor retreated down the hall.

Hodai went back to studying the hated face, looking for signs of—what? Death? Awakening? Hodai knew what he hoped for, what he feared—and they were one and the same.

Time passed. Hodai listened to the regular breathing, loud in the stillness of the paneled chamber. He fidgeted, shifted from foot to foot, tugged at his robe, all the while wondering when Tsiru would return.

Then he realized that Tsiru hadn't lit the evening incense before leaving in such haste. Sighing in annoyance, Hodai went to the room's altar and, with flint and steel, struck a shower of sparks onto the bed of dried sweet grass that held the disk of incense. The grass caught; tongues of flame sprang up in a mad dance of red and yellow, only to die down almost as quickly. But the smoldering embers were enough to set the incense alight. A wisp of fragrant white smoke rose in the still air of the room.

He returned to the bedside. Once more he studied the hated face. No change; none at—

The eyes opened. Haoro smiled up at him with a skull's evil grin. "Hello, Hodai." The voice was hoarse with disuse, and weak, but it held all the old cruelty, all the terror in it. "Come to see how I'm faring? I'm touched."

Strangled screams caught in Hodai's throat, threatening

to choke him, as he fell back from the bed. His hands beat uselessly against the air.

Haoro laughed a thin, terrible laugh.

Don't even think of telling the emperor what happened.

Nama sat unmoving as Zuia fussed around her, readying her for the emperor's summons. *I am empty inside*, she thought. *There's nothing left to feel with.* She retreated into the place in her mind where nothing touched her. It was a place she'd found during the living nightmare she'd endured. Let Zuia do what she would. . . .

A hissing in her ear brought Nama back to herself. She jumped a little, startled, and looked to Zuia. "What is it?"

The look of angry frustration on the maid's face puzzled Nama at first. Then she understood. Of course; Zuia dared not slap or pinch her lest she leave a mark that the emperor might see. Seeing Zuia so confounded lightened Nama's despair, if only by the weight of a grain of millet. Little enough, true, but Nama clung to any victory she had nowadays.

Zuia thrust her fan at her. "Don't forget this," the maid snarled. "And don't forget what is hidden in it."

Ah, yes; the tiny blade with which she was to cut herself slightly, so that she would bleed as a virgin would. Nama took the loathesome thing from Zuia's hand, handling it as gingerly as she could.

"Above all," Zuia went on, "don't forget to use it. The emperor has bedded virgins before; he knows what to expect."

Somewhere deep inside a spark of rebellion leaped up. "And if I tell the emperor what was done to me?"

Zuja laughed at her, a cruel, cold laugh. "My lord will deny everything. After all, it wouldn't be the first time that a girl who'd played the whore and found herself with child claimed she'd been raped. And even if you were believed, it was your duty to kill yourself when your family's honor was so besmirched. You didn't. So you would be cast out as a ruined woman. Perhaps you could find a brothel to take you in—one that caters to those with . . . exotic tastes. Some men, I've heard, find pregnant women exciting. Or perhaps you would just starve on the street.

"And if that's not enough for you, remember this: if all comes to naught because of you, your family dies. So keep your mouth shut, and play the game my lord Jhanun has set you to. Succeed, and you will be richly rewarded."

Nama shut her eyes in pain. Zuia was right; there was no way out for her. It was even too late to die. Phoenix help her, she was so cold and empty inside. . . .

The little maid in charge of airing out the bed silks appeared in the doorway of the sleeping chamber and bowed. Her eyes were huge. "Lady Nama," she said breathlessly, "the emperor's eunuch is here to take you to the Phoenix Lord." She stared at Nama in awe.

For a moment Nama thought she would faint. Only the thought of her family sustained her. "Tell him I'm coming," she managed to say.

The girl disappeared on her errand.

Refusing Zuia's hand, Nama stood, smoothing her elaborate robes. She looked down at the fan in her hand for a long moment.

She could "forget" it here. Or drop it on the way. Then it would soon be all over. . . .

"Come," ordered Zuia as she left the sleeping chamber.

The fan now tucked securely into the sleeve of her inner robe, Nama followed.

Shima stood by the banks of the Moth, the little river that flowed from the Vale. In its course, it would join two other small rivers, the Yellow Dog and the Crying Woman, to become the Red Horses, which would become the Tiensha when it reached the land of the Jehangli.

Dusk was turning into night, and the air grew colder. But the scent of spring drifted on the breezes at last. Shima wrapped his *jelah* closer, shutting out the cold, shutting out the memories of the day. They haunted him anyway.

What of this matter of the ship coming early? What if it

never came again? There weren't enough mulberry trees yet in the Vale. All the hard work of his people would go for nothing.

Then there was his own problem, petty as it might be in comparison to the possible disaster facing the Vale. The attacks of the Feeling were getting stronger and, worse yet, coming more frequently—much more frequently—of late. Despite Zhantse's reassurance, Shima still wondered if he were going mad.

This was not a thing to bear alone. So he called into the night, "Miune! Miune Kihn! Can you hear me?"

The night breeze teased through his long hair, tugged the fringe of his boots. At his feet, the Moth flowed on.

Somewhere a little desert owl hooted. He watched the river intently, but the water was dark, and hid its secret well.

It was his ears rather than his eyes that gave him the first warning. The sound of the placid rippling changed ever so slightly. Had he not been listening, he would have missed it.

Then the waters at his feet swirled. Bubbles appeared, and suddenly a head many times the size of his own broke the surface, stretching up and up on a long neck and body. Water streamed from the lacy, weedlike fringes that surrounded the head, and two large, round eyes regarded him. From each side of a long snout sprang a feeler the length of a man's arm. One reached for him.

Shima put out a hand and caught the feeler. It curled around his fingers. He sighed in relief. "I'm glad you were close by, Miune."

As am I, my friend. I feel that thee are troubled—what is it?

Shima sat on the bank and told his friend of all that had happened that day.

They entered the imperial chambers at long last. Nama was so frightened that she had passed beyond it into a kind of numbness. So she barely noticed the room around her; later she would remember only an impression of *gold*. Sheets of hammered gold in the image of the Phoenix on every wall, gold silk against dark woods, the golden sashes of the eunuchs who descended upon her, cooing over her like a flock of doves.

The only thing that pierced the fog she walked in was the sight of Zuia being forced into a corner as the eunuchs crowded around. It brought a tiny smile to her lips.

"Ah! How pretty," the oldest eunuch said, clapping his hands in pleasure. "Lips like the petals of a rose! The emperor will be pleased."

It seemed that she passed their inspection, for most fell back from her. Only the three senior eunuchs stayed.

Then the eldest took her hand and led her into the emperor's sleeping chamber. The others followed at her heels like well-trained dogs.

The room was huge, filled with exquisite treasures, but all she saw was the bed in the shadows. It seemed to fill the chamber. Her knees turned to water at the sight of it, and she trembled.

The eunuchs, thinking hers were the fears of a maiden, spoke softly to her, patted her cheeks with smooth, gentle hands. They whispered little encouragements as they slipped the heavy outer robe from her shoulders and bore it away. The door shut behind them.

A man stepped from deep shadows beyond the bed; he came forward slowly. Nama almost screamed at the sight of him. Her uncle's agents had done their work well; the Demon might be twin to this man who stretched out a hand, who ran a finger down her cheek, down her neck, and into the front opening of her robe. Who teased that robe slightly open and traced the curve of her breast. . . .

Was she truly in the emperor's bed chamber, or back in the house of nightmares?

The other hand joined the first, parted her robe, and, with its brother, cupped her breasts.

She could not go through with this. She couldn't! There

was no Zuia to keep her from striking this time. She would scratch his eyes out, she would—

She thought of her family and did nothing.

The hands withdrew. "You're very pretty," the emperor said, his voice soft. "Just as your uncle said. Don't be afraid, little butterfly. I know this is your first time, so I will be gentle."

She knelt before him, accepting all that was to come, her heart a lump of ice within her breast. Her fingers closed upon the fan in her sleeve, and she retreated to the haven within her mind.

Linden studied the gelding as Raven, lead line in hand, trotted it back and forth before him in the stable yard of the inn.

Lleld, sitting on the edge of the watering trough, asked, "So?"

Much as he hated to say it, Linden admitted, "The swelling is gone, and so is the lameness. He's fit to travel again."

"Good. We've been delayed long enough. Tomorrow we set out for Nen dra Kove." She jumped down and dusted the seat of her breeches off. "I know that ship has orders to wait for us, but I want this over with."

Don't we all, Linden thought bitterly. *Don't we all.*

Thirty-two

After a journey of few rests and hard riding, the troupe entered Nen dra Kove in the teeth of a ferocious storm.

"I don't believe it!" Maurynna yelled as the wind tried to snatch her words away. "First Taren's horse, now this!"

"Never mind all that—let's find that inn," Lleld yelled

back. "We'll worry about the weather later. After all, how long can this last?"

"Days!" Maurynna shouted.

A chorus of groans greeted her words. Soaked and weary, the troupe rode through the great port city in search of the inn used by entertainers waiting to board a ship to the Phoenix Empire.

Maurynna slitted her eyes against the blowing rain, and wondered how long the storm would last.

I can't stand this waiting much longer; I want this over with. Then, *I want to go home.*

General V'Choun halted his troops at the eastern bank of the Tiensha, the narrow, shallow river—now barely more than a stream in the long drought—that marked the border between the Western Plains, ruled by the Zharmatians, and Jehanglan proper. Sometimes emperors had pushed the border farther west; sometimes the Zharmatians had forced it back and into Jehanglan. Back and forth the wars raged. Only the boldest or most desperate farmers tried to wrest a living from the fertile soil. This earth was watered with blood.

The soldiers stopped in a jangle of armor and harness. They had covered the distance in little more half the time it usually took. Men and horses were weary to the bone. Their breath steamed in the early morning chill as they formed three lines facing the river. Mist snaked around the horses' feet as they waited, and there was fog before and fog behind. Many of the men looked around uneasily; V'Choun couldn't blame them. If ever there was a perfect time for an ambush, this was it. Two scouts splashed their horses across the river and disappeared into the fog.

V'Choun beckoned. At once Captain Chiand-Tal rode alongside and saluted.

"I'm ready, sir," the captain said. The hand that gripped the staff bearing the green banner of a messenger was steady.

The old general studied the man before him. Every inch

a soldier, V'Choun thought. Just what he liked to see; some of the younger officers nowadays . . . The army was not what it once was. But then, the emperor was not the man his father was. V'Choun regretted that old Xalin had not passed on his own fire and wisdom. He loved Xiane like a son, but Xiane was not—

Bah! Enough of this maundering. That Xiane was now sending for Lord Kirano proved there was hope for him yet. Maybe he would make right the mistake his father had made; it was the only thing Xalin had done that he and V'Choun ever argued over.

V'Choun said, "I thank you, Chiand-Tal, for volunteering for this mission. It's not an easy thing to ride alone into the land of the People of the Horse. But you're a man of the western lands; you've dealt with the Tribe before, have you not?"

A crisp nod. "Yes, sir. I will do my best to—"

The thunder of hooves cut him off. At once the archers split off from the rest of the troop, to flank it with bows drawn and arrows nocked. Javelins were readied and swords came out. V'Choun cursed the fog that kept him from seeing what approached.

Then, riding out of the mist, came the two scouts. They plowed through the waters of the Tiensha and back up the eastern bank.

"General! The Horse People come!" one gasped as he brought his mount to a rearing halt before the general.

"What banners do they bear?" V'Choun snapped. The answer decided whether they lived or died this day. If the Zharmatians came in war, they would be as a twig against a flood.

"The horsetails are white!"

V'Choun let loose a gusty sigh of relief. All around him he heard other sighs to match his. They would live one more day, at least.

But had the horsetail banners been red . . .

"Thank the Phoenix," he said quietly. "Now we wait." He motioned the soldiers back so that he waited alone on the bank. His horse, an old hand at such games, stood with only the occasional swish of his tail to show that he was not a statue.

From out of the fog came a ghostly piping, fading in and out like a fever dream. A moment's fear seized V'Choun; then he recognized the tune. It was not one of the war songs. Rather, this was the music announcing the presence of Oduin the *temur*, the leader of the People of the Horse. And that could only mean one thing.

How did they know? V'Choun asked himself in astonishment. *No—old Ghulla cannot* still *be alive!*

She was. For the first figure to appear wraithlike from the mist was the old Seer of the Zharmatians upon a blood bay mare. Withered and wrinkled and older than the bones of the earth Ghulla was, the stories said, half hag and half demon. Her thin grey hair wisped onto hunched, bony shoulders clad with the skins of wolves and wildcats. Though V'Choun made no sound, her milky, sightless eyes turned unerringly to him. All around him V'Choun heard the mutterings of the spell against the Evil Eye.

"General V'Choun," she cackled. "Old enemy. We meet once more."

V'Choun saluted her. "An honest enemy," he said, "is truer than a false friend."

Once again Ghulla's cackle sounded. "For a young pup you show much wisdom," she said. "I have hope for you yet—especially since you're here."

"You know why, then."

"Of course." The arrogant confidence in those two words would have filled an oxcart to overflowing. But beneath it, V'Choun, experienced with all that was *not* said at an imperial court, heard a note of uncertainty. So, Ghulla Saw part—but not all. It was what she didn't See that frightened V'Choun. But there was little he could do about shadows.

The ghostly pipes grew louder. Then, by some trick of the fog—or Ghulla's wiles—one moment V'Choun looked at empty mist swirling over the grass; the next, the vanguard of the People of the Horse materialized as if out of the air.

Twenty young warriors, men and women, armed to their very eyebrows faced him. But their bows were safely tucked in their cases, and each bore in one hand a long staff from which hung a white horsetail. They sat straight and still in the saddle as their horses advanced at a slow, high-stepping trot.

From behind he heard some idiot's ribald comment about the kind of war he would like to wage upon "women who played at soldiers." There was a solid *thump!* and a harsh whisper of "If you ever meet the Zharmatians in battle, you horse's ass, pray it's the men you fall prisoner to! Now shut your filthy mouth—I've no wish to lose my balls!"

At some signal V'Choun didn't see, the line suddenly split, with the horses, ten to a side, stepping sideways to open a passage through the center.

Through that opening rode Oduin, *temur* of the Zharmatians; to his left to guard his shield side rode his eldest son, Yemal. To his right, riding in the place of honor under the protection of the *temur*'s own sword, came the banished Lord Kirano. They stopped by Ghulla so that she was to Kirano's right.

V'Choun bowed low in the saddle to hide his shock. He'd no idea Oduin was so ill! Phoenix, the man looked like Death incarnate. Oduin's face was drawn and grey; lines of pain etched deep furrows around the sunken eyes and the shriveled lips; his tunic of fine white leather hung from once powerful shoulders like a sack draped over one of the stick men the farmers used to scare birds from the fields.

He's being eaten from the inside by a demon, V'Choun thought. He'd seen it before, this evil. It ate its way through a man the way a worm ate through an apricot, and what the demon didn't destroy of a man's mind, the pain did.

Beside Oduin, Yemal looked a vision of the perfect warrior, healthy and hale, bursting with vigorous life. He smiled thinly when he saw V'Choun; with a sinking heart

V'Choun saw death in that cold smile. The Phoenix help them all; for now, the young stallion was kept on a short rope. But the day the hand holding that rope faltered . . .

It would mean war—and Yesuin's death. V'Choun knew well there was no love lost between the two brothers, sons of rival wives.

His thoughts took but an instant. He raised his empty hands in token of peace. Oduin did the same.

"You know why I have come, great Horse Lord," V'Choun said.

"So I do," Oduin said. Even his voice sounded frail. But there was still the heart of a warrior in it; Oduin would fight this enemy to the last. "This man has been my guest and my friend. What do you want with him?"

"To bring him back to the Phoenix Court," V'Choun said.

"Will he sit in the place of honor in the Emperor's tent?" came the first ritual question.

"He will."

"Will the Emperor feed him, clothe him, give him a fine horse and a tent of his own?"

"The Emperor will." Seeing the effort this cost the *temur*, V'Choun broke in against custom. "Old feuds will be forgotten. All the Emperor has, he will share with Lord Kirano as a brother—or, should I say, as an almost father-in-law?" he dared to jest.

Oduin smiled faintly at that. There was relief in his face, though whether it was for the reminder that his guest was grandfather to the heir and so would be revered now as an ancestor-to-be, or to have the long ritual shortened, V'Choun wasn't certain. There was only one question remaining. . . .

Oduin turned to the grey-haired Jehangli man by his side. "And you, elder brother of the heart? Do you go of your own free will?"

For the first time Kirano spoke. "I do, for this is the Way." The words rang with an inner peace that V'Choun envied.

"Then travel with the wind at your back, my friend, and a swift horse beneath you. I will miss you," Oduin said. His voice shook; he wheeled his horse away.

The Zharmatians followed him, disappearing back into the fog as if they were no more than a dream. For a long moment Kirano looked after them. Then, taking up his reins with a resolute air, the old lord set his horse to ford the shrunken river.

"Let us go," Kirano said when he once more stood upon Jehangli soil. "There's much to be done."

"More than you know, my old friend," V'Choun said. "More than you know."

A few days later, Maurynna stood on the shore, her cloak wrapped tightly around her as the wind lashed the waves into a white-foamed frenzy. Her hood fell back, and long strands of her hair whipped in the wind. She ignored them, her head thrown back so that she could sniff the salt-laden air, and watch the dark clouds scudding across the sky. Gusts of rain blew into her face from time to time.

Footsteps crunched in the sand behind her. She knew who it was even without looking. She turned and smiled.

Linden peered out from inside his hood, a doubtful expression on his face. "Is this standing about in storms something all sailors do?" he asked. "It seems a damned uncomfortable thing."

She laughed at him. "No, silly. Don't you smell it?"

He sniffed the air. "Salt?" he finally guessed.

"There is, but that's not what I meant. The storm's finally ending; I can smell it on the wind. *That* is something sailors do."

The expression in his eyes turned bleak. "So we can leave?"

"Yes," she said. "Tomorrow, perhaps."

He looked away; she saw the muscles in his jaw work.

She went to him, and he opened his cloak. She stepped inside the shelter he offered, and wrapped her arms around him. He held her close. Laying her head upon his shoulder, she said, "I don't want to leave, either, Linden. But—"

"Yes?"

"I just want to get it over with. I can't stand having this thing hanging over us any longer." To her dismay, her eyes burned. *I won't cry,* she told herself fiercely. *Tears will do nothing!*

He pulled her tighter. They stood together, letting the last of the storm sweep around them.

It was all they could do, Maurynna thought.

For a time, it seemed he wandered in a fog; sometimes it cleared, and Haoro knew what happened about him. Other times, his surroundings made no sense, and the voices talking over his head spoke gibberish. Worse, he was trapped inside his head, unable to speak, unable to tell the ones who washed him, dressed him, and fed him, what he wanted.

But each day the fog receded a little more. Each day, the periods of lucidity lengthened. Soon, he told himself, soon the fog would be gone for good. Soon he would move against Pah-Ko.

Linden was awakened the next morning by the sound of an Assantikkan curse scorching the air like lightning. Alarmed, he threw the covers back and jumped out of the bed.

"What the—" he started, then saw Maurynna, clad only in a tunic, leaning precariously out of the tavern window.

She pulled back inside and turned a face so full of fury on him that Linden stepped back, hastily wondering what he'd done to deserve *this*.

"It's the bloody, bedamned *wind*," she snarled as she stalked off to retrieve her breeches from the foot of the bed.

Oh, by the gods—were they now becalmed? No, now that he listened, he could hear the wind blowing, and blowing constantly by the sound of it. Baffled, Linden peered out of the window; sure enough, the branches of the almond tree in the courtyard swayed to and fro. "But it's blowing, and steadily, too," he said, unable to understand what the problem was.

"Just so," Maurynna snapped. "As you say, it's blowing, and steadily. *But it's blowing the wrong way!*"

"The wrong way?"

"Yes, the wrong way! It's blowing straight into the harbor. We're trapped here just as surely as if someone built a wall across the harbor mouth."

He sat down on the bed as the full meaning of her words struck him. "How long will it last?" he asked.

She stood before him, her breeches still clutched in one hand. "That's just it. There's no way of telling. It could end tomorrow. Or it could go on for days, even tendays! And there's not a damned thing we can do about it, either."

Just, Linden thought bitterly, *what we do not need—another delay.* He knew Maurynna was close to breaking with the need to get this over with. How much longer could she bear it?

Thirty-three

The Phoenix help her, the pain was unbearable. Shei-Luin clenched her teeth on the strip of silk Tsiaa had slipped into her mouth when the birth pangs had begun in earnest. She wrapped her hands tighter in the loops of silk rope tied to the bedposts at the head of the bed.

She hated this. Hated the pain, the stink of her own sweat-soaked body, the feeling of her waters bursting, flooding the silken sheets with bloody liquid. She glared up at her maid.

Tsiaa clucked sympathetically. With a cloth wrung out in cool, jasmine-scented water, the older woman wiped the sweat from Shei-Luin's face. Their gazes locked; as ever

Tsiaa's eyes held only serenity. Shei-Luin clung to the peace she saw there. It was her only reassurance that all was well. The baby was coming too early. She should have gone at least another two spans of days.

Outside, the thunder of an early summer storm rolled yet again. Rain hammered furiously at the shuttered windows. The junior maids huddled together, twittering in fear at the fury of the storms outside and in.

Useless idiots. She would have them all flogged.

Only Tsiaa remained a bastion of calm. *Sweet Tsiaa; I will reward her richly when this is over.*

The ominous rumble had hardly died away before another spasm wracked Shei-Luin's already tormented body. She arched against it, fighting to keep control, but an animal cry of pain and fear escaped her.

She was being torn in two! Pain lanced through her again. She shook her head, dazed now. What was happening? Xahnu's birth had been so easy! "Like spitting a melon seed" had been Tsiaa's description. It had made her laugh.

Damn it! Wasn't the second supposed to be easier? Her head swam as her senses faded in and out.

As if from far away she heard Tsiaa say, "You! Illomened one! Go see what delays the midwife. She should have been here long ago!"

Yes. Where is the midwife? Shei-Luin's battered mind echoed. *I will die without her.*

Fear tried to claim her. But Pain had her first and would not let go. If she could have, Shei-Luin would have laughed.

Instead she screamed as yet another contraction threatened to tear her apart. A woman wailed in panic; dimly Shei-Luin heard Tsiaa driving someone from the room with kicks, blows, and curses. Then the maid was bending over her again, crooning encouragement.

Contraction after contraction ripped through Shei-Luin, in rhythm with the storm outside. Time ceased to have any meaning. She wandered through a forest of pain illuminated by the savage lightning, and pushed at the babe caught in her womb. Pushed and pushed yet again. Nothing happened. She fell back against the sweat-soaked sheets in exhausted despair.

She was dying. She knew it. She was dying and the child with her.

Forgive mé, my son.

Running footsteps wove a path through the fog engulfing her mind. Thank the Phoenix—the midwife at last! Hope returned. Shei-Luin pulled herself back from the brink of darkness and forced herself to look to the door.

But no. This was not the sturdy, competent woman who had attended her only yesterday. This was a frightened girl, one of the kitchen maids by her clothes, sent with a message to the one place where no male—not even a eunuch— might go: an imperial birthing chamber.

The girl babbled something, panting between the words. At first Shei-Luin could hardly make out her barbarous country accent. Then she understood, and only exhaustion kept her from crying out her fear.

"Th' bridge—washed out!"

Shei-Luin resigned herself to death. The Phoenix Pavilion stood on an island in the center of a lake. The only access was the bridge that stretched from the shore to the pretty pebbled beach that ringed the island.

Since the birth had not seemed imminent, the midwife had retired last evening to the village on the mainland, where all but a small, select group of servants went each night. Shei-Luin cursed the tradition that ordained the practice.

The bridge was gone. And no little cockleshell of a boat could survive this storm. There would be no help for her.

As if to underscore her abandonment, the skies roared once more. The maids screamed in terror. Then the floor undulated like a snake.

"The Phoenix is angry!" someone shrieked. "Run! Run before the building falls upon us!"

A bolt of lightning illuminated the room even through the closed shutters. Shei-Luin saw the maids trample each other in their panic to get outside. A moment later, only she and Tsiaa were left.

Once again Shei-Luin fastened her eyes on her senior maid. She spat the shredded strip of silk from her mouth. "Tsiaa," she begged. Her voice was but a ragged whisper. It was all she could do. "Help me."

"Lady," Tsiaa said. "I will do my best."

Nira Pah-Ko sat on his throne in the hall of the Iron Temple, receiving the adulation of the pilgrims who had made the hard and dangerous journey to Mount Kajhenral. The pilgrims—mostly men, but with a few women among them—knelt in a line before him as they chanted the Thousand Praises of the Guardian, touching their foreheads to the floor between each verse.

"Holy One, you are the rock of the Empire. We praise you."

Pah-Ko shifted slightly on the golden throne, a smaller version of the great Phoenix Throne that only the emperor might use upon pain of death. As always, Hodai, mostly recovered now, sat at his feet. He'd collapsed the day Haoro came out of his long illness; Pah-Ko thought that the shock of seeing one who'd been considered lost return to life had been too much for the boy.

Hodai was better now, but the boy was still too pale, tired too easily. Pah-Ko fretted as he glanced down at the back of the sleek black head bowing in weariness, and wished the pilgrims would hurry.

"Holy One, you are the strength of Jehanglan. We—"

The chant broke off as Hodai's head snapped up, and his hands clawed at the air.

"Aiieeaahhhhhhh!" he wailed like a soul in torment. "Aiieeaahhhhhhh!" again and again and again.

It was the voice of the Phoenix.

The agony stretched on forever. Dimly Shei-Luin heard Tsiaa call to her, encourage her, curse her for giving up. It was all that kept Shei-Luin tied to this world. She clung to the voice, hardly understanding the words.

Now and again, the ground shook. It seemed the Phoenix was still angry. Yet the walls did not fall upon her, crushing her for her sacrilege.

Shei-Luin took what heart she could from that. Then she heard, "Just a little more. A little more! One more push, my brave lady—I can see the head!"

Shei-Luin drew a deep, painful breath and bore down with her last shreds of strength. It would be the last time. She could do no more.

The pilgrims cast themselves facedown on the floor, covering their heads with their hands and wailing in panic. The temple guards jumped forward. "Silence! Silence, you dogs!" they yelled as they lashed out with their staffs of golden bamboo. One by one the pilgrims' cries died out into whimpers of pain.

"What is this?" Pah-Ko cried. "Hodai, what—" He knelt by his Oracle and seized the slave boy's shoulders.

It was plain that the child was in the grip of a prophecy. But such a prophecy! Pah-Ko had never seen anything like it. His heart hammered in his chest with fear.

For there were no words to this prophecy that held Hodai in such a grip; only scream after scream of mixed fear and crazed longing. But the true horror was that it was the voice of the Phoenix, the beautiful, golden tones twisted and perverted. Even the temple guards, stalwart as they were, grew ashen-faced as they listened.

Then, all at once, it stopped. Hodai fell to the floor. The silence rang in Pah-Ko's ears.

Unbearable pressure, intolerable pain—then, release!

A thin cry split the air. Shei-Luin slumped back against the pillows, spent. Her heart fluttered in her breast like a hummingbird's wings. She mouthed, "What sex?"

Tsiaa held the child aloft in triumph. Its blood-slick body

glistened in the light of the single oil lamp. "A boy, lady! Another heir for the Phoenix Throne!"

Shei-Luin closed her eyes in relief. Another son! Now nothing could stand between her and the empress's throne. Knowing that Tsiaa would see to the child, she drifted on a sea of happy scheming.

Until she heard Tsiaa's gasp.

Shei-Luin's eyes flew open once more. Her gaze fastened on Tsiaa's stricken face as the maid stared down at the child she held in her arms.

Shei-Luin's heart froze. "What?" she whispered. "What is it?"

Phoenix, don't let there be anything wrong, she prayed. *Please, let my baby be whole.*

The priests would kill even the emperor's own child, were it deformed.

Trembling hands held the infant out to her. "L-look at his leg," Tsiaa said.

Shei-Luin looked down at the infant in her arms—and moaned. There, for all the world to see, was the proof of her infidelity; proof of her treason.

For her newborn son bore on the side of his thigh the same kind of birthmark that his father did: a darker patch of skin as if someone had splashed brown ink on the child while still in her womb. It was small, no larger than a silver coin, but it held her death warrant.

Xiane, of course, had no such blemish. But one look at "his" newborn son, and even that besotted fool would know who the father was.

For once Shei-Luin's agile mind refused to work. She could only stare beseechingly at the only woman she had ever named "friend."

"Tsiaa," she whispered. "What shall I do?"

The ground shuddered once more.

The maid's expression hardened. "There's only one thing, lady. Give him to me."

Wondering, Shei-Luin did as she was bidden. Tsiaa gathered the child to her breast, crooning to him, her eyes filled with adoration. Then Tsiaa turned away, head bent over the infant in her arms, and crossed the room to the window. She threw open the shutters. Then she went to the brazier and knelt before it.

Shei-Luin nearly choked. She suddenly understood what Tsiaa meant to do. Emotions warred within her; every instinct she had as a mother screamed for her to protect her child from harm. Yet to save him—and herself—from death, she must let Tsiaa do this thing.

Tsiaa looked over her shoulder. Her iron calm broke at last. "Lady, do not let them torture . . ." The sentence died in a sob.

"I won't. I promise, Tsiaa; it will be quick."

The maid nodded. One hand stretched out, trembled, clenched for the space of three heartbeats. Only when that hand was steady did it continue its journey to pick up the small tongs. Then Tsiaa selected a coal from the brazier. Carefully, so carefully, she pressed the glowing coal against the betraying birthmark and held it there for long moments.

The baby screamed. A whimper she couldn't contain escaped Shei-Luin.

Tongs and coal fell back into the brazier with a sound like an executioner's sword striking home.

"Lady," Tsiaa said tonelessly. She stood. Her face was grey; she crossed the room like a sleepwalker and handed the wailing baby to his mother. From outside came a distant rumble of thunder. "Lady, I regret my clumsiness. I was merely trying to relight the lamp that had gone out when the shutter blew open. But the ground shook and I stumbled, and— Raise him, Lady." A tender hand caressed the down-covered head. "Raise him to be a good man, a strong shield for his brother's back." She sank to the floor, eyes closed, kneeling with her hands folded quietly in her lap.

"I will. Thank you," Shei-Luin said softly. "Thank you, my friend." She gathered her son to her breast. She—and he—were safe.

A final surge of lightning lit Tsiaa's face. Already it was the face of a corpse.

*   *   *

Somehow, despite his aching bones, Pah-Ko reached Hodai before anyone else. He cradled the young Oracle's head in his hands. "Hodai," he called gently. "Hodai."

The boy's eyes fluttered open, but their gaze was unfocused. Hodai was still in the grip of prophecy. Words faint as the beating of a butterfly's wings breathed past his lips; it was the voice of the Phoenix, but never had Pah-Ko heard it so faint, so subdued.

"The way is open. Follow it." The eyes shut once more as Hodai slid down into sleep.

Pah-Ko wrinkled his brow. *What way?* he thought, puzzled.

Then his eyes grew wide. *Of course! The* Way!

And it was the Word of the Phoenix.

It was always the same in the Garden of Eternal Spring, Yesuin thought. Flowers might bloom and fade, green leaves might turn brown and fall to the earth, but never did it happen all at once, never was the garden sere and brown in the grip of winter. Always there were fresh buds to take the place of those just past. Far off in the distance he heard a storm raging, but not here. The skies above the Garden were as blue as ever.

He gazed out from the pavilion where he sat with Xiane over a game of *ulim-choi*. A pair of tiger butterflies fluttered past, dancing from flower to flower. From somewhere deeper in the garden he heard a wren singing merrily.

Every time he was in the garden, he saw and heard the same, or something very like. It depressed him. Nothing changed.

Especially Shei-Luin. He wondered if she would ever forgive him for encouraging Xiane to follow the Way. Maybe if he tried after she returned, she would finally relent and unlock the secret door to her chamber. . . .

Stop telling yourself lies. A woman who would sacrifice a country to save her children, will sacrifice you as well.

Yesuin sighed and turned his attention back to the game.

Xiane was scowling fiercely at the circular game board as he considered his next move. Yesuin saw his dark gaze dart here and there, seeking opportunities, weighing moves.

"Hah!" the emperor said at last. He beamed and clapped his hands in glee. "See if you can best this, cousin! I— What is it? I left word that I was not to be disturbed."

The last was snapped at a young man carrying the brown horsetail whip of a junior cavalry officer in one hand. In the other was a sealed message.

Shaken, Yesuin dragged his thoughts from the grey mire they wallowed in of late. Phoenix! He should have noticed the man long before this! What if he'd been an assassin?

The young officer paled. He stopped and bowed, then came on as if every step might be his last. "I apologize, Phoenix Lord," he said as he entered the pavilion, "and the eunuchs tried to stop me, but you once left word to bring you any messages from General V'Choun. If this unfortunate person has offended, Imperial Majesty, then let my blood wash away that offense."

With that, the officer fell to his knees and, letting the whip dangle by its cord from his wrist, offered the letter to Xiane in both hands. Yesuin stared at the whip as it swayed, the long rough, red-brown hairs hissing softly as they rubbed against each other, remembering with sudden, over-whelming clarity the horsetail banners of the Zharmatians.

Xiane took the letter. "You did well—Captain."

The young officer looked up in confusion. "But, Majesty, I'm only a— Oh!" His face split in a huge grin.

"You did the right thing in bringing this to me, despite the possibility you would be punished. Go back to your barracks and trade your sergeant's whip in for the grey of a captain's."

The officer knocked his forehead against the floor three times. "Thank you, Phoenix Lord. Thank you!" He stood, backed the required three steps, then turned and strode off with a now jaunty step.

Yesuin smiled. "That was well done, Xiane."

Xiane looked embarassed, but pleased. "That was a brave

man who did his duty. He could have been killed for his presumption and he knew it. Some chicken-heart of a superior officer dumped the task on him, no doubt. Now let's see what we have here." He broke the seal on the folded sheet and read.

Xiane's long face gave away little. But Yesuin saw the tiny widening of his eyes, heard the faint catch of his breath. Then Xiane crumpled the letter in one hand, his face suddenly grim. He stared off into the distance.

Yesuin blinked. Angry, happy, baffled, hurt—he'd seen Xiane in all those moods. But not once had he seen Xiane look like this. A chill ran down his spine. "What is it? Is Kirano dead?" he dared to ask at last. The Phoenix help Jehanglan if it were so; Yesuin was certain that Kirano was the only one who could convince the emperor of the rightness of the Way.

At first Xiane seemed not to hear. Then he shook his head like a diver surfacing, and said, "Kirano? No, Kirano is well enough. V'Choun says they must travel slowly, but there is nothing amiss with him."

Was there the faintest emphasis on "him"? Yesuin held his breath.

"But V'Choun sent a fast messenger ahead with other, less welcome news. Yesuin—cousin—I'm sorry, but V'Choun writes that your father is very ill. There's death in his face, V'Choun says."

Of all things, this was the last that Yesuin expected. He had not seen his father in years; his last memory was of a hale, hearty, and powerful man who seized the cup of life with both hands and drank deeply of it, then roared joyously for more. Why, he'd seen his father lift the corner of a wagon by himself so that a new wheel could be slipped on the axle! How could such a man be deathly ill?

His head spun. Suddenly nothing seemed real. As if from a great distance, he heard a voice that sounded like his say, "If my father dies, then my brother becomes *temur*. As soon as Yemal can call the tribes together, he'll break the treaty. The treaty that I'm the bond for. And then I will die."

How calm the voice sounded! Dazed, Yesuin wondered if he'd somehow fallen into a play; the actor who read his speech did the part well. So very brave . . .

Or had he eaten poppy gum somehow, and dreamed now?

A hand clamped onto his wrist so hard it hurt. But the pain brought Yesuin back from the wilderness of grief he'd wandered into. He stared into Xiane's eyes, eyes that burned and held his so that he couldn't look away.

"It will not happen," Xiane said. "Do you hear me? *It will not happen.* You've been my friend, Yesuin. No matter what your brother does, it won't break that friendship."

You've been my friend.

Yesuin nearly wept at those words, at the purity of what Xiane had given him all this time.

No, he wanted to confess, *I've been your betrayer.* He dared not. Not because it might cost him his life, but because it would break Xiane's heart to know that both he and Shei-Luin had tricked him. Yesuin was weak, yes; but he was not cruel.

He placed his hand over the one that still gripped his wrist. "Thank you," he whispered.

Xiane's mouth twitched in a wry smile. "It's the least I can do. Have you any idea how good it's been to have someone I can talk honestly to? Who understands the things my mother taught me?

"But you won't be able to stay here, cousin. You know that. You'd be a target for some fanatic who'd blame you for the breaking of the treaty."

Xiane released his wrist and leaned back in his chair. "I will make certain . . . arrangements against that time. You must be ready to move on a moment's notice."

Yesuin nodded. "I understand. Thank you, Xiane. For everything."

"Where will you go?"

"I dare not go back to my own people. Yemal will kill me, I'm certain of it." Yesuin rubbed the bridge of his nose as he thought. "Perhaps the Tah'nehsieh. I remember their

Seer, Zhantse, coming to visit ours when I was very little. He was a kind man, and once told me that I might visit him for as long as I wanted. I wonder now if somehow he knew that this day would come."

Xiane stood; he stared down at their forgotten game. Yesuin rose as well.

"Well, 'that day' isn't here yet," the emperor said, his voice rough. "But when it does come, there'll likely be no time for farewells. So I'll say them now, cousin."

To Yesuin's surprise, Xiane caught him in a fierce hug. Yesuin returned it, nearly undone by the sudden realization that he would miss this unpredictable, sometimes foolish, often exasperating man.

"I'll miss you, Yesuin," Xiane said as if reading his mind.

"And I shall miss you, Xiane. May you be happy," Yesuin replied.

"And you," Xiane said, releasing him. "We must go back to the palace. I wish to begin those 'arrangements' I spoke of." He glanced once more at the abandoned game. "I've no interest in finishing. Have you?"

"No," Yesuin admitted.

"Thought not." Xiane led the way from the pavilion. "Besides, I know who would have won."

"Oh?" said Yesuin, rising to the cocky certainty ringing in the words.

"Of course. I would have."

Yesuin snorted. "With *that* defense?"

"Cousin, you didn't see what I had planned for you," Xiane said. He grinned.

They argued all the way back to the throne room, much to the scandal of the eunuchs and lords who heard them.

Haoro leaned upon the arm of his attendant as the younger man led him into the hall.

"You've been ill and abed a long time, Holy One," the acolyte said. "You must go easy at first. Each day, the leech said, you can go a little farther."

Haoro nodded and set his teeth. By the end of the short hallway, he was so exhausted, the acolyte half carried him back to his bed.

He slept then, and when he awoke, he called the acolyte to him. "I would walk again," he said.

"But Holy One—" the young man began, frightened.

Haoro waved him to silence with a curt gesture. "Help me up—now."

This time he went three steps more before his strength gave out. Well enough, he thought when he lay on his bed once more; he would rest again, get up, walk three more steps than before, rest, and so on, until he had his full strength back. By the next full moon, he vowed to himself, he would walk unaided to the main temple.

After a time, he beckoned the acolyte to him. "Again," he said.

Thirty-four

The old priest heard the news in consternation. "The emperor did *what*?" He shook his head in horror.

The kneeling messenger, a junior priest from one of the lesser temples, bowed his head. "As soon as the way had been cleared after the earth tremors, he went to the Phoenix Pavilion where the concubine Shei-Luin was recuperating from the birth of their second son. It's said she nearly died giving birth."

Nira Pah-Ko frowned. "That doesn't matter. He was wrong to have visited the woman during her period of purification. And she was not put to death?"

"No, Holy One. Xiane Ma Jhi covered her with the hem of his robe. He even gave her Zyuzin the Jewel, of the Songbirds from the Garden of Eternal Spring, for her own."

The frown grew deeper. The messenger quailed visibly before it. Plainly the man feared he would be blamed for the bad news he brought. To ease him, Pah-Ko signaled Hodai to bring the man a cup of tea, likely an honor beyond anything this lowly priest had ever expected.

The man touched forehead to floor again and again in a frenzy of thanks. He took the cup in trembling hands and waited.

Pah-Ko nodded approval at the courtesy; lesser priest and stripling youth though he was, this one had manners. The *nira* accepted a second cup of tea from Hodai and drank.

The young priest bowed slightly over the cup once again and sipped. His eyes widened in delighted surprise at the taste of a tea fine enough to grace the emperor's own table.

Pah-Ko drank in silence and thought. Who would have thought that Xiane would flout custom so! And he the son of such a pious father. It seemed everything the young emperor did was in error. He had been wrong to seek the woman out during her purification, and wrong to have kept her from the proper punishment. Did it matter that she had given the Phoenix throne another heir? She was still impure from the birth. Xiane Ma Jhi had much to answer for. For if the emperor was not righteous, what hope had the empire?

Pah-Ko shook his head sadly.

The Way is open. Follow it.

Yes, it was time to follow that path in truth.

It was a most auspicious day. First the sun had risen strong and clear, a golden phoenix driving away the wispy morning clouds known as "dragon's breath" from the sky. Then round-faced Zyuzin, now Murohshei's "little brother," saw a paradise bird in the garden. It had seized a jasmine blossom in its beak and flown to the west, the same direction Shei-Luin would journey this day.

A very auspicious day, praise the Phoenix.

Her period of confinement and purification was over at last. She had thought the first one unbearable; this one, though it was cut short, had seemed interminable.

But, she exulted in the private fastness of her heart, she had borne yet another son! None would dare challenge her now as First Concubine. And, if Xiane kept his word, soon-to-be empress.

Shei-Luin sat in state in the audience hall of the Phoenix Pavilion, awaiting the escort the emperor would send to bring her back to the palace, back to the heart of Jehanglan. Attendants went to and fro, arranging trunks and travel cases of gilded bamboo and camphor wood.

The scarlet silk of her robes was heavy with embroidery; images of the Great Phoenix and its symbol, the sun, worked in gold bullion covered the outer robe so thickly that it could almost stand without her in it. She ran fingers over the ridges formed by the thick thread and wondered if anyone had managed to supplant her in Xiane's affections during her absence. She didn't think so, considering the great risk he'd taken in breaking custom and visiting her here in the Phoenix Pavilion before her time was over, and in calling her back early.

She frowned at the memory of that visit. Fool—she could have been killed for that. She'd never known such terror as when that long ass's face of his had peered through her door that cursed morning.

So it would be all the more annoying if he'd found some-one else. The last time she'd returned from her sequester-ing, she'd had to bribe one of the lesser eunuchs to falsely denounce the pretty twins, brother and sister, who had caught the emperor's fancy in her absence. Then there was all the trouble to see that the eunuch met with a suitable . . . accident. Another fool, that one; he should not have tried to blackmail her. Had he been faithful, she would have rewarded him richly.

She folded her hands in her lap and smiled very slightly. There were always some who thought to take her place— like Jhanun, and the niece he'd sent to Xiane. Shei-Luin remembered the empty face, and knew she'd find no real rival there. That bloodless rabbit hadn't enough fire to hold Xiane.

But she did. She might be years away from the People of the Horse, and only half of the blood, but she was still Zharmatian in her soul. What she took she held—as she had the emperor's heart. And she was the only one to give Xiane children, and strong, healthy sons at that.

Healthy sons. On that thought she had to press her lips together to still the smile that grew there. Soon she would see Yesuin again, and tell him she forgave him. Her heart thrilled at the idea. She couldn't stay angry with him— especially since she'd never heard that her father had been sent for. Yesuin must have heeded her at last and talked Xiane out of that bit of idiocy.

Murohshei approached, a cup of tea in his hands. He knelt and offered it to her. "Lady, some refreshment before your litter arrives?" His light eunuch's voice fluted above the bustle in the hall.

Shei-Luin took the proffered cup. It was a delicate thing, fine white porcelain so thin it seemed ready to float away, with golden phoenixes sporting around it. A tea cup that only one of the imperial family, or an esteemed favorite, might use. Her mind saw one like it in Yesuin's tanned hand, remembered the nights he'd come in secret to her chambers.

Shei-Luin drank. The taste was clean and slightly bitter under the sweetness of jasmine flowers. She looked over the cup's edge at Murohshei. His eyes smiled at her. It was the same kind of tea she and Yesuin always shared after . . . He would be so surprised when she came to his chamber from the tunnels.

If only she could bring little Xu with her; but he was already sent with his wet nurse and his brother to the hills to escape the summer fever demons that would rise soon.

But at least she would be returning to court. True, there would be those old sticks who were sure to be scandalized that Xiane called her back before her time of purification was over, but she would risk their wrath. She thought she knew why Xiane took this gamble.

Shei-Luin allowed herself the luxury of a tinkling laugh of delight at the thought. Certain of her women paused in their ordering of boxes, turning to look in surprise. The younger ones smiled, thinking, no doubt, that their mistress was as happy as they to return to the palace and the pageantry and excitement of the imperial court.

If only Tsiaa were here. . . .

"Murohshei, do you still burn incense for Tsiaa's soul each day?"

Murohshei nodded, serious again. "And a phoenix of yellow rice paper as well, that the Phoenix may know she gave the empire her life."

"That is well." A coldness crept through Shei-Luin's spirit. *Did Xiane know how Tsiaa served the empire, we would pay with our lives—and the empire would be torn apart by the warlords as a lamb is by hungry dogs. I will not allow that. Xiane's blood is weak. Not so my sons'. The Phoenix Throne shall be theirs and their sons' after them, a new dynasty strong and vigorous.*

Someday Tsiaa would have better than one eunuch burning incense to her memory on the sly. Shei-Luin would see to it.

"Lady Shei-Luin!"

Zyuzin's sweet, high boy's voice rang through the audience room. He ran the length of the long room, soft white hands hiking up his robes, his patterned slippers twinkling across the polished floor. "Lady," he called. "The litter is here and it is the emperor's best, the one inlaid with gold and ivory and jade!" His moon face beamed with excitement. "And there are many, many soldiers to escort you, and drummers and singers and flute players. There's even a tiger on a leash!"

"Thank you, Zyuzin," Shei-Luin said and smiled a tiny, satisfied smile.

There would be no inconvenient rivals awaiting her this time.

* * *

The troupe gathered around the fireplace in Lleld and Jek-kanadar's room to hear the news that Lady Mayhem brought them. Outside, the wind whistled around the eaves of the inn. It was, Linden thought as he poured wine for everyone, a maddening sound.

"I spoke with Captain Okaril again," Lleld reported. "He's as frustrated as we are, and said that the instant this damned wind dies down, we're to get down to the dock as—"

She broke off as Otter broke into a fit of coughing. When it was over, he said, "Your pardon—some wine must have gone down the wrong way."

Linden frowned at him. "I hope that's all it is; I noticed that one of the serving maids was coughing last night. If you get too sick to travel—"

The bard waved a hand. "I'll be fine, boyo, don't go fussing over me like a mother hen, now," he said, holding out his goblet for more wine. "I'll be on that ship with the rest of you."

"You'd best be," Lleld said, much too sweetly.

Otter blew her a kiss and drank. "See? The cough's gone. Go on, Lleld."

"Not much more to say. He'll send his cabin boy, Eustan, for us, and we're to move our asses like never before, he said."

As if to mock her, a particularly powerful gust shrieked around the corner of the inn. They listened glumly as it went on and on.

"I don't know about anyone else," Lleld said, "but I'm beginning to hate that sound."

Ah, to be in the palace, the home of all elegance, once more. Glittering courtiers in their fantastical robes and sea-shell belts, drinking and dancing; poets dedicating subtle verses to their patrons, scribing poems of moonlit trysts and lightning passions; conceits like jewels, such as the Garden of Eternal Spring, the Garden of the Moon, the Hall of

Amber. A thousand, thousand things to delight and enchant.

Shei-Luin stood as her women disrobed her, lifting a hand or holding out her arms as they respectfully asked, but making no move to help them. When she was naked, one led her to a carved bench by the bathing pool; she sat and the woman took the jeweled pins from her hair and began brushing it.

Shei-Luin watched as the other women prepared her bath. One dribbled scented oil into the gently steaming water and swished it around to disperse it. The delicate bouquet of gardenias filled the air like a dream. No doubt the oil had been distilled by one of the lesser concubines as part of her household duties. Shei-Luin silently rejoiced that, as the mother of the heir, she no longer had any such responsibilities. She'd hated making the ginger soap Xiane favored. All too often the lamb's fat sent up from the kitchens was rancid—courtesy of a well-placed bribe to the cooks by one of her chief rivals at the time, a rival who knew how sensitive Shei-Luin's sense of smell was.

But now that childless rival comforted the soldiers of a distant barracks while she basked in Xiane's favor. As for the cooks—well, good cooks were harder to come by than concubines. She'd forgiven them after they'd been beaten. It had been Murohshei's inspired idea to force them to eat a millet bowl each of the same foul stuff they'd inflicted on her. They would never cross her again; they knew how lightly they'd gotten off and were grateful.

"Lady." The soft voice interrupted her memories. "Lady, your bath is ready. Will it please you to enter it now?"

Shei-Luin nodded. The woman brushing her hair hastily pinned it up again to keep it dry. Shei-Luin stood, ran a hand over her flat stomach; two children and still the figure of a maiden.

"When Murohshei returns, send him in to me," she ordered as the bath attendants handed her down into the bathing pool. She sank into the hot water and sighed with pleasure. This was one of her chief delights; as a lesser concubine from a noble but exiled family, she'd had to share a bathing tub with at least two other women. Since no one else liked a bath as hot as she did, she was always outvoted, and the water was always too cold for her.

I don't think I shall move for a long, long time, she thought with lazy indulgence and leaned back, closing her eyes.

It was some time later that Murohshei returned to her chambers—not until the women were almost through toweling her dry. Zyuzin followed him; the boy carried his *zhansjen* under one arm. Murohshei touched the younger eunuch's cheek lightly. Zyuzin smiled and fluttered his eyelashes a moment at his lover before sitting down. He ran delicate fingers over the strings.

"And?" Shei-Luin asked.

"A messenger was sent to the Phoenix Lord at the Temple of Ancestors this morning. It's only the second day of offerings, Lady; you have ample time to prepare for him," Murohshei said. His voice betrayed nothing.

Good; I have until tomorrow night, then, for my reprieve. He must finish the ceremonies there and they are long and tedious, Shei-Luin thought. *Then I must enchant him. I wondered if he bothered to visit the boys while he was there; their pavilion is near the temple.*

"I await that auspicious moment eagerly." Her eyes said, *Go. Find out everything. Find out what I want to know.*

Murohshei bowed and left once more.

Shei-Luin stretched languorously on the table in the bathing room, reveling in the feel of the slave's strong fingers as the woman kneaded fragrant oils into her skin. Zyuzin sat nearby, fingers seducing a tune from the *zhansjen*, his voice raised in a love song, his plain, round face transformed with the joy of singing.

His voice is a gift of the Phoenix, Shei-Luin thought sleepily. Though Zyuzin was now sixteen, he still had the beautiful, clear tones of a younger boy. It was what the eunuch masters hoped to preserve each time a boy singer was castrated. More often than not something changed in a boy's voice as he aged, the precious clarity slowly blurring with the turning of the seasons until it disappeared like a snowflake in the hand. That Zyuzin was here was but further proof of the Phoenix Lord's favor. Now the Jewel sang just for her.

And it pleased her that Murohshei had found a lover in the boy. Faithful heart that he was, he deserved this happiness—however long it lasted. Shei-Luin was all too familiar with the shifting loves among the eunuchs. For Murohshei's sake—and Zyuzin's—she hoped this was one of the rare matches that held.

The slave found a particularly tight knot in her muscles. Shei-Luin made a noise of protest and the talented fingers gently eased the stiffness out.

She heard the door to the outer chamber open, but there had been no rapid tip-tapping signal that warned it was Murohshei or another servant. This was an intruder.

Who dares? she thought, waving the bath slave off, raising herself angrily onto her elbows. *Who dares disturb me at my bath?* She took breath to order the interloper whipped.

A startled chirping of her women's voices from the outer chamber, and a sudden terrified silence brought her sitting upright upon the table, the words stillborn on her tongue. Zyuzin's song ended in mid-note.

"Precious Flower," the despised voice called and the Emperor of Jehanglan surged through the doorway. The bath slave and Zyuzin, *zhansjen* hastily set aside, went to their knees and bowed, foreheads touching the teak wood of the floor again and again.

No—it couldn't be. Astonished fury seethed within her breast. She fought it down before he could see it.

Her emotions now under iron control, Shei-Luin gracefully descended from the massage table, deliberately heedless of her nakedness. She knew what effect it would have on Xiane. He would see only that—not the anger that she knew she could not keep out of her eyes.

A flush rose along the high cheekbones of his long,

-horsey face. "Out," he said. "All of you—out."

The servants scuttled from the room, their eyes averted from the Phoenix Lord. Shei-Luin waited, eyes cast down now with girlish modesty, a tumble of black hair falling over her shoulder to conceal her breasts. "My lord," she said.

Xiane held out a trembling hand. "Here—come here. It's been too long, Precious Flower."

She laid her hand in his, forcing herself not to wince when he crushed her fingers. "August Lord, I thought you were at the temple of your ancestors this day." *Thrice a fool! Xiane, not even you could be stupid enough to cut short those ceremonies—could you?*

His presence was answer enough. Did not Jhanun and his coterie hate her enough that this idiot must give them more reason? She ground her teeth behind her soft smile.

"Most High, you must have ridden hard to return here so quickly from the Khorushin foothills."

Which was easy enough to guess; the Emperor of the Four Quarters of the Earth and Phoenix Lord of the Skies stank of horses and sweat like a slave from the stables. Xiane hadn't even stopped to bathe before coming to her.

She breathed through her mouth. But she couldn't help asking, "Have you seen our sons? Is little Xu's leg—"

He pulled her impatiently into the next room. "Yes, yes, I saw them," he said as he yanked at his robes. "They're well. But Xu will bear a scar on his leg. Stupid woman, to let a burning coal fall on him like that."

The outer robe tore free under the wrenching fingers. The inner robe was more resistant; when she went to help him, Xiane pushed her down onto the bed amid the fragrant silks. He knelt by her feet and hiked the offending garment up. She watched him, unmoved, as he loosened the drawstring on his baggy breeches.

He continued, "You were too easy with her, Precious Flower. Strangling was a mercy; she should have been given the death of a thousand cuts." Then he fell upon her, toying with her hair, running possessive hands down her body, fondling her small feet.

As he murmured idiocies over each delicate toe, Shei-Luin thought, *I know how Tsiaa should have died, pig, if she had truly been clumsy. I promised her as gentle a death as possible. May it not raise suspicion and undo me—but what else could I do? I could not let her suffer. She was mine.*

She would pay him back. She smiled and opened her arms to him. "Come to me, my lord. Perhaps we can make another son to prove your glory to the world."

Silence hung over the Zharmatian camp like a shroud, broken only by a faint sound of drumming. Even the horse herds ringing the camp were quiet, as if they knew that something was wrong. Somewhere among the horsehide tents a baby suddenly squalled; just as suddenly, the noise stopped. Though it was nearing dusk, no cooking fires were lit.

Here and there some of the People gathered together, tight little knots of men or women, their heads together, whispering. The knots made way for Yemal as he strode through the camp, his hunting leathers stained with the sweat of a fast, hard journey. Wary faces turned to watch him and the young men who walked behind him.

Yemal saw knowledge in the eyes that looked down in submission when they met his.

The old wolf is dying.

Here walks the new leader and his pack-brothers.

Here walks power.

Those eyes were right. Yemal reached the door of his father's tent, his foster brother Dzeduin on his heels. From behind the closed flap came the drumming he'd heard. On either side of the door sat his father's lesser wives, blood dripping from self-inflicted cuts and scratches on faces and arms. Some sobbed in honest grief; most merely looked lost or frightened. One or two of the young ones eyed him boldly.

And sitting among these lesser wives was the mother of his brother, Yesuin. Yemal smiled coldly at her. She stared back, her face hard. But behind the hardness was fear.

She was wise to fear; unlike her son, Yesuin's mother was no fool. Yemal's smile widened as he pushed aside the flap to the tent and went in, Dzeduin following.

The stench of sickness hit him like a blow. Yemal nearly gagged, controlled it with a fierce effort; it would not do to show weakness before the ones waiting here.

Especially before the dying one. His father lay on his sleeping furs, swaddled in blankets like a baby despite the mildness of the evening and the stuffy heat inside the tent. Oduin's eyes burned with pain; one of his foster brothers, Kiu, supported him while he drank from a horn that Mejilu, his chief wife and Yemal's mother, held for him. A thin trickle of white *mharoush*, the fermented milk drink of the tribes, dribbled from the corner of his mouth. But from the way his father's eyes cleared, Yemal knew there was more in the horn than *mharoush*. Poppy, no doubt, and enough to send a healthy man into the realm of dreams—or death. To a man wracked by the demon that ate Oduin, it merely brought a temporary respite. When the horn was emptied, his mother wiped the milk away, and Kiu helped Oduin settle back against the pile of cushions that propped him up slightly.

"Father," Yemal said, "I am here." He glanced at his mother; she rose quietly and withdrew to the half circle of watchers ringing the walls. This was men's business.

For a moment he thought his father didn't hear him. Then Oduin turned to look at him. How did he still live, Yemal thought. The demon inside Oduin had eaten him away until his head looked like a thin, worn drumskin stretched over a skull. Yemal knew that were he to tear away the blankets, the ravaged body beneath would look the same. Only the eyes, glittering fiercely in the light of the oil lanterns hanging from the roof poles, looked alive—at least until the poppy wore off once more.

Those eyes regarded him. Yemal bowed to his father,

then moved to kneel at the foot of the bed. He sat back on his heels and waited.

"So you shall have your wish at last," his father rasped. "You will be *temur*."

"As you have raised me to be," Yemal countered.

Oduin snorted; it turned into a hacking cough. When the paroxysm was over, he said, "And what will you do when you are *temur* at last?"

Yemal smiled slightly. "You know well what I will do, Father. What you should have done years ago."

Shriveled lips drew back in a wolf's snarl. "So—you still intend to wage war upon the Jehangli? And what of your brother?"

"My brother has turned Jehangli," Yemal said with a sneer. "You've heard how he lolls in the palace with the emperor, living a life of decadence fit only for a eunuch, not for a man! If he dies, it will be only a Jehangli that dies—and that is as nothing."

Oduin sat up a little straighter and raged at him then, in a thin, wheezing voice that had no force behind it. Yemal sat through it without moving. When it was over, his father's eyes were glazing once more with pain.

"Lie down, lie down," Kiu urged. The old man flashed a reproachful look at Yemal as he settled his foster brother against the pillows and drew the blankets up. "Rest now."

Oduin closed his eyes. Soon the tent was quiet, save for the sound of his final battle: each wheezing, rattling breath as the *temur* fought to hold on to life.

A pounding on the door of their sleeping chamber brought Linden out of bed with a curse. Maurynna was right behind him.

"Who is it?" he growled. A quick look at the window told him that it was still far from dawn.

"It's Eustan from the ship," a boy's voice called. "The cabin boy—remember? The captain sent me to tell you that the wind's shifted, and if everyone hurries, we can be off on the morning's tide."

For a moment Linden was too stunned to speak.

"Hello?" the voice called. "Did you hear me?"

Linden pulled himself together enough to answer, "We heard. Have you told the others?" He tossed up a globe of coldfire.

"Not yet. Now that I know you're up for certain, I'll rouse them as well." The sound of quick footsteps faded away down the hall.

Somehow a cold pit had opened in his stomach. Linden turned to find Maurynna standing in the middle of the floor. She was deathly pale.

But the look in her eyes was calm and resigned, and when he opened his arms and she stepped into them, only the rapid beating of her heart hinted at her fear.

He held her tightly, unwilling to release, until she said, "There's still much to do."

"Aye, there is. We'd best . . ." He let her go, and they set about packing as quickly as they could.

A wild howl of grief snapped Yemal out of his half doze, sitting by his father's feet. It was followed an instant later by more howls and long, quavering cries. Yemal rubbed his eyes and looked at the still figure in the bed.

His father's eyes were open and glassy, staring unseeing at the ceiling. Yemal heaved himself to his feet, stiff after the long deathwatch. He drew his belt knife and made the first of the ritual cuts on his arms, then his cheeks.

As if his movement were a signal, other knives came out, and other arms, other faces were slashed. Blood flowed like red tears.

Then Yemal went to kneel by his father's side. As he shut the open eyelids, blood dripped down his arm and hand to streak Oduin's face.

"Good-bye, Father," he murmured. "I am *temur* now. And as soon as your death rites are over, so is the treaty."

The sweet morning song of a bird woke her. Shei-Luin grimaced at the weight of Xiane's arm across her chest, crushing her breasts. She eased it aside, pausing as the tone of his snoring changed. For a moment she thought he would wake. But though he snorted and snuffled and groaned, Xiane slid back into sleep. Shei-Luin crept from the bed. Casting a silk robe about herself, she left the sleeping chamber.

She wanted a bath.

Murohshei tended a teapot in the other room. Without a word he offered her a cup of fragrant *soonan* tea, its smoky scent tickling her nose as she breathed it in. Let the courtiers turn up their noses at it, she thought, because the Zharmatians drink it. This was the tea of her childhood. It comforted her.

She drank, long and deep. "Ah, thank you, my Murohshei. That was good. Now, what news have you for me?"

He told her of the many little scandals that were the underlife of the court and made her laugh. Then, taking a deep breath, he quietly gave the news that Yesuin's father, old Oduin, who had been *temur* of the Zharmatians for as long as anyone could remember, was rumored to be gravely ill, even dying.

Shei-Luin went very still. She knew what that meant. "If Oduin dies, then Yemal leads the tribes." Fear wove a cold knot in her stomach. Yemal free upon the Western Plains, fretting at the treaty forced upon the Zharmatians in his father's time. Yesuin here in the palace, hostage to that same treaty—and no love lost between the brothers. All that stood between them was their dying father. "Yemal will break the treaty."

Of what use is a hostage then? Shei-Luin's mind said. *Yesuin will be—*

She could not say the words even in her mind. They hung on the air like an executioner's spear and pierced her heart.

"But there may be worse, Lady," said Murohshei.

Shei-Luin could only stare; what could be worse than a threat to Yesuin's life?

The eunuch took the empty teacup from her cold hands. "Do you remember the Lady Nama, Favored One?"

Shei-Luin frowned, thinking. "Ah, yes; the niece that Jhanun foisted upon Xiane for a concubine. A pretty little thing with the heart of a rabbit. What about her?"

Murohshei met her eyes. "She's with child. It was confirmed this morning."

"That's impossible!" Shei-Luin blurted. "Xiane cannot father a child!"

She stopped. No, Xiane couldn't father a child. At least that was how she interpreted the prophecy that had brought Lura-Sharal and her to the palace: only her sister could bear a child by Xiane. Her mind darted back to the feast of Lady Riya-Akono. Jhanun must have guessed her secret that day, and decided her game could be played by two; she would never believe that little rabbit would have had the nerve to seek out a lover on her own—not with the punishments awaiting an unfaithful concubine. Likely Nama's uncle had forced some Zharmatian, captured just for this purpose, upon her. Shei-Luin wondered if the poor wretch's body would ever be found now that his job was done.

And the crowning irony was that she couldn't denounce the girl, not without giving herself and her own children away. No, she and Jhanun would dance around each other, each keeping the other's secret though it was bitter as bile.

Shei-Luin clenched her teeth in frustration. Remembering how she had been guarded throughout her pregnancies, she knew it would be impossible to do anything to Nama— soon to be Nama *noh* Jhi.

Yet she had to. While she had been the only one to bear an heir to the Phoenix Throne, there had been no question of who might wear the robes of the empress someday. But now, if Nama bore a son . . .

What contest would there be between a woman of one of the great noble houses and the daughter of an exile? A daughter born, no less, of a Zharmatian concubine.

Already many of the ministers feared her for her influence on Xiane. If she—and her sons—became expendable, and the ministers supported Jhanun . . .

I will kill Nama, Shei-Luin swore. *For the sake of my children, I will kill her and her babe with her.*

"Hurry!" Captain Okaril bellowed. "We need to make this tide!"

"All's ready!" Linden yelled back from the hold. "The horses are settled."

Okaril's face disappeared from the open hatch. "Cast off!"

Linden heard a flurry of activity from the deck. Then he felt the current catch the ship, felt it slip away from the dock.

They were on their way to Jehanglan at last.

Thirty-five

Maurynna stood with Linden by the railing of the ship, looking into the night sky. For once the mysterious fogs that swept across the straits had dissipated. The creaking of canvas and the slap of waves against the hull filled the darkness around her. Linden must have sensed her mood, for he said nothing, just watched the black water as the ship knifed through it.

Once she'd stood like this on the deck of her own ship, studying the stars, reckoning a course. But tonight that responsibility was someone else's. For the first time, she was glad of it. She had no idea where they were.

There were constellations that she'd never seen before on the horizon ahead; she wondered, if they sailed south long enough, would these strange stars take the sky, chasing away the ones she knew from childhood? Already the figure of the Sky Sisters was half lost beneath the northern sky-line. Would *everything* in this strange land be alien to her?

A sudden rush of longing to see Dragonskeep again took her. Unable to bear the strangeness any longer, she said, "Let's go below."

She caught Linden's hand as they went down to the cabin they shared with Lleld and Jekkanadar, and wished this was over.

The next morning, there was nothing in the water that Linden could see, no reefs or rocks, yet the ship took another unexplained tack, this time heading to—damn—which was it? Port, that was it. Left was port. He leaned on the rail and looked down into the blue water rushing past, and thought he'd have to tell Maurynna he'd finally remembered.

Lleld joined him on the rail. Her red curls blew in the wind; she pushed them back when they fell in her face.

"We've changed course again," she said. "Was there anything there this time?"

"No," Linden said, "not that I can tell in this damned mist that keeps blowing around us, anyway. I wonder if that odd globe Captain Okaril has guides him despite this fog? Maurynna said last night she'd not care to try this dodging about when she couldn't see. Seemed to raise her hackles, it did."

Lleld pushed a handful of curls back from her face once more, then grabbed a few of them and tugged, considering his words. "I'll wager anything you're right," she said at last. "Did she get a good look at that globe thing? The captain certainly warmed up to her as soon as he realized she knew something of the sea. Clever of her to tell him she had uncles who were sailors."

"It's no more than the truth, after all. And she got a better look than Okaril wanted her to have. He wouldn't let her too close to the thing, but what's that to a Dragonlord?" he said with a grin.

Okaril, thinking they were but traveling entertainers, would not allow them any privileges, such as standing on the quarterdeck with him and the steersman. But he'd unbent a little when he'd realized that Maurynna had more than a landsman's knowledge and appreciation of ships and the sea. So a short while ago he'd allowed Maurynna onto the quarterdeck briefly, but wouldn't let her anywhere near the mysterious globe that the steersman watched with unnerving intensity. Indeed, when he saw her looking at it, even from across the deck, he'd hurried her from the quarterdeck. As if chastened, she'd gone down belowdecks to their quarters.

He wondered, though, why she'd not mindcalled him yet to tell him what she'd seen. So he reached out to touch her mind, tapping his forehead with the two middle fingers of one hand to let Lleld know what he did. When Maurynna answered him, she sounded worried.

What is it, love? he asked, letting Lleld "listen" in.

That blasted cough Otter picked up in the inn is worse. He has a fever now, Raven says, and we've no medicine.

Damn, Linden thought to himself. That wasn't good.

Maurynna went on, *Taren says that when we make Jedjieh, he can find an herbalist and get something for him. But until then, the best we can do is make him comfortable.*

Lleld broke in. *Find Jekkanadar and ask him if Fiaran gave him any useful herbs. We usually take some simple things like willow bark and dried mint when we travel. If we're lucky, there'll be some sweet elm bark in there as well. That's good for coughs.*

I'll do that right now, Maurynna said and withdrew.

It took Linden a few moments before he realized he'd never asked about the mysterious globe. But that could wait until later. He stared out once more into the thick mist that had descended upon them two days out of Assantik and had stayed with them ever since. No matter what Taren said about there being no magic in Jehanglan, this fog had the feel of magery about it.

Then all thoughts of mist and magery were driven from his mind by two words shouted down from the crow's nest.

"Land ho!"

As he looked, the mist parted, and before him lay the land of Jehanglan.

Shima sat at the foot of Zhantse's pallet, tapping a soft, hypnotic rhythm on the drum he held between his knees. His younger brother, Tefira, Zhantse's apprentice, sat at the head, making certain that the dried twists of sweet grass in their little clay bowls on either side of him kept burning.

He watched the rise and fall of his master's chest. Most times a Seeing came upon Zhantse unbidden. Other times— such as now—the Tah'nehsieh shaman went into trance to seek them. There was a tingling in the air this night, and Shima knew that Zhantse had found something, if not what he sought.

Then the twin curls of white smoke from the bowls of sweet grass swayed though there was no breeze, and the rhythm of the shaman's breathing changed, becoming lighter and more rapid. Zhantse was close to waking.

His head turned from side to side, and he mumbled like a man talking in his sleep. By degrees, Shima changed the pattern he tapped out, then stopped. He shook his hand to loosen fingers and wrist. Tefira picked up the bowls of smoking sweet grass and took them outside. A moment later he came back in and, taking a gourd dipper from its hook on the stone wall, scooped up some water from the big glazed jar near the door and brought it to the bed.

Zhantse pushed himself up onto his elbows. "Feh," he said, making a face. "That was not an easy one." He drank the water.

"Did you find Pah-Ko?" Shima asked.

Zhantse looked troubled. "No. I sense something worries him, but not what. But while I was in the Grey Lands, I Saw Amura sneaking out to meet Nathua."

Shima perked up at that. Amura was one of his cousins, and one of the many Tah'nehsieh who had slipped into the slave camp at the Iron Temple over the centuries to explore and map the caverns and tunnels beneath Mount Kajhenral. "Oh?"

"It's done."

Simple words to mean so much. Shima caught his breath and knew his brother did the same.

"The map? The map is done at last?" Tefira said.

The shaman sat up. "It is, indeed. I will turn it into a chant to be memorized."

Said Shima, "Then that means—" He couldn't finish.

"That the time of the prophecy is upon us. Now we await the one from the north."

The skies turned dark with storm clouds as they made port. Linden looked up at the threatening clouds and wondered if this was somehow also the work of the Jehangli priest-mages, or just more bad luck. He hoped it would hold off until they had the horses unloaded, for the wretched official who met the ship at the dock wouldn't allow the others to take Otter on to the hostel that foreign entertainers were assigned to.

"No, no," the Jehangli insisted in wretched Assantikkan. "All stay together. Not ahead does anyone travel. All stay together—is order."

Their luck held until Taren's gelding—the last horse—was lifted from the hold. Then the skies opened up and the rain crashed down upon them.

"By the gods!" Lleld complained as she led Miki up the street. "Did someone up there kick over a giant's bath? This keeps up and we'll all have to grow gills!"

But at last they made the hostel and got Otter inside by a fire. There was another group of northern entertainers huddled by it, including a man with a little monkey on his shoulder, but they made way when they saw Otter's red cloak and heard him coughing.

After a round of quick introductions, and the other group's offer to help carry packs upstairs, Taren took Linden and Lleld aside.

"I'm off to look for something for that cough," he whispered. "*Quala* root, if I can find it. May take a while, though. Not all the herbalists carry it."

"Are you certain? It's pouring out there, and that officious bastard warned us to stay in here," Lleld said.

Taren winked and gave them a conspirator's smile. "I'll borrow something to wear from the porter—he'll be willing to look the other way for a bit of coin. And don't worry about me; I know my way around Jehangli cities. But remember—don't leave the hostel yourselves! It's forbidden at night."

With that, he slipped out of the common room. Linden and Lleld looked at each other and shrugged.

"Unlike us, he does know Jehanglan," Lleld said.

"So he does," Linden agreed. "Let's see to Otter and find out more about our fellow entertainers."

Shei-Luin smiled to herself as she slipped through the tunnels of the palace. The Phoenix smiled upon her this night! Xiane gone away hunting, and Yesuin left behind.

Soon she would be with him once more. . . .

Her heart raced like a maiden's on her wedding night as she turned into the tunnel that led to Yesuin's chamber. Light streamed through the peephole from his room; he was still awake!

But as she neared the secret door, her footsteps slowed. Voices—Yesuin was not alone. Her disappointment sitting like a stone in her stomach, Shei-Luin crept up to the nearest peephole and peered through.

Yesuin sat bent over a game of *ulim-choi*. Opposite him was one of the many young lords of the Jehangli court. By the number of pieces still on the board, she knew that they had just begun, and that with skilled players, a game could easily last half the night.

She turned away and retreated down the tunnel, holding back her tears by will alone.

Thirty-six

The poor quarter of Jedjieh was threaded with narrow canals doubling as stinking trails through the warrens of poverty. Dressed as he was in the foul-weather garments borrowed from the hostel's porter—voluminous grass cape and a broad-brimmed hat to hide his foreign features and clothing—Taren had no fear of being attacked or even noticed. Why should one of the numberless poor attract attention?

Still, he hurried through the rainy evening. He could not take the chance of being gone too long; the pretext of searching the market for *quala* root for the old bard's cough was not to be abused. He patted the pouch hanging from his belt, running fingers over the hard lump of root he'd purchased from the shop of herbs not far from the inn. A pity they'd been out of ague bark for him. A shiver that was not from the rainy chill danced in his bones.

He found the house he sought and stopped before it. The door was the only opening at street level, no doubt heavily barred on the inside; windows in this part of Jedjieh were set high, well out of the reach of thieves. These were no different, and shuttered now against the rain. Still, he saw faint gleams of light peeping between the thin bamboo slats when he stepped back a few paces.

Taren pulled the cord. From somewhere inside he heard the soft ringing of a bell. He pulled it twice more, paused, then twice more again.

Silence. Taren wiped his forehead; the skin felt hot and dry even in this wet. Then came the sound of feet scuffling down the stairs. He heard a wheezing cough, then a scraping that told of heavy bars shifting. The door swung open, and a hand bearing a paper lantern appeared. Next came the wizened face of an old woman. "Who is it?" she demanded, squinting into the darkness.

Taren pushed the brim of his hat back so that the light of the lantern fell upon his face.

"Baisha! You've returned!" the old woman gasped.

"Just so. Now get out of my way, foolish one. I must send a message to Lord Jhanun and I don't have much time." He pushed by her and cast hat and grass cloak onto a nearby bench.

"The writing brushes and inkstone are in the first room," she wheezed after him as he climbed the curving stairs. "There are strips of paper already prepared."

"Good. There's no time to waste."

His teeth chattering now, Taren hastened to the room. By the far wall was an old lacquered table, splints around two of its legs, the pitiful castoff of some wealthy household. The poor found a use for everything in Jehanglan.

But shabby as the table was, the brushes and inkstone upon it were of the finest quality. So were the thin strips of paper cut to fit around a pigeon's leg. There were even strips of heavier oiled paper to protect a message against weather such as this night's. By them lay a scattering of silk threads, blue to show that the messages they tied came from Jedjieh.

Xiane rode into the courtyard at nightfall and looked up at the elaborate building that towered over him. His great grandfather had built it as a "simple hunting lodge." Hah. It was so big, as Xiane remembered from childhood, he was afraid of getting throroughly, and frighteningly, lost in it.

Hunting lodge, indeed. Palace was more like it. Still, as far as imperial residences went, it *was* small, and better yet, relatively isolated and private. A perfect place for a guest that Xiane did not want everyone to know about. Not just yet, anyway.

Xiane swung down from his horse and tossed the reins

into the hands of a bowing groom. With a wave of his hand, he dismissed his escort of soldiers. The house steward came to meet him.

"General V'Choun is within?" Xiane asked.

"Yes, Phoenix Lord. So is your other guest. They await your coming."

Xiane nodded. He pulled his riding gloves off and absently slapped them against his thigh, raising a puff of dust.

Phoenix knew he didn't want to do this. But he had to; he had no choice. Squaring his shoulders, Xiane walked grimly to the door. First he would bathe, rest, and eat.

And then . . . He would see.

"Where the hell is Taren?" Linden said. He paused by the window for what seemed the hundredth time in the last candlemark. And as he had done every other time, he opened the shutter and looked out into the rain. "He should have been back long ago."

"Perhaps the nearest simpler's stall didn't have what he needed," Raven offered. He fed the fire in the brazier another lump of charcoal.

"Taren did say he might have to search for it," said Lleld, "because not all herbalists have it."

They sat in the little sleeping chamber Raven shared with Otter—in the one chair, on the floor, at the foot of the bed. The bard lay half-propped up on the bed, sipping weak tea to soothe his throat, raw from coughing.

From her spot on the floor Maurynna said, "But that was well before dusk. It's nearly full night now."

"Just so," Linden said. "I don't like this." He jammed his thumbs into his wide leather belt in frustration.

Said Jekkanadar, "And we've missed our chance to look for him ourselves beyond this area."

"What do you mean?" Linden asked, suddenly alert. " 'Beyond this area?' We were told we were not to leave the hostel at night at all."

Jekkanadar shook his head. "I talked a bit with Brinn, the man with the little monkey, Toli. He told me that even as outsiders we may go beyond this small area around the docks; not very far, true, and only during daylight. After dark, we're confined here to this quarter. He and some of the others have been out, ah, seeing the sights, now and again since they got here about two tendays ago."

Who has the right of it? Linden wondered. *Taren or Brinn? And either way, what are the Jehangli so afraid of that they confine outsiders to certain quarters?*

"Linden, who told you that we couldn't go out at night?" Maurynna asked.

He answered, "Taren. He told Lleld and me that it's forbidden to leave the hostel after dark." Shrugging, he said, "Perhaps it's changed since he was last here."

"Would the innkeeper send someone to look for Taren?" Otter rasped.

"Save your voice," Lleld said, turning from her perch on the foot of the bed to glare at him.

"I'll go see," said Jekkanadar, and left.

When he returned, he reported, "Our host won't go. Nor would he send for the city guard when I asked him to. The impression I got is that he's somehow considered responsible for us. I'll wager he wouldn't want the city guard to know that one of 'his' foreigners is on the loose."

Linden peered out the window again. "We'll give Taren a while longer," he said. "Then I want to look for him as far as we're allowed. He may have just had to look farther afield than he thought, or he may be in some kind of trouble."

To Xiane's frustration, Kirano refused to interpret the significance of the giant serpent.

"In time, my lord, in time," the old scholar said as he poured tea.

V'Choun met Xiane's frustrated look, smiled slightly, and shrugged as if to say, *humor him.*

Xiane sighed, took up his cup, and leaned back on his cushions. V'Choun did the same.

At last Kirano ceased his endless puttering with the teapot and said, "So tell me, Lord of the Four Quarters, what you know of the Phoenix that you owe your throne to."

Why, Xiane wondered, had he asked *that*?

Kirano settled himself more comfortably upon his cushions. He smiled gently; immediately a thousand wrinkles sprang into being. Save for his long grey mustaches and wispy chin beard, he looked, Xiane thought, like one of the carved, dried apples that poor children used for the heads of their dolls. A comforting face for a man who asked disturbing questions; questions that had earned banishment.

"You know it as well as I," Xiane countered.

"Humor an old man whose wits wander these days," Kirano said. His eyes were anything but those of a feeble-minded dodderer. Instead they watched him with a hawk-like intensity.

Grumbling, and feeling like a student again, Xiane dutifully recited, "Michero, the last of the northern emperors, held the Lotus Throne of his ancestors in an iron hand. By his will, the dragons ravaged the land, and the land bled and died.

"His lords begged my august ancestor, Xilu, to save them from the emperor and his dragons, for Xilu was the only noble strong enough, brave enough, and righteous enough to win the favor of Heaven and defeat the vile emperor. At first Xilu refused, for he was at heart a simple man. But the lords—and even the common people—begged him unceasingly to take the throne. But Xilu was a man of peace and he knew such a course meant war.

"Overwhelmed by their demands, Xilu fled into the wilderness so that he might meditate upon the proper path to take. At the advice of his brother Gaolun's Oracle, he went to the forbidden mountain of Rivasha, where the phoenix built its pyres. With him went Gaolun, he who became the first *nira*, and the Oracle."

Xiane paused and drank some tea. The truth was, he'd always hated this part of his lessons. Again and again and yet again had his tutors hammered into him tales of the greatness, the glorious sacrifice of Xilu the Beneficent until

Xiane, crumbling under the weight of such an ancestor, wanted to scream. For he, the son of a mere Zharmatian concubine taken in war, had had no real worth. So had they told him a thousand, thousand times until he'd believed it.

No worth, that is, until his only brothers—both sons of the First Concubine—were executed along with their mother for plotting against the old emperor.

Xiane stared down at the delicate cup clenched in his hands, a cup with golden phoenixes sporting around it. A cup that only the emperor, and perhaps his favorites, might drink from. His cup.

He went on. "But when they reached there and descended into the bowl of the dead volcano of Rivasha, they found that it was the time of the phoenix's death and arising. They knelt before it, overwhelmed by its beauty, and fearing for their lives, yet knowing those lives were properly forfeit. They had broken the law.

"But the Phoenix looked kindly upon them and merely bade them witness its rebirth. So Xilu, Gaolun, and the Oracle watched as the Phoenix laid the last sticks of fragrant wood upon its pyre. Their hearts ached to think of the death of such beauty as the Phoenix settled upon the pyre and allowed the enchanted fire to fall from its feathers upon the logs."

Another sip of tea. "The wood burst into flames. And because the fire was the Phoenix's own, it also blazed up. They wept as they watched it die.

"But as they watched it burn into ash, a voice like nothing they'd ever heard before, a voice of unearthly beauty, rang in their minds. It was the phoenix, and because of their tears, and because the land of Jehanglan was dying under the rule of the wicked emperor and his dragons, it would aid them. Xilu, because of his righteousness, would become the next emperor of Jehanglan. Gaolun, ever devoted to his elder brother, would become the first high priest of the phoenix. The phoenix would seal itself inside the sacred mountain, lending its power to them in exchange for the worship of the people.

"And that," Xiane said, drawing a deep breath, "is how the Rule of the Phoenix came to Jehanglan." Pleased with himself, he drank the last of his tea, cold now; he had remembered everything and told it, he thought, very well.

"No," Kirano said, shattering Xiane's pleasure. "That is not how the Rule of the Phoenix came to Jehanglan. It is but a lie. Your father would never let me tell you the truth. Xilu was a warlord, greedy and ambitious, and his brother an equally greedy user of magic—the sort of magic that is forbidden in Jehanglan since their time. The Phoenix never consented to be used. It is a prisoner."

The cup fell from Xiane's hand and shattered on the floor. He stared numbly at it. From one snowy-white fragment a golden phoenix's head stared back at him. "I—I don't believe you," he stuttered as he pushed himself to his feet.

"You will."

The calm certainty struck Xiane to the heart. He fled from the truth in Kirano's face and all that it meant.

Taren ground the stick of ink against the stone, mixed the resultant powder with water and dipped the tiny brush into it. Steadying his shaking right hand with his left, Taren wrote as clearly as he could upon the tiny paper strip.

Meet at Rhampul. The troupe with—

His hand shook uncontrollably as he wrote the character for "horses." Muttering a curse, he examined it, decided it could still be read. But now the shaking fever had him in such a grip that he dared not write more lest he smear the entire message. It was no matter; he'd warn in person whichever lieutenant Lord Jhanun sent that he'd been forced to teach the outlanders Jehangli, and that the Dragonlords, at least, had been terrifyingly apt pupils.

Taren pressed his thumb first against the wet inkstone, then at the end of the message, getting as much of it upon the paper as he could. He examined it. Good; the impression was a clear one. Lord Jhanun would recognize it. He blew gently on the ink to dry it.

"Old one!" he called, drawing a hand across his forehead. It remained dry. If only this fever would break! "I need you to bind this to the pigeon's leg for me."

A rapid shuffle of feet was his answer. The old woman appeared in the doorway. "I saw, I saw," she bleated. "You have the shaking sickness, don't you, Baisha? I saw." Gnarled fingers reached for the message and a protective strip of oiled paper, plucked one of the silk threads from the table. "Come, Baisha. I know just the pigeon to use; one of the imperial breed. She's never failed."

Taren nodded his assent and wrapped his arms around his body in an effort to ward himself against the shaking. He followed her from the room and down the narrow hall to a ladder leading to a trapdoor in the roof. For all her years the old woman climbed nimbly, thrusting the trapdoor aside with surprising strength. Taren followed more slowly. Rain spattered into his eyes as the old woman gained the roof.

"Close the trapdoor," she called to him as he heaved himself up. She didn't wait for him but went straight to the pigeonloft, cooing all the while like some giant, elderly pigeon.

Taren did as she bade and followed, wishing he'd kept the grass cape and hat; If any of the others asked, he'd have trouble explaining how his clothes came to be soaked. Besides, the cold and wet just made him feel worse.

When he reached the pigeonloft, the old woman held one of the sleepy birds in her hands. It was as she said, a dove grey beauty with black across its silvery breast feathers, one of the imperial breed known for speed and strength.

"Hold her," she ordered, "while I bind the message to her leg; it's easier with two."

He wrapped his cold fingers around the bird, feeling its warmth, aware of the heart beating quickly under the soft feathers. The old woman bound the strips of paper around the pigeon's leg with a speed and deftness he would not have thought possible of the misshapen fingers. She took the bird back from him once more.

She caressed its head a moment, and sang to it, then raised her hands, and with a gentle toss sent the feathered messenger winging into the rainy night.

"So it's done," Taren said with a sigh of relief.

"It is," the old woman echoed. "That one will not fail of her charge."

"Then I'm off," said Taren. "I must be back at the hostel before the others become suspicious."

He hurried back to the trapdoor and heaved it aside, leaving the old woman to lock up her birds once more. Shaking as he was with cold and fever, it was harder to go down the ladder than it had been to go up, but he made it without falling.

But the effort made his legs tremble so much he couldn't stand. Taren sank to the floor, his back against the wall, his teeth chattering as the shivering took him with a vengeance. "Ha-ha-have you—" he gasped as the old woman descended the ladder.

"Ague bark? Yes. Sit you there, Baisha, while I brew some for you." She scuttled off.

Taren cursed as well as his chattering teeth allowed him. Damn it all, this was taking too much time! The others might begin wondering, worrying.

And that could be dangerous.

Linden, Jekkanadar, and Raven stood at the door to the hostel, looking out into the rain. Still no sign of Taren.

What's taking him so long? Linden wondered.

Trampling on the very heels of the thought, Raven said, "Where could the man be? He should have been back long ago."

"Indeed," Jekkanadar said. He rubbed the scar on his cheek, a sure sign that he was worried. "What do you think?" he said to Linden.

The landlord squalled something in a mixture of vile Assantikkan and Jehangli. It was a moment before Linden could translate it as, "Shut the damned door!"

"I think," said Linden, obeying, "that we'd best get our

cloaks and go look for the man. I know that he said he knew his way around, but a footpad needs only a moment to rob and kill if he finds a victim off guard, and Taren is not a robust man. Let's go."

On their way to fetch their cloaks, they came upon Brinn, one of the other entertainers, in the upstairs hall. "No sign of your friend yet?" he asked. The monkey riding on his shoulder pulled a wry face at them.

Linden couldn't help smiling at the droll creature and held out a finger to her. She wrapped one clever little hand around it and chattered at him before she let go.

"No," Linden said. "We're just going out to look for him."

Brinn shook his head. "Not the wisest thing to go out alone here. This place is like a maze and who can you ask for directions? I sure don't speak their bird's jabber." He paused, then looked over his shoulder before continuing in a lower voice, "Hate to say it, seeing as you're looking so worried about Taren and all, but I heard a story or two on the voyage that would curl your hair, about what these Jehangli barbarians do to foreigners who go outside this quarter without leave. Why—"

A door opened and Dorilissa, the other troupe's leader, came out of the chamber.

"Seeing as how they're looking so worried about Taren and all, Brinn," she snapped, "why don't you stop wasting their time and help them look for the poor man? Rouse the other men—it's not safe for the girls out there, get snatched for brothels, they might, the innkeeper said—rouse the other men still here, I say, and go look for him!" She held out her arm and chirped to the monkey. The monkey jumped from Brinn's shoulder to her new perch. "Toli stays here; I don't want her catching a chill," Dorilissa said as she went back into her chamber, alternately muttering imprecations at Brinn and cooing endearments to the monkey. Her door slammed shut once more.

"Yes, ma'am," Brinn said meekly to the door. He slunk off to do her bidding.

"Meet us in the tap room," Linden called after him, glad of both the reprieve and the help.

"I like that," Jekkanadar said with a chuckle. "The menfolk can go out and get soaked unto death on a night like this—but not the monkey!"

They reached the door to the room Otter and Raven shared. Linden laid a hand on the latch. "Now comes the worst part."

Jekkanadar looked startled, but only for a moment. "Oh," he said. "Indeed."

"Indeed," Linden echoed, and opened the door.

Taren tried to crawl down the hall to the stairway. But after only a few feet he had to give up; his shaking limbs threatened to spill him onto his face, and bruises would be too awkward to explain.

He sat back against the wall once more, cursing in frustration.

"We'll go, too," said Lleld after Linden announced their intention of looking for Taren. She glanced over at Maurynna, who nodded. "I'm sure Dorilissa or one of the other women will stay with Otter. Would you mind?" she asked the bard.

Otter shook his head. "That would be fine," he croaked.

"No," Linden said. When both Maurynna and Lleld glared at him in astonished anger, he said, "Dorilissa just told us this quarter isn't considered safe for women, especially at night."

"I'll remind you that I'm in charge, Linden," Lleld said. "Not you."

In the moment of frozen silence that followed, Maurynna asked, "Is it not safe for women because of thugs who capture women for brothels?"

"Just so. We can't go in a group to look for Taren because we won't be able to cover enough area fast enough; we'll need to split up. You'd both be too tempting as targets."

"Oh, Linden—I've heard that tale in every port I've been in, and never met anyone who actually knew someone it happened to! It's always been 'a friend of a friend's cousin's aunt' or some such foolishness," Maurynna said.

"Rynna and I are more than capable of handling filth like that, Linden—or are you forgetting that we're also Dragon-lords?" Lleld said, her voice icy.

"Or are you once more coddling me nigh to smothering?" Maurynna asked far too quietly and calmly.

"Blast it, Lleld, I haven't forgotten anything. Nor am I trying to protect you, Maurynna. But think! Even if you each came with one of us, it still might invite an attack, and I know both of you well enough to know you won't—indeed, *can't*—stand by and play the helpless female.

"So then what? What if word got back to the authorities that there are two women here who are far stronger than any woman should be—especially a woman as small as you, Lleld? Can we afford the questions that would be asked? Can we afford the attention?" Linden ran a hand through his hair in frustration. He looked at Maurynna, silently begging her to understand.

"Blast you," she said at last. Her eyes burned with anger. "Why do you have to be right?"

Lleld cursed. "He is, isn't he? Very well, Linden; this shall be a military operation. You're in charge—for now."

Would the damned old hag never get here with that tea? Taren's teeth chattered with a sound like bamboo stems rattling against each other in a storm. He had to get back to the inn!

He heard slow footsteps coming back up the stairs.

"Revien, Willisen, and Vaden went out earlier, right after Taren left," Brinn reported when all the searchers were gathered in the taproom. "They was looking for a dice game—least, Willisen and Vaden was. Revien's likely found a whore to stay with; he usually does. So it's just me and Laeris to help."

"That's still more searchers than we would have had," Linden said as he slung on his cloak. "We'll divide up the market and look."

Maurynna stood silently at his side. She chewed her lower lip.

Linden bent his head so that their foreheads touched. "Don't worry, love. We'll find him," he said quietly.

Just as quietly she replied, "I'm more worried for you. I wish we could go with you; Dorilissa could stay with Otter." She sighed. "But I understand—barely—why we can't."

He stroked her hair and gave one lock a gentle tug. "We'll be fine, though I do wish you could come along. We could use another Dra—" He broke off; Laeris was looking at them. "Take care of Otter for us, love."

"I shall."

The innkeeper eyed them all sourly as he wiped down a table. "You drink or look?" he demanded in his bastardized Assantikkan. "Take up space, you buy."

"We're off now," Jekkanadar replied. "Do you have lanterns we could borrow?"

Linden nodded to himself. Good thinking, that; they couldn't use their coldfire here.

"Cost you extra," the innkeeper said. His eyes glinted.

Jekkanadar smiled, and said sweetly, "What do we care—since it will be whatever lord hires us who pays our board. We'll be certain to tell him of this." As a look of dismay passed over the innkeeper's face, Jekkanadar added, "Ah! You weren't thinking of overcharging our prospective patron, were you? I don't think whoever he is would be at all pleased at that."

The innkeeper paled. "Take them and go," he spat. He yelled for a potboy to bring the lanterns and handed them out along with curses to see the "dirty foreign dogs" out the door.

"Good luck to you," Maurynna said, and squeezed Linden's hand. "Find him quickly."

*   *   *

Taren drained the last of the tea. Whether it was the warmth or the medicine itself, already the shivering had eased. He closed his eyes, willing the fit to pass completely. The moment he knew his legs would carry him, he stood and took stock of his condition.

No, he was not as well as he might be. He still shivered, but it would have to do; he'd been gone far too long.

"We'll split up," Linden said, "and quarter the market." He gave directions to the men. "Understood?"

The others nodded.

"Good, then; we'll meet back here in about a candlemark. Let's be off."

The men hurried off into the rainy night.

Taren hurried as quickly as he could down the stairs to the front room and threw the grass rain cape over his shoulders. Next he jammed the hat onto his head, letting the strings dangle.

Moments later he was back in the street. He trotted along, staggering a little when a particularly bad spell took him, but keeping as steady a pace as he could. Sometimes, though, he had to stop and rest, cursing every moment he wasted.

A little more than a candlemark later, Linden held up his lantern; the men straggled one by one out of the darkness. He counted as they came to the light. Just four men besides himself; Taren was still missing, then.

He swore under his breath. "No sign of him?"

"None," came the tired answer.

"Then we try again."

Someone groaned; the cloaked figures turned away from the light and disappeared like ghosts into the darkness once more.

Soon Taren was just outside of the outlanders' quarter.

He came to one of the many small, arching stone bridges

that spanned the canals. He slowed then, not wanting to lose his footing on the rain-slick pavement; hearing quick footsteps behind him, Taren moved to one side to allow the other to pass.

"Taren? That is you, isn't it? What are you doing here?"

Taren hesitated a moment, then turned, a long, slender, needlelike blade now in his palm. He kept it hidden under his grass cloak. "I might," he said, when he saw who it was, "ask the same of you, eh?"

"I thought you were looking for something for Otter's cough."

"I did, and a cursed lot of trouble I had to find it," said Taren, pointing under his cloak with his free hand. "It's right here. And look what else I found."

Another spasm of coughing took Otter. Maurynna supported him through it; at last it ended, leaving the bard limp and weak. He leaned back against the wall.

Lleld hurried up with a cup of tea. "Here, drink this; perhaps it will help."

"It hasn't yet," Otter wheezed good-naturedly as he took the crude cup. "But it's certainly better than nothing." He drank. "Gods, what I'd give for a glass of good Pelnaran wine right now. Or better yet, Elenna's ale."

"Indeed," Maurynna said. She sighed. "That would mean we were home again."

Lleld sat on the edge of the low bed. "Where are they?" she complained.

Curiosity aroused, the other wanderer came forward. "Oh? What—"

"Hist! Quiet! Is that a guard coming up behind you?" Taren whispered.

The man spun around, searching the rainy darkness. If he got into trouble—

An arm slid around his neck. *What!* his mind screamed. His desperate fingers scrabbled at the iron grip that choked him but to no avail. Gasping, he sank to his knees. With a final effort he reached behind and tried to claw his attacker's face. But all he succeeded in doing was knocking Taren's hat off. He saw it fall over the side of the bridge.

Taren's voice snarled something in his ear but the man's mind was too frozen with fear to understand. White-hot pain blazed through his skull.

Xiane rode away from the hunting lodge with the uncomfortable feeling he'd played the coward, refusing to let Kirano speak any more of Xilu, insisting when he returned to the room that they speak of anything but that.

Yes, it had been cowardly. But Phoenix help him, he was not ready to hear Kirano's "truth" about his ancestor and the founding of their dynasty. He wasn't certain he'd ever be ready to hear it.

Because if everything he'd been taught all his life *were* a lie, Xiane knew there was only one thing he could do.

And it was the one thing he couldn't bring himself to do. Not so much for his own sake, but for Xahnu's.

No, he could never do such a thing to his son.

But if it were the only way to right an ancient wrong?

Xiane dug his spurs into his horse. Startled, it leaped into a gallop, leaving their escort to scramble after.

He would think about it another time. Now he wanted to lose himself in Shei-Luin's charms.

Ironic, Xiane thought, how the father could frighten and the daughter entice.

"Linden! Linden! I found him!"

Linden turned back from the stinking alley he was just about to search with a sigh of relief. He saw two figures hurrying to him, one helping the other along. Linden ran to meet them.

"Good work, Laeris. Taren! Are you well?" he called.

The face that peered up at him when he reached the two men was deathly pale, and the eyes glittered with fever. The rain sluiced down his face.

"I apologize for being so much trouble," Taren said with

a smile that was but a tired shadow of his usual sweet one.
"I had to go much further than I thought I would. Then a
bout of this old sickness took me and I had to sit in a
doorway and rest for a very long time. But"—he patted his
beltpouch—"I have Otter's medicine. Shall we take it to
him?"

Magic. Magic walked through his dreams, a magic of a
kind he'd not felt in far too long.

Northern magic. Dragon magic.

The old dragon stirred in his sleep, twisted and turned
as he had not done for many lives of men. Far above, the
surface of the lake swirled angrily; waves threw themselves
against the shores.

Those of humankind who lived along those shores stared
in wonder as their placid lake tossed as if in a storm—but
the night was still.

"Ah," they told each other. "It's the Old One. He stirs."

Far below, the old dragon sank back into his dreams.
The time of his awakening had not yet come.

But soon.

Thirty-seven

*A **fruit seller, rising early*** to get the best place by the
gate, caught sight of a straw hat bobbing in the water by
the pilings at the far end of the bridge. Whistling with
delight, he wheeled his laden barrow across and, after making certain no one was about to steal his melons, leaped
the parapet and scrambled down the steep bank.

Ah, it was a fine hat—at least compared to his own,
which was frayed and tattered at the edges. He reached for
it eagerly, one hand gripping a projecting stone to support

himself, the fingertips of the other just grasping the hat. He tugged at it.

It was caught on something, something under the bridge. He sighed; was nothing in his life ever to be easy? Grumbling, the man leaned out a little farther and looked under the span.

It took some moments before he realized what he gazed on. Then he was up and climbing the bank as fast as he could. Grabbing his wheelbarrow once more, he hurried to the market. Some of the city guard would be there even this early. Let them deal with a drowned body. He wanted nothing more to do with it—or the hat.

Raven, in his guise as servant, was the first downstairs the next morning. He walked into the main room of the inn to find it filled with men dressed alike in red and gold, wearing helmets and bearing weapons—the first he'd seen in Jehanglan.

Soldiers! We've been betrayed, he thought in a panic. His knees almost gave way; suddenly it was hard to breathe. He stopped, one hand on the newel post, hoping they wouldn't turn around and notice him.

Idiot; of course they will. You stick out as badly as a purple sheep in a flock. Still, he could hope. He carefully eased one foot onto the lowest stairstep, intending to sneak back upstairs.

They noticed. Or, rather, the innkeeper pointed him out to the soldiers. One came toward him; it was easy to see this one was in charge. He stared at Raven's hair and eyes, then made some comment Raven could make no sense of. The other guards looked uneasily at each other.

The man spoke again, slowly; he paused, as if expecting a response.

Raven could only stare down at the Jehangli. His breath came short and fast. He'd never been so frightened in his life; part of him stayed aloof enough to despise himself for it.

The soldier—*Captain?*—Raven's mind named a rank—

frowned and spoke once, more sharply this time. He gestured impatiently.

Raven started as footsteps came down the stairs behind him. He turned to see Jekkanadar. As always, the Dragonlord's dark, lean face was calm. Raven went weak with relief; Jekkanadar would know what to do.

The soldier repeated his earlier words. To his shame, this time Raven could make them out; the words were badly pronounced, but they were Assantikkan. Had he not been paralyzed with fear, he would have understood them.

And he was the one they all depended upon to guard Maurynna? Gods help him, he was nothing but a coward.

Then the meaning of the soldier's words sank in.

"Have body—you look. All look."

Everyone into Otter's room! Otter—pretend to be much sicker than you are; Maurynna, tend to him. We've unexpected company.

Jekkanadar's mindvoice burst into his mind; Linden cursed and sprang for the door, Maurynna and Lleld right behind him. He didn't question Jekkanadar. The other Dragonlord would not have dared mindspeech unless the need was extreme.

In moments they were in the room Otter and Raven shared. Otter was burrowing under the quilts on the bed as they entered. He sagged back against the pillow, feigning weakness; his sudden pallor, however, was real. Footsteps— too many footsteps—echoed down the hall.

Lleld tugged a kerchief from her belt pouch. "Get that bowl of water and bathe his brow," she whispered, tossing the kerchief to Maurynna.

Maurynna grabbed the bowl and sat on the edge of the bed, wiping Otter's pale face with the damp kerchief. Linden sat on the opposite side from her.

The door flew open, and Jekkanadar and Raven entered, followed closely by Jehangli soldiers. As ever, Jekkanadar's expression betrayed nothing. But Linden took one look at Raven's ashen face and was sick at heart.

Look at him—he's well-nigh fainting with terror! And this boy is the one to guard Maurynna? Bitterest of all, he could say or do nothing. Raven was the only one they had.

"Fool boy!" he snapped. "What kind of trouble have you brought us?"

The harsh words had the effect he'd hoped for. The color came back to Raven's face, and the glassy-eyed stare of terror turned into a burning glare of hatred.

"That's better, lad," Linden said quietly in Yerrin. "Stop worrying; things may not be as bad as they seem."

At first he thought Raven didn't understand his mountain accent. Then the gamble paid off; at the sound of his childhood language, surprise replaced hatred in Raven's eyes. "Now take a deep breath; we'll get out of this yet," Linden continued. *I hope.*

Raven's chest rose in a long, slow breath and the boy nodded slightly in understanding.

Linden stood up, pretending a calmness he didn't feel. "What is this about?" he said to Jekkanadar. He walked casually around the bed, putting himself between Maurynna and the soldiers as if by chance.

"They've found a body," the other Dragonlord said. "They think he has something to do with us."

Linden frowned; who could it be? Taren was back with them, so it wasn't— "Bloody hell—does anyone know if Willisen, Vaden, and Revien came back last night?"

"Damnation," Lleld breathed so softly only another Dragonlord might hear her.

One soldier, evidently the leader, snapped, "Quiet!" and continued in broken Assantikkan to Jekkanadar, "What that one say? You all come. Now."

Linden switched to Assantikkan. "We're traveling entertainers. Our singer is ill," he began, gesturing at the grim-faced Otter. He gave up at the look of frustrated incomprehension on the Jehangli's face.

He's getting maybe one word in three, Linden thought in frustration. *If only we dared speak Jehangli! I'm certain we could make ourselves understood.* He didn't even consider waking Taren; the man had been near collapse last evening.

The man turned to one of the other soldiers. "Find an interpreter who speaks Assantikkan," the Jehangli ordered. The soldier saluted and left smartly.

Thank the gods; the man has some sense. Linden exchanged a relieved glance with Jekkanadar.

He considered asking Jekkanadar in *arolan* what was afoot, but the captain looked in a temper already; no sense in annoying him. If only he dared further mindspeech to find out what Jekkanadar knew. Who could it be? And what did this mean for them?

He ground his teeth in quiet frustration.

The captain snapped a low-voiced order to his men and the interpreter. Four of the soldiers left the room.

Although the man had spoken too quickly for Linden to catch all he said, Linden was certain of the gist: "Round them all up. Bring them here."

That he'd guessed right was confirmed a short time later when some of the members of the second troupe were herded in, Vaden stumbling and with red-rimmed, squinting eyes that spoke of too much raw wine.

It must, an irreverent voice in the back of Linden's mind noted, have been some dice game.

The interpreter, a merchant's clerk who spoke Assantikkan—of sorts—translated the captain's tidings about the body found that morning. "Are any not here?" the translator finished.

Dorilissa looked around. "I don't speak much Assantikkan; will you tell him that we're not all here yet, but—" She looked over at Vaden.

"Left Willisen at the dice game with the sailors from our ship," he mumbled. "He was dead drunk, so was the sailors; I couldn't get him and me back."

"Revien?"

"Found himself a whore to stay with—as usual." Vaden groaned and held his head in his hands. "M'head hurts."

Jekkanadar told all this to the clerk, who passed it on to the Jehangli commander.

The order came. "Captain Riushi wishes all to come."

"No," Linden said immediately. "Of our people, the two young ones and the old man stay." At all costs Maurynna must stay out of the hands of the soldiers; she *was* the mission. If something went wrong, and the soldiers cast them into jail after viewing the body, he could at least mindspeak her to get away.

The captain's head snapped around to look at him, no doubt wary at his tone; the soldiers still with him came to full attention.

More of the other troupe filed in along with more soldiers. The latter came alert at the sight of their fellows standing at ready.

"You see," Jekkanadar said placatingly to the interpreter, "our singer is ill, and these two are but servants." He waved at Maurynna, who still bathed Otter's forehead, and Raven, who now brewed tea over the brazier. Otter coughed pitiably. "We don't need them. He does."

The interpreter, a merchant's clerk, took a moment to compose his thoughts—or steel himself to pass on their refusal—then spoke rapidly to the captain.

The captain's black eyes glittered with anger. But before he could say anything, the door opened once more and the rest of Dorilissa's people squeezed into the crowded room along with Taren, who looked tired and ill. The soldier accompanying them went straight to the captain and whispered something in his ear.

The captain was a stalwart man; his face betrayed nothing. But Linden saw the man's gloved fist close convulsively on the hilt of his sword.

Then, to Linden's relief, after a long moment of reflection, the captain's hand dropped and he nodded. But the look he turned on Linden said he had not forgotten—or forgiven—the defiance. The Jehangli smiled coldly and pointed to the door.

Linden understood. He was to go and view the body as

a punishment. He had no doubt that he had barely escaped worse.

But what had held the man back?

"I'd best go as well," Dorilissa said, pushing her way to the front. "It might be . . ." She bit her lip. The others murmured, "Avert," behind her.

The soldiers herded them out of the room without even a chance to say good-bye. Linden looked back and almost wished he hadn't at the sight of Maurynna's stricken face.

They were out in the street before anyone realized that another had joined them. Somehow Lleld had slipped into the group. Linden glared at her; she thumbed her nose in return.

As they passed through the streets, Jehangli everywhere stopped to stare. There were comments about Linden's size, his Marking, and the color of his hair. None were looked upon favorably. "Yellow ox" was one of the least insulting observations. Dorilissa's florid complexion also drew a number of scathing remarks.

But most of the comments were about Lleld's red hair. A few mothers even covered their children's eyes as the little Dragonlord passed.

They went much farther than Linden had supposed they would, past a placard that he suspected marked the border of the foreigners' quarter, and into a section of shabby buildings separated by canals. As they went over one bridge—a good walk from the hostel—the captain pointed to the water and said something to the clerk that Linden couldn't catch.

"He found there," the clerk said in his pitiful Assantik-kan.

Linden exchanged a surprised glance with Lleld. Why so far away? And who was it?

Gods, but it was hard not to use mindspeech! Linden nearly cursed aloud in frustration. But looming over the lesser buildings were the gilded towers of a temple, or so he guessed it to be by the images of a great golden bird upon them; they didn't dare use mindspeech again so close to a priestmages' lair.

The captain led them to a wooden building a short distance beyond the fatal bridge. Guards stood on either side of the door. They snapped to attention as the captain pushed the interpreter inside first, then went in himself, the Dragonlords and Dorilissa close on his heels. The guards followed, bringing up the rear.

Inside was lit with smoky torches stuck into rings in the walls. The room looked to be a warehouse of sorts; there were wooden boxes that had, judging by the marks in the dirt floor, been shoved aside to clear a space.

The reason lay upon a straw mat in the center of the room. It was the body of a man, his face uncovered, a rough canvas sheet pulled up to his neck. Thin brown hair, coated with some substance, hung in stiff rattails; in the torchlight the sallow skin looked like wax.

Although it was what they'd expected, they all stopped short. The captain looked at them.

"Oh, gods," Dorilissa said weakly. She swayed; Linden caught her arm. For a moment Dorilissa clung to him, her eyes locked on the corpse before them. Then she drew herself up and stepped away from Linden.

"It's Revien," she said. Tears shone on her cheeks. "Revien, you pain in the ass, what were you—" Her voice broke. Dorilissa turned away, her face buried in her hands.

"He one of yours, then?" the interpreter asked.

"Yes," Lleld said grimly in Assantikkan. Her childlike face was bleak. "Or rather, one of Dorilissa's. His name was Revien."

"What he doing wandering Jedjieh?" the captain demanded through the interpreter. "Only foreign quarter allowed, all else forbidden to outlanders."

"I don't know," Lleld replied shortly.

The captain had enough Assantikkan to understand that. Linden could see more angry questions burning in the man's eyes. Questions that for some reason the man did not let slip past lips pressed in a hard line like the slash of a knife.

"He—he didn't like the food at the inn," Dorilissa hurried to say. "So he . . . He must have gotten lost; he left us while it was still light out."

The clerk relayed this to the obviously disbelieving captain. Linden bent over the body, listening with half his attention to the discussion between Dorilissa, the interpreter, and the captain as they all spoke in the worst Assantikkan he'd ever heard. Lleld joined him at Revien's side.

Revien's eyes were still open, staring into eternity; Linden shut them and studied the expression on the dead face. Death had blurred the lines there but not yet erased them.

<<He died in pain,>> Linden said in an undertone, speaking *arolan*. He knelt on the mat by the body.

<<There's fear there, too,>> she replied as softly, joining him on the floor. <<Was it his heart, do you think?>>

<<Perhaps, though I don't think so. He's the right age for it, but he seemed healthy enough. I'll wager it was robbery.>>

He drew back the canvas sheet that covered the body, exposing Revien's naked torso to the waist. No, no stab wounds in the chest. Not that he'd expected it; a robber would strike from behind. Well and well; he would soon see.

Wondering if Revien had tried to save himself from the water, Linden drew each hand in turn from under the sheeting. But the skin was not scraped and torn as it would be from clutching at the rough stone the bridges were made of. So Revien was either dead or unconscious when he went into the water.

Linden noticed a thin sliver of something under one grubby nail. *Dried grass? From where in these city streets?*

He gently rolled the body onto its right side so that he could see the back. Nothing amiss there, either. He frowned, perplexed. *Did the robber use a club, then?*

His gaze traveled up to the head. Through the clumps of thin brown hair he could see that no blow had been struck.

He fingered one of the caked strands of hair; a vile-smelling green powder came off on his hand.

Of course; scum from the canal, dried now. He wiped his hand on the matting.

Then something caught his eye. He looked a little more closely and let the body down again, sick with an ancient memory.

All this drew the attention of the captain. He gestured Dorilissa to sit on one of the boxes, then crossed the room. The merchant's clerk lagged behind. It was plain the sight of the dead man repelled him.

"Bah," the captain said to him in their own language. "Do you think a body will hurt you, chicken-hearted one?"

"There may be a ghost," the clerk insisted. "How do I know what the spirits of these foreign dogs might do? I would not have it follow me. Besides, he looks like the belly of a fish. They all do, save the Assantikkan back at the hostel." He rubbed his own honey-colored skin. "And the little female has hair like a demon. Maybe she is one."

The captain shook his head in disgust. "Ask the yellow-haired barbarian what he does."

It was hard to hold his tongue, Linden found, and pretend ignorance—especially of the insults. Then, too, the time taken in the translations was annoying—all the more so since it was poorly done. But he forced himself to wait while the clerk—stubbornly ensconced as far away from Revien's body as he could get—translated the captain's question with painful slowness.

"Looking for wounds," Linden said slowly in Assantik-kan. "I thought perhaps he'd been robbed." He waited patiently through the translation.

To the interpreter, the captain said, "There are no wounds. He was found in the canal; he drowned. Perhaps he was drunk and fell off the bridge. It happens frequently. Tell them the man's clothes and pouch are in that basket over there."

Linden started to rise, intending to examine Revien's belongings; a sharp jab in the ribs stopped him. Lleld blinked innocently at him and he nodded, realizing what he'd almost done. He swallowed hard, feeling a little sick; he'd have to play the game better than this.

When the translation finally came, Lleld passed it on to Dorilissa. "Do you want to see his things?"

Wiping her eyes, Dorilissa shook her head. "No," she whispered. "I mean, I do, but I can't. Could ... would you—"

"Yes," Lleld said gently, and went to the basket. She tugged the lid off and pawed through the contents. Her hand came up holding Revien's belt pouch. She shook it and was answered with the clinking of coins.

<<He was right; it wasn't robbery,>> she said in *arolan*. She opened the pouch and rummaged in it, then held up a carved stone for all to see.

"That's a luck amulet," one of the other guards said. "A cheap one; it's for gambling and love. They're sold in the eastern end of the market, where all the trinket dealers are."

"Then he was far from the stalls of the food sellers," the captain replied idly, smiling in amusement as the interpreter translated. To the guard he said, "Looking for a whore with the money he won, you think?"

The guard grinned, showing crooked teeth. "Maybe it was too much for his heart."

The clerk didn't bother translating.

Linden frowned. Then why ... He made a decision.

"The man must have been drunk," Linden said to the interpreter. "Why else fall off the bridge?" He drew the canvas sheet up once more. From the corner of his eye he saw Lleld about to protest. He willed her to say nothing, wishing again for mindspeech.

Somehow it worked. Also speaking in Assantikkan, Lleld said, "Likely. Now what happens?"

Once this was translated, the captain smiled with grim amusement and said, "Now you'll come with me and answer questions."

*　　*　　*

"What happened? Who was it?" Maurynna demanded the moment Lleld and Linden were back in Otter's room at the inn. "Why were you gone so long?"

"Give us a moment to catch our breath, love," Linden said as he sank wearily onto the edge of the bed; Lleld did the same beside him. "We spent too damn long answering questions for that blasted captain of the guard. That's why we're so late." He stretched his long legs out with a groan. The little room where the guard had taken them for questioning had been too small for him to extend his legs without kicking someone—as he had been tempted to a few times. Still, in the end the guards had seemed satisfied and let them go.

Yet beneath it all he'd felt questions the captain had wanted to ask, and didn't, like a water snake swimming below the surface of a pond.

Otter took the chair facing them, Raven on the floor at his feet. Maurynna sat cross-legged on the woven grass matting near the bed.

Linden was glad to see the bard feeling well enough to get up. But that still left one of their band unaccounted for. "Where's Taren?"

"Back to bed," Raven answered. "That soaking he got last night didn't do his shaking sickness any good."

Linden nodded absently. Something tugged at his mind; something that hadn't seemed quite right. . . .

Otter said, "It was Revien, wasn't it?" and drove the thought from Linden's mind.

"Yes. How did you know?" Lleld asked.

"Because Willisen returned not long after you left. And since we were keeping watch at the window, we saw Dorilissa's face as the lot of you came up the street. What happened to him? Robbery turned to murder?"

"No; he wasn't robbed. The captain thinks he was drunk," Lleld said, "and fell off the bridge and drowned. I wonder if it could have been his heart."

"He was murdered," Linden said shortly.

"What!" the others exclaimed. A confused babble followed.

When it died down, Lleld demanded, "What do you mean? I examined Revien's body the same as you. There were no wounds, and the money was still in his belt pouch. Do you think he was poisoned?"

Linden rubbed the back of his neck, trying to ease his tense muscles. It had been hard during the questioning not to betray what he knew. He wasn't surprised the guards hadn't seen the evidence; it would have been easy for true-human eyes to miss in the poor light.

He sighed. "There was a tiny triangular tear in the skin at the base of the skull below the left ear. I looked a little more closely; it was a small hole, hard to see, but notable because of its shape. If his hair hadn't been hanging in clumps as it was, I wouldn't have noticed it.

"But I saw something like it once before, long ago. When we—the Wolfkin, that is; Bram and Rani's mercenary band—were hired by Prince Khirin of Kelneth, there was a traitor in his camp. Some of our people died mysteriously—by poison or magic, we thought at first. It was our herbalist, Tiglin, who discovered the truth."

He frowned at the floor, lost in his thoughts for a moment, remembering the first death. Tall, grizzled Stoat, a warrior to his calloused fingertips. Stoat, who'd taken pity on a sixteen-year-old boy fool enough to run away from home in the dead of winter, and taught that same young idiot what he needed to know to survive in a mercenary camp and in a war. Even now he could hear Channa's heartbroken wail when she found her husband's body that grey morning. It still haunted him down the centuries.

Linden shook himself back into the present. "It's done with something like a long awl, something pointed and narrow. A sharp thrust here"—he touched the base of his skull—"drives it up into the brain. Death is instantaneous. And all there is to give it away is a tiny puncture wound that can barely be seen. How Tiglin ever guessed . . ."

"That's no soldier's trick," Otter said. His lip curled in disgust. "That's a thief or—"

"An assassin," Lleld finished. "Revien wasn't robbed, so it wasn't a thief. But why would an assassin seek him out?"

"Worse yet," Jekkanadar said, "who would hire one? And was it meant for Revien or one of us?"

"If so," said Maurynna, "then which of us is next?"

Thirty-eight

Yesuin woke as a hand clamped over his mouth and a weight fell on his chest, pinning him to his bed. He struggled, but it was no use; his unconscious habit of wrapping the bed silks around himself like a cocoon meant he could neither strike nor kick. Panic seized him.

He felt lips move against his ear. After a moment, he understood the words they whispered: "I come from the emperor! This is the time you said your farewells against."

Yesuin went limp to show his visitor that he'd heard. At once the hand was gone from his mouth, and the weight pinning him disappeared. Shaking, he sat up, pushing the silks away with a whispered oath.

The room was dark; he saw Xiane's messenger as only a deeper blackness moving through the shadows. Looking out of the window, he found he could still see stars. He picked out the one called Bright Princess; she was halfway between zenith and setting. It was still some time before dawn, then.

A tiny light flared in the room. Yesuin threw up a hand to shield his eyes. When they were used to the sudden glow, he looked once more. A man stood watching him, a little lamp in his hand.

Yesuin recognized him at once. "You're the one who brought the emperor the message that day!"

The young officer nodded. "Yes. Since his Imperial Majesty promoted me, I've enjoyed nothing but good fortune. I would do anything for him. But you must hurry. On my way here, I heard some of the senior officers making plans for your arrest. All that's holding them back is the fear of disturbing the emperor so late at night—they know your rooms are near his. Still, I'm afraid they may not be far behind me."

He bent and picked up a bundle from the floor by his feet, then tossed it onto the bed beside Yesuin. It landed heavily. "The dress of an imperial messenger," the officer explained as Yesuin clawed the bundle open, "along with passes for the outposts, tokens for horses, money for supplies once you reach the border towns—everything you need. There's a horse waiting for you in a secret place."

He described the place; Yesuin knew it. More than once Xiane had sent a private messenger off from there. And there was a way there from the tunnels. . . .

Now that his first fright was over, Yesuin was strangely calm. It surprised him. He pulled on the sturdy breeches and short robe, then the thick felt-and-leather boots with steady hands. "Does Xiane know?"

"He does. The day he gave me this commission, he gave me permission to approach him day or night the instant a message came that your brother had broken the treaty."

The officer's hand slipped into his sleeve and came out once more. Before it went back into hiding, Yesuin caught a glimpse of a token that few were ever given.

Almost done. He jammed the felt cap low over his forehead. At last he stood up and slipped the strap of the message pouch that completed his disguise over his head so that it went diagonally across his chest. The pouch was heavy against his hip; Xiane had been generous.

As he always has been.

"I'm ready," he said at last. A thought came to him. "You said that there were officers planning to arrest me."

"Just so. The messenger went first to General Guanli. He's the one who's so afraid to disturb the emperor." The look of disgust on his face told Yesuin who had been responsible for the appearance of this man in the garden that day.

"If they come for me, can you distract them, send them off on a fool's chase?" *Let him say "yes".* . . .

The officer nodded. "Easily. Tell 'em some eunuch said you were off with this female slave or that lady's maid—it would work. Guanli doesn't want to set foot in this part of the palace if he can help it. But how will you—"

"I have a way," Yesuin broke in. It was stupid what he planned—pure idiocy—but he had to try. "Go. Lead them astray."

The officer nodded. He went to the door, but paused. "I will. Go as quickly as you can. And go with the emperor's blessing; he said to tell you he loved you like a brother."

Yesuin's throat grew tight. "Tell him I wish he was, for he was better to me than my brother ever was, and I loved him as I never loved Yemal. Tell him I wish we were sitting at a campfire, telling each other lies about the hunt."

The next moment Yesuin was alone. He locked the door, then ran across the room to the hidden door to the tunnels. As he slipped through and latched it behind him, he suddenly realized he'd never asked the officer his name, so that he could burn incense to the man's ancestors. With practiced fingers, he lit the small lamp he kept just inside the tunnel, dropping the flint and steel in his pouch. It would be useful later.

It was just as well, he realized, that he didn't know the man's name. *That way I can't name him if I'm captured and tortured.*

As he might well be if he went through with his foolish plan. But even as he argued with himself to go straight to where the horse was tied, his feet led him down the tunnels to the quarters of the First Concubine.

For once he didn't care about moving quietly. He ran like a man chased by demons.

* * *

So it had come at last. He'd known it would, but that didn't ease the pain. He was about to lose the closest thing to a true brother he'd ever had, his only friend, and it hurt.

Xiane paced his sleeping chamber. The slapping of his bare feet was the only sound. For once he was alone; his eunuchs, having seen the token carried by the hooded messenger, had retreated to their own beds. This was no business of theirs.

If only he could say farewell. . . . It was best not to go; he might change his mind and beg Yesuin to stay. And Yesuin would. He would stay—to be the emperor's only friend until the day a swift dagger between his ribs ended his life.

No—he had said his farewells already, sent a final message with the captain. It would have to do.

The night air was cool against his bare skin. Xiane raked his fingers through his long black hair, freed for the night from the topknot every Jehangli man wore in public.

If only, if only, if only . . .

It came to him that he now understood how the tiger in its cage in his private zoo felt. Back and forth, back and forth it would pace, just as he paced now, snarling and lashing out at the bars that imprisoned him, as Xiane wished he could do. But there was nothing to strike out against.

But he could not stay here alone. Not this night. As he passed the bed, he caught up the robe he'd thrown off when he went to sleep earlier. Shrugging it on, he threw open the door of his sleeping chamber and strode through the outer rooms, a bevy of surprised, sleepy, and half-dressed eunuchs staggering from their beds and running to catch up as he walked swiftly down the hall.

Besides, Xiane thought, old Guanli the Chicken-hearted could not arrest Yesuin until officially informing him of the breaking of the treaty. And Guanli would *never* dare roust him from where he went now. Never.

Xiane smiled broadly at the thought.

* * *

The startled trilling of her maids' voices woke Shei-Luin from a deep sleep. She sat up, listening, her heart pounding.

Who could it be at this hour? Is something amiss with the boys?

But there were no wails of grief as there would have been had ill befallen her children. Instead there was silence. The door to her sleeping chamber opened, and Murohshei entered, a lamp in his hand. He wore the expression of a man who didn't believe what he'd just seen. Without a word, he set about lighting the lamps in her room.

When she opened her mouth to demand an explanation, he shook his head violently at her.

The answer appeared in the doorway. Xiane! She hissed under her breath. How dare he—

She blinked. Xiane's hair was loose, hanging over his shoulders and down his back. Shei-Luin sat up straighter, feeling as bewildered as her eunuch looked.

The emperor of Jehanglan had walked the halls of his palace with his hair loose like some Tah'nehsieh barbarian? What was happening? And his expression . . . Shei-Luin had never seen Xiane look sad before.

"What is it?" she asked. "The children—"

"Are well," Xiane finished heavily. To Murohshei, he said only, "Out."

Murohshei lingered barely long enough to bow. When they were alone, Shei-Luin got out of bed. Xiane, she saw, didn't even notice she was naked as she walked past. He sat on the edge of the bed, staring at the floor.

Confusion warred with concern. As she pulled on a light robe, she asked, "What's wrong, my lord?"

Xiane took a deep breath before answering, "I came to tell you because I know you and Yesuin were friends as children. Oduin must be dead. Yemal has broken the treaty."

And that meant—Her knees turned weak. Somehow she made it back to the bed. She sank down next to Xiane, unable to say a word. Her heart pounded, and roared in her ears.

"Yemal broke the treaty," he said, almost to himself, "and so I lose my only friend."

Shei-Luin swayed as the world turned grey around her. Somehow she kept from fainting. "Yesuin?" she whispered. "Yesuin is dead?"

Xiane looked up at her in surprise. "Of course not!" he said, exasperated. "Didn't I just say he was my friend? Do you think I would let my friend—my only true friend—die for another's actions?"

She said faintly, "Then Yesuin—"

"Is on his way to the border, disguised as an imperial messenger. I arranged it all when I first got word that Oduin was ill."

Relief flooded her. She drew a long, trembling breath. "You arranged his escape? Even for you, my lord, that's a risky thing. There are those lords who will be furious at being cheated of 'revenge' for Yemal's actions."

And Xiane had chosen to defy them for the sake of a powerless, expendable hostage. No—for the sake of his friend.

By the Phoenix, she'd never thought she could ever respect Xiane, or anything he did. She'd been wrong—very wrong.

On a sudden impulse, she leaned forward and cupped his face in her hands. As his eyes widened in surprise, she kissed him—and meant it.

Nor did she mind when he reached for her. She knew that he wanted—needed—comforting. This night he would have it ungrudgingly.

At last—the tunnel that led to the First Concubine's sleeping chamber! Yesuin slowed to a walk, breathing through his mouth to make as little noise as possible.

But what was this? There was light streaming through the little peepholes in the wall. Surely Shei-Luin was asleep by now?

But if she were awake, perhaps he could get her attention. . . . He pressed one eye against the nearest peephole.

Shei-Luin was awake. So was Xiane. They sat side by side on the edge of her bed, talking intently, but too far away for him to hear what they said. Both wore only light robes against the night chill.

Suddenly Shei-Luin leaned forward and, catching Xiane's face between her hands, kissed him.

Yesuin turned away, empty inside. He had seen the look on her face; the kiss was no sham.

Once more he broke into a run, heedless of who might hear. He knew what he must do.

Shei-Luin opened her eyes to darkness, wondering what had awakened her. A deep sigh from the other side of the bed, and she knew. She propped herself up on one elbow and turned to where she knew Xiane lay, although she couldn't see him.

"Did I wake you, Precious Flower?" he asked.

"It's nothing, my lord. Can't you sleep? What is it?"

Another sigh. "I keep dreaming about Yesuin and waking up, wondering how he's faring." A silence, then, "Have you ever lost a friend, Shei-Luin?"

Unexpected tears stung her eyes. "Yes," she whispered huskily. "The only woman besides my sister that I named friend. Tsiaa, my maid."

She felt him shift in the darkness. "Tsiaa? Isn't that the one who— Oh, Shei, I'm sorry. I never knew."

And with that an arm reached out for her, wrapped around her, and drew her close so that her head rested on Xiane's shoulder. He stroked her hair as she cried, for Tsiaa or Yesuin or for herself, she didn't know.

When the tears had ended, she didn't move away. *What has happened to Xiane?* she wondered as he continued stroking her hair. The answer came to her a moment later.

He's growing up at last.

*   *   *

Late the next morning, as Murohshei combed his hair and pulled it up into a decent topknot, Xiane listened idly to the soft chatter of Shei-Luin's maids in the next room.

One was insisting that the palace was haunted. "Two of Lady Mienya's maids heard someone running through the palace late last night, and so did Lord Siachun's footmen. And many others heard as well, even some lords and ladies, I heard. But when anyone peered out into the halls to see who it might be, there was no one there!"

An excited murmuring broke out among the others. "Ghosts!" they told each other. "What else but ghosts?"

I've lived in this palace all my life and I've never heard of any "ghosts," Xiane thought. *I wonder what it was?*

"Done, Phoenix Lord," the eunuch said quietly.

Xiane turned in the chair to look at the bed. Shei-Luin still slept. He considered joining her again, but he supposed he'd best put old Guanli out of his misery. So he stood and stretched, saying, "My thanks, Murohshei."

The eunuch bowed. "May I be of any other service, Your Majesty? Do you wish to break your fast here?"

Xiane shook his head. "No, I shall go to my chambers for that. Just give me my robe."

When he was dressed, Xiane left the sleeping chamber with Murohshei in the lead. At once the gossip ceased as the maids fell to their knees and touched their foreheads to the floor. He passed through the group. Murohshei opened the door and bowed him out.

As he'd expected, an agitated General Guanli waited for him in the hall, surrounded by a group of officers and soldiers. Xiane caught the eye of one particular captain and was rewarded with a tiny nod. An invisible weight disappeared from his shoulders. He said gaily, "General! What are you doing here so early in the morning?"

It was, Xiane knew, almost noon.

Guanli, who no doubt had never gone back to sleep after getting the news of Yemal's defiance, nearly choked at "early." But he rallied and said, "Majesty, I have grave news. The Zharmatian dog Yemal has—"

"I am half Zharmatian, General," Xiane reminded him softly.

The general turned the color of bleached silk. Stuttering apologies spilled from his lips, and his knees shook. Xiane thought the man would faint.

"Go on," he said wearily, more from a wish to get this over with than from any sense of mercy. "What has Yemal done?"

"Broken the treaty, my lord," Guanli managed to say. "And that means . . ."

Here the general paused to take a deep breath. It was well known, Xiane reflected, that Yesuin was a constant companion of his. But there was no one Guanli could dump the giving of *this* news upon.

"That means the hostage's life is forfeit," Guanli finished.

The hostage's life. Not *Yesuin's life.* Not one trace of regret, either. And Guanli had gone to Yesuin for advice when buying horses.

How quickly one went from "person" to "thing."

"So it is," Xiane agreed. "Have you arrested him yet?"

"No, Phoenix Lord. For that we must have your permission."

"We give it." Xiane stared blandly back at Guanli's surprise, daring him to say anything.

But Guanli was not the man to pull the tiger's whiskers a second time—not when he'd escaped so narrowly the first. "Thank you, Phoenix Lord." Gathering officers and soldiers alike with a glance, Guanli barked, "March!" and led them down the hall at a brisk military pace.

Xiane tagged along behind, enjoying the furtive, backward glances as they marched through the elegant halls.

It seemed no time at all before they stood before the carved and lacquered door to Yesuin's chamber. At Guanli's nod, a soldier tried the door. It was latched from the inside.

Xiane started in surprise. By the Phoenix, was Yesuin

still here? He dared a glance at the young captain. The man looked as baffled as he.

He waited in an agony of suspense as Guanli called to Yesuin to open the door.

If Yesuin is still inside, there's nothing I can do to help him. . . .

There was no answer. Xiane didn't know whether to be relieved or frightened. When they finally entered, would they find empty rooms, or the body of a suicide?

Unable to stand the suspense any longer, he snapped, "Break it down."

Two burly soldiers rammed the door with their shoulders again and again and again. It was thick, as befitted a door in the royal quarters, and yielded reluctantly.

At last the way was clear. Before the soldiers could storm the opening, Xiane shoved past them and crossed the threshold, ignoring the cries of "Majesty! Be careful! He may have a weapon!"

Yesuin would never hurt him, Xiane knew. Never.

Linden and Maurynna were sitting in the hostel's common room, talking over a shared plate of food, when Taren entered.

"Good day, my friends, and good news," he called to them.

"What's that?" Linden asked, beckoning Taren to join them.

"While I was walking through the bazaar, I happened upon the official who matches up the troupes with patrons."

Linden heard Maurynna's breath catch. His own heart had begun beating harder. "And?" he finally said.

"We have a patron, and there's a well-guarded merchant train that we may travel with for safety."

That was well, Linden thought. He had no proof that bandits preyed upon travelers here in Jehanglan as they did in the northern countries, but he'd wager they did. "When do we leave, and who's our patron?"

Taren grimaced. "Tomorrow morning. We'll be hard put to be ready in time, but we've no choice."

Linden looked at Maurynna in dismay and saw that the color had drained from her face. She reached for his hand; he caught hers. Cold fingers wrapped around his; but when she spoke, her voice betrayed none of her anxiety.

Maurynna asked, "Who is our patron?"

"I'll go warn the others. Why don't you finish your meal?" Taren stood up and walked away. Then, as if belatedly realizing he hadn't answered Maurynna's question, he said over his shoulder, "Oh, a noble I heard of during my time in Jehanglan. A Lord Jhanun."

Silence greeted him. Xiane went a pace or two into the room, looking from side to side. The room was empty of any living thing, the air heavy and still. Xiane listened; he heard nothing but the breathing of the men behind him, the faint chink of armor against armor.

He sighed in relief. He'd feared to find Yesuin dangling from a beam, or crumpled on the floor with his dagger thrust into his heart. Another two steps into the chamber, and the soldiers had room enough to enter without shoving him out of their way.

They fanned out, searching the room in growing frustration. Xiane nearly laughed as one pawed through a box of clothes. The soldier mumbled curses as he pulled out robe after robe, but no hidden hostages.

Xahnu might hide there—but a grown man? Xiane hid a smile behind his hand.

He had one bad moment when he remembered the window. Had Yesuin jumped to his death? He caught his man's gaze and jerked his chin at the window. The officer took his meaning and looked outside.

"He didn't get out this way," the young captain announced to the room at large. "There's no rope, no ladder, and no body on the ground."

"So how *did* he get out?" Guanli roared. "Look! Look

harder!" He lashed his men with his horsetail whip as if they were recalcitrant ponies.

Xiane stood, an island of calm in a whirlwind of destruction. Drawers were pulled out and emptied, boxes of clothes overturned, their contents a rainbow of silk across the floor, the bed pulled apart and swords run through the mattress.

Yesuin, he thought, *I don't know how you managed it, but well done!*

It wasn't until the soldiers were reduced to looking behind the scrolls hanging on the walls that inspiration struck. As innocently as he could, Xiane said, "The door was latched from the inside, so he couldn't have left that way. He didn't leave by the window, either."

At his first word, all activity had ceased, and all eyes focused on him. Now Guanli and his men waited for the next pearl of imperial wisdom.

"Perhaps," Xiane said slowly, rubbing his chin, "the ghosts got him."

More than one face turned pale. "Ghosts, Phoenix Lord?" Guanli asked.

"Oh, yes," Xiane assured him as he picked a way to the door. "Ghosts. Many people heard ghosts running through the palace last night—didn't you know?" He looked back over his shoulder.

"No, my lord," said Guanli, shaking his head. If he'd looked terrified when he'd inadvertently insulted Xiane, he looked doubly terrified now. Everyone knew that hungry spirits were worse than angry emperors.

"Now you do," Xiane said, and left. As he walked back to his own quarters, he thought, *If that doesn't throw them off your trail, cousin, I don't know what will. I've done all I could. It's up to you now. Good luck, my friend.*

Freedom and safety lay far to the north in Nisayeh, the red land of the Tah'nehsieh. All he need do was reach it.

But now that his fellow tribesmen had broken the treaty, and roamed the lands between here and Nisayeh, getting out of the imperial palace might prove to be the easy part,

Yesuin thought. *Curse Yemal! May he be eaten by demons.*

As his sturdy horse trotted along the road, fellow travelers made way for him in his guise as an imperial messenger. Yesuin made his plans.

They were simple: avoid other messengers. Avoid any army units that he could; they might have an officer who'd seen him in the capital city, or they might think he was a Zharmàtian spy who'd killed a messenger and stolen the blue-and-gold uniform. Get to Rhampul, the last military outpost before Mount Kajhenral. He'd risk being recognized, but it was the last place to get a good horse; the military had the best animals after the nobles and the imperial household.

Then a last, furious ride to the mountains between Jehanglan and Nisayeh—all the while praying that his false brother was elsewhere with the warband.

One step at a time; first, Rhampul. Damn Yemal for starting this. Someday I'll kill him as he tried to kill me.

Someday; but first, Rhampul.

Thirty-nine

"I don't understand this," **Linden** muttered as the troupe broke camp for yet another day of hard travel. "We keep passing through village after village, but even when we stop at one for the night instead of camping, we're never allowed to put on a show. Don't these lords expect the entertainers to earn something on the way to their holdings?"

Lleld shrugged. "Perhaps they're afraid it will lessen the value of the show, somehow."

Maurynna shook her head. "That we're not allowed to perform isn't so odd. But I'll tell you what is: that these merchants picked a road that goes only through unsettled land or these little villages. And when we do stop in a village, they don't settle down for a few days to trade. We're on the way the next morning, barely enough time for them to sell anything save what's at the top of the mules' packs and is easy to get at."

"Could it be that they don't think the villagers have enough money to buy their goods?" Otter offered. He stood by Nightsong's head, stroking her nose as Raven saddled her.

Maurynna shook her head. "It's not adding up, Otter. If you take a route like this one, through little villages, you pack less-expensive goods, little necessities, no luxury items—and you stop and trade. You make no money if your wares stay in a mule's pack. I asked Tar—" She broke off and looked around, an odd expression on her face.

So did everyone else. All there was to see was what they'd seen every morning of this cursed journey, thought Linden: the merchants camping as far away from them as they could get, and the guards surrounding them all.

"What's wrong?" he asked. "Did you hear something?"

"No." She squirmed a little as if her back itched. "This may sound mad, but . . . Has anyone else had the feeling we're being watched?"

"The guards always seem to keep more of an eye on us than the merchants," Lleld said, "but I think that's just because we're 'cursed outlanders.' Is that what you mean?"

"No," Maurynna said vaguely. "It's not that. I know they watch us, but—It's worse near water."

"Water?" Linden asked in bafflement. This was making no sense.

"Yes, everytime we cross a stream. . . . Oh, forget I said anything. Here comes Taren; he's probably coming to tell us to hurry."

And so it proved; they quickly finished breaking camp and made ready for another long day of journeying.

Xiane sat with Imperial Minister Musahi in one of the smaller garden pavilions, this one a simple affair consisting of an arching frame of giant bamboo overgrown by honeysuckle. It was where he and Musahi, then his favorite tutor, had had many lessons when Xiane was younger. Both were still fond of it.

Xiane listened, resting his chin in his hand, as Musahi, sitting across the little table from him, read from various reports, boiling them down to the simple facts, and reading between the lines for what was left out.

"Tchah, tchah," Musahi said in his dry, reedy voice as he shuffled between sheets of rice paper. "I fear Lord R'sao is up to something, Phoenix Lord. Here he requests more wagons for shipping the salt from the White Flower mine. But these figures *here* show that the yield is down, due to 'unexpected cave-ins' that are mentioned nowhere else in this report."

Xiane sighed and plucked a honeysuckle blossom from the nearest vine. "He's diverting it again, isn't he?" He bit the end from the blossom and sucked the single drop of sweet nectar from the flower. Musahi had taught him that as a boy.

"I'm afraid so, Your Majesty. And this time, something will have to be done. It's much worse than before."

"He's gambling again, I'll wager. See to it, Musahi. Now—what else?"

The older man nodded as he skimmed through the various reports before him, mumbling to himself. Xiane leaned back and closed his eyes, letting the sweet scent of honeysuckle wash over him. The air was warm and heavy, and Musahi's barely audible drone as he muttered to himself nearly put Xiane to sleep.

But he woke instantly when Musahi said, "How strange. How *very* strange," his tone much sharper than usual.

"What is it?"

Musahi read a little further, then set that report down on the table, tapping it with one finger. "Lord Jhanun has suddenly left the capital—"

Xiane shrugged. That was nothing unusual. Jhanun traveled a great deal, most often to the Iron Temple where a nephew was a high-ranking priest. The stiff-necked prig was well-known for his militant piety.

"—and the composer of this little report says that Lord Jhanun is on his way to Rhampul, according to a groom with a loose tongue."

That was a surprise. "Rhampul? There's nothing there; it's a small military posting—"

"Led by an officer with ties to Jhanun. And the oddest thing of all is that a number of those who hold with his views—"

All the ones with their topknots done up too tightly, in Xiane's opinion, but he said nothing.

"Have also left the capital." Musahi glared down at the papers in his hands as if they deliberately kept secrets from him.

Xiane blew a long breath out through his lips. It was no coincidence that the most adamantly conservative Jehangli lords were all absent at once. Something was up; there was no doubt of that.

He needed to find out what. But the other side of the coin was that, with those same lords away and unable to raise objections, *he* could advance his own secret plans.

It would have to be done quickly; days of preparation would only mean that word could get to those lords quickly enough for them to turn back to the capital. It wasn't fair to Shei-Luin, but she would have to be content with what could be arranged in only a day or two.

And the throne of Lady Riya-Akono, he thought, would make up for much.

Shima! Shima!

Shima, on his way home from delivering a message to the Vale for Zhantse, reined up his horse. The little mare, grateful for the unexpected rest, dropped her head to look for stray bits of grass. Shima closed his eyes and concentrated. *Miune—what is it?*

I have found another like thee! Is this not wonderful? the mindvoice bubbled.

Are you certain?

Oh, yes. I'm following her. She has hair much like thine, but the others! Never have I seen such people. They travel in a merchant train with many guards.

Traveling entertainers from the north countries, no doubt, Shima thought to himself. But "many guards"? That was not usual. Some guards, yes; enough to make a merchant pack train less attractive to bandits. But what merchant would pay for "many guards"? *Miune, be careful! If the guards see you—*

I am always careful. Thee would like their horses, I— Oh! The noon rest is ending and they are making ready to move on. I must go!

The contact ended as abruptly as it began. Shima shook his head, worried. *I hope Miune knows what he's doing. If he gets too excited and sticks his head up at just the wrong time . . .*

Still, the thought that there was someone else like him was a comfort. Urging the mare on again, he hoped Miune brought him more news, and soon.

Forty

The temples at the four Points of Warding might be larger, and the temple at sacred Mount Rivasha might be holier, but none was grander than the temple of the Phoenix in the imperial capital. It was here the emperors—and now the first empress in more than a hundred years—were crowned.

For the first time since she'd entered Xiane's harem, Shei-Luin passed through the city's streets unveiled and in an open litter. Crowds thronged the way, calling to each other in excitement, bowing at the sight of Xiane in the litter ahead of her, bowing to *her*.

Only the soldiers with their wooden batons kept the crowd from spilling into the road as they pushed and shoved and jostled each other for a better view. Parents held their children up to see the spectacle; Shei-Luin heard one mother shrilly bidding her child to remember this auspicious day. Many people waved burning sticks of incense and chanted, "A thousand, thousand years to our emperor! A thousand, thousand years to our empress! Children of the Phoenix, rule us forever!" A heady mix of sandalwood, pine, rose, and myrrh wafted over her as her eight bearers marched steadily through the streets.

Step by solemn step they came to the temple and her destiny. She had a moment's anxiety at the steepness of the stairs, imagining herself sliding ignominiously out the back of the litter. But the bearers knew their business; the four sturdy men in front dipped their shoulders as the four behind lifted their end of the carrying poles, and the heavy litter stayed level as they mounted the stairs. Shei-Luin heaved a small sigh of relief. Today must be perfect.

Xiane's litter disappeared into the huge entrance of the temple as her own reached the top stair. Before her stretched the wide expanse of the forecourt, its white marble shining in the sun. Lesser priests lined the way, watching in awe as she passed.

The entrance loomed before her like a huge, open mouth. She raised her chin in defiance, ready to embrace the destiny that was hers.

There it was again; the itching between her shoulder blades as if someone watched her. Maurynna looked quickly over her shoulder, hoping this time to catch whoever it was.

But as always no one was there. There was just the empty, grassy sward leading to the banks yet another nameless little river. The feeling intensified. *Damn it all*, she thought, clenching her fists in frustration, *if I only knew* how *to look, I know I'd see him or her or it.*

"Again?" Linden asked just as it faded away.

"Yes; gone now, though, as always," she answered. Could someone be trailing them? But the land was wide and flat, with nowhere for a rider to hide.

A hand on her shoulder made her jump. She whipped around.

"Easy, love," Linden said. He looked worried. "Are you, ah—"

"Feeling well? Yes," she said in exasperation. "It's just that I keep getting this feeling as if there's someone just outside the range of my vision. Someone who wants to talk to me. I even feel it in my dreams sometimes."

Linden swore. "May the gods preserve us from dreams like that," he said with a fervor that surprised her. He pulled the horses' brushes from the packs. "I'll take care of the four-foots," he said, "if you'll pack our blankets."

He went off in haste, calling Shan and Boreal to him. She stared after him in surprise, blankets clutched to her breast. Otter, whistling a leisurely way through the camp, stopped.

"Leave it open like that, Rynna, and something's sure to jump in," he teased, one finger nudging her dropped jaw shut. "Something amiss?"

She told him of the exchange with Linden, finishing with, "And why should dreams like that bother him so much?" as she rolled her blankets.

Otter tugged at his beard. "Oh, yes; that would do it." He paused; then, leaning close so that no other sharp Dragonlord hearing might catch it, the bard asked, "Has he ever told you about Satha?"

Maurynna searched her memory. As she went back over every time she'd teased another tale of his life with her heroes, Bram and Rani, from him, she realized that while Linden was eager to tell her everything he could remember about them, he rarely spoke of the undead harper who had played such a role in the Kelnethi war. A quick mention of his name, nothing more, even that much avoided if possible. She shook her head. "No, nothing."

And she, remembering the advice Otter had once given her, never asked for more. Should she, Maurynna wondered as she rolled up Linden's blankets next, have insisted on knowing all?

Otter dropped onto one knee by her and continued, "That's how it started with Rani, you see—Satha reaching into her dreams. That was how she first knew about him, how he called her to release him from his tomb.

"It frightened her and drew her at the same time. Satha was a harper, dead long before Rani was born, famed through the Five Kingdoms for both his voice and his beauty. Princes and princesses, kings and queens, even Dragonlords traveled to the Kelnethi court to hear him. His legend had not dimmed with the years after his— Ah, now, I can't say death, for Satha didn't die. His would-be killer failed. But neither was he alive."

The early morning chill made her flesh creep; at least, Maurynna told herself it was the chill. She rubbed at the goosebumps along her arms. She now understood why Otter had always refused to tell her and Raven more than the barest details about Satha when they were children. She wasn't certain she wanted them now.

"But that wasn't what she found in that tomb, was it?" she asked anyway. "Someone young and beautiful, I mean."

"Not by a pig's ear," Otter said. "I don't know how he worked it, save that it was strong magic, but Satha was neither completely alive or completely dead. He *was* a horror to all." A faraway look came into his eyes. "A horror to all save Rani. She both saw and heard Satha as he was in her dreams, Linden told me once, as well as what he'd become. The greatest harper who ever lived, his voice lost for all time—except for one woman who heard him sing nearly two centuries after he should have died. Gods, how I envy her," he said softly, shaking his head.

"Beautiful voice or not," Maurynna said, shivering, "I don't want any dead harpers in my dreams, thank you."

Otter smiled. "I don't think you have to worry, Rynna."

They both turned to watch Linden brushing out Shan's

tail. The tall stallion hated having his tail handled and kept pulling it out of Linden's hand. After one particularly violent twitch, Linden responded with a string of curses and threats that came near to scorching the air as he grabbed the offending tail once more.

Shan looked over one shoulder at his rider, his eye ringed white with astonishment. Maurynna thought she had never seen the stallion look so surprised. He submitted meekly to the relentless brushing of his thick black tail, as unlike Shan as might be.

"No, you don't have to worry," Otter repeated. "Linden's doing it for you."

Two priests helped her from the litter as a chant rose around her. They led her up the nine steps to the lower altar, then past it to where Xiane waited at the high altar. He turned, offering her his hand to aid her up the high step, and smiled at her as she joined him.

It was a sweet smile, so like Xahnu when he was happy that Shei-Luin smiled back without thinking. Xiane's fingers closed around hers in a brief squeeze. Then he turned to face the altar once more.

Shei-Luin did the same, and her breath caught in her throat. For resting on the altar before them were the imperial crowns of Jehanglan. Each nestled inside a shimmering hemisphere of pale golden light. She knew, if she stretched out her hand to take one, that that hand would burst into flame the instant it touched the light, and burn with a fire that would consume her very bones.

For this was the fire of the Phoenix that burned here, the fire that protected Jehanglan's greatest treasures. It was said that the crowns were found in the ashes of the last pyre the Phoenix had built before it consented to become the guardian of the land. They were used only at the crowning of the rulers, then returned to their places.

Xiane had told her the night before, "That's because everyone says they're too precious and holy to wear for every occasion. *I* think it's really because my revered ancestor found his too damned uncomfortable to wear every day. The wretched thing was heavy!"

Heavy or not, uncomfortable or not, they were the most beautiful things Shei-Luin had ever seen: gold of many different shades, wrought like flames, formed the circlets, while from the brow of each crown rose a phoenix of the purest white gold. The eyes of the phoenixes were emeralds, and there were more emeralds scattered throughout the flames of the emperor's crown. Moonstones dotted the crown of the empress.

Now the high priest of the temple took his place on the other side of the altar from them. His voice soared up in a chant; from all around the temple, other voices rose to meet his as the chorus of priests called upon the power of the Phoenix.

At first Shei-Luin noticed nothing unusual. Then chant turned to song, and that song rose and fell like a surging ocean, thundered in her ears like a storm, roared around her like the wind that runs before a forest fire.

It will be like nothing you've ever experienced before.

Xiane had not exaggerated, she thought, shaking. There was power here, power of a kind and magnitude she'd never dreamed of. It sang in her bones and burned in her veins, carrying her before it like a river of fire; it was both beautiful and terrible beyond belief. She imagined herself stripped of flesh, a creature of flame and light. Dream or truth? She couldn't tell.

Then the voices died away once more until only the head priest's was left. Softer and softer it became. Shei-Luin came back to her body, once more able to feel Xiane's fingers on hers. Her vision cleared, but her head ached, and the world wavered like a fever dream.

Her thoughts muzzy and slow, she looked at the altar again as, with the ending of the priest's song, the light guarding the empress's crown flickered and sank into the white quartz of the altar. It sparkled in the crystalline stone like a ring of fire beneath ice.

Beside her, Xiane shook his head like a man waking

from a deep sleep. She saw his hands reach out, close upon the smaller crown, and raise it from the altar. He turned to her, the crown held high, and she pivoted to face him with no more will than a puppet; it was as if someone else guided her body, and she was dimly grateful for it. She wasn't certain she had enough wit left to place one foot before the other.

She stood immobile as Xiane lowered the crown. Just before it touched her, Xiane whispered, "Be ready, Shei— this will be uncomfortable."

The imperial crown settled on her brow, fitting itself to her head as if it had been made just for her. Xiane dropped his hands like a man exhausted from heavy labor.

Not even the thick fog wrapped around her mind could stifle the quick blaze of exultation that shot through her as she balanced against the sudden weight. She was the Empress of Jehanglan!

Then she felt it. The crown was alive—she would swear to it! It hummed against her head like a hive of bees, the vibrations digging deep into her skull. A soft gasp of pain escaped her, and she swayed.

Xiane, frowning with concern, caught her hand and turned her to face the nobles and priests who filled the temple. She clung to his fingers, anchoring herself against the madness and pain that threatened to take her.

"Behold my First Wife!" Xiane cried. "Behold the Empress of Jehanglan, the Lady of the Phoenix!"

Though her vision played tricks on her—faces from the crowd rushed at her, then retreated; colors swam, and shapes faded at the edges—Shei-Luin saw the congregation bow. Bowed to *her*, daughter of a despised exile, the afterthought when her sister was sent for. The taste of victory was sweeter than any honey.

But if she must wear this accursed crown any longer, she would faint.

Somehow, Xiane guessed. He all but snatched the crown from her head and set it carefully in its place on the altar once more. At once the sensation of bees drilling into her skull vanished, though she was still sick and faint. She thought the priest looked troubled, but her eyes played such tricks on her that she wasn't certain. She closed them.

While she concentrated on staying upright, the priest's voice rose in a chant once more. She listened as the others joined in and the air grew heavy with power, pressing against the back of her neck like an unseen hand.

"The crown is sealed again," Xiane whispered as the song died down to a soft chanting. "We may leave. Precious Flower, can you walk?"

She nodded, her eyes still shut. She would do whatever she had to do. A deep breath, then another, and she looked once more upon the priests and nobles filling the temple. Suddenly she was glad that the ceremony had been arranged so quickly that it had to be kept simple, unlike Xiane's own coronation, as he had described it. She had reckoned herself cheated; now she thought herself fortunate.

Only Xiane's hand beneath her elbow kept her from stumbling; he supported her until they were at her litter. The same two priests as before helped her. Though her head still spun, Shei-Luin felt better as soon as she sat.

Xiane returned to his own litter. He must have said something to his bearers, she thought, for almost before he was settled, the bearers hoisted the litter and started for the door.

Then it was her turn. As they passed down the wide aisle and past walls covered with gold and amber and ivory, Shei-Luin kept her gaze fixed on the daylight ahead.

She would never invoke the power of the Phoenix lightly again. Like fire, it could both warm and kill. But now she had a claim to that power. She was empress, and her sons the acknowledged heirs. She was content—for now.

Damn it, there it was yet again! Maurynna turned in the saddle, looking.

Nothing—nothing at all save the green, rolling grass-

lands and the glitter of a little stream nearby. Muttering to
herself, she faced forward once more.

At once, the skin between her shoulder blades prickled
once more.

Forty-one

To Shei-Luin's surprise, only a few days after her crowning, Xiane left to go hunting. It struck her as odd, since
he'd lost his favorite hunting companion when Yesuin escaped.

Even odder, in many ways, was that she was sorry he
was gone. Truth be told, she missed him. So she filled her
days with reading the reports Xiane had Lord Musahi prepare for her, and questioning the former tutor about the
state of affairs in Jehanglan. To what was probably the
astonishment of both, they got on well together, and Shei-
Luin quickly saw why Xiane valued this pedantic, precise
man so much.

When she was not talking to Musahi, she walked in the
private gardens of the empress—*her* private gardens—and
fed the carp that lived in the lotus pond. Against all custom,
she ordered Xahnu and Xu brought back from the pavilion
in the Khorushin Mountains, and taken to her quarters to
live, rather than the royal nursery. She played with them in
the gardens; at last, she thought, she could finally see
enough of her children.

When evening fell and the boys were in bed, Zyuzin sang
to her until she fell asleep.

But each night, she woke in the darkness, and wondered
when Xiane would return from hunting.

*   *   *

As an "imperial messenger," Yesuin was entitled to food and lodging at any way station upon his route, or at any inn if there was no way station. He avoided the way stations whenever possible, stopping at one only when he had to change horses, lest someone recognize him from the palace, or ask awkward questions about what route he used to ride.

Even the inns made him uncomfortable, but when he ran out of food, he would stop at one to rest himself and his horse. At least at inns, the sight of his uniform, with its horse badge upon breast and back, kept the curious away from him. Ordinary folk, it seemed, avoided any kind of imperial entanglement whenever possible.

This night, his saddlebag was empty again, he'd not eaten for a day and a half, and his horse was nearly spent. He rode into a little town and down its only street, making for the sign with its sheaf of millet and rice stalks bound to it, the symbol for an inn throughout the countryside. As he passed the tiny temple, a pigeon winged past overhead, the last light of the sun flashing on its white wings, and landed upon the rickety wooden tower by it. He saw the swirl of robes as the pigeon keeper scurried up the tower ladder to welcome the bird and strip the message from its leg.

Did it say *Seize any imperial messenger who looks Zharmatian?*

Were he not so tired, the thought would send chills down his spine. But he'd seen a score of messenger pigeons on his ride, and none had aught to do with him. None would, he was certain in his heart; Xiane would find a way to stop it. The only thing he must worry about was avoiding his own people, and reaching Nisayeh, the land of the Tah'nehsieh.

One night, perhaps a second, to rest, then on to Rhampul.

The thought of Rhampul made him uneasy. He'd no wish to stop at the fort, but it was the only place to get a good horse. All that was available from the countryfolk were broken-down nags.

At last he was in the courtyard of the little hostel. He tossed the reins at the stableboy and, after dismounting and taking his saddlebag, growled, "Care for him well—brush him and feed him the best you've got."

"Yes, sir!" the boy said, ogling the uniform. "The very best, sir!" He led the tired horse away.

Yesuin went to the inn and pushed aside the hanging over the open doorway. A miasma of equal parts onion, garlic, asafoetida, and unwashed bodies rolled over him. Yesuin paused to gather himself, then plunged into it. The sooner he was part of it, the sooner he'd get used to it. Heads turned as he entered, then looked quickly away again at sight of the badge of the golden running horse upon his tunic. The owner hurried up to him, wiping his hands on a stained apron.

"This way, sir, this way! A table just for you!"

Yesuin followed. Conversation died as he passed, springing up again only reluctantly. The owner rousted two drinkers from a small table in the back. They slunk off without a word. With a sigh of relief, Yesuin sat down.

"Tea," he said, knowing the wine in this place would be vile, "and a bowl of stew and millet. And make certain there is nothing *but* stew and millet in that bowl, do you understand?"

"Yes, sir! Right away, sir!"

The innkeeper scuttled off. Yesuin buried his face in his hands, thinking, *The boy outside* must *be his son.*

With a pang, he thought of his own two sons. He'd never even seen Xu; the boy had been taken straight to the Khorushin mountains to the imperial pavilion there. All he knew was what Shei-Luin had told him: the boy looked just like him, even down to the birthmark on the thigh, hidden now by a burn scar.

Poor, brave Tsiaa.

He wondered if Shei-Luin would ever find another maid she could trust the way she'd trusted Tsiaa. Then he wondered if he'd ever see those dearest to him again—Shei-Luin, Xiane, his sons—and a darkness settled in his soul.

He shook it off with an effort. First he would get past Rhampul, then reach Nisayeh. After that, he would see.

When his meal arrived, Yesuin ate, hardly tasting the watery stew. Someday, he promised himself, someday he'd return.

But first, Rhampul.

As V'Choun poured tea for the three of them, Xiane found enough courage to ask the question that had been tormenting him. "If the Phoenix did not give himself to Jehanglan, Lord Kirano, how did Xilu and Gaolun capture it? It could not have been an easy thing."

"No, it took great preparation, preparations that had begun years before when Gaolun found a young girl-child who was considered mad by her fellow villagers. Although she was weak of wits and could only grunt, now and again, she fell down in fits and spoke in a clear voice of things the villagers couldn't understand the meaning of. But Gaolun could. He bought her from her parents, who were only too glad to get a good price for such a useless girl-child, and brought her to his brother.

"Now, Gaolun was a priest in a minor temple dedicated to Kirahi, goddess of mercy and justice, a goddess we no longer worship. Xilu was the warlord—'king' he called himself, though he was little better than a bandit—of a little kingdom on the fringes of a much smaller empire of Jehanglan.

"The prophecy was this: there would come from the north two dragons of a kind never seen before. If they were captured and chained, their power could be used in turn to capture the phoenix, the symbol of Jehanglan. And when the symbol was captured, so could the country be taken, as well. It took years for the preparations to be complete, including the seeding of false Oracles who prophesied the sacrifice of the phoenix. Both Xilu and Gaolun were charismatic men and many flocked to their cause and did their bidding without truly understanding it. At last, all was ready."

Here Kirano paused to drink his tea. He looked expectantly at Xiane, who nodded slowly.

"You mean the four Stones of Warding," Xiane said, "that were all cut from a single huge boulder of white quartz found in the caverns under Mount Kajhenral."

"As were the smaller warding stones," said Kirano, "used around the bowl of Mount Rivasha. Then came the day they were waiting for: two dragons unlike any ever seen in Jehanglan were found."

V'Choun interrupted, "Kirano, I never understood—there were dragons in Jehanglan already. Why didn't Xilu and Gaolun try to capture one of them?"

"Because our dragons were of a very different kind. Ours were gentle creatures that lived in water; and when they were old enough and powerful enough, they could turn to mist. No chains could hold them then!

"But the northern dragons were different. They were creatures of the air, like the phoenix; and, like the phoenix, creatures of fire."

"Fire?" Xiane asked.

"They were seen to breathe it," Kirano replied, "when the soldiers went to capture them. Both had been badly wounded when they were caught in a typhoon, and the smaller died of his wounds before he could be chained in the place prepared for him at the southernmost point of the warding. The larger was taken into Mount Kajhenral and never seen again.

"But the trap was now set, and when the phoenix returned to Mount Rivasha to build its pyre, Xilu and Gaolun, now at the head of a small army of fanatically dedicated priest-followers, were ready for it. As the new, vulnerable phoenix emerged from the ashes, Gaolun and his minions bound it within a magical barrier.

"And since that day, Jehanglan has tapped the magical power of its poor prisoner." Kirano drained the last of his tea from the cup. His head drooped slightly, and Xiane noticed a bluish tinge to the thin, wrinkled lips.

"Forgive me, Phoenix Lord, but I must rest."

Xiane stood. But one last question occurred to him. "What truly happened to the dragons of Jehanglan?"

Old eyes gazed wearily up at him. "Xilu had them hunted down and killed after he overthrew Michero, the last Lotus Emperor. They were gentle creatures; it was a slaughter of innocents. Xilu has much blood on his hands to answer for, my lord."

And how much of that blood has stained his descendants? Xiane wondered bitterly. All his life had been a lie. All of *Jehanglan* was a lie.

He didn't want to believe it, Phoenix knew. But Kirano's words were the truth, he was certain of it. It was there in the calm, old eyes. It was even in the depths of his own heart.

Everything was a lie.

"I will talk more with you in the morning, Kirano," he said.

"What's this place, Rhampul, we're making for?" Linden asked Taren as they sat around the fire while Raven and Maurynna, as "servants," made dinner. "I don't remember it from the map."

Taren said, "My apologies, Linden. I'd forgotten it. It's a little . . . settlement on the Black River. I asked the merchant in charge of the caravan what his plans were. He said they planned to rest there for a few days."

Raven looked up from stirring the pot of stew. "A damned good thing, too," he said with a frown. "This pace is killing their animals! What's that idiot thinking of? Even the Llysanyins will be better off for a rest."

"More importantly," said Lleld, "is when will Maurynna and Raven be able to make their break? If I remember the map correctly, the Black River leads south to the capital city. But Mount Kajhenral is in the north. You've been telling them to hold off and hold off, Taren. So when will be a good time?"

Linden stiffened at Lleld's words. He'd been grateful to Taren for putting off the time he and Maurynna must separate. Yet Lleld was right; this was what they had come to Jehanglan for. . . .

He looked at Maurynna, who stared down at the fire now, chewing her lower lip. *Maurynna,* he dared in mindspeech, and put everything he felt into her name. She looked at him with a small, brave smile.

We knew it had to come, she said.

The worry beads appeared as if by magic. "At Rhampul. Once we reach the Black River, Maurynna and Raven can follow it north until they find a place to cross. Then all they need do is follow that bank north; that will put them on the same side of the river as Mount Kajhenral."

Linden closed his eyes to visualize the map in his mind's eye. "He's right. How far to Rhampul?"

"A little more than a day, less if we push on."

So little time. . . .

The hell with what the guards said; this night he and Maurynna were going for a long walk—alone. Their tent was not quite private enough.

Once more he faced Lord Kirano across cups of tea. As always, the older man wore his serenity like a mantle. It surrounded him, sheltered him, kept the storms of emotion from battering him. No fear touched Kirano, no doubt shook him, no uncertainty caused his feet to stumble on the path he'd chosen. So complete was his armor that he could look in the eye the man who held his life in one hand, and challenge that same man's deepest beliefs without a qualm.

But this time Xiane knew he had the final argument. This time he would see that almost supernatural calm shaken.

"You said that Xilu and Gaolun used false Oracles. Do you say, then, that the Oracles are false?" Xiane challenged. "That they're all liars?"

"No, not at all," Kirano said. "True, there have been false Oracles, but most times they've been quickly found out and dealt with. No, a true Oracle, like a Seer among the Zharmatians and the Tah'nehsieh, speaks only the truth. We may not always *understand* that truth," Kirano admitted with a wry smile, "but in time it will be seen what that truth was."

Good—Kirano had himself stated the foundation of Xiane's argument. Now to lay the next course. "Was the *nira*'s old Oracle a false one?"

"Myan? No. He was a true Oracle before he outgrew his gift. Not as powerful, perhaps, as Pah-Ko's present one, but strong."

"Hah!" Xiane slapped his leg in glee. Now came the keystone of his attack. "So what of Myan's prophecy that one of my seed and yours would save Jehanglan from calamity? Was that false? I have two fine sons by your daughter Shei-Luin. Surely that's enough to hold the Phoenix and keep the disasters that Myan saw at bay."

He grinned in triumph. There! Let Kirano find a way around that, he crowed to himself as he sipped his tea.

Kirano set his own cup down on the low table, then composed his hands in his lap. He was, Xiane considered, taking his defeat well. But then, his own father—the old emperor—had never denied that Kirano was the quintessential gentleman, even while cursing the man for a heretic.

Then Kirano spoke. His voice was as calm and reasonable as always, but his words cut to Xiane's heart like a sword.

"Seed they are of yours, but your sons are no seed of mine."

Xiane suddenly felt lightheaded, as if he'd stood up too quickly, and the world was grey around the edges. Somehow he managed to set his cup down without spilling it. "What do you mean?"

Kirano blinked at him like a wise old turtle. "Don't blame Shei-Luin. I never told her, and I doubt very much her mother, my second wife, did. I'm not Shei-Luin's father."

The next morning, as Raven attended the horses, he found that Nightsong had cast a shoe. She led him to where it lay in the beaten-down grass around the campsite. With a heavy sigh, he picked it up and went back to the smoldering remains of their campfire. Nightsong followed him.

"Bad news," he announced, and held up the shoe. "We can't leave just yet."

Linden looked up. Raven expected a glare of annoyance. Instead a look of guilty relief flashed across the big Dragonlord's features. "Give it here," Linden said, rising and leaving his saddlebag on the ground.

Taren came up as Linden examined the shoe. "What is it?" he asked. When told, he shrugged and said, "So throw it in her saddlebag and let's be off. The others will be ready soon." He jerked his head at the merchants' camp.

"Absolutely not!" both Linden and Raven said at the same time.

Raven explained, "The road is hard and stony, Taren. That's not good for a horse's hoof."

"Raven's right. Nightsong's not going anywhere without a shoe," Linden went on. "We've spares for each horse for emergencies like this, and I know how to put a new one on her."

"We must leave *now* if we're to make Rhampul tonight," Taren insisted.

"Which you said could be done by hard riding, and that would lame her," Linden said.

"We'll have to take that risk," Taren said.

Nightsong bared her teeth at him.

Linden snapped, "No, we're not. I won't have anything that endangers our mounts. Now get over there and tell that horse's ass of a merchant who's in charge that we're not ready to leave yet. If he objects, tell him that we don't think this Lord Jhanun would be happy to find that he's paid all this money to bring us here and that one of the star performers can't perform—and we'll lay it at his doorstep that she can't. That should shut him up."

Taren hissed in frustration. For a moment Raven thought the man would argue further, but Taren turned abruptly and strode away. Linden looked after him a moment, frowning, before going off to find one of Nightsong's spare shoes.

Raven stared after Taren, surprised at this sudden change in the man. He'd *never* seen Taren lose his temper before.

Raven was even more surprised when Taren never went to speak with the merchant they all thought lead the caravan. Instead the former slave went straight to the head guard. Moments later, the guard shouted orders, and the preparations to leave ceased.

Now why would that guard listen to Taren? He takes his orders from—

But his train of thought was broken when Lleld came up and asked, "What's afoot? Why aren't we getting ready to go?"

Xiane rode back to the imperial palace hardly knowing what he did. His mind chased itself in circles, and his thoughts twisted like a nest of snakes. He felt sick to his very soul as the memory of his conversation with Kirano played over and over in his head like a song gone awry.

"*What do you mean?*" he'd managed to say through the shock that threatened to overwhelm him.

"*Her true father was a Jehangli scholar who came to study under me even though I lived with the People of the Horse then. He was young and handsome, and I was neither. Nesilyu was given to me as my second wife by her father, a minor chief among the Zharmatians, for a small service I'd done him. It was his way of thanking me. She wasn't happy at being the wife of what was to her an old, old man. But my student found favor in her eyes, and she in his. It's an old story, and a sordid one. And yet I could understand why it happened.*"

Here Kirano had paused and looked so sheepish that Xiane doubted what his eyes told him. Kirano *less than utterly composed?*

"*Truth was, I didn't want another wife,*" the sage said frankly. "*I was quite content with Lura-Sharal's mother. But I couldn't offend Nesilyu's father, and he was adamant I take her. So I did, but neglected her, I'm afraid. How could I blame her when she found comfort with another*

*man who did appreciate her? The inevitable happened.
Since it would have been an innocent child who suffered
the most, I pretended that Shei-Luin was indeed my own,
and didn't denounce her mother."*

Xiane shifted his reins from one hand to the other. How
like Kirano to be so generous. Most men would have turned
the woman and her babe out to starve.

Or had the reknowned sage simply not wished to be
laughed at as a cuckold? There had been an odd look in
those black eyes at the end. . . .

It made no difference why Kirano had accepted Shei-
Luin as his own all those years before, Xiane decided. What
mattered was *now*, and what *he* must do. As when he
helped Yesuin, he must do what was right, not what was
easiest.

He must take the first step upon the Way.

Forty-two

Dusk was falling as the caravan leaders swung off the
road and headed for a relatively flat patch of ground in the
rolling plains. Taren, riding to one side of the caravan to
avoid the dust the mules kicked up, clapped his heels to
his gelding's side.

When he caught up with the head guard, he snapped,
"Pig and son of a thousand pigs! Why are we stopping
here? We should push on to Rhampul—we started late this
morning!"

"We're stopping because it's nearly dark and the animals
are ready to drop! And if we keep on, all will know that
something isn't right. Do you want to warn the ones who
travel with you? Shall I have one of my men beat a gong
and shout out 'Ho—you're prisoners and don't know it

yet!' " The guard rubbed wearily at his eyes. "Now go before they notice us talking." He turned his horse away and began shouting orders.

Damn the man; he was right. Taren wheeled his horse around and set off along the length of the caravan, fighting to get his temper under control once more. He'd slipped badly this morning.

When he reached the rest of the troupe, Lleld hailed him with, "Thank the gods! I thought that madman would never stop for the night! I hate setting up a camp in the dark."

Taren made himself smile and agree. He went through the evening like a sleepwalker, responding only when spoken to, pretending to be more tired than he was. At last everyone retired to their tents, save Linden and Maurynna, he noticed as he slipped into the one he shared with Raven and Otter. Once again the two soultwins went off, blanket rolls tucked under their arms.

There was little talk. Otter was tired, and soon fell asleep. Raven seemed thoughtful, but Taren struck up a conversation anyway as they settled into their blankets.

"There's one thing I never understood, my young friend," he whispered, though it was likely nothing less than a shout in his ear would waken the gently snoring bard. "Why it was that Maurynna was the one chosen to go to Mount Kajhenral, and why you're with her instead of one of the other Dragonlords, especially Linden."

He'd never dared ask before, lest someone think too much about it and grow suspicious. But now . . . Now they were so close that it made no difference. By the time anyone—especially this fool boy—added two and two and got five, he would have the soldiers from the fort at Rhampul down upon them.

Raven pulled off his tunic. "I'm going because I'm true-human, and the priestmages won't sense me," he said as he folded it and laid it to one side.

"They'll sense *her*, won't they? She's a Dragonlord, after all," Taren pointed out.

Raven slid down into his blankets, yawning hugely.

"That's just it," he said sleepily. "There's something different about her. They don't know why she's different, either, but she is. Maybe it's because she can't Change like the others. But even Linden has trouble sensing her; he once said it was like she was hidden in a fog. They think the priestmages won't 'see' her, either."

Hidden in a fog . . .

A memory of a rogue Oracle prophesying in the midst of her death throes came to mind, and once again he heard her words.

One alone—the Hidden One—means the end of the Phoenix. But four will give you the throne—

So Maurynna Kyrissaean was the key, the one who must be captured at all costs. The riddle was solved at last. Fierce exultation filled Taren, and he knew what he must do that night.

"Taren? What is it?"

"Nothing, my friend. Go to sleep. Tomorrow will be a busy day."

A few candlemarks later, Raven slitted one eye open as a faint noise brought him half awake. When he saw it was just Taren disappearing out the tent door, he shut it again and pulled his blanket closer, glad that *his* bladder was behaving. He sighed and drifted back into sleep.

The evening incense still hung sweet and heavy on the air. Shei-Luin lay on her side, watching the flame guttering in the lamp as its oil ran low. Xiane ran his fingers up and down her back as he talked about whatever took his fancy. Long accustomed to the habit, Shei-Luin listened with only half her attention, her eyelids growing heavier.

Xiane babbled on. Suddenly she was wide awake.

"My lord, what did you say?" Shei-Luin said slowly. She turned and sat up in the bed.

Xiane pushed aside a strand of hair that hid a breast. "You're so beautiful, Shei-Luin, and just think! We shall have more time for each other when I'm no longer emperor, and you're not empress." Xiane smiled up at her, his head resting on his pillow. "Come, lie down with me again."

"One moment, lord—please! Tell me what you mean by these words. I'm but a weak woman, and wish my lord's wisdom."

Phoenix help her, if she had understood this fool correctly, all she had risked these years was for nothing! And her sons . . .

This would mean the lives of her children.

"Very well, Precious Flower. I have spoken long with your father recently, and—"

Too stunned to remember imperial protocol—and too angry to care—Shei-Luin interrupted, "My father? How could you speak with him? My father is with the Zharmatians on the western plains."

Xiane squirmed and grimaced, looking unnervingly like Xahnu when she'd caught him sneaking candied melon from the bowl in her chambers. "Um, well—no, he isn't. With the Zharmatians, that is. I invited him to speak with me after—after something strange happened. He's staying in one of my hunting lodges."

She stared at him, adding things up in her mind. At last she said, "So you did send for him after all. And when I thought you were hunting lately . . ."

"I was talking with your father about, about . . ." He swallowed.

She could just imagine what they spoke of. She knew her . . . father and his obsession only too well.

Ah, Xiane, you fool, you idiot! Why couldn't you have been with another woman?

Another woman she could deal with easily. Poison, or an "accident"—the possibilities were endless. Her father's heresies, though . . .

Captain Tsuen paused a moment to reshape the hairs on his writing brush. Damn, but there wasn't a decent brush to be found in this place, and Lord Jhanun hated a sloppy report.

Still, while this waiting in Rhampul was not the most

comfortable assignment the great lord had given him, it was not the worst, either; at least he didn't have to room in the barracks with the common soldiers. The inn he stayed at wasn't of the best, but the wine was surprisingly good even if the straw mattresses were thin and lumpy. And the river that flowed beneath his chamber window soothed him to sleep at night. He paused a moment to listen to its rippling music.

A soft knock at his chamber door startled him. It was late; who could be— Ah! The chambermaid must have reconsidered his offer. He smoothed his long mustache and smiled; he'd known she would. The report could wait until tomorrow. But smile turned to astonished gape when the door swung open.

For it was no maid, but the outlander who was one of Lord Jhanun's most trusted servants, one whose words were to be regarded as the lord's own—and this one did not do his own errands. Tsuen had expected the man to send a messenger.

Then he saw the light of triumph in the man's face and knew this game of waiting was over.

"Is Lord Jhanun here yet?" Baisha demanded.

"No—he stopped to confer with the other members of the Four Tigers, Kwahsiu said, at Lord Hwaene's estates," Tsuen reported. "He'll be here later."

"Kwahsiu and Nalorih came ahead, then?"

When Tsuen nodded, the outlander said, "Good—send a servant for them."

When Lord Jhanun's other men arrived, Kwahsiu said, "You have them? The dragon-creatures that will anchor the new wardings?"

"I do. They're camped a half day's ride from here. I must rest for a time, but if we leave at dawn and ride hard, we can take them."

A soft splash caught everyone's attention. "What was that?" Baisha asked, going to the open window.

Tsuen joined him. There was nothing but the darkness of the river flowing past. "A fish," he said. "Nothing more."

* * *

Maurynna suddenly pulled the blanket that had been pushed aside up over them. "Oh, for—it's back!"

Linden said, "What is?"

He saw her blush in the pale moonlight. "That feeling of being watched! It went away when—a while ago. But now it's back. If I only knew what it was—and why it's following me!"

"My father wants you to free the Phoenix, doesn't he?" Shei-Luin said quietly. Too quietly; Yesuin would take the warning. Would Xiane?

"Yes. He told me the true history of the Phoenix, the meanings of the portents, why so many priests died when those creatures attacked—he explained everything. The Phoenix needs to die so that it may be reborn. All things have a Way they must follow, and that's the true Way of the Phoenix," Xiane said.

"Those priests died because their faith was weak. As for the rest— My lord, my father was banished for his heresies. He lies! The Phoenix must stay within Mount Rivasha, else Jehanglan falls into chaos. Send him away, my lord," she begged, leaning over him, willing him to forget everything but her as she ran her fingers lightly down his chest and beyond.

Xiane drew her down for a long, smoldering kiss. "But Kirano *doesn't* lie," he said when he released her.

Released her, not rolled onto her. That, Shei-Luin thought, was a bad sign.

Xiane went on, "So how can you say he lies? He's a follower of the Crane Hermit. He won't lie."

"Then he's mistaken. Whichever it is, send him away, my lord," Shei-Luin said, desperate now. "He's dangerous."

Xiane caught her hand and frowned. "We will not discuss this anymore," he said. There was an edge of anger in his voice she'd never heard before—not for her. "While I've not yet made up my mind, I am leaning toward his way of thinking. And if I do decide it's the proper thing to do, I shall abandon the throne of Jehanglan because I have no right to it, and you and I and the boys will retire to an estate in the country where we may live simple lives as country nobles. Now—come here, Precious Flower." He pulled her to him.

She went. Had she any other choice? But as she went through the motions she knew so well now, her mind raced in circles.

At last Xiane was done. When he had fallen asleep next to her, Shei-Luin lay awake and wrenched her thoughts into order.

Does this fool truly *think we would be allowed to live quietly in the country? By the Phoenix, the country will fall into factions the moment Xiane abdicates. Can't he see that? Can't he see that we'd be a threat to those factions? He and I would be killed, and the boys—*

A chill went through her as she contemplated the future that lay before them if Xiane pursued his mad plan.

The worst that she could imagine was that the children would be slain at the same time as she and Xiane, so that no one could snatch them to use as figureheads.

And that led to the best she could foresee: her children used as puppets by some lord claiming to reestablish the legitimate dynasty. He would install himself as regent to the "poor little orphaned princes" and, as soon as that lord—Jhanun, most likely—was securely ensconced as the true power in Jehanglan, Xahnu and Xu would fall victims to some unfortunate accident or mysterious illness. Then Jehanglan would have a new emperor, and a new dynasty. At least in this future, the boys might have a few more years of life.

But they would still die.

She couldn't allow that. Xiane must die before he abdicated. But how? He was a young man, and healthy. Such rarely just dropped dead. An accident? As the night wore on, Shei-Luin came up with one plan after another, discarding each almost as soon as she thought of it.

With the first light of dawn came the answer. She was

half asleep when she heard the drone of a fly in the room. It swooped here and there, buzzing industriously as it searched for food.

That sound . . . A memory stirred at the very edge of sleep. Something about that sound . . .

Shei-Luin snapped awake, then had to bite her knuckles to keep from crying out. Yes, that was it. That was how it would be done—if Xiane persisted in his mad plan.

She hoped with all her heart he would turn from this path.

The next morning Raven sat staring at the wall of the tent as if he would find the answers to his questions scrawled upon the dirty canvas. Where did Taren go last night? It couldn't have been just to water the ground; he'd have been back by now.

Raven was certain Taren hadn't realized he'd been awake—if just barely—at the time. It was only later, when he was truly awake, that he realized Taren had been fully dressed.

So where was he? It was clear Taren meant to come back; his blankets lay where he'd stretched out the night before. Raven sighed and rolled them up so that there would be no further delay.

And why weren't the merchants moving on? All during the journey, the merchants had pressed on as if any delay cost them gold by the candlemark. Yet when he'd gone outside a little while ago to look for Taren, he saw that while they were packed, they'd made no move to travel on. Instead they clung to their camp, small groups huddled together talking, their faces anxious.

Nor had anyone seen Taren.

And biggest question of all, why had Taren suddenly looked as if Raven had handed him the key to a chest of treasure last night? Belatedly he remembered that Maurynna had said not to speak of her inability with anyone. With a sinking feeling in the pit of his stomach, Raven took out his anger at himself and Taren by throwing Taren's blanket roll to the back of the tent. Gods curse it, why had he opened his big mouth?

The rolled blanket struck Taren's belt pouch, left behind on the ground, and sent it flying, scattering Taren's things. Raven shut his eyes and clenched his fists, fighting the urge to break into a string of curses.

Just my bloody, damned luck. Muttering under his breath, he knelt to pick up Taren's belongings. The way his luck was running, Taren would pick *now* to return, and this was not something Raven wanted to explain.

Among the items was one that caught Raven's eye: a small, heavy awl of darkened steel that had fallen from its sheath. But it was like no leather awl that a traveler might carry that Raven had ever seen before. *How very odd*, he thought. The metal portion, a narrow, three-edged blade, was perhaps the width of a hand long; the point . . .

Raven incautiously touched it. Bright red blood welled out; he stuck his pricked finger into his mouth, grumbling. The damned thing was dangerous!

He examined the handle. While the end was flattened as he expected an awl's to be so that one could push it through leather with the heel of the hand, it was not the traditional bulbous shape that would sit secure in one's palm. And it was wrapped in twisted wire like a—

It's not a handle. It's a hilt.

Licking suddenly dry lips, Raven examined the edges of the blade. They were honed to a killing edge.

Linden's description of Revien's death wound came back into Raven's mind: *There was a tiny triangular tear in the skin at the base of the skull below the left ear. I looked a little more closely; it was a small hole, hard to see, but notable because of its shape.*

And hard on the heels of that memory came another like a wolf leaping upon a stag: *It's done with something like a long awl, something pointed and narrow.*

Taren had been out that same night, had come back much later than had been expected. And Taren owned a mysterious knife, kept carefully hidden, that looked at first sight like an—

Sickened, Raven almost cast the vile object from him, then reconsidered. The others should know of this. He had no idea why Taren had killed Revien; had the man seen or overheard something dangerous to Taren?

No matter; let wiser heads riddle that one out. His hands shaking, Raven shoved the awl-knife into his belt pouch and bundled Taren's things together again.

Then he picked up his own bundle and walked out of the tent into the late morning sun. He forced himself to walk with unhurried steps to where Stormwind waited with the other Llysanyins; he nearly melted with relief when he saw that all of them were already saddled, and all save Stormwind had blanket rolls in place. Linden, most likely, may the gods bless him for once.

Raven sauntered up to Stormwind as if he hadn't a care in the world. He even managed a jaunty whistle as he lashed his blanket to the back of the saddle.

"Be ready," he told Stormwind in a cheerful voice and patted the stallion's shoulder for the benefit of the Jehangli guards walking nearby. "We may have to make a run for it. I think treachery walks this camp."

Every Llysanyin's ears swiveled around at that, but only Stormwind turned to him. Raven wondered how much the animals truly understood.

Stormwind fixed a dark eye on him and bobbed his head once.

Satisfied, Raven strode off to find the others.

The lotuses gleamed white in the early morning sun. Lost in thought, Shei-Luin stood on the edge of the magnificent pool that was the center of the gardens of the empress, staring without seeing at the expanse of fragant white flowers that covered the marble-edged pond. A soft breeze teased at the heavy red silk of her robe. She ignored it.

From behind her came the sound of Xahnu's laughter as he played with his nurses, and a soft lullaby for Xu. And from barely a pace behind her, she heard Murohshei's even breathing, a balm to her tumbling thoughts. She focused on a blossom a bow-length from the marble edge, and watched the delicate flower sway as the breeze abandoned her and danced across the pool.

It surprised her that what she contemplated bothered her so much. She'd thought she hated Xiane. To her surprise, at some point that had changed. She despised him most of the time, yes; truly hated him—no. Not anymore.

He was a bumbling, inconsiderate oaf, but he meant well. He'd proven it in such a way that Shei-Luin blessed him for it.

If Xiane had not let him escape, Yesuin would have died when his brother broke the treaty. And though Xiane's position saved him from taking Yesuin's place in death, it was still a risk.

And that was why she found this hard, may the Phoenix help her. She knew well it was only because of Xiane's affection for his hostage-friend that Yesuin still lived. For angry as she'd been with Yesuin, she'd never wanted him dead. Never that. Though she would never see him again, the knowledge that he was alive and free gave her comfort, gave her the strength to accept the gilded bars of the cage she lived in.

But despite all he'd done for Yesuin, Xiane was a threat to her sons. She listened once more to Xahnu's bubbling laugh; to think of that beloved voice stilled before its time . . .

She would do what she had to do, as she had always done. Thank the Phoenix that it need not be irrevocable. She could set the stage; but need not perform the play if Xiane saw sense.

"Murohshei," she said softly, not turning her head.

"Yes, Favored One?" the eunuch answered, keeping to his position one pace behind her shoulder. If anyone watched from the palace, they would not be seen with their heads together, plotting.

"Have you thought about what I told you the emperor is considering?"

"Yes, my lady."

"And considered my fears of what it would mean for my sons?" The words came hard. Did speaking them give them power?

"Yes. And I fear that you have the right of it." The eunuch's voice was soft and worried. "For when I was a boy in the palace, long before you came, I listened many times to the young lords' tutors as they lectured on the history of Jehanglan. Such killings have happened many times in the past. It *would* happen again."

A coldness filled Shei-Luin. Though Murohshei was certainly no Oracle, his words had the ring of a true foreseeing. Why couldn't Xiane understand? Could anyone truly be so naive?

If anyone could, it would *be Xiane*, she thought wearily.

"I can't allow Xiane to abdicate," she said. "If I can convince him otherwise, all will be well, life will continue as it has, and one day Xahnu will inherit the throne.

"If Xiane will not see reason, then I have no choice but to take the throne as regent." She paused; she had never said the next words aloud. With them she placed her life in Murohshei's hands. If he chose to betray her, she would die a long and agonizing death.

Taking a deep breath she finished, "Which means that Xiane must die."

The breeze strengthened, tugging at the sleeves of her heavy robes, rippling the water of the lotus garden, setting the white flowers bobbing. Murohshei waited at her shoulder. He said no word of reproach, nor called for the guards. Instead he said quietly, "I understand, Beloved of the Phoenix. What do you need of me?"

Relieved, Shei-Luin said, "You must send word to Zyuzin's family." Then, unable to keep still any longer, she set off along the white marble edge of the pond. Murohshei followed like a shadow. As she walked, she told him what must be done.

When she finished, she added with a fervor that suprised her, "Let us hope it will not be needed."

"May the Phoenix hear your wish, my lady."

As he waited with the others for Raven and Taren, words slammed into Linden's mind with the force of mountain falling. *Thee* are *the ones he spoke of—I feared so! Run! Run!* With them came fear and images of the Dragonlords dragged off in chains to suffer for eternity.

He reeled under the onslaught; shaking his head to clear it, he looked to his fellow Dragonlords and knew they'd experienced it as well. They looked stunned. Only Otter was untouched.

That was a dragon, Linden's mind faltered as he instinctively looked for Taren to explain this; supposedly all the Jehangli dragons were dead. Even as he wondered whether to believe it, there came a sight that decided him.

Taller than the Jehangli, he caught a glimpse of the man he looked for. But not a Taren as prisoner, no; this Taren wore an air of command and rode at the head of a squad of—

"To the horses!" Linden bellowed. "It's a trap!" With a curse, he threw himself into the crowd of merchants between them and the Llysanyins, striking out left and right, clearing a path. The other Dragonlords fell in behind him, Otter in the center. He heard the Llysanyins scream in anger as they realized the danger.

So sudden was the attack that panic broke out among the Jehangli. Many threw themselves to the ground, wailing in fright; Linden had no mercy for those either too slow or too foolishly brave to get out of his way.

Guards ran to stop them. Linden ducked under the pike of the first to reach him, picked the man up and hurled him into his fellows. Using the pike as a flail, he battered his way on, none able to stand before his fury. The shrieks and moans of injured and dying men rent the air, doubling when the furious Llysanyins charged into the crowd, laying about them with teeth and hooves in a storm of death. The stench of blood and urine and voided bowels filled the air.

And all the while Linden heard the traitor yelling orders to "Take the creatures alive!" to the soldiers following him.

The guards fell back to regroup; Linden knew what would happen next. They would charge in a mass so thick that the Dragonlords would be overwhelmed and taken. He made ready to take as many as he could down and, remembering the images the unknown mindvoice had sent them, thought it might be best to die here. It would at least be a clean and honest death.

Then the Llysanyins plowed their way to the little group. Linden looked over his shoulder long enough to see Jekkanadar heave Otter onto Nightsong's saddle, and to make certain that Maurynna was on Boreal. He leaped to Shan's back; all were mounted now. "Ride!" he ordered and wheeled Shan around.

But Maurynna cried, "Raven!" and turned in the opposite direction at the same instant Taren bellowed, "Get the black-haired girl! She's the key!"

Linden cursed and tried to go after her, but the soldiers swarmed into the gap she'd made and blocked his way. Gods help him, he'd forgotten the boy, and now Maurynna might have to pay for it. His heart went cold.

She reached Raven the same instant Stormwind and the Two Poor Bastards did. As Raven flung himself into the saddle, Lleld's mindvoice ordered *Split up! Run!*

Linden hesitated long enough to be certain Maurynna and Raven broke free. Then he gave Shan his head; as the stallion leapt forward like a battering ram, Linden laid about him with the pike. For one terrible moment he feared he'd waited too long. Hands grabbed at his legs; the butt end of another pike thudded against his ribs, nearly unseating him.

Then he and Shan were free. He cast the pike aside and raced after the others across the rolling plain.

Maurynna clung grimly to the saddle as Boreal cleaved through guards and merchants like a living sword. Behind her, Stormwind neighed a challenge as he followed on Boreal's tail. All the while she heard Taren's voice exhorting the soldiers to take her, to take all of them alive.

She wanted to kill him.

Suddenly Boreal was clear; Stormwind raced up alongside, and together they left the camp behind, the Two Poor Bastards following.

As she looked wildly around, trying to see Linden and the others—but especially Linden—Lleld's mindvoice crackled in her head.

Ride for Mount Kajhenral.

But— She had to know if all was well with Linden; she had to at least say good-bye. Tears forming in her eyes, she reached out for him with her mind.

The force of Lleld's shout nearly felled her. *No! Do not mindspeak Linden! Go—I order you in the name of the Lady.*

Never had she heard such steel in Lleld's voice. She knew why the little Dragonlord forbade her to speak to Linden. But to not have even that much!

Love warred with duty. Duty won.

Ride north, then west, else thee will ride straight into the fort of Rhampul.

It was the voice that had warned them. She had no choice but to trust it. Maurynna turned Boreal. "This way," she called to Raven. "This—" Her voice broke.

She settled down to outrun the soldiers who pursued them.

They had not been riding long when the others crested a low rise and disappeared down the other side. When Linden, lagging a little behind, reached the top, he saw the others waiting down below. Otter was leaning on the high pommel of his saddle, trying to catch his breath. Jekkanadar lay on the ground, ear pressed to the earth, listening.

"I think we've lost the soldiers," Linden reported as he joined them. He ran a hand gingerly along his ribs; none broken—he thought. "We wait here for Maurynna and Raven, then?"

Jekkanadar would not meet his eyes. But Lleld—

Lleld sat up straight as a spear in the saddle. The harsh sun of Jehanglan cast its light on a face grimmer than he had ever seen it.

All at once he was afraid he understood why. "Where is she?" Linden said, his voice fierce and low.

Lleld said, "Gone. I mindspoke Maurynna, ordered her and Raven to leave for Mount Kajhenral."

He stared down at her, perilously close to wringing her neck. Otter must have read his thoughts in his face, for the bard made to push Nightsong between them.

Lleld stopped him with a wave of her hand; then she crossed her arms across her chest and met Linden's eyes without flinching.

"How dare you," Linden said, choking back his fury. The coldness he'd felt when he thought Maurynna might be caught by the soldiers came back tenfold. "Gods damn you, Lleld, couldn't you give us a chance to say good-bye?"

"There was no time, Linden," she said.

"You had no right!" Linden yelled, overcome by anger at last.

"I had every right!" Lleld yelled back. "Or did you forget that the Lady made me the leader of this mission? And the mission comes before any of us, or any of our feelings. Nor will you mindspeak her. The gods only know what hornet's nest we've heaved a rock into. Our job is to play decoy and stay just ahead of the soldiers. Now, after a run like that, even Llysanyins need to rest a bit. But be ready to ride at a moment's notice."

Linden snarled a curse and dismounted. When Lleld brought him a waterskin and some dried meat, he nearly slapped her hand aside. Instead he glared up at her from his seat on the ground.

"You have to eat, Linden. We don't know when we'll get another chance."

She was right, of course; it was one of the first things a

soldier learned. Eat when you could, rest when you could—
and do anything else that you could, when you could. He
remembered last night and his heart ached. If he'd
known . . .

So what if Lleld was right? It didn't help one bit.

Now and again the Dragonlords took turns listening for
the thud of hoofbeats in the ground. It came sooner than
they expected.

"Mount up," Jekkanadar said grimly during his turn.
"They're coming." He jumped up and mounted Hillel once
more.

A few moments later they were all in the saddle again.
Lleld set her heels to Miki's sides. At once the little Llysanyin was off again. Jekkanadar and Otter followed, letting
the shorter-legged Miki set the pace.

Linden fell in behind. As he rode, he kept looking over
his shoulder, even though he knew it was futile. Maurynna
would be well on her way by now.

Forty-three

"*Maurynna! Maurynna—hold up!*"

Maurynna looked back over her shoulder. Stormwind
had stopped and Raven was jumping down. "What is it?"
she called as Boreal slowed and turned. Fear seized her, for
Raven was picking up one of Stormwind's forefeet.

"Stone, I think," Raven said. "All of a sudden he stumbled and stopped."

Stormwind nodded. Raven straightened and dug into a
saddlebag. "Well enough, then, boy—we'll have that out
faster than my Uncle Fox can down a mug," he said as he
pulled out a hoofpick. The tension in his voice belied his

flippant words. Once more he bent over the foot Stormwind lifted for him, and set to work.

After looking all around like a nervous owl, Maurynna sat and watched as Raven worked.

The moments slid past. "Damn," he snarled, "the little bugger's wedged tight."

Then Maurynna heard the sound she'd been dreading: the chink of armor, a low rumble of men's voices. Their pursuers were some distance away, but they had lost valuable time. "Raven," she said, her voice low and tense. "*Hurry.*"

"I'm trying," he snapped. Then, "There!" in triumph.

He dropped Stormwind's foot. The stallion took a careful step or two. Even Maurynna could tell he limped slightly. But the Llysanyin nudged his rider and swung toward him. Raven took the hint and mounted.

"We'll have to go slowly," Raven said, and set off.

Maurynna dropped behind, letting Stormwind set the pace. Although the Llysanyin did the best he could, she fretted. Now and again, the breeze brought the sound of the troop following them; once she even thought she recognized Taren's voice. And each time, the noise was closer.

They rode on slowly. Too slowly; their enemy followed like hounds on the trail of a wounded deer.

At last it happened. As they reached the top of one of the rolling swells of land, a harsh shout went up behind them.

Stormwind broke into a limping run; Boreal came up beside him. On they went, the Llysanyins held to the speed of ordinary horses by the sore hoof.

It was like something from a nightmare. One where, no matter how you tried, you could never move faster than a crawl, while the fiendish thing behind you moved like the wind, and each time you looked over your shoulder, its dripping fangs loomed closer. Maurynna had had nightmares like that, and hated them. Now she lived one.

Another backward glance; she saw Raven do the same.

Their pursuers whipped up their horses. It was only a matter
of time now.

Raven fumbled at the long dirk hanging from his saddle.
"Get away while you can!" he yelled over the sound of
pounding hooves. He drew the reins back.

"Stormwind, keep running!" Maurynna ordered, then,
"Don't be stupid—what good is a dirk against swords? You
stop, and so do I."

"You stubborn—" He looked back. "They're nearly on
us! Ride!"

Stormwind did the best he could, but it was, Maurynna
knew, futile. Any moment the Jehangli soldiers would have
them. She reached for her own dirk. If nothing else, either
she would force them to kill her, or she would take her
own life.

Just as her hand closed on the hilt, it happened again. A
sense of a ribbon of wet, glittering darkness snapped into
Maurynna's mind. With it came a sharp order: *Due west
and cross the river!*

She clapped her heels to Boreal's sides. "We have one
last chance!" she cried.

Stormwind matched her pace; Maurynna prayed that the
river they sought was not far off. She'd no idea how long
the gallant Llysanyin could last. Longer, she hoped, than
their pursuers, who were once more dropping behind, judging by their yells of frustration.

It seemed like forever, but she knew it couldn't have
been much more than a mile before they saw the river.

"Now run for it!" Maurynna yelled.

The Llysanyins raced across the flat, open floodplain.
Maurynna could hear Stormwind grunt with each stride, but
the stallion kept up. Closer, closer came the dark water and
its nebulous promise of safety.

Then they were plunging into it with a terrific splash.
The black water fountained up, soaking them. Maurynna
shrieked in surprise; she hadn't expected it to be so *cold*.
A moment later she felt Boreal swimming strongly beneath
her. She clung to the saddle; she was a good swimmer, but

she'd no wish to test herself against the current tugging at them.

Still, she nearly jumped out of the saddle when something brushed against her leg. It must have touched Boreal as well, for the stallion neighed in surprise and redoubled his efforts. Nearly sick with fright, Maurynna told herself over and over that sharks did *not* live in fresh water, that she'd never heard of a freshwater fish large enough to harm a horse and rider, and river weed did not eat meat.

But that was in the north; who knew what lurked in Jehangli waters? She shut her mind to the thought.

At last they were to the other side. The stallions scrambled up the bank with difficulty. They stood a moment, sides heaving, then set off at a trot.

Though what good it would do, Maurynna didn't know. The land around them was as flat as a table, and they the only beings upon it. They must stand out like two lone chessmen on a board. All too soon the soldiers would cross the river after them.

It came even faster than Maurynna had feared. Yells of triumph told them they had been discovered. Maurynna glanced at Raven.

"Can he run anymore?" she asked quietly.

Raven shook his head.

"Then we fight here," she said, and drew her sailor's dirk. "I'll not be sport for them any longer."

A fierce grin lit Raven's face. "Just like Bram and Rani, eh?"

Maurynna laughed. "Just so. Though they were better armed."

They turned the horses to face their enemies. A strange calm took Maurynna. She thought only of how many enemies she could take with her. Her sole regret was that she dared not mindspeak Linden; if he was safe, she'd not be the one to somehow lead the Jehangli priestmages to him.

The first soldiers drove their horses into the water. Soon the whole troop was swimming across. Maurynna imagined she could see the glitter of blood lust in their eyes. Only one figure remained on the shore.

"Damn," Raven said. "I wanted Taren's head." He spoke as mildly as if he talked of a new bridle, and Maurynna knew the same strange calm rode him as well. *So this is what it is to die,* she thought.

And Death came.

How are you faring? Linden mindspoke Otter as they rode.

Well enough, Otter answered, but there was a tired note to it. Tired, and worried. *Linden, I've been too afraid to ask, but— Did they . . . ?*

Get clear? I think so; I hung back to make certain. And if something had happened, I'm certain I would have felt it. Frustration with not truly knowing ate at him. But he had to cling to that belief or go mad.

Thank the gods. They can drive a man mad, but . . . I love them both.

Linden smiled sadly. *Aye,* he said, *I understand.* Then, *Tell us when you need to rest, Otter; we'll soon have a safe distance between us and those bastards.*

A mental snort of indignation. *I'm good for a while yet, boyo.*

Linden smiled in truth this time. Then he stared out over the rolling grassland, and settled himself a little deeper in the saddle.

Death came—but not for them. Before Maurynna's astonished eyes, the black water roiled, and horse after horse vanished beneath the surface or was thrown into the air to land among its fellows. The yells of triumph turned to cries of panic in the blink of an eye as soldiers tumbled from their saddles and slid beneath the deadly waters, doomed by the weight of armor and weapons.

Maurynna and Raven watched, transfixed by the slaughter before them, unable to move or look away. Some of the Jehangli soldiers, those closest to the far shore, turned their horses in time and retreated. There were pitifully few of them; they milled around Taren, who stared across the river as if he could fell them with a glare, the sunlight glinting in his white hair.

Then one of the soldiers broke and ran. As though his flight were a summons, the others followed until only Taren was left. At last even he turned away from the deadly waters and rode off.

Raven slid down from Stormwind. "Wha—what happened?" he said, his voice shaking. His icy calm was breaking at last.

Maurynna's followed. She whispered, "I don't know. It felt . . . I thought . . ." But she no longer knew what she thought. What they had seen was impossible; there was no rational explanation for it. All she knew was that it scared the daylights out of her.

"Raven, let's get away from here." And even though Boreal didn't need the rest, she also dismounted to lead him, for she wanted to feel the solidity of earth beneath her feet, needed an anchor in a world gone mad.

"What about the Two Poor Bastards?" Raven said. "They were following us."

"They know what they're doing; they'll find either us or the others before long." She lifted her head, feeling the breeze on her face—and, for the first time, the tug of the imprisoned dragon. Was it because she was now the only magical being for miles?

"This way," she said, and set off across the rolling grasslands.

Yesuin dozed in the saddle as he rode. He should make Rhampul today, he thought drowsily, as the horse trotted steadily on.

He slipped into a half-waking dream. He was running so hard that he felt his heart hammering in his chest like a drum, each beat reverberating in his blood.

Like a drum, like a drum . . . He came awake with a gasp.

Those *were* drums he heard! Cursing, Yesuin halted his horse and listened. His heart went cold within him as

he recognized a rhythm he hadn't heard since his childhood.

He was in the path of a Zharmatian warband.

How can they be on this side of the Black River?

His first instinct was to dig his heels into his horse's sides
and race away. But his horse was already tired from the
long days of traveling; he must husband its strength for as
long as he could.

He set off, keeping to the hollows as much as possible.

At last Lleld slowed Miki to a walk.

Linden, riding rear guard, was glad of it. Even a Llysanyin couldn't gallop for candlemarks on end, although the
greathearted creatures would run themselves to death if
their riders' lives depended on it. But there was no such
need, he thought; they had kept the mad pace for a good
two or three candlemarks now. Whatever horses of their
enemies hadn't been ridden into exhaustion would still be
far behind.

But not far enough to discourage them from the chase,
he hoped.

Otter slumped over his saddle. Nightsong looked back at
him and nickered in concern. Then the mare stopped; by
the way she planted her feet, Linden knew she wasn't going
another step.

She had the right of it, anyway. Otter needed a rest. Linden called "Hold up!" to the others, and dismounted.

Lleld turned in her saddle. "We rest here," she said, "at
least for a time."

The bard groaned as his feet touched the ground once
more. He patted Nightsong's shoulder and allowed himself
to be led off to the side. More groans followed as he lowered himself slowly to the ground.

"You're not hurt, are you?" Linden asked, suddenly
afraid that Otter had taken some wound during the escape
and not said anything.

"Not permanently," Otter complained. "But I don't think

I'd be bedding any lasses even if one were here and throwing herself at me."

Linden laughed in relief. "Lie down and rest, you silly ass. One of us will see to Nightsong."

They made a rough camp in one of the hollows, not intending to stay more than a few candlemarks, just enough to eat a little and sleep. Then they would be off again, the gods only knew where, their mission to draw as many Jehangli soldiers as possible away from Maurynna and Raven.

"We can't keep going south as we have, or we'll run into more settled lands," Linden said as he chewed on a strip of dried meat. "Maurynna and Raven will be traveling north and west—we don't want to follow them. Northeast brings us back to Rhampul. Well, Lady Mayhem? You're in charge."

Making a face at him, Lleld said, "I should toss this back at you as something military. But I say, south a little more, then west across that river Taren spoke of. Show ourselves on the rises as often as we must to keep them after us, lead the soldiers on a merry chase for as long as Maurynna needs, then lose 'em and ride like hell for the north. Once the power of the priestmages is broken, one of us can Change and search out Maurynna and Raven." She lifted her chin at him in defiance. "What do you say to that?"

"That it's what I'd do. I'll take first watch. The rest of you try to sleep even though it's still day."

He left the others unrolling blankets. Again and again as he circled the camp, his mind and heart turned to his soul-twin. Was all well with her? He remembered his confident words to Otter earlier; may the gods grant he was right, that the strange "fog" that kept him from sensing Maurynna clearly wouldn't hide the mind-pain of her death.

But Taren said to take us alive. It was small consolation, yet it was all he had. He clung to it.

And as he walked, he found that he had forgiven Lleld. He knew her well enough to know that she wasn't deliberately cruel. She had seized their one chance without hesitation; Gifnu's hells, he would have done the same in her place. And the restrictions she now laid upon him made good military sense. It did not make them any easier to bear.

He glanced up at the sun, and wondered how Rani and little Lady Mayhem would have gotten along.

Likely very well indeed. It was a frightening thought.

A couple of candlemarks or so later, he roused Lleld and sought his own blankets.

Trot, walk, trot; Yesuin pushed his horse on mercilessly, cursing it when it stumbled from weariness. Yet with every step, it seemed, the drums drew closer. Then came the sound he'd been dreading: a shrieking, eldritch howl that froze his blood.

He'd been seen. Yesuin looked over his shoulder and saw a waking nightmare—riders spilling over a rise, red horsetail banners flying. It wasn't a large band, but he saw one rider turn back, no doubt to tell the main warband of the prey to be had.

Yesuin lashed his tired mount into a heavy gallop, crouched over its neck as it ran, and prayed.

He was mad, flying in such a storm. But there was nowhere Linden could see to land and Change so that he might seek shelter in his human form. The thunder rolled over him, nearly deafening him with its peals, and the turbulent air tossed him about like a butterfly in a gale. Lightning stabbed the air around him. The thunder grew louder and louder. . . .

Curse it! That wasn't thunder! Linden shook himself awake and pressed his ear against the ground for an instant, then threw his blanket aside and jumped to his feet. "They're coming!"

Lleld took only a moment to wake up. Then she was on her feet and lashing her pack together. Otter was only a little slower. Jekkanadar ran back into the camp from his patrol of the perimeter; the Llysanyins followed at a smart trot.

Each worked with grim efficiency and soon they were on their way. Lleld held Miki to a fast trot; Linden approved. It would keep them ahead—but not too far ahead. When the time came for more speed, the Llysanyins would still have it to give. And so they would play with their pursuers until it ended, one way or another.

They had been riding for some time, keeping to the dips in the land as much as possible, when he heard it: the sound of hoofbeats—but in front of them, and close.

How the hell did they circle around us so quickly? Linden thought in astonishment.

Lleld pulled Miki up. "It's not possible!" she cried.

The others stopped as well. Then came a sound that raised the hair on the back of Linden's neck. A ululation like a pack of wolves on a blood trail, a nightmare sound that drew ever closer, riding on a wave of thundering hooves. The hair on the back of his neck rose. He knew that sound—or one very close to it. It was so like the war cry of Bram and Rani's warband that, for the space of a heartbeat, he was lost in time.

But it was certainly not those he would have welcomed.

Then a single rider crested the rise in front of them, his horse staggering with weariness. It slipped and slid down the shallow slope. When he saw them, the rider cried out in despair.

As if it were a signal, two things happened almost at once. The exhausted horse fell, pitching the man from the saddle. He rolled the rest of the way down the slope, coming to rest almost at the feet of the Llysanyins.

As the stranger got to his knees, a small group of horsemen spilled over the brow of the low hill, the strange, eerie cries echoing from rider to rider. Some carried long staffs with red horsetails streaming from them.

One look, and Linden knew these were not the Jehangli soldiers who chased them. These were much worse.

And the damned dirks were all they had for weapons. Useless as it was, Linden drew his anyway.

Haoro entered the temple council room and took his seat. This was the first time the council had met since his recovery. He looked around.

There were many empty seats, not to be filled until priests of a suitable rank could be brought in. And of those empty seats, most were of those who had agreed to support him in his bid to become *nira*.

He didn't have the time to cultivate more. His uncle's latest message, destroyed just before coming here, allowed no more time for subtlety.

The words danced in his mind as if written in fire: *I will have the northern creatures soon. Do your part.*

He would have to move—and quickly.

The riders swirled around them like leaves in a storm. The horsemen rode small, hairy ponies, big in the barrel and heavy-boned, and rode them as if they were part of the ugly little brutes. The galloping circle drew closer and closer until at some unknown signal they stopped, the ponies rolling back on their haunches to face in.

Long, narrow faces with high cheekbones leered at them. *So these are Zharmatians*, Linden guessed, remembering things Taren had let drop.

He looked from them to the man they'd chased. He was dressed somewhat like the Jehangli soldiers that had pursued them, but his face was not like other Jehangli he had seen. This one looked more like the riders. He was young, Linden saw, but haggard with exhaustion.

There were only eight horsemen. And overconfident to boot; Linden read it in their wolflike smiles at the helpless prey they had found.

The poor wretches have no idea what they're up against, do they? So it's two-to-one; the Llysanyins alone could take them, Linden thought, though he still wished for his greatsword, Tsan Rhilin. To the others he said, *Otter—let Night-*

song fight for you; just hang on to the saddle. She'll get you clear first chance she has. Lleld, Jekkanadar, you do the same. Shan and I will follow once I've grabbed this poor beggar. Once we're clear, the Llysanyins can outrun anything they've got.

The man opposite Linden yelled a demand as he pointed with his sword and gestured. Although Linden couldn't understand the language, the meaning was as plain as a sunrise: drop the weapon and get off the horses.

"No," Linden said in Jehangli. "And get out of our way."

A surprised babble of rapid speech filled with clicks and trills.

"You speak Jehangli?" the man said in that language. His own version was so heavily accented that Linden could barely understand him.

"Yes," said Lleld. "We all do. Now do as the big man says. We've nothing to do with you or you with us. Let us go our own way and we won't hurt you."

Shouts of laughter and derisive hooting. One bold fool spurred forward and snatched at the front of Lleld's tunic. Before Linden could intervene, she grabbed the fellow's arm and heaved. He flew through the air over her head.

Linden had seldom seen anyone look so surprised. *Poor wretch; no doubt the last thing he was expecting was a child-sized woman who's as strong as he is. I could almost feel sorry for him.*

The man landed, tucked, rolled, and sprang to his feet. He picked up the sword that had flown from his hand and rushed at Lleld. Nightsong's head shot out like a striking snake's as he passed her; she caught the man's forearm in teeth that could easily crush through skin and bone.

The man knew it as well. He stood like a stone, his face impassive, but fear writ large in his eyes. Nightsong shook her head gently. Nothing. She shook her head again, harder this time and, judging by the sudden grimace of pain that shot across the man's face, tightened the viselike grip of her jaws. He dropped the sword. Nightsong put one large hoof squarely atop the blade and released the man; he ran for his horse.

"What goes on here?" a new voice asked in Jehangli.

Linden turned to see a rider approaching at the head of a band of horse archers, a mixed group of men and women. At a signal, the archers fanned out and around so that the Dragonlords, Otter, and the stranger were enclosed within a double ring of Zharmatians for a moment. Then their original captors slipped back through the archers' ring so that their comrades had a clear field.

Linden's hopes sank when he saw the archers. Not even a Llysanyin could outrun an arrow. They'd lost their chance for escape.

Heavy scars, newly healed, slashed across the man's cheeks, straight and deliberate as the blade that had made them. His expression, like the other Zharmatians', was impassive, but his eyes were full of speculation. The man held up empty hands in token of peace.

In return, Linden rested his dirk across his saddlebow.

The man nodded, and the archers relaxed. "This was an ill-chance for you, to meet this one." He jerked a thumb at the man standing quietly by Shan. "You're *baishin*, outlanders," he said. "More of the northerners the Jehangli bring in, yes?"

Linden nodded.

"I am Dzeduin, foster-brother to Yemal, *temur* of the Zharmatians. This dog is Yesuin, the *temur*'s half brother."

"Must have been one hell of a family argument," Lleld murmured.

"Why are you hunting him?" Linden asked.

For the first time the hunted man spoke up. Staring at the ground, he said in a voice heavy with weariness, "Because my brother has hated me since we were children. My mother was our father's favorite wife, though Yemal's mother was his First Wife." Then he looked up at Dzeduin. "And when I was given as hostage to the Jehangli, my father grieved. Grieved, and wished it was Yemal in peril, didn't he?"

There was no answer. The hunted man bared teeth in a wolfish grin. "I always admired that about you, Dzeduin. You won't lie."

The other Zharmatians murmured at that. Dzeduin's hand clenched on his sword hilt, but that was all.

"Your brother wants you," Dzeduin said. "You'll come with us. So," he added, his gaze taking them in, "will the four of you."

Linden ground his teeth. There was nothing they could do, not with archers surrounding them. To fight would be suicide. "What would your *temur* want with a stray band of traveling entertainers? Let us be on our way." He made ready to snatch Yesuin if the ruse worked.

Now Dzeduin smiled, a bare curving of his thin-lipped mouth. "Traveling entertainers who have horses that think for themselves. Traveling entertainers of unusual strength— such as a small woman who can toss a man like a kitten. Traveling entertainers who are so important to Lord Jhanun, one of the most powerful Jehangli lords, that he sends a troop of soldiers under the direction of one of his most favored servants to take them. So Ghulla has Seen."

Dzeduin's pony danced backward; he raised a hand. At once a Zharmatian rider swept in and pulled Yesuin up behind him. Then the archers' bows were up once more, arrows nocked and drawn, each wickedly barbed head pointed at the little band.

"Yemal will see you," said Dzeduin. "Come." His pony sat back on its haunches and wheeled around, then sprang into a run.

They had no choice but to follow.

Raven stopped ahead of her. "We're safe. Even if there are any soldiers left, they'll never catch us now." He rubbed Stormwind's nose, and ran a critical eye over both horses. "Look at them! Not even sweating after a run like that!" he said, grinning in delight. Raven slapped Stormwind on the rump and bent to examine his hoof.

Nodding, Maurynna halted by him and sat down, grateful

for both the respite and that she was still in one piece.
Never before had she ridden the stallion at a flat-out run.
Indeed, she'd never ridden any horse at that pace; she
thanked the gods that her first try had been on a Llysanyin.
Boreal wouldn't let her fall if he could help it. Even so,
the high cantle and pommel of the saddle had been all that
saved her when they'd zigged and zagged to avoid little
gullies and large rocks in the race to the river. More than
once she'd grabbed leather and hung on for dear life.

She lay back on the grass, breathing hard, and realized
it was done. She was on her own. Where Linden was right
now, she didn't know, and didn't dare find out. The effort
needed for mindspeech from this distance might be enough
to alert the priestmages.

She didn't even know if he was still alive. Had he and
the others been able to elude Taren's soldiers? And what
had that miserable traitor Taren meant, anyway, by calling
her "the key"? More to the point, who was behind the mysterious mindvoice, and the images it had sent?

She remembered the one of Linden in chains and shuddered.

*Damn Lleld anyway, not letting me bid Linden farewell
even by mindspeech!* Maurynna thought bitterly. *What
would it have cost?* Tears flowed down her face.

The answer came unbidden in her mind: mere moments
and all of her resolve.

She couldn't stay here. She'd turn back if she did.

Forcing the words out, Maurynna said, "Can Stormwind
go on?" At Raven's nod, she said, "Then we'll keep walking for a few more candlemarks."

"I want to find a stream where Stormwind can soak his
foot."

"Well enough. When we find one, we'll rest, set up a
rough camp, and stay the night perhaps, if we're not disturbed. Come dawn, we can be on our way again." She sat
up. A breeze sprang up and dried the tears upon her cheeks.
With a muffled oath, she stood up and set off to the north,
walking quickly. Boreal followed.

Behind her, she heard Raven exclaim in surprise. Then came the heavy thud of Stormwind's hooves upon the hard ground as man and stallion followed.

Raven trotted up and fell in beside her without a word; she was grateful for that. All that was left to her now was their mission. She was the least of the Dragonlords, but she would do the best she could or die in the trying.

The hot scent of blood raced through the turmoil of his dreams. He'd not felt such chaos since the dark years. It woke long-buried memories of woe and dread to haunt him once more.

The old dragon moaned.

Forty-four

Their three days of walking to give Stormwind's foot a chance to heal had slowed them badly. Maurynna had chafed at the delay, but couldn't argue with Raven. Better to lose time now, than have Stormwind's hoof fail when they needed a burst of speed. Stormwind had, by constantly stepping in front of Raven and presenting his near side for mounting, conveyed that his foot was better. Raven had insisted on one more day of easy walking.

To make up for the delay, they'd ridden steadily since then. Two days ago, they'd left the rolling plains. Now they were in a land of grass yellowed by the blazing sun and scrubby pines twisted by the wind blowing incessantly over the flatness stretching all around them. But ever before them loomed the goal that Maurynna's dreams now urged her to: mountains that jutted up from the flat plain like a row of dragon's teeth.

Maurynna marveled at those mountains, bare and stark

against the sky. At times they looked as solid as the mountains that she called home now, standing tall and proud since the earth was young. At other times they seemed as insubstantial as a dream; she need but stretch out a hand and they would dissolve like mist.

She had never seen anything like it back home. It was, she realized, a trick of the light. And even that seemed different here in this part of Jehanglan. It poured around them, lucid and clear, like water running over them. She was tempted to catch some and pour the light from hand to hand like a juggler before casting it back into the air to splash around them once more.

And over all stretched a turquoise sky that seemed but a stone's throw overhead. She had seen such expanses of sky while at sea. But never had it seemed so close before; they must be far, far above sea level by now. Nor had she ever seen so much sky while ashore; this was a country of vast distances, a place for giants to stride freely in. She felt like an ant.

Yet mile by mile, the ever-changing mountains drew closer as the Llysanyins covered the distance with their ground-eating trot. It had been pure torture at first, posting for candlemarks at a time, but now Maurynna's muscles had adapted. It was, she reflected with grim amusement, a case of either get used to it or curl up and die; as Raven had explained, trotting was the most efficient way for horses to cover long distances.

A pity she couldn't quite convince her sore rear of that— especially at the end of a long day. But Boreal's pace was smooth, thank all the gods, a big, long stride that was easy to ride.

It could be much worse. Remember that pony you and Raven took lessons on so long ago? A short, clippy trot that damn near rattled the teeth out of you. Even Raven *had trouble riding it.*

Maurynna shook her head, remembering those lessons. No, give her a Llysanyin any day if she had to ride for candlemarks on end.

A memory of one of her early riding lessons with Linden came back to her: "Don't jump up out of the saddle; you don't need to do all that work. Just let Boreal drop out from beneath you, and be there when he comes back up." When, one day, she'd wailed in frustration that she'd never catch the trick of it, Linden had simply said, "You will."

So she had—finally. And Linden wasn't here to witness her triumph, small as it was; he was . . . The gods only knew where he was right now. She prayed he was safe. As tears pricked the back of her eyelids, she clamped down on the turn her thoughts had taken. Down that path was only misery. Maurynna fixed her mind on the journey.

One morning, as Murohshei slid an embroidered slipper onto her foot, he said quietly, "Lady, Zyuzin had word from his family. All is made ready as you wished."

Shei-Luin went cold inside. It was one thing to plan this, another to take this first step. The stage was set now.

May the actors never set foot upon it.

"Thank you, Murohshei," she whispered.

"I'm sorry, Favored One," he said softly.

She smiled, a sad, wistful smile. "As am I, faithful friend. As am I."

Linden looked grimly around as they rode into a large camp. As they passed through it, Zharmatians stopped whatever they were doing to stare at them. An astonished murmur arose at the sight of Yesuin.

At first Linden thought this might be the main camp of the tribe, as Yesuin had described. That hope died when he realized that there were no children here, no old people; and hanging from every tent was a red horsetail, the Zharmatian symbol of war, he now knew.

Dzeduin led them to a large tent. "This is where you will stay while word is sent to Yemal."

Still astride their horses, their captors watched while they dismounted. Other Zharmatians brought them ropes.

Linden saw the Llysanyins look at each other. They knew what was afoot.

Sure enough, the instant saddles and bridles came off, the Llysanyins bolted, knocking the smaller Zharmatian horses aside. Linden watched as they raced into the middle of the small herd of horses the Zharmatians kept as remounts, then tried not to smile as the astonished Zharmatians picked themselves up.

Well enough; the Llysanyins would be close by if needed. And as soon as the Zharmatians called off the archers and relaxed their vigilance . . .

Come hell, high water, or anything else, he was off to find Maurynna. Until then, this was as good a place as any to hide from whatever plans Taren had had for them.

Forty-five

"There's a nice little spot hidden by that copse of trees a bit downriver; a quiet little backwater with a sandy bottom," Raven announced as he returned to camp one evening, his hair soaking wet and dripping over everything. "Might want to take a quick bath; I just did and it felt wonderful."

Maurynna peered blearily up from her blankets. "Does sound wonderful. I'll wait till morning, though. It's getting dark now, and I won't risk coldfire."

Besides, she was too sore to move. *So much for the vaunted strength of a Dragonlord*, she thought wryly. *A pity it doesn't include an iron butt.*

Shima yawned as he swung down from Pirii, his little mare. It had been a long ride from the Sandy Ridge *mehanso*, and he wanted nothing more than to give two of the rabbits he'd shot on the way home to Zhantse, then go to his mother's house and fall into his bed; he'd been awake since dawn.

But when he went inside, Zhantse wasn't there. His brother Tefira was, though. The boy was stuffing supplies into his saddlebag, a sour, angry expression twisting his features.

"What's wrong?" Shima asked, dropping down beside his brother, though he thought he knew.

"I went into a Seeing trance, but—" Tefira broke off, and threw the saddlebag against the far wall. In a voice thick with unshed tears, the boy said, "I'm to go to the little hut in the meadow again."

"More fasting?"

"More fasting. I don't understand, Shima. I had visions, true ones, when I was little. I Saw them even with my eyes open. Why won't they come to me now when I can go into a Seeing trance? Did Zhantse make a mistake, taking me for an apprentice?" The tears finally spilled over.

Shima held his little brother as he cried. "For what it's worth, I believe in you, Tef. The visions will come again— you'll see. Now dry your eyes."

Tefira obeyed. "But they won't come, so I have to stay here and study harder, and meanwhile you get to travel and do exciting things."

Shima snorted. "Traveling to Sandy Ridge is hardly exciting."

"That's not what I meant. *Zhantse* had a Seeing while *I* was in trance. You're to travel south, to meet the one that Miune's been talking about."

Confused, Shima asked, "Why?"

"Because she's the one from the prophecy."

"Oh," was all Shima could think of to say.

The next morning, Maurynna found the pocket of sandy beach that Raven had spoken of, and knelt by the river. She scooped up a double handful of water and splashed it over her face.

Ohh, that feels good. She pulled a wooden comb from her belt pouch and untied the thong holding her hair. Her gaze drifted back to the water. A frond of some aquatic plant she hadn't noticed before drifted hypnotically to and fro in the current.

She worked the comb through her hair, dreamily watching the plant as it undulated in the water. First she'd get all the knots out, then give her hair a good washing while she bathed.

It was a moment before she realized something was wrong about the rippling frond; when she did, she sat up straight, one hand reaching for the dirk at her belt.

The river's current in this little backwater wasn't powerful—but it was brisk. Certainly strong enough to cause anything to flow in one direction only: downstream. This plant, or whatever it was, moved against the current. Suddenly, as if aware of her changed regard, it disappeared.

Maurynna jumped to her feet. The water heaved and bubbled about a spear length from the shore. She scrambled backward, never taking her eyes from the water, but missed her footing up the earthen bank and stumbled to a halt.

A large head burst from the water, rose up and up. Maurynna opened her mouth to scream.

Do not be afraid, a voice said inside her mind. There was the boom of a river in spate in the words and the merry tinkle of a mountain stream singing over rocks. *I would not harm thee.*

With a shock, Maurynna realized she faced a dragon. But it was like no dragon she had ever seen or heard of. She shut her mouth and studied it as it studied her.

It was blue and green as she was in dragon form, something that gave Maurynna a feeling of kinship. But where she was the deep iridescent shades of a peacock—or so she'd been told; she had little memory of her one flight, Kyrissaean, of course, having been in charge—this dragon was all the blues and greens of turquoise, its scales edged in black. Two feelers grew from each side of its wide muzzle and numerous lacy streamers that looked like river weeds sprouted from around its face and along its neck and back.

But that made no sense. Then she realized that, though this dragon had short, stubby legs, he had no wings. In fact, she wasn't certain where his neck ended; his body was long and narrow like a snake's or—

An eel. My gods, he's a water-dwelling dragon!

Yes, he said. *I am. I live in the rivers and lakes of this land. But what, pray tell me, are* thee?*

Maurynna asked, "What do you mean?"

I have been following thee and the others for some time now—since before thy party split up. With thee now I sense a human such as dwell in this land. But others of thy companions, those who are not here now—I sensed those who are both dragon and human. Is such a thing possible? His mindvoice squeaked with excitement.

He was also, Maurynna saw upon closer examination, not as large as surprise had made him. A sneaking suspicion crept into her mind.

She also thought she now knew the source of her feeling of being watched.

Not waiting for an answer, the waterdragon continued, *But thee—thee I do not sense at all. It is as if thee move through a fog. I see thee before me but there is nothing in my mind when I search for thee. I have a friend like thee.* He waited, feelers and streamers quivering, for her answer.

Another waterdragon, but one who shared Maurynna's odd "invisibility"? She said slowly, "Some of my friends—such as the one who is with me—are indeed what we call truehuman. And others of us—myself included—are known as Dragonlords in our lands."

Dragonlords? the waterdragon asked.

Maurynna nodded. "Yes. We're weredragons."

The waterdragon reared up a little higher and came down once more, splashing water everywhere. *So it was true what the strange dragons told my parents!* He danced in the shallows, excited as a puppy.

Maurynna jumped back as a small wave threatened to

swamp her feet. Then the import of what the waterdragon said struck her. Could he be speaking of Pirakos? Wait— he'd said "dragons"; could he mean Dharm Varleran as well? "The strange *dragons*?"

Yes. Once, two strange dragons appeared by my parents' lake. I was still in the egg. My parents, who told me this story, greeted them in wonder, for they had never seen dragons with wings like a bird's.

Maurynna thought to herself, *That's fair enough. I've never heard of dragons who live like fishes!* And the dragon's words confirmed her suspicion. *He's a youngling— nothing more than a baby by a truedragon's accounting.*

They told my parents of the northern lands they had come from, and the mountains that were their home. But one said that the one he loved had died. The urge to explore came upon him, so he wandered far from his home, and the other joined him. My parents told them of this land, of the great phoenix that lives a thousand years and dies in fire only to be born once more from its own ashes. They desired to see the phoenix and flew farther inland. It was near the time of the phoenix's rebirth.

The mindvoice turned sad. *My parents never saw the winged dragons again. Then one day the priests came with soldiers, and killed all the waterdragons that they could find. My kind are not warriors and many died. My parents hid my egg. They said they would come back. . . . *

The tale broke off in a hiccup of grief.

"And they never did," Maurynna said aloud, catching her breath at the lonely pain in the young dragon's mindvoice. "I'm sorry—" She tilted her head.

Miune Kihn, said the waterdragon.

She wondered if all the Jehangli water dragons had had two names like Dragonlords, or if Miune was the only one. "And I am Maurynna Kyrissaean," she said.

Are thee a winged dragon like the journeyers?

She forced a smile. "Yes. Here; I will try to make you a picture in my mind."

She concentrated on an image of Linden. Slowly she

built in her mind the memory of him on their trip from
Cassori to Dragonskeep last summer. The glint of sunlight
on his deep red scales, the powerful arch of neck and wing
as he crouched upon the flower-strewn meadow where they
had stopped. She remembered how he'd gathered himself,
suddenly springing up, his wings flashing out and down as
he rose into the sky.

Then, before she could stop remembering, Linden's
words, cheerfully ignorant of what was to come: *Your turn!*
She pushed the memory of her failure to Change from her,
holding instead the image of a red dragon suspended
against a sky of molten blue.

"Do you see the red dragon that I'm thinking of? That's
my soultwin, Linden, in his dragon form. He's the big
yellow-haired man who was riding the black horse."

Miune Kihn huffed in excitement; clouds of vapor billowed from his mouth. *I saw him, I saw him! But what
do thee— Hwah! What is this?*

Maurynna staggered as Kyrissaean surged to the fore.

I am Kyrissaean! Who are thee? her draconic half pro-
claimed imperiously, much to Maurynna's surprise. She
was even more surprised that this time her wretched draconic half did not seem intent on suffocating her.

Miune Kihn did not answer right away. He dropped
down onto the sandy beach so that the end of his broad
snout nearly touched Maurynna's nose, and stared into her
eyes. When he did speak, Maurynna wanted to laugh despite the pain of Kyrissaean's intrusion. For Miune Kihn's
tone was exactly the same as she remembered Breslin using
from his lofty status as a seven-year-old to her lowly five-
year-old self years ago.

Thee are rude, Miune Kihn stated. *Thee have no
manners at all.*

Kyrissaean lashed out at the waterdragon with a blast of
anger. Maurynna reeled under the onslaught, and fell to her
knees.

Brat! Miune Kihn yelled, and mentally "thumped"

Kyrissaean. *Thee are causing thy human pain,* he scolded.

Kyrissaean snarled in wordless surprise, but Maurynna felt the pain in her head recede to a mild ache. She wanted to applaud but thought better of it; Kyrissaean would no doubt throw another tantrum.

Tantrum. By the gods, that was just what her draconic half had been doing all along. The revelation was blinding.

Miune Kihn must have caught the thought from her mind, and all the attendant images and feelings, for he said, *Thee are but a babe, Kyrissaean, one that was woken too early—but even a youngling may have concern for others. Thee were frightened and hurt but thee should not be hurting thy human in return; thy human half is not at fault. I know from her mind that thee should be sleeping for many long years yet. Rest easy, little sister. Leave thy human in peace.*

A rumble of emotions bubbled through the back of Maurynna's mind: anger, surprise, remorse, and, most amazing of all, meek compliance. Then, for the first time since her one and only Change, Maurynna was completely alone in her mind. She sat down in astonished relief.

"What—" she began. Then, "She would never speak to another dragon." She told Miune Kihn how Kyrissaean had refused to speak to Linden, what had happened the day Morlen the Seer had tried to speak to her. "How did you—?"

The waterdragon curled back on himself, one feeler tucked into his mouth as he thought. Finally he said, *I think she was afraid of the others. What happened in the meadow with this Morlen the Seer—I would guess he was too old, too powerful; he frightened her and she was already frightened. Even thy soultwin is older. But I am a dragonchild like her. I also saw from thy mind how thee first became what thee are. I think it was too soon—for both of thee. And there was bad magic to hurt thee.*

Maurynna stood up once more. She moved gingerly; it felt as if her body didn't quite fit anymore. "I think you're right," she said, marveling. How simple it had been—and no one had thought of it save another dragonchild. "My thanks for this, Miune Kihn."

Thee are welcome, Maurynna Kyrissaean. And my friend calls me just Miune. Will thee do the same? The feelers waved in the air.

To herself, she thought, *Like a Dragonlord's names.* "Of course."

Running footsteps sounded in the grove of trees behind her. Before she could stop him, Miune whirled and leaped for the river.

"No—come back! It's just my friend!" she cried.

But Miune did't heed her. For the first time, Maurynna got a good look at all of the waterdragon as he slid into the water. He was small even for a youngling, she thought, not much more than two spear lengths long, and sleek, save for a noticeably distended stomach. His legs emerged not from beneath his body like a horse's, as the dragons she knew, but from the sides so that his elbows and knees jutted out. Maurynna guessed he must waddle on dry land. But in his own element Miune was graceful, slipping into the water like some giant otter, disappearing as she watched.

Raven emerged from the grove of trees and ran down the slope, dirk in hand. "Who were you talking to?" he demanded, his face pale and worried.

Maurynna pushed the hair back from her face and shook her head. "You'll never believe this, but a baby dragon found me. Then he spanked Kyrissaean soundly and sent her to bed."

Startled, Raven swore and looked up, his eyes searching the skies.

Maurynna laughed aloud. "Not there." Pointing to the river, she told him, "There." At his disbelieving stare, she said, "He was a waterdragon. His name is Miune Kihn."

Scowling, Raven said, "Is this a jest? I've never heard of a waterdragon."

For an answer, Maurynna pointed to the wet sand near her feet. Two unmistakable dragon footprints showed clear in the sand, four long toes to the fore, one to the rear, all tipped with claws. A long, shallow trench—where the young dragon's body had rested—gouged the sand and disappeared into the river.

Raven knelt and ran his fingers over the footprints. He whistled, and said softly, "By all the gods. . . . This is a strange, strange land." He stood once more and dusted off his knees. "And I can't wait to finish the task and go home." He turned sharply to face her. "Does this mean you can Change now?"

Maurynna put a hand to her mouth. "I don't know. I could try—no! I can't!"

"Why—oh, gods. That's right. Damn those priestmages. They'd likely sense you. Blast; it would have made finding pasture and water so much easier when we enter those badlands ahead." He swore, long and hard.

"Keep that up, and I've hopes of making a sailor of you yet," Maurynna said, laughing. "Here; help me erase these. I don't want to chance the wrong person seeing them."

Together they scuffed out the telltale prints. When they were done, Raven said, "I came to tell you that we're ready to move on now."

It wasn't until they were well on their way that Maurynna realized she'd never gotten her bath.

The sun was past the nooning and slipping into the west, casting long shadows from the tents across the ground.

At least, Linden thought, they were able to walk around the Zharmatian camp while they waited for this Yemal, who was, according to Dzeduin, elsewhere leading raids on the Jehangli. If they'd had to stay inside, he would have gone mad by now. The amount of freedom they were given astonished him; only Yesuin was confined to the tent.

The only thing they were not allowed to do was approach the herds where the Llysanyins ran free among the tribe's horses, eluding every attempt by the Zharmatians to catch them. That they were kept from the Llysanyins was of no real concern; all he had to do was bellow orders for their mounts to meet them at such and such a spot, and the Llysanyins would crush anything or anyone in their way.

The problem, he knew, was getting out of range of the archers long enough for the Llysanyins' superior speed and endurance to ensure their escape. Whenever any of them left the odd, circular tent given over to their use, they were shadowed as they walked through the encampment. One move toward escape, and a cry would go up.

Damnation. If only one of us could be in a large enough open area for long enough, I'd say the hell with the priestmages and Change! It would scare the daylights out of the Zharmatians, if nothing else, and the others could escape.

A lovely plan, and no chance of executing it.

Grumbling, he wandered to the center of the camp and found Lleld and Jekkanadar there, watching as Otter tuned his harp. Some stout sticks with dried grass bound into their cleft ends lay at her feet.

"What's this?" he asked, joining them.

"We're supposed to be entertainers, yes?" Lleld said quietly as Otter began a song.

Linden nodded, watching as some of the Zharmatians drew near in curiosity. They settled down around Otter, listening intently to the unfamiliar music. More joined them.

"So we entertain, and perhaps they'll figure they made a mistake and let us go. These people are at war; what use is a troupe of entertainers to them?"

Hm, Linden thought. Not likely, but it was certainly worth a try.

Otter played for a long time. When he finished, Lleld bent and caught up four of the sticks. She tossed two of them to Jekkanadar. They walked to an open area and, after jamming the solid ends of the sticks into the ground, lit the dried grass with flint and steel from their belt pouches. When the torches caught and flared up, they pulled them from the ground and tossed them into the air.

"Light the others, Linden," called Lleld as she and Jekkanadar threw their torches back and forth to the squealing delight of thc Zharmatians, "and at my signal toss them to us."

Linden did as she bade, and when her sharp *Now!* rang in his mind, he tossed the new torches in, first to one, then to the other, watching as the burning brands joined the elegant dance. The Zharmatians slapped their thighs and yelped in approval.

"I would be more impressed," a dry voice said in Jehangli from behind Linden, "did I not know that your kind is immune to fire."

Linden spun around. Before him were three people on horses. Dzeduin, he knew. And he had a feeling he knew who the other man was, a cold-eyed man, with a scarred face like Dzeduin's, who sat his shaggy little horse like a king.

But it was the third who made the hair on the back of his neck rise. First glance said she was but an old woman, eyes white and sightless, who looked as if she should have been on her death bed long ago. But those blind eyes followed every move, and Linden felt the power within that frail body.

She cackled. "I know what you are—*Dragonlord*," she said.

It had been an easy thing to get Xiane to wander off deeper into the gardens for another evening walk with her. An offer to show him something new she'd found, coupled with a look from beneath her lashes, and Xiane grinned, showing long white teeth like a horse's. He'd led her from the pavilion without another word; he knew how these expeditions ended. She'd taken care that he should, and hated herself for the lie.

So off they went. Shei-Luin knew that many eyed them knowingly, smiling behind their hands. What did she care for their laughter? This was life and death.

They talked of little things as they walked deeper into the garden—court gossip, the latest rumors, a new poem.

Eventually they reached the little woods. "It's in here, my lord," she said. He followed her in.

They walked between the trees, through glades filled with moss and sunshine, and down a faint path. The little deer that roamed this forest watched, unafraid, as they passed. Birds sang overhead, and the rich, humus scent of forest surrounded them like incense.

Her thoughts roamed ahead to their destination. *Soon the day will end; they will be settling down, but not yet asleep, and will be there if I need them.* Despite the warmth, the thought sent chills down her spine.

At last, when she and Xiane neared her goal, Shei-Luin said, "My lord, have you considered what I asked you?"

"To reconsider abdicating?" Xiane nodded. "I've thought about it, Precious Flower, many times. But I've truly come to believe that letting the Phoenix go will be best for Jehanglan. The Way must be followed."

"It will mean chaos, my lord," she said. They were only steps away from the place of reckoning now, marked by a scrap of silk so that she could not miss it. She was sickened by what she planned for him. He trusted her; she suspected that he even loved her in his own way.

They stood now, facing each other in one of the mossy little glades, so like the others; they might have been anywhere in the forest. But there was a difference, one important difference: a steep-sided ravine ran through it. The edge was only a few paces from them.

And at the bottom of that gully—

Everything hung on one final question, a question she never wanted to ask. But ask it she must.

"If you do abdicate, Xahnu and Xu will die. Whatever lord takes power after you will not suffer such potential rivals to live. Surely, Xiane, you won't sentence them to death?"

She no longer had the hypocrisy to call them "your sons" to his face. If she could not be completely honest with Xiane, she would be as honest as she dared.

He placed his hands on her shoulders and smiled down

at her. "Precious Flower, they will be well," he said, teasing
a lock of her hair free so that he could run it through his
fingers. "No one will harm them, or us. Why would they?"

His long, horsey face glowed with sincerity. Xiane truly
believed his words. He couldn't understand why she
thought otherwise. She offered him one last chance.

"History says otherwise." *Wake up, Xiane, and see the
mortal danger you place us all in! Put aside your rosy
vision of the world! Setting the Phoenix free may be the
right thing to do, but is it the wisest? Nothing is black and
white, my poor, naive emperor, no matter how you wish it
so,* she thought sadly.

He considered that, and her hopes soared. Once she
dreamed of being free of Xiane; now . . .

"That was in the past, Shei-Luin, and a time of troubles.
The world has changed. This is a decision that all will accept and respect. You'll see."

She must be as a sword, hard and cold, cutting away the
infected limb lest the rot spread and the body die. Weeping
inside, Shei-Luin reached up and gently undid the ties of
Xiane's robe, for it was of heavy silk, and would offer too
much protection. All the while he smiled at her like a child
expecting its favorite treat.

The five of them stood before Yemal and some of his men,
including Dzeduin, in a tent new to the encampment. It was,
Linden noted, larger and painted with strange symbols, unlike any of the others. Bundles of herbs hung from the
ceiling ribs, and the fragrant smoke from the lit brazier in
the center tickled Linden's nose. The old woman who Linden now knew was Ghulla, Seer of the Zharmatians, sat on
a low, carved stool to one side. She stared straight ahead
as if in a world of her own. Linden suspected this tent was
hers.

"First," said Yemal, speaking Jehangli, "I shall attend the
matter of these . . . traveling entertainers. Is Ghulla right—
are you indeed *Dragonlords*"—he stumbled over the unfamiliar word—"from the north?"

"Don't be silly," Lleld said. "Why? Just because we juggle torches? That's an old trick where we come from. Don't Jehangli jugglers have the nerve to try it?"

"Fire doesn't hurt Dragonlords," the old woman said in a voice that creaked like branches in a wind. "And three of you here are Dragonlords—I Saw it." Her head turned; the sightless eyes fixed on Linden. "The fourth one nears Nisayeh, the Red Lands."

The breath caught in Linden's chest.

The robe fell to the ground in a puddle of gold. Xiane's lighter underrobe followed. He stood before her now, clad only in breeches. She stepped away from him, to the edge of the ravine, as if to tease him, and undid her own outer robe. Though it would shield her somewhat from what was coming, its weight would slow her down too much.

As her robe fell to spill across the moss in its turn, Shei-Luin glanced into the ravine as if by chance. Though she had planned this moment a thousand times, her resolve nearly failed her.

There, below her, was another scrap of silk marking a hole in the ground. A stray gleam of sunlight glittered on flashing insect wings hovering above it. "My lord," she said, hating herself, "what's that?"

"What is what?" asked Xiane, coming to see.

He stood beside her at the edge of the little ravine and peered down. She took a careful step back.

"What did you see, Precious Flo—" He broke off with a gasp of fear. "Shei! We must—"

"I'm sorry, Xiane," she whispered, and pushed him.

With a bloodchilling scream, Xiane disappeared into the ravine. Nearly fainting, Shei-Luin fell back a few steps. She heard the sickening thump as Xiane hit the ground, heard him frantically calling her; then she heard the deep, angry buzzing, rising in a wave of sound that drowned all other noises—all save Xiane's panicked, agonized screams that went on and on, piercing her heart like a knife.

Then even those stopped. Shei-Luin fell to her knees,

crying, tearing at her hair, raking her face with her fingernails, cursing the cruel fate that made her choose between
her children and the man she was just discovering the
depths of.

A pain like a hot pincer seared her cheek. She cried out
and clapped her hand to her face. When she withdrew it,
the body of a red bee fell to the ground.

She heard Xiane's words once again: *If the others smell
their dead sister, they'll be after us.*

And if she died here as Xiane had died, her sons would
be alone. Shei-Luin sprang to her feet. Kilting up her robe,
she fled through the forest.

How does she know? Linden thought in an agony of apprehension.

"You're certain these are the ones you Saw, Ghulla?"
Yemal asked.

"Yes. There's power about them, like to the power of
Miune Kihn. If they—and the other one—stay free, the
reign of the Phoenix Lords will end."

"And the Way will be restored," said Yemal. He rubbed
his chin thoughtfully, eyeing them. "The answer is simple,
then, isn't it? You shall remain the guests of the Zharmatians."

"True guests—not prisoners?" Lleld demanded.

Yemal raised his hands. "I swear it by the Mother of the
Herds. The four of you shall be honored guests of the People of the Horse."

"I witness it," Ghulla said, "and I shall hold his word in
the name of the goddess K'rahi, whose servant I am."

Lleld turned to Yesuin, her head tilted in question.

"No Zharmatian would break that oath," he said, "especially not when a Seer holds his word."

"Done, then," Lleld said brightly.

Linden turned to her in dismay. "Are you ma—"

"Linden, think about it! That bastard Taren and his soldiers are hunting for us up and down the length of Jehanglan even now, I'll wager. If we leave, we'll have to spend

our time and strength running from him, and he knows the countryside and we don't. What if he captures us? If something happens to you, Maurynna will know—I've heard you talk about how 'aware' she is of you. And quite honestly, I don't trust her not to abandon her mission if that happens." She paused, staring at Jekkanadar. "I know I would," she finished quietly.

Jekkanadar caressed her cheek with his fingertips. "As would I," he admitted. "I'm with Lleld on this, Linden. We're safer here."

"So be it, then," Linden said heavily. Then, glancing at the former Jehangli hostage, he said, "What about Yesuin? Is he part of this?"

"No," Yemal said shortly. He sauntered the few steps to stand before Yesuin. "Brother," he purred. "It's good to have you back from the Jehangli."

Yesuin rolled his eyes. "Give over, Yemal. We both know it's a lie. Why don't you kill me and have done with it?" he said wearily.

Would Yemal really kill his brother? Linden thought, sickened. *Yesuin certainly seems to expect it.*

"I'd thought the Jehangli would take care of that for me," Yemal said. "But I should have known Xiane would be too weak for that."

"He is a true friend," Yesuin said quietly. "Would that *he* had been my brother."

Yemal struck his brother a powerful backhanded blow across the face, nearly felling him. But Yesuin kept his feet; he said nothing, merely stared at Yemal. Blood from a split lower lip trickled down his chin.

"Think you to return and take the tribes from me?" Yemal challenged.

"What use? They won't follow me. They no longer know me; they know you. No, Yemal, I was on my way to the Tah'nehsieh."

Ghulla's head turned sharply to him. "Why there?" she said.

"Because long, long ago, before I was given as a hostage

to the Jehangli, Zhantse said that when the time came—
and it would—I might live with the Tah'nehsieh if I
wished," Yesuin answered.

The sightless eyes fixed on him as if they would bore
through to his soul. "You speak the truth," she said at last.
Then, "Yemal, if Zhantse wants him, you must not kill
him."

"I will do as I please, old woman. Remember that, and
all will be well."

Dzeduin and the others drew sharp breaths. They looked
uneasily from Seer to *temur*.

Ghulla cackled like a mad hen. "*Temur* you may be, boy,
but *you* remember that *I* am Ghulla, servant of K'rahi.
Never forget it's bad luck to threaten a Seer, especially in
the *ham'sul*."

Yemal snorted at that and turned his back on her, but
Linden suspected the disdainful gesture was nine parts
bluff; he'd caught the troubled look in the *temur*'s eyes.

"Yemal," Dzeduin said in an urgent undertone, "it's bad
luck to cross a Seer. Hurt Yesuin, and you'll be crossing
two. If Zhantse wants Yesuin, let him have him, by the
Mother! We've just started a war—we don't need any
curses upon us!"

Ghulla cackled, revealing a mouthful of crooked teeth.
Her head bobbed on her bony shoulders. "A wise pup are
you, Dzeduin, and so young! Listen well to him, Yemal,
now and always. When the way is clear, let Yesuin go to
Zhantse. Until then, I claim him; he shall stay here in the
ham'sul with me."

Linden heard a tiny sigh of relief escape Yesuin, and saw
Jekkanadar's lips twitch as if he hid a smile.

Yemal turned a glare of angry frustration from Seer to
foster brother. At last he growled, "Very well, then." Turning to the Dragonlords and Otter, he said sharply, "Come!"

The news of Xiane's death plunged the imperial palace into
chaos. Weeping servants ran to and fro, wailing that now
the marauding Zharmatians would kill them all.

Shei-Luin, striding through the public portion of the palace like a tiger, caught one of the lesser ministers by the sleeve as he ran past. When he turned to her, wailing, "We are lost! We are lost!" she slapped him across the face as hard as she could.

Only then did he truly see her. "Phoenix Lady!" he gasped, and sank to his knees.

"Worthless one," she snapped, though it was painful to talk with her swollen cheek, "find the lords and ministers of high rank and bid them to the audience hall, do you hear? Bid them come on pain of death. Go!"

Clearly terrified, the man wobbled upright and ran off. Shei-Luin turned to Murohshei and Zyuzin, who had shadowed her since her return from the garden.

"Murohshei—see that he obeys, then come to me. Zyuzin, go to the nursery. Have Xahnu brought to my quarters."

It was late when Shei-Luin entered the audience hall she had dared moons earlier. This time though, she swept in as empress, not as an importunate concubine. Behind her came Murohshei, a sleepy and confused Xahnu whimpering in his arms.

Shei-Luin noted the faces as she passed: who looked upon her with hate, who looked to her for guidance, who looked merely confused and afraid. Step by sure step she came to the stairs leading to the dais. At the top were the thrones of Jehanglan. She paused to gaze at them a moment before turning to Murohshei and taking Xahnu from him.

Then she started up the stairs. Hugging Xahnu, she whispered in his ear, "Don't cry, my little phoenix. All is well. Be brave. I will let nothing hurt you."

By the time she reached the dais, Xahnu was quiet in her arms. She turned to face the mightiest lords of Jehanglan.

"Your emperor is dead," she cried. "But your empress and your next emperor live. The barbarians howl on the borders, and Jehanglan is in peril. Seek to take the throne, each man for himself, and Jehanglan falls to the wolves."

Silence greeted her words. She felt the panic beneath it; they knew she spoke the truth. Cradling Xahnu against her, she turned and walked to the thrones. She paused before the throne of Riya-Akono—her throne.

A quick movement, and before anyone could cry a protest, she sat upon the Phoenix throne, Xahnu on her lap.

"I claim this throne for my son," she said, her voice ringing throughout the room. "I claim this throne as regent. Who shall follow me and save Jehanglan?"

No one moved. Xahnu squirmed in her lap, uneasy at the mounting tension. Shei-Luin counted her heartbeats.

Then old General V'Choun came forward to stop at the foot of the stairs. His eyes were red, and he looked years older. Shei-Luin remembered that Xiane had spoken of him with affection. She held her breath, waiting for his words; they were life and death to her.

"I would not see my country torn apart, lady. I will pledge my fealty to the next emperor through you." He knelt and pressed his head to the floor.

Lord Musahi was next. One by one, the other lords and ministers followed.

Shei-Luin sat upon the Phoenix throne of Jehanglan and accepted their homage, her son asleep now on her lap.

"Do you think Yesuin will be safe?" Linden said in an undertone as they followed Yemal and Dzeduin back to their tent. During the journey to the Zharmatian camp, he'd come to like the escaped hostage.

"Oh, yes," Jekkanadar replied in a tone of absolute conviction. "Perfectly safe."

Surprised, Linden asked, "How can you be so certain?"

Jekkanadar turned to him and smiled. "Ghulla's tent is a Mousehole."

Raven lay on the far side of the dying fire. Unable to sleep, Maurynna pushed aside her blankets and sat up. Her thoughts whirled through her mind. Ever since meeting Miune, she wondered one thing over and over.

Could it really be something that simple? That Kyrissaean had been frightened all this time?

It couldn't be. She would scream if it was. But if . . .

Only one way to find out; moving as quietly as she could, Maurynna stood up and slipped out of the camp. When Boreal made to follow her, she waved him back.

At last she stopped. She tried to let her mind empty as she'd heard Linden and the other Dragonlords talk about. Then she willed herself to Change.

For a moment she thought it was about to happen; her joy was so great she nearly cried aloud. But then a thread of memory came back: her First Change, and the pain . . .

Panicking, she pulled back. She found herself on her knees in the coarse grass, her chest heaving as she fought for air. She still couldn't Change.

The gods damn it all, she was sick of this! She slammed her fists against the ground, heedless of the pain, past caring if she injured herself. What did it matter? She wasn't a real Dragonlord. Again and yet again she pounded the hard-packed earth, ignoring the jarring pain up her arms, her teeth clenched against the howls of frustration that tore at her throat while hot tears spilled down her cheeks.

Why? Why me? WhywhywhywhyWHY am I like this? Why, damn it—why?

How long the frenzy lasted, she didn't know. But when it was over, she sat back, hiccuping as she looked at her sore hands. They ached, and were black with dirt and stained green from the grass. Lost in a false calmness born of exhaustion both emotional and physical, she wiped her cheeks with a sleeve and studied her hands again. Stray thoughts ran through her numbed mind.

I'm going to regret this tomorrow.

I still can't Change.

Hope I didn't break anything. She flexed her fingers; everything still worked.

That was stupid. I guess Miune was wrong . . .

Then a little voice at the back of her mind asked, *Was he? Or was all this because of Kyrissaean's fear—or your own?*

Too exhausted to care anymore, Maurynna pushed herself to her feet. She walked slowly back to the camp; Boreal met her halfway.

"Thank you," she whispered as she twined the fingers of one hand into his long mane.

They continued on together until they reached her blankets. Suddenly cold, Maurynna sank down and pulled them around her. She didn't bother calling up a heat spell; she knew it wouldn't help. This was a coldness of the spirit, not the body.

Boreal touched his nose to her forehead before wandering off. His breath was warm and somehow comforting. Maurynna closed her eyes to wait for the dawn. It would be a long time coming.

Forty-six

Far-off thunder rumbled among the low clouds clinging to the top of the nearby, triple-peaked mountain. Maurynna paused as she laid the fire and looked up. Lightning danced along the craggy peaks.

"Wonder if it'll come this way," Raven said as he dumped a meager load of firewood by her. "This was all I could find; wood is scarce in these parts."

Boreal and Stormwind wove back and forth along the sandy floor of the dry streambed, heads held high. They stared at the storm on the mountain, watching the lightning intently. Their noses touched.

As if that were a signal, they trotted back to where the two-foots had set up camp. Maurynna reached up to rub Boreal's nose; to her surprise, he caught her hand in his strong white teeth and tugged gently.

She stood, baffled. "What is it?" she asked as he released her fingers. "Is there something you want to show me?"

For an answer the grey stallion wheeled around and seized her saddlebag in his teeth. With a grunt, Boreal heaved it from the ground and surged up the wall of the streambed. Stormwind did the same with Raven's.

Maurynna and Raven gaped at each other in surprise, then ran to catch the Llysanyins.

"Boreal!" Maurynna said, catching the stallion's mane, "what are you doing? This is where we're camping."

But Boreal ignored her as he heaved his way up the crumbling banks. Maurynna had to let go or be dragged along. She looked up at him, fuming. The light was fading fast and she had no intention of fumbling in the dark for a new campsite. "Get back here—both of you!" she shouted, for Stormwind followed close behind his herdmate.

Boreal dropped the saddlebag and neighed from the top of the bank. He danced back and forth along the bank, plainly urging her to join him. Stormwind also dropped his burden; but instead of joining Boreal in his dance, the grey-maned stallion stood still, looking into the distance—at what, Maurynna couldn't see from her lower vantage point. After a few moments Boreal joined him. Together they watched . . . something.

"What are they looking at?" Raven asked.

"I don't know," Maurynna said uneasily. Yet whatever it was, they allowed its approach. It wasn't dangerous, then; the Llysanyins wouldn't be so complacent.

Her curiosity was soon satisfied. The Llysanyins, who had stood shoulder to shoulder against whatever approached out of the deepening gloom, now moved apart. The next moment, a horse and rider appeared on the bank.

Maurynna gaped up at the interloper. In the dimness even she was hard pressed to make out details. Man or woman? The figure wore a short kilt topped by a kind of wrapping made of gaily woven wool that revealed nothing of the rider's form.

But if their visitor was male, he wore his hair longer than any man she'd ever seen, black and arrow-straight to his waist. The stranger stared calmly down at them and shook—his? her?—head slightly, the Llysanyins on either side.

"Are you truly planning to camp there?" the rider called down to them.

While not as deep as Linden's, the voice was definitely male. Him, then.

"We are, indeed. I'm not going any farther tonight, thank you," Maurynna snapped.

Her next acid comment died in a confused gasp. She stared, open-mouthed, up at the stranger.

Here, deep in Jehanglan, someone had spoken Yerrin to them. She turned to Raven; he looked just as stunned as she felt.

"Then your horses are wiser than you are," the stranger retorted, still in that language. He pointed at the three peaks of the distant mountain. "When the Storm Brothers dance on the mountains, it's death to be caught in the washes."

Raven recovered before she did. He said, "How do you speak Yerrin?"

The stranger made an impatient gesture. "I'll tell you if you'll get your fool selves out of that wash. Any time now, it'll turn into a river with the rain off of D'sah'nii'joos, the Three Sisters."

Maurynna looked to the triple-peaked mountain. Yes, the Three Sisters would be a good name for that one. And the stranger's words made sense. Even from here she could hear thunder. She nodded to Raven. They hurried to gather the rest of their things together. The Llysanyins slipped and slid down the banks.

Maurynna tied the little bundle of wood with a length of twine from Boreal's saddlebag. No sense in wasting it; as Raven said, the stuff was scarce. Raven quickly saddled the Llysanyins. She tossed him the bundle and he bound the wood to the back of Stormwind's saddle.

They mounted once again—Maurynna with a groan—and set the Llysanyins to the bank. The powerful animals heaved themselves up it a second time.

The stranger slid off his small, shaggy horse and tossed

their saddlebags up to them before jumping back into his own saddle.

"Away from here," he ordered. "Sometimes the banks crumble when the flood comes through." He wheeled his horse away. It sprang into a gallop. Boreal and Stormwind followed at an easy lope.

They had only gone a short distance when a far-off rumble caught Maurynna's ear. It drew closer, growing louder with each heartbeat. She halted Boreal and looked back at the wash, curious.

With a roar, a wall of water thundered through the wash, surging over the banks. In a kind of horrified fascination, she watched the bank they'd stood on such a short time before melt into the rioting flood. The sudden river had a new, wider bed to rush through.

A chill ran down her spine. *We would have died in that.* Sailor that she was, the thought of a watery death frightened her.

Boreal pirouetted once more and leaped after Raven and the stranger. She didn't try to hold him back. Instead, she held on to her saddlebag as well as she could, letting the reins fall onto Boreal's neck, concentrating on keeping her aching body in the saddle.

She caught up with Raven and the stranger a short time later. They had stopped, waiting for her. Boreal halted before the stranger's shaggy mount.

Caught between fear and curiosity, Maurynna studied the man; he returned the compliment. Finally she said, "Thank you. We're strangers to this land and would have been caught in that like rabbits in a snare."

"You're welcome, Maurynna Kyrissaean." He laughed at her start of surprise. "Yes, I know both of your names, lady. A . . . friend told me about you and asked that I look out for you." Mischief glinted in his eyes.

"A friend?" Maurynna began in confusion; her heart was still hammering in fright at hearing her full name. Then she laughed. He had to mean the youngling waterdragon; who else in Jehanglan knew?

The stranger smiled; a wide, friendly smile that called forth an answering grin from her, it was so infectious. "I see you understand of whom I speak. I'm Shima, spirit drummer to Zhantse, shaman of the Tah'nehsieh."

"That doesn't explain how you come to speak Yerrin," Raven said roughly.

"Your pardon; I should have introduced myself in your fashion. I'm Shima Larkson of the Wolf Clan."

"Your father"—here the man shook his head—"your mother, then, is Yerrin? How is that?" Maurynna asked.

"Indeed; how did a Yerrin come to be here?" Raven said with a scowl, his voice full of suspicion. He turned to Maurynna. "And who is this friend, anyway, that you both seem to know?" he demanded.

"To answer your first question, O Man-whose-name-*I*-do-not-know, my mother, Lark Hollydaughter, was ship-wrecked on these shores," Shima said. "I take my Yerrin clan from her." He looked pointedly at Raven. Courtesy now demanded that Raven identify himself.

The look was wasted. Raven merely glared back at him, unsatisfied, his lips pressed together in a stubborn line Maurynna knew only too well.

Said Raven, "That still doesn't tell me who's making so free with Rynna's names." He locked his arms across his chest, looking prepared to wait until dawn for his answer.

Maurynna smothered a sigh. "Shima, tell him. He won't be satisfied if I say it; he'll think you're only agreeing with me to lull our suspicions."

Shima nodded slowly. "Fair enough, that. The friend of whom we speak is Miune Kihn, one of the last waterdrag-ons in Jehanglan. He may well *be* the last; I've never seen another. But Miune says he can feel others deep asleep under their lakes far away. I hope for his sake it's not merely wishful thinking."

Raven turned to her. "The dragon at the river—?"

"The one who freed me of Kyrissaean's interference," Maurynna said shortly. "Therefore, yes, I deem him 'friend.' May we please be done with this farce? I'd like to camp sometime before morning, please. I'm not the rider you are, and I *hurt*, damn it."

Raven bit his lip. "I'm sorry; I forgot." To Shima he said, "Raven Redhawkson, Marten Clan," all belligerence gone.

Shima nodded. "Well met, Raven Redhawkson. Follow me, please; I know a good place to camp not far way."

Shima's idea of "not far" was certainly not Maurynna's. It was, in her painful opinion, too damned far. She remembered Linden's tale of how, when he was sixteen, he'd run away from home to join his cousin's mercenary band. Fearful that his father would catch him first, Linden had ridden so hard and long that he'd arrived with bleeding saddle sores. Maurynna fervently hoped she was not about to share the same fate. But at last they reached their destination.

The campsite was a pocket in one of the red rock formations that thrust up from the earth with such abruptness. Shima led them around the base of the tower of stone to a crack in the living rock, barely wide enough to admit a horse and rider. But when they followed him inside, they found it expanded into a large open area surrounded by the towering rock. At the far end a spring bubbled out of the rock into a pool hewn from the stone. Coarse grass grew around the precious liquid. Above them, the stone swept up like a chimney; framed in the opening high above was one of the strange southern constellations. After the first glance, Maurynna refused to look at it again. That even the very stars were alien made home and everything she loved seem farther away than ever.

Boreal halted at the edge of the grassy patch. Letting her saddlebag tumble from her tired hands, Maurynna attempted to lift herself from the saddle; her muscles screamed in protest and refused to respond. She bit back a whimper of pain.

But somehow Raven heard. He dropped his saddlebag next to hers. "I'll be right there to help you," he said as he untied the bundle of firewood and tossed it to the ground.

Maurynna watched sourly as he swung down, moving easily despite their candlemarks of riding. She considered boxing his ears out of sheer temper and jealousy; further reflection told her he'd likely refuse to help her down after that and she'd be stuck atop Boreal for the night.

That would hardly be fair to the stallion, so Maurynna gritted her teeth as Raven dragged her out of the saddle, her aching body complaining with every pull and tug.

The moment she had both feet on the ground, Boreal turned, planted his nose in the small of her back, and shoved gently. He repeated the action, a little harder, when she didn't move.

"Boreal's right, beanpole," Raven said. "Go sit down before you fall down. I'll take care of him."

Maurynna opened her mouth to protest. But her shaking legs barely held her up as it was, and common sense told her she would indeed fall down if she tried to unsaddle the Llysanyin. She limped off to sit by the pool, pausing to salve her pride by snatching up the bundle of firewood. At least she could start the fire while the two men set up camp.

Her hands shook so much she nearly couldn't work the flint and steel; she wished she could set the fire alight with a word as Linden had shown her, but she dared not use a Dragonlord's magic. It seemed forever before the shower of sparks caught and the flames danced merrily against the night.

She sat by the fire, forehead on knees, sore of body and of heart. Of the two, the latter was the worse. Tears pricked her closed eyelids. The questions that tormented her every waking moment came back. What had happened to Linden and the others? Had they escaped Taren's soldiers?

She was certain she would know—somehow—if something was truly wrong. But that didn't make not knowing beyond a doubt any easier to bear.

Gods, Linden, I never knew I could miss someone as much as I miss you.

Her breath caught in her chest. Willing herself not to cry, she pressed her forehead against her knees until it hurt.

"Hungry?"

Maurynna looked up. Arrows rattling together in his quiver, Shima squatted beside her, a few leaf-wrapped bundles clasped one-handed to his chest. He offered her one.

She took it and turned it over in her hands to study it. It was long and narrow and heavy for its size. The fibrous leaves forming the covering were coarse, tied at the ends with strips of the same stuff. She picked open the bundle and found a small, sticky "loaf" of what looked like cooked grain of some sort. It looked a dull greyish brown in the firelight and not very appetizing at all. She looked up at Shima.

"*Pyamah* cakes," he explained. "It's a staple of my people. A man can live a long time on *pyamah*. The grain's mixed with water, and sometimes a little honey, left to ferment a bit, then wrapped in leaves from a plant called spice grass and boiled or baked in the ashes of a fire. The spice grass preserves the cakes and flavors them as well." He broke off a bit and ate.

Maurynna gingerly followed suit. The stuff was dense and chewy, with a flavor like hazelnuts. On the back of her tongue she caught a hint of—cinnamon?—and another taste she didn't quite recognize, but whatever it was, it was *good*. She'd thought she was too tired to eat, but the *pyamah* was tasty; she was suddenly ravenous. Besides, however it tasted, it would have been a welcome change from the millet she and Raven had been subsisting on. She ate eagerly.

Raven joined them by the fire and Shima handed him one of the cakes. Raven regarded it dubiously, then shrugged, unwrapped it, and bit into it.

While they ate, Maurynna studied Shima by the firelight. He was shorter than either of them, though taller than most Jehangli she'd seen. The firelight picked out reddish glints in his black hair. Every other Jehangli she'd seen had bluish highlights in their hair.

His Yerrin blood, no doubt, Maurynna thought. *That might also account for that high-arched nose like a sea eagle's beak; I'll wager anything his mother was from the north of Yerrih.* But the dark honey of his skin and the doelike dark eyes could only be from his Tah'nehsieh father.

She finished her cake, listening as Raven and Shima talked, too tired to contribute. Like a wayward boat that wouldn't answer to the helm, her mind continuously drifted back to thoughts of Linden no matter how hard she tried not to think about him. She rested her head once more on her bent knees. She would not cry; she and Linden weren't the only soultwins who had ever been separated, after all. Besides, she'd feel a fool crying in front of a stranger.

"Is something amiss, lady?"

Shima's gentle voice was nearly enough to break her resolve. She swallowed hard before answering, "I miss my soultwin, Linden. I don't even know what's happened—"

She broke off, listening. Had she really heard— Yes; there it was again. A strange shuffling noise, growing closer with each passing moment.

"Raven, get your dirk out," she said tensely. "Someone's coming." Her weariness evaporating at the hint of danger, she jumped up and drew her own dirk with a speed that brought a gasp from the Tah'nehsieh.

Shima leaped to his feet, bow in hand.

They stood shoulder to shoulder, facing the entrance to the campsite, Maurynna and Raven with dirks out, Shima with arrow nocked and drawn.

Now Maurynna could hear soft grunts and heavy breathing. Whatever it was, it was large; an animal of some sort? She braced herself.

Shima, did thee have *to choose this place? Thee knows these twists and turns are—oh, bother! I scraped another scale!*

Hard on the heels of the plaintive mindvoice came Miune's head peering around the last turn in the passage, feelers waving in annoyance. The rest of him followed in a waddling shuffle. He huffed his way to stand before them, blinking in mild surprise at the weapons.

Weak with relief, Maurynna sheathed her dirk and

laughed. While he didn't relax, Raven lowered his own dirk; he stared and stared at Miune, who in his turn appeared to be fascinated with Raven's red hair.

The dragon shuffled a hesitant step or two forward, and stretched out a feeler to play delicately with a lock of it. Raven stood, eyes wide in astonishment, still as stone.

Shima carefully relaxed the draw on his bow and returned the arrow to his quiver. He wiped his forehead. "Miune!" he said. "Have you any idea how close I came to shooting you? Next time—"

Miune turned a ruby eye on him. *Next time do not come here,* the waterdragon said mildly. *I cannot talk while I'm trying so hard not to scrape my scales.* He looked mournfully at his sides. The bulge Maurynna had noticed before had lessened, but was still apparent.

"You shouldn't have eaten so much that day," Shima said cryptically.

Maurynna wondered what he meant, but it seemed ill-mannered to ask.

A feeler waved the admonition away. Then Miune turned his attention back to Raven. *Thee are Raven, are thee not? Thee are not a, um . . . * The feeler twisted its way into the youngling dragon's mouth.

"No," Raven snapped, his bemusement gone. "I'm not a demon. I just have red hair."

"Of course he's not a demon," Shima said in exasperation. "Zhantse wouldn't send me after a demon."

Miune did not look convinced.

Shima threw his hands in the air and turned back to the fire. "We were eating. Come join us, stubborn one."

Maurynna and Raven joined him; Miune waddled along behind.

Pyamah cakes? the young dragon asked.

"With honey," Shima replied. "Just the way you like them. My mother made them."

Then I forgive thee for my scraped scales.

Maurynna covered a smile at the magnanimity suffusing

the little dragon's mindvoice; it barely hid the hungry anticipation. Shima merely snorted.

As the two settled down she watched and marveled at the easy friendship between them. Save in a bard's tale, she'd never heard of such a thing between truehuman and dragon. For without a word passed between them, Miune curled himself into a half circle and Shima sat in the curve of the eel-like body, resting his back against the dragon's scaled side as if against a chair. A feeler wrapped around the man's shoulders the way one truehuman might drape an arm over another. Shima unwrapped a *pyamah* cake and placed it in Miune's waiting mouth. The dragon chewed greedily.

The meal was long over. Maurynna lay with her head pillowed on her saddlebag, tired yet unable to sleep. She gazed into the fire, letting thoughts drift through her mind like wisps of smoke in the wind, chasing one from time to time. The others talked quietly; the waterdragon's words were a mere whisper in her head.

A drifting thought jumped out at her. "Miune," she said into a lull in the conversation, "when I first met you, you were hiding in a good-sized river. But Raven and I came across nothing like that today. Did you walk overland all this way?"

No, he said with a delicate shudder. *That would hurt my feet too much. Thee do not remember the stream—little but deep—that thee crossed before thee came to the wash?*

Maurynna pushed up onto one elbow, intrigued. "Yes, but you're much too big to hide in something that small." She waved a hand to take in the younling dragon's length.

But hide there I did. I saw from thy mind how big thy soultwin is, Maurynna, and I remember what my parents told me of the northern dragons they met. By rights the northern dragons and thy kind should not be able to fly; thee are all too big. But it is part of thy magic to be able to, Miune said. *Likewise, it is the magic of my kind that we can change size to fit the water we wander in if needed.*

"Do you mean that you could shrink to fit in a tiny puddle?" Maurynna said. The thought fascinated her.

No; there are limits, just as there are limits to how high thy kind can fly. Even fresh from the egg I could not hide in a puddle. Now I find that there are streams whose water I could hide in when I was younger that I cannot hide in now. When I am at my full growth, I will need at the least a very large stream—nay, a small river—or a lake to conceal myself fully. The old ones, the most powerful among my kind, passed beyond that need. They could travel as a cloud travels.

Now Maurynna sat upright. "What do you mean?"

Just as I said. They could turn themselves into mist and ride the wind as clouds do.

Turn themselves into mist . . . Surely that couldn't be possible. Then Maurynna bethought herself of the times she'd seen her fellow Dragonlords Change. First they dissolved into a sparkling red mist that spread until it took the form of a dragon. Then, in the blink of an eye, the dragon solidified.

If a Dragonlord could do it, why not a truedragon? And halt the process at midpoint? Not the kind of truedragon she knew, certainly; but the Jehangli waterdragons were clearly a different breed altogether. Why shouldn't their magic be different as well?

"Gods help us," she breathed. "It could be done."

Shima said, "They were called *Djahn N'Tsina*—Lords of the Rain. It's said that in times of drought, they sometimes took pity on humankind and brought gentle rains to water the fields and fill the wells and rivers. But now—" He held up a hand, then let it fall as if casting something away. "But now, of course, they're all dead save Miune, and this is the third year of a drought in many parts of Jehanglan. The Phoenix has not seen fit to send his people—or the rest of us—enough rain for the fields."

Miune shook his head vigorously. *The Rain Lords are not all dead! I have told thee this thing already. Oolan Jeel sleeps at the bottom of his lake!*

"And you once admitted to me that even your parents had only heard stories of Oolan Jeel," Shima said, gently. "I'm sorry, my friend, but he may be only a legend of your kind."

The waterdragon fixed his gaze on Maurynna. His eyes burned as if he must make her believe him. *Oolan Jeel is not a legend. And there are others of my kind who have hidden themselves away to dream in deep lakes until the time of the Phoenix is ended.*

A torrent of longing ran through the words. Maurynna swallowed against sudden tears; the waterdragon's pain cut like a knife through her soul. The broad-snouted head came around to lean against Shima's upraised knee and rested there, feelers quivering. The man laid a hand above the thick eye ridges and stroked gently.

Maurynna remembered what Shima had said earlier. She hoped with all her heart that the youngling dragon was right. It hurt to think he might be the last of his kind. *I'm sorry,* she said to him and stretched out a hand; a feeler wrapped lightning-swift around it, squeezed, and was gone again.

Thee are lonely, too.

"Yes, I miss my soultwin. I've no idea where he is or how he and our friends fare."

Then I shall look for thy soultwin and friends, Maurynna. If they are near a stream or river, I should be able to find them for thee, I hope.

"Thank you," was all Maurynna could say without crying.

"That would be well done," Shima said. He wrapped his arms around the young dragon's neck and hugged him fierce and hard, then sat upright once more. "Now let us tell stories, talk as friends with no cares in the world, before we sleep. For tomorrow we must return to my *mehanso*."

He fed another stick into the fire. It blazed up, illuminating his face in its ruddy light. "Listen now, and I shall tell you one of the stories of my people," he said, and began his tale.

Maurynna sat and listened and lost herself in the tapestry of Shima's words as he wove them amid the dancing flames.

She wasn't certain what woke her. One of the others murmuring in the midst of a dream? The cry of a night bird, if such lived in this desert? Maurynna rubbed her eyes, propped herself up on one elbow, and looked around, wondering if the sound would be repeated.

The fire was now a small bed of coals glowing dark red. By its dim light, her sharp eyes could make out the sleeping shapes around her. Raven and Shima on the other side of the fire, looking like well-wrapped logs within their blankets, Shima with his head pillowed on Miune's tail. The waterdragon sprawled on his side, scales gleaming dully in the faint light.

Could Miune have been right? As always, the thought ached in her soul. *If only—*

A movement by the entrance caught Maurynna's eye. Even as a cry of warning sprang to her lips, it died; Boreal, she thought, was allowed to swish his tail as he stood guard. Stormwind lay on the ground nearby.

As she watched, Boreal approached his herdmate and touched noses. Stormwind's head came up; he nodded once. Then the black Llysanyin scrambled to his feet, shaking his head and neck as if to banish the last dregs of sleep, sending his long grey mane flying. Boreal lay down as Stormwind ambled off to stand near the entrance to their holt.

As Maurynna looked back at the figures on the other side of the fire once again, the young dragon grunted and snuffled, and she recognized the sound that had woken her. She smiled once more as the tip of one feeler came up and quivered like a reed.

What a funny little creature he is, she thought as her gaze ran down the length of him, admiring the color of his scales. *Hardly like a dragon at all. I wonder if it's because he's spent all his life with humans?* As her eyes came to his slightly bulging middle, she remembered how greedily he'd gobbled the *pyamah* cakes earlier. *Just like a chi—*

The realization hit Maurynna with the force of a ship striking a reef. Her breath caught in her throat.

It had been Miune in the river that day. Miune, the funny little dragonchild who made her laugh; who had reassured Kyrissaean, and given them both peace at last. The memory of the roiling, bloodstained waters, the dying screams of terrified men and horses made her stomach turn.

Part of her mind wondered, *How many horses did he—* She squashed the thought.

She sat up, shivering, but not from the cold night air. Taking slow, deep breaths, Maurynna pushed back her horror.

He fights in a war begun long ago, and not by his kind.

Wherever it came from, the thought reassured her. Miune Kihn had killed not for bloodlust, but because he'd had to. There had been no joy in the killing; of that she was certain. He had done it to protect her and Raven. And protect them he had, else they would be dead now—if they were lucky. The thought of how close they'd come to being Taren's prisoners made her shudder.

Suddenly, with such an ally, the mission before her seemed not quite so impossible. It was not a rational belief, she knew that; the little waterdragon would not be there to help her in the end. But it comforted her nonetheless. Maurynna bowed her head for a moment and breathed a quiet prayer that all would be well, then lay down again, wondering what the next day would bring.

The funeral was a nightmare. Shei-Luin went through it like one caught in a fox ghost's spell.

General V'Choun had not let her see Xiane's body when it was retrieved from the little ravine, and the priests had carried it off immediately. "Remember him the way he was, my lady," the old general said through his tears, and gently guided her away.

Now the earthly husk of the emperor of Jehanglan lay

upon the lower altar in the temple where, so short a time before, Xiane had helped her get through her coronation. For nine days it would lie here, preserved by the power of the Phoenix, covered by a mantle of heavy gold silk. The costliest incenses burned at each corner of the altar.

For nine days she kept vigil before the altar, beginning at dawn, and ending at sunset; for, at dawn on the tenth day, Xiane Ma Jhi would go to the Phoenix, and his ashes, would be interred with those of his ancestors in the vault beneath the altar.

The days had been the peaceful times. Shei-Luin knelt by the side of the altar, near Xiane's head, and let her mind empty.

The nights . . . The nights had been hell. For night after night, Xiane came to her in her dreams. Sometimes he looked as she remembered him, with his long, horselike face and big teeth. Other times, the worst times, his face was swollen and lumpy, as if someone had slipped rocks under the skin. His eyes bulged grotesquely as they focused on her, and she knew this was the ruin that V'Choun had tried to spare her.

But fair or foul, each dream was the same: Xiane, standing in a mist that swirled grey fingers around him, wept, and said to her, "Why? Why did you kill me, Precious Flower? I loved you—didn't you know it?"

"I had to, Xiane; I'm sorry, but I had to. What you planned would have cost the boys their lives." Each time, she wanted to cry, but no tears came forth. Each time, she tried to beg his forgiveness, but the words died on her tongue.

He would fade away then, though his voice stayed long enough to say, "All would have been well, Shei-Luin; all would have been well."

She would awaken then, too wracked with grief and remorse to sleep again.

And now it was almost over. On this, the tenth morning, Shei-Luin went to the temple for the last time. She came before dawn, startling the priests who kept watch during the night.

The head priest himself came to her, all obsequious sympathy. "Imperial Majesty, you need not stand vigil this day, you know. In fact, you need not be here at all today." He looked annoyed that she should make such a mistake.

"I know," Shei-Luin said. Her voice shook; for once she didn't care that someone saw a weakness. "I came to bid Xiane farewell."

"I'm sorry," the priest said, his voice suddenly gentle. "I didn't realize that— Of course you may bid him farewell."

He led her to the altar and shooed the other priests away. "I will leave you alone, Phoenix Lady."

For the last time, Shei-Luin stood by Xiane's body. Despite the priests' spells and the clouds of incense, she caught the first hint of the sweet, sickening smell of decay.

Ignoring it, she bent over the shrouded lump that was Xiane's head. "I'm sorry, Xiane," she whispered, "truly sorry. Please . . ." The words that would not come before, came to her now. "Forgive me. I didn't want to kill you, and I wish I could have loved you the way you loved me."

She remembered how, the night of Yesuin's escape, he had looked, sitting on her bed, his black hair hanging loose upon his shoulders. That was how she would remember Xiane Ma Jhi. "Perhaps—perhaps one day I could have." She bent and kissed the silk covering his brow.

"Phoenix Lady."

The words were the merest whisper. She turned.

The head priest stood at the bottom of the stairs. "I'm sorry, my lady, but the dawn comes, and we must give him to the fire."

The first tears coursed down her cheeks. "I understand." She was still crying when she returned to the palace.

Morning came, and with it, company.

The first to hear the intruders was Miune. *Horses,* he said. He heaved himself from the ground.

After listening a moment, Maurynna said, "I hear them

now, as well. Your people, Shima?" She looked to the Tah'nehsieh. "Whoever it is, they come openly." Still, she kicked back her blankets and stood up.

"No one should be seeking us," he replied, frowning. "And the Jehangli don't ride this land. Not openly. Not unless they come to rai—"

A soft neigh from the depths of the winding entrance cut him off. Stormwind answered it and trotted quickly across the grass. He disappeared into the gap in the rock.

Raven, crouching by the fire, laughed as he fed twigs into it. "Rest easy. Hear how happy he was? Must be the Two Poor Bastards."

"Who?" Shima asked with a quick shake of his head as if uncertain he'd heard correctly.

Maurynna debated trying to explain and took the coward's way out. "You'll see."

She watched the opening. Both Shima and Raven came to join her. A short while later Stormwind appeared once more, followed closely by Jhem and Trissin. They neighed a greeting and went straight to the pool.

As they passed Shima, Trissin swiftly turned his head. For a moment Maurynna feared that the Llysanyin thought Shima was Jehangli and would attack him. But the danger passed in a heartbeat, and Trissin followed his brother to the water.

Shima stared after them. At last he asked, "They're more of your horses, aren't they?"

"Llysanyins, yes," Maurynna answered.

"They're beautiful," he said. There was an odd note in his voice.

"Hm," said Maurynna as she eyed the Poor Bastards with a critical eye. Where they weren't covered in mud, they were plastered with the red dust of this land. Their thick manes and tails were filthy and tangled, and the feathers of their feet were a mud-caked disaster. Beautiful? Hardly.

Then she recognized what she'd heard in Shima's voice: the same longing as in Raven's when he'd first seen Boreal.

I daresay a horseman can see beneath the dirt, she

thought. Then: *they look like Shan did the first time I saw—*

No; she would not let her thoughts stray there. But useless tears pricked her eyes anyway.

Calling herself sixty kinds of a fool in every language she knew, Maurynna cursed under her breath and knelt to roll up her blankets. She yanked the lacing tight with a savage tug.

If only this were over.

"As soon as the Poor Bastards are cared for and have rested and eaten, we move out," she said.

She must have spoken more vehemently than she'd meant to, for Raven and Shima looked at each other and went meekly to tend to the newcomers.

They came into the village late in the afternoon three days later. Maurynna leaned back against the high cantle of the saddle. While she guessed that, as the crow flew, the distance from where they'd camped that first night to Shima's village was not that great, the roundabout route they'd taken had added miles and candlemarks onto the journey.

Shima had apologized for it. "Because we fear invasion by the armies of Jehanglan, there are no direct trails to my *mehanso*," he said. Then, with a wry smile, he added, "Not that there are any direct routes anywhere in this country. It's not an easy land, this."

Maurynna remembered those words now at the end of the ride. She thought of the stark beauty of this country, the mountains rearing abruptly from the desert soil to stand proud against the turquoise blue bowl of a sky that went on forever, the tough, scrubby, needle-leafed vegetation grey-green against the red of rock and sand. A young land this, angry and proud, its hard edges not yet worn to gentleness by wind and rain. Even the mountains around Dragonskeep, high as they were, were not so fierce as these.

No, not an easy land at all. But one where the gods might walk.

And now they were come to Shima's home. She'd guessed "*mehanso*" meant village. With growing wonder, she saw how wrong she was as they entered the valley at one end. For rank after rank of mud-brick houses lined the cliff walls, most tucked back into caves like gouges in the stone, perhaps twenty feet deep or more, and running the length of the cliff on both sides of the valley. Judging by the number of houses, there were enough people here to populate a fair-sized city in the Five Kingdoms.

Remarkably few people came out of their houses to see the strangers, though. Perhaps, Maurynna thought, they were occupied with other things. But there should be more children than this, surely? Younglings always knew something was afoot even before it happened.

"Shouldn't there be more people?" she asked as Boreal followed Shima's little Pirii along the hard-packed trail that ran between the cliffs. Stormwind came close behind, with Trissin and Jhem trailing him. Their destination seemed to be a kind of large oval courtyard encircled by a low wall with openings at the narrow ends.

Shima waved a hand at the mud-brick houses above them on either side. "The valley can't support all those who could live here, were they here all the time; many of these homes are empty most of the year. Their owners are away with the flocks," he answered as he brought his pony to a halt in the courtyard, "or working the fields scattered throughout the land. Only a few of the farmers who tend nearby fields, and many artisans, live here year round. The rest of us come back for the four Great Fesitvals. Then the *mehanso* is crowded indeed."

And now the first of the valley dwellers met them: the children, in the lead here as they seemed to be the world over when there was something new at hand. They pranced around the horses, caroling greetings—(Maurynna assumed from the happy faces)—and shouting questions that Shima answered with a laugh. The Tah'nehsieh man jumped down from his horse. Children swarmed over him.

A few detached themselves to stare at the strangers. Maurynna dropped the reins on Boreal's neck, steeling herself to dismount. Would she never get used to riding the day long? To put off the dreaded moment a little longer she studied the children gathering around the Llysanyins.

They were slightly darker of skin than Shima, with hair the blue-black hue Maurynna had seen throughout Jehanglan. All, regardless of sex it seemed, wore only a short, kiltlike garment. Their soft voices fluted like tiny birds as they whispered among themselves, dividing their attention between humans and horses. They giggled behind their fingers when she greeted them in Jehangli.

She smiled back at them; the smile froze a little when she realized she really couldn't put off dismounting any longer. Not unless she wanted to eat and sleep atop Boreal. Ah, well; might as well get it over with. She raised herself in the saddle and swung her leg over the high cantle.

To her surprise it was easier today. *Maybe there's hope for me after all*, she thought, as she gently lowered herself to the ground.

Shima moved to help her; Raven jostled him out of the way. Maurynna stood a moment, shocked and angry.

That wasn't just rudeness. How dare he assume that only he's allowed near me?

"I don't need *any* help, thank you," she snapped, glaring at Raven.

He stared back sullenly for a moment. She braced herself for an explosion. Then he turned and strode back to Stormwind.

"They're with my mother now, resting before the feast this evening."

Shima sat with his back against the rear wall of his master's house in the village. The side and front walls of the house were built of mud brick; but this wall was the living rock of the mountain itself, the house itself tucked under an overhang in the cliff. In his hand he held a clay beaker filled with cold, sweet water from the upper spring, and sighed. He wished they were at the hut tucked away in the tiny meadow on the mountain.

Or that Raven was. It didn't much matter to him who

was where, as long as there was a ridge or two between them. He shook his head and grimaced, then drank.

Zhantse looked up from tipping the last of the chopped roots into the pot. He smiled, turning his face into a maze of sun-carved wrinkles like a dried riverbed.

"I should be doing that since Tefira's not here," Shima said, and made a halfhearted move to get up.

"But I cook better than you do," the shaman retorted as he waved him back. Zhantse picked up a spoon and stirred the thick stew.

Shima snorted. *That* was a matter of opinion. He had learned his cooking from his mother, acknowledged one of the best cooks in the villages. It was part of what had won her an honored place among the Tah'nehsieh when she came shipwrecked to the shores of Jehanglan so long ago and was sold inland as a slave. That, and capturing his father's heart.

Zhantse chuckled. "Well, then—perhaps I don't. But I won't poison us, either, so don't worry. I want to hear what you think of our visitors, and it would be a shame for dinner to burn because you became distracted with talking."

"Then let us hope you don't become distracted with listening. Give me the *pyamah* dough; I can shape loaves in my sleep."

"Be warned; I moved things about while you were gone—or, rather, my sister and two youngest nieces did," Zhantse said. "They decided this house was a disgrace and needed cleaning." His tone spoke eloquently of his martyrdom. "The honey jar has a red cord now; Yallasi broke the old tie and she insisted on that color. No matter what I said, she insisted on red; said it was 'cheerful' or some such idiocy," he said as he passed the rough earthenware bowl to him.

"A Seer is a person of awe to all but his own family," Shima repeated the old proverb in a lofty tone and heaved himself up. "We're lucky she didn't break the jar," he grumbled as he grabbed the bowl. Pottery everywhere trembled whenever Yallasi came near. And to lose that much rockbee honey would have hurt; he'd taken too many stings in the acquiring of it.

He went to the line of storage jars by the side wall. There were the jars with the colored cords he was familiar with: white for *pyamah* meal, blue for dried spotted beans, yellow for pine nuts. But with them were *two* jars with lids tied down with brownish cords; one should have been blue and white for the chunks of sun-dried pumpkin.

Shima frowned. "Zhantse, which did you say?"

"The red. Remember; to you it will look— Oh, bother the girl! She didn't tell me she'd broken the cord on another jar. And did she think to use one of the same colors as before? Of course not. I'll tend to that tomorrow. For now, Shima, the honey jar's the second from the left."

Said Shima, "You didn't tell her . . . ?"

"No," Zhantse replied. "I know you don't like it spoken of."

"Thank you," Shima said. "What color is the second cord, anyway? It doesn't look the same shade of brown as the other."

Zhantse glanced over. "Green."

"Ah; thank you." It was silly to be ashamed of something he couldn't help, especially when his mother had told him his inability to see certain colors wasn't unknown in the northern lands. Rare, perhaps, but not unknown. But since when did common sense have anything to do with such things? He was still sensitive about it. To his relief, he was no longer teased as he had been as a child; either the others had forgotten or, as adults, they now had other concerns. Either reason was fine with him. He had no wish for the teasing to begin again because of Yallasi's gossip.

He untied the narrow woven cord that held the lid down—*what does red look like? And green? I wish I knew*—and used a small wooden spoon hanging on the wall behind the jar to scoop out some of the honey inside and drizzled it over the *pyamah* batter. He replaced the lid and tied it down carefully with the methodical neatness of a man who spends much of his time in the wilderness.

He licked a stray bit of honey from his fingers. Ahh, that was good; wild honey, stolen from the rockbees that lived in the cliffs, all the sweeter for the stings taken in the harvesting. He began stirring while he collected his thoughts.

"They're the ones you Saw; no doubt about that," Shima finally said. "The woman—Maurynna Kyrissaean—is indeed a Dragonlord like the one in the legend. I like her; she's honest and open, no guile in her eyes. And Miune vouches for her as well." He paused, thinking of the stories his Yerrin mother had told him, and imagining soaring among the clouds. It seemed so real that for a moment he could almost feel wings sprouting from his back—

"Did you fall asleep?" Zhantse asked.

Shima came back to himself with a start. "What?" he said, startled.

"You were staring at the wall as if you saw your heart's desire there. I expected you to drop the bowl."

Shima gave an embarrassed laugh. "That would have been a crime, wasting good *pyamah* dough, wouldn't it?" He brought the bowl to the fireside and made a fuss over arranging the dough on the broad leaves of spice grass and folding the bundles.

Zhantse said, "And the other, the man with her? You've said nothing of— Ah; you don't like him."

Shima didn't bother to erase the betraying frown. "Raven? No. I could forgive his first rudeness to me; that was but apprehension of a stranger. But now, though . . ." He told his master what had happened in the square. "You would've thought I was trying to seduce his wife away instead of helping a tired woman who is soultwinned to someone else entirely. He has no more right to her than I.

"Nor," he continued with a certain vindictive relish, "does she appreciate his possesiveness."

"Damnation," said Zhantse. "He's jealous; that's bad."

For a moment Shima didn't know what the old shaman meant. Then he understood and groaned. "Spirits, I hadn't thought of that." He turned a stern glance on his master. "I'll not be the one to tell him."

Zhantse smiled once more. He ladled some stew into a small bowl and handed it to Shima. "Here; have something to hold you until the feast tonight. You must be hungry after your ride." The smile broadened. "And of course you're the one to tell him, and no other, since your brother is still at the hut in the upper meadow. That's what apprentices and spirit drummers are for—to do the dirty work."

Shima glared at his master, who laughed. He ate the stew and fumed in silence. Easy enough for his master to say, "Do this thing," and not face the consequences.

Which Shima was certain would include an angry fist when Raven found out that he would have to stay behind.

Grumbling, Shima laid the *pyamah* bundles on a tray woven from bundled maize leaves and took them outside to the beehive-shaped clay oven. The air above the smoke hole shimmered and danced, making all behind it as insubstantial as a dream. Shima squatted and carefully pulled aside the flat stone that served as the door to the oven's firebox and peered inside. Glowing red embers greeted him.

"Are the coals ready?" Zhantse called from the doorway.

"Just right."

Replacing that stone, Shima then slid the upper stone— that which served as the door to the oven proper—to one side along the narrow ledge that ran across the front of the oven. He pushed each leaf-wrapped bundle into the oven with a long stick. All the while he hummed one of his favorite planting songs; he enjoyed baking. In this he was truly his mother's child, he thought.

When the *pyamah* loaves were arranged to his satisfaction, Shima replaced the stone. A thought came to him as he brushed away stray bits of leaf and twig from before the oven.

"Zhantse," he said, "have you Seen yet how Maurynna is to accomplish this thing?"

The silence that answered him was so deep that Shima looked up in dread. His master suddenly looked old, as ancient and worn as the stones around them.

Shima went cold inside.

"Yes," Zhantse answered at last. "This morning. It—it will be hard." He paused; when he spoke again, his voice was the merest whisper of sorrow and pain. "I Saw what must be done. But, Spirits help me, I don't see *how* she can do it."

Lord Jhanun sat in his chamber in the inn at Rhampul. To one side sat Kwahsiu and Nalorih; before him, forehead touching the floor, knelt Baisha.

"You failed me," Jhanun said to him.

"Lord, the creatures are in Jehanglan," Baisha said, raising a desperate face. "We need only capture them—"

"Fool!" Jhanun roared. "The Zharmatians have them now—didn't you hear the soldiers' report? How did you let them get away? You should have had them."

Baisha cringed and touched his forehead to the floor once more.

Jhanun seethed. Three of the creatures in the hands of the Zharmatians, and a warhost between him and the one Baisha said was the Hidden One. Baisha would pay for—

"Lord."

The quiet voice broke into his thoughts. Surprised at the interruption, he snapped, "What is it, Kwahsiu?"

Kwahsiu fidgeted under his glare, but went on. For once he wasn't smiling. "Lord, Nalorih and I saw what happened. It should have been easy to take the creatures; we even saw them standing together, talking. Then all of a sudden, they struck out like madmen, and their horses came for them. It was as if they'd been warned somehow, my lord. They *knew* something was wrong; I don't know how, but they did."

All during his partner's sober recitation, Nalorih had nodded in confirmation.

"Very well. The three of you, take the troops here and keep searching for the creatures. Perhaps they'll evade the Zharmatians as—"

Once again he was interrupted, this time by a knocking at the door. "Enter!"

Captain Tsuen entered. "This just came, my lord. The messenger apologizes for the delay. He barely evaded capture by the Zharmatians."

Jhanun took the folded note and broke the seal. He read the message again and again, unable to believe it. At last he said, "Xiane Ma Jhi is dead—and that bitch has declared herself regent! She dared to sit upon the Phoenix Throne!"

Stunned silence greeted his words.

Unable to contain his fury, Jhanun ripped the note to shreds. "Kwahsiu, you take the troops and hunt for the werecreatures. Nalorih, you shall return with me, as will Baisha." He fixed the outlander with a venomous glare. "Perhaps if you're under my eye you'll do better." He rose from his chair.

Baisha rapped his forehead against the floor again and again.

"Enough. We ride for Mount Rivasha," Jhanun said. "We'll raise troops from the officers in the army who are members of the Four Tigers, and hold the holy city against that bitch. Get the horses."

Forty-seven

As they sat outside the next day, enjoying the afternoon sun, Maurynna asked, "How many brothers and sisters do you have, Shima?"

"Two sisters, one older, one younger, and a younger brother."

Raven said, "Where are the others, and your father? Don't they live here?"

"Keru, my younger sister, lives here as I do," Shima said.

"My father and other sister are with our sheep. My younger brother, Tefira, though . . ."

Seeing his worried look, Maurynna said, "Is something amiss? Where is he?"

Shima shrugged. "Fasting in an isolated hut. He's Zhantse's apprentice, and training to be the next shaman. Zhantse took him because, when Tefira was younger, he had visions—little things, for he was but a child, but true. Yet, since then, nothing."

He glanced over his shoulder at the house, where they could hear Lark singing. "My mother's worried about him."

"I'm sorry," Maurynna said.

Raven stood up, dusting the seat of his breeches. "So am I. I'm off to see to the horses, beanpole. Coming?"

Maurynna shook her head. "No," she answered, blinking in the sun, "I think I'll just enjoy sitting in one place for a while." Then, moved by a sudden spirit of mischief, she added, "But why don't you go, Shima? I know you'd like to see the Llysanyins again."

Raven flashed her a sour look, but made no objection.

She watched them walk off together, settled back against the wall, and closed her eyes. In a little while she'd go for a walk of her own. But for now, the sun felt good on her face. All too soon she would be riding into the gods only knew what danger; she would enjoy this simple pleasure while she could.

The sun-baked brick lent a dry, dusty scent to the air. It was a good smell, warm and welcoming, singing of the little, everyday things that meant home.

Like hearing Linden's breathing when I wake up at night . . . She tried not to think about Linden, not to wonder if she could now Change. She would only drive herself to tears or madness.

Luckily Lark came out at that moment, her arms full of something that looked like long strips of some kind of leaf. A small basket dangled by its handle from one finger. She smiled when she saw Maurynna. "Mind if I join you here? This is my favorite place to work."

"Of course not." Maurynna shifted. Lark eased herself down and scooted back so that she also rested her back against the wall. Maurynna watched curiously as the Yerrin woman spread her leaves upon the blanket before her. "What are you doing?"

"Making a basket. It's very soothing—once you know how," Lark said dryly. She drew a bone needle with a large eye and some little bundles of dyed lacings from the the basket. The lacings, Maurynna saw, were narrow ribbons 'of flexible reed. After poking through them, Lark chose one of a soft blue and threaded a length of it through the eye of the needle.

Maurynna picked up one of the long strips of leaf and tugged it gently. Though dried, it was strong and flexible. "What are these?"

"Maize leaves. Makes wonderful coiled baskets. Watch." Lark picked up three strips, bundled them together, and folded one end back upon itself. Taking up the needle, she wrapped the folded section tightly with the cord, careful to catch the loose end under the wrapping. "This is the center; from here I work in a spiral that the maize leaves form the core of."

Maurynna watched, fascinated, as the other woman's nimble fingers deftly wrapped the lacing around the leaf strips. Every couple of finger widths along the ever-growing spiral, the needle would slip into the inner row and out and around the working row once more to bind them together. When she reached the end of the leaves she worked with, Lark fanned them out and slipped three more in so that the ends overlapped. Then she wrapped them tightly and continued.

It looked easy enough. With a glance at Lark for permission, Maurynna picked up another needle and a length of lacing, and some strips of the core material. She settled herself to work.

Bundling the strips was easy; so was folding the end. Nothing very hard about this. But then came the lacing. Then somehow the narrow reeding went one way and the core another, the strips separating and fluttering gracefully to the ground like mocking butterflies.

Maurynna eyed them and the errant lacing. Hm; yes, this *could* be frustrating. And she, the gods knew, was frustrated enough. So she returned lacing, needle, and leaf strips, deciding to save her temper. She'd watch Lark.

The Yerrin woman's deft fingers worked steadily. "The bottom's big enough now," Lark announced after a time that Maurynna lost herself in. "Time to change the angle so that the working row sits on the old one and begin the sides."

Sure enough, as the wrapping and stitching continued their magic, row by slow row the sides of the basket spiraled gracefully up. Twice Lark changed the color of the cord, using a green one for a while, then switching back to the blue.

"It's beautiful," Maurynna marveled. "Can you use anything else for the core of the spiral?"

"Oh, yes—long pine needles or grass, any sort of flexible plant stalks, I would imagine. Spice grass makes a wonderfully fragrant basket; a bride-to-be makes spice grass baskets for her future husband's mother, grandmother, and sisters as tokens of respect and affection."

Her voice grew wistful. "I wish that sweet woodruff grew here in Jehanglan; I've always thought that it would be as nice as sweet grass for a basket. It grew all around the cottage where I grew up; I still remember the lovely fresh hay scent of my old mattress. My mother had stuffed it with sweet woodruff for me, and the scent grew stronger as the woodruff dried. I used to think it was magic of some sort."

Maurynna wished there were some way Lark could go back to Yerrih. Maybe she should suggest the woman return with them when the ship returned. But would Lark leave the life she had made in Jehanglan? Maurynna thought not.

"How did you come here?" she asked. "And where are you from in Yerrih?"

"I came from near Gull Rock Port in the north. My family were farmers, but the first time I went into the port and heard the crying of the gulls, I knew the sea was for me."

A warm feeling of kinship glowed in Maurynna's breast. This was talk she could understand. She nodded at Lark to go on.

"When I was old enough, I signed on as ship's cook on board the *White Seal's Dream*, a trim little cog out of Gull Rock Port. I was happy on her; she was a good ship with a good captain, old Skua Hareson who could smell a storm coming three days off, and we saw the world.

"But one ill-omened day we took on a new man in Tanlyton, a Kelnethi who said that he'd gone a-traveling after his girl cast him off, and was now down on his luck and would work for passage. Skua took pity on him, and that was the beginning of our troubles."

Ater his girl cast him off. . . . That joggled a memory Maurynna couldn't quite place—but one that bothered her. Annoyed because she couldn't remember, she tugged a strand of her hair as if that would drag the memory out from its hiding place in her head. "What do you mean?"

"The man had a soul blacker than the pits of hell, and a tongue that mixed truth and lies with every breath until you didn't know which was which. Gave us the name his mother called him, not the one he grew up with, and told us he was Kelnethi. Oh, he spoke the language like one born there, I'll grant you that. Looked like one, too; took after his mam who was from near Bylith. But for all that, he was a Yerrin born to Eagle clan." Lark's voice vibrated with hate.

Confused, Maurynna said, "But surely you saw the clan braid—"

Lark shook her head. "Cut off; he was *parna*, outcast. Without it, he was indistinguishable from any man from the other kingdoms. May the gods curse the day that scum lied his way on board the *Dream*!

"For he hadn't been 'cast aside'—not he. The girl he'd wanted was his half brother's betrothed. When she wouldn't change her mind, and his brother caught him try-ing to rape her, he killed them both."

Here Lark shuddered, her eyes full of old ghosts, and Maurynna couldn't blame her. A kinslayer was a vile thing in any of the kingdoms. But to the Yerrins, who held the ties of blood sacred, they were a special abhorrence. The worst torments in Gifnu's hells were for kinslayers and kill-ers of children. To give such a one hearth-room, even un-knowingly, could well bring down the wrath of the gods.

Despite the pain of old memories that rang in her voice, Lark went on like a ship plowing through a storm. "He was to be hanged after being outcast, of course, but somehow his mother drugged the guards and freed him. The boy slain hadn't been *her* child, after all," Lark said bitterly.

"To make a long story short, after we took that filth on board, a madness seized Skua. He had an ancient rutter his great-granda won off a drunken, broken-down old pilot. Skua kept it only as a curiosity; he had his own. But in the other was a chart that claimed to show a safe route here. And that was how the gods chose to punish us."

"Skua tried it?" Maurynna asked, appalled. To trust one's ship to a book of charts unknown and unproven! The gods had been angered indeed to muddle the captain's wits so.

But it raised a question that had bothered her since hear-ing of House Mimdallek's "enterprises." She asked, "How do ships travel here safely? For those of House Mhakkan and certain . . . others do. The Straits are said to be im-passable because of magic. How do they get through?"

"Magic that the priestmages say doesn't exist." Lark snorted. "*They* call it the Will of the Phoenix, but magic it is, pure and simple.

"There's a safe course through their wizardry; it twists and turns and, worse yet, changes from time to time. I'm told the ships from House Mhakkan each carry a small image of the Phoenix given to them by the priestmages. It floats within a globe of crystal mounted by the ship's wheel and points out the safe route."

Ah, yes—that must be what she'd seen on the ship they'd taken from Assantik.

"That's one way. Another is to use a magic sniffer," said Lark. "I suspect that's how—" She clamped her lips shut on whatever she was about to say.

Maurynna didn't pursue the slip. Instead she said, "A magic sni—? Oh, of course! Someone whose 'little talent' is sensing magic." So that was how the House Mimdallek ship got through. . . .

The other woman went on. "Some ships have made it through by sheer luck or by following sailing directions that another smuggler used and was willing to share for whatever reason. Of course, once the course changes . . ." Lark's shoulders hunched against remembered pain.

"That's how you were caught."

"Aye, caught we were, in a magestorm spawned in hell," Lark said heavily. She passed a hand over her eyes. "One moment all was clear; the next— That storm was sent for us. I know it. *Dream* was stout and strong, but even she couldn't weather the savage beating she took; I've never seen anything like the fury of that blow, and I've ridden out many a winter's gale in the northern seas. We fought it for candlemarks. Then in one mighty blast, wind and wave picked our poor ship up and cast her upon the rocks as a man might throw down a stick. She broke her back and spilled us into the water like beans from a jar.

"Those that didn't drown right away clung to the wreckage and tried to ride it out. But one by one I watched my shipmates go under until there were but five of us left clinging to the mast: myself, Skua, Raene Sailmaker, Corby, Skua's little grandson and our cabin boy—and the kinslayer."

A tear slid down Lark's cheek. "Corby lost his hold and drifted away. His grandfather went after him. I saw them both sink beneath one giant wave, that hellstorm's final blow. It was like a thing alive, that wave; it knew we were there and wanted us dead.

"But Raene, the kinslayer, and I—we all held on, more

dead than alive, and me with a broken arm. We were washed ashore and found by one of the tribes that live on the fringes of Jehanglan proper. We were taken as slaves." Her lips shut in a grim line upon the last words.

It was a line Maurynna knew better than to cross. So she asked, "How do you know all this about the kinslayer? Surely he didn't tell you while on board the ship—Skua would have tossed him overboard." For *she* certainly would have, or faced a mutiny. No sailor would risk the ill luck one so cursed might bring to ship and crew.

Lark shook her head. "Raene and I only found out later when we nursed him through a fever and he began raving. Even delirious, he sounded quite pleased with himself.

"When we heard the tale and understood why our fate had befallen us, why our comrades had died, Raene tried to smother him. The guards pulled her off before she could finish and took her away. I never saw her again. And the kinslayer—" She laughed bitterly. "The last I ever heard was that the filth had found a master to match him. He became a favorite of Lord Jhanun, another with treachery in his heart. They were well-matched." A long sigh. "If only he'd died of that illness; but no, the shaking sickness torments you but it doesn't kill. So he continues to hide his foulness under that sweet smile of his and wreaks the gods only know what misery upon innocent folk."

Sweet smile ... The unease that had been prodding at Maurynna since Lark began her story crashed down upon her like a mountain of ice. A sweet smile. The shaking sickness. She remembered where she'd heard of the tale of a man cast aside by a woman. ...

It was hard to breathe. "Lark," she said, "what was the kinslayer's name?"

The Yerrin woman began indignantly, "One does not name a—" Their eyes met; Lark broke off. "His true name," she said quietly, "was Lynx Willowson."

There's still a chance. ...

"But—"

Maurynna sat still as death for Lark's next words.
"But he called himself Taren Olmeins."

After Lark went back inside to start the evening meal, Maurynna sat lost in thought. She couldn't bear to be the one
to tell Raven. Bad enough that the man he'd called friend
at one time was a traitor, but to have helped a kinslayer . . .

No, she wouldn't tell him. Not yet. Not until they were
well clear of Jehanglan, else he'd worry every moment
when doom was to fall. Perhaps when they were home in
Dragonskeep, she'd tell him.

Dragonskeep . . . She shivered. Oh, gods—*Dragonskeep*
had given hearth-room to a kinslayer. Were the gods even
now planning revenge upon her home?

Avert, avert, avert!

She ate little that evening, and went early to bed, pleading a headache.

Forty-eight

"There's going to be a celebration for you two tonight,"
Lark announced at breakfast the next morning. "It's not
often we get visitors."

Maurynna, feeling better after a night's sleep, said,
"Truly? How kind! What kind of celebration?"

"The usual feasting and dancing," Shima replied. "But
first, while Raven is still seeing to your horses, Zhantse
wants to speak with you before you go to the celebration.
I'm to take you to him; he'll be waiting for us in the desert
near the foot of the mountain called Zunest'sha'sho. It
means the Lonely One."

"I see," Maurynna said, quietly. *This is where I find out
why Morlen insisted I go.*

She wished the day was over already.

* * *

"Any news?" Linden asked as Jekkanadar entered their tent again.

"Nothing much. There have been some battles, but it seems it's mostly quick sorties in and out."

Linden nodded. It was a kind of warfare he was familiar with.

"Have you . . . ?" Jekkanadar waved a hand.

"Felt anything of Maurynna? No," he answered grimly, and let his mind empty again to see if he could feel her.

Nothing, as always. He kept trying; he had to believe she was still alive.

It had been an ordeal to convince Raven that he didn't need to go with her.

"One of us needs to go early to the feast," she insisted. "We can't both be late; that would be an insult."

At last he'd capitulated, though with no good grace. Maurynna saw him set off with Lark and Keru, Shima's sister.

Now she rode behind Shima through a landscape made more alien than ever by moonlight. She looked around and shivered as they wound a way through gullies and past rocks that towered over her head.

Then Shima led her through a narrow passage that opened into a wide, flat gully. A man stood on the far side of a campfire.

At first Maurynna thought the man facing them was old, but still hale and hearty. Then she realized that he was probably younger by a decade or two than Otter, his lined and weathered face making him seem much older. By his side stood Miune. The waterdragon's feelers quivered at the sight of her.

"Hello, Miune—I'm happy to see you again," she said.

A feeler waved happily.

She dismounted and left Shima to remove Boreal's tack. Standing on the opposite side of the flames, she said in

Jehangli, the only language they would have in common, "I greet you, Zhantse."

The seamed face smiled. "As I greet you, Maurynna Kyrissaean. Shall we sit by the fire?"

She nodded, and sat. In a short while, Shima joined them. For a time, no one spoke.

The desert night was cold; Maurynna was glad for both the fire and her cloak. The Tah'nehsieh men wore the thick, woven wraps that she had learned were called *jelah*. She thought they looked like narrow blankets split down the front.

"There is an ancient prophecy, its words handed down from Seer to Seer of the Tah'nehsieh, the People of the Red Desert," Zhantse said, breaking the silence. "My master had it of his master before him, and so on, even before the dawning of the Phoenix Kingdom. Jalla, it was, who Dreamed the words in the long ago."

The shaman's eyes closed; in the flickering light of the fire he looked like a wise and ancient tortoise. "All listen! For these are the words of his Seeing," he chanted.

The shaman's voice suddenly deepened, and the next words rolled out like the thunder that had rumbled among the distant mountains all evening.

" 'The blade of the north is the key. Give it human hands to guide it, dragon spirit to drive it. Only then shall what is bound, be unbound.' "

The red firelight played over Zhantse's wrinkled face; he looked at each of them in turn. "For many, many years no one understood what those words meant, not even Jalla. He died never knowing what his Seeing meant. What was the 'blade of the north,' and what was it the key to? How were human and dragon to work so together? While our kinds were not enemies, such a thing was unheard of."

"And now you think you know," Maurynna said, surprised at how calm her voice sounded. It was a calmness she did not feel inside.

"Yes," Zhantse replied. "The first piece of the puzzle came long ago when two northern dragons found their way to this land." He nodded at the waterdragon. "Miune? Here it is your tale, I think."

Thee truly wish this, shaman? Miune's eyes shone.

"I do, Miune. I bid you speak," Zhantse said.

Shaman and dragon locked gazes; then Zhantse held out a hand. Miune brushed the waiting fingers with the tip of one feeler and nodded.

Yes, this is my part of the tale, the coming of the northern dragons; my parents told me of it. The young dragon raised his head and tucked his forelegs a little more tightly beneath him.

"Your pardon, Miune," Maurynna said, "but this is a thing that's confused me for some time. You said once before that your parents . . . disappeared before you were born. So how could they have told you . . . ?"

They sang to me when I was still in the egg. It is the way of my kind; our songs are powerful. I heard them and although I did not understand then, I remembered and understood later. If I listen very hard, sometimes I can still hear them singing in the cave they—and now I—live in. The rocks remember. Miune looked down and his mind-voice grew soft. *Sometimes the songs are very beautiful but sad, like the fading of autumn into winter. But most bring joy. Those are like the singing of a stream over stone. Those are my favorites.*

But listen and I will tell thee what my parents told me. When they first came, one of the winged dragons of the north carried a bundle that he did not speak of, nor did he open it. It lay in a corner of the cave he took to live in. My parents did not ask about it. They simply made both dragons welcome. After a time, he spoke to them of the life he had led before, and he showed them the few keepsakes he'd kept from that time.

They were amazed, for he said that he had lived as a man, that in his young years he had not even known what he was. But a great grief had come upon his human form and that part of him determined to leave this life, to seek the one who went before. So the dragon told them, saying

*that his human half slept deeply and would soon slip
away.**

"What was his name?" Maurynna asked at the same time
Shima demanded, "What was in the bundle? Wretch, you
never spoke of this to me," and tugged a feeler.

**Ouch!* Thee are the wretch, Shima, for that hurt. Thee
must blame Zhantse's kind; it is a great secret of the shamans and I promised long and long ago never to speak of
it, lest some mischiefmaker seek to thwart Jalla's Seeing.**
To Maurynna he said, **His name was Dharm Varleran,
and he died later in a storm. Does this mean aught to
thee?**

"So Dharm and Pirakos were together," she mused aloud.
"Miune—what *was* in the bundle? Is it still secret?"

A fine thing it would be if even she—if indeed she was
the one spoken of in the prophecy—could not be told. The
gods would laugh long and hard at that. Such jests delighted
them too much, she thought sourly.

For a space of time Miune lay silent, motionless save for
the slight quivering of his feelers. Then he stretched one
feeler out to her and brushed her hand.

It is time, he said in a tone that brooked no argument.
We go to the Lonely One. He heaved himself to his feet
and marched away.

So quickly and unexpectedly did the waterdragon move
that Maurynna and the others were caught by surprise. They
scrambled to their feet. Both men picked up torches and
thrust them into the fire. When the torches caught, they
started after Miune.

Maurynna found herself walking behind Zhantse and
ahead of Shima as they followed the youngling dragon
through the moonlit gully without speaking. A haunting
tune in a wailing, minor key ghosted through her mind. It
fit so well with the eerie, barren landscape around her that
at first she didn't notice it was there. When she did, goose-
flesh prickled her arms as she wondered where it came
from; she felt as though she walked along some border in

the dream world where the weight of a sigh would tilt the scales between nightmare and enchantment.

Then she realized that it was Miune she heard in her mind. Could this be one of the songs his parents had sung to him when he was still in the egg? If she listened very hard, there were words shimmering on the edge of her mind. She almost had them. . . .

Instead, she stubbed her toe on a rock and stumbled. A tiny bat flitted past her as if mocking her with its airy grace. Maurynna ruefully decided she'd best pay attention to the winding path or risk landing flat on her face. The flickering light of the torches threw confusing shadows on the trail; she wished she dared send up a ball or three of coldfire.

Then they were climbing out of the gully and up the slope of Zunest'sha'sho, the Lonely One.

Revelation made her stumble again. "Oh my gods," she breathed. " 'The Lonely One.' "

So this is where Dharm Varleran buried his sorrow—for a time. Then he died and Pirakos fell into a hell beyond imagining.

The thought made her shiver. She whispered over her shoulder to Shima, "Have you been here before?"

He closed the distance between them. "No. I'm merely a spirit drummer; this is a matter for shamans."

She looked up at the rock towering above them. "Do we go to the top?" Her legs felt tired even thinking about it.

Shima laughed softly. "No, thank the Spirits. This much I do know: what we seek is kept in a cave not very far from here."

He sounded so guilty that she looked over her shoulder. "Oh?"

The younger Tah'nehsieh flashed her a wry grin. "It's forbidden to come to this place, but it's also a boy's dare to follow the shamans as far as you can when they travel here. I was lucky; I was never found out. My friend Teira couldn't sit for days after he was caught, his father was so angry," he whispered.

The trail grew sharply steeper, and the humans in the

party waited as Miune huffed and waddled and sometimes backslid his way along it until it became level again. Then it was the turn of the two-foots.

It was not as bad as Maurynna, still a sailor at heart, feared it would be; her new Dragonlord strength made all the difference. The men seemed not to notice the climb. Perhaps, Maurynna thought, they were so used to this rough country that a few hundred feet up or down made little difference to them.

Then the path was level once more. They followed Miune closely as the trail clung to the side of the towering rock. There was a breeze up here; it carried the night scents of the desert to Maurynna: the still-hot smell of dust, a delicate fragrance of flowers that hid from the searing heat of the sun and showed themselves only to Sister Moon and the creatures of the night.

In here.

The words came a bare instant before the waterdragon turned sharply to the left and disappeared with a flick of his tail. Zhantse followed.

When Maurynna's turn came, she found that the trail led to a wide crack in the rock face. One side of the opening jutted out farther than the other and curved in slightly. She guessed that, from below, it would look like merely a fold in the rock.

Curious, Maurynna stepped into the opening. Wide as it was, she thought that Miune must have had some difficulty slipping through; the youngling dragon would not be able to come here much longer.

Then she realized that, after this night, he might well have no reason to come here anymore. The "key" would be gone—and she would be the keeper of it. The thought froze her feet to the ground.

Somehow Zhantse must have sensed her hesitation, though he mistook the reason for it. The shaman turned and said, "Come. A little more and the way opens out."

Then he looked beyond her and spoke to Shima in their own language, a question, by the sound of it. It seemed to

Maurynna that there was a note of concern beneath the quick words. But whatever those fears were, they appeared to be laid to rest by Shima's cheerful reply, for while Zhantse's skeptical expression seemed to say, "On your head be it," the shaman nodded and went on.

And what was that about? she wondered as she made her way deeper into the mountain. She glanced back over her shoulder at Shima. His face betrayed no fearful secrets; he merely looked intent on picking a safe way along the uneven floor.

No answers there, then. She continued on, one hand slipping along the wall. Her gaze strayed above her head and she noticed that the walls and ceiling of the tunnel were black with soot. *How many generations of shamans have come this way*, she mused, *over how—*

Before she could complete the thought, she entered a large stone chamber. After only a few steps, she had to stop. The walls and ceiling were painted, an explosion of bright, intricate designs that, she swore, moved whenever her eyes settled on any one. A wave of vertigo washed over her.

"Good gods!" she exclaimed, and dropped her gaze in self-defense. The floor, she was relieved to see, was the dull red of the mother rock.

When she looked up once more, either the designs had decided to behave, or her eyes had adjusted, for the rapid swirling stopped. Still, the chamber was not a comfortable place. A quick look around told her it was empty save for a stack of fresh torches and wall brackets to hold them. She fixed her eyes on Miune and Zhantse standing together by another, much narrower, exit on the far side of the chamber.

Shima's startled, "Hwah!" from behind her reassured her she was not the only one affected. He stumbled as he thrust the torch he carried into the nearest bracket.

"Were you not with us," Zhantse said, gesturing with his free hand first to Miune and then himself, "you would even now be lying on the ground, certain you were going mad. And if you did not leave quickly enough, it would become so. For beyond here are things that are not for all to see."

"That which the dragon brought?" Shima asked.

"And other things," replied Zhantse evenly. His dark-eyed gaze snapped to his drummer like a sword coming to point.

"I understand, master," Shima said, humbly. "No word will I speak of this."

Good, else I should have to thump thee. Miune sounded only a little disappointed that he was not to have revenge for the tugging of his feeler.

"From here I must go alone," Zhantse said. "No one but a shaman or Miune may go beyond this point, and he's now too large to attempt this passage."

Maurynna watched as the shaman laid a hand on one side of the mysterious opening and chanted softly, his head bowed. In answer there came a hum like the whisper of wind through harp strings. When it died away again, Zhantse entered the passage, his voice rising and falling in the chant. She saw the light from his torch and heard him for a time; then, abruptly, both ended as if the shaman had stepped out of this world and was beyond all perception.

In this strange land, mayhap he did. A shiver ran down Maurynna's spine at the thought.

He will be some time, Miune said as he crossed the chamber. *There are places where he must pray and offer the sacred pollens he carries.* The waterdragon settled to the floor.

Shima joined him. Maurynna held back a sigh and sat down. This room made her twitchy; she wanted the night sky above her once more.

No one spoke. And as the silence grew, Maurynna became more and more aware of the magic imbued in the stone around her. It *itched*. But she could no more scratch inside her head than she could walk across the sea. So she set her teeth and willed herself to endure.

Raven clapped in time with the drummers as he sat with Lark and her neighbors, watching the two lines of dancers weave intricate patterns around each other. Their stamping feet raised puffs of dust, shrouding the great bonfire in a haze of red, even as their song spiraled up to the stars.

Song and dance came to an end in a final, triumphant "Hyah!" The dancers halted, laughing and catching their breath. But the drummers had little mercy; with a challenge that Raven recognized by tone if not words, the lead drummer beat out a fast, complicated rhythm. The others joined in.

The rhythm put Raven in mind of one he'd learned for his role for the troupe. One thought led to another; he stood up, swaying slightly.

Surprised, he thought, *Whoa! Best take care, boy. That mesta is more potent than it tastes!*

Lark looked up at him, eyebrows raised in question.

"There are others who'd like to dance, I'm thinking," was all the explanation he gave her along with a grin. He turned his back on the leaping bonfire and set off into the darkness.

The magic thrummed in her bones now and felt like sand fleas inside her skin. She wanted to run away. Instead, Maurynna pulled her cloak a little closer and hunched into a ball. Something dug into the side of her face; her fingers went to it to see what—

Her cloak pin. Or, rather, Rani's cloak pin. Maurynna locked her fingers around it and the little vixen pressed into her palm, solid and comforting. It brought back thoughts of Linden. She wrapped herself in that remembering; it kept the magic around her at bay—at least a little. She could endure now.

So of course at that moment, Zhantse returned. Maurynna rubbed the vixen's nose with her thumb and raised her head.

Now she would find out what Dharm Varleran had left for her. Worse yet, now she would find out just what she would have to do.

*   *   *

"Hunh," Raven grunted as he paused at the top of the path that led to the small patch of grassland the Llysanyins had taken as their own. Stormwind and the Two Poor Bastards stood, ears pricked, facing the sound of the drumming. From the way their tails twitched from side to side and Jhem's hind feet shifted, Raven knew he'd guessed right.

But where—Once more his gaze swept the nook. Still only three Llysanyins, and none of them was Boreal. "Rynna's not back *yet*?"

Was something amiss? Should he go look for her? That seemed a good idea until a part of his mind, less fogged with *mesta* than the rest, asked, *Where?*

He shook his head. "Damnation," he swore again and again, all his frustration bubbling up. He stood, fists clenched and feet wide apart, as the Llysanyins came up. As Stormwind snuffled his hair, Raven made a vow deep in his heart.

Then he jumped up to Stormwind's back. Jhem and Trissin crowded in behind.

Zhantse bore a cloth-wrapped bundle in his arms as he strode across the painted chamber. His black eyes glittered with excitement.

"Come," he said. "This is not the place for you to see your destiny, Maurynna Kyrissaean. Come away."

Maurynna stood. Gods, but she wanted out of this place. The magic buzzed in her ears now, making it difficult to hear; vertigo snatched at her and retreated. Her only consolation was that Kyrissaean remained quiet. Had her dragon half been awake . . . Maurynna shuddered at the thought; then she took a deep breath, stumbling after Zhantse. The shaman lit a fresh torch from the pile and led the way into the tunnel to the outside.

This time she was second in line, with Shima behind and Miune bringing up the rear. With each step, the thrumming in her bones faded until it was but a disquieting memory, like a bad dream that one doesn't quite remember upon waking. As she stepped out of the passage and was under the night sky, Maurynna let her head fall back, and filled her lungs with the cool, sweet air.

"It's not a comfortable place, is it?" Shima said quietly as he stopped beside her.

"You've never been there before?" she asked.

"No, I'm not training to be a shaman," he replied. One hand came up to rest gently on her shoulder, to both comfort and urge her on.

She obeyed. Shima continued, "Tefira may enter the chamber, for he is Zhantse's apprentice. He'll discard the used torches we left there and replace them with fresh ones."

His sympathetic—but amused—tone said that it was just one of many boring duties his brother performed.

They went on, the dry scraping of Miune's claws following them along the trail. Zhantse didn't stop at the bottom as Maurynna half expected him to; instead the shaman set off briskly for the gully, his *jelah* swinging jauntily from side to side.

Ah, well; she supposed the suspense wouldn't kill her. It would just torture her a little more.

Stormwind paced along the canyon floor to the dancing ground, moving in the *shallinn*, the high, slow trot that paused between each beat. When they were within sight of the celebration, the Two Poor Bastards came up on either side and matched Stormwind. Given their size and the precision of their steps, Raven knew the Llysanyins would set jaws to dropping.

Nor was he mistaken. Already they had been spotted; as friend called to friend, more turned to see. Raven slipped from Stormwind's back. He jogged to meet Lark, now standing.

"D'you think anyone will mind?" he asked.

"They can truly dance?" Lark said as if she hadn't heard him. And perhaps she hadn't; she was gaping at the Llysanyins who cantered slowly in a circle. Now and again, at some signal Raven couldn't see, they would rise up on their hind legs and reverse direction.

Then Lark gasped, and answered her own question. "Dear gods," she said in awe. "They *can* dance! Watch— whenever the rhythm changes. . . ."

She was right. There were patterns in the drumming, and whenever the pattern changed, the Llysanyins moved with it. Raven stood, as captivated as the first time he'd seen them dance. More and more people crowded around them to watch.

Someone pushed a drum into his hands. As if bewitched, he began drumming one of the Assantikkan rhythms the Llysanyins knew, *Takka nih Bahari*, "Dance of the Red Ghost." Their impromptu dance flowed into the one they knew so well.

Trills of wonder filled the night air. Raven drummed, and as, one by one, the Tah'nesieh drummers joined in as they caught the rhythm, the Llysanyins danced in the firelight.

Maurynna knelt by the dying campfire. Zhantse went stiffly to one knee before her, with Miune on one side and Shima on the other. The shaman laid his burden in her lap.

"It's for you to open it—*Dragonlord*," Zhantse said, hesitating only slightly over the unfamiliar northern word. At his gesture, Shima laid more fuel upon the fire. The young flames stretched up like scarlet towers reaching for the heavens.

Maurynna stared down at the lumpy, cloth-wrapped bundle; she rested one hand upon it to keep it from sliding off. It was perhaps the length of her arm, slightly wider at one end than the other, and narrow. Grass string crisscrossed the length of it. It shifted under her fingers; she heard the faint scrape of metal against metal.

Feeling vaguely as if she commited some kind of sacrilege, Maurynna pulled her small belt dagger from its sheath and slid it beneath the bindings. They parted easily before the sharp blade. She ran her fingers over the rough brown cloth; then, taking a deep breath, she eased the cloth back from the wider end of the bundle.

A thick, round disk of iron appeared. *What?* she asked herself, and answered it in the next heartbeat: *a sword pommel.* That it was still unrusted told her much about how dry this desert was.

But—a sword? She was no warrior. Morlen had chosen wrong; surely Linden was the one to wield this.

Yet the burden had been laid upon her. Pressing her lips together in determination, she wrenched the covering back, revealing the hilt with its wrappings of leather so dry it disintegrated as the coarse fabric brushed against it.

The wrapping caught on something entwined around the quillons. Maurynna freed it and found herself staring at what seemed to be a large, incomplete ring of black metal. The ends, she saw as she teased it loose of sword and cloth, were worked. A tiny glint of red winked at her.

Her breath caught in her chest and she couldn't speak. She scrubbed at one of the ends with the cloth; she knew now what she held. Her eyes stung with tears.

Gradually a silver dragon's head revealed itself from the tarnish of centuries. One of the ruby eyes was missing, but the other shone bravely in the leaping firelight.

The tears slid down her cheeks. From all she'd heard, the humansoul Dharm had planned to renounce his hold on life, leaving the dragonsoul Varleran to live as a truedragon. So why had Varleran carried these bits of Dharm's life with him? Truedragons didn't cling to possessions as humankind did. Had Dharm changed his mind? Or was the releasing of a soul for her kind not like the shutting of a door, quick and final, but instead a slow drifting away, as one might slip into dreaming?

She traced the curve of the torc with her fingers. This had been old when Linden was born more than six hundred years ago. Compared to her paltry two decades of life it seemed as ancient as the earth.

She held it up before her face and studied it. What stories would it tell her if it could speak? What hopes and dreams died so long ago? She could almost feel the echo of them.

Shima stirred, laid one slender log in the fire, then another; the flames leaped higher. Neither he nor the others asked questions, demanded answers. The vast stillness of their land echoed in them. She was grateful for it.

But *she* had a question. But not—her courage failed her—quite yet.

There was a thing that must be done now, and no way to do it, save to pass through the other side of hell. She wondered if the Tah'nehsieh would accept it. Maurynna drew herself up straighter. The warmth of the fire dried her tears.

"This was Dharm Varleran's—" Her mind could not find the Jehangli word for "torc," if indeed there even was one, "badge of rank."

"Ah. So that's what it is. Miune and I had always wondered," the shaman said mildly. He and the youngling dragon nodded at each other as if to say *Now we know.*

Would they take her next words so calmly? "It must go back to Dragonskeep."

Of course, Miune said.

Zhantse nodded. "I understand."

She must have gaped at him, for he continued, "This bundle has never been one of the holy things of my people, but a charge laid upon us. We have merely been its guardians until the proper time."

The proper time. No more hiding, then.

She swallowed hard. "Zhantse—just what is it that I must do?"

It was midnight in the Iron Temple. Hodai went to Pah-Ko's chamber to see if this night, perhaps, the *nira* felt well enough to go to the ceremony.

But Pah-Ko slept, and Hodai was unwilling to disturb him. He patted the blankets into place and slipped out of the room.

As he entered the *nira*'s private balcony, a figure detached itself from the shadows. It was Haoro.

Hodai grunted in terror. What did the priest want now? He fell back a step, his hands raised as if to fend off a blow.

"Why so afraid, little Hodai? I come to tell you that this night, I shall keep my part of our bargain. After the midnight ceremony, come to the north tower, for tonight I give you your voice."

Stunned, Hodai stood transfixed as Haoro swept past him. A faint echo of a beautiful voice chimed in his ears.

It was to be his at long last. . . .

Hodai could barely wait for the ceremony to be over.

Instead of answering immediately, Zhantse stood up and tossed a handful of what looked like rough pebbles into the fire. They sizzled and flared, hissing as they burned.

Some sort of tree gum, Maurynna thought, *like myrrh.*

As Zhantse chanted softly, thin white smoke rose and hovered above the fire. Maurynna's nose twitched at the spicy, mysterious scent, and a chill ran down her spine as she watched the smoke collect.

It's as if there's a giant, invisible hand catching it.

Zhantse passed his hands through the smoke, gesturing first east, then west, then south, and then, last of all, north. At each motion a fragrant tendril broke off from the main column of smoke and floated horizontally in the indicated direction. Maurynna watched in astonishment and awe as one passed directly over her head. She tilted her head back to follow it, giving up only when she was in danger of falling over backward.

She turned back to Zhantse. "Wh—what . . . ?"

"To drive away any evil spirits that might bring ill luck," the shaman said, "did they know our plans."

Urk. Now *there* was a comforting thought.

Zhantse remained standing and stared beyond her into the darkness, his face grim. Maurynna resisted the impulse to look over her shoulder; there might be something there. The firelight lit the shaman's face from below, turning the kindly, seamed dark face into a terrifying mask.

Then the mask moved. "For many, many lives—almost since the beginning of the reign of the Phoenix—there have been a few brave men who have slipped into the slave camp below the Iron Temple. At the risk of their lives, they have mapped the caverns and tunnels beneath the Mountain of Nightmares, seeking the anchor of the power that kept the Phoenix imprisoned, gathering that information piece by painful piece. Many became lost and died slow deaths in the darkness under the mountain, or died under the hands of the guards before they could escape with what they knew.

"But enough lived. Enough that we know the way to the cavern where the dragon lies."

He fell silent. A little voice in the back of Maurynna's mind whimpered, *Why do I get the feeling that finding Pirakos will be the easy part?* She chewed her lower lip.

A moment later she realized one hand was clenched upon the hilt of the sword. She forced her fingers open and turned her hand palm up; her palm was smeared with something that, for one heart-stopping moment, she thought was blood.

But it was merely a trick of the firelight and the dust from the rotting leather that bound the hilt. She'd seen its like on old books in her Aunt Maleid's library. Still, she found it disquieting and rubbed her hand clean on her breeches.

"And once I find Pirakos?" she asked.

"Then you use the key that you hold. For the one you seek is chained by a magic that will fall to the touch of cold iron wielded by more magic."

Maurynna tilted her head. "That doesn't sound too impossible. So that means there's a reef in these waters somewhere, doesn't it?"

A look of bafflement replaced the masklike expression. Shima spoke rapidly in their own tongue.

"Ah!" Zhantse said, smiling. "We say 'a boulder in the path.' " He drew a deep breath, serious once more. "The 'reef,' as you say, is that in order to free Pirakos, you must get close to him. Close enough that, once the final chain is loosed, he will be able to reach you."

Oh, gods, why does Zhantse sound so grim . . . ?

"And that is where the danger lies. For Pirakos is mad, Maurynna Kyrissaean, mad with hate and rage and pain and bloodlust, all focused upon those who walk on two feet."

As she was forced to do. Damn Kyrissaean, anyway.

Maurynna wanted to kick something in frustration, or weep in terror. Instead she just asked, "Must I go alone?"

"No," Zhantse said. "We could not ask that of you."

Thank the gods, she thought, nearly undone with relief. *So Raven and I will go on to—*

The shaman said, "You'll leave at the dark of the moon; that will give you a few more days to rest—and, since he's memorized the route in a chant, Shima will go with you."

"Where were you?" Raven demanded when Maurynna finally got back to Lark's house. He looked down at her from the opening to the upper floor. "You missed the dancing. The Llysanyins finally got to perform."

"Talking with Zhantse, Shima, and Miune," she answered wearily. She shifted the bundle she carried to the crook of her other arm and started up the ladder.

"What's—"

"Raven—please. I'm tired. I want to go to bed. I'll tell you in the morning."

For a moment she thought he would block her way until she told him. But he retreated; she heard his feet scuffle along the dried clay of the floor. When she got to the top of the ladder, she was alone. Trying not to think of all she'd learned that night, she went to her own sleeping pallet behind a screen of plaited reeds, slipped the sword and the torc under her pillow, then undressed and got into bed.

She pulled the blankets up to her chin and lay staring up into the darkness. Bad as this night had been, worse was yet to come. Wait until they told Raven he couldn't go with her. . . . She groaned and rolled over.

* * *

Hodai knelt on the floor, the blindfold Haoro insisted he put on before coming into the room bound tightly around his head. He clenched his hands together so hard they hurt. As unobtrusively as possible, he turned his head from side to side, trying to make sense of the faint sounds he heard.

There were more people in the room than he and the priest, he was certain of it; but how many there might be, he had no idea. Although it frightened him to sit in darkness while all those around him walked in the light, he could understand the why of it. This was forbidden magic, he suspected, and the less he knew of who took part, the safer they were. Not everyone had a powerful uncle to protect them.

But what was that scuffling noise, those grunts? Forgetting himself, Hodai turned his head toward the sounds. Someone cuffed him sharply on the ear. Hodai shrank away from any more blows.

Then came words that drove all else from his mind: "We're ready, Holy One," a soft voice said.

He heard the fizzling sound of incense catching, and a few moments later the sweet scent tickled his nose. Then a voice started a soft chanting; other voices joined it, and Hodai felt a kind of pressure building in the air. It pressed on him, dug tendrils into him the way ivy dug into a stone wall. It sang inside him until his head spun, and he was afraid he would be sick.

Dizzy now, he dimly heard a final voice join the chorus—Haoro's, the only one he recognized. It reverberated in his head, on and on, until it seemed he'd knelt here forever.

Then he became aware of a pressure building in his chest, rising up and up to his throat, and catching there, as if every song he'd ever heard dwelled within and now tried to escape. He held his breath in wonder and excitement.

Yet the songs were trapped as they always were; he wanted to scream his frustration. Then came a muffled whimper and a soft thump, and then a finger traced a line across Hodai's throat with something hot and wet.

And then it happened. The lock on his throat was gone! Hodai opened his mouth and sang a high, clear note.

There were murmurs of astonishment, and a hand clapped over his mouth, but gently. Haoro laughed softly and said, "Not so loud, little Oracle! Someone might hear. Now sit there, and leave the blindfold until I tell you otherwise."

Hodai nodded, waiting in a fever of excitement. Mysterious noises surrounded him; then he sensed that the room was empty. He raised his hands to the blindfold, but waited.

"You may remove it now, Hodai."

He yanked it off. Haoro stood before him; the priest looked tired, but pleased. "Is it well, little Oracle?"

Hodai took a deep breath. "It's well."

The voice that belled forth from his lips nearly made him swoon with its beauty. He wanted to burst into song.

Haoro must have guessed, for he said, "I think the first thing you sing should be the Song, Hodai, to thank the Phoenix for this gift. But if you sing with the others, there will be awkward questions asked; let me first set the stage for a 'miracle' by the Phoenix.

"It's nearly dawn. If you hurry, you can get to the eastern edge of the plateau before the phoenix of the sun rises. Sing there, Hodai, in the wilderness, and only there until I give you leave, do you understand?"

"Yes," Hodai breathed.

"Go then, little Oracle, and remember—this voice is yours for as long as the Phoenix shall live."

Hodai threw himself upon Haoro's sandaled feet and kissed them. Then he sprang up and ran for the door, wild with joy.

This day he would greet the Phoenix.

After Hodai left, Haoro wearily ran his hands over his face. One last thing to do in what was left of this night of nights. He would have a while, he knew, before Hodai returned, but he wanted this done with.

Despite the fatigue weighing him down, Haoro walked

swiftly through the passageways of the temple until he came to the door that led to the *nira*'s chambers. The guard before the door was one loyal to Haoro; he looked straight ahead as the priest slipped into the room.

Once inside the door, Haoro paused to listen. Soft snores came from the other room. Satisfied, Haoro went to the little cabinet that held teas and other such things. Opening it, he searched until he found the laquered canister of ground rice flour; Pah-Ko, he knew, was fond of rice gruel when he couldn't sleep.

Haoro reached into his sleeve and withdrew a folded packet of rice paper. Opening in, he poured the contents into the rice flour. As he'd thought, they were much the same color as the rice. One would have to have a sharp eye indeed to see the addition.

Satisfied, Haoro returned the now-empty packet to the pocket in his sleeve, and left. Now it was only a matter of time.

Forty-nine

Lightheaded with excitement, Hodai watched the eastern sky change color, glowing gold and apricot. Any moment now, the rim of the sun would show above the distant horizon.

Wait, wait—just a little more. . . . He saw it!

In the instant between the opening of his mouth and the first notes of the morning hymn, a whirling disorientation he recognized washed over him, the herald of a prophecy.

Then, before he could stop it, his new voice poured forth, and the world snapped back into focus. Too overjoyed to wonder what he might have Seen, Hodai poured his soul into the paean to the sun.

And when he sang the first notes of the Song, he knew that this was what the Phoenix sounded like, and tears of happiness rained down his cheeks. He was complete now.

The argument had gone on for far too long. Shima's head was aching, and the northerner showed no signs of giving up.

"Who the hell are you to tell me I can't go?" Raven bellowed. "Of course I'm going. Maurynna needs me."

He did not, Shima noticed, look at Maurynna as he said that.

Shima sighed. It would be very long indeed before he forgave Zhantse. This hothead might have accepted the shaman's word; he certainly wasn't going to take the word of a potential rival. Groundless as it was, Shima saw suspicion in the bright blue eyes. Mustering what was left of his patience, he said yet again, "I told you: the skin dye won't work on you. Not with those freckles; they'd show through. No Jehangli or Tah'nehsieh has them."

He silently blessed all the spirits that he had not inherited his mother's fair northern skin—and freckles— else they would truly have a problem. "Besides," he continued, "Zhantse has nothing to turn that red, curly hair of yours straight and pure black, either. You would look *wrong*, Raven. Wrong enough to bring a guard over, and all he'd need then is one look at your northern eyes. We'd be captured before we could begin."

"Rynna has 'northern eyes' as well," Raven snapped.

Shima waited for Maurynna to speak, but she just sat, staring at the floor as if the answers to all her questions might be found there.

"True, but her hair is black and straight enough—and long enough—to pass for a Tah'nehsieh. And she has no freckles to betray her beneath the skin dye. A quick glimpse of *her* won't attract closer attention from a guard. All she has to do is keep her gaze lowered."

"He's right," his mother said. "Believe me, Raven. I've tried the dye and it doesn't work." She held out a curl of her fiery red hair, and said with mock sadness, "I never even tried to disguise *this*. Miracles are for the gods."

She looked so woebegone that even Raven smiled, albeit reluctantly. But it was clear he was still not convinced. Shima saw fury smoldering unabated in the other man's eyes.

Before Raven could erupt again in anger, a voice from the other side of the blanketed doorway of the outer room called, *"Hoh neshla,"* the traditional Tah'nehsieh greeting at the door of a dwelling.

Zhantse! Shima's shoulders sagged in relief. Thank the Spirits that the Seer was here. Maybe he could talk some sense into this stubborn northerner. Otherwise this argument would chase its own tail into tomorrow. And the day after that, and the day after *that.* ...

"Enter, Grandfather," his mother called in Tah'nehsieh and went to greet him.

Maurynna, who until now had sat quietly to one side, cocked her head at Shima. "Zhantse?"

"Yes."

She nodded and fell silent again. Shima wondered again at her silence. He'd not thought her one to sit passively by while others decided her fate. Indeed, if—as had been revealed in conversation with his mother earlier this morning—she'd once been the captain of her own ship, she was used to making decisions and taking charge of her own life. Yet here she sat quietly, arms clasping her folded legs, though at times during the morning it looked as if she struggled with something, some idea or decision.

What could it be? Before he could chase down the possibilities coursing through his mind like so many rabbits, Zhantse entered the inner room. Shima readied a folded rug for his master to sit upon; stone floors were hard. He heard his mother fetching a beaker of cool water from the water jar for their new guest. He held himself ready to translate; Zhantse had precious little Yerrin, and Raven had barely more Jehangli.

The Seer sat down with a nod of thanks. But before

Zhantse could speak, Raven snapped at him, "Is this your idea, that I stay behind?"

Both Shima and his mother gasped. This was rudeness, speaking so to an elder and speaking first. Shima reluctantly translated the ill-mannered words as if doing so tainted him with Raven's discourtesy. Zhantse listened and studied the younger man challenging him.

It was Raven who looked away.

Only then did Zhantse speak. "Yes," was all he said, his voice mild as ever. "I Saw it. I Saw that this mission will fail if you're with Maurynna. You will be discovered, and you will die, as will Maurynna and Shima. Without you they have a chance." He spoke Jehangli, Shima noted, so that Maurynna could understand.

His mother caught her breath and left the room.

Shima translated for Raven. But his mind raced over Zhantse's words.

Without you, they have a chance. Not *Without you, they will succeed.*

That the future was veiled from Zhantse's Sight did not bode well. Shima felt the first clutch of fear he'd known since he'd heard that the one from the prophecy was coming.

Yet if the land was to survive, the risk must be taken.

He prayed. *Shashannu, Lady of the Sky, help us.*

A torrent of objections spilled from Raven's lips. There was no time for translation. Not that Zhantse seemed to expect it; again he sat, letting the younger man's anger flow over and around him, never allowing it to ruffle him.

Yet there was another it touched. For now Maurynna roused herself from her earlier withdrawal; her odd-colored eyes blazed. Shima braced himself for a battle worthy of the gods. Even Zhantse betrayed a flicker of nervousness.

But her voice was quiet—dangerously quiet—when she spoke. "Raven." That was all; the single word, no louder than a sparrow's wings in the dawn.

Still, it stopped Raven. He stood, watching her, fists clenched tight against his sides.

"Don't make me say it, Raven," Maurynna said. She might have been discussing the weather.

Say what? Shima wondered.

Raven tossed his head back. Impossibly, the knuckles of the clenched fists turned whiter. "It's the only way I won't, Rynna," he said. Then, challenging: "Are you certain you want to?"

Say what? Shima wanted to scream.

"No, I don't. You know that." The words were soft. She looked as if they hurt her.

"Then I'm going."

Sorrow replaced pain, and in its turn gave way to stern majesty. Shima held his breath.

"You're not going, Raven." A catch of breath, then: "Dragonlord's orders."

The words meant little to Shima but clearly much to Raven. For the other man's face went deadly pale; he shook as if with fever. But when he spoke, his voice matched Maurynna's note for calm note.

"As you wish . . . Dragonlord." And Raven walked out, a terrible calmness wrapped around him.

Maurynna put her head down on her knees and cried.

It was not until the evening that Shima was able to speak to his mother without one of the northerners, his sister, or a member of the tribe present. He found her in the store-room, looking over her supplies of dyed grass and reed lacing for making baskets. At least, that was what she seemed to be doing. But by the look on her face, Lark's mind was miles upon miles away. It wasn't until he cleared his throat a second time that she came back to herself.

"Oh—I'm sorry, Shima. I—I didn't notice you. I was . . . busy deciding what colors to use for a new basket." But it was not indecision that filled her eyes.

"You were worrying," Shima said bluntly. "Because of what Zhantse said this morning."

"Yes," she admitted, and looked away. "I'm—" She shook her head and wouldn't finish.

But Shima knew what she refused to say. "Afraid? So am I. But it must be done. You know this."

"I know. But I'm a mother, and you a child of my body. It's my right and my burden to fear for my children." Once more she met his gaze; her eyes begged, *Let us speak of other things.*

Shima was only too happy to agree. "What Maurynna said to Raven—'Dragonlord's orders'— Is she one who must be obeyed as the Jehangli obey their emperor?"

A smile twitched at his mother's fear-thinned lips. "Not quite the same; I've never heard of a Dragonlord ordering anyone to death for not obeying—but I've also never heard of anyone ever disobeying, either." The smile broke through. "I think folk consider it most . . . unwise to anger someone who can turn into a dragon—and sit on you."

"Ouch," said Shima, unable to repress a smile of his own at a sudden memory. He'd *had* a dragon sit on him. Luckily, never very hard.

"Besides, like bards and Healers, Dragonlords are considered the favored of the gods in the Five Kingdoms. And only a fool annoys the gods."

"So people obey," Shima said, thoughtfully.

"The wise do," said Lark. "Remember that."

"Where are you going, Maurynna?" Shima asked from behind her.

Maurynna stopped and turned, shading her eyes with a hand. Shima was striding down the steep trail that led to the little cliff house that was Zhantse's. Today he wore sandals of woven grass that slapped against the rock, raising a little puff of red dust with each step.

She waited for him. "Down to the pasture to visit Boreal. Would you like to come?" she asked, knowing the answer.

His face lit with delight and he rushed down the last quarter of the trail; she laughed and set off again.

After a time, Shima asked, "Where is Raven this morning?"

"Riding, I suspect. It's what he does when he's upset. It

will . . . It will take him a little while to accept that he has to stay behind."

"So he's sulking?"

"Not really, he's just . . . You have to understand—we've always gotten in and out of trouble together," Maurynna said plaintively. "We've always looked out for each other."

"Ah. And now that you're getting into the worst trouble of your life—" Shima let the sentence hang.

"Just so. Raven can't be there, and I know it hurts him. Even after this is over, he won't be the one I count on, because . . ."

Because everything in my life turned topsy-turvy a few months ago. And through no fault of his own, Raven's suddenly standing at the door looking in—and not just with me, but also with his own family.

Not that Raven was making life any easier for anyone. Maurynna sighed, reflected she'd done quite a lot of that lately, and caught herself sighing again. "Oh, blast it all," she snapped at no one.

Shima wisely said nothing.

Shei-Luin left the audience hall after hearing the day's latest petitions and giving orders for the defense of Jehanglan against the invading Zharmatians. Minister Musahi walked at her side; Murohshei, as always, was one step behind.

"Arrangements must be made to send the heirs to the mountains to avoid the fevers," Musahi said.

Shei-Luin frowned. "I would keep them with me a while longer," she said, "for the people to see Xahnu, their emperor-to-be. But make the arrangements, Minister, for them to travel there from Rivasha. They can go after Xahnu and I make sacrifices to the Phoenix in the temple there."

Musahi bowed. "As you wish, Phoenix Lady," he said, and left her.

When they were alone, Shei-Luin said to Murohshei, "There is yet one more thing I must do to make all safe for my sons. Escort me to the chamber of Lord Jhanun's niece, Nama."

"As you wish, Flower of the West. This way."

As they entered the little meadow with its spring-fed pool, Maurynna could see only three Llysanyins standing hands above the tribe's smaller horses. It was as she'd guessed; Raven had taken Stormwind out. She couldn't blame him, she thought, as she stuck two fingers in the corners of her mouth and whistled. During his ride, Raven would come to see the sense of their objections. At least, she hoped he would. He *could* be sensible at times.

As the shrill blast of the whistle echoed off the valley walls, Boreal shouldered his way through the little herd; the Two Poor Bastards followed. Once clear, Boreal tossed his head and kicked up his heels like a yearling colt as he ran, finishing by prancing to a halt before her.

Maurynna rubbed his nose. "Silly," she said affectionately, her good humor restored. Beyond him she could see Trissin and Jhem coming up.

Boreal snorted, the noise almost covering up the small, wistful sound behind her. Maurynna looked over her shoulder.

Shima was staring at Boreal like a hungry little boy at a tray of sweets that he wasn't allowed to touch. A thought came to her.

"We'll have to ride to Mount Kajhenral, won't we?" she asked.

A nod was all the answer Shima spared her.

"And if— and *when* we make our escape, we'll have to ride like hell to get away, yes?"

Shima came back to himself at that. "Spirits, yes! They'll try to ride us down."

"They won't ride Boreal down. But your horse will never be able to keep up with him," Maurynna said flatly.

Shima drew himself up. "Pirii will do what she can," he said. But she heard the faint note of defeat.

This is probably useless, Maurynna thought as she

looked once more at the Llysanyins. *If Linden couldn't convince them before . . . Ah, well, they won't trample me for asking.*

Yet before she said a word, Trissin nipped at his brother to chase him away, and strode up to Shima. The iron grey Llysanyin rested his nose on the man's shoulder. When Shima—whose eyes were huge—didn't move, Trissin nudged him sharply and swung broadside to him.

"Mount up," an astonished Maurynna said to the stunned Shima. "You've been chosen."

"The child you bear is a danger to mine," Shei-Luin said. "Whose is it?"

"I never knew his name. He wouldn't tell me, so that I couldn't curse him and his ancestors." The pale, bloated face turned to her, eyes red from crying.

Nama was oddly calm; surely she must know why Shei-Luin was here, and what it meant. Calm—or too exhausted to care.

Nama pushed herself up from the bed and staggered to her feet. Her swollen belly dragged at her; she shuffled across the floor to stand face-to-face with Shei-Luin. Her lips pulled back in a terrible parody of a smile.

At last, Shei-Luin, thought with contempt, the rabbit stands up for herself. But she suppressed a shiver. For an instant, with her red-rimmed, bloodshot eyes and grimace, Nama looked like one of the demon masks actors wore onstage.

The burning eyes fixed on Shei-Luin. Said Nama, "I don't know who he was, or where he came from. All I know is that he looked like Xiane, and that was why my uncle had him brought to the imperial city—so he could get me with child."

The voice, harsh as a crow's with weeping, rose to a shriek with the next words. "He raped me—again and again and again! He would tell me he was sorry—hah!—then force himself on me. For moons it went on, no matter how I begged, no matter how I fought, until I was pregnant.

Only then did it end!" There was no longer any trace of the pretty young girl in the contorted face.

Nama turned sharply, nearly falling. She showed none of the heavy grace common with pregnant women; it was as if she hated the child within her so much that she could reach no compromise with what it did to her body. She pointed at her maid huddled at the foot of the bed, her finger stabbing the air. "And she helped! When I fought too hard, she held my hands down! Always she watched me so that I might not kill myself to escape my torment and my shame."

The maid cowered from that accusing finger. Apologies and pleas for mercy poured from her lips, a tangled jumble of words that made no sense.

Shei-Luin swallowed hard to keep from vomiting. This was not what she had expected. She had thought to confront another player for the throne. Instead, she found a victim.

It was the sight of Yesuin and me together that gave Jhanun the idea for this atrocity, she thought. *I will never be able to remember the joy I had with Yesuin without remembering what this poor child went through.* And she would never see Yesuin again to forge new memories.

Jhanun would pay; Shei-Luin vowed that. But there was justice that could be dealt out now.

"Do you wish mercy for this woman?" Shei-Luin asked.

Nama looked over her shoulder. "Are you mad? No! I don't! Give me a knife, and I will cut Zuia's throat myself!"

"Cutting her throat would be merciful," Shei-Luin pointed out. To Murohshei she said, "Call in two guards. Tell them to take this woman to the executioner. She is to die the death of a thousand cuts."

Murohshei bowed and left the room.

The maid screamed and threw herself at Shei-Luin's feet. "Mercy, have mercy upon me, lady!"

"Why?" Shei-Luin asked coldly. "You, a woman, aided in the rape of another woman. You had no mercy then."

The maid wailed in terror.

Two of the women guards of the harem entered. Shei-

Luin stepped aside, glancing at the guards' faces. One look at their hard expressions as they each seized an arm told her that Murohshei had informed them of Zuia's crime. Good; there would be no taking of bribes to look the other way while the maid escaped. It had happened, she knew. It would not this time.

The hulking women picked the maid up from the floor. Zuia screamed and fought like a madwoman. She was a strong woman, but the guards were stronger, and trained warriors. They dragged the maid to the door.

"Wait," Shei-Luin said.

The guards stopped. They frowned, no doubt fearing a reprieve for the prisoner, a mercy they did not agree with. Zuia fell silent, her eyes filled with hope.

"When it's over," Shei-Luin said, "her head is to be struck from her body and nailed to the city gate as is the custom. Throw her body to the dogs."

Zuia fainted. The guards smiled grimly; their eyes said, *It is no more than she deserves.*

"We hear and obey, Empress," they said. There was a respect in the words Shei-Luin had never heard before.

After Murohshei closed the door once more, Shei-Luin turned back to Nama.

"Thank you," the girl said.

Shei-Luin nodded. "Where's the man who did this to you?"

"I know not. Once it was certain I was with child, I never saw him again."

"Lady," Murohshei interrupted, "I remember some moons back, there was talk among the lower servants that a body had been found in the river. There was no head, and it was the body of a young man. They had heard it from the farmers who brought the vegetables."

"He was young," Nama said. "Younger than Xiane. The head will never be found. At least *he* is dead." Her fingers dug into her belly as if to rip the infant from her womb. "Must I bear this child?" Her gaze challenged Shei-Luin.

"You cannot," Shei-Luin said as gently as she could. "You know why."

Nama turned away a little. "Yes. Even if it was killed as it came from my womb, there's the chance that one day a pretender would come, claiming to be that child—Xiane's child—who was saved, and another infant killed in his stead."

Silence filled the air between them. At last Shei-Luin said, "I'm sorry." And she was. The girl deserved better, and she could not give it to her. Not when it meant danger to Xahnu and Xu someday.

Nama nodded, then drew herself up to stand as proudly as she could. "I would end my shame," she announced. Only a glimmering of tears betrayed her fear. They did not fall.

I was wrong. This is not a rabbit. This is an eagle. "I will help you."

"How?" whispered Nama.

"Poppy juice. You shall sleep, and . . . never wake."

Relief set free the tears that fear could not. "Thank you," the girl said. "That is a gentle death. And after . . . ?"

"I will order your ashes set in the altar of the Phoenix. The priests will burn incense to your memory every day, and I will burn it myself each year upon this day for as long as I live. I promise you that."

"You're generous, Empress. Again, I thank you." She smiled a little.

"You're brave, Nama, and I had thought you a coward. I was wrong." With that, she surprised Nama—and herself—by bowing to the girl.

Nama returned the bow as best she could. "Please—let it be soon. If I have too much time to think . . ."

"I understand." Shei-Luin nodded at Murohshei. He bowed to both of them, and left. When they were alone, Shei-Luin took Nama's hand and led her back to her bed. "Sit down," she directed.

The girl obeyed. Shei-Luin placed a chair opposite her and sat. They waited.

Soon Murohshei returned, a flask of the best rice wine in one hand. "It's already mixed," he said softly. In the other hand he held a large goblet. It was gold and studded with pearls—one of Xiane's. Shei-Luin nodded her approval. Murohshei poured out the wine and set the flask aside.

After catching Shei-Luin's eye, he bore the goblet to the bed. Going down upon both knees, he raised it above his lowered head and presented it to Nama. She took it; he bowed, touching his forehead to the floor as if she were the empress.

Shei-Luin saw a spark of color bloom in the pale cheeks at the honor. Nama licked her lips; she stared at the death she held in her hands for a long moment. "Let my uncle know that I did this willingly to erase the shame he laid upon me." Then she raised the goblet to her lips and drank.

"Eh!" she said, grimacing. Then she smiled a little, explaining sheepishly, "It makes the wine too thick and sweet," and gulped the rest down.

After a time, Nama said, "My head is heavy." Her eyelids drooped.

"Lie down," Shei-Luin bade her in the same gentle voice she used for Xahnu or Xu.

When she and Murohshei had made the girl comfortable, Nama, her voice barely above a whisper, asked, "Will you stay with me? Please?" and held out her hand.

Shei-Luin took the cold, trembling hand in both of her own. "I will."

"Thank you." Nama's eyes closed.

A little while later, her lips curved in a smile. "No one can ever hurt me again." The words were slurred and her eyes didn't open.

"No," Shei-Luin answered. "Never again."

The smile remained. Shei-Luin noticed that the girl's breathing was slow and shallow. She felt for a pulse; it was weak, but steady. Shei-Luin stroked the small hand.

There was nothing to do now but wait.

*   *   *

The explosion that Maurynna half feared never came.

She came upon Raven some time later, sitting on the wall that encircled the dancing floor, a flock of children squatting on their heels around him as he cleaned Stormwind's tack.

At hearing that one of the Two Poor Bastards had agreed to bear a truehuman, all he said was, "A pity we lost their saddles. Nothing the tribe has will fit Trissin," and went back to his task.

Maurynna threw her hands into the air and left him sitting on the wall, the children laughing and handing him things as he pointed to them and tried to name them in stumbling Tah'nehsieh.

But the moment she was out of his sight, she leaned against the nearest wall. "Thank the gods," she muttered under her breath. One less thing to worry about.

She didn't know just when it happened. One moment Shei-Luin heard the shallow breathing. The next, it had stopped. Once again she felt for a pulse. Nothing. Nama *nohsa* Jhi, last concubine of Xiane Ma Jhi, late emperor of Jehanglan and Phoenix Lord of the Skies, was gone.

Shei-Luin tucked the limp hand she had held for so long under the blanket covering Nama. "May you find happiness where you've gone, poor child," she said. "I will send your uncle after you to be your slave." She stood up, stiff after sitting for so long.

To Murohshei, she said, "Send for her women to wash her and prepare her body. When she's ready, have the eunuchs carry her to the main audience hall so that the chief ministers may witness that Nama is dead and her child with her. Let them set their thumbprints to that.

"And when that is done, bid the priests come, and tell them her ashes are to be interred in the temple. She's to be given the honors of a *noh*. She's to have a shroud of the imperial golden silk, just as . . . just as my sister did."

Her voice almost broke then. Had things been different, could she have been friends with Nama?

She had no time to dwell on might-have-beens. She was the empress of Jehanglan, and there was much she must do.

And the first was to issue a proclamation for the death of Lord Jhanun as a traitor.

Trissin stood with legs braced as Raven and Shima clambered over him. He snorted from time to time, and his skin twitched as the two young men worked over him with a blanket and a long length of grass twine as they measured around his broad barrel, but otherwise the stallion was as steady as stone.

"Sorry, boy," Raven said after one particularly violent twitch. "Didn't mean to tickle you."

"Hunhh," Trissin rumbled deep in his chest. "Hunnhhh."

Shima looked startled. From her patch of shade, Maurynna said, "I've heard Shan make that sound, as well. And I swear he 'chuckled' once. Somehow, you just don't expect a horse to answer you like that. At least, I don't." She grinned. "But then, I'm a sailor, not a horsewoman."

"No," said Shima. "You don't expect it—not quite like that." He eyed his new mount with, Maurynna thought, both pride and trepidation.

"Have you thought of a name for him yet?" she asked.

"What do you mean? Trissin is his name, yes?"

"That's just his pasture name," said Raven. "The master of the stables at Dragonskeep told me that they're given those so that the grooms don't have to keep saying things like 'the sorrel mare with the white sock on her near foreleg and the blaze' or 'the bay stallion with the snippet on his nose.' Gets cumbersome. Their person picks a name for them."

"Sometimes," Maurynna said wryly, remembering the naming of Boreal. "If they don't like it, they won't answer to it. Be prepared to haggle."

Trissin nodded, sending his heavy mane flying.

Shima's eyes were huge now. Maurynna almost burst out

laughing, the look in them was so easy to read: *What have I gotten myself into?*

Poor Shima, she thought, *but like swords, most things do have two edges.* She hid a smile behind her hand. Then, "Name him," she ordered.

"Hm." Shima pinched his lower lip between thumb and forefinger. "What . . ." He reached out, ran his fingers lightly along the stallion's powerful neck, then held out his hand. Trissin buried his nose in the cupped hand and exhaled. They stood so for a long moment.

"Je'nihahn." The word came out suddenly.

Trissin tilted his head in question.

" 'Hahn' is 'west' in your tongue, isn't it?" Maurynna asked. "What does 'Je'nihahn' mean?"

" 'Wind-from-the-west,' " answered Shima. "West is lucky." His expression turned sheepish. "I was thinking of the names of your Llysanyins, you see, and . . . and that's what came into my head. So—will you accept it?" he said to Trissin.

Once again the big head nodded.

"Welcome, Je'nihahn," Maurynna said, and raised her hand in salute. Raven echoed words and gesture.

The stallion touched his nose to his person's shoulder. Shima threw his arms around the Llysanyin's neck and buried his face in the thick mane.

"Hunnh," rumbled Je'nihahn deep in his chest. "Hunnnnh."

Hodai looked up from the finches' cage to see Pah-Ko shifting restlessly in his chair. Ever since the news had come of the death of the emperor and the new empress's sacrilege in daring the Phoenix Throne, his master had been restless every night. He waited, knowing what was to come.

It did, a little while later. "Hodai, a bowl of hot rice wine, and another of rice gruel, please."

Forcing his fingers to say "Yes, master," instead of singing his pleasure to serve, Hodai trotted to the tea cabinet and withdrew what he needed.

When all was ready, he presented it to his master, and watched him eat and drink, dreaming of the day he could tell Pah-Ko his wonderful news.

Fifty

A cry of agony woke Hodai. Terrified, he ran into Pah-Ko's chamber, where he found the *nira* writhing on his bed, hands clamped to his belly.

Forgetting Haoro's injunction, Hodai cried, "Master! Master, what's wrong?"

Pah-Ko turned pain-maddened eyes upon him. "How—" he gasped.

The habit of obeying was too strong to break. "Haoro," whispered Hodai.

"Hao—Hodai, what have you done?" Pah-Ko cried. "Why did you do this to me?"

Hodai shook his head in fright and bewilderment. "But I—"

Pah-Ko thrashed on the bed, whimpering like an animal, unable to hear him.

"Didn't," Hodai said. Then, unable to stand his master's pain anymore, he fled.

Zhantse knew the instant his dreams turned from fantasies of his sleeping mind into Truth. For there before him lay the familiar swirling grey mist that he must pass through. He approached along the stone road that appeared before his feet. Soon he would pass through the mist and walk through the Place of Dreamings.

Suddenly he stopped and peered intently at the fog. Had

he truly just seen a dark shape through the mist? Yes; yes, he had. Not that that was so strange. He often found Pah-Ko or Ghulla waiting for him, though he'd not seen either of them lately.

But this figure, dimly seen through the fog, stumbled and doubled over as if in pain. For a moment Zhantse wondered if he had fallen back into ordinary dreaming. He paused, reaching out with his senses.

No, this was indeed a true Dreaming. Could it be some unfortunate that he saw, one who traveled here by mistake because of illness or injury? Such happened sometimes, he knew. He hurried forward to give what aid he could to the inadvertent Journeyer. Silken fingers of mist caressed his face and hands as he pushed through them.

But it was no stranger who stood before him. The hunched figure wore a robe that he knew well, scarlet with golden dragons and phoenixes embroidered upon the heavy silk. A face grey with pain lifted at his approach.

"Pah-Ko!" Zhantse cried. "What's wrong?" He caught the *nira* in his arms, supporting the priest when the man would have collapsed. His heart filled with dread. Adversary, this man had been, yet friend as well. Many claimed to seek the Truth. Pah-Ko was one who did. "Tell me what's wrong!"

"Poison," said the Jehangli priest, his voice a whisper of agony. "Tiger's whiskers."

"Who?" Zhantse demanded, sickened. This was the work of a sadist, not just a murderer. Ground tiger's whiskers didn't kill at once. A victim writhed in agony as the bits worked their way through the body like a thousand tiny knives. "And why?"

"Haoro wishes the feathered mantle," Pah-Ko gasped, clenching at his stomach. "It must have been him."

Zhantse was aghast. Haoro? *That* one upon the little Phoenix Throne? The land was doomed. "Surely the Phoenix would never choose—"

"The Phoenix has no voice," the *nira* said. Tears flowed

down his cheeks; clearly this pain broke him as the other, merely physical, could not.

Zhantse nearly brought a hand up to wipe them away, then remembered that in this realm, the tears were not real, but simply a manifestation of grief. Then the full meaning of Pah-Ko's words became clear. "Hodai . . . ?"

"Hodai is no longer my Oracle."

So the servant had died before the master. No wonder Pah-Ko wept; Zhantse knew he loved the boy as the grandson he would never have. "When did he die?"

A short bark of laughter, a terrible sound of pain and betrayal. "Hodai still lives. The desire for a voice was too much. He betrayed—" The tortured voice broke and Pah-Ko wept bitterly once more.

"The Phoenix itself told me to follow the Way," the *nira* whispered. "If I had lived, perhaps we could have convinced the emperor—did you know that he sent for Lord Kirano? Perhaps Kirano can convince—no, I forgot. Xiane Ma Jhi is dead."

"What?" Zhantse demanded, shocked. "When?"

But Pah-Ko was too far gone to answer. Instead, he said, "I always knew you kept a secret from me, my friend. Tell me, does it mean danger for my country?"

"No. Here—let me show you," Zhantse said. He wrapped an arm around Pah-Ko's shoulders, and concentrated.

In an instant they hovered above the Vale.

It stretched out below them, a valley shaped like a wide, shallow bowl, an emerald jewel glowing against the red earth, protected within a ring of mountains. At one end of the valley, one mountain rose higher than the others. Once a volcano, thousands of years before, its crown had collapsed, leaving a deep hole that was now a placid blue lake.

Trees of all ages lined the terraced slopes of the green valley; small figures moved among them, tending them. Their leaves rippled in a breeze that did not penetrate the Place of Dreams.

"It's beautiful," Pah-Ko breathed, his eyes wide, forgetting his pain at last. "What are the trees?"

"Mulberries," Zhantse said, "for the silkworms. Someday we'll have enough to trade."

Pah-Ko smiled weakly. "How do you get enough water?"

"The lake; it's never run dry," Zhantse said.

"Never?"

"Never."

Pah-Ko said, "There's a dragon hiding in that lake."

Cautious, Zhantse said only, "That's the old tale."

"And it's a true one, my friend. The dragon is in a sleep so deep, it is like unto death. That's why I can feel him, I who am at death's door." Pah-Ko slumped heavily against Zhantse's arm. "Lay me down, my friend. I can hold on no longer."

The Vale dissolved; they were back where they started. Zhantse did as he was bidden, and knelt by his friend's side. He held Pah-Ko's hands, wincing as the gnarled fingers clenched on his with each new spasm of agony. The air whistled harshly though the *nira*'s teeth as Pah-Ko awaited his release. Zhantse prayed to Shashannu, Lady of the Sky, that it came soon. Inured as Pah-Ko was to pain, this was a thing no being should have to endure.

The Lady heard. A short time later, the deep, gasping breaths turned shallow and Pah-Ko's eyes became vague and unfocused. Then, from one heartbeat to the next, the light went out of them.

For an instant longer, Zhantse held the twisted fingers, then laid them upon the still breast. He watched the color fade from the dream-form that once held Pah-Ko's spirit, leaving it as grey as the mists that surrounded the Place of Dreamings. Zhantse blinked as tears stung his eyes. When he looked again, Pah-Ko was gone.

The shaman rose. "I thank Shashannu that you were able to see the Vale, my friend. It was hard keeping such beauty from you. But alas! for your land and mine, Pah-Ko. Evil walks them, and yet more evil may follow!"

For they had run out of time. Shima and Maurynna must leave at once for the Valley of the Iron Temple.

Zhantse began the long journey back to his body.

* * *

Shima dropped the bundle of kindling by the clay oven near the door, and stretched. His sister, Keru, came out of the house, balancing a basket of spice grass leaves on her hip. Shima's stomach growled in anticipation. Baking day was always a good time to be home.

As Keru passed him, Shima lightly dug a knuckle into her head. "Bzzzzz," he said, imitating a rockbee.

Keru laughed and swatted at his hand. "Why couldn't I have had all sisters?" Her eternal complaint, and only rarely meant. She set her basket down by the kindling. Straightening, she began, "Nathua brought back dried persimmons from the Vale, and gave some to— What's wrong with Zhantse?" she finished sharply, looking beyond Shima's shoulder.

Shima spun around. One look told him something *was* wrong—very wrong. "What is—"

Zhantse cut him off. To Keru, he said, "Get Maurynna Kyrissaean. Now!"

Keru ran into the house.

A coldness born of fear fell over the little yard. "Master?" Shima whispered.

"My sister will be here shortly to dye Maurynna's skin. While she makes the Dragonlord ready, get food and water and anything else you need. You must leave as soon as possible."

For a moment Shima could only gape at the shaman. At last he managed to say, "But we were to wait for the dark of the moon!"

"There's no time. Pah-Ko is dead. So is the emperor." The shaman's voice was grey and flat.

Simple words, and full of ill-omen. Shima caught his breath as their full import struck him. "To whom does the feathered mantle fall?" he asked.

"Haoro," said Zhantse.

"Spirits help us," Shima said, fear threading its cold way down his spine. "I go." A moment later he was running along the dusty paths through the *mehanso*.

*   *   *

"Who are they?" Maurynna murmured to Lark as they watched the three women who had invaded Lark's home. Each had a wide-mouthed pot to which she added water drop by drop, stirring briskly after each addition.

"The older woman is Zhantse's sister, Chanajin. With her are her daughters Zelene and Yallasi."

The women paused in their work and smiled as Lark spoke to them in their own language. Maurynna nodded in return, assuming introductions had been made.

"And as for *what* they're doing," Lark went on, "they're preparing the dye for your skin."

Maurynna chewed her lip. Yes, she had been warned of this, but it was not supposed to happen for at least a hand of days yet. But Zhantse had had Lark roust her and Raven unceremoniously from their beds, and hurried off before Maurynna could wake up enough to ask any questions. Nor did she like the worried look in Lark's eyes, although the Yerrin woman spoke cheerfully enough.

Now Raven's voice drifted in through the window; he'd been chased outside earlier. He still sounded confused. Maurynna sympathized. But before she could ask Lark what in blazes was going on, the Tah'nehsieh women, finished with their preparations, descended upon her.

Moments later Maurynna found herself stripped to the waist, her hair hastily pinned on top of her head, bits of it coming down already, with her arms held out to the sides at shoulder height, enduring the cold touch of dye and early morning air as the three Tah'nehsieh women dabbed at her with rough bits of cloth, working the thick sludge into her skin.

I wish there was a fire in this room.

Goose bumps prickled along her skin and she shivered. Another strand of hair came loose; it fell into the stuff coating her shoulders. Despite the injunction against using any of her magic, Maurynna finally called up a heat spell. A very little one, she told herself. Hardly noticeable. It would do no good catch her death of cold, after all.

The spell helped—a little. *If only the dye weren't so thick and slimy as well as—Ugh!*

Chanajin swirled the disgusting stuff into Maurynna's right ear, working the daubing cloth into every nook and cranny. Maurynna grimaced. Next came her left ear. Zelene and Yallasi were finished with her torso and were each working down an arm. Maurynna's gaze met Lark's. The other woman smiled wryly in sympathy.

I can't complain they're not thorough, Maurynna told herself. *I just wi*—"What the—!" She grabbed the waist of her breeches just in time.

Chanajin tugged at the drawstring of her breeches again, and said something. When Maurynna wouldn't let go, the woman turned to Lark and began a vigorous complaint, waving the dye cloth as she spoke. Lark essayed a reply, and the flood of words and gestures began anew.

Suddenly Maurynna thought she understood, and was appalled. Did the woman truly think that she would wear one of the men's short kilts? Gods help her, not even the shortest of her nightgowns exposed so much leg!

When Lark looked at her and opened her mouth to speak, Maurynna interrupted with, "I know what you're going to say—and the answer is *no!* I, I—I won't."

Damn it all, she could feel her face burning. Maurynna was certain she was blushing furiously.

Lark laughed. "I told Chanajin that. But she says that if you're trying to pass for a Tah'nehsieh man—wait; I just had a thought."

She said something to Chanajin, who started to protest, then fell silent, frowning thoughtfully. Lark spoke again and pointed to Maurynna's breeches. Grumbling, Chanajin gave in; Maurynna could see it in the jut of her lower lip.

She nearly melted with relief. "What did you say to her?" she asked Lark.

"That you have the height of a man, and the free stride of a man, but that you most certainly do not have a man's legs." Lark grinned. "They'd give you away in an instant. I then pointed out that your breeches are similar to those worn by the Zharmatians, and that some Tah'nehsieh wear them, especially when riding long distances. And that's when most of us are captured, so many of the slaves wear them."

"Most of us"—she thinks of herself as one of this dark-haired, dark-skinned tribe. Strange words to be uttered so calmly by a woman whose fairness was alien to this land.

No, not so strange, Maurynna realized. *She's spent most of her life here, after all. And will I do the same someday, think of myself only as a Dragonlord rather than as a member of House Erdon? Will I forget who I was?*

Before she could be swept away by a flood of unformed doubts and fears, Lark went on, "You will, of course, have to change those stiff boots of yours for ours." Lark pulled up her long skirt enough to reveal a soft boot made of split leather, gartered to the knee with narrow strips of more leather. Gay-colored fringe ran down the sides.

As long as she could keep her breeches, Maurynna didn't care if she went barefoot, and said so fervently.

Lark chuckled. "Shima has an old pair he kept to use as a pattern. I'll get them and one of his *tevehs*"—Maurynna recognized the word for the kind of sleeveless tunic the Tah'nehsieh men wore—"for you to wear. And just to warn you, you'll have to stay like that a while longer for the dye to take. But in a little bit, one of the girls will bring in a hot infusion to wash that stuff off with; it will also set the dye."

With that warning, Lark disappeared. Zhantse's kinswomen sat with their backs against a wall. They had the look of people settling in for a long wait.

Maurynna gloomily increased the strength of the heat spell.

At last they were ready to go.

"It's late in the day to start a journey," Maurynna said quietly to Shima as she pulled Boreal's girth snug.

"Have we any choice?" he replied. "Look at Zhantse. I've never seen him like this."

Maurynna glanced over at the shaman. Zhantse paced back and forth, snapping at Lark and Keru as they packed food and skins of water into the saddlebags.

"Hurry! They must be away!" Zhantse urged over and over.

At last the bags were full; Lark and Keru each brought one to where the Llysanyins and their riders waited.

Without a word, Maurynna and Shima took them and tied them to the saddles. It was too hard to talk, Maurynna discovered.

"The—the scrips are packed inside," Lark said, her voice quivering. "You'll need them to carry the food once you leave the horses."

"Thank you, Mother," Shima managed to say at last. He caught his mother in a hug. "Stay well."

"Stay out of the way of soldiers," she retorted. "Both of you." Tears shone on her cheeks.

"You must go now," Zhantse said, a worried frown creasing his forehead. "Get as far as you can while the light lasts."

They nodded, and mounted. Maurynna looked around.

No Raven. She urged Boreal on; Shima quickly caught up with her. They turned again and again to wave until the others were out of sight.

"Now where to?" Maurynna said as they rode. There was a hollow feeling in her stomach that had nothing to do with hunger.

"There's a back trail out of the valley. It's narrow and steep, but it will put us closer to Mount Kajhrenal than the main route."

Before she could reply, there came a thunder of hoofs after them. Maurynna turned.

It was Raven. She pulled up; so did Shima, though his face was a mask of disapproval that lightened only when he saw that Raven rode bareback.

As the cantering Stormwind pranced to a halt, Raven said, "No, I'm not trying to go with you—not like this. I just thought I'd ride with you while I can." He looked from one to the other. "Well enough?"

"Well enough," Maurynna said. Then, "I'm glad you came, Raven. I didn't want to leave without saying good-bye."

"You wouldn't be so lucky, beanpole," Raven said.

They rode on quietly, side-by-side when the path was wide enough, single file where it narrowed. Shima led them into a little side canyon that, to Maurynna's inexperienced eye, looked like any of a hundred others they'd passed.

They came to where another path branched off the one they traveled.

"This is where you must turn back, Raven," Shima said. "Only Maurynna and I may go on from here." He gestured at the path, his hand rising in the air.

Maurynna looked up and swallowed hard. True, Shima had warned her it was steep and narrow, but by the gods, she hadn't expected anything like this! The first part ran along the canyon wall; then, when it ran out of wall, it turned in a switchback, back and forth, back and forth, until it reached the plateau high above. She hoped there was enough room for the Llysanyins' broad hooves.

I've seen wider hair ribbons, she thought wildly as Shima set Je'nihahn to the path. She'd never again complain about the trail to the meadow back at Dragonskeep.

"Beanpole," Raven said, staring up at the trail, "drop the reins on Boreal's neck, hang on to the saddle, and by all the gods, *stay the hell out of his way.*"

She did as he bade her, letting the reins fall onto the stallion's neck, especially since Boreal was nodding hard enough to send his mane flying. Her fingers locked onto the high pommel of her saddle, she said, "I'm ready."

Boreal began climbing.

I wouldn't mind if I could go up a rope ladder—then I could just pretend I was climbing a mast. Or if I could fly up and send Boreal on alone; that wouldn't be bad, either. Damn Kyrissaean, anyway.

Fifty-one

That night, Lark had trouble sleeping. Every time she closed her eyes, images of Shima and Maurynna in the hands of the temple guards tormented her. Each time the images ended with them trembling upon the lip of the Well of Death.

She rolled over yet again, and propped herself up on her elbows, her heart hammering.

It was in the darkest part of the night that the noises she'd half expected came. Holding her breath, she listened as the stealthy footsteps crossed the lower floor, heard the rustling of baskets being opened.

She thought he'd given up too easily. Flopping back on her bed, she waited for the sounds to end, for him to come back up the ladder. When she heard his breathing turn deep and regular, Lark rose and quietly went about her own preparations.

A scratching at the tent door brought Linden awake instantly. "Who is it?" he called softly.

"Dzeduin. May I enter?"

Linden looked around at the other Dragonlords and Otter, now awake also; they nodded, sitting up in their blankets. "Yes."

The Zharmatian slipped inside and crouched just inside the doorflap. "Word just came that troops bearing the crest of Lord Jhanun are within a day's ride, and that they're led by one wearing the garb of a merchant. Perhaps it's the one who betrayed you; if we ride out soon, we'll be able to tail them."

Linden grunted. "I'll go. I'd like to get my hands on that

bastard Taren; I want to know what his game was." He pushed back his blankets and stood up, wearing only his breeches. As he reached for his tunic, the others kicked off their own blankets. In a ragged chorus they announced that they, too, wanted to find Taren.

Soon they were dressed and following Dzeduin through the dark camp, their cloaks wrapped tightly around them.

Lark waited where the trail came out onto the top of the cliff. Crouched behind a thick saltbush so that she couldn't be seen from below, she pulled her *jelah* closer against the predawn cold. The land of the Tah'nehsieh drank up the heat of the sun during the day like a miser hoarding up gold, she thought, and spent it in the night like a wastrel in a tavern. Behind her, her horse nibbled the dry, spiky grass that grew in tufts between the rocks. Somewhere a bird sang a few tentative notes as if uncertain whether it should be awake this early. Lark yawned in sympathy.

He would be coming. She was certain of it; just as certain as she was that the sun would rise this day.

The bird's song came again, less hesitant this time, and with a jaunty trill at the end. Lark smiled; it was a rock wren, one of the saucy little birds that lived near the *mehanso* and would dash in to steal the grain from the great mortars as it was being ground.

Now the wren burst into full song. The sound echoed cheerily among the rocks. Lark shut her eyes to rest them, knowing her feathered serenader would play sentry for her.

As it did a short time later. The song ended with an indignant chirp and an explosion of flapping wings. Lark looked up in time to see the small, reddish brown bird rise above the cliff and fly off, still scolding the intruder below.

She inched closer to the cliff edge and waited for her eyes to become accustomed to the gloom below; the light of the newborn sun was not yet bright enough to reach down between the cliffs.

He rode up the trail just as she'd known he would. She watched him until he was hidden by a switchback. Lark stood, groaned a little at the stiffness in her limbs, and mounted her horse. She rode it along the upper trail as it twisted and turned between the boulders that covered the plateau like an army standing watch. When the boulders became walls that towered over her head, she went on until she came to a narrow gap blocked by brush.

Here, she knew, was one of the tribe's lookout points. From here, a sentry could look out over the plateau and see an invading army long before it reached the trail to the valley. One could also see a goodly portion of the trail from the valley to here. Lark pushed the brush aside and sent her horse up a short slope to a point behind the left-hand wall. Satisfied with her view, she settled herself to watch her backtrail.

She waited with the patience of a hunter. At long last, she heard the ring of iron horseshoes on stone and saw rider and horse surge out of the ravine onto the plateau and stop. He squinted against the sudden brightness and raised a hand to shield his eyes. His hair flamed in the young sunlight, and the years of her exile fell upon her like a snowcat upon its prey.

Gods help her, how long had it been since she'd seen a fellow countryman? Not since her ship went down in the Haunted Straits, and she had washed ashore more dead than alive nigh thirty years ago. Six hellish years a slave, traded from tribe to tribe, until Kuthera of the Tah'nehsieh took her to wife. Now she was content with a place in both family and tribe, her only regret—and it was a mild one now, she admitted; it had faded with the years—that she would never see her homeland again. So she'd filled her children's heads with tales of the northern lands. Of the four, only Shima, the oldest boy, longed to see Yerrih, with her broad, grassy plains like an ocean of shimmering green and pine-clad mountains wreathed in mist and clouds.

This man was an image out of the past. Red hair, blue eyes, freckles splashed across his nose; so had her own father looked, her brothers, her uncles. He turned in the saddle as if to make certain of his saddlebag, revealing the clan braid that hung down his back like a ribbon of pale fire.

His clan braid. Her hands went to her own, one at each temple in the manner of Yerrin women; stroked them. Even after all this time, she couldn't bring herself to abandon them. She was still Yerrin. She would be until she died— as any true Yerrin was.

And that truth was a weapon.

It seemed all was well with the saddlebag, for her quarry now urged his horse on. Lark watched until he was lost from view at the turn. She closed her eyes then, the better to listen.

At first, nothing. Then once again the ring of metal-shod hoof on stone. She waited as the sound drew closer, then pressed her heels into her horse's sides. They trotted back down the slope and out onto the trail, blocking it.

She had timed it well. Raven was not yet in sight. Lark wrapped her *jelah* a little closer and waited. The other horse came on steadily; she could hear the stallion snorting softly. Any moment now . . .

The rider pulled up short and exclaimed in surprise. One hand flashed to the dirk hanging at his side, then dropped. He stared at her. His mount bobbed its head, iron grey mane falling over black neck.

"Good morning, Raven," Lark said pleasantly. "Going somewhere?"

He said nothing, but his eyes were hard and angry. Lark settled the *jelah* about her shoulders a little more comfortably. She wondered if he would try to push past her—and if the Llysanyin would agree to it. If yes, there was little she could do to stop them. Her rangy Tah'nehsieh mount would go down before the massive northern horse like a pin in a game of draughts.

But the Llysanyin—Stormwind, she remembered, rolling the Yerrin word in her mind, delighting in its sound—stood like the rocks around him, solid and unmoving.

After what seemed a hundred years Raven said, "I'm going for a ride."

"Indeed?" She guided her horse forward until the two animals stood facing each other, with Stormwind slightly to her left. "And if I asked to look in that saddlebag you were so concerned with before, I wouldn't find the dyes for skin and hair, now would I?"

A wave of pink passed over Raven's face, then ebbed. His chin went up as he answered, "Very well, then; you know where I'm going."

"Even though Zhantse warned you that if you went, they would fail?" Her *jelah* slipped a little; Lark drew it closer once again.

Raven's legs closed around Stormwind's sides, urging him on. "I don't believe him. Or you."

But the Llysanyin clearly did, for the stallion ignored his rider's command. Instead he turned his head so that one eye looked back at Raven. Now Raven's face turned nigh as red as his hair and stayed that way.

"Well, I don't," he said to the horse.

The Llysanyin snorted and turned back to Lark.

"Everything will be for naught," she said to the horse. "They will all die. Zhantse has Seen." She should feel silly, she thought, appealing to an animal. But there was too much *knowing* in the great dark eye that regarded her.

The Llysanyin backed up a few steps, his meaning as plain as if he spoke words: *No. We go no farther.*

Lark gently touched her heels to her horse's sides; it stepped forward to close the gap.

"Stormwind!" Raven cried. "We have to—"

But there was no arguing with the Llysanyin who backed one more step to drive his point home, then stood like a statue.

Frustration twisted Raven's face. "Damn you," he said to Lark. "She needs me."

"Does she?" Lark countered. "For what? Do you know how to live off of this barren land as Shima does? Do you know the trails, the hiding places? What could you do for her save betray her with your curling hair that will still glint red in the sunshine even with the dye? And there's one other thing. . . ." She swung her head slightly so that her braids fell forward, and saw his eyes go to them.

"I still have them," she said, her voice even.

"So I see." He sounded wary as if unsure where she would lead him with this unexpected opening. "Grey and black binding. Wolf Clan."

"I'm still Yerrin in my heart although I've lived these many years in Jehanglan."

The wariness increased. "As am I, although I spent most of my life growing up in Thalnia."

"As to where this trail is leading . . . Have you seen a single Jehangli or a Tah'nehsieh with anything even remotely resembling a clan braid?" she challenged.

First came confusion, then annoyance. "Of course not! After all, they're not— Oh, gods."

Comprehension at last. The freckles stood out starkly as Raven's face paled to a sickly white.

"Just so," Lark said, left forefinger jabbing the air for emphasis. "Will you hack off your clan braid, declare yourself outcast? Is simple jealousy worth that? For that's all it is, isn't it? You want to be with Maurynna; you resent that it must be Shima who goes instead.

"Well, my young friend, believe me when I say I wish it was you with her," Lark continued vehemently. "Think you I like sending my son into such danger? Better he bide at home and tend to his drumming for Zhantse.

"Yet did I think that your going would help them, I would keep your clan braid in reverence. I would even return with you to declare you a hero before Marten clan's elders, tell them that you sacrificed your braid to aid a Dragonlord—and I've no wish to leave Jehanglan anymore. My life is here now with my husband and children; if I left, I might never be able to return past the Straits. But I would do it." She leaned back slightly and wrapped her legs about her horse's barrel. "So, young Raven—what shall it be? Will you try to pass me? Or will you go back with me to the *mehanso*?"

Raven snorted. "I've not much choice, have I? Storm-wind won't go—will you, boy?"

The Llysanyin shook his head.

"I didn't think so." For a moment, he scowled at the horse's mane then, raising his eyes, asked, "What chance would I have afoot?"

"As a stranger in this country? None," Lark said frankly.

He nodded at that, accepting her word. Thank the gods, beneath all the foolish, romantic, youthful notions, the boy had a solid streak of common sense.

"Then I'll go back with you." His shoulders slumped in defeat.

"Raven," she said, her voice shaking with relief, "You've no idea how happy I am to hear you say that. I did not want to have to use this."

And now she flung the *jelah* back from her shoulders, revealing the long sailor's dagger—almost a short sword—hanging at her right hip.

"Ah," Lark said as Raven's eyes grew wide. "You didn't think I'd do such a thing, did you? But I'm a mother, Raven; I would do anything to save my son from certain death, even if it had come to killing you—for Shima would die were you to follow him and Maurynna. And I could have done it, too. You didn't know I was left-handed, did you? You wouldn't have been expecting to be struck by a weapon and from that side."

Stormwind's head had come up at the first sight of the sheathed blade and he sank down upon his haunches. Lark held her breath, but the stallion's forefeet stayed on the ground. Still, she kept her hands where the Llysanyin could see them until he accepted that she meant his rider no harm after all. She relaxed only when the stallion did.

"Shall we return to the *mehanso*?" she asked, a little shaky from how close she'd stood to death from those deadly hooves.

For his answer Raven signaled Stormwind to sink down upon his haunches once more. But the big stallion merely pirouetted in place on the narrow trail. Then man and horse set off at a fast walk back along the way they'd so recently traversed.

She wanted to call to him, tell him she was sorry but this was for the best. Yet she knew there was no consolation for the way he'd been outguessed and, yes, tricked into letting her get so close to him. Instead, she followed without a word. It would do no good to rub his nose in his failure.

Still, she couldn't help thinking, *Thought you'd nothing to fear from a middle-aged woman like myself, did you, boy? Never underestimate a mother, my fine lad—or any woman for that matter.*

Maurynna shifted in the saddle, trying to ease her sore muscles. Boreal whickered softly to her as he felt her move. She leaned forward and patted the dappled grey shoulder. "I'm well enough, boy. Someday I'll get used to this."

And pigs will dance. Well and well, she could always hope.

Ahead of her Shima rode easily, following a trail that was invisible to her, but plain, it seemed, to him. To take her mind off of her physical discomfort, Maurynna began wondering what they would face once they reached their goal: the mines in the valley of the Temple of Iron.

And once there, how was she expected to get away again? Surely the soldiers would be hunting her and Shima. To the best of her remembrance, that little detail had never been discussed—or at least not in *her* hearing. Even Zhantse had not Seen how they were to do it; he just blithely assured her that they would come up with some idea.

How comforting, she thought with a scowl. As comforting as finding one's ship aground on a reef with a hole the size of a bear through the hull, and a storm from the depths of hell on the way.

Perhaps she'd think about how much her rear end hurt instead.

* * *

The sun had gone down perhaps a candlemark or more ago before they caught up with the Zharmatian scouts who trailed the troop.

"They're over that rise," one of them said, "riding along the road as if they own it. We let them see us earlier; they've been trailing us ever since, but they're all in armor and are too slow." She grinned as if this was the best game in the world.

"Shall we go see?" Dzeduin said. "I suggest we leave the horses down here; they'd show up on the ridge."

"Good idea," said Linden.

Soon they were lying in a row, only their heads peeping over the hill. Below them on the other side was an empty road winding between the ridges.

"Listen," whispered Lleld. "They're coming."

Sure enough, the vanguard of the troop came into sight. At their head rode a man dressed in a dark Jehangli robe.

"Damn!" the four northerners said at once.

Dzeduin jumped.

"It's not Taren," Linden explained.

"Still, they're with the lord who's with that bastard Taren," Lleld pointed out. "Wish we could put their noses out of joint somehow."

"Dzeduin," Otter said slowly, "once, when talking to Taren, he told me about some Jehangli legends. Do you know of the things called 'corpse lights?' "

"Oh, yes; they're very bad luck to meet. If one touches you, you'll die before a year is out," Dzeduin said.

Linden listened with half his attention, vaguely wondering what Otter was getting at. The soldiers on the road below would soon reach where the Zharmatian scouts had turned off. There was no way, Linden knew, their trackers would miss the trail, not with so many torches holding back the night. The men below knew their business.

Otter persisted in his questions. "What color are they? How large? How do they act?"

"Blue as a corpse's lips, the stories say. As for size— perhaps a man's fist?" Dzeduin replied in puzzlement.

"They dance in the darkness, around and around their prey, seeking souls to join them. Otter, why do you—"

Linden began laughing quietly the same time Lleld and Jekkanadar did. "Shall we?" he said to them.

For an answer, three balls of coldfire sprang into existence above the road ahead of the troop.

Dzeduin hissed in surprise. He scrambled back as if he would run.

"Don't worry, lad," Otter said, putting out a hand to stop him. "It's nothing to be afraid of."

"Hunh," Lleld grunted softly. Her brow furrowed in concentration. "It's not easy creating them from this distance."

"Indeed," Jekkanadar agreed. "There!" Six balls of blue coldfire now danced in the darkness.

They were right. Until now Linden had always called coldfire into existence from the air around him. This was much harder; but once created, even from this distance it was easy to control them. He sent his coldfire to join the others.

"Let me have them," Lleld said. From the wicked glee in her voice, the men below were in for a bad time.

Linden gave control of his coldfire over to her. Immediately, the glowing blue lights spread across the road as if to contest the soldiers' coming. Then they advanced, first one, then another, darting forward with the speed of a striking snake, stalking the soldiers like cats.

And now the Jehangli saw them. Startled yells carried up the hillside. The band pulled up short, some soldiers hauling back on their horses' mouths so hard that the poor beasts sat down. Linden winced, remembering the harsh bits the Zharmatians used; these looked like more of the same.

The line of coldfire lashed out, curling around the soldiers like the length of a whip, trapping them within a slowly revolving circle of lurid blue "corpse lights." Now and again, one would dart in at a rider, veering off just short of touching him.

The shouts of alarm now held a note of panic as the

soldiers dodged the ill-omened lights. Then their leader bellowed orders, telling them to form up once more. Lleld swore as they slowly obeyed, drawing strength from their leader.

"Ah, bother him," Lleld said. Her hands swept through the air as if the coldfire were puppets and she the puppeteer tugging their strings here and there. The coldfire leapt in response. "Give me more," she demanded, her eyes intent on the scene below.

Linden obeyed. So did Jekkanadar. More coldfire burst into light.

The newcomers were too much for the soldiers. One trooper, wielding a torch like a mace, swatted frantically at a light darting at him. He missed the coldfire, but a companion wasn't so lucky. The second man caught the blazing torch full in the face. His scream of agony pushed his fellows over the edge into mindless panic.

Lleld thoughtfully left a gap open and the troop was not long in noticing. There was a frenzied scramble to turn the horses; some of the animals nearly went down. Then the troop fled back down the road in a terrified rout.

To his credit, their leader was the last to leave; one light of a particularly sickly blue flung itself after him, touching down light as a feather between his shoulder blades, illuminating the man's back for a moment before rejoining the other globes of coldfire.

Linden frowned. That last bit was a nasty touch he wouldn't have thought Lleld would stoop to. It disturbed him. She had a wicked sense of humor, yes, but not cruel. At least the poor beggar hadn't seemed aware of what had happened.

"That was uncalled for," Jekkanadar snapped.

At first Lleld said nothing. Then, in an odd, strained voice, "Both of you—bid your coldfire to go out. I'll do the same with mine," she said.

Baffled, Linden did as she asked. A blink of an eye later, only one dancing light was left—the one that had touched the Jehangli. It wandered along the road as if seeking something, hesitating at the place the scouts had turned off.

"That one," said Lleld far too calmly, "is none of mine." She jumped up and ran down to Miki as the ghastly blue light inched along the scouts' path, like a hound baffled for the moment, but sure of its trail in the end. She flung herself into the saddle and wheeled the little mare around. "I suggest we get the hell out of here," she yelled, "because that one's real!" The little Llysanyin mare raced off.

For once no one argued. As he helped Otter down the slope to the horses, somewhere in the back of his mind Linden wondered if this was the first time in her life everyone agreed with Lleld wholeheartedly. Without further ado, the rest of the party scrambled into their saddles; the next moment they thundered over the crest of the next gentle hill, following Lleld and Miki down the other side.

While they rode, Linden wondered if corpse lights ever haunted a large camp. He sincerely hoped not.

Kwahsiu caught up with his men and, with a generous dose of whip, curses, and threats, stopped them some three *ta'vri* down the road. They huddled around him, their faces masks of terror in the light of the torches they carried.

The Dragonlords had been out there—of that, he was certain. This was some trick of theirs; he'd never heard of that many corpse lights at once.

He looked from man to trembling man, and decided he might as well call off the search for the northern weredragons. These dogs would refuse to hunt that quarry any longer.

"Back to the barracks," he said. "Tomorrow we start for Rivasha."

Fifty-two

For lack of anything better to do, the morning after being foiled by Lark, Raven decided to explore the land around the *mehanso* on foot. So he went out, picked a direction, and began walking.

Soon he found himself among the garden plots of the Tah'nehsieh. To his northern eyes they looked odd; instead of large fields of grain, there were strips running along narrow irrigation canals. Laid out between the canals were little gardens thickly planted with crops both known and unknown to him. He recognized gourds and beans, but what were the tall, thick stalks that supported the vines? They bore a long fruit tightly wrapped in its own leaves. Walking carefully along the path worn between the vegetation, Raven decided on a closer look.

He examined one of the strange fruits. There seemed to be only one or two per plant, and they grew directly from the thick stalk. A tassel of silky threads protruded from the pointed end. They were turning from a soft golden color to a brown. Gingerly he squeezed the odd growth at its thickest part. It was hard beneath his fingers.

"Not ripe yet, I guess," Raven murmured.

"On the contrary," a voice piped up from behind him—in Yerrin. "See the color of the tassel? That means the maize is nearly ready to pick."

Raven jumped and whirled around, one hand on his belt dagger. "Who's there?" he demanded.

From the next garden plot, a hand waved from what appeared to be an impenetrable tangle of vines. "One moment."

A crouched body scuttled sideways from under the jumble of vines and unfolded itself, revealing a long, lanky boy of perhaps fourteen years. The boy pushed a stray lock of hair back from his forehead with one hand; the other held a clump of weeds. He had an air about him that made him seem older than his years. "You must be Raven."

If the language hadn't already given him away, the nose would have. The boy's parentage was stamped on his face as it was on Shima's. And there were only two of Lark's brood Raven had not yet met, and one was female.

Raven said, "And you're Tefira, yes?"

Tefira's face lit in startled appreciation. Then he sighed. "It was the nose, wasn't it? You're not another Seer."

"No, thank the gods," Raven said fervently.

"Ah. I thought you might help me."

Raven wondered at that a moment. If the boy had a question, why didn't he just ask his master, Zhantse? Why would Tefira need help from another Seer?

He caught himself before he asked. Of course—this was the one that Shima was worried about. What had he said about him? That Zhantse had taken Tefira as an apprentice Seer and— Damn; he couldn't remember the rest.

"Mmph," Raven said instead.

Tefira tilted his head to one side. "But I might be able to help you."

"Oh?" Raven asked, his interest piqued. "How?"

Dark eyes narrowed, watched him steadily. "You wanted to go with my brother and the Dragonlord, didn't you?"

"I *should* have gone with your brother and my friend," Raven corrected with no good grace. "But your master decreed otherwise. I still don't believe his so-called vision."

And if he said it enough times, he might even convince himself of it.

The boy shook his head, sending his long black hair flying. "Oh, no—trust Zhantse's Seeings. He Sees true. And I hear in your voice that you know it as well."

Raven scowled. He didn't need some snot-nosed brat—

Ah, hell—he might as well be honest. He was angry because the boy looked so much like his brother Shima, may that bastard get saddlesores in the worst spot. "So how can you help me?"

Now Tefira looked sly, and Raven saw that he was holding back a smile. "Zhantse said that you weren't to go with them, yes?"

Raven shrugged, annoyed. Why bother to ask? Of course the boy knew the answer already. The whole damn tribe knew, no doubt. "Yes."

"Just so." The smile blossomed. "But he didn't say you couldn't *follow* them, now did he?" With that, Tefira gazed at him, all doe-eyed innocence.

Raven stretched his lips in something that wasn't even meant to resemble a smile. "I already tried that."

And if it hadn't been for your *damned mother* . . . It still riled him how she'd anticipated his clever plan. It was even more infuriating that he'd left himself open to a possible attack by her. Some bodyguard.

"So you did. But you see, had you succeeded then, you would have caught up with them, and gone with them. That would have fulfilled Zhantse's vision. But if you leave now . . ." Somehow Tefira managed to look even more innocent. "Interested?"

Raven caught his breath, thinking. The boy was right. True, it was splitting hairs as finely as any lawspeaker in a court of clan elders. . . .

Never mind that. The boy was right, damn it all.

"I'm interested. Now, what's in it for you?"

The startled look on Tefira's face made him laugh. "Don't ever try to trade horses, boy," Raven said. "At least, not with me. When I see someone looking at me more innocently than a newborn baby, I know there's something afoot. Out with it, Tefira. It can't be money; I don't have much, and what I do have wouldn't do you any good."

The air of maturity that had so impressed Raven slipped at last. "Shima gets all the adventures," Tefira complained, "and I never get to do anything. Just fast and go on vision quests that . . ."

"I . . . understand," Raven said at last into the sudden

quiet. A Seer—even a Seer in training—who couldn't See wasn't much use to anyone. No wonder Shima was worried about this one.

As if he'd never interrupted himself, Tefira went on, "Shima is the one to go hunting if we need it, he's the one to carry messages to the different *mehansos* or to the plains tribes. Me, I have to learn what plants to use for a thousand and one ailments, where to dig the sacred colored clays and the prayers for each one, and memorize chant after chant after chant. I never do anything exciting. I've never even seen the ship that brings the trees for the Vale."

Tefira scowled horribly at the weeds he still held as if just noticing them. "Oh, I forgot. I also get to weed the gardens," he said, and pitched the offending tangle of greenery as far as he could.

"So your price is to go with me," said Raven.

"Just so. You need me, you know. I can get supplies; you can't—my mother will be watching you. Also, you'd never survive this land alone."

"So your mother warned me."

Tefira dusted his hands on the seat of his kilt. "She spoke the truth. So you'll take me with you as your guide when you go?" he said eagerly.

"*If* I go," Raven said.

Crestfallen as a puppy with a slapped nose, Tefira asked, "What do you mean?"

Knowing it was silly—he'd walked, after all—Raven still looked over his shoulder. There were other Tah'nehsieh working in other gardens but that didn't concern him. None of them could understand Yerrin even if they were close enough to overhear. He beckoned Tefira closer.

"There's a slight problem . . ." Raven began.

Haoro stood before the priests' council. "We must have a *nira*, and quickly," he said. His gaze swept the men sitting at the table. Only three were of sufficient rank to challenge him, and of those three, one was already sworn to him. Of the two left, he knew one for a coward; Kuulu would never seek the feathered mantle.

That left Remui. Haoro met his eyes; was that a challenge he saw there?

Then the floor shook. And even though none of them was sealed to the beast below, pain lanced through them all. Haoro forced himself to stand firm even as the others bent beneath it.

His face grey, Remui said, "I will begin the preparations for the ceremony, *nira*."

That evening, in the cool of the dusk, Raven rode Stormwind out beyond the *mehanso*. As was their habit morning and evening, they went a mile or so to a dry wash; its sandy bottom was perfect for a long gallop. From there they often spent the day exploring the surrounding countryside.

But this time was different. A figure wrapped in a colorful *jelah* sat atop one of the many low columns of red stone at the head of the path leading to the dry riverbed. It was as motionless as the stone beneath it.

Stormwind slowed and turned his head to examine the mysterious being with one eye as they approached it.

"I don't see any weapons, boy. Do you?" Raven said, fighting to sound natural. He must have succeeded since Stormwind only shook his head and kept trotting.

Damn; who *was* it under that blanket thing, anyway? He wouldn't put it past Lark to have guessed this one, too.

As they drew even with it, the shrouded figure held up a hand.

"I have a message for you." The *jelah* fell back.

Raven strangled a sigh of relief barely in time. "You're Zhantse's apprentice Seer, aren't you?" he said. He saw Stormwind's ears tilt forward in interest.

"Just so," the youth said. His voice was cool and distant. "I am Tefira. And this is my message: you are to travel to the valley of the Iron Temple to aid the newest Dragonlord. I shall be your guide. This is a needful thing; be ready at dawn tomorrow."

With that, Tefira stood up in a a single graceful motion. He said no more, nor looked back as he jumped down from the column and disappeared among the boulders. A few moments later, Raven heard a horse's whicker of greeting and then hoofbeats moving away.

"Sooo—this is a change, boy, isn't it?" said Raven. "Looks like we're going on that journey after all." To his relief, Stormwind nodded after a moment's hesitation.

Thank the gods, we've put that one over Stormwind. Clever of Tefira to phrase things that way; made it sound like one of Zhantse's prophecies without actually saying so and lying. And speaking of prophecies—damn, but the boy has the intonation down pat, doesn't he? If I didn't know better, I'd swear that oracular tone was real.

Raven smiled a little as Stormwind started down the trail to the wash. *My, my—wouldn't Maurynna be surprised? Served her right, too; if everyone else had been sensible from the first, he would be with her and Shima now. Hell; the gods only knew what they might be facing and only two knives between them against who knew how many swords.*

What good a *third* knife would be against those swords, he refused to consider. He'd find a weapon; perhaps he could jump a guard. He turned Stormwind back to the *mehanso*. They both needed a good night's sleep. He and Tefira would have to ride hard if they were to catch up with Maurynna and Shima.

Fifty-three

It was nearly dark when Shima pulled up Je'nihahn. Maurynna stopped beside him, lost amid this land of stone canyons. They dismounted.

He called out something in his own language. "Now we

wait," he said to her. From somewhere nearby, Maurynna heard water gurgle; a spring, she thought.

Then came the sound of leather on stone, and two shadows stepped away from the walls. Even though she'd been expecting it, she still drew a sharp breath.

The shadows turned into young Tah'nehsieh men. They spoke quickly and urgently with Shima.

He turned to her. "Zhantse sent a fast messenger on ahead of us, and everything's arranged. My cousin Amura in the slave camp is expecting us; Rasse," he tilted his head toward one of the the men, "got a message to him earlier. Rasse and Omasua will care for the Llysanyins until we get back. They've been warned about them."

"Did you hear that?" she said to Boreal.

The Llysanyin nodded. She passed the reins to Rasse, then dug into her saddlebag for Dharm Varleran's sword. She belted it around her waist, glad the long-ago Dragonlord hadn't carried a greatsword as Linden did. Her *jelah* covered this one nicely. "How far?" she said, picturing a long, long walk ahead of them.

"Not very," Shima said. At her startled look, he explained, "The temple soldiers don't like to come out here; it isn't safe for them in these winding little canyons."

Maurynna looked around; she could well believe it. This was wonderful country for setting ambushes.

"Then let's get started. The sooner this is over, the happier I'll be." *And I can find Linden again, which will make me happiest of all.*

"This way, then," Shima said, and set off. She followed.

It wasn't much more than two candlemarks later, she guessed, that they came out on a ridge looking down into a narrow valley strewn with enormous boulders. Across it, the valley wall rose up into a high plateau. Below them were low buildings of stone; barracks and the slave quarters, she guessed. A road ran along the floor of the valley; it ended at a huge set of doors in the opposite side of the valley.

Gods, they're big enough to get a dragon in—

Suddenly she realized she looked upon Pirakos's prison at long last. She went cold inside.

"Hsst!" a nearby voice said.

Maurynna turned as a man crawled out of the darkness.

"Hello, Amura," Shima said.

"Hurry," Amura said in Jehangli. "They've been as nervous as cats since the Zharmatians started raiding—not that they'd raid here. We never know anymore when a patrol will come past. And there's a rumor that the priests have chosen a new *nira*—and that means they'll be going into the main tunnel soon."

Amura spoke quickly as he led his cousin and the mysterious northern stranger along the valley road. "There's a small opening down this way. We've found it's the safest way to the caverns under Mount Kajhenral. A recent earth tremor ripped away the rock concealing it. There are unlit torches waiting for you just inside."

"Thank you," the northerner whispered. The message had said she was a Dragonlord; Amura remembered his aunt's tales, and wished he could see this woman Change. Lark had said the northern dragons were nothing like Miune.

They were scrambling over the rocks to the opening when they were spotted by a patrol. At the first shout, Amura yelled, "Go around that rock and straight ahead. I'll lead them away."

He turned and ran, making certain the patrol saw him. He didn't dare look to see how his cousin and the Dragonlord fared. He could only pray that they made it safely; and when a second and third patrol joined in the chase, he prayed that *he* would make it to a hiding spot before the Jehangli soldiers could catch him.

Maurynna stooped and snatched at the torches; they were right where Amura, bless him, had said they'd be. But they didn't dare stop and light them; the patrol would be sure to notice a light where no light should be.

There was, she realized, enough moonlight filtering in

for her dragonsight to see for a fair distance. Passing a torch
to Shima, she said, "Grab hold of my shoulder; I can see
enough to lead you in for a way. We'll light the torches
when they can't be seen."

Shima did as she bade him, and they set out into the
bowels of Mount Kajhenral.

They were well into the mountain before the second torch
sputtered and died. Maurynna stopped. The dark here
seemed solid as a wall; she thought that if she stretched out
a hand she would bruise it on the utter blackness before
her.

She slid a foot forward, questing. "Ow!" Then, before
Shima could worry, she explained, "Stubbed my toes."

She steadied herself with one hand on Shima's shoulder
and rubbed her aching toes. Damn these soft boots, she
thought. If only they had more torches . . . Ah, well; no use
whining over a missed tide as her old first mate used to
say. At least this was something she could remedy.

Whether it was a good idea or not . . . She would *not*
think about that.

"This is stupid. We'll kill ourselves stumbling through
here in the dark, and what good would we do Pirakos then?
This place already reeks of magic because of him; I'm going to risk some coldfire. No one will notice it," she said,
and hoped she was right.

She raised a hand and drew a small ball of coldfire from
the air. The Tah'nehsieh gasped. Maurynna set the coldfire
to hover close to the ground. It revealed a path strewn with
rocks and crevices, all waiting to turn an unwary ankle.

Rank stupidity indeed to try this trail blind. Maurynna
called the coldfire to her and held it out to Shima. "Would
you like this one?"

She had to smile at the wonder revealed on his face by
the faint glow. No doubt she had looked the same when
she'd first seen coldfire. The memory brought with it an
ache of longing. To be back in her aunt's garden once more,
Linden by her side . . . She pulled herself back to the pres-

ent. This was no time to lose herself in wishes and memories.

"Go ahead, take it," she urged. "It won't burn you."

Shima's dark eyes were huge as he stared at the coldfire. He reached out, hesitated; then, after a quick glance at her, stretched out a hand with more confidence. He cradled the glowing ball in his hands. The light pulsed with his heartbeat and shone through his fingers, the glow red with his living blood.

"Beautiful," he whispered.

Her hand twisted again in the air, capturing another ball of coldfire from nothingness. Maurynna paused, listening, though for what, she could not have said.

All was silent; the mountain did not cave in on them; no army of priestmages appeared behind them. They were safe, thank the gods—or at least as safe as they could be. "I wonder how far away Pirakos is," she said. "I hope Zhantse is right and that this is the way."

"He is," Shima averred. "You'll see."

Maurynna stared down the narrow tunnel revealed by the coldfire's light. *Like walking down a whale's throat.* Ah, well; nothing for it but to go on.

But before she had gone three paces, Shima pushed in front. "I should go first," he insisted. "If there's something evil in these tunnels, better that you have some warning." He was away before she could protest. . . .

Or ask him about the tremor she heard in his voice. Did he know of something lurking in these tunnels that Zhantse had not warned her of? Her hand sought the sword hidden beneath her Tah'nehsieh garb. The feel of the hilt reassured her.

Not that a short sword would be much use against, say, a mountain troll from one of Otter's stories—

Stop that!

She followed Shima.

Surely they'd been walking for days already. And here was yet another turn in this cursed, unending tunnel; this one was so sharp they couldn't see beyond it. Maurynna sent her globe of light around the bulge of rippled stone that forced the detour. It bobbed warily around the obstacle, the light growing softer as it advanced a short way along the route. Then—

The coldfire died. Just—died. To Maurynna it felt as if it had been swallowed.

But by what?

"Why did you—" Shima began.

"That was none of my doing," Maurynna whispered, shaken. "Something . . . Something . . . *ate* it."

They clasped hands instinctively, listening. Maurynna held her breath, knew Shima did the same so that whatever had taken the coldfire would not find them. She thought of retreat, but her limbs would not obey her. All she could do was hold to the slight comfort of the hand gripping hers and wait.

A thought struck her. What if whatever it was sought light? She doused the coldfire Shima held lest it draw evil upon them.

The darkness fell, a thousand times heavier than before. Shima gasped; his grip tightened convulsively. The moment stretched on and on until Maurynna feared she would go mad from the suspense.

But nothing came for them.

She drew in a deep, shuddering breath. The air in the tunnel, so dusty and stale before, was sweet in her lungs. She leaned against an outcropping of stone, gasping. Shima's fingers slid from her hand; she heard him sit down.

Part of her mind railed at her, *Coward! You're a Dragonlord—you shouldn't be afraid!*

But, her fears argued, *What good does being a Dragonlord do me in here? There's no room to Change.*

Another thought ghosted across her mind: *Even if I could Change . . .* She crushed it and the wave of self-loathing that always followed it, but not quickly enough.

Only her will made her face that feeling and name it for what it was. *So I'm the least of the Dragonlords; so be it.*

That's as the gods will. But being a full Dragonlord wouldn't help me here; there's no room to Change—not even for Lleld.

If she couldn't Change, she could at least do what any other Dragonlord could do. She would go on. In defiance, she called forth another globe of coldfire.

Her heart nearly stopped at the sight before her. For Shima lay curled tight as a hedgehog on the uneven floor of the tunnel, shaking violently. She dropped down on one knee beside him. Gods help them—what had happened to him?

"Shima!" She laid a hand on his shoulder; the skin was cold and slick with sweat. He made no answer.

Nearly sick with fear, Maurynna wondered what had befallen her companion. A poisonous snake? No; one wouldn't go this deep underground. Something else equally deadly?

"Shima! What's wrong?"

Against all hope he answered. "The walls . . . They're falling."

His voice was so weak and muffled, she could barely hear him. Even so, the stark fear in it made her blood run cold.

What was he talking about? Had he heard something she missed? Terror rose in her to answer his; like a gale wind it threatened to overwhelm her.

Then, from somewhere deep inside, simple common sense rose to save her. *Silly goose*, it said. *How on earth could a truehuman hear something that a Dragonlord couldn't? Especially something as loud as rocks falling!*

Simple truth; it saved her. "The walls are not falling, Shima," she said firmly, gripping his shoulder. The skin beneath her hand was still cold and clammy. "They've been here since the world was born, and will be here when it ends."

He uncurled a little, though he still shivered. Now his words came clearer. "The feeling . . . Help me."

She stared down at him, puzzled. The 'feeling'?" What on—

Suddenly Maurynna understood. One of her cousins' friends had the same fear of enclosed spaces; poor Romnis couldn't sleep in a room with a closed door without panicking.

For a moment Maurynna felt sorry for Shima—then exasperated. Damn it all, the man must have known what he was getting himself into with this route! And if he didn't, Zhantse certainly must have.

She burst out, "Then why did you come with me if you're afraid of being trapped? You must have known!" In pure annoyance, she grabbed him by the shoulders and pulled him upright so that he sat against the wall. "Look at me!"

He opened his eyes; his face looked grey in the coldfire's glow. Shaking his head as one throwing off a daze, Shima said, "It doesn't always happen. It will pass."

"But if you've been like this all your life, surely—"

He cut her off. "But it hasn't been all my life, I tell you," he said, fear and anger—anger at himself, Maurynna realized—edging his voice like a knife. "It's happened only recently—the past two seasons—and strikes without reason." He struggled to his feet. "See? I'm well now."

He *did* look better, Maurynna conceded. Like a newly dead corpse instead of one a few days old. She had a good mind to send him back. Then she remembered the patrols they'd left behind them.

No, she was stuck with him and he with her, and they both were stuck with this tunnel. "Are you well enough to go on?"

"Yes. Just," he said, then hesitated. Maurynna waited. The next words spilled out in a rush and made Shima sound much younger than he was. "Next time—please warn me first?" he said.

Maurynna smiled. "Fair enough. If I can, I shall. Come."

This time she insisted on going first. Shima argued briefly but futilely. Maurynna was not in a mood to be gainsaid; thank all the gods, the man had sense enough to recognize that and recognize it quickly.

If only Linden would be so sensible . . .

Once again she sent the coldfire around the bulge of stone. But this time she followed it closely, not letting it get more than a few steps away from her. After squeezing around the obstruction, Maurynna paused and poured more energy into the coldfire. It blazed up.

The light showed only more tunnel like the path they had already journeyed through. There was nothing that might explain what happened to her other globe of coldfire. Had she somehow extinguished it by accident? For a moment she almost convinced herself; then she remembered what she'd felt as it had disappeared. She shivered.

But there was nothing for it but to go on. Step by cautious step, they advanced; the coldfire glowed steadily.

There was only an instant's warning—but it was enough. This time Maurynna was ready. She felt the coldfire flicker even before she saw it happen, and poured more energy into it, willing the glowing ball to stay lit.

It was a battle like no other she'd ever faced. Once, while serving as second mate on Aunt Maleid's ship, she'd helped fight off pirates, and she'd defended herself against footpads more than once. But this was no battle of the flesh; this was of mind and will alone. She gritted her teeth against the unaccustomed strain and wished for a sword in her hand and a simple fight.

Die! The command beat at the coldfire and through it, at her. The coldfire flickered and dimmed.

Live! she ordered, recklessly pouring yet more energy into the coldfire. It was, damn it all, *her* coldfire and would go out when *she* bade it do so.

And. Not. Till. Then.

The coldfire blazed up like a tiny sun under the lash of her anger. She felt the other will retreat, sensed something like confusion, then it was back, slamming into her like a wall of hate. She pushed back with every bit of strength she had.

Dimly, she felt Shima's hands on her shoulders; somehow she knew that he lent her his own strength, knew that he sometimes did this for Zhantse when the shaman went into a trance. She seized that strength and wielded it against the Other.

It was unbearable, like being buried under a fall of boulders, each burning hot and all jagged edges. She struggled to hold from heartbeat to heartbeat.

Just when she thought she would fail, it stopped. The Other was gone. Maurynna went to her knees in relief. The coldfire hung in the air before her, glowing softly as if nothing had happened.

She shook her head, dazed. Had she imagined the whole thing? She looked back over her shoulder at Shima. By the look on his face, it had been as real as the rock beneath her.

He said, "What—what was that?" His voice shook with weariness as he held out a hand to her.

"I don't know," said Maurynna. She refused his hand. "Not yet; I must rest." She leaned back against a smooth bit of wall and closed her eyes. Gods help her, she'd never felt this tired—nay, exhausted—before. This was not just a weariness of the body; she knew *that* feeling well enough. This was of the mind and spirit as well. She wanted nothing more than to curl up in Linden's arms and sleep for a year. She wrapped her arms around her bent legs and rested her head on her knees. "Just a little while," she said. She shut her eyes against the world.

Too short a time later, Shima touched her hand. "We must be away," he said. "I don't know if it's safe in these tunnels."

Oh, gods. Move? She was still so tired. Even the tiny effort to keep the coldfire alive was a drain. Still, she wavered to her feet.

"Are you well?" he asked anxiously.

"Well enough," Maurynna said. Even to herself she sounded miles away. "Let's go on for as long as I can."

So on and on they went. The tunnel twisted now like a

snake and was no longer the relatively smooth path it had been. Where before the floor had been solid—if strewn with rocks—now they had to jump from rock to rock and scramble up, down, and around. Many times it narrowed so much that they had to turn sideways and exhale before working a way through.

Once Maurynna thought she was caught. But she found that she could empty her lungs just a tiny bit more, and she squeezed through, thanking the gods all the while that she was not a big-breasted woman. Still, it was hideously uncomfortable.

Her head swam as she escaped at last. Dazed and gasping, she looked around as Shima emerged behind her.

Here the tunnel opened out into a good-sized "room." That was good; she needed to sit once more. But to her horror, the coldfire's now faint and wavering light revealed numerous exits from the room.

Panic nearly claimed her. Then she remembered that Zhantse had warned them of this place; at least, she hoped it was the spot he'd told them about. Behind her she heard Shima counting.

"One, two, three," he said. He sounded unutterably weary. "Four. . . . There; that must be the exit. Shall we see if the blazes are there?"

They supported one another in the seemingly endless journey to cross the room. At last they reached it.

"Right hand wall," Shima muttered. "There should be—" He stopped.

The wall was blank.

Maurynna's stomach churned. Had they taken a wrong turn somewhere? If so, could they ever get out again? An image flashed across her mind: she and Shima wandering lost beneath the mountain until their food and water ran out. Would some other brave Tah'nehsieh explorer find their bones someday?

"Let's look again," she said, suddenly glad she was so tired. Otherwise, she'd be in hysterics.

They looked. Nothing. They even went down the low-ceiling tunnel a short way, although Zhantse had told them the blazes were just inside the opening. But the walls were as nature had left them.

"Where did we go wrong?" Maurynna said at last. Then, "Shima, I must sit down. Now."

She leaned on his shoulder as he led her back to the center of the room. It was the only clear spot large enough for them to sprawl in exhaustion.

Shima opened the pouch hanging at his side and pulled out a *pyamah* cake. He carefully broke it in half and held it out to her. Their eyes met; Maurynna nodded, understanding the reason for the meager rations. It made her skin crawl. As she reached to take her portion, a wave of faintness spread over her and the coldfire flickered alarmingly.

All at once Maurynna remembered last summer, when she'd found Linden felled by an attack of combined sorcery and poisoning. She recalled now how Kief Shaeldar had taken the little globe of coldfire Linden had conjured up before the attack and returned it to him. For even the tiny expenditure of energy to keep the coldfire lit, the older Dragonlord had said, was too much for the stricken man.

She closed her eyes and concentrated as she ate. Yes; now that she paid attention to it, she could feel the drain. She could not keep the coldfire lit.

But neither can I douse it; what will that do to Shima?

Two impossibilities to reconcile; she wanted to howl her frustration and weariness to the world. Instead, she made herself say calmly, "Shima, I can't keep the coldfire lit. Not now; not after . . . what happened back there."

He swallowed hard, she saw, as if the last mouthful of *pyamah* cake had turned to ashes on his tongue. Then, slowly, reluctantly, he nodded. "I—I understand. It must be near dawn by now. We should try to sleep, I suppose. . . ." His voice trailed off miserably.

Sleep. Somehow the word had never sounded so beautiful before. Had the lord of all demons appeared before her and offered her gold and pearls, Maurynna would have told him to take such trash away and bring her a feather bed instead. Swallowing the last bit of *pyamah* cake, she curled up on the dusty floor of the cave, and drew her *jelah* closer.

Shima did the same. "Ready?" she asked.

A long pause. "Yes." He squeezed his eyes shut.

She bade the coldfire go out, hoping that "tomorrow" she'd have the strength to bring it forth once more.

Yet even if she did, they were still lost. Her heart quailed at the sudden reminder. Resolutely, she thrust the knowledge from her. Things would work themselves out when she woke.

She hoped.

"This is a good place to camp," Tefira said. "See the *dilanqui* vines? We can get water from them."

Raven looked around and nodded; the spot was sheltered, with plenty of vines crawling over the rock. "Well enough," he said and swung out of the saddle. He rested a hand on the Llysanyin's shoulder while he stretched the kinks out of his back.

"And a good place to leave the horses," Tefira continued as he jumped to the ground.

"What?" Raven demanded. Leave Stormwind?

Stormwind stamped a foot as if echoing his thoughts.

Tefira nodded. "From here on the trail is too broken and narrow for them; remember, I've listened to the scouts talking. And see that big rock there? The one like a woman wearing a *jelah* and carrying a basket on her head?"

With a jut of his chin, the boy indicated a rock formation about a half mile away from them. After a moment Raven remembered that pointing was considered impolite among the tribe. It took him a moment to tell which rock Tefira spoke of, for he was unused to seeing images in the bones of this land the way the Tah'nehsieh did. But then something in his vision shifted, and he saw it clearly.

"That means that we're nearing the rim of the valley. On horseback, we would be silhouetted against the sky—and those silhouettes would be wrong. We don't look like Jehangli soldiers, and our mounts don't look like Jehangli horses, especially Stormwind."

Raven met the Llysanyin's gaze. "He's right, boy," Raven said reluctantly.

Stormwind's ears went back.

"You know he's right."

Stormwind looked away. He snorted, a sound of pure and unadulterated disgust.

Thank the gods he can't talk, Raven thought. *He's just said plenty, and I don't think I'd like to hear it in words.*

Maurynna woke to a darkness so complete that for a moment she thought she'd gone blind. But before she had time to panic, she remembered where she was—and that was enough to bring on a second rush of fear.

She forced it away and sat up, hugging her knees. The unnatural fatigue was gone; she must have slept deeply indeed to feel this rested. It was time to go on—if they could.

At a word from her, a globe of coldfire appeared in the air, spinning slowly. As its light fell on Shima's face, he awoke.

He blinked up at her, then, as he remembered their plight, sat up as well, his expression grim.

"Shima, I hate to ask this, but are you certain you remembered correctly?"

He nodded. "The tunnel that goes to—" He stopped, his eyes unfocused. Then, so suddenly it startled her, he jumped to his feet. "I didn't count the tunnel we came in through, did I?"

Maurynna pointed. "It was that one; I remember the knob on that little outcropping." She sent the coldfire to him and watched, holding her breath, as the Tah'nehsieh strode along the wall, counting.

Stopping before another opening, Shima seized the coldfire and examined the walls. One look at the grinning face he turned back to her, and she was on her feet. Scooping up their shoulder pouches, she said, "Let's get out of here."

They set off down the tunnel.

* * *

"So where will they be?" Raven whispered as he and Tefira scuttled among the rocks.

"They would have gone to my cousin Amura," Tefira answered. "He knows the entrance."

"So where's Amura?"

Tefira didn't answer. Alarmed, Raven said, "Don't you know where—"

"No! All I know is that he's in the slave camp, but I don't know where that is. This is further than I've ever been before." The boy scrambled ahead.

Raven stood rooted to the ground in shock. "You mean we've come all this way, and you don't even know how to find—"

With something that sounded suspiciously like a sob, Tefira broke into a run and disappeared around an outcropping. Desperate not to lose the only guide he had, Raven raced after.

As he came around the outcropping, he heard Tefira cry out, but it was too late. He ran straight into the Jehangli patrol. An armored fist caught him on the side of the head; he went to his knees, hearing the cries of "Dakka! Dakka!" that he'd heard too often in Jehanglan whenever someone saw his hair or Lleld's for the first time.

Dazed, he saw the glint of sun on metal, and rolled. The spearpoint meant for his heart sliced through the flesh of his upper arm instead. He cried out at the pain.

He heard Tefira yelling that he wasn't a demon. Then a harsh voice barked orders that he couldn't understand, and two men hauled him to his feet.

Then came an order he *could* understand. "March!" The spear pricked him in the back, and Raven felt blood running down as he fell into a stumbling walk, Tefira by his side.

Was this what Zhantse feared? Raven wondered as they walked. If he caused the mission to fail, and Maurynna's death . . .

He shut his mind to the thought, and concentrated on

keeping his feet. Somehow they had to get away; he had to stay alert.

As they walked, Maurynna became more and more aware of a strange, uneasy feeling. She stretched out her senses, wondering what it was; then she knew, and her breath caught.

Pirakos. Pirakos, pulling at her, willing her to him. The feeling made her flesh creep; there was a darkness there, unclean and evil, that made the simple darkness of the tunnels beyond the coldfire's light seem like a friend.

She was so caught up in her discovery that she walked like one in a dream. It wasn't until Shima cried, "Light!" that she looked around.

Sure enough, from a jagged opening above and ahead of them, daylight poured in, warm, cheerful, comforting. She drank it in.

A thought came to her. "Shima—does the direction chant say anything . . . ?"

"No, yet I know we're going the right way—see the mark there? I wonder if that tremor Amura spoke of opened this, as well."

"No matter, as long as we're going the right way. But Shima, I must look outside. I—I hate this darkness."

With that, she ran to the tunnel wall below the opening. To her relief, there were hand and footholds. She began climbing, Shima right behind her.

It wasn't far, and there was a ledge as if some considerate being had arranged for one so that they could crouch side by side and look out upon the world.

True, she thought wryly, all there was to see was the red rock and hard-packed soil of a steep slope, and the needled plants that grew everywhere in this land, but the sunlight was pure joy, and the air fresh. She breathed it in, her eyes closed, her face raised to the warmth and light, enjoying this little miracle—until she heard Shima gasp, "Tefira!"

"What?" she said in confusion, opening her eyes once more.

Then she saw them, and the world froze around her.

Fifty-four

"Oh, dear gods! Shima—you've got to help them!" Maurynna gripped the rocks in front of her at the sight of Raven, wounded and bleeding, stumbling along the valley floor as Tefira supported him on one side. The valley guards herded them along with jabs from their spears and pikes.

Yes, he was a fool to disobey and follow you—but if everyone who'd ever played the fool died for it, there would be precious few people in the world. He doesn't deserve to die.

Tefira, they would make a slave; Raven, they would kill as an outlander demon. She was as certain of that as she was of the tides. Her blood turned to ice at the thought of it.

"Shima," she pleaded when he didn't move.

He turned to her, emotions warring in his face. "What would you have me do?" he said. "My duty is to you. They've brought this upon themselves."

Harsh words that the misery in his eyes belied. That was his brother down there. And while he might not care much for Raven, Shima certainly didn't wish Raven's death, either. The anguished look on his face told her that.

"Go," she said. "Distract the guards—there aren't too many of them. Give Raven and the boy at least a chance to get away. I'll . . . I release you from my service. I can go on alone, truly I can, Shima. I can *feel* Pirakos; that will guide me."

He made no move to leave her.

Her fists clenched. If she had to drive him away from her by force, she would. Then, without her willing it, words sprang unbidden to her lips. "Dragonlord's orders!" she snapped. "Go!"

How stupid; the words would mean nothing to Shima. He'd not been raised on legends of—

But the Tah'nehsieh was scrambling out of the hole and slinking between the rocks and scrubby bushes that clung to the sloping canyon wall before she could blink. He moved like a shadow, slipping from one impossible hiding place to another, making his way downhill faster than Maurynna would have believed possible.

She glanced at the canyon floor once more. The guards marched their prisoners along with harsh words and an occasional blow. One guard poked Raven with his spear; Maurynna heard Raven's faint cry. Blood welled up, staining his tunic.

She raged in silent fury as prisoners and guards passed by below. Helplessness sat ill with her, but she must leave this to Shima. That, or break her oath to Morlen. And that she would not do.

At least, not while there was another way.

She looked once more for Shima. But there was no sign of him. Only sheer will kept her from jumping to her feet to search the slope below for him. Had he run away? No, if he were the kind to break, Zhantse would not have chosen him as her companion. Though she'd known him for only a few days, she trusted the Seer. Why, she wasn't certain. But trust him, she did.

Then a flash of movement caught her eye. Had she been truehuman, she doubted she would have seen it. Shima seemed to flow across the ground like a shadow.

Then he was at the base of the slope and out in the open. She chewed her knuckles as Shima raced across the canyon floor behind the unsuspecting guards and started up the other side.

Thank the gods the canyon is narrow here. But what is he planning?

While she watched, he changed direction. Now, instead of heading upslope, he traversed it in the same direction that the five guards herded Raven and Tefira. He moved quickly. No doubt, she thought, he depended on the guards not thinking to look up.

Now he had nearly caught up with the little group. Maurynna thought she could see where he was making for: a point where the canyon narrowed even more. She still could not guess Shima's plan, but whatever it was, she hoped it worked. And now she must be away—or else be forsworn. It was all up to Shima.

It was one of the hardest things she'd ever done. But she turned her back on the scene below and returned to the darkness that waited to swallow her once more.

Shima darted from boulder to boulder, *kaqualla* bush to *kaqualla* bush, their sharp grey-green, needlelike leaves pricking him each time he slid into their shelter. Once, while out in the open, he slipped on a loose stone and dislodged a shower of pebbles. They tumbled down the slope. To him it sounded like an avalanche; he froze, afraid even to breathe, hoping that his dun-colored breeches and sleeveless tunic, and his dark skin, would blend in with the colors of the canyon wall should one of the guards look in his direction.

None did. Indeed, it seemed they hadn't heard a thing. He exhaled shakily. He'd been lucky this time. Yet now he must hurry even more if he was to reach his goal in time— and that meant more chances to catch the attention of the guards.

But it had to be done. He set off again, moving as fast as he dared.

It wasn't good enough; the group below already had a lead on him. Now it had increased, and he didn't think he could close it once more. He cursed under his breath.

I must *get ahead of them before they reach the exit to this canyon. If only they'd slow down!* He drove himself on, straining every nerve and muscle in a nightmarish— and likely futile—scramble across the treacherous slope.

Just when he was certain he'd fail, something happened

below. Shima paused long enough to see that Tefira was down and clutching one ankle. Raven knelt beside him; bloodstains spread across his tunic from numerous small cuts, dark against the pale cloth. The guards clustered around them with curses and shouted orders. Shima seized the opportunity and flung himself across the slope without any effort at concealment. If he could just make that group of boulders just ahead . . .

There! He collapsed among them, breathing hard. Thank the Spirits he'd made it without attracting notice from below.

Then the world went mad—or he did. Suddenly, the desert scents he'd known all his life overwhelmed him. The dry, dusty smell of the rocks and sand, the sharp, resinous smell of bruised *kaqualla* that clung to his clothes, a thousand other subtle scents, all hammered at him. He bit his lip to keep from crying out.

And, Spirits help him, he should not be able to hear so clearly the curses the guards heaped on the unfortunate Tefira.

His eyes betrayed him next. One moment his vision was normal; the next, everything stood out so clearly it was painful. He could see details of the group below that he should not have seen from this distance, not in a thousand years.

A botched darn on one guard's tunic caught his stunned attention. His gaze fastened on the uneven stitches as if nothing else mattered in the world.

Is this what an eagle sees like? he wondered. His mind tumbled over itself in a welter of confused sights and sounds and smells. Was he stricken with a sudden fever? Or just gone mad at last?

Yet mad or not, he had a mission. Staggering, Shima rose to his feet once more. He pushed his fear away and darted out from the shelter of the rocks. Once more he made his way across the slope. He drew ahead of the men below, their pace slowed by the limping Tefira.

As he slid and slithered from hiding place to hiding

place, the world receded to normal almost without his noticing it. He sighed in relief even as he ran. All was once more as it should be.

Or was it? Were things just a bit sharper, colors a bit brighter? He refused to think about it.

For now his goal lay ahead of him: a large, round boulder balanced precariously by a few small rocks. It was a wonder the recent tremors hadn't dislodged it already. He hoped he had better luck.

Now, he prayed as he covered the last stretch to the boulder, *let Raven and Tefira stay ahead of the guards; those bastards can't want to get too close to a potential demon. . . .*

He was in place. Pressed against the boulder, Shima looked around it to the canyon floor below, watching the group below. With a shock he saw that Tefira, under the guise of talking to Raven, was instead searching the slope. Darting a quick glance to make certain none of the guards were also interested, Shima dared to raise a hand for the briefest of moments. Tefira lurched and came to rest against Raven, one hand now grasping the Yerrin's arm as if seeking to steady himself; Shima saw and knew the motion for what it was: an exaggerated nod.

But how had the boy known he was here?

Now Raven and Tefira were almost abreast of his position. On a hunch, Shima raised his hand once more. Tefira started running, dragging a surprised Raven after him. There was no sign of a limp now.

Shima almost laughed aloud. The boy had been faking a twisted ankle all this time!

Still, just *how*— A thought struck Shima. Maybe the boy was meant for a Seer after all.

Enough of that. He still had work to do. From sheer surprise, Raven and Tefira had gained a fair headstart. They ran swift as hares as they coursed among the rocks.

But now the guards were after them. Staying out of sight behind a rock, Shima cupped his hands to his mouth and bellowed in Jehangli, "Sergeant!"

The guard with the most braid on his armor stopped in confusion; he looked wildly around.

"Those two are just a diversion, you fools! There are Tah'nehsieh warriors up here, curse them. Hurry!"

The sergeant hesistated. Shima let loose with flood of curses that he'd heard once from a thwarted Jehangli general who'd picked the worst route to try to invade the *mehanso*. The soldiers below him blanched and started up the slope without further delay.

Shima watched from a narrow crack between two rocks. He waited as the armored men grunted their way toward him. Just a little more would see the guards into the trap. "Come along, little idiots, come along," Shima whispered as if he talked to his family's flock of sheep.

But unfortunately the sergeant had somewhat more wits than any of the woolly idiots Shima had once herded. The man stopped, waved his squad to a halt, and called, "But, sir, where are the Tah'—"

Shima cut him off. "Over the ridge, of course, you idiot," he raged like a man in a towering fury. "The others are holding them at bay. Now *move*, you sorry donkey turds, else I charge you with cowardice!"

At that, the men started climbing once more and at a much smarter pace. Better to face armed Tah'nehsieh than the punishment reserved for cowards, no doubt. Shima had counted on that fear.

Closer . . . closer . . . a few more steps . . . Now!

Shima set his shoulder to the stone and heaved.

The great boulder teetered—but nothing more. Cursing in frustration, Shima tried again. He *must* send it tumbling! Else they would be upon him and he would be a dead man.

Frantic, he heaved again. The stone wouldn't move.

And now he could hear the heavy breathing of the soldiers as they labored up the steep slope.

Shei-Luin went up to the altar in the Temple of the Phoenix in Rivasha, the holiest of the temples of Jehanglan, and lit nine sticks of incense. She placed them in the gold stand, and bowed her head in prayer.

She prayed for Jehanglan, for Tsiaa, for her children's safety, for Yesuin's safety, and for Xiane, that he might shelter beneath the Phoenix's wing. She prayed for the strength to do all that needed to be done, to guide an empire until her son was old enough. She prayed for Lord Jhanun to fall into her power; she would revenge the wrongs done Nama.

When she was done, she turned to the waiting head priest. "I would see the palace of the Phoenix," she said.

For a moment she thought he would refuse; she was, after all, only a woman.

But she was also the empress of Jehanglan. He bowed, saying, "This way, Phoenix Lady," and led her from the temple through a passage behind the altar.

They came out upon a stairway of white marble that stretched up the last of the slope of the holy mountain of Rivasha. At the top of the stairs was a tower, also of white marble. She had taken a litter to the temple; the walk from the bottom of the mountain to the temple had been a long one. She knew better than to ask for one here; even emperors went afoot to the Phoenix. She lifted her robes and began the long climb. When the priest would have stopped Murohshei, Shei-Luin turned to him.

Their gazes met, battled; the priest dropped his hand. Shei-Luin went on; Murohshei followed.

At last she stood upon the tower. Before her was the Palace of the Phoenix, the sacred heart of Jehanglan. Mount Kajhenral was a necessary evil; this, she'd been told, was all beauty and goodness.

From her father's teachings, she knew that this mountain was one of the dead volcanoes that dotted Jehanglan. Like many of them, its top had sunk in to form a bowl. Set all around the crater were boulders of white quartz glinting in the sun.

Yet while many of those other dead mountains held lakes in their craters, this one held light—a pure, white light that swirled with gold at the base defined by the quartz boulders.

It looks just like a giant, upside-down bowl! She nearly giggled at the thought. Somehow, she'd always pictured a palace like the imperial palace, with the Phoenix perched upon a tower. This was, she had to admit, somewhat of a disappointment—just an upside-down bowl of light, like the smaller ones that held the crowns, that hid whatever was—

Something moved inside the light. Shei-Luin gasped. Whatever it was, it had been huge. No, not a whatever—she had seen the Phoenix. She bowed to it, but the shadow was gone.

When she returned to the temple, Shei-Luin said to the high priest, "I wish my sons to see this, to receive the blessing of the Phoenix. I will await them here. Murohshei, go to the palace and bring Xahnu and Xu to me when they awaken from their naps."

The head priest bowed to her and said, "This way, then, Phoenix Lady. There's a set of chambers for the use of the imperial family when they visit; I shall bring you there."

As Murohshei departed on his errand, Shei-Luin followed the priest.

The tunnel ended in a huge cavern. Maurynna jumped down to the cavern floor. She held the coldfire before her, but the space was so huge that its light was but a feeble glow that revealed nothing.

Then, once again, the will of the Other slammed against her, and the coldfire died.

Fifty-five

Once more Shima set his shoulder to the round boulder. This time he pushed so hard that his joints cracked and his vision swam.

Nothing.

Perhaps it was the almost superhuman effort; perhaps not. But suddenly the world was too sharp, too clear once more. Startled, Shima heaved one last time.

The boulder tumbled from its precarious base with an ease that sent him reeling. He went down on hands and knees. Somehow he kept his wits about him long enough to look below.

The boulder picked up speed as it hurtled down the slope. With a sound like thunder, it swept other boulders and rocks before it. In moments, the single stone had become an avalanche.

The looks of horror on the faces of the leading men cut Shima to his soul. The poor wretches barely had time to scream before they were crushed like insects.

He felt sick. This was not the first time he'd killed a man; even though he was no warrior, he'd once fought to defend himself, his family, and the others in the spring pilgrimage to the Holy Mountain of the Lady when they'd been attacked by a stray patrol of Jehangli warriors. But that time it had been face-to-face. This . . .

He shook his head. He'd had no choice but to use whatever weapons he could lay hand to; now he'd best take thought to saving his own skin. With the boulder gone, so was his concealment. And not all of the Jehangli had been caught; he could see at least two who, being lower down, had cast themselves to the sides and safety. Now the faces that turned up to him revealed animal fury and a lust for revenge; a lust that would not be satisfied until they had spitted him on the ends of their spears and watched his blood flow while he thrashed in a lingering death.

Shima jumped to his feet and ran.

Murohshei sat in the nursery, waiting patiently for the children to waken. He knew from bitter experience that, if woken early, Xahnu would be cranky for the rest of the day. He smiled down at the little emperor-to-be, sleeping peacefully with his thumb in his mouth, the dark fringe of his lashes like crescent moons upon his cheeks. His brother lay beside him, a smile on his plump-cheeked face.

Zyuzin plopped down on the cushions beside him. "It will be a while," he whispered ruefully, "because we just got them settled a short time ago." He nodded at the children's nurses, who sat a little ways off, gossiping with their heads together. "Took me *ages* to sing them to sleep."

Murohshei shrugged. "So? The temple will still be there, and our lady understands."

Malevolence lurked in that darkness; if she took one more step into it, it would be on her like a snowcat on its prey. She dared not create another ball of coldfire. Until she had a better idea of what was in here, she would not reveal her position. She had never been afraid of the dark before, but this terrified her. If only Linden was here with her . . . If only *someone* could be here with her.

But the darkness was not the worst of it. For now the stench of the place attacked like a living, malignant thing. It nearly overwhelmed her; she clapped a hand over her mouth and fought her rebellious stomach down. The acrid reek wound around her and brought tears to her eyes. She wondered if she'd ever be able to scrub the stink off.

Gods help me, she thought, wiping her eyes, concentrating on breathing through her mouth, though it was little better, *has poor Pirakos lived in his own filth all this time?* Her stomach did another slow flip.

She took a cautious breath, shallow and experimental. The stench of excrement was nearly overwhelming, but, worse yet, under it she could smell festering flesh and old, rotting blood. She breathed through her mouth again, sickened. Morlen had been right; Pirakos's chains had dug into his flesh as a rope knotted around a young tree is covered by the growing wood. The thought of his agony made her knees tremble.

Still, there was no gain in standing here. She shuffled a little farther into the cavern.

Something caught Maurynna's foot; she stumbled. In catching herself, her foot came down heavily on a lump that splintered with a dry crack and threw her off balance. She staggered and fell.

Her hand came down on a round rock. But when her fingers closed over it, they slid into two openings. Holding her breath, Maurynna explored farther.

It wasn't a rock. It was a skull. A human skull.

"I must see how my brother fares," Tefira insisted. "I know which way he went. Even I've learned the ways through this badland. I listened when the scouts talked, studied the maps they scratched in the dirt. I—just never learned where the slave camp was."

Raven knew it was dangerous. Worse, it was useless. Unarmed as they were, they could give Shima no aid. But neither could he gainsay Tefira's right. This was a matter of kin. So he nodded sharply and said, "So be it."

Tefira was off like a racehorse. Raven scrambled after him, only his long legs enabling him to keep up with the boy. Up and down and around they ran, dodging boulders and prickly plants, until they reached a ridge. There they hunkered down among the rocks so that they wouldn't stand out against the skyline. Below them, the earth formed a rock-strewn hollow. Raven cleared a space of some sharp stones and laid down on his stomach, careful to keep his head in a patch of shadow so that the sun wouldn't flame in his hair.

"See the path that runs just below the ridge on the other side? I think Shima will make for that; it leads down to a maze of trails that the Jehangli won't go through if they can help it. Sometimes our young warriors hunt there. We can reach it from this side as well."

Tefira did not, Raven noted, say just what the warriors came to hunt. He suspected it wasn't rabbits.

"Here he comes!" Joy and relief flooded the boy's voice.

Raven saw Shima crest the ridge and slither down to the trail. One moment all was well; the Tah'nehsieh ran along the path like a mountain goat. The next, Shima was tumbling down the slope in a cloud of dust.

Then Raven heard the faint sound of shouted orders and knew that the soldiers would be there any moment.

"Thank you for letting Yesuin ride with us again," Linden said, reining Shan alongside Dzeduin's horse as they rode on the banks of the Black River.

The Zharmatian shrugged and smiled ruefully. "Since Yemal's not here now . . . It just seems cruel, making him stay in Ghulla's tent all the time. Even she enjoys riding still," Dzeduin said, glancing over at the ancient Seer, who kept up easily with the group.

Lleld said something to her, gesturing to Jekkanadar and Otter, and the Seer burst into cackling laughter.

"How old is she, anyway?" Linden asked.

"Old. Very old. I don't think she's changed since I was a child." Dzeduin shivered. "I don't ask how she does it. I don't think I want to know."

They rode on a little longer side-by-side. Then Dzeduin burst out, "I wonder when she's going to tell Yesuin—she won't let me do it."

"Tell him what?"

"That Xiane Ma Jhi—the emperor, the one who saved his life; his friend—is dead. She said he needs to find Zhantse in Nisayeh first."

Linden looked over at Yesuin, who had joined the laughing group in their joke.

"Poor beggar," he said.

* * *

It happened as he jumped over a small crack in the dried ground. Shima's foot came down on a loose rock and he tumbled down the slope in a painful tangle of sharp little stones and sand. He fetched up at the bottom of the basin with a painful thump that knocked the wind out of him. His head spun.

He sat up, shaking his head, then took stock. Bruises, yes; scrapes, yes—even a deep cut or two. And a bump on his head that hurt like blazes. But there was nothing broken or even sprained.

"Hwah!" he said as he lurched to his feet and limped off. "That was lu— Ouch!" He'd found a new bruise.

He scuttled across the bottom of the basin as fast as he could, intending to be over the far ridge before the Jehangli soldiers climbed the one he'd fallen from.

But the basin was wider than he'd thought, and the way was so broken that he was only partway up the other side when he heard the clash of armor. Ahead was a tiny "cave" formed by a tumble of boulders. Shima threw himself at it and wormed a way inside, fervently hoping there were no snakes hiding there from the sun.

He curled up, turning so that he could look back the way he came, the opening etched stark and bright beyond the darkness that sheltered him. At once his body began to complain. Shima ignored it, concentrating on breathing lightly so that he might hear the soldiers.

Let them take the path! he prayed over and over.

At first all he heard was a distant murmur of voices. Then, once again, his hearing played tricks on him.

"HERE! A TRAIL!"

The words clanged in his head. For a moment he thought they would shatter his skull. He moaned and clutched his head against the pain.

"WHAT IF HE WENT DOWN?"

Then it was upon him again, worse than ever. The Feeling thrashed within his chest like a hawk throwing itself against the bars of a cage.

OutOutOutOutOutOutOut!

Even knowing it was Death that drove him, Shima
scrambled frantically for the opening.

Bones. The floor of the cavern was littered with cracked
and shattered bones. Maurynna's hands searched around her
almost without her willing it. Her head spun; had the Jehangli priestmages fed Pirakos on criminals and those suspected of harboring a dragonsoul? She licked dry lips.

Gods, what that must have done to Pirakos, forced to eat
human flesh. She prayed that the unfortunates were dead
before they'd been thrown in. Her mind quailed at the
thought of what terror they'd faced otherwise. Then she
realized: these were the ones that got away, only to die a
long, lingering death in the darkness.

She had to have a light; she'd been lucky before. Some
of the fragments she'd touched were sharp as a spear. If
she'd landed wrong . . .

Cupping her hands, Maurynna called up a tiny flicker of
coldfire, barely more than a candle's flame. It cast the fee-
blest of glows.

Yet it was enough, with her dragonsight, to reveal that
an arched opening lay before her, and that the cavern she
followed curved away beyond it.

She stood up once more and held the coldfire cupped in
her hands. What she sought lay beyond that arch, and seek
it she must.

From nowhere a voice hissed through her mind like a
wind of cold evil.

Truuuuehuuuuumaaaaan.

She walked through the archway as one bespelled.

Shima staggered as the harsh desert sunlight beat down on
him. The brightness seared his eyes as if someone had
thrust a torch into them. He groped his way along the rock-
strewn ground, the Feeling driving him into the open. On
he went, hearing the triumphant cries of the soldiers, but
as if from a distance, as if they had nothing to do with him.

But they did, and part of him knew it and fought to get away. The war went on in his mind but his feet led him unerringly to the center of the basin.

He saw the Jehangli soldiers reach the bottom of the slope—and he could do nothing. The Feeling ruled him, devoured him, would kill him.

Spirits—no! This is madness! They'll kill me—please let me go, he begged it.

One soldier's arm drew back; Shima saw the sunlight blaze along the spearhead. In another instant it would bury itself in his heart. But there was nothing he could do.

For he—he was melting! Shima cried out in terror as the world faded, but there was no sound.

Maurynna went forward, step by slow step. Bones blanketed the cavern floor. She never knew at what point she became aware of the slow, heavy breathing. At first it seemed to be the ebb and flow of her own heart's blood in her ears. Then she realized the sound came from without, but that it demanded her heart match its rhythm even as her feet moved to its time.

Then she was past the turning and climbing up a wall into a cavern even larger than the one before, and shaped like a long, deep bowl, blackened in places. A narrow path, level with the entrance, ran around the sides. At the far end were four pillars hewn from glittering quartz, their tops level with the path, each surrounded by a nimbus of golden light; in the center of the square they formed was a huge, oddly shaped rock. Two of the pillars were beyond the rock; but of the two that she could see, the heaviest chains Maurynna had ever seen led from their bases to the rock in the center. She walked along the path, looking down into the bowl and wondering at the strange scene, forgetting all else: her fear, the terrible stench of the place, the malevolence that flooded this hollow heart of the mountain.

Then, with a rattle of those cruel chains, the strange rock moved. A great eye opened, glowing red and insane in the light of the pillars as the huge head peered up at her. Long white fangs shone as Pirakos laughed silently, horribly.

Thee are mine, girl.

Tefira cried out as his brother dissolved into red mist. "Shima! Shima!" he screamed.

A quick glance at the boy's terror-stricken face told Raven that Tefira didn't understand what was happening to his brother.

But he did. And he knew what it would mean if the spearhead—cold iron—should pierce that mist: Shima would be unmade.

He had only the instant of the soldier's surprise and hesitation to do something. Raven snatched up a heavy stone and flung it even as that moment's reprieve ended and the soldier's arm went back once more to hurl the spear.

Raven forgot to breathe as the stone hurtled through the air. Had he aimed true?

Jhanun arrived at his compound in Rivasha as leader of a much smaller force of men than he'd hoped for. Many troops were away fighting the Zharmatians and their lightning raids. He left the men outside the city for now, and rode in with just a few trusted men as escort. Before he did anything, he wished to pray to the Phoenix for guidance.

But when he entered his family's shrine, he found the altar draped in grey, the color of mourning, and the steward of the house burning incense in a bowl the same color.

"Who's dead?" Jhanun demanded.

The steward whirled around, one hand clasped to his breast. "My lord! You startled me!" He bowed, then said, "Didn't you know, my lord? Your niece, Nama, concubine to the late emperor, is dead, and her unborn child with her."

Jhanun could only stare at the man, unable to face the fact that his second plan had crumbled to dust.

Mistaking stunned silence for grief, the steward hurried to say, "But the empress honored her, my lord! She was given the honors of a *noh*, and her ashes placed in the altar of the imperial family. And it's said that, while she's here, the empress burns incense for Nama in the—"

"Shei-Luin *noh* Jhi is here? In Rivasha?" Jhanun demanded.

The steward blinked. "Shei-Luin Ma Jhi, my lord," he corrected in mild reproof. "Yes—she and her sons are here."

Her sons . . .

He would never get control of his niece's child now, to set it up as a claimant for the throne. But—

Her sons . . .

With the swiftness of a tiger, Jhanun spun around and ran from the shrine.

Come closer, girl, the voice wheedled. *Come closer, let me see thee.*

Maurynna clutched her head. The syrupy voice slid around her mind, carrying with it hints of blood and violence, desperation beyond measure, the taint of madness, and a sick delight in it all. *No,* she said, *I don't trust you.*

Yet go closer she must; how else to free him? She crept forward.

Come closer, I promise that— Pirakos threw back his head and howled as he fought against his chains. The sound slammed into Maurynna as it boomed and echoed in the cavern. She went to her knees, crying out at the pain in her ears.

I will eat thy liver! shrieked Pirakos in her mind. *I will tear thee apart piece by piece and scatter the foul bits to rot, truehuman filth. I will kill all the truehumans,* he raged as he hurled himself as far as his chains allowed. The shackles dug into the flesh festering beneath them. A sweet, sickening stench filled the air.

Maurynna vomited. Sick and shaking, she wiped her mouth with the back of her hand and huddled on the path as a maelstrom of thoughts and images and emotions raged through her mind.

. . . The caress of sunlight on her wings, the taste of the winds . . .

Maurynna began crawling.

I used to hunt rabbits when I was a youngling dragon, thee should know. I would catch them as they came out of their burrows.

The voice slid around her mind, giggling insanely, poking at her, prying, howling in agony, carrying with it the seeds of madness. Most horrible of all was the mind she sensed within—the merest glimpses, but there—trapped and wailing in despair. She concentrated on moving opposite hand and knee, hand and knee, working her way along the path. Sharp slivers of rock cut her as she crawled; she welcomed the distraction from the mindvoice that babbled and bounced within her head.

But now they hide inside—dotheeseethem—and I can't get in anymore, and they wait for me. They wait and wait, their fangs fierce and long and dripping venom. Waiting to tear me apart as—HATEHATEHATEHATE—I will tear thee apart!

He can't reach you, she told herself over and over again, the chains won't let him get out of the bowl, they're too short. Get to the spell stones.

And when she shattered the enchantment? What then?

It didn't matter. She couldn't think about that; she would not think of anything save the ground just ahead of her and how to avoid the worst of the stones. It was the only way. She crawled along the path, inch by painful inch, while the ravening Pirakos flung himself against his chains, her mind closed to all but the burden of forcing her unwilling body forward.

The journey went on and on; then, so suddenly it startled her, Maurynna knelt by the first of the spell stones. It was the one that bound Pirakos's right foreleg.

Golden light washed over her. She raised her face to its gentle warmth, remembering what it felt like to stand beneath the sun. Before she could wonder if she ever would again, Maurynna drew the short sword from its scabbard. Gripping the hilt as hard as she could lest it turn in her blood-slick hands, she drove it into the nimbus.

* * *

It is time! Thee must throw down the Stones of Warding!

Linden halted Shan, shocked. The strange voice that had warned them of Taren's treachery was back in his head. He wondered if he'd imagined it. Or if he was going mad.

But no, that couldn't be; Lleld and Jekkanadar had also stopped, and both wore the same startled expression. Otter, Dzeduin, and Yesuin, on the other hand, had obviously not heard anything. They rode on a few steps before bringing their mounts to a halt and looking back, surprised.

But Ghulla reined her horse in, and sat watching the Dragonlords, smiling slightly.

"What is it?" Otter asked.

"Who—" Jekkanadar began at the same time Lleld said, "That's the voice that warned us, isn't it?"

"Yes. You agree, then, that it's a dragon?" he said. He'd been certain of it, the other time he'd heard it, but what if it were a trick of the priestmages?

Lleld nodded. "Oh, yes; it's definitely draconic—at least, I think it is," she said with an uncertainty utterly foreign to her.

So she'd had the same thoughts of trickery.

Jekkanadar said, "What, discretion at last, Lady Mayhem? Now I've seen everything." His smile was wry. "But I agree. We can't be certain."

Lleld didn't favor him with a glance. "But what does it mean by the 'Stones of Warding?' " She looked over to Ghulla. "Do you know?"

The Seer nodded, still smiling slightly. "They're an abomination, part of the enchantment that keeps the Phoenix prisoner against the natural order of things.

"There are stones, surrounded by temples, at three of the four quarters. They help anchor the power that keeps the Phoenix in Mount Rivasha. The focus is the northern dragon, held under Mount Kajhenral. That's the place that only your soultwin may enter, Linden Rathan. But the others are important as well; unless all are cast down, the Phoenix may not be able to break free. It's possible that the priestmages could summon enough power to hold the prison in place if one falls. They might be able to hold the Phoenix for a time even if three anchors of power were destroyed. Yet I think it would be for only a short time. All their power could not hold the Phoenix long once all the foundations of its prison were swept away."

Hurry! Thee must hurry! Thee endanger Maurynna Kyrissaean with thy delays. It will take time for each of thee to reach the Stones—time that she does not have to waste.

The golden light exploded, hurling her back. Her head struck the ground so hard that stars swam before Maurynna's eyes.

It was Pirakos's roar that brought her back to herself. The truedragon threw himself against his chains with renewed fury. For one heart-stopping moment, Maurynna thought the links would give. But they held, tribute to the long-dead smiths who had worked them. She took a moment to thank them.

Then she was running along the hewn path to the next spell stone.

He—He was solid once more! Yet what had happened to him? Shima shook his head, then stopped, dizzy; his neck was far too—

In one blinding instant he understood; the answer was in the terrified faces before him. Roaring, Shima lashed out with a clawed forefoot. The Jehangli soldiers flew through the air like the pebbles the children threw at the crows to keep them from the young maize. Nor did they move again.

Shima reared up in the hot sunlight, his wings spread wide, overwhelmed by what had happened to him, the wonder of this moment. He stared down at what had been his arms. The light glinted on black scales.

A blur of motion caught his eye. Shima dropped to all fours once more and swung his long neck around, ready for battle.

But it was Tefira and Raven who scrambled down the slope to him. The Yerrin bent and picked up a spear lying on the ground. As if from years ago, Shima remembered that same weapon pointing at him. His mother's tales came back to him, and he understood how close he'd come, not just to death, but to annihilation.

And he knew who had saved him. *Thank you*, he said to Raven. He stopped, startled at using his mind to speak. How had he known . . . ?

There was much to learn, he decided, about being a Dragonlord.

"You're welcome," Raven said. He leaned on the spear. "Now what? And where's Rynna? Why did you leave her?" he demanded.

She ordered me to help you. Dragonlord's orders, she said, Shima replied.

The Yerrin threw back his head and whooped. "To another Dragonlord? Oh, I like that!" Then he sobered. "But we have to find her."

Yes. But, Shima thought, *where?*

Haoro lay prone before the image of the Phoenix while the choir chanted. Though the tile below him was cold, he hardly noticed. Soon he would rise and they would lay the feathered mantle about his shoulders. Soon he would be the *nira*, second only to the emperor in power—and that emperor would be Jhanun.

He smiled, his cheek pressed against smooth tile, while around him the power grew.

Linden reeled in the saddle. The voice rang in his head like a Jehangli temple gong. It was angry and frantic and . . . very, very young, somehow. Close to tears, even, if a dragon could cry.

Danger to Maurynna . . . Trick or no, he couldn't take the chance. He had to Change—now.

He swung a leg over Shan's neck and slid out of the saddle. "Room!" he yelled.

Shan spun on his haunches and raced off. Miki, Hillel and Nightsong followed, ignoring their riders, and herding the Zharmatians' horses with them.

"Linden, wait!" Lleld yelled as Miki bore her to a safe distance. "You don't know—"

"I'll take that chance." He threw his head back and let himself dissolve into mist. From somewhere far away he heard terrified yells; Yesuin and Dzeduin, he thought. Nothing would surprise Ghulla.

A heartbeat later he stood, solid once more, claws digging into the earth, wings half unfurled, his hindlegs tensed for the leap that would take him into the sky. He swung his long neck around to face Lleld and Jekkanadar. *I'm going,* he said to them. *Are you with me?*

For answer, they both swung down from their saddles and moved a safe distance from the horses and each other.

We are echoed in his mind as they flowed into Change. A small red dragon and a larger black one faced him moments later.

Where? Linden asked of the voice he could still feel in the back of his mind. Images blossomed: temples, open in the center, ringing glowing stones vibrating with a power that repelled him.

No, wait; *he* was not the one repelled. It was the one—the *dragon*—who spoke to him. He knew it now beyond all doubt.

And with the images came the knowledge of *where*. Linden hurled himself into the air.

You're the fastest, Lleld said in his mind as he climbed. *Take the tower beyond the city. We'll take the other two.* Lleld and Jekkanadar made their leaps into flight.

Linden wheeled against the sky and raced south.

The next stone. Once more Maurynna gripped the sword; she took a deep breath and lunged forward. And once again the explosion knocked her to the ground. But this time she let herself fall as Lleld had taught her, muscles loose and relaxed.

Now up once more and on to the third. But here the hewn walk narrowed; she must tread a path barely more than two handspans wide, while below her a mad truedragon screamed for her death and flung himself at her.

Step by careful step she went, hardly daring to breathe, sweat trickling down her face. At last the third stone was before her.

The chorus ended on a last, ringing note of triumph. Two priests came to help him up. Haoro stood as two more laid the feathered mantle upon his shoulders. It was surprisingly heavy. He looked down at the golden feathers surrounding him like a nimbus.

"The litter waits, Holy One," one of the priests murmured.

Haoro felt for the little knife in its sheath in his sleeve pocket. Once at the creature's prison, he would cut his arm and sprinkle the vile thing with his blood, sealing the bond between them. His searching fingers found it tucked securely away.

"I'm ready," he said.

They brought him to the litter of the *nira*.

Linden felt the image of the temple with its glowing stone form in his mind once more. With it came the feelings of fear and loathing; from deep inside he felt the beginnings of an answering rage. A draconic rage. Rathan, his dragon half, was stirring.

Linden took that rage and used it. He raced through the sky like a comet.

There was barely room to kneel before the third stone. Maurynna settled herself carefully, trying not to think about what would happen if she fell.

Though Pirakos was quiet now. She risked a glance at him, and wished she hadn't.

He crouched below her like a cat waiting for a mouse to come out of its hole. Glittering, bloodred eyes followed her every move. Smoke drifted from his nostrils.

For the first time she thought to wonder why Pirakos had not tried flaming her. He could easily reach her; she was certain of it. So why hadn't he? And why hadn't he melted the chains—

Her gaze fell on the blackened rocks she had noticed but not truly *seen* earlier. Pirakos had tried his fire, then. A suspicion formed in her mind. She studied the dragon below her as he studied her.

Yes; now that she knew what to look for, she could see the signs: ropes of thick scar tissue running down throat and chest, the scales twisted and deformed.

Pirakos had indeed tried fire to free himself. But the stone had held and reflected the deadly flames back onto the dragon. How many centuries of torment had he endured while he healed? And how desperate had he been to attempt such a thing in the first place? Surely he'd guessed what might happen.

She would never forgive the priestmages for driving another creature to such measures. Cursing, she slashed at the third stone in cold fury.

It was nearly her undoing. She rolled and half fell from the ledge. She caught herself, legs dangling. At once Pirakos threw himself at her and she heard the scream of tortured metal. Terror seized her. The chains were failing!

She scrambled frantically to pull herself back up to the path, certain she felt long fangs snap shut inches below her feet.

Then, somehow, she was back on the path. Her hand closed once more on the sword hilt. Maurynna whispered a prayer of thanks that it had not fallen to the floor below. Sick and shaking, she closed her mind to what had nearly happened and crept along the path.

Just one more . . . And then what?

Knowing he'd never be able to walk among the stones in this form, Shima concentrated on turning back to a man, praying it would work. He felt himself dissolving once more. . . .

The next instant, he stood upon two feet again. He rounded on his brother and Raven. Hands on his hips, he announced, "You two are going home!"

They nodded meekly.

The last stone.

It lay before her, the golden nimbus surrounding it pulsating wildly as if mourning the loss of its fellows.

Maurynna raised the sword once more. Her arms shook with weariness, and she hoped she'd have the strength for this last task. She drew a deep breath.

The sword slashed down into the magic warding the stone. The stone wailed like a soul in torment; Pirakos howled in triumph. Maurynna cast Dharm Varleran's sword aside—it would do her no good now—and threw herself past the stone, her hands clamped over her ears.

She ran along the path circling the bowl to its end as Pirakos threw himself against his chains. The screaming of tortured metal was like a lash across her back, urging her to hurry, hurry, hurry. She forced her weary body to obey.

A harsh grinding told her that Pirakos had succeeded in pulling one chain loose from its anchor. Could the others be far behind? Desperate, Maurynna looked down into the other cavern. It was a jump, but one that she thought she might dare.

Rather, had to dare if she had any hope of reaching the tunnels before Pirakos caught her. Maurynna jumped.

She knew it was only a few heartbeats, but it felt as though she fell for ages before her feet slammed against the cavern floor. Maurynna dropped and rolled, ignoring the stones digging bruises into her back and shoulders.

An instant later she was up and running. Behind her she heard Pirakos roar in triumph as another chain broke. She must find the tunnels—or die.

Then came the sound of the third chain snapping. Maurynna threw all caution aside and ran as hard as she could.

As she reached the entrance to the second cavern, she heard the final chain break, and heard the nightmare scrabbling of Pirakos's talons upon the rock as he clawed a way out of the bowl of his prison.

Now!

The word rang through his entire being, a command that could not be ignored. It was time to wake from this little death.

The old dragon began the long journey to life.

Fifty-six

Maurynna raced around the stones jutting out into the cavern. Her heart hammered in her chest; she ran now in blind panic, searching for a tunnel to lead her out of this charnel house. She was certain this was where she had come out of earlier.

It wasn't. It was but another bay off of the enormous cavern. A stray breath of air teased against her face. She came to a skidding halt in the center of the big open floor and looked desperately for a way out. On three sides she was trapped by walls of stone. If she could get back out, hide among the rocks . . .

Pirakos filled the opening, the stench of his rotting flesh nearly overwhelming her. A mad light filled his eyes.

Thee has been rare good sport, truehuman, but now I shall kill thee—kill thee as all of thy kind should die.

The mindvoice was mild, and even friendly. But the edge of bloodlust and hunger for human flesh that lurked behind it made that friendliness all the more terrifying. She was to die for no better reason than insanity's whim.

But I'm not truehuman, Pirakos! I'm a Dragonlord, as

your friend Varleran once was, she cried, snatching at reason like a drowning man snatching at a rope of straw, knowing it was just as futile. Inside her mind she grasped at another forlorn hope: *Kyrissaean* . . .

Shima saw his brother and Raven to the hidden trail that led to where Boreal and Je'nihahn waited with Rasse and Omasua.

"Find them," Shima ordered. "Raven, they know you; I'm certain they'll take you and Tefira back to Stormwind and Zinluta if you explain."

Raven, one hand clamped over the deep cut in his arm, turned sharply to him. Their gazes met, warred. A hard-fought battle, then Raven nodded, wavering a little where he stood. Shima hoped he wouldn't faint before they reached the horses; Tefira was too little to carry such a tall man.

Raven must have seen the worry in his eyes, for he inhaled deeply and said, "I'll get there."

"Thank you for being sensible," Shima said, knowing how hard it was for the other man to do this.

"About time, don't you think?" Raven said with a harsh laugh.

Shima half smiled and turned away. Tefira grabbed his arm.

"And you?" his brother asked in alarm. "Aren't you coming with us?"

Shima shook his head. "I'm going back to find Maurynna—if I can." He thought with dread of the impossible task ahead.

Raven, his eyes squeezed shut in fierce concentration, as if by will alone he would put his weakness to flight, said, "Mindcall her."

Mindcall her. By all the Spirits, he could now, couldn't he? Shima closed his own eyes and let his mind range.

At first, nothing. Then . . . there! Sudden caution held him back from directly touching her mind; who knew what might be happening. He could feel her presence, a whirlwind of impressions, then . . . Anger. Fear. Danger.

His eyes snapped open. "I don't know just where she is," he said, "but Pirakos is free—and about to attack her!"

He couldn't face Pirakos in this form and live. Shima didn't even think about what he was doing. He ran. Behind him, he heard Tefira cry out, "Shima, where— Let me go!" and Raven's reply: "He needs room to Change."

To Change. For one heady moment, Shima thought he'd fallen into the tales his mother told on still summer evenings. But when he stopped, knowing instinctively that he'd gone far enough, the hot, rough stone beneath his feet said to him, *This is no dream.*

Shima let his mind empty, let himself flow into Change. Moments later, he sprang into the turquoise blue sky, rising like an arrow to the sun.

The crazed truedragon's head wove back and forth, daring her to try to get past him. A deep *houf! houf! houf!* rumbled through the bay, a spine-chilling echo of Lleld's laughter so long ago. Another stray puff of air wisped around her, conjuring images of a flower-strewn meadow and lying naked in the sun with Linden. . . . Maurynna burrowed into the comfort of the memory. Why not? She was doomed.

Something stirred in her mind even as another tiny breeze tickled past her cheek.

Pirakos's long neck swung around. *Air . . . clean, sweet air . . . outside*—* The naked longing blazed in Maurynna's mind as Pirakos frantically sought the source. His head darted to and fro.

Then once more the truedragon remembered her. The big head swung around. *I taste freedom in that air*, he said, *and I will take it. But first*—*

With tormenting slowness, he stretched out one taloned forefoot; the coldfire gleamed on the long, sharp claws. His eyes gleamed with sadistic anticipation.

The forefoot paused barely an ell from her face.

*   *   *

The litter jounced down the trail to the great doors barring the entrance to the cavern. Incense wafted back from the thuribles carried by the acolytes before him. It was sweet, but not as sweet as the hymns of praise the priests sang in his honor.

Haoro balanced himself against the jolting and smiled. True, soon he would face the beast itself and take on some of its pain. But now he was second only to an emperor in honor; soon the tribute trains would bring riches to his impoverished family, and as soon as Jhanun took the throne and the four Dragonlords were in place . . .

The ground shuddered. The singing wavered, but recovered an instant later when nothing else happened. The procession continued down the path to the floor of the valley, past the village of the slaves and the barracks of the soldiers.

All were out, kneeling along the road that led to the great doors, bowing again and again as the litter passed. He deigned to glance at them.

The faces of the soldiers held careful respect; here and there one glowed with fanatical devotion. Haoro made note of those; they might prove useful someday.

The slaves . . . Bah. Cattle not worth noticing. A few held the light of rebellion in their eyes even yet; Tah'nesieh and Zharmatians for the most part, with one or two Jehangli who had not yet learned their places.

They would. All of them would. He was not the weakling that Pah-Ko had been.

Then the gates loomed before him, and Haoro dismissed the trivialities of rebellious slaves from his mind. For now he would come into his power. They had come to the great doors.

Swinging their censers and chanting, the priests and acolytes stood in two lines before them, waiting as slaves hauled on the chains hanging from the enormous handles. Slowly, ponderously, the great bronze doors swung open inch by inch. When they were finally open, other slaves ran to bring the waiting priests lanterns and torches.

*   *   *

Shima rose straight up into the sky until he was certain that he would not be easily spotted from the ground, then caught a current of air beneath his wings, riding it like a hawk. He watched the ground below in an agony of suspense.

But there was only the land itself, hard, red earth with wind-carved rocks jutting up like parched bones.

Damn it, where were they? Shima cursed silently in frustration. Surely, even from this distance he would be able to see—

His breath caught. Lady have mercy, what if they were still underground? There was no place to run, nowhere for Maurynna to hide from Pirakos. And if, by some miracle, she did escape the dragon, she would be lost in the caverns.

Shima's blood ran cold at the thought.

There came a sound in the distance, a sound that Maurynna couldn't quite recognize though its familiarity danced in the back of her mind. At once the tang of fresh air grew stronger. Pirakos shuffled back, his head weaving as he sought the origin. A sound like a whimper of desperation escaped him.

Knees shaking, Maurynna wondered how long the reprieve would last. Could she get past Pirakos while he was distracted?

Kyrissaean, I must Change! Maurynna begged, *just as I did the night Linden was in danger!*

The night that Linden faced the mage Kas Althume and fought Althume's blood magery with only the magic that bound his human and dragon souls. The night that she had risked drowning when she jumped from her ship and swam to shore, not understanding why she was so driven, but knowing that Linden needed help—help that she alone could give him.

Suddenly she was lost in time; once more she stood with that sultry summer night wrapped around her, caught between dark magic and light as they warred over her, pulling her one way, then another. Fear washed over her like storm-born waves swamping a ship.

She was drowning in fear. . . .

Then dark magic once more burned her soul, tearing it apart, just as on that terrible night. *Gods help me*, Maurynna begged. *Not again! Please—not again!*

But the dark magic burned deeper and searing pain ripped through every fiber of her being, unraveling her mind, unraveling *her*. Layer upon layer of pain like thundering cascades of molten metal and rock buried her, crushing the breath from her lungs. This time she would not live through it. This time she would die . . .

No—that was before! Thee remembers what went before—and what should never have been!

A wordless outpouring of repentance flashed through her mind like water gushing from a spring; then, *I give thee both of us*, the voice said, and faded like mist.

Maurynna shut her eyes and let herself fall into nothingness.

The first of the priests marched into the yawning mouth of the cavern, their hymn now a song of triumph. The litter swayed after them as the sturdy priests bearing it strode forth. Haoro settled the feathered cape and sat up a little straighter so that all might see him in his moment of glory.

He blinked as they entered the dimness of the cavern, leaving the bright day behind. Then they were pacing down the huge tunnel, the martial chant of the priests thundering in his ears like the roar of a waterfall.

Pirakos remembered her once more. But no sooner did the big head swing around to her than he reared back in surprise.

Maurynna flung herself at him. They met, breast to breast, their scales clashing and hissing as they slid against each other. Though she was much smaller than he, Maurynna bowled Pirakos over by sheer surprise. She lashed out with fang and claw.

*   *   *

Deeper and deeper into the mountain they marched. Haoro gave in to curiosity and glanced quickly over his shoulder.

The opening looked smaller than he'd thought it would; they had come a fair distance already. A shudder ran through him at the knowledge of what lay only a short distance ahead now: a bend in the tunnel. Once beyond that point, they would be engulfed in darkness, with only the torches between them and eternal night.

This was what she was meant to be! As with the only other time she'd Changed, Maurynna's dragon body knew by instinct what to do. But this time, her human mind guided her as well. She remembered watching a mother swan defend her cygnets against a hungry dog, how the bird had struck the dog blow after powerful blow using her wings. The dog fled in the end, but not before the swan had broken one of its legs. Though it went against all instinct to risk her precious wings so, she did the same to Pirakos, slamming the joint of one wing into the side of his head.

Ow! That was worse than hitting a funny bone!

Pirakos roared in astonishment and fell back from her. The mad light in his eyes faded to bewilderment. He looked so lost in that moment, like a child who'd wandered away from his mother at a fair, that she felt sorry for him. It didn't stop her from slashing at his throat with her fangs to drive him off.

Pirakos stumbled away from her. Before she could attack once more, his head came up, and he sniffed the air with pathetic eagerness. She held back; it was plain the truedragon had once more forgotten that she was there.

Air! Fresh air! Freedom! Pirakos babbled over and over, all the while testing the air like a hunting dog. *There-therethere!* He set off at a lumbering run, chains dragging behind him. *This is the way, I know it, I know it,* he whimpered frantically.

A whirlwind of images leaked from his mind: the long candlemarks when there was nothing to listen to but the beating of his own heart or the rattle of chains. Screaming criminals thrown into the cavern for punishment: the lucky ones died immediately under his claws, the unlucky ones somehow dodged him only to go mad in the dark caverns and slowly starve to death. The unimaginable foulness of eating human flesh, he whose best friend had once been human himself—but it was that or starve. But bitterest of all was the memory of richly clad men who came down this very path from time to time over the centuries, bearing one man on a litter, one who wore a mantle of golden feathers about his shoulders. A man who stood at the edge of his prison, looking down at him, before opening a vein in his arm and dripping blood down upon him to seal the twisted bond between them.

For that man was the focus of the magic that kept him here. But now Pirakos was going to mend that, *Ohyesoh-yeso*hyessss.*

Maurynna followed as the dragon's lumbering gallop turned into a clumsy, clanking run. This moving on four feet was trickier than she'd guessed it would be; if she thought about it, her feet tangled. So she kept it from her mind, concentrating instead on what she gleaned from Pirakos's hate-filled memories, although much of it turned her stomach. She let that revulsion fuel her rage over how the dragon had been treated, and swarmed through the tunnel after him.

Amura stood with the other slaves, watching as the last of the procession disappeared into the tunnel. He slid a glance sideways at his friend and partner here in the slave camp, Chuchan the Dwarf.

Chuchan was doing the same. Their gazes met, worried. What if Shima and the northern girl—Maurynna—were still at the dragon's prison? Would they be able to complete their mission? Or were they lost inside the mountain?

Thousands of questions and no answers.

So he stood in the sun, in a line with the others, baking as the sun rose higher and higher in the sky.

*   *   *

Wisps of a vile odor slipped past the heavy scent of the incense. Haoro nearly gagged; only steely determination kept him from clapping a hand to his nose. He would *not* show such weakness.

Others were not so strong of will. The chanting faltered. All around him came muffled gasps of, first surprise, then muffled choking. The sounds bounced off the stone and echoed around him like something from a bad dream.

Then a single determined voice rose above the others; at first it quavered, but moment by moment it grew stronger. As if it were a call to arms, the other voices rallied and once more the hymns that he'd waited so long to hear filled Haoro's ears.

He let the sweet praise drive away all apprehension.

The feel of moving air grew stronger by the moment. Still hard on Pirakos's tail, Maurynna craned her neck, hoping for a glimpse of daylight beyond the truedragon. She opened her mouth to draw in a huge draught of fresh air, heady as wine with the promise of freedom.

Augh! What was *that*? Something tickled the back of her throat, some kind of smoke, she thought, but sweet. She stopped, coughing. Pirakos rounded a curve in the tunnel and she lost sight of him.

Then the screaming began.

Haoro's litter fell to the ground with such force that the air was knocked from his lungs. Gasping, and half-stunned from the fall, he saw legs running past him as he sprawled on the tunnel floor, and wondered what was happening. How *dare* these dogs ruin—

A sound of metal dragging across stone penetrated his mind. He looked up to see a huge mouth filled with long, sharp fangs diving at him.

"No! No!" Haoro shrieked, awakening at last to his doom. He tried to crawl away, but the feather cloak had twisted around his legs. "Noooo!"

The great jaws caught him; it seemed a thousand knives stabbed him—and stopped short of the mercy of death. As the dragon's head came up, Haoro begged and pleaded and screamed for a quick death.

It was not granted.

Fifty-seven

Shima angled his wings and veered. Something far below had caught his eye. It was not Pirakos, that he knew; but it still bore investigating.

Men—armed men. At least fifty, perhaps more, and riding for the pass into the valley beneath Mount Kajhenral.

Oh, Shashannu—why does the damned relief troop have to come now!

He had to stop them before they reached the temple. Hoping that these soldiers had no arrows tipped with dragonsbane, Shima folded his wings and dove.

The sudden, shocking sounds made Maurynna fall back on her haunches. Dear gods, what—

A roar of triumph, then a voice bellowed in her mind, *Now I have thee! I will rend thee limb from limb, true-human filth! Now die!* The last word skreeled in her head like a paean of hate.

Maurynna raced around the bend in the tunnel. The horrific sight before her brought her to a stunned halt.

Broken figures lay strewn across the tunnel floor. For a moment, Maurynna couldn't believe these had once been human. Surely these were just toys smashed and torn apart by a deranged child in a tantrum. Weren't they?

Please don't let it be real. . . . Her mind retreated from the carnage before her.

Then the hot scent of fresh blood assailed her nostrils, clearing her head like a whiff of burning vinegar, and once more she heard the screams. There were far fewer voices now to cry out. She raised her head and saw Pirakos stopped ahead of her. Beyond him, she caught a glimpse of daylight. A rumbling, chest-deep growl brought her eyes back to Pirakos.

The truedragon's long neck whipped back and forth, and there was something clutched in his mouth. He looked for all the world like a puppy playing with a rag doll. But rag dolls didn't shriek like damned souls and wave their arms.

A flutter of gold caught Maurynna's eye, and she recognized the cloak of feathers that had garbed the hated figure in Pirakos's ravings.

Then came a wet, muffled crunch. Blood ran down the truedragon's jaws; the rag doll went limp. With a howl of triumph, Pirakos cast it aside.

What had once been a man wearing a cloak of sun-colored feathers slammed into the wall and slid down it, to become a crumpled pile of offal.

Talons closed on it, swept it up and threw it to land against the other wall, again and again and again, Pirakos jumping from one side to the other to scoop up the body and throw it.

Maurynna wondered if a dragon could be sick to its stomach. If she watched much longer, she would find out. Besides, there was that glimpse of daylight she'd seen before; if she could edge past Pirakos . . .

No. He was too big, filled up too much of the tunnel, even without the mad leaping from side to side as he batted the dead man about; now he looked like a cat playing with a dead mouse. Frustrated, Maurynna looked once more at the daylight beckoning to her.

There was less of it.

For a moment, Maurynna couldn't understand what was happening. Then she knew.

Pirakos! They're closing the doors! We'll be trapped in here—

Forever.

*   *   *

"What's that?" Chuchan dared whisper.

Amura woke from the standing half doze every slave learned. He immediately glanced at the soldiers near them, ready to throw up an arm to ward off a blow.

Was Chuchan mad? He knew better than to—

But the soldiers ignored Chuchan's transgression. Instead, every soldier's attention was focused, as well as Amura could tell, on the entrance to the tunnel. Uneasy looks passed between them.

Amura shuffled a little closer. The soldiers ignored that, as well. He listened so intently it felt like his ears were growing as long as a Jehangli donkey's. Yet he heard nothing, nothing at—

Wait! That was a scream; it had to be. No chant he'd ever heard held such panic, such . . . terror . . . in it.

By all the Spirits, what was happening in there? And where were Shima and the northern girl in all this?

More screams; this time there was no doubt what they were. Then came a low, rumbling growl that sang of death. Amura felt the hair on his arms rise.

"Close the doors!" the sergeant of the door guards yelled. "For the sake of the Phoenix, close the damned doors!"

Even as he spoke, he rushed to the enormous door panel closest to him and tugged frantically, futilely upon it. It was far too large and heavy for a single man to move. After an instant's paralyzed surprise, his remaining men ran to help him. Even those guarding the slaves forgot their charges and threw themselves upon the door.

At first, nothing happened. But with panic came inhuman strength. The doors began to move, infinitesimally at first, then more and more. The men pushed and shoved, cursing the weight; the doors moved ponderously upon their hinges. Soon only a gap the length of a man's arm from elbow to fingertips remained; then only the width of a man's hand. Men ran to fetch the massive crossbar that would seal the doors forever if need be.

Amura held his breath. Did he wish them luck or wish

them to hell? In a matter of heartbeats it would be all over; the crossbar was in position . . . it was almost home. . . .

Then the doors burst open once more with a violence that tore one portal from its hinges, and nightmare incarnate burst through them with a hideous roar.

The soldiers had seen him; so much for his chances of landing and surprising them. Not that Shima had had any real hope that something as large as he was now would go unnoticed. He heard shouts of surprise, fear, disbelief; perhaps they would run? He could always hope.

But no—the commander shouted orders, rallying his men. They would stand and fight, and Shima knew he must face them.

Wait; the *men* might stand and fight. . . . If he could have smiled in this form, Shima's grin would have well-nigh split his face in two.

Yes, the men might stand—but the horses certainly wouldn't. Shima waited until he was just beyond the range of the powerful bows, and roared as he passed overhead.

Green fire sparkled and flashed in the harsh sunlight. Amura stood like a man bespelled as a huge creature hurtled through the open portal, the sun glinting off its scaled hide. As it cleared the doorway, great wings unfurled as if to soak in every bit of sunlight possible. The soldiers unlucky enough to be close by fell beneath its taloned forefeet and snapping jaws. Their more fortunate comrades ran and hid. The dragon ignored them.

So *this* was one of the northern dragons his aunt had spoken of! Who could have dreamed of such terrible beauty? Maurynna had seemed such a quiet girl. All around him men hurled themselves to the ground; Amura remained standing, transfixed by the sight before him.

The scaled head stretched up to the sun, eyes almost shut as if the bright light burned them. Jaws stained with blood opened; a high keening filled the air.

"Get down, you fool!" Chuchan whispered, and an arm

across the back of his knees brought him down. "Do you want to get eaten?"

Amura rolled onto his stomach and behind the rock Chuchan crouched behind. "Maurynna wouldn't—"

"Dolt! Look again. That's not the northern girl. This beast wears shackles."

Shaken, Amura did as the dwarf bade. By the Spirits, Chuchan was right! This, then, was the dragon that had been chained beneath the mountain for untold lives of men.

So Maurynna and Shima had succeeded. But where were they?

Concerned, he stuck his head above the rock to look for them—and found himself staring into a red eye gleaming with bloodlust. The big head swung toward him and the great jaws opened.

It worked even better than Shima had hoped. Horses raced in every direction, their riders either dumped unceremoniously in the dirt, or clinging desperately to their saddles. As he'd thought, the horses had more sense than their riders. *They* had no intention of becoming dinner.

A fine sight indeed, Shima thought, laughing to himself. Then he sobered again, and flew back toward Mount Kajhenral.

Damn Pirakos! He had paused just outside the wretched doorway, blocking her. Maurynna snarled deep in her chest; she wanted to see the sky once more, and she wanted to see it *now*. She'd had more than enough of these cursed tunnels; even now there still came faint mewling cries behind her that caused both hackles and gorge to rise. She tried to mindcall the other dragon, but he was so stunned by his sudden freedom that she couldn't reach him. Nothing for it but to shove Pirakos out of her way.

She backed up, then lowered her head like a bull.

There was the temple. But what was this? Priests streamed forth from the buildings like ants from a disturbed hill.

Shima watched from high overhead as they ran for the narrow road that led to the valley.

Amura's blood ran cold. This was a death he'd never imagined, and he was too paralyzed with fright to even attempt escape.

Not that there was really any place to hide on this barren slope, besides a few stray boulders.

He only hoped it would be quick. Suddenly the dragon roared, nearly deafening him. Now it would strike—

But no; instead it jumped and slewed around quick as a snake, turning upon . . .

Another dragon that had charged from the tunnel and run into it from behind. Amura rubbed his eyes.

The second, smaller dragon shone like a peacock's tail in the sun, all iridescent blues and greens. This, then, was the girl he'd led to the tunnels. Now she was completely in the open and facing the shackled dragon—a dragon that was larger, stronger, more experienced . . . and mad. He watched the larger dragon's head snap back as it made ready to strike.

Linden no longer needed the mysterious mindvoice's guidance. For miles now, he had felt the power ahead pulling at him like a lodestone, magic calling to magic.

And now it was below him. He circled over a magnificent structure arranged in a square around a huge central courtyard of white marble paths and gardens. Within that courtyard, in the exact center, sparkled a column of white quartz, the height of two men, stretching up to the sky. With a scream of rage, Linden dove at it.

At the sound, small figures wearing saffron robes spilled out from the temple, looking all around. At last one looked up; with his sharp dragonsight, Linden saw the tiny figure pointing at him. Then all looked up.

He roared again, and spat forth a long gout of fire to warn them. Now he was close enough to hear shrieks, and the priests ran in panic. None, he was certain, would stand against him.

He landed and, letting the rage that burned deep within him—Rathan, his dragonsoul's rage—fuel his strength, Linden wrapped his tail around the column and heaved.

It came free. Though it was heavy, he flung it into the columns that supported the roof of the walkway around the courtyard. The roof collapsed, burying the stone under a pile of rubble.

Then Linden leaped into the air, knowing where he must go next.

It was silly what irrelevant detail could catch your attention when you faced death, a detached part of Maurynna's mind observed. The hot dust stirred up underfoot tickled her nose, just as the dust in the riding arena did during the practice bouts. She wanted to sneeze.

With the dust came a memory: *If your opponent has the longer reach, get inside it if you can.*

Before Pirakos could strike, Maurynna sprang forward, snapping at his throat. She missed—just barely—as he scrambled back.

Pirakos snarled and sprang into the air. Startled, Maurynna hesitated, losing her chance to stop him.

Thee will not again prevent me from slaying truehumans. With the taunt came an underlying image of city after city bursting into flames. *I will cleanse this la—*

He stopped in mid-word. His wings beating furiously to hold him in place in the air, Pirakos cocked his head as if listening to someone else.

This was her chance. Despite knowing she had no more likelihood of stopping Pirakos than a kitten had of stopping a snow cat, Maurynna took wing, straining to close the distance.

A roar as sudden and loud as a clap of thunder surprised her so much that she ducked and almost forgot to fly. A thought raced across her mind: Pirakos had seen her and was attacking.

But when she looked, the green dragon paid her no attention. Instead, he still listened to a voice only he could hear. His eyes glowed with excitement.

If that wasn't Pirakos, then who—?

The first stone falls—I feel it! Pirakos howled in her mind with mad glee. **I go—I go!**

Maurynna watched in bewilderment as Pirakos raced away. Then she remembered the mysterious roar and searched the heavens.

There! A black dragon dove out of the sky. Maurynna's heart beat faster. There was only one such dragon in Jehanglan. And if Jekkanadar were here, Linden could not be far behind. Wild with excitement, she flew to meet the new dragon.

There it was! A column of white quartz in a temple courtyard.

How to do this . . . Lleld knew she might not be strong enough to pick the thing up. Besides, she didn't want to land—what if they had spears?

Yet strength wasn't all in a fight. She dove at the glittering stone. At the last instant, she spread her wings, slowing herself just enough so that she wouldn't break every bone in her body. She hit the top of the column at a sharp angle, all four feet together.

The thing went over like a toy soldier. Lleld tucked her wings and rolled, then came out of it, winging for the sky before anyone could even think of stopping her.

Jekkanadar! Maurynna cried as she neared the other dragon. She looked eagerly beyond him, but neither Lleld nor Linden were in sight. *Where are the others?*

Her gaze returned to the black dragon swooping down to her level. Wait; something wasn't right. . . . Her breath caught. This wasn't Jekkanadar. This was a dragon she'd never seen before.

Who are you? she demanded, baring her fangs for battle

as the other closed inexorably on her. When the answer came, Maurynna nearly fell from the sky in astonishment.

A snuffling brought Murohshei out of his half doze. He went over to the bed.

Xahnu and Xu smiled up at him; Murohshei returned the smile, saying, "Awake at last, little Phoenix Lords? Good; your mother wants to see you. She has a wondrous thing to show the both of you."

He stood up and clapped his hands. The nurses hurried over.

She wanted to soar into the sun in pure joy. For if both she and Shima had been unheralded Dragonlords, how many more might there be? Their kind still had a chance. She had a thousand questions for Shima, and all of them danced on the tip of her tongue at once.

Instead she said, *Shima, Pirakos intends to lay waste to this land. I must follow, try to stop him, and I've already waited too long. But there are still soldiers here—*

My cousin and the others can deal with them. This land is mine. I go with you.

It will be dangerous. . . .

So is living, replied Shima and dropped lower. Maurynna followed. Shima mindcalled, *Amura!*

Poor Amura nearly jumped out of his skin. "Yes, Sky Lord?" he called. His voice shook.

Shima's mindvoice was pure exasperation. *Amura, you ass, it's Shima. But never mind that. We go to follow the mad dragon. The first Stone has fallen, cousin; you know what must be done.*

Maurynna thought that if the poor man's jaw dropped any more, a horse could walk right in. But Amura rallied valiantly and raised a hand in salute. "This one falls as well! Go!"

Maurynna turned beneath the vast blueness of the Jehangli sky and set off after Pirakos. Shima followed.

*   *   *

"Arm yourselves!" Amura yelled. He seized a pike from a fallen soldier and waved it above his head. "We must destroy the altar in the inner temple."

The Tah'nehsieh and Zharmatians rallied to him. Even a few of the Jehangli came. Some snatched up weapons from the ground and used them against the soldiers yet standing. Others caught up rocks and pelted the troops as they tried to form ranks. Here and there a soldier dropped under a well-thrown rock and someone would dart in to seize his weapons—and cut the man's throat.

It was not the way Amura liked to do battle, but they must fight this one however they could. They had numbers, but the enemy had armor and weapons and, more deadly yet, training. Even now, a few temple soldiers were beginning the formation Amura recognized as the "turtle." If the soldiers succeeded, the rebellion was lost.

"To me!" Amura bellowed. Then, "Charge them!"

The men wavered; most were not armed yet, and to strike against those who had opressed them for so long . . . Amura despaired. Had they had the heart beaten out of them?

Defeat hovered in the air like a vulture.

Then another slave, Mad Senwan, driven insane long ago by the slaughter of his family, threw himself upon the soldiers, screaming the names of his wife and children over and over as he swung his mattock around his head like a whirlwind. Soldiers went down before him like grain to a sickle, their helmets crushed or faces smashed to pulp. Hot blood gushed onto the thirsty dust. In his frenzy, Mad Senwan penetrated deep into the still-forming "turtle." The shock of his attack was so sudden that many soldiers retreated, crying out that a demon was upon them.

The fear in the soldiers' voices was the goad the slaves needed. "Now!" Amura cried. The men roared their hatred, their rage, their lust for vengeance, and surged forward.

Some were not yet armed; it made no difference. Their bodies were their weapons. With bare hands they flung themselves upon the soldiers, gouging eyes, staying the swing of swords, dragging shield arms down so that their comrades could plunge a blade past the gaps in the armor. That they died themselves meant nothing; they had been dead men for years.

The end came suddenly. One moment the tumult of battle was all around him, the sound of sword against sword, the quiet, desperate grunts of men fighting for their lives, howls of anger and pain; then came a silence so profound that for the space of a heartbeat Amura wondered if he were dead or deaf.

Then the moans of the wounded broke upon his ears. He came to himself. Too many of the men who had become his friends lay dead or dying in the hot, red dust of the valley. But among them were the soldiers left after the dragons' onslaught—all the soldiers.

Moving stiffly, Amura dropped his pike and picked up a sword and shield. "Take their weapons. We storm the temple."

Unbelieving faces stared back at him. Storm the temple, their eyes asked. But that was sacrilege unheard—

"Yes!" someone roared, and the others took it up. They swarmed over the bodies like ants. Amura watched as they armed themselves.

Mad Senwan lay at the bottom of the largest heap. Though his body was hacked almost beyond recognition, a peaceful smile lit the ruin of his face.

"He's found them," Chuchan said. "Tiala and the girls." His voice faltered; he cleared his throat noisily. With a glare that dared Amura to say anything, the dwarf clapped a helmet on his head and stumped away.

They flew as fast as they could after Pirakos. At one point they saw him far ahead, but no matter how they pushed themselves, they couldn't close the distance. Instead, their wings grew heavier; each stroke came slower and the distance between them and their quarry grew until Pirakos was but a speck on the horizon. Then even that disappeared.

His madness gives him strength, Maurynna realized at last, trying to ignore her aching wings, *even though he*

*hasn't flown in a thousand years and more. But we're too
new to fly for so long at such speed.*

Indeed, not long after, Shima's wings missed a beat and
he "stumbled" in the air. He caught himself, but Maurynna
knew it was only a matter of time before one of them fell
to a horrible death.

Glide! she shouted, hoping to break through the veil of
exhaustion dulling Shima's eyes. *We must land and rest.*

Shima snarled, but agreed. Wings outstretched, they spiraled down to the ground. Just before they landed, Maurynna said, *Don't Change.*

Why not?

*Because we might not be able to Change back to this
form. Linden once told me that if a Dragonlord is too ill
or tired, he can't Change. It's our magic's way of protect-
ing us.*

Nor did she dare risk not being able to Change back to
a dragon. She didn't quite believe that bit of hell was truly
over.

They both settled with a jarring thump. Maurynna
groaned softly and sank to the ground. Morlen's tale of the
truedragons' ill-fated attack came back to her; she imagined
them sprawled over the ground, exhausted and wounded
and heartsick. Her mind turned away from the images.

It was the better part of a candlemark later that she broke
the silence. She still had a thousand questions for Shima,
but only one had to be answered now: *What did Pirakos
mean, "The first stone falls?"*

*One of the others—your soultwin or the other two—has
toppled one of the Stones of Warding, I think. If the others
fall as well . . .*

The Phoenix is free. Maurynna considered that, added it
to what she knew of Pirakos. *Do you know where the Phoenix is imprisoned? Because I think Pirakos intends everything to end this day.*

Shima nodded. *I think you're right. As for where, the
Phoenix is held at Mount Rivasha. I know what direction
it lies in from here, but . . .*

Just get us near there, Maurynna said grimly. *I think we'll be able to "feel" Pirakos once we're closer.* Even now she could dimly sense him. She heaved herself to her feet and crouched on her haunches. Shima did the same; Maurynna thought he looked as tired as she still felt—and she felt as if she'd run the length of Thalnia and back five times. Although it would put them well behind Pirakos, they would have to rest now and again, or risk overtaxing themselves and possibly damaging their wings. She remembered how afraid Linden had been that she'd done just that with her first—and heretofore only—flight a little over a year ago. Now she and Shima had already exceeded what she'd done that day, and they had much farther to go.

Their only hope of catching Pirakos was that he would be so unused to flying after a thousand years of captivity that he would be forced to rest eventually as well.

Yet he'd already left them far behind; that, Maurynna thought, did not bode well. Her fanged jaws clenched in determination, she leaped heavily into the sky once more.

Up the steep, switchbacked road they marched, clad in a motley assortment of armor and armed with whatever weapons they could scavenge. What they would find at the top, Amura didn't know. He remembered his aunt's tales of the spells of the northern mages, and speculations that the Jehangli priests were in truth users of magic. He could only hope that none of them knew how to turn a man into a toad.

Beside him, Chuchan began singing. It was one of the marching songs popular in the soldiers' barrack, but the words of the chorus had been subtly changed. Ripples of laughter ran through the band; Chuchan sang on, the rest joined in on the chorus, and the infectious rhythm invaded their feet. Soon they were marching, proud as the Phoenix Emperor's elite guard, ready to fight—and win.

Amura squared his shoulders and stepped out boldly. Whatever faced them—mages, monsters, or more soldiers— they would prevail.

They had to. This was their chance to make the Vale truly live.

Fly, rest, fly. The world narrowed: to periods of increasingly painful flying; to shorter and shorter times of rest as her sense of urgency grew. Maurynna knew that that same urgency affected Shima as well. With each rest he fidgeted more and more, just as she did.

And they *were* getting closer. Pirakos must have stopped to rest as well—or to lay waste to the countryside, though she'd seen no evidence of that, thank the gods. May he be so consumed by his goal that he leaves the innocents of Jehanglan alone, she thought.

Still, they were catching up. He was not that far ahead of them; she could feel it. The link between their minds that he'd forced upon her now served her purposes.

And when they caught him? She would answer that question later.

At long last, Jekkanadar reached his quarry. It lay in a courtyard below him; groups of saffron-robed priests tended the area surrounding it. He saw some sweeping the marble paths, others tending to small gardens of flowers.

He roared to warn them off; they looked up, screamed, and scattered like leaves in a storm.

Jekkanadar landed beside the column. Rearing up onto his hind legs, he set his forefeet upon the top, and pushed. Slowly, slowly, the stone tilted. He snarled and pushed harder.

Just as it crashed to the ground, Jekkanadar felt a searing pain in his wing. He whirled, roaring in a draconic rage. Before him stood a young priest—a boy, really—wielding a sharp hoe. Though he was plainly terrified, the boy waved the hoe at him again.

Impressed by the boy's courage, Jekkanadar merely knocked him lightly out of the way, and jumped into the sky. But at the first beat of his wings, he fell to the earth again.

Only then did he realize that the membrane of skin that stretched from spine to spine on his wings was torn. He was trapped.

Desperate, Jekkanadar bellowed, *Lleld! Lleld! Help me!*

Saffron-robed priests and acolytes were everywhere. Some cowered in little groups as they frantically searched the sky, afraid, Amura soon realized, that the "demons" would return and destroy them as well. Others ran back and forth, for all the world like a flock of chickens with a fox among them. Their cries and prayers filled the air. Some—mostly the very young and the very old—stood weeping in bewilderment. Amura saw one old man trying to comfort the three crying little boys clinging to his robes. The old man watched them approach, his eyes half defiant, half fearful. He wrapped his thin, stringy arms around the children as if to make of them a bulwark against all harm.

Amura led his men around the little group; he did not war with children and elders. He looked back once. The old man had caught up the smallest boy—a child of perhaps four years—and was hustling his charges away, his chin on his shoulder as he watched the former slaves. Relief filled the seamed face, relief that did not quite believe the reprieve.

The slave band marched on, heady with their newly won freedom. Most of the priests fled before them. Sometimes one of the older boys, or the more vigorous of the old men, tried to bar their way. They were swept aside, not by sword and pike, but by a force as inexorable as a river freed from a dam.

At one point Amura thought he saw the old *nira*'s Oracle, half hidden behind one of the many prayer pillars that dotted the huge courtyard before the temple. But the boy scuttled away like a frightened beetle when he saw Amura looking at him.

Amura forgot about him in the next instant. For the temple doors opened, revealing a small group of sturdy men, all in their prime, all clad in robes of saffron and scarlet.

Whispers flew through the slave band; these were the priest-soldiers of the Phoenix. They bore no swords, for it was forbidden to shed blood in the temple precincts, but each held a stout quarterstaff. And each slave knew only too well what these priests could do with those deadly staves. They had seen condemned prisoners die beneath the whirling staffs before being fed to the dragon.

And those were the lucky ones, Amura thought. He remembered the screams of the others as they were thrown into the Well of Death. He took a deep breath and raised his sword. "Shield men—to the front! Pikes ready!" he shouted.

A moment later it was done. "Now—*charge the bastards!*"

"Here they are, Phoenix Lady."

Shei-Luin turned from her contemplation of the Palace of the Phoenix. It had drawn her from the comfort of the imperial rooms in the temple; she'd hoped to see the great shadow within it again.

Murohshei smiled at her; by his side was Zyuzin, his eyes wide in his round face. They stepped aside to reveal the rest of the little party.

Shei-Luin held out her arms to Xahnu, taking him from his nurse, and held him so that he could see into the crater. Xu's nurse held her charge so that he might see, as well. He gurgled at the sight.

Then Shei-Luin saw it again. "Look! Look! Do you see that shadow? That's the—"

The bowl of light shimmered wildly. Streaks of gold raced across it, forming a pattern of—

Cracks. The Palace of the Phoenix was dissolving before her very eyes. Shei-Luin watched, numbly, as the glowing shield dissolved, revealing a huge golden bird beneath it. Enormous eyes of emerald green blinked up at her, glittering with mad fury.

People screamed around her, but Shei-Luin hardly heard them. Only one thought filled her numbed mind.

Xiane, you died for nothing. I'm sorry.

Then someone was tugging at her sleeve, taking Xahnu from her nerveless arms. A voice bellowed in her ear, "Lady! We must flee!"

Below her, the great wings spread.

Fifty-eight

Somehow they were down the stairs from the tower. She remembered none of it. Behind her, Shei-Luin heard a wild singing. She looked back once.

The Phoenix was rising on wings of flame. One brushed against the tower; the wooden shelter topping it burst into flames. Then Shei-Luin looked no more. With her little family around her, she ran.

The old dragon opened his eyes at long last. Water swirled around him. High, high above, he could see a faint brightness that he knew meant the sky. He rose up to meet it, swimming strongly, eager to feel the air once again.

Brighter and brighter the water around him grew, until—

His head broke the surface of the lake, and Oolan Jeel tasted the wind once more. He lay a moment upon the surface of the water, basking in the sunlight.

But great things were happening. Sending out a call to the few others he knew slept at the bottoms of their lakes, he let himself dissolve into mist, and rose from the lake like a cloud.

The city of Rivasha burned. As they ran down the streets, part of a panicked crowd, Shei-Luin could see the Phoenix passing overhead. Flames sprang up wherever the fire that dripped from its wings fell.

She heard horses—a troop of cavalry! They were saved! "This way!" she cried and, snatching up Xahnu from his exhausted nurse, ran down a side street, the others following.

They came out almost in the middle of the mounted group; there were only a few of them. She cried to their leader. He turned in the saddle—

"No!" Shei-Luin tried to turn back, but it was too late. Jhanun's horse spun around and leaped at her. She fell back, dodging him. He cursed.

But she couldn't avoid the second man. She stared up into an alien face, yellowed with the sun, topped by a fringe of white hair. He laughed at her in triumph, reaching for the child in her arms.

Then Murohshei was between them. A small blade flashed, and the rider clapped a hand to his leg, howling. Together, Murohshei and Zyuzin dragged him down from his horse.

Shei-Luin fell back against a building, Xahnu clutched against her chest, her heart pounding in her ears. Yet it was not enough to drown out Jhanun's triumphant cry.

"Leave them—Nalorih's got the other boy! Split up—you know where to meet!"

With a scream of anguish, Shei-Luin ran into the road after them. But they were mounted, and she was not; and she bore the weight of a sturdy, screaming child besides.

She watched in despair as the riders disappeared into the smoke, her son and his nurse their captives.

Turning, she saw Murohshei haul their captive to his feet. Blood ran down the man's leg.

"I recognize this one," Murohshei said. "He's one of Jhanun's servants—Baisha."

"Bring him," Shei-Luin said, coldly.

When Linden reached the former prison of the phoenix, he saw a city in flames, but no phoenix, only an empty crater topping a low mountain. The place reeked of magic.

Then he heard an unearthly singing and looked around.

Rising from behind a palace came the most beautiful thing Linden had ever seen. The phoenix burst into the air, fire dripping from its wings. It was the size of a truedragon, with a tail of long, flowing feathers.

Golden feathers, golden talons, golden beak; the phoenix shone like a small sun. Only the eyes were green and filled with hate. It rose above the palace only to stoop down again like a striking hawk. Fire streamed out behind it. At the last possible moment, the phoenix pulled out of the dive, skimming just above the palace and the temple. It blazed through the air like a fiery comet, screaming in mad fury.

Fire sprang up in a hundred places. Linden could hear the terrified screams of those within as each refuge turned into a charnel house. The phoenix swung round for another pass; this time it struck at the towers with beak and claws. They shattered under the onslaught like dried reeds. Again and again the phoenix struck the palace, seeking revenge for its centuries of imprisonment.

It wants to burn the world, he thought. Then, *I have to stop it—there are too many innocents in this city!*

With a roar, he dove at the phoenix. His fiery breath passed over its head, and the phoenix looked around. It left its assault on the city and came after him.

He dodged it, trying to draw it away from the city again and again. But it returned after every attack. He tried to reach its mind, but stopped when he realized that, unlike a dragon, the phoenix's mind was that of an animal.

He kept after it, not daring to close with it, though the fire that dripped from the actual phoenix's wings and tail wasn't as deadly as that of the Sending Morlen and the truedragons had faced. He tried blasting it with dragonfire, but it was too quick.

As he wasn't, once. A tip of that fire brushed across his tail, and he roared in pain. It was only a matter of time, he knew, before it caught him. He'd come to this fight already tired.

As if sensing his fears, the phoenix dove at him, shrieking its rage to the skies.

*   *   *   •

Lleld flew through the blue Jehangli sky, forcing her wings to beat as hard as they could. She should be in Rivasha now, helping Linden. But Jekkanadar needed her. She could only pray she got to him in time.

Linden veered away from the phoenix as the screams of rage assaulted his ears again and again. Then, over that sound, came a bellowing roar. Rolling, he turned his long neck to look over his shoulder to the north. The sight that met his eyes made his wings falter and sent a cold grue down his spine.

The sight of the chains dangling from fetters on all four legs was bad enough. But then he saw the raw, oozing flesh around the fetters and his stomach roiled.

Yet worst of all was the look in the strange dragon's eyes. Gods help him, no dragon should look like that, eyes blazing scarlet with madness and blood lust. That was not the nature of dragons; that this one should have been so twisted from its true self . . .

This must be Pirakos, his shocked mind said. *By Gifnu's nine hells, what have they done to him?*

He almost forgot the phoenix. Only the rush of wind through the golden feathers warned him. Linden frantically dropped and rolled again. The fiery trail barely missed him as the phoenix flew through the space where he'd just been.

But he was not the phoenix's target, he realized the next moment. He had simply been in the creature's way; he mattered no more than an insect to it now.

For it had also seen Pirakos. Its shriek of rage as it flew over Linden well-nigh deafened him. *This is my true enemy,* that wordless shriek said.

And Pirakos thought the same. *Thee!* Pirakos raged. *Thee are the cause of all my suffering!* The dragon's mindvoice rang in Linden's head, threatening to shatter his skull: *This one is mine! Stand aside or I slay thee, too.* Pirakos howled insanely and dove. Scarlet flames erupted from his open mouth.

The phoenix flew to meet him, fire dripping from wings and tail, its green eyes burning with the same madness. From it came images and feelings that scorched the mind: the torment of being buried alive in a cavern filled with molten rock, fury at being trapped, the desperate need to immolate itself upon its nest-pyre. And above all, a towering rage at the dragon that it perceived as the cause of all its tortures.

Linden fell back before their combined fury. He wanted to cry out that neither was to blame, both had been used, it was all the fault of men greedy for power, men dead centuries ago and beyond revenge. Yet he knew neither would listen; both dragon and phoenix alike were too consumed by their madness and hatred. He could only watch. All the while, the violent emotions of the combatants beat at him.

Dragon and phoenix met in a burst of scarlet and gold fire. Golden feathers shriveled and blackened as dragonfire scorched them. A sickening odor filled the air. Then Pirakos banked and slashed the phoenix across the breast. A shriek of rage and pain rent the sky. The wound dripped blood the color of the sun at dawn.

Pirakos screamed his triumph, but it was short-lived. For the phoenix swept around and lashed its foe across the face with its blazing tailfeathers. Pirakos turned his head at the last moment, taking the blow along his neck.

It was all that kept the battle from ending that instant. Had the blow landed across his vulnerable eyes, Pirakos would have been blind, and easy prey for his enemy. But his tough neck scales took the brunt of the blow; now those same scales were curled and blackened by the intense heat of the magical fire. As Linden watched in horror, a few of the scales crumbled away, revealing burned and blistered flesh beneath.

The wind shifted. Linden had thought the smell of burning feathers nauseating; this was ten times worse.

Though Pirakos did not fall from the air, he faltered. It was clear that only instinct kept him aloft. His eyes were glazed with pain, and the great body shuddered. Linden knew that the truedragon was nearly done.

The phoenix rose in the sky, a triumphant scream bursting from its throat. Its eyes glittered like emeralds. It climbed higher, stroke by powerful wingstroke. Yet it had not escaped unscathed: though the slashing blow Pirakos dealt it had failed to still the great wings, the breast wound bled golden ichor like liquid amber. And the flight itself was slower than before, and wobbled.

The loss of those wing feathers is throwing it off balance, Linden thought. *Perhaps there's still a chance—*

With a fierce cry, the phoenix stooped like a hawk upon a rabbit, arrowing straight for Pirakos. The dragon hung in the air, motionless save for the heavy beating of his wings. His chains dangled like hangman's nooses.

Chains. Iron . . .

Shei-Luin's band wandered the burning city, seeking a way out. Once Shei-Luin looked up, and saw a creature from a nightmare fly overhead, a great red beast that did battle with the Phoenix.

She had but one thought in mind: get her son back.

Then they entered a part of the city that wasn't burning yet, and before them was a soldiers' barracks. Exhausted as she was, she found the strength to break into a run, Xahnu heavy in her arms. She would let no one else take him; she'd already lost one child.

She cried out to the soldiers she saw. When they recognized her robes, they ran to meet her, their captain among them.

As quickly as she could, she explained what had happened.

The captain drew in a harsh breath. "Phoenix Lady, we will do what we can, but it will take time. This barracks is all foot soldiers. We must send to another for a mounted troop, and I fear it will be a small one, for most are searching the city to lead people out. But go inside and rest, my lady."

Numb, Shei-Luin did as he bade. They led her to the officer's quarters. She gave Xahnu to Zyuzin, saying, "Find a place for him to sleep."

Then she remembered their prisoner. She turned to him.

An idea danced at the back of Linden's mind, but he could spare it neither time nor attention. *Pirakos,* he bellowed, *damn you—don't give up without a fight!*

To give Pirakos time to recover, Linden flung himself at the phoenix, turning at the last instant before the fiery wings lashed across him. Even so, the heat from those wings was so great, Linden felt as if a burning whip lashed across his wings. He gasped in pain, but retaliated with fire of his own. His ploy worked; the phoenix veered away.

Yet not for long, Linden knew. He mindcalled Pirakos, *Help me, damn it! That thing will set all the countryside aflame!*

What care I for this land? came the bitter reply. **The death I have wished for all these centuries is here. This thing will take me, and it may burn the world for all it matters to me. I will not help thee.**

Gods help them both; the phoenix was returning. Linden knew it would be his death to close with it alone; he had neither the strength nor the old magic of the truedragon. But neither could he let the fiery bird set the land ablaze.

Bloody coward! he hurled at Pirakos.

Pirakos's eyes blazed red hatred at the insult. He raised his forelegs as if he would slash Linden's wings to shreds. The chains rattled.

And the errant idea burst forth like a shooting star.

It's magic—and you've cold iron! Help me!

For a moment the truedragon simply stared. Then a light filled his eyes, a terrible mix of joy and bloodlust. He threw back his head and roared a dragon's laugh. **Thee are wise, little cousin. Yes, I die this day—but I take* that *with me!**

Before Linden could move, Pirakos hurled himself upon his enemy. He met the phoenix breast to breast; it screamed in surprise. Ignoring the flames that devoured him, Pirakos threw one foreleg around his enemy and clasped it close, like a lover embracing his beloved. The other foreleg ground the shackle that tortured it into the wound in the feathered breast. The iron bubbled and hissed as the phoenix's blood melted it—and the phoenix screamed in agony as the infection of cold iron entered its body. The blazing wings faltered.

Pirakos roared again, agony and victory twisted together in a last cry as he and the phoenix fell through the air. Somehow the dying dragon bent his long neck around; a torrent of scarlet flame took the phoenix even as it burst into a holocaust of golden flames. Their bodies were but black shadows within the fire.

Linden watched, numb with shock, as the two enemies tumbled through the air faster and faster, a flaming ball of whirling gold and scarlet fire. There was nothing to be seen in the heart of it now but a brightness that hurt the eyes.

Then they crashed to the earth, into one of the temple buildings. The ancient, lacquered wood burst into flame like oil-soaked kindling. Fragrant smoke, smelling of camphor, rosewood, sandalwood and more, billowed up even to where Linden hovered.

May the gods have mercy upon them, Linden thought. Suddenly every wound ached, every burn tormented him, and he was tired beyond belief. He spiraled downward slowly.

"Where is Xu?" Shei-Luin demanded.

Baisha frowned at her, one hand pressed to the wound in his thigh. "It's not your place, concubine, to question what a lord—"

Shei-Luin exploded in fury. *"Where is my baby, damn you?* What have you done with my little one?" she screamed. Her long, painted fingernails slashed across Baisha's face. "Outlander! It's not your place, foreign filth, to dictate to the empress and the mother of the heir! Beg for mercy or I shall have you killed."

Baisha clapped a hand to his bleeding cheek. His face

worked, emotions tumbling across it: hate, anger, then . . . fear. He darted a look at the impassive eunuch standing at Shei-Luin's side and the color drained from his face. He shrank into himself.

Shei-Luin knew what he saw. Murohshei, eyes like flints, still as a statue, hands tucked into wide sleeves. Hands that at her word would draw forth twin daggers and slit this pig's throat. And Baisha knew it; knew that Murohshei would take as long as she wanted to kill a certain henchman of Jhanun's slowly and carefully, eking out every bit of pain with loving malice for the theft of her son.

In a voice as soft as chrysanthemum petals drifting across silk, Shei-Luin said, "I will ask you only once more. Where's my baby, my little Xu?"

Baisha heard the razor's edge behind the silk as she'd intended. Even more color leached from his face. He was now a grey creature, indeed; grey of hair, grey of robes, grey of face.

"I . . . I don't know," he whispered.

Shei-Luin dropped a hand in a chopping motion. Like a tiger, Murohshei sprang before the wounded man could move. In the blink of an eye Murohshei was behind Baisha; he seized the man's hair in one hand and jerked the terrified prisoner's head back. The other hand held a small but deadly dagger to the exposed throat, its point pressing into the pallid skin.

"Don't move," Murohshei breathed. "Don't struggle. Don't make a sound, pig." The dagger pressed a little harder. A drop of blood appeared.

"Now, filth," Shei-Luin said, "Let us see if your wisdom has increased. You know where they're taking my son, Baisha. You will tell me." She trembled, barely containing white-hot fury. She let Baisha's death fill her eyes, let him see it there.

Talk or you shall die.

Baisha tried to stare her down. Fool; did he think she was any woman? She was the empress of Jehanglan.

Sweat broke out on Baisha's forehead. His lips quivered,

and Murohshei slowly, slowly rocked the dagger so that the edge lay against the exposed throat.

Jhanun's creature voided himself in his terror. The dagger moved—just a little. So very little.

"Rhampul!" Baisha squealed like the pig he was. "They bring him to Rhampul!"

"Why there?" Shei-Luin shot back.

"The soldiers there are loyal to Jhanun, and some are mountain men. If you send troops for Xu, they'll hide him where you'll never find him."

All at once Shei-Luin understood. Xu was to be a hostage, just as his father had been. But Xu would have no kindly captor as Yesuin had. Let her move against Jhanun, and her son would die.

"Kill him!" she screamed.

The knife flashed across the pale throat and blood spurted out. Dead eyes wide with disbelief, Baisha crumpled to the floor like a pricked bladder. Murohshei wiped the blade on Baisha's robe and returned it to his sleeve.

Her mask of calmness shattered like thin river ice under a heavy blow. Frightened for her child, Shei-Luin forgot *when* she was for a moment. "Get Yesuin. Tell—Phoenix help me, I forgot," she wept, sinking to her knees in despair. "He's not here anymore.

"Murohshei, Murohshei—what shall I do? My baby; they have my . . ." She cried as she had not cried in years, her heart frozen with a mother's grief.

"Lady," he said, "we can only go on."

The temple and its grounds were theirs. They were patrolling it, looking for stray bands of priests, when they heard a sound of unearthly beauty.

Amura and his band followed the singing. Never, Amura thought, had he heard such a voice. It filled his heart until he thought he would weep; such splendor was more than mortal man was meant to know.

Though it was long past dawn, the voice rose now in the solo passage from the Song. Amura had heard it a few times when he'd chanced to be in the temple on early errands; never had it held such beauty or such power. He led his party beyond an outcropping of rock and stopped in amazement, for the singer was Hodai.

So—the rumors were true. By some miracle—or magery—the old *nira*'s Oracle had found a voice. And such a voice!

The boy stood close to the edge of the cliff, facing them and the east, his hands clasped to his thin chest. He seemed not to see them as he sang. The ancient words flowed like liquid gold from his lips, soaring up and up into the final triumphant paean. This was the crowning glory of the Song. This was beauty to break the heart.

But just as it reached the final note, the crystal purity of Hodai's voice shattered. Amura cried out. His sword fell from suddenly nerveless fingers, and he covered his ears against the terrible betrayal.

A moment later he recovered himself. He almost couldn't bear to look at Hodai; what must the poor child be feeling?

But Hodai's face was blank; then sad wonder filled it. His lips parted. "Gahunk?" he said softly, to himself. His shoulders slumped. More animal-like sounds followed, all in that same tone of resigned sorrow. The now-pale lips closed once more.

For the first time, Hodai seemed to notice he was not alone. His eyes met Amura's, and Amura hoped he never saw such despair in a child's face again. He walked forward slowly so as not to frighten the former Oracle, his hand outstretched. Zhantse would find a place for the boy in the tribe.

Hodai bowed his head; his hands spread in a gesture of defeat. Then, before Amura could close the distance between them, Hodai drew himself up as proudly as if he stood before the Phoenix Throne and turned away. Three quick, decisive steps brought him to the edge of the cliff—and beyond.

Amura cried, "No!" as the boy disappeared from view.

Too stunned to move, to do anything, he stared at the spot Hodai had stepped from.

He should go look. He couldn't. Not for a hundred sheep and a hundred horses—wealth untold to his people—could he stand to look upon the small, broken body now lying far below. It would break his heart. Instead, Amura spun on his heel and led his men away. They followed without a word; one or two—fathers, they were—wept quietly, perhaps imagining their own children sprawled upon blood-stained rocks.

Amura glanced up at the sun; vultures dotted the sky already. He broke into a trot. It was long past time, he thought, to see the Vale again.

Linden came to rest on the ground some distance from the pyre that consumed both Pirakos and the phoenix. Yet even from this distance the heat of the towering flames beat against him, and it came to his mind that this was no natural fire. For, in his dragon form, he was immune to a natural blaze of any size; he'd once flown through the wind-whipped flames of a forest fire and felt nothing more than a pleasant warmth. Only a fire born of magic could cause the discomfort he felt now. And where the intense heat licked at his wounds, there came short, stabbing flashes of pain that he ignored. He was too exhausted—and saddened—to care.

They had done what they'd come to do. And failed. Never again would Pirakos see the mountains of the north. *But he died the death he wanted, Linden.*

Linden's head snapped up. The mindvoice had a clarity to it he'd never heard before, but he knew that voice as well as his own. He just couldn't believe he heard it now. How had she gotten here so soon after Pirakos? Not even a Llysanyin could come so far so quickly. *Maurynna-love?* he said in disbelief.

The voice in his mind went on, *He died cleanly, not like a wounded animal trapped in its own filth.*

It *was* Maurynna! The darkness lifted from his heart.

Forgetting his wounds, Linden reared up onto his hind legs, wings fanning to hold him upright. He looked wildly around. No, there was no Llysanyin with a beloved figure upon its back racing through the ruins of the city.

Look up, silly, the laughing mindvoice said. The love in it washed over him like springtime after a long, bitter winter.

Linden did as she bade. In the distance he saw a dragon silhouetted against the sky. Scales the iridescent blues and greens of a peacock's tail flashed in the sunlight. With a roar of pure joy, Linden sprang into the sky and raced to meet her.

By Maurynna's side flew another dragon, this one black. For a moment Linden thought it was Jekkanadar, and wondered where Lleld was. Then he realized this was no Dragonlord he'd ever seen before. A young truedragon, then, wounded in the ill-fated rescue attempt and left behind? No, Morlen would never abandon one of his kinswyrms; the old truedragon would have stayed.

So who—and what—was the mysterious stranger?

In the first flush of excitement, Linden hadn't noticed how Maurynna and the strange dragon's wings trembled with weariness. But now he did, and said to them, *Land before you both fall from the sky.*

It was also, he realized, damn good advice for himself as well. He angled back toward the place he had just left. Once more he landed, but this time with a lighter heart. The others followed, the black dragon in the lead.

Linden studied the strange dragon as it landed. It was black, like Jekkanadar, but didn't have the brownish blotch on its right hind leg that the Assantikkan Dragonlord did, and was, Linden thought, a little larger than Jekkanadar.

Was this a youngling truedragon, left behind, or could he dare hope . . .

Then he forgot all speculation as Maurynna landed and stretched out her neck to him. Wishing they were alone— and in human form—so that he could be more . . . demonstrative, he laid his scaled cheek against hers.

Heart of my heart, he whispered in her mind.

But before she could answer, a wild singing brought them all around. It was equal parts of pain and joy, and more terribly beautiful than anything Linden had ever heard. It raged through heart and mind, and he knew he'd hear it in his dreams for the rest of his life.

At first he couldn't tell from where it came. Then his dragonsight caught a movement in the blaze that consumed the enemies, a darker gold amid the towering yellow and red flames.

The song came from the very heart of the fire.

The priests were getting bolder, and he didn't dare flame them. Jekkanadar knew the walls would just reflect his own fire back at him—the one kind of fire that could hurt him.

But the priests had found spears somewhere, and crept closer and closer. The sharp heads glinted wickedly in the sunlight.

Damn, he'd no wish to be stabbed to death. Jekkanadar drew breath; this would be quicker.

Flames washed over him then, blue-green flames like a cool mountain stream. Yelping in surprised relief, Jekkanadar sprang into the air, his wing whole once more.

Damn it all! a voice yelped in his mind. *Watch where you're going! Now let's get out of here.*

Higher and wilder the song became. There were no words to it, just notes like liquid gold shimmering in the air, rising upon the fragrant smoke to the heavens. And still the dark form moved within the flames. Indeed, it seemed larger now, and more substantial. After a moment, Linden realized that it moved in rhythm with the singing.

He also realized that the flames were dying down faster than he would have expected. The building that Pirakos and his enemy had crashed into was large enough, he'd thought, to burn far longer than this.

Then two things became clear at the same time; the knowledge hit Linden like a blow. For with each heartbeat the fire died a little more. And as the fire died, the figure within the blaze became more distinct.

The phoenix— a strange mindvoice gasped in Linden's mind.

He knew it was the stranger. As one part of his mind wondered that the unknown one spoke Yerrin—although with a trace of an accent he didn't recognize—Linden finished, *Is renewing itself.*

Moment by moment, the song of the phoenix turned from pain to joy. The last of the flames died away, revealing a giant golden bird like the one Linden had just confronted—and helped send to its death. He braced himself for another attack.

The bird's head turned so that one scarlet eye stared at them.

Linden caught his breath. Scarlet. Not green, but scarlet—like a dragon's.

No. Not death. Release.

The mindvoice was tentative, as if unsure of how to use words. Indeed, Linden wasn't certain if he really heard words, or just fitted them to the emotions that suffused the mindvoice.

Friends. Guard. Not let . . . capture again.

Fear filled the mindvoice. The phoenix held out its wings as if in supplication.

Its feathers need to harden, the stranger said. His eyes were huge as he watched the phoenix.

Yes. Help.

We will, Linden answered with the others. He sprang into the air first and flew the short distance to the young phoenix. He landed, careful not to get too close to the wings. The others did the same.

The young phoenix spread its wings, fanning them gently, then stretching out first one, then the other. The color of the feathers rippled, changing from the purest yellow to red-gold. At last the colors settled to a rich gold like an old coin, with the wing and tail feathers tipped with a ruddier gold. And when the phoenix raised its wings as if paying homage to the sun, Linden was certain he saw a greenish tint underlying the feathers of its throat. A tint he had *not* seen on the phoenix he'd fought.

Then the wings swept down and the phoenix rose lightly from the earth. *Free now!* it sang.

Indeed, yes, Linden thought as they watched the phoenix fly swiftly into the sky and disappear. They were all free now, especially those two who had suffered the most.

Linden?

He turned to Maurynna. Long fangs greeted him; startled, he flinched back. Blue-green flames washed over him.

At once his wounds ceased hurting and the ache disappeared from his muscles.

You've no idea, Maurynna said smugly, *how long I've been waiting to do that.*

Lleld and Jekkanadar settled to the ground to rest. *I'll mindcall Linden, tell him what's happened.*

Jekkanadar was only too happy to agree. Since they'd landed in an uninhabited area, he laid his long neck on the ground and closed his eyes. Lleld spread a wing over him.

He was almost asleep when he heard Lleld shriek, *By the gods!*

He sprang up, looking wildly around for enemies. *What's wrong?*

Linden said there's nothing we can do in Rivasha; both Pirakos and the phoenix are free, though Pirakos died—he thinks. He said to return to the Zharmatians for Otter, Yesuin, and the Llysanyins.

None of which was cause for nearly frightening him to death. *Lleld—what aren't you telling me?*

Her mouth opened in a dragon's grin. *Maurynna wasn't the only one no one felt! There's another new Dragonlord,* she caroled in joy.

All Jekkanadar could find to say was, *By all the gods . . .* Then he threw back his head and roared with happiness.

*   *   *

Ending the conversation with Lleld, Linden said, *We must do something about the fires.*

But what? Maurynna fretted. *There's no way we can bring enough water to—*

A voice like gentle rain broke into her mind. *Thee cannot—but we can.*

She looked up in astonishment and gasped. For drifting in the sky were six ghostly dragons, long and slender like Miune. They were the color of fog, glittering here and there like mother-of-pearl.

A soft rain began to fall. All around them the flames hissed and died.

The Rain Lords, she thought in wonder.

Miune had been right.

Fifty-nine

The first message raced through the *mehanso* like the wind before a storm: *Strangers approach. Many strangers.* It came with the running feet of the children, who spread the word as they raced to their homes. While Shima translated it for them, Linden watched from the rooftop as mothers hurried out of the stone houses and hustled the children deeper into the canyon.

"Where are they going?" he asked.

"To the Pillar," Shima answered from behind him. "It's an island of rock rising from the canyon floor. My people retreat there during invasions. No enemy has ever taken it."

Linden looked over his shoulder. "Do you think this is an invasion?" He pushed away from the low wall he leaned on. "We'll need room to Cha—" He looked up at the sound of flapping wings. "What on . . . ?

A small—as dragons went—fiery red dragon glided in circles above the canyon.

"Lleld!" cried Linden, Maurynna, and Raven together.

"Ah," said Shima. "This is the Lady Mayhem you told me of?"

Maurynna nodded. "The same."

Linden changed to mindspeech and greeted Lleld, letting the others "listen" in.

Lleld rolled in the air. *What a lovely place to fly—the currents are strong! I saw the children being herded away, but everything's well. It's only our party approaching.* She rolled again. Silvery laughter bubbled in Linden's mind.

How long? he asked.

Four, perhaps five candlemarks. The three of us and Shan could be there sooner, but the Zharmatian horses can't match the Llysanyins. Oh, and speaking of Llysanyins, Shan is a . . . tad annoyed that you never came back for him, Linden.

The last was said far too innocently for Linden's peace of mind. He could just imagine Shan's temper; a "tad annoyed" his ass. Making a mental note to stay out of reach of hooves and teeth, Linden slid a snake-eyed look over his shoulder as Maurynna and Raven burst into laughter.

"I'll remember that," Linden muttered at them.

I must return, said Lleld. She banked out of her lazy circling and flew back the way she had come. Then, faintly, came, *Do remember to dodge, Linden.*

"Shima," Maurynna said, wiping her eyes, "does your mother have a good supply of bandages to hand?" Once again, she and Raven dissolved into laughter.

A puzzled Shima looked in mute appeal at Linden.

"Ignore them," he growled. "They think they're funny. Shan has a bit of a temper sometimes, that's all." Linden stalked off down the stairs hugging the outside wall, pointedly ignoring Maurynna and Raven.

Above him he heard Shima ask in a worried voice, "Bandages? Temper? Are all Llysanyins like that?" and the others trying to reassure him between bouts of laughter.

No, Linden wanted to yell back. *I was just the lucky one.* Damnation. Maybe he could find an apple somewhere.

Jhanun would pay. For now he had escaped her but, by the Phoenix, he would pay for the theft of her child.

Dressed in tunic and breeches of Zharmatian cut, but made of Jehangli imperial brocades, Shei-Luin rode at the head of a troop of soldiers as they galloped along the main road to the capital. Xahnu rode pillion behind her as a Zharmatian child would. When he tired, Murohshei would take him.

Once I am in the capital again, I must consolidate my power, for there will be war—I know it. Jhanun will fight me to the death for Jehanglan, for he is a man. But I am a mother—and will hound him beyond the gates of Death for my youngest son should any harm befall Xu.

Jhanun did not yet know what he faced. But he would— if it took her the rest of the both of their lives, he would learn.

It wasn't quite as bad as he'd thought it would be. Linden and the others stood with the Tah'nehsieh leaders as Lleld, Jekkanadar, and Otter, with the whooping Zharmatians ranging behind, cantered into the valley. Leading them all was Shan.

When the stallion saw Linden, he neighed angrily and broke into a dead run. Linden stepped forward and held his ground. He heard gasps behind him as the charging stallion closed the distance with no sign of stopping.

Linden hoped Shan knew what he was doing. Hell—he hoped *he* knew what he was doing. If Shan didn't stop in the next few heartbeats, it would be impossible for him to end the lethal charge.

He's gone too—!

Somehow Shan did the impossible. At what Linden would have thought beyond the last possible instant, Shan skidded to a halt in front of him, nearly sitting in the dust to do so.

The next thing Linden knew, strong white teeth snapped in his face and at his chest, once, twice, a half a dozen times almost before he could blink. Finished, Shan turned his head so that one angry eye was fixed on Linden. The stallion's ears were pinned tight against his head.

"Are you quite through?" Linden asked mildly.

Shan snapped once more at Linden's face.

"Look what I found." Linden reached into his belt pouch and held aloft his prize—a dried apple.

One black ear twitched forward, then the other. They quivered with anticipation.

For one moment, Linden considered teasing Shan with the apple, then decided that he'd no wish for a broken foot or worse, even if Maurynna could Heal him now. He held the wrinkled morsel out on his palm. "Here."

The apple disappeared with a loud crunch.

"Friends again?"

"For an apple," a dry voice said, "Shan would be friends with the Black Troll of Cavralen. Wouldn't you, you greedy guts?"

Linden looked up to see a tired and dusty—but smiling—Otter approaching, Nightsong close behind. For a long moment the mare regarded Shan happily munching, then snorted in disgust. *Stallions*, she seemed to say. *Walking stomachs*.

"Gods, but it's good to see all of you again," Otter said, catching Linden in a kinsman's embrace. Then the bard held his arms open, and Maurynna and Raven leaped into them.

"Ooof! Have mercy on an old man!" But the bard was laughing and giving back at least as good as he got; Linden swore he could hear Maurynna's ribs creak. "Truly, I thank the gods we're all together once more and all safe."

From the corner of his eye, Linden saw Zhantse meet Yesuin and lead him away.

"Shima," Maurynna called. "Come meet Otter."

Shima came forward shyly, but was soon drawn into the group.

A tug on his sleeve drew Linden's attention from the reunion. He looked around—no one there—and then down.

"He's the new Dragonlord?" Lleld asked, her eyes fixed on the Tah'nehsieh.

"He is," Linden replied. "Shima Ilyathan."

Lleld heaved a sigh of pure happiness. "Oh, good—he's still much taller than I am."

It was only a few days later when word came that the last of the magic was gone from the Straits. It was time to find their ship once more; Lleld claimed the errand for herself.

"No one knows where Miune is, and I want to stretch my wings again," Lleld complained. "They won't let me fly over the canyon anymore to tumble in the air. I make the flocks and herds nervous, they say—can you imagine?"

"Yes," said Linden, who'd been in the common pasture hammering down a loose nail in Boreal's shoe as Lleld practiced her aerial acrobatics one day. If the Llysanyins hadn't formed a barrier around him when the Tah'nehsieh horses had panicked . . . "I can imagine. Easily."

"Hmph," Lleld sniffed. "Anyway, I'm off." She ran down to the wide dancing floor. As always, a crowd of children raced after her to watch her Change.

As they watched Lleld fly away, Linden turned to Maurynna standing behind him. "So it's back to the sea again for us, Maurynna-love. And since you can Change now, I don't think the Lady will object if you choose to spend some time away from Dragonskeep and onboard a ship once more."

For a moment he wondered if she heard him, for her eyes looked beyond him to the canyon wall opposite. Their gaze was dreamy and unfocused as if she saw something else entirely. A half smile played over her lips. Then her gaze shifted to him, and her smile widened.

"Do you know, Linden," she said, "I think I would like to see mountains again. Our mountains."

Linden held out his arms and Maurynna stepped into his embrace. She hugged him fiercely.

"I want to go home," she said quietly.

He rested his cheek against her hair. *Home*. The word had never sounded so beautiful before. "So we shall, love," he answered and pulled her closer. "So we shall."

Epilogue

The mist hung over the land like a blanket. The clank of armor and weapons came eerily through it, one moment clear, the next cut off as if by a giant hand closing over the sound. Soldiers moved among the corpses carpeting the ground, appearing and disappearing in the thick greyness, now and again turning a body over, disturbing the ravens at their feast. The midnight birds flapped off, slow and heavy, cawing their indignation to the grim sky.

The men ignored them. For the most part, they were silent as they went about their grim business; orders occasionally passed back and forth, the words falling like stones into the heavy air.

All at once there was a flurry of excitement. A young lieutenant called out, "Here, Kwahsiu! The message was right! They're here!" He stood aside, stiff and proud, as his superior hurried to him. The foot soldiers crowded along behind as close as they dared, everyone following the grey shadow ahead of him.

Kwahsiu looked down. Nalorih stared back at him with sightless eyes, surrounded by soldiers that bore Lord Jhanun's crest, unlike the others on the field. Yes, this was the party he'd been sent to find. Pray the Phoenix that he found the one he was looking for. The others didn't matter, and he would grieve for his friend later.

"Search," Kwahsiu snapped. The mist swirled around him.

The soldiers examined the bodies to no avail. They began ranging up and down the bank, cursing the thick fog as they stumbled along the uneven ground.

A thin, eerie wail cut through the air. A fearful babble

answered it. "Quiet!" Kwahsiu roared, turning his head to locate the sound. It came again, distorted by the fog, but recognizable. Ah—ahead and to the left. "That's no ghost, you fools—don't you know a baby's cry when you hear it?"

He hastened toward the water and followed the bank to a copse of trees looming out of the grey dimness. As if to urge him on, the baby cried again. Well ahead of his men, Kwahsiu climbed over fallen branches and trunks, eager to reach the infant hostage.

A thicket of brambles lay between him and his goal: a basket cradle on a little beach of pebbles and sand, the body of woman sprawled before it. Barely glimpsed through the leaves, a gaping wound in her back told of how she'd come by her death; it was a miracle she'd been able to run so far with her precious burden. Kwahsiu found a moment to wonder where they'd found a cradle after they'd fled Rivasha; likely raided a farm, he thought.

The babe inside the cradle wailed its hunger and indignation at being alone. Kwahsiu chuckled; no more than his father or mother was Xu Ma Jhi used to deprivation. Pray the gods that the child would be more biddable than the female parent. Kwahsiu drew his sword and hacked a way through the brambles to the cradle.

He was preparing to cut the embroidered ribbons holding the child within the cradle when it happened. One moment the river beside him flowed swift and silent. The next, it erupted with a roar of fury. Kwahsiu screamed in terror for the first time in his life as a huge head adorned with feelers and streamers towered over him. The mouth gaped open, revealing long, sharp teeth like knives. Even as his paralyzed mind said "Dragon!" Kwahsiu was sent tumbling by a vicious sideswipe of the great head. Then, to his horror, the monster swooped down on the infant and seized the basket cradle in its mouth.

Like the cracking of a whip, the scaled nightmare reversed on itself and disappeared into the river. The last glimpse Kwahsiu had of the only thing that could keep the imperial troops from his lord's walls, was the cradle between the dragon's jaws, its head well above the water as it disappeared into the fog.

Between the pain of body and soul, Kwahsiu realized he had failed his lord. There was nothing left for him but to make reparation the only way he could.

He braced his sword in a tangle of tree roots and placed the tip against his heart.

"What is it you have, Miune?" said Zhantse.

Miune Kihn set his burden down gently on the grass, glad to be home once more at the head of the Black River. *It is a youngling, a human youngling,* he said. *A soldier was going to kill it.*

Zhantse raised his eyebrows.

He was, I tell thee! Miune insisted. *He was standing over the cradle with his sword drawn.*

"I see," Zhantse said. "Then I think you did well, Miune. There's a madness among the Jehangli these days; I don't doubt they would kill a babe. Let us see what you've brought me." Picking up the waterdragon's precious bundle, the shaman carried it to the fire over which a rabbit roasted on a spit.

Miune waddled awkwardly behind. *When we know whether it is a boy or a girl, I would like to name it,* he said.

"That seems only fair," Zhantse agreed. "You did save its life."

Setting the basket cradle down, Zhantse drew his knife and cut the embroidered straps that held the baby in. He wrinkled his nose as it became evident that the baby's swaddling clothes had not been changed in far too long.

Faugh! the dragon said and sneezed.

"Agreed," said Zhantse. Holding his breath, Zhantse undressed the baby. He examined the fine clothes briefly. Miune watched him and knew what he thought; some would call such things riches, but such were of no consequence in Nisayeh.

Still, they were his infant's only birthright. *Keep them,* he urged.

Zhantse gave him a long look, but did as Miune asked. Still, he set the fouled brocaded silks to one side. Then, with the baby in the crook of his arm, he moved upwind of them. "We will ask Yesuin about them when he returns from tending the horses."

The shaman laid the baby—a boy child—on the long grass, and fetched a bowl of water from the river and an old, soft cloth from his pack. Miune stood guard; though he had given up care of his youngling to Zhantse, he still felt protective toward the helpless little creature—protective and fascinated.

Zhantse returned and washed the baby. It squalled the entire time. "Healthy," the shaman noted, wincing at a particularly outraged shriek. "Good lungs. But what's this?"

He was, Miune saw, looking at the baby's thigh. *A burn?* the dragon said.

"Yes. An old one, well healed. We need not worry about it. Now, my dragon friend, tell me why you brought this baby to me."

Miune waved his feelers guiltily under the shaman's stern gaze. Perhaps, just perhaps, Zhantse wouldn't think his splendid plan to be quite as splendid as he did. The dragon tucked a feeler into his mouth and nibbled it.

Zhantse studied him for a long while. Then a smile creased the wrinkled face. "You brought me a new spirit drummer, didn't you? To take Shima's place."

Relieved, Miune said, *He is healthy and strong, and has no one else. I think he will make a good drummer for thee when he is older.*

"Oh, you do, do you?" the shaman said, but there was a laugh in the stern words.

Yes. And his name will be Khivran after thy—

"What do you have there, Zhantse?" a voice asked.

Yesuin! Come see my youngling! I saved him from a soldier, Miune said.

The waterdragon watched as his new friend came up and peered over Zhantse's shoulder. *His name is—*

"Xu!" Yesuin cried, his face suddenly pale. "Miune, Zhantse, that's—that's my younger son! See the burn? Shei-Luin told me . . . How did this—What has become of Shei and Xahnu?"

Yesuin staggered and would have fallen had not Zhantse reached up and steadied him. The shaman helped Yesuin kneel by his son's side. Yesuin took the child up in his arms; tears streamed down his face. "I never thought I'd see him," the Zharmatian said softly.

Does this mean I may not name him? Miune asked Zhantse. Though moved by the sight of father and son, he was still annoyed at having to give up his youngling after all that trouble.

"Hush. You've done a good day's work here," Zhantse whispered as he jabbed Miune with an elbow. "And the child already has a name."

I liked mine better. Miune grumbled, but only to himself.

Yesuin raised his head. "One day, Xu and I will seek his mother and brother. Until then, if you agree, Zhantse, I will raise him as a Tah'nehsieh."

"I agree," the shaman said. "You are both welcome here."

At least his youngling wasn't to be taken away from him completely. Mollified, Miune said, *And when that day comes, I will go with both of thee, and we will have a great adventure.*

About the Author

Joanne Bertin lives in Connecticut and is currently working on *Bard's Oath*, the third novel in the *Dragonlords* series, and attempting to put together a harp.